Ted Heller is a senior writer at *Nickelodeon* magazine and a contributing writer for *GQ* magazine. His first novel, *Slab Rat*, received widespread critical acclaim. He lives in New York City. *Funnymen* is his second novel.

ALSO BY TED HELLER

Slab Rat

FUNNYMEN

TED HELLER

ABACUS

An *Abacus* Book

First published in the United States of America by Scribner in 2002
First published in Great Britain by Abacus in 2002

Copyright © Ted Heller 2002

The moral right of the author has been asserted.

A CIP catalogue record for this book
is available from the British Library.

ISBN 0 349 11499 4

Printed and bound in Great Britain
by Clays Ltd, St Ives plc

Abacus
An imprint of
Time Warner Books UK
Brettenham House
Lancaster Place
London WC2E 7EN

www.TimeWarnerBooks.co.uk

*This book is dedicated to the memory of my parents,
who also met in the mountains.*

ACKNOWLEDGMENTS

Once again, I wish to thank Chuck Verrill, my agent, and Jake Morrissey and Nan Graham of Scribner.

I also would like to acknowledge the following people: Laura Galen and the crew from *Nickelodeon* magazine, Richard Beswick, Patricia Schultz, Iris Johnson and the Johnson family, Michael Hainey for the martinis, Susan Mitchell for her incredibly sharp eye, and, with the hopes that he doesn't sue me, Ken Lipman, hopefully not the only person who will like this book.

Now we are all sons of bitches.

—Kenneth Bainbridge,
Director of the Trinity test,
July 16, 1945

A complete list of important people who appear in this text
begins on page 411.

I

ARNIE LATCHKEY [co-manager of Fountain and Bliss]: It's sad to say, but the funniest that Harry and Flo Blissman ever were was on the night that they were too dead to perform. Best thing that ever happened to Ziggy, his parents dying the way they did. Best thing. From a professional standpoint, of course.

SALLY KLEIN [Ziggy Bliss's cousin and co-manager of Fountain and Bliss]: When Harry met my Aunt Florence, she was one of the old Garrity Gaiety Gals; she had a wonderful figure, a fabulous face, but she was only five feet tall. Harry had two inches on her. But Flo could really belt it out; "a lion's roar coming out of an ant" is how someone once described her voice.

If Harry and Flo were passing through Philly, they'd stop over at our place. We had a front porch and Harry would go on the porch and sit on a swinging seat. He'd gaze off into the distance and he'd be mumbling and swaying. My mother told me he was doing their act in his mind, trying to get it right. Well, he may have been doing that or he might have just been talking to himself. With entertainers you can never tell.

My parents took me to see them once. Harry and Flo came on toward the middle and did a sketch about a wife who couldn't cook. The audience took this time to go to the bathroom or smoke cigars in the lobby. I really don't remember much about the act.

LENNY PEARL [comedian]: Instant amnesia, it was like—as soon as they went offstage you forgot what you'd just seen. I was on the road with them for *years*. They were strictly a bottom-of-the-barrel, low-rung vaudeville act. A cough in the audience was like a standing ovation for them. They were the two tiniest things you ever saw, if you ever saw them.

Now, let's tell the truth here: the act failed. Before they signed with the Bratton circuit, they were on the Pantages circuit and they also had toured with the Keith and Albee companies. California, Oklahoma, Chicago, Florida—they failed everywhere. But at least they got to see the country.

Archie Bratton [president of A. C. Bratton Theater Ventures] wanted to bill them as the Mirthful Midgets, did you know that? Well, Harry stood up to him and said, "Hey, we ain't midgets!" But Bratton did it anyway.

There was this magician with our company and his name was Ferdinand the Fantastiq. The reason there were no letters after the *q* was because Archie Bratton was so goddamn cheap, he'd even save money on the ink on the handbills they passed around.

If you ask me what Ferdinand was, where he was from, I couldn't tell you. Some people thought he was Maltese or a Gypsy. His hair was jet black. He put a lot of paprika in his food, I remember, so he might have been Hungarian. He was a damn good magician. Did the best disappearing act I ever saw. Let's see someone else *really* disappear like that!

SCARLET ROBIDEAUX [Ferdinand's assistant]: Ferdinand had a thin handlebar mustache and he waxed it with black shoe polish, and his shiny black hair was parted in the middle. He was always polite to me and to the other girls. He never tried to lay a hand on us and that was rare—if you were an entertainer there were all kinds of things said about you. But he was a gentleman.

All I really did was go on the stage and hold up things for him or slip backstage and get props. That was quite a costume I had! I looked like a peacock. All those blue feathers. Ferdinand would do the routine, saw me in half, make me disappear, levitate me. He never worked with birds though—he told me he'd often had "artistic differences" with them.

I realized that there was something going on between him and Florence Blissman. I heard rumors. I would see them walking down the hallway together in the hotels. And you just knew. She was very lonely and I couldn't blame her.

LENNY PEARL: Oh, there was all kinds of gossip. But this was the life we led. Did I know about Flo and the magician? Sure I did. It was like *The Wizard of Oz* with the Munchkins. You put all these munchkins from the world over on a set together and suddenly it's the ancient Roman baths all over again except a lot shorter.

When Flo got pregnant I slapped Harry on the back and congratulated him. He was so small I nearly knocked him over. He didn't seem very happy for it being his first kid. 'Cause maybe it wasn't really his kid.

SCARLET ROBIDEAUX: In the act I got into a box and Ferdinand sealed it shut. He spun it around and then opened it and I was gone . . . there would be nothing but my feathers wafting around inside.

One night Ferdinand told me he was going to change the act. *He* was going to disappear, he said. He told me he had a brand-new box and all I had to do was stand there and look very pretty. Well, I could not believe my eyes! This new box was quite grand. It was real mahogany. There was gold and pearls and floral inlay and it was very magnificent.

At the end of the act Ferdinand bowed to the audience and then went into the box and tipped his hat. I closed the door and walked around it. Then I opened the door and he was gone.

As far as I reckon, he was never seen again.

SALLY KLEIN: After Ziggy was born, my mother told me, Harry just devoted himself to the act. That was when he started rehearsing to himself and mumbling and staring off into space.

• • •

CATHERINE RICCI [sister of Vic Fountain]: Codport [Massachusetts] was a fishing town, right on Buzzard's Bay. Papa [Bruno Fontana] worked on the piers, in the fish market. He was an assistant manager there. He couldn't ever get the smell of fish off him, even on weekends. Nobody would sit too close to us at the movies because of the smell. But nobody really liked to sit too close to anybody. Most people smelled of fish in that town and everybody pretty much kept to themselves.

Mamma [Violetta Fontana] was like a lot of Italian mothers. She stayed home and took care of the kids. You couldn't walk in that house without tripping over a baby. Vic was the youngest, so I think he had more people tripping over him than the rest of us. Maybe that toughened him up.

My father was very quiet. He'd give you a look and you shut up for a while. He'd always be yanking Vic's hair or his ear, especially his ear—it's amazing Vic could even hear with all that yanking. But make no mistake: Mamma ran the family.

ARNIE LATCHKEY: Vic hated fish, would never eat it. Not even caviar or lobster. You couldn't pay him to look at it. Once we had him all set to do a swashbuckler movie with Rhonda Fleming, but he wouldn't do it. I tell him, "Vic, you know, it's not like you're really on the high seas; you're on a soundstage and they got a big bathtub," and he says, "No, but when I see the movie it'll be like I *was* on the high seas." As though he would go to see one of his own movies.

[Vic's mother] had a little dash of Madame Defarge about her. Cooking, cleaning, and knitting, but plotting to take over the world. Vic got his looks from Bruno, the hair, the height, the eyes. Bruno, who could make

Calvin Coolidge seem talkative, had those scary blue eyes—like looking at ice. And his hands were as big as catcher's mitts.

RAY FONTANA [Vic's older brother]: Pop worked his way up at the fish market, lifting crates of cod and clams. Crates it took two guys to carry, he did it on his own. Once I saw him carry an armoire down the stairs without resting it. The armoire alone weighed two hundred pounds. And after he put it down, what happens? Three of my sisters and my brother Sal come running out.

TONY FERRO [childhood friend of Vic]: Rocco Straccio was a terror. Everyone in Codport was scared stiff of him. He had dark skin and all the kids called him Rocky the Nigger. Not to his face, mind you. He had black eyes. And his teeth were black, his teeth and his gums. There was all kinds of stories about him. He'd come over from Sicily on steerage when he was six. Alone. The immigration people in Boston saw that he was covered with rat bites, and he bragged to them he'd bitten back. They didn't believe him, but then they found two dead rats on the ship with tiny human teeth marks on them.

Straccio took the money in three cuts. From the fishermen themselves; if they didn't pay Straccio up front, they couldn't fish. From the market, where the fish was hauled in and then distributed. And finally when the fish was transported out of New England.

He'd do this thing—he'd put his hand on your nose and twist it really hard and say, "Got your nose." And then he'd have his thumb wiggling between his fingers. Now, my uncle did that to me too and it was no big deal, but when Straccio did it, for the next five hours you made sure you still had your nose.

[Vic and me] both dropped out of school and wound up working at Jiggs's Pharmacy over on Governors Street. Jiggs was Jiggs Cudahy, a big Irishman with a big round red face, like an apple. I was a stock boy and a soda jerk and Vic jerked sodas and did deliveries. He made good ice-cream sundaes and malteds. The both of us, we had those white uniforms—like a Norman Rockwell picture—and it made us look like we was doctors except we had those meshed paper hats and not too many doctors wear meshed paper hats. Vic was always fussing, smoothing out the wrinkles, sneaking looks at himself in the mirror behind the counter. And he delivered stuff—you know, cough syrup, bromides, elixirs, that kind of stuff. I kept wondering, why's Vic so anxious to do the deliveries? You got a nickel a run sometimes, while if you was behind the counter you could sometimes clear fifty cents in that time.

Well, in a fishing town the men are gone most of the day and there's no chance of them popping in. Vic's a strong handsome kid and we were what?—seventeen, eighteen years old at the time. Well, what do you *think* Vic was doing? Why do you think it took an hour to deliver a tin of cold cream two streets away? That sonuvabitch'd be making a big fancy banana split with his left hand and sniffing the fingers on his right. Jiggs didn't care—as long as Vic told him everything blow by blow afterward, old Jiggsy didn't care.

RAY FONTANA: The women in town, all the girls—they loved Vic. The one word they used to describe him was "luscious."

•   •   •

SEYMOUR GREENSTEIN [neighbor of the Blissmans in Echo Beach, Brooklyn, and childhood friend of Ziggy's]: After Ziggy was born, Flo would leave him with my parents when she and Harry were on the road, and my mother would take care of him. When Flo was back in town she'd take him back. But there were times, my mother said, when they'd be out touring and Ziggy wasn't with us. I don't know where he was then.

My mother also told me that when the Catholic mothers in the neighborhood saw her with Ziggy in the baby carriage, they'd cross themselves. He was always weird looking.

There was this one time that Ziggy was completely forgotten about. Harry and Flo left him with a neighbor, who then left him with us, and my mother left him with—well, somehow he got lost during all those handoffs. It *was* like football: you keep lateraling and doing all sorts of razzle-dazzle and flea flickering, you're going to eventually fumble. So one time he got fumbled and for about three weeks he was on his own. A ten-year-old kid, all alone.

I saw him perform years later. If you knew how poor and lonely he was as a kid, then the way he performed made sense. He wanted, he *needed* you to love him. He'd do anything for it.

SALLY KLEIN: My father's ladies' undergarment business was doing well and we had a small cottage in Delaware, nothing too fancy. Ziggy was with us for a few weeks there. He was around seven, I'd say. A year older than me. He didn't know his way around the house, he'd always walk into the wrong room or he'd fall down the stairs.

He'd "go" everywhere. He'd run around the house and bounce off the walls and he'd be holding himself nervously, trying to keep it in. It was pretty funny but then it wasn't funny when you found a puddle in the kitchen or you'd open a door and he'd be going against the couch. My mother didn't know how to handle it. I remember this one Sunday morning in the summer. My father was lying down on the love seat with a newspaper over his head. When he woke up he howled, he really howled. Ziggy had had an accident on his feet.

• • •

RAY FONTANA: Vic was my mother's favorite kid, there was no question about that. I got hand-me-downs from Sal. But Vic always got new clothing. That kid was the best-dressed second grader you ever saw. His diapers were tailor-made—I ain't kiddin'—by this Milanese tailor downtown. And the crease was always in the right place.

It was not a musical family, no. There was no piano, nobody ever took violin lessons, nothing like that. The thought of one of us going into show business? Forget it. The thought of anybody in that town going into any business other than fish . . . you might as well talk about getting elected president.

CATHERINE RICCI: Vic really got the looks. My mother used to tell him that angels had dipped him in a lake of honey and then brought him to our house.

And the hair. Under the light sometimes it could look blue . . . it was just like Superman in the comics.

At the dinner table Vic sat closest to Mamma and half the time she had her hand in his hair or was pinching his earlobe and saying, *"Faccia bella."* She would then wrap her big arms around him and pull him into her chest and he'd stay in there for a while.

As a kid, Vic liked listening to the radio. Bing Crosby, Russ Columbo, Basil Fomeen. Fritz Devane, "the Grand Forks Golden Boy," was his favorite. He hated Vaughan Monroe, the man who sang "Racing With the Moon" and sounded like a hound being strangled.

Father Claro was the priest [when] Vic was about ten or eleven. He came to our house one night and asked Mamma if Vic could join the choir. My mother and father went into the kitchen to talk about it—I think Papa thought that any boy who sang in a choir was an *effeminato*, a sissy. They came out of the kitchen and Mamma says to Father Claro, "How did you know my boy can sing? We never hear him sing. Can Vic sing?" And Father Claro says, "Signora Fontana, with a face like this, he could honk like a dying goose but we'd still want him."

A few weeks later, every woman leaving the church would tell Father Claro how much better the choir sounded now that Vic was in it. You couldn't find a seat in that place. The women and the girls all loved to watch Vic sing.

TONY FERRO: He really stood out in the choir. All the other boys wore these wrinkly gray choir uniforms but Vic's was sky blue—his mother saw to that—and not a wrinkle to be seen. And the other thing was, he didn't sing, he mouthed the words. He told me he wasn't supposed to sing; Father Claro had told him to just move his lips.

ARNIE LATCHKEY: The first time Vic ever had to lip-synch a song, the director asked him if he needed help or instructions. "Are you kiddin'?" Vic said. "I did this for three years in church!"

• • •

LENNY PEARL: Archie Bratton fired me one day when we were in Columbus, Ohio. I went back to the hotel to pack and I was thinking, Okay, *bubeleh,* now what? You're eighteen years old and your mother's a cripple and your father sells used tea kettles on Orchard Street and your sister's married to a door-to-door comb salesman who stutters.

It turns out that Bratton did that to all of us, fired *everyone* one by one. The Beaumonts, a tap-dancing and tango act, Billy and Mary . . . he calls Billy Beaumont in and says, "Billy, hit the road. You're out. You're a cancer on the show. Go. Mary stays, you're gone." Then a few minutes later Bratton calls Mary in, told her she was fired and that Billy was staying. Now, he could've done the brave thing and lined us all up and said, "Guys, gals, the company is bankrupt, it's kaput. I'm sorry. Good luck." But he had to get one last shot in.

So I'm on the train that night back to New York and when I get to Grand Central the next morning I pick up a copy of *Metronome* and read to my great relief that Archibald J. Bratton had been shot three times in the head at the Southern Hotel in Columbus.

Whoever did it, God bless 'em.

SALLY KLEIN: Harry and Flo went back to Echo Beach. My mother told me Harry was humiliated, distraught . . . she thought it would kill him.

Years later, Ziggy told me it was the happiest he'd ever been. For the first time, he had his parents around for a long stretch. And I found that strange. Because, if you think about it, Uncle Harry and Aunt Flo were devastated—they'd been performing their whole adult lives and now they had absolutely nothing. But Ziggy remembered it as a great time.

SEYMOUR GREENSTEIN: Kids from all over Brooklyn would come to our neighborhood just to see this kid Sigmund Blissman. He was a sight to behold, all round and red. And that wild Brillo hair of his, even back then.

Kids from Coney Island, Brighton Beach, Flatbush, wherever. One social club from Poseidon Avenue had a contest called Count Ziggy's Freckles. I think he was about ten at the time. They called Ziggy into where the club met and they stripped Ziggy down. They started counting his freckles and Ziggy stood there patiently. As it was dawning on them that they weren't ever going to be able to count them all, Ziggy says, "Wait. You forgot to count *these*." And he pulled down his underwear.

ARNIE LATCHKEY: Some of the showgirls in Vegas used to call him "the Hose." Or maybe it was "the Horse." His real last name should've been *Blessed*-man.

•   •   •

CATHERINE RICCI: No girl ever had to worry about whether Vic's mother was going to like her when he brought her home because after a while, Vic never could bring a girl home. Mamma would've gone after her with a chopping knife or her infamous rolling pin.

If he'd brought home the Virgin Mary, Mom would've complained about her having a bad reputation.

RAY FONTANA: Vic always had a ton of girls around. All the dates I ever had, I think it was just 'cause they wanted me to introduce them to my good-looking kid brother. I dated this girl Ann McGee maybe two dates. My mother loved her, thought she was terrific. Her family was from Flounder Heights, the ritzy lace-curtain-Irish section. A few months after I took her out, she drops by. I say, "Hey, Annie, where you been?" She brushes right by me and heads toward Vic.

And then my mother tells me that Ann McGee is the biggest *puttana* in America. All 'cause she was now with Vic.

TONY FERRO: He was working half the women in Codport. A lot of these women, Vic was pals with their husbands around town. Guys at the pool hall, at Jiggs's, on the piers. Vic would joke around with them and all but meanwhile he was givin' it to their wives.

I remember once he told me to pick him up outside of Joe Ravelli's house. Joe was a good guy; he used to sell Italian ices in the summer for extra dough but he'd always give the kids ices for free. He was off fishing and the wife was home. The door opened and I saw Mrs. Ravelli in the doorway, in the shadows, adjusting the belt of her robe, which was green. Vic gave her a nice love slap on the ass—you could hear it twenty yards away. He come outta there with a little smile, he straightened his hair out with a comb, and then he flashed me a crisp new ten-dollar bill.

ANGELA CROSETTI [friend of Vic Fountain in Codport]: My mom and me would go to Jiggs Cudahy's soda parlor almost every day after school. We'd sit at the counter and Vic would make us an ice-cream soda or a malted. My mother would apply her lipstick and eye shadow for an hour beforehand at her vanity table, till everything was perfect. When she was ready she looked gorgeous. People always compared her to Rita Hayworth.

She and her friends called Vic *il ragazzo con i capelli blu come la notte.* The boy with the hair as blue as the night.

TONY FERRO: The storeroom was between Jiggs's office and the soda fountain. But Vic had set it up so's there was a nice space on the floor in there. He used about a mile of cotton for a mattress. Actually it was Jiggs who set it up. 'Cause there was a hole in the wall that divided Jiggs's office from the storeroom. One afternoon Vic is in there doing his thing—I think it was Angie Crosetti's mom, who was a real hairy cow—and I walk into Jiggs's office and there he is, this fat red Irishman with his *cazzo* in his hands, peekin' through the hole in the wall.

"We could charge money for this view, Tony," Jiggs said to me.

One day Jiggs's wife is sick, she's got an upset stomach. Jiggs comes over and says to me, "Hey, Tony, can you run these pills over to my wife on your way home?" I tell him, "Flounder Heights ain't on my way home, and besides, I don't deliver the stuff ever. That's Vic's job. Have him do it." He rubs his chins a couple times and says he'll just bring it over himself when he goes home.

So I've got an hour left in the day and I notice that Jiggs just isn't concentrating. Then Vic leaves to deliver the pills to Mrs. Cudahy, he takes off his white mesh hat and is on his way. Jiggs waits two minutes and he says, "Okay, Tony. Out! We're closing up!"

I says, "Huh? It's five o'clock, how are we closing?" And he says, "'Cause we just are!"

He locks up and puts the CLOSED sign on the door. I see him start walking up the hill toward Irish Town and he was huffin' and puffin' 'cause even though it was April it was still cold out and the smoke was coming out his mouth.

That night, Jiggs flipped his lid. He set fire to the drugstore . . . nothing was standing except the soda fountain and the chrome stools at the counter. Everything else was ashes. And Jiggs sawed his wife's head off in her sleep. How they know it was in her sleep, I don't know—you'd think that would wake her up. That was the end of her and the end of him too.

•   •   •

SALLY KLEIN: One day my mother gets off the phone and she's looking very sad and I ask her why and she says, "It's bad news, Sal. The Battling Blissmans are back in business."

There was a hotel in the Poconos called the Baer Lodge. Rosie McCoy was an old-time hoofer who'd married "Big" Sid Baer, who owned the place, and she and her husband opened up a nightclub there called the Den. Rosie was the entertainment director and she contacted all her old friends from when she was a dancer. Singers, actors, all kinds. The Beaumonts, Smith and Schmidt, the contortionist act Twyst and Tern, Lenny Pearl. And, of course, Harry and Flo.

They moved into our cottage in Delaware for a while and rehearsed their act. I'd see them in the backyard going through their paces. The only time I ever heard anything was when Flo sang. What a belter. The furniture would rattle when she sang, like there was an earthquake.

Ziggy was not staying with us at the time. You know, it might make us sound cheap but to save money to reupholster and recarpet all the places where Ziggy had "gone," well, as I said, my father manufactured brassieres and girdles and corsets—he just used lace from the factory. For ten years our entire house looked like one big brassiere-and-girdle set.

Some psychologist might say this is where Ziggy got his big-boob fetish. But I really don't know.

DR. HOWARD BAER [Rosie McCoy Baer's nephew]: Aunt Rosie booked the Blissmans on a bill with the Beaumonts. I was young then and I had a big crush on Mary Beaumont. She would lean over and hand me candy in her dressing room; it was and still is the most exciting thing that's ever happened to me. The bellhops called her Mary Cantaloupes.

The Blissman act lasted maybe twenty minutes . . . I couldn't tell if it was supposed to be funny. Aunt Rosie had once booked this actor named Lionel Gostin who had done Shakespeare and was very respected. Gostin would get onstage dressed in black and the lights would dim until you could see only his face. He'd do scenes from *Hamlet* and *Othello*. He'd play to the thousandth row, but there *was* no thousandth row. There was usually a plant in the crowd, some guy who'd stand up and yell "Bravo! Bravo!" and get five bucks for it. Now I knew that Lionel Gostin was not onstage to get laughs. He was doing drama. But I never could figure out what the Blissmans were doing.

Except at the end. Florence would sing. It was as if she was punishing the audience. "Okay, you made it through our lousy comedy act. Think you're so tough? Now I'm going to puncture your eardrums and shatter your eyeglasses."

•   •   •

HUGH BERRIDGE: I was a vocalist in a Boston trio called the Three Threes. [We wore] woolen vests that had the trey from a domino on them and would play at social functions such as balls, weddings, and once in a while we opened up for big bands—Basil Fomeen and Isham Jones and the like. We had regular jobs or were going to college. Rowland Toomey worked in insurance and was quite the expert at death benefits, Teddy Duncan had a degree in law from Harvard. I too was studying law at Harvard.

One night we were in Codport performing, and a rather middling ten-piece band was supporting us. Unbeknownst to us, the theater manager had written on the advertisements that there would be an "open mike" contest—the Three Threes would take on anyone willing to sing with us. Most of our audience that week was comprised of kids, teenagers only a few years younger than ourselves. And they were quite shy and therefore reluctant. A few did come onstage, and they'd never been on that side of a microphone before . . . they sang a few bars and then trotted off, quite red in the face.

Suddenly this handsome boy with a mop of dark, curly, and almost preternaturally bluish hair was being pushed by friends into the aisle. He was, as they said back then, "togged to the nines." He brushed back his hair, adjusted his tie—which was turquoise, I believe, to match his eyes—and walked toward the stage. He already had that now-famous Vic Fountain walk, that combination swagger and strut, a little bit like John Wayne. Very cock-of-the-walk, I must say.

As he got on the stage I heard a sighing and some sort of commotion—the girls in the crowd really thought that this boy was very handsome.

We didn't even have to nudge him toward the mike . . . he just walked up and grabbed it. I turned to Jarvis and Teddy; we had no idea if this dark, handsome boy could sing, but we were quite sure he had charisma.

The band started up "Ain't She Sweet," and we began singing. Vic mouthed the words for a few bars but then he realized that, as he was only inches in front of the microphone, everyone could tell.

He stepped back a few feet and whispered to me, "What do I do?"

"You sing," I whispered back sternly.

So he began singing.

Vic was a natural baritone who made himself into a tenor. He sang "under" the lyrics, behind them. He phrased a shade behind the beat and got beneath the lyric. It was instinct, I suppose. Either that or he didn't know the song we were singing. While we sang, he sang around us . . . it was almost scatting, one could say, but was, I guess, *lazier* than that, more Perry Como than Ella Fitzgerald.

He was the only one that night who did an entire song with us; it was "Always" by Irving Berlin. He got applause. *We* got applause.

The next night there was an open mike again. The first person on the stage was none other than the boy from the previous night. He showed up for all five nights, each time dressed better.

By the fifth night he had memorized the two songs he performed with us. Within a month he was part of the act.

GUY PUGLIA [friend of Vic Fountain]: "What would you think if I became a singer or something?" Vic asked me. We were shooting eight ball at Kitty's Korner Klub on Perch Street.

"You?" I says. "Vic, you ain't sung since that candy-ass choir. And you didn't even sing *then*."

Well, he proceeds to tell me about that trio, the Three Threes, and I says, "Yeah, but come on . . . what about the actual singing part of it, when it comes down to making the words come out your mouth in the form of some kind of melody?" He waves his hand at me and says, "Hey, anything Bing Crosby can do, I can do."

And I understood that. Vic was six-one, had big shoulders and muscles . . . and you ever see Crosby? He looked like a twig that someone hung a tweed hat on and handed a golf club to. So to me that made sense.

There was only one voice teacher in the town. His name was Enzo Aquilino and he'd sung opera in Milan decades before. Or so he said. Walking past his house you sometimes heard opera playing on the Victrola, pouring out the window. It was beautiful. But sometimes you heard his students tryin' to sing opera and that wasn't so beautiful.

CATHERINE RICCI: My mother called Mr. Aquilino "the little skunk" because of his silver and black hair. Well, he simply refused to give any lessons other than in the operatic style. But Mamma knew that was not the kind of singer Vic wanted to be. "Okay, okay," my mother says to him and then leaves. Twenty minutes later she's back with her rolling pin. Aquilino locked his door but she busted in through the window and started smashing all his framed Enrico Caruso pictures to pieces. "You teach my boy to sing or I'll eat your piano!" she tells him.

Now, I slept with [my sisters] Connie and Dolores, in the room next to

Vic's. Vic was the only one of us who had his own room. Ray and Sal shared too, upstairs.

One night I hear yelling and I rush to Vic's room . . . I had no idea what was going on.

I couldn't believe what I saw: Papa had pinned Vic to his bed with one arm—Vic was flailing around like crazy, trying to break free. And my father was jamming a big haddock down Vic's throat in one piece. He was just shoving it down Vic's mouth.

"You wanna sing, sissy?" Dad was hissing. "*Femminuccia!* Big-band sissy boy want to sing? Trying singing now, eh? Sing now. Sing like that sissy boy Crosby! Sing now!"

In five minutes the whole haddock from the head down to the tail was down Vic's throat.

But Vic kept at it. Every day he took the lessons.

Oh, did I mention that the haddock was still alive?

HUGH BERRIDGE: Vic asked me for a way to reach us in Boston, and I gave him the number of our manager, Jack Enright. I did not think we would ever hear from him.

On the train back to Boston, Rowland Toomey started imitating the way that Vic had vocalized, the sonorous, oily swirling around the melody. Teddy Duncan turned to him and said, "Rowlie, perhaps we *could* use another voice. He certainly did have a presence."

"But we're a trio," Rowlie said. "We've always been a trio."

And as the world knows, soon Vic climbed aboard our little caravan, and we became the Four Threes.

* * *

SEYMOUR GREENSTEIN: When a teacher called on him and he didn't know the answer, Ziggy would give his wrong answer in cockamamie accents and dialects, like Yiddish, Chinese, German, Japanese. And so there was a lot of laughing because he *never* knew the right answer. We were once reading *Romeo and Juliet* aloud and when it was Ziggy's turn, he really hammed it up. I don't know if he got one word right but it didn't matter, not with that hilarious British accent. He was the class clown to end all class clowns.

SALLY KLEIN: It was summer and the Blissmans were booked for the Baer Lodge for July. Ziggy was, I'd say, seventeen. He'd never seen them perform. They'd never taken him on the road. But this time—for whatever reason—they brought him to the Poconos.

DR. HOWARD BAER: I was at the desk when they came in. Ziggy looked nothing like his parents. He was a teenager, had bright red hair and a round nose, and he looked like a brand-new basketball.

The three of them walked into the lobby and approached Allie Gluck, who worked the front desk. Allie indicated Ziggy and asked, "Harry, what's this?"

Ziggy squirmed in that babyish way he used in the act and he pinched his crotch and said, "*I'm* this." The way he said it . . . you had to be there.

I remember thinking it was strange: Harry had booked only one room. So you had a husband, a wife, and a seventeen-year-old staying in one room. Not even a suite.

Allie said to Ziggy, "You sure you don't want a room for yourself?"

"Yeah, I'm sure," Ziggy answered him.

Allie asked him, "Are you scared of the dark?"

"Oh yeah. I'm a-scared. Very a-scared. But not of the dark."

Allie asked, "Of what then?"

"Oh, lots and lots of things," Ziggy said.

By now you've got two dozen or so people in the lobby and they're all paying attention.

"So you want to be with Mommy and Daddy?" Allie asked.

Ziggy looked at Harry, made a weird face, then he looked at Flo and made the same face.

"On second thought," he said to Allie, "I think I'm a-scared of them too."

I'm not kidding when I tell you that Ziggy Bliss already had about fifteen people in the palm of his hand.

When Harry's face lit up, it looked like it was the first time that had ever happened.

It was a double bill. Harry and Flo were opening up for the Beaumonts. You had a hot weekend in July and a packed hotel. The Beaumonts could have been the next Fred and Adele Astaire or Vernon and Irene Castle. They were in *Staten Island Serenade* with George Raft but I think that was it, film-wise. They really were such magnificent dancers.

The routine the Blissmans were doing was that Harry is jealous because Flo, he finds out, had been working as a small-size model behind his back and, it turns out, she's making more money than him. They're five minutes into it and—no exaggeration—half of the crowd had filed into the lobby or was in the bathroom.

All of a sudden Ziggy comes onstage. It was like *that*—he was just there. His first time ever.

Now most people in the club had never seen Sigmund Blissman before.

They'd never seen anyone who *looked* like Ziggy Blissman. They couldn't tell if he was five or fifteen or fifty-five years old. Right away there's a big hush.

He's on the corner of the stage. One hand is nervously clutching the curtains and the other is holding an ashtray.

"What are you doing here?" Harry asks him. And he's apoplectic. Coming onstage during his act . . . you simply don't do that.

"I'm watching the show, Poppy," Zig says.

"Go upstairs! *We're performing!*"

"Don't look like much performing to me, Poppy."

People are tittering already, they're coming in back from the lobby.

"Zig," Harry says, "your mother and I—"

"What? You're finally gonna get married?" Ziggy says.

Ziggy lifts up the ashtray and then lets it drop. And it breaks. He says, "Hey, Mommy, now you don't have to sing tonight."

The place is in hysterics by now.

Ziggy goes into the audience, grabs an ashtray. He breaks that one too and says, "And now you don't got to sing tomorrow neither."

"Sonny, every ashtray you break will come out of our paycheck," Harry says.

"But you work for free, don't you, Pops?"

"For free?"

"Yeah, you always say that Rosie Baer don't pay you nothing. Hey, Ma, can I dance with Mary Beaumont tonight?"

"*You?*" Flo says. "With Mary Beaumont? Dance? Why, you can hardly walk!"

"Oh, I can walk," Ziggy says. And then he breaks out the physical gags, he tries to walk but it's as though he has his ankles tied together. He reels around the stage, goes into the audience, falls down, even starts jumping from table to table. "See, Ma, I can walk. I wanna dance with Mary Beaumont!" Whining like a three-year-old.

"Now now, Ziggy," Harry says, "that's what Billy Beaumont is for."

"Yeah, you're right, Poppy. They're the best pair there is in dancing. And you know what? Billy Beaumont, he ain't bad neither."

Flo sang the closing number and Zig did this thing, as if he was going insane from the noise, covering his ears and reeling around like a boxer getting his brains knocked out.

It didn't end there. After a twenty-minute break, Billy and Mary took the stage. Ziggy let them do a number and, well, he couldn't resist. He bounced onto the stage during a tango and asked Billy if he could cut in. Now, poor Billy, he could not say one word onstage because of the mincing, effeminate manner in which he spoke. So he just shook his head. Ziggy whipped out a pair of scissors and cut Billy's bow tie. Then he started flitting around like a butterfly for a few seconds and grabbed Mary and began to tango, if that's what you want to call it, with her.

Billy would have murdered Ziggy, and Mary would've grabbed those scissors and castrated him. But in show business, I guess, if the crowd is going with it, you go with it too.

So Mary and Ziggy did a tango and during one dip he buried his head in her cleavage and when he got up out of it, his eyes were bulging out . . . it really looked like they were going to pop out of their sockets. He careened around the stage and bounced off the walls. When he finally "recovered" himself, instead of dancing with Mary, he started dancing with Billy instead.

The crowd loved it.

SALLY KLEIN: Rosie Baer said you could see it physically, literally dawn on Harry: *After years and years, I've finally found my meal ticket!*

The problem with Harry and Flo was that for thirty years, it was basically two straight men. Well, now they finally had their funnyman.

• • •

RAY FONTANA: Aquilino told my mother he wouldn't give him any more lessons. And this rumor got spread around town that my mother destroyed—that she *ate*—his piano. Now, it is true that he did get a new piano several weeks after the lessons stopped. But that my mom ate it . . . that's just a lie.

CATHERINE RICCI: When Mamma came back from Mr. Aquilino's the last time, she looked really bad. I went to the bathroom door and asked if I could help her but she said no. An hour later she's in the kitchen preparing our dinner. I notice she keeps picking things out of her teeth and throwing them out into the little trash can. They were splinters. She kept taking these white and black splinters out of her mouth.

HUGH BERRIDGE: Our manager Jack Enright phoned one day and said that a fellow named Victor Fontana was calling. The name meant nothing to me, I told Jack. He said that Vic had claimed that we—Teddy Duncan, Rowlie, and myself—had promised to secure a position in the trio for him. Jack was upset. "A trio does not have four people in it, Hugh," he told us, quite unaware in his fit of pique that, yes indeed, not only could I sing but I could count as well.

I told Jack about what had happened in Codport and he told me that he would—the words are his—"lose the wop."

But Victor was not so easy to get rid of.

MAEVE CLARITY [Jack Enright's secretary]: Our office was very small; there was a reception area, which was where I worked, Mr. Enright's office behind me, and there was [his partner] Timothy Flynn's office and a small meeting room. We were on Boylston, only a few streets away from Our Lady of Victories Church, where I would go every day before work and at lunch.

On that fateful day, I was typing up a contract for Mr. Enright and there was a knock at the door. We had one of those doors with a small pane of glass in it—the glass was frosted and you could only see shadows behind it—and our company's name was on the door: FLYNN ENRIGHT ENTERTAINING AGENTS. When I heard the knock I said, "Come in!" but nobody did. I saw a shadow behind the glass and there was another knock. "Come in! The door is open," I said again, very nicely I might add.

Suddenly there was a loud noise, a crash . . . the little window in the door was being smashed in by—I couldn't believe my eyes—it was a rolling pin! Some of the letters on the door were gone and the ones that were left now spelled out FRIGHTENING GENTS.

Then in a flash the entire pane of glass was gone.

It was a short stocky woman dressed completely in black and there was a tall boy maybe eighteen years old . . . his hair looked blue to me under the light and he had clear blue eyes, almost turquoise. There was another man, very short and wiry. I was so scared. I was eighteen years old.

They burst into the reception area and they started jabbering all at once—I couldn't understand what was going on, not one word. When I reached for the phone to call the police, Guy, the short wiry one, yanked the phone out of the wall.

All the time I thought that the lady was going to start clubbing me with the rolling pin.

[They sat] down and waited for Mr. Enright to return from lunch and I kept looking at the clock. Those ticking sounds were sounding very loud, let me tell you. I knew he would be back at 1:30 and he was never late. He was a kind man, he always took care of his family, and he was seldom intoxicated during the day.

At exactly 1:30 he walked in and was about to say, "Maeve, what happened to the glass in the door?" But then he was struck on the head by the rolling pin. They dragged him into his office and closed the door. The short wiry man told me not to get the police. Well, that wasn't going to happen anyway as Victor's mother had used the phone cord to tie me to my chair.

HUGH BERRIDGE: Teddy Duncan and I were going over some charts in our rehearsal space when Jack Enright called. He said, "You know, boys,

I've been giving it a lot of thought. A trio with four people in it is a *capital* idea! Why not give this Fontana lad a shot?" Well, at that second Rowlie walked in, and when we told him about this, he said that if we let Fontana in, he would quit. Rowlie got on the horn and I heard Jack's voice on the other end. Rowlie kept saying "no" and "I don't think so, Jack." Then I heard a woman's voice on the other end—she was rattling away, talking a mile a second, sometimes in English, sometimes in Italian.

Rowlie hung up and said, "You know, perhaps we *could* use a new direction in our sound."

• • •

ARNIE LATCHKEY: Zig related to me that after that first show they went back up to their hotel room. Rosie Baer is in there too with a bottle of champagne and a tray of chopped liver and crackers.

Now Harry and Flo had no idea if Ziggy was gonna do this again. No idea at all. The old man's probably thinking, If the kid don't do this thing again, I'll disown the bastard! So he looks at Zig and says, "Sonny, how would you feel about maybe doing this again?"

"You want me to go onstage again, Poppy?" Zig says.

"Didn't you hear all the people laughing?"

"Yeah sure, I heard," Zig says. "But you were mad at me at first."

"At first, yes," Harry says. "Now, why do you think they were laughing?"

"On account of you and mom and the act?" Playin' real dumb.

My guess is that Rosie Baer is thinking, *Oh, Jesus God, the freckled fat boy isn't gonna do it again.*

Harry says to Zig, "Well, they were also laughing at *you*. They thought you were very funny."

"Me?" Zig says. "They thought I was funny?"

Flo chimes in with her two cents and says, "They thought you were hysterical, Ziggy."

Ziggy puts his shoes up on the coffee table and says, "Did anyone ever say that you was hysterical, Mom?"

Flo says, "To be honest, no . . . nobody has ever said that."

"Did anyone ever say *you* was hysterical, Poppy?" Zig asks.

"No, Ziggy. No one," Harry says. Not an easy thing for a comic to admit.

Ziggy puts his hands behind his head, leans back against the couch, and says to Rosie: "I get fifty-two percent, they split the rest twenty-four/twenty-four. Plus I want an additional ten percent of the take from the box before you take your bite."

"You three split it thirty-three percent down the line and I give you five percent," Rosie says.

"Then you can all go to hell," Ziggy says, "and burn rye toast there."

Rosie says, "Okay, then, have it your way."

And they shook hands all around and in a minute Ziggy was dipping his stubby red fingers into the chopped liver.

SALLY KLEIN: I saw Ziggy in the hotel coffee shop the morning after the first performance. I hugged him—he *was* my cousin after all—and I said, "Congratulations! I'm so happy for you!"

"Little did you know, when I did a number one on your couch pillows where I'd be today, didja?" he said with kind of a twisted smile.

"No. I guess I didn't," I said to him. "I hear you were hilarious."

"Was it hilarious when I wee-wee'd on your father's socks?"

I kept trying to congratulate him but he just wouldn't let me. He kept bringing up other things.

DR. HOWARD BAER: On the poster stand advertising the show, the one that stood in the hotel lobby, Ziggy's picture was up the next day. The next day! There was a black-and-white glossy of the Beaumonts at the top and beneath them it said: "Also appearing, the Blissmans. Plus: Ziggy!" The picture of Harry and Flo was just of them, smiling pleasantly. But Ziggy— his hair was wild, his eyes were crossed and bulging out, and his tongue was sticking out.

If you ask me, Ziggy already had a dozen of these pictures when he checked in.

There was a serious incident very late one night. The house detective told Allie Gluck, who told me. Strange noises were coming from Mary's room—she and Billy didn't sleep in the same room—and the detective was summoned. Ziggy, apparently, had tied Mary's wrists and ankles to the bed using hotel towels, which had a bear logo on them. She was naked and so was Ziggy, who was swaying back and forth in the chandelier over the bed. "The Lord in his mysterious ways," the house dick told Allie, "had blessed this young Hebrew mightily."

Ziggy, Allie was told, merely wanted one kiss from her. That was all.

•   •   •

MAEVE CLARITY: Looking back, I guess I resented that we were now representing a man who had tied me up in my seat and whose mother had threatened to bash my brains in. But I must say, being tied up . . . it was thrilling at the time.

HUGH BERRIDGE: Vic had a pleasant voice; his was a relaxed, ambient timbre, but he was terribly unpolished. It was going to take some time to meld him into our own sound. He was, we also realized, going to stand out on the stage. Our performances were live, in small ballrooms or at social functions, and Rowlie, Teddy Duncan, and I were all on the short side or of average height and had short, straight blond hair (Rowlie had sandy brown hair but after a summer at Newport it would be dirty blond). But Vic was a lot swarthier. And taller. The cut of his clothing was—dare I say it?—gangsterish, and his hair was curly and terribly unruly.

Mr. Enright tried and tried and ultimately got Vic to agree to dye his hair blond for our first performance together.

"Okay, so what do I do?" That's what Vic asked at our first rehearsal. I remember thinking, What you *ought* to do is please comb back your hair, but naturally I did not say that aloud. He'd brought a chum along, that diminutive scrappy fellow named Guy.

Working feverishly, over the course of several weeks we incorporated Victor into the act. I think he and Guy were staying at a hotel near Hanover Street. He was, I must allow, very eager to learn and was quite punctual.

Vern Hapgood was our arranger. He was a New Haven man, had taught choral music there, and had the reputation of being a martinet. He was a perfectionist, yes, but was not ill-tempered.

He ran us through the songs and played the piano. He wasn't happy with Vic—not with his voice, not with the way he looked or his manner, the way he spoke and dressed. There was very little about Vic that he liked.

GUY PUGLIA: The poor kid'd work himself silly with these blue-blood candy asses, day in, day out. But at night, he had stomach cramps real bad. From the worrying. He had the runs and the chills and the sweats. He thought—he said it many times—"I can't cut it, Gaetano. I'm no good." I said to him, "Hang in there, Vic, it'll come. It's just singing." He said, "Uh-uh. I can't do it. I'm out of my element." I says to him, "Hey, what the hell is singing anyways? It's talking but with a melody, right? You can talk, can't you, Vic?" And he'd say, "Yeah, I can talk." But meanwhile he's doubled up with his hands over his guts, shivering and sick.

He dropped about fifteen pounds—he couldn't keep food down, he couldn't keep food up, he couldn't keep it anywheres . . . so why eat? And he didn't.

His mom would call the hotel three or four times a week to check up on us. There was no phone in the room so Vic would have to go to a phone booth out on Salem Street and he'd call her back. She kept telling him to eat, eat, eat. Then she'd put Bruno on the line and Vic'd say, "Hey, Pop," and then you didn't hear nothin' on the other end. Bruno was on the other end and not saying one fuckin' word.

"Okay, Pop, I got you," Vic would say. "Put Mamma back on."

Violetta told me on the phone once: "You take care of my boy."

Well, I wound up doin' that for the next sixty fuckin' years.

CATHERINE RICCI: Mamma sent me up to Boston with a few slabs of veal Milanese and some lasagna, about thirty pounds of food. She said to me, "Make sure it gets into that boy's stomach. And if it don't go down his mouth, you get it into him some other way . . ."

HUGH BERRIDGE: Slowly but surely, he got the hang of it. This was not *Rigoletto,* of course; this was the kind of music the Pied Pipers or the Ink Spots were singing. And he started to fit in. His voice, even Vern admitted it, was malleable. But it was just eating Vic alive at first. "I'm tryin', guys, I'm tryin'," he'd say. He looked sickly at times.

[Vic] had trouble remembering the lyrics. Teddy Duncan—he always thought on his feet—had the clever idea to write the lyrics on Vic's shirtsleeves. So we had Jack Enright's secretary write the lyrics in red ink on the sleeves of his shirts.

Unfortunately we had not noticed how much Victor was sweating.

●　●　●

SALLY KLEIN: You couldn't pay to keep people away. They came from as much as fifty miles away, which in those days was a big deal.

Harry and Flo already had engagements lined up in Camden, Newark, and Buffalo, and Rosie booked them back into the Baer Lodge for after that.

DR. HOWARD BAER: The shows at the Lodge were great. It always started the same, making it look as though Ziggy was interrupting Harry and Flo's show in progress. Ziggy would later tell interviewers that he was the first to introduce the whole Pirandello angle into modern comedy, something about a fourth wall being torn down.

Each night their show got funnier and each night the show got a little longer. He'd really get that audience going when he went into the crowd and sat on laps and starting playing with people's food and drinks and cigarettes.

By the time the Beaumonts came on, the crowd was exhausted. Ziggy had wrung them dry. So the Beaumonts would be dancing but nobody was paying attention. And you know, it was sad. Poor Mary Beaumont was a mess. She was drinking heavily, I heard. And Billy was no help. Neither of them ever knew exactly when Ziggy was going to bounce onstage; sometimes he did it in their first number, sometimes he waited till the end. But those two, they were dancing skittishly, like a guillotine could fall on them any second.

On the last night, it all went wrong. Billy was off, Mary was way, way off. You know how when a figure skater falls and you *cringe?* Imagine twenty minutes of that.

The band was playing *Tales of the Vienna Woods,* I think. This was their closer. And on comes Ziggy.

Well, he didn't come on. What he would do is, he'd clandestinely creep into the pit where the band was and he'd take one of the musicians' instruments. This night it was a trumpet. So while the Beaumonts were waltzing, all of a sudden there was this loud strident noise. The spotlight then caught Ziggy in the pit and he was blowing the horn and his eyes were bulging, completely crossed.

Billy said, "Hi, Ziggy. You're here to interrupt us again?"

Ziggy said, "You two could use an interruptus, it looks like."

Mary said to him, "Well, get on with it then."

Ziggy said something to the effect of "I'd like to waltz with Mary if I could, Billy." And he was sucking his thumb, standing knock-kneed and pigeon-toed like a shy child.

He hopped onto the stage—he was in his baggy red flannel pyjamas. Just the sight of him holding that trumpet, the fifty or so people left in the room were giggling.

"Will you blow my horn, Billy, while I take a spin with the missus?" Ziggy asked him. "You like blowing on things, Billy, that's what your wife told me."

Billy blushed, turned beet red . . . he looked down, stared at his shoes. Ziggy readjusted his pyjama bottoms in a comical way, in preparation to dance with Mary.

"Boys, if you will," Ziggy said, trying to get the band to resume.

"No. No more," Mary said. "No more of this."

"Hey, that's not what you said last night in your room, Mare," Zig said.

"You sick Jewboy," Mary said to him. That's when people knew it wasn't a joke anymore, that it wasn't a routine. There were gasps from every table, from every Jewboy in the place, from ten years old to seventy. "You want to tell people what you were saying when you begged me to kiss you and you were jerking yourself off in my room? Why don't you tell everyone that!"

Well, the lights came down real fast. You can imagine.

Aunt Rosie never booked the Beaumonts after that.

• • •

GUY PUGLIA: After four weeks Vic was sounding just like Crosby, [Bob] Eberly, or Fritz Devane. Jesus, he looked funny in that stupid domino vest. Enright's "girl" had knitted it for him but then he lost all that weight. It was one of those pullover deals, straight out of a Henry Aldrich movie. And it was hanging on him like a collapsed parachute.

He'd started seeing Lulu [Louise Mangiapane] back home—but this was Vic and he could never get enough tail. So I don't think he was missing her too much.

MAEVE CLARITY: The Four Threes Trio was booked into the Lynn Palaestra on Cape Ann for four nights. They would be singing with the Noel Galen Orchestra. The Galen band was opening for the Floyd Lomax Orchestra—Connie Bishop and Dick Fain were their singers then.

Before that, however, Vic had asked me out on a date. I was still living with my father and my brothers Jimmy and Tom. I knew they wouldn't approve of Victor, but . . . well, he and I went to the movies and had dinner a few times and we took walks along the Charles.

Now, I wasn't "that kind of girl." I'd never been out on a date before, never even held a boy's hand. I was very demure. Vic was charming, very funny, but I had to explain many things to him, such as about time zones, what a vice president was, and what kidneys were for. But he caught on quickly to everything.

He had such crazy dreams back then . . . he just used to talk and talk. It's funny to think about it now. We'd be walking along the river and he would tell me he was the next Fritz Devane, how he was going to eventually try out for the Dorsey band or Benny Goodman. Walking around with him, I'd get such looks from the other girls. He was so dark and big and handsome and here I was, this pale skinny Irish girl.

But I think I was letting him down. He once tried to hold my hand and I snatched it away. I was very scared. What if one of my brothers ran into us? A few nights later he tried it again, and again I wouldn't let him do it. So he said, "How's about this instead, Maeve?" and he took my hand and put it on his pants. "Is this any better?" he asked me.

Now I was eighteen and very shy and . . . well, I didn't know much. This was all very new to me. I didn't know anything about boys. So I said,

"Yes, Vic, this is better." Because my hand on his pants seemed a lot cleaner to me than it being in his hand.

"Oh!" he said. His face lit up. "So leave it there."

HUGH BERRIDGE: The first show we did was seamless. Vern Hapgood had drilled us well. Backstage, however, Vic was a mess. Teddy Duncan said he'd seen Vic upchucking on a box of reeds belonging to a tenor sax man from the Floyd Lomax band.

Vic had promised us he'd dye his hair blond or light brown. But he didn't do it. Rowlie was very upset by that and so was I, frankly.

I remember that Jack Enright's secretary had accompanied us up to Lynn. Rowlie really had a case on her, really thought she was quite the dish. Backstage she'd seen how oversized the vest was on Vic and she quickly went about doing some tailoring.

"Let Me Call You Sweetheart" went off without a hitch. We were clicking. But Vic was—as some Mediterranean types are wont to do—he was sweating. The lights were hot, there was no air-conditioning. It was his first time performing. He was sweating profusely.

Oh no! I remember thinking. The lyrics!

By the third song—I believe it was "The Song Is You"—the lyrics were gone. Vic would lift his arm and occasionally snap his fingers just to sneak a look at his sleeves. But by now each of his sleeves had become one long red blotch.

GUY PUGLIA: I'm backstage and this bald guy who plays trombone for the Lomax band is saying, "Hey, someone call a doctor! That guy's arms are bleeding all over!"

[The] girls, though, they ate him up. They wanted to mother him, that's what it was . . . they just wanted to drag him home or into a bush somewheres and adopt him.

"Are his eyes turquoise?" I heard a girl ask another girl. And the second girl said to her, "Eyes? Who's looking at his eyes?"

• • •

ED SMITH: I was the assistant manager of Herbie's Duplex [a nightclub in Camden, New Jersey] right before the war. Herbie was Herb Shipman, who'd been in the record business in New York in the late twenties . . . but the real owners of the joint were the Pompiere crime family. We lined up some good acts but the bigger names in the area would play New York, Philly, Atlantic City, places like the 500 Club, the Hacienda, or the Mosque. We'd book a band or two and some comics. George Simms played the place a few times, Mackie Brine too. And Lenny Pearl. The food? Well, let's just say I always made sure to eat at home before coming to work.

The Blissmans had played the Duplex maybe a year before and had died, just died. But you felt sorry for them—they'd tried hard.

Now, the second time we booked the Blissmans it was to open for the Jorge Estrada Orchestra. There was the whole hot Latin scene going on then; you know, Ray Lopez, Cesar Romero, Carmen Morais, Jose Iturbi—they were coming out of the woodwork. But Jorge Estrada was as Spanish as a bialy—his real name was Joey Eisenberg. He dyed his hair black and he used some lotion on his skin to give it a darker tone.

We got this publicity picture in a few days before the Blissmans came. That was the first time I'd ever seen Ziggy Bliss, I guess. I thought, This kid is *human*? His head was like a scouring pad, like Brillo after cleaning up a big mess of catsup. I showed the photo to Herb and he took a look at it and he just grunted.

I remember, it was Jimmy Canty, he was the road manager for the Jorge Estrada Orchestra. We're going over some business stuff maybe four hours before the first show. And Ziggy Bliss walked in.

Jimmy Canty said to me, "What the hell, Herb's letting baby rhinos into the joint now?"

Ziggy comes over, introduces himself. He told me he wanted the first pick of dressing rooms and Jimmy laughed out loud. I told Ziggy there were only two dressing rooms: "The band gets the bigger one and you and your family get the smaller one, behind the kitchen." Jimmy made a crack, like that'll be enough room 'cause the opening act was a midget act. Ziggy said, "They ain't midgets. They just act like they are."

I say to him, "You're getting the smaller room. Case closed, kid."

Ziggy—this is something I'll take to my grave—looked at Jimmy Canty and said, "You better tell Señor Joey Eisenberg that he better play real, real good *esta noche*. 'Cause we're gonna wipe him off the stage otherwise. Ta, gentlemen."

"Well, that just beats anything I ever stuck my finger in, Eddie," Jimmy said.

Five nights later, we'd reversed the billing. The Estrada band was opening up for Ziggy Bliss and his parents. And you know what? It was Jimmy Canty whose idea it was. 'Cause there wasn't one of the guys in that band who wanted to come on after the Blissmans had torn up the crowd.

And they got the bigger dressing room too.

• • •

HUGH BERRIDGE: By the fourth show at the Lynn Palaestra I really felt that we'd become a trio again. Vic calmed down, he was rolling with us . . . there was a sense of unity in the vocalizations. He'd still perspire—but not as much—and it wasn't until the fifth song of the set that the lyrics became indecipherable.

MAEVE CLARITY: Victor was staying at a small hotel in a town just north of Lynn. Beverly, it was. And I stayed with my father and brothers in South Boston, but each night I came up by train to watch Vic perform. My father was not too pleased with that but Mr. Enright had promised him that it was work-related and that no harm would befall me.

"I'm nervous, baby," Vic would say to me about an hour before he went on. Nobody had ever called me baby before. Or since. It was thrilling.

"There's no reason to be nervous, Victor," I would assure him.

"Make me not nervous, puddin'," he would say. "Come on. Calm me down."

I always felt myself blush when he said that . . . I would get all red and prickly.

Mr. Enright and his partner, Mr. Flynn, had sent me up to Lynn every night to ensure the success of the Four Threes trio. As I wanted to do my job and perform all duties required of me—this *was* the Depression, you must remember, and times were tough for everyone—and as I wanted to satisfy everyone, I did as I was told, and Victor was no longer nervous.

TONY FERRO: The last night he was performing, I drove a bunch of us up there—me, Cathy, Lulu, and Ray—in my old Ford. We were all excited. By then Lulu had a very serious thing for Vic. She had made enough manicotti for an army and was bringing it up for him.

So we pull into Vic's hotel and we're a little early. We climb up the stairs and we open the door to the hallway, right? And from the end of the hallway I heard something. I think I thought someone was moving furniture around. Lulu said, "Some place they got Vic at, huh?"

By now it's clear that it wasn't furniture being moved around. And it was coming from Vic's room.

The door's already open just, like, a slit. I didn't know what to do. I had no idea what it was, right? Then I think it was either Ray or Lu nudged the door open.

The first thing I seen was a naked broad on a bed. This broad was whiter than white by two shades. Like a piece of chalk. And then in the other corner of the room was Vic and Guy, both with just their boxer shorts and socks on. And the two of 'em was kicking some guy in the ribs . . . this blond guy was on the floor and they was kicking him.

The next thing I heard, Lulu had dropped the big vat of manicotti.

Guy came over to the door and says to me, he whispers, "What the fuck you doin' here, Tony?"

I says, "What the fuck are *you* doing?"

Guy says, "It's business . . . something in the group, the trio." He told me I wouldn't understand and then he closed the door.

LULU FOUNTAIN [Vic Fountain's first wife]: Wanna know what I think? I think that Guy and Vic were banging the girl. Is that what the world wants to know? One of the other guys in that trio was seeing her, dating her. He heard them banging her and then tried to play hero. He didn't know she was begging for it from Vic and that Guy was part of the deal. So he tries playing Jack Armstrong and Guy beats the daylights out of him while Vic watches. Happy now?

HUGH BERRIDGE: On the final night at the Lynn Palaestra, there was a most unfortunate mishap. Rowlie—or so he told us—had been playing shuffleboard in Marblehead with some fellow Cantab alums when a boom from a yacht caught a frightful gust of wind and swung toward him. It sounded dreadful, the way he described it to me. Five broken ribs. He was quite shaken.

Suddenly the Four Threes had become the Three Threes again. Now it was just Teddy Duncan, Victor Fontana, and myself.

• • •

SALLY KLEIN: Before the Blissman act left the Lodge, Rosie had a talk with Harry. She and Harry agreed that, with Ziggy now in the act, they might want to consider changing management. Jerome Milton was handling them. He was a real old-timer and was big on long-term deals, contracts for ten years or longer, so Harry told Rosie that getting out of the deal wasn't going to be that easy. But Rosie Baer was a smart cookie.

She called Jerry Milton up and they shot the breeze for ten minutes. And she says, "Miltie, I got some news for you. And I don't know how you're gonna take this. Harry and Flo aren't too happy with the deal." So there's no noise on the phone for a half a minute and Rosie says, "Are you still there?" And Jerry says, "Yeah, still here. They're not happy? Gee, that's too bad." And Rosie tells him—never mentioning Ziggy—that no, they weren't at all happy and they wanted out. And I think she's envisioning lawyers and fees and contracts and all that tsuris when she hears paper being ripped up on the other end.

"Okay, Rosie," Jerome Milton says, "they're out of the deal."

So now Rosie was handling the act. She called up the Bursley-Bates publicity outfit in New York and got some tips from someone there. She gave me $400—the most money I'd ever seen up to then—and told me to travel around with Ziggy, Harry, and Flo, make sure everything was always on the level. "Some of these places," she said, "some of these people . . ." She knew the whole nightclub scene.

She told me to watch out for Ziggy, to keep him out of trouble. Apparently something had happened with Mary Beaumont at the Lodge, but nobody ever told me anything.

I was worried. I think Harry was too. Let's face it: it was wall-to-wall Jew at the Lodge. But now they had to play to *goyim*. I was thinking, If they get so much as a titter out there in *shaygetz*land, it's an act of God.

It didn't take me long to see that there was nothing to worry about. They played Herbie's Duplex in Jersey and the only word that comes to mind is "electric."

ED SMITH: I was closing up [Herbie's Duplex] and it was dark—all the chairs were up on the tables—and I was counting the take. Out of the bathroom comes Jimmy Canty. It was customary for a band's road manager to be the last guy out of the joint. He pours himself a shot of something and I probably had a drink too. It's maybe two or three in the morning now.

I offered to drop him at the Statler, where the band was staying. I locked up the place and we're about to pile into my car when Jimmy gets sprayed all over with something. Seltzer it was, coming from one of those old bottles with the nozzle. We looked up 'cause we could tell it was coming from the roof. But we didn't see anybody.

We get into my car and we drive a block and I smell something. And Jimmy smells it too.

There was urine in that bottle. It was piss mixed up with the seltzer.

Jimmy didn't ever figure out who it was. He didn't put two and two together.

I did but I kept my mouth shut. Until now.

• • •

HUGH BERRIDGE: "I guess the trio's down to three, huh, guys?" Vic said in the rehearsal studio. He was drinking coffee and smoking a Chesterfield.

The weekend after the Lynn shows we had our first radio appearance. It was *The Cecil Newcombe Newcomer E-Z Oil Hour*. Nobody remembers Newcombe nowadays; he was one of those amateur-hour hosts such as Major Bowes or, later on television, Ted Mack. Several noteworthy performers got their start with Cecil Newcombe, whose show was sponsored by a lubricating company, E-Z Oil. Jerry Talbot, the comic, and Peggy Clements, "the Twangy Torch from Tyler, Texas," were Newcombe Newcomers, and so was Sasha Deckel, the violinist.

Vern worked us particularly hard that week. He told us that a live show, such as the one we'd performed in Lynn, though it was important, was ultimately ephemeral, but that a radio show was something for posterity. I remember Vic asking me what "ephemeral" and "posterity" meant.

GUY PUGLIA: Happynuts—that's what we called the arranger—was really giving Vic the business. Yellin', screamin', stompin' his foot down. See, on account of that, uh, "shuffleboard" accident I did, they was down to three singers and had to kind of readapt their sound.

I remember Vic saying to Vern Happynuts, "So, uh, why aren't I featured more?" He just out-and-out asked. Well, you could tell this went over like a belch at a funeral. They just looked at each other and didn't say nothing.

So I piped in. I says, "Yeah. Why not?"

Happynuts said that this was something that'd have to be okayed with Mr. Enright—and then he tried to pull a fast one on Vic. Quickly he says something like, "Okay, from the top, one-two-three." But I was wise to it . . . I says, "Whoa! Hold your horsies, pal. If this is something that's gotta be okayed with Enright, *then why don't we okay it with Enright? Like, right now.*"

I picked up the phone and Happynuts—he's maybe five foot four, about two inches taller than me—he walks over to me and I dialed the phone number for him, just in case he tried to pull another fast one on me.

I was looking out for Vic . . . that's what I always did.

MAEVE CLARITY: I picked up the phone in the office. Mr. Enright and Mr. Flynn were out at that moment celebrating the fact that the windowpane in the door had been repaired.

It was Mr. Hapgood on the other end.

He said that it had dawned on him and on the trio too that, what with Rowland Toomey having quit the group so abruptly, why not feature Victor more prominently? And it made perfect sense. Furthermore, as Victor had been perspiring less, his command of the material was becoming more mature. At one point in the conversation it seemed that somebody was telling him something and that perhaps Mr. Hapgood had stubbed his toe violently.

Well, I did something that to this day I'm not particularly fond of, seeing as I was brought up by my father and by the nuns at school to never lie.

I told Vern Hapgood to wait. And I kept him waiting for about two minutes. I filed my nails and counted to sixty. And then—oh, I still get embarrassed thinking about it—I got back on and told him that Jack Enright had thought it "a brilliant idea."

When I did that I felt so—I don't know. I got a squishy feeling all over.

GUY PUGLIA: We rigged it up with the Irish broad in the office. The whole thing. And if she didn't go for it—and believe me, she went for it—then Enright would've gone for it. I would have seen to that.

ARNIE LATCHKEY: If you couldn't make it as an amateur on the Major Bowes show, then there was the next level down; that was *The Owen Atkins Spotlight*, brought to you by some Martinizing outfit. Now if you were so lousy that you couldn't do Owen Atkins, the next rung down the ladder was doing a show in your living room with two Dixie cups and a string. And below *that*—twenty rungs down this ladder—was Cecil Newcombe's Newcomers. The man once had three Portuguese jugglers go on and do a four-minute bit and this was on the radio! All you heard were bowling pins dropping.

HUGH BERRIDGE: I had never been on the radio before. Neither had Teddy. This was something new and exciting for us, a dream come true. We had a week to polish ourselves, to get our act down pat. Victor was now the featured singer and Teddy Duncan and I were moved to the background. Looking back from a remove of some six decades, it makes sense. But Teddy was very upset at the time. Vern tried to placate him and I told Ted, "We really ought to do what Mr. Enright asks of us."

The show was on a Sunday night . . . we'd been booked into the Newburyport Lounge, a rather smallish nightclub near New Hampshire. We would do two songs and then Mr. Newcombe would chat with us for a minute.

GUY PUGLIA: Happynuts was going to drive us to that club where the radio show was; he was gonna take Vic and the other two guys.

The Irish broad pops in just when we're all about to leave.

What an operator she was.

MAEVE CLARITY: I offered to drive Teddy Duncan, Victor, and Guy to the Newburyport Lounge because I felt that . . . well, it was raining that night and Mr. Enright did not like all the boys traveling in one car, particularly Vern Hapgood's, which was really some old crate.

The rain had become torrential and I was never so frightened in all my life.

Ted Duncan . . . he was the life of the party. The other boy, Rowland, he used to bother me; somehow he'd gotten into his head that I was his girl. But I was no such thing. But as for Mr. Duncan . . . there never would have been a trio if it hadn't been for him.

He was sitting in the back with Guy. We hit a puddle near a sign . . . then that terrible noise . . . Teddy Duncan went right through the window and there was glass all over his head.

I stopped the car and Victor said, "We're supposed to be at the Lounge in five minutes."

I saw a house, a two-story home, and there were lights on. I told Victor and Guy that I had no idea where a hospital was and that they had to be at the nightclub now in *four* minutes. Mr. Duncan's forehead was bleeding . . . I said that whoever lived in that two-story home would have to summon a doctor.

Guy got out of the car and—I guess in the accident the door had broken because he couldn't open the door—he pulled Ted Duncan out right through the window. This was much harder than it sounds because all the glass was broken and a lot of the glass was scraping his skin as he was being wriggled through it.

Then Guy and Vic helped Teddy up the pathway to this house.

I checked my watch and called out, "Two minutes, boys!"

It was still raining out and very dark and I lost sight of them. And they were only maybe fifteen yards away. I heard a noise . . . it was the thud of the people opening the front door. And then a few seconds later Victor and Guy emerged from the rain and fog and were back in the car.

I felt just like a bandit, like Bonnie Parker or Ma Barker. Because I really "stepped on it," as they say, and we made it to the Newburyport Lounge with about thirty seconds to spare.

HUGH BERRIDGE: Backstage I pulled Jack Enright's secretary aside immediately. "Where's Teddy?" I demanded of the girl. I have to tell you: months before when I'd met her in Jack Enright's office . . . she would chase Rowlie around, wait for him outside his house at all hours of the night, had somehow got into her head that he was going to marry her. But in these last few weeks she'd really fallen into disfavor.

"Teddy just quit," she told me.

I looked around. Vic had slipped his vest on. A clarinetist was licking his reed, the tenor saxophonist was screwing the mouthpiece in. I noticed something about Vic's vest. Instead of there being three domino pips on it, now there were only two.

"He quit?" I asked the girl, understandably incredulous.

"Here," she said. "Slip it on quick." And she handed me a new vest, also suddenly with but two pips on it.

Good God, it was all a devious scheme!

"We got a minute before we're on, Hugo," Vic said to me. "I think some polo horse may have kicked Duncan in the head. It's too bad."

Hugo. He'd forgotten my name.

Quickly, I had two belts of scotch—one for Rowlie, one for Teddy—and then a third, for all of Humanity itself. And I joined Vic onstage.

RAY FONTANA: Cecil Newcombe comes on the radio and says something like this: "Folks, we were supposed to have an exciting new trio, the Three Threes, sing tonight, but I'm afraid we have some news . . ."

Sal and Tony [Fontana] and Pop had to restrain Mom. You know how those old-time radios, they had cloth covering the grille? Where the noise comes out? When my mother hears Newcombe say he's afraid he has some news, she starts clawing the cloth off the grille . . . it was confetti in three seconds. She's yelling, "I'll kill you!" and I asked Cathy, "*Who's* she gonna kill?" but then I remembered that Mamma always thought the tubes inside the thing were little men.

But the news was just that the Three Threes were now the Two Threes.

CATHERINE RICCI: They sang three songs and then Cecil Newcombe interviewed them. When we heard Vic talking on the radio it was just amazing. It was the first time Papa ever really paid attention to the radio other than to shut it off or listen to Mussolini or *NBC Symphony*. He was so proud.

Cecil Newcombe asked Vic about the group and then that man Hugh started to say something, but Vic jumped in and explained how they'd gotten together. The audience chuckled when Vic spoke . . . not just 'cause Vic was funny but because he was funny-sounding. They'd never heard the son of a fisherman talk before, I guess. Newcombe asked another question and Hugh began to answer it and then Vic interrupted again and he got more laughs. But this time because he *was* funny! Cecil Newcombe asked why [Ted Duncan] had quit the group and Vic said he'd had a croquet accident. Except he pronounced it "croquette." Newcombe asked what the future held for these two young singers. Vic told him that a nightclub act was ephemeral but that being on the radio was really for posterity.

Mamma was in tears. Papa was smiling but also crying.

• • •

SALLY KLEIN: We took a bus from Camden to Trenton and then from Trenton to New York. They had a two-day break before an engagement in Buffalo and wanted to spend some time at home.

I had dinner at home with Harry and Flo. Ziggy went out . . . he didn't tell us he was going anywhere, he just went. And he didn't come back until the next morning.

I was asleep when he came in, asleep on the couch in the living room. It was maybe eight in the morning and he looked like hell.

I said, "Where've you been? Is everything okay?"

"No, Sal," he said, "everything is *not* okay . . ."

Well, he'd done a few things. He went to Jerome Milton's office and demanded to look at the contract that Milton had with Harry and Flo. When Milton told him he'd ripped the paperwork up, Ziggy went nuts and grabbed Milton by the collar. Now, I know Ziggy was only eighteen years old and on the fat side but he was always very strong. He was *much* stronger than Vic Fountain and that's a fact. Vic never got in a fistfight in his entire life unless he had Guy Puglia, Hunny Gannett, or Ices Andy around.

I asked Ziggy, "Why do you care so much about the paperwork? You should be glad Milton ripped it up."

"I just wanted to make sure he ripped it up, Sal," he told me with that mischievous baby grin he had. You know, smiling with one corner of his mouth.

He had turned over file cabinets, flung open every drawer in the office, just to make sure.

"I asked one of the girls in the office to have dinner wit' me," he said. "And she said no dice."

I told him, "Well, you'd just ransacked their office and made a spectacle of yourself! Do you think that's the way to make a nice impression?"

He didn't hear me. Some things filtered in but if he didn't want to hear something, it went straight in the other direction.

He told me that after leaving the Milton office he made a few rounds. He went to the Bursley-Bates publicity agency and met some people, including [publicist] Bertie Kahn. Then he went to a bunch of newspapers. He demanded to see Walter Winchell, he demanded to see Westbrook Pegler, he wanted to see Grayling Greene and Lee Mortimer and Bud Hatch. All the *ganzer machers* on Broadway and in gossip. He wanted to spread the word around, tell them he was going to play Buffalo in a few days.

"I just cannot see," I told him, "Grayling Greene or Westbrook Pegler getting on a train to Buffalo to see the Blissmans!"

"Get out, Sal," he said.

I didn't think he was serious and so I didn't budge.

He yelled at the top of his lungs. "Get the hell outta my house!"

Harry and Flo ran out of the bedroom. They were in—they had to wear kiddie pajamas because that was the only clothing that would fit them.

"Ziggy! Why are you yelling at your cousin?" Flo asked him.

Ziggy said to her, "Don't you ever raise your voice at me."

"I will raise my voice as loud as I want to," she said back. Which, believe me, was a frightening proposition . . . I started thinking, Uh-oh, I might have to get a new pair of glasses.

Harry said, "Can we all go back to sleep here?"

And then Ziggy really let them have it. He shouted and shouted, he called them every name in the book. He called them "old vaudeville midgets." He said he was ashamed to know them. He said one day he was going to sleep with Betty Grable, Rita Hayworth, Hedy Lamarr, and Myrna Loy. I remember Harry saying, "What the hell's Myrna Loy doing on that list?" Ziggy just cursed them out some more.

I tried to tell myself, Okay, he's eighteen years old, he's talking about conquering the world. But he's also Cousin Ziggy. Years and years later [husband] Jack said to me that the child part of him which should have been underdeveloped was overdeveloped, and the adult part of him which should have been overdeveloped had never developed at all. So he was way, way off-kilter.

I was young too, so I don't know if I realized it then . . . that Ziggy was lonely, he was very, very lonely. He absolutely *craved* love. And attention, which he often mistook for love. He never had much of either when he was a baby or a child. He just wanted to be loved. And here he was, alienating the only two people who cared about him.

Aunt Florence was weeping and Harry had to hold her up.

"Look what you did to your mother!" Harry said. "Look what you did!"

Ziggy stormed out.

"What did we do so wrong?" Flo was asking Harry.

He shook his head and muttered something I didn't understand: "That goddamn magician."

DICK HARVEY [assistant manager at the Erie Lounge]: The week before the Blissmans played Buffalo, Dick Fain and Connie Bishop had performed with the Floyd Lomax band. We'd had a hard time of it, those of us working there, because Mr. Fain was not easy to deal with. Ever try and stop a guy from sticking his finger in a wall socket? People used to call him the Prince of Pain.

The Blissmans had performed at the club before and hadn't done too well. But now with this fat kid with the crazy red hair, they really had a strong show.

Their final night was the broadcast night. The Blissmans were opening for the Dick Saxon Orchestra. There were some reporters, entertainment reporters from the local papers, there that night.

The first few nights Ziggy had gone into the audience and done some gags—but on *this* night? It was as if his life depended on it. The house was in stitches. He even got a bunch of waiters and busboys involved! It was hilarious.

The mother sang a song at the end. Someone from the radio station had to put up a screen in front of the mike so people at home wouldn't have their fine china busted. In the club, people's ears were ringing. Then everybody thought the show was over and the lights came up. The radio announcer was about to go to a commercial and all of a sudden Ziggy was back on the stage.

He wrested the mike away from the announcer and started talking about his parents. He said that though they were short of stature, they were giants where it counted, in their hearts. They'd risen up from nothing, from nowhere, he said, they'd done vaudeville and burlesque and eaten cold soup and stayed in hotels that no rat should ever be caught dead in.

He was almost weeping. His parents were right next to him.

An hour later Ziggy came out of the dressing room. He goes over to Bud Hatch, the old *Globe* columnist, and says to him, "I hope you newspaper guys got all that Mommy and Poppy stuff."

• • •

HUGH BERRIDGE: We got back to Boston and everything started happening so quickly. Jack Enright's secretary called to say that Jack had lined up a few more engagements. There was one in Boston and one as far away as Camden, New Jersey, opening up for Floyd Lomax's band.

But then it all fell apart.

Vic and I had a rehearsal at the studio. We waited outside in the corridor but Vern didn't show up. Vic forced open the door. Nobody was there. More startlingly, neither was Vern's piano. From what I understand, both had abruptly moved to Texarkana, Texas.

Several days after that, I made a decision that I have not regretted for a single day: I retired as a vocalist. I devoted myself to the law and time has proved that this was the smart thing to do. For I'd come to feel that being an entertainer was not advantageous to my health. I feared, I admit, waking up one morning with a badminton shuttlecock embedded in my midbrain.

MAEVE CLARITY: I showed up one morning at the office and let myself in. I sat at my desk, put on some lipstick, and waited for Mr. Enright and Mr. Flynn to show up.

At about noon I started getting worried. I went into Mr. Enright's office and saw that the room was stripped bare, no desk, no chairs, not even a lightbulb. It was the same with Mr. Flynn's office.

I went home and the next morning it was the same thing, except now my desk and phone were gone.

I came in for two weeks more but Mr. Enright and Mr. Flynn never showed up. I tried calling them at home, but their numbers had been disconnected. I gave up on my job there and started working at Filene's. The next time I heard of Victor Fontana he was Vic Fountain and was performing with Ziggy Bliss.

Years later in the fifties, I ran into Mr. Flynn in a tavern in South Boston. When he saw me coming toward him, he quickly drained his glass and ran out of the place.

• • •

ARNIE LATCHKEY: It's funny the way things work out. Murray Katz at WAT [Worldwide American Talent agency] was doing the bookings for the Floyd Lomax Orchestra. The Lomax band had played Camden the week before Ziggy and his tiny parents performed there. If Murray had booked us in one week later—*one week!*—Vic and I and Zig would have met then and who knows what would've happened? It really does makes you dwell on kismet.

Entertainment is in my blood.

This goes back years and years, to the old country, and if you think I mean France, what UFO did you just desaucer from, my friend? My grandparents on one side used to make woodwinds back in Poland or Russia or Moldavia or somewhere, and on my father's side my grandparents would take the guts out of cats, sheep, and cows and turn them into strings for violins and cellos. You ever wonder, Hey, who the hell is so desperate for money that they turn animal guts into strings? Well, now you know. That's what they did, when the czar and czarina and their henchmen on horseback weren't too busy taking a Zippo lighter to their hovels, might I add?

So they came over in a boat and believe me, they weren't playing shuffleboard in beaver coats and drinking brandy out of gold flasks on the poop deck of the *Mayflower*. They came over on a vermin-infested tub and settled in the Bronx and they didn't miss a beat; it was violin strings again. One thing about a poor neighborhood, no matter where it is: lots of stray cats. Now, when some people look at a stray cat, they see a pet. My family sees one, they hear Brahms.

My mother sewed costumes for the old Yiddish theater big shots downtown, people like Luther Adler and Robert Weitz, Morris Carnovsky, Lionel Gostin, and the great Zelda Gutterman, the "Sarah Bernhardt of

Second Avenue." These were important people, noble, respectable, almost *regal* people . . . *and they spat on her!* Never a penny in tips or a kind word, those lousy *momzers*. And her sister, my Aunt Ruthie, she played the organ at the Orpheum on Gun Hill Road, for the silent pictures. They had it all mechanically rigged up: the lights darken, the organ and Aunt Ruthie slowly rise out of the floor and she starts playing; when the picture is over she slowly sinks back into the floor. Well, one day—it was the day before *The Jazz Singer* opened—she sank back down into the floor and nobody ever saw her again. It was the end of the Silent Era and the end of Aunt Ruthie too.

My father, Hyman Latchkey, started a music and record store with his brother-in-law Sy Lowe, and if you think they had enough business savvy to call the store Hy's and Lowe's, then think again. Not even Hy and Sy's they could come up with. No. There was a sign above the door and it said MUSIC STORE. They sold sheet music and 78s and worked seven days a week and had nothing to show for it. Did they ever complain? Did you ever once hear them gripe or curse their fate? Yes. They did. All the time.

My older brother Marvin was a concierge at Heine's [Resort] in Loch Sheldrake and got me a job as a *tummler* in the Catskills one summer when I was about sixteen. I was a very klutzy busboy by night and by day I'd run Simon Says games or I was a lobby comedian in a bellhop's suit. An insult comic, like Rickles or Jack E. Leonard. But I didn't have the finesse for it. I'd stop people and say, "May I take your luggage? Your wife has the face of a horse." I got in trouble when I pinched some fourteen-year-old girl's cheek and said to her father, "She's gonna break a lot of hearts in a few years but I'd like to have sex with her right now." So I was fired, but whether it was 'cause I wasn't funny or 'cause I broke a lot of dishes, I don't remember.

All I know is this: Marvin—he ran dice games up there too—got a girl in trouble. A seventeen-year-old, the daughter of a rich family staying at Heine's. I make a couple of calls to New York and we get this girl taken care of. I saved my brother's neck.

"I owe you one," Marvin told me as I was getting on the bus to go back to New York after I was fired.

"You sure do," I said to him. "Big time. And I ain't forgetting it."

Slow dissolve. Manhattan. I start working at the [music] store, sweeping up, doing inventory, and occasionally stealing a few *centavos* from the cash register. Well, I might not have been the brightest stripling on the Great White Way but I knew I didn't want to work in that crummy store the rest of my life. I wanted out. So I turned on that irresistible, infectious Latchkey charm and wheedled my way into the hearts and minds of some of these Broadway big shots. Irving Berlin. I met Irving Berlin a few times.

A doll. I hit him up for three bucks once and he gave it to me and said, "Kid, here. I don't wanna see you again." So I go back the next day and asked for four. Didn't get it. Gershwin? Cohan? The Schuberts? Jerry Kern? I met 'em all. Larry [Lorenz] Hart? Great lyricist. Lousy tipper. Cole Porter once was signing something for me at the Waldorf Towers and with the other hand he tried to put his hand on my fanny—I shooed it away like you would a butterfly.

My old man, he fired me from the store. There was a minor discrepancy problem with the inventory. And I was the fall guy and rightly so.

So now it's time to take advantage of some of my contacts. Murray Katz, who years later was Executive VP in Charge of Doing Very Little at Worldwide American, takes me under his somewhat foul-smelling wing and before you know it, I'm twenty years old and I'm the road manager of the Floyd Lomax Orchestra.

If I don't take that Lomax job then I don't manage Fountain and Bliss. Kismet again.

Floyd says to me on my very first day on the job: "Latch, this job is about reeds, reefers, and roast beef sandwiches." Had he told me I'd be reaming out spit valves too, I might not have taken the job. That and running girls in and out of hotels. Well, to tell you truthfully, he did mention the latter and that's why I leapt at the opportunity.

[Looking at photograph of the Floyd Lomax Orchestra, taken at the Luxor Ballroom, White Plains, New York, 1938.] Okay, let's start here. This pianist . . . look real close . . . that's Larry and Stu Morrell, the Siamese twin pianists. Larry was actually the real musician of the two; Stu just played along with their left hand. He was a real highbrow, read tomes the size of train cars. Their deal was, Larry would be in the band for two years and then Stu would teach philosophy for two years while Larry hung on. I once said to him, "You know, you're the only sideman who *has* a sideman." Yeah, it was some outfit.

This fellow is Mr. Harry Bacon, he blew alto sax for us. Does he look strange? A little . . . *different*? No? Well, nobody else thought so either. But one day it turns out that Mister Harry Bacon is actually *Miss* Harriet Bacon. *Nobody ever knew!* For years that dyke traveled around with us, nobody knew. She'd pal around with us, smoke cigars, and go to the track and chase tail just like the rest of the boys. And she was married too! Figure that out. Had a wife out on the island, in Bay Shore. We were all completely fooled. It all came out one day when Roy Lindell, one of our horn men and a big bowl of fruit salad, had a few too many one night in Baltimore and he came on to Harry. They started wrestling and roughhousing and the guys are standing around in a circle, cheering them on—this is in a parking lot, I think it was at the old Hippodrome—and Roy's now got

Harry Bacon's pants down and then he pulls his boxers off. Well, the applauding stopped on a dime, believe you me. I say, "Gee, Harry, uh, you're hung like a tick." "I ain't hung at all," Harry says. "I'm a broad. Get a load of this . . ." And then she unbuttons her shirt. We were all of us, to a man, astounded. Harry stands up and says, "You tell my wife about this, I'll cut yours off too." And after that, she was just one of the guys.

But poor Roy, when he got an eyeful of that crotch or lack thereof—the fact that he'd made a pass *at a broad!*—it really sickened him.

This guy over here, behind Harry . . . Sid Gibson . . . he blew tenor sax. A hophead. This bald head belongs to our trombonist, Cueball Swenson . . . he did a couple of years for something but he straightened out his act somewhat. This is the guitarist, Pip Grundy. Look at his hands. Seven fingers on his left hand, about nine on his right. Anne Boleyn with a gee-tar. I tell you, the Pipster didn't always hit the right note but he could hit more wrong ones *at one time* than any other guitarist around at that time.

And this is Floyd Lomax. Looks just like Humpty Dumpty, don't he? He was from some town outside Detroit, he played trumpet. Kept a pearl-handled Colt in his trumpet case for absolutely no reason whatsoever. Ypsilanti, that's it. Six foot seven, weighed 350 pounds jaybird naked. Could he eat? He'd down more sausages in one meal than Warsaw does in a year. And the man loved cooze. Craved it. If he couldn't score it was a nightmare—he'd just break down and cry his fat heart out, Floyd would. You ever see a six-foot-seven, 350-pound whale in boxer shorts holding a trumpet and weeping like his puppy just got run over by the ice-cream truck? Christ, on all his undershorts he had sewn in gold threads—and you could've moved a family of ten into Floyd Lomax's boxers—the words "'Tis all pink on the inside."

The kind of music they played . . . Floyd was aiming for the High Society sound, sort of like Eddie Duchin or Griff Williams; it all sounded like you'd just chowed down on a Vassar sophomore, which are Floyd's words, not mine. Now, we knew we could never crack that market. It just wasn't gonna happen. So we aimed lower, a lot lower. *Billboard* even called it "the Low Society sound."

We'd play a set and then we go back to our hotel and Floyd gets his fix of you-know-what, and I got to make sure that [vocalist] Dick Fain is all tied up in his bed with manacles so he don't electrocute himself, and the boys are playing pinochle and drinking and just playing their horns . . . and that's what we did. It was a hard life, it didn't pay too good, the hours were lousy as hell, but, boy, did we have a ball.

• • •

SALLY KLEIN: It was at the Mohican Club in Teaneck when Ziggy broke the news to us. Harry and Flo and I were in the dressing room and Ziggy walked in. He pulled a chair up, loosened his tie. It was a jokey tie, orange and a yard wide.

"I been thinkin' about the act," he said. He's got that impish face on—you've seen it a million times in the movies—what Arnie called his "Uh-oh, I think I may have driven your Mercedes off a cliff" look.

Harry asked him, "What about the act?"

Ziggy just comes out and says, "I think Flo should cut a song or two from the act, maybe drop the number at the end."

Now, I'd sensed this coming. Because Flo always ended with a song and Ziggy was always interrupting it. But for the last couple of shows he was barely allowing her to begin it. The act ended with Ziggy being Ziggy and the audience loving it.

Flo said, "You want me not to sing? This is what my son is telling me?"

"This is what I'm telling you, Flo," Zig said. By now he didn't call them Pop or Mom anymore except when they were onstage.

"But I got my start singing," Flo says to him. "That's how your father and I got started."

"Look, if it was up to me, you'd belt out thirty songs up there. And there wouldn't be an ashtray or a pair of eyeglasses intact within a hundred miles. But this is business."

Harry said, "I think this is something your mother and I should talk about."

And Zig said, "Okay. Then talk about it." And he—knowing quite well that Harry had meant talking about it *alone*, in private—just leaned back in his chair.

Flo turned to Harry and said, "All right, Harry, all right. No more singing then. Fine."

Harry said to her, "You sure, darling?"

She nodded and Ziggy said, "I'm glad you seen it my way," and then walked out.

When he left the room, it was like Himmler had just left after an interrogation. We could breathe again.

"Uncle Harry," I said, "are you sure you just did the right thing?"

He said, "The right thing? No. The *right* thing would be to ship him off to a nuthouse, that would be the right thing. What we just did, Sally, was make sure we have our next few meals and a roof over our heads and can afford to be buried properly. *Which might be any day now!*"

SNUFFY DUBIN [comedian]: I was offered the emcee's job at the Mohican Club and I grabbed it. It was a good house, two hundred seats and the three b's: bands, booze, and broads. Johnny Nelson's band was the house band, Tina Mitchell sang for them, and Benny Lampone was the owner on paper. But Big Al Pompiere and a few other Jersey characters were the real owners.

I met Ziggy at the Mohican and, man, we just *clicked*. Same age, same backgrounds—him from New York and me from Chicago—we grew up poor and my father was in show business too. He was a cantor—Pavarotti with *payess*, no shit. Ziggy and me were friends, but there was a mutual jealousy thing maybe too: you know, he was a performer already and was flat-out hilarious and he just destroyed people up there, so yeah, I envied that, sure. He was a comic genius, even at that age. See, some people, some comedians, they just have that raw comic instinct. They're born with it. Me, I had to work and work and teach myself that instinct.

But, yeah, jealousy. I was—back then, at least—a slim guy and there were girls around, and I went out and had a good time. I don't think that Ziggy had even kissed a girl yet.

Well, we fixed that.

Zig and I are hangin' at the bar one night and it's me, him, and this col-ored cat named Jimmy Powell. He cleaned up for us but let me tell you, that man could dress. Silk and satin all over the place and the fucking shiniest white shoes you ever saw, a real hepcat, and where he got the money for his threads . . . well, who knew?

It's way after hours and me and Zig are telling jokes and shooting the shit and the subject gets onto girls. As in, where do you get one in this town?

I told him, "Ziggy, it's four in the A.M.—any girl you get right now, you don't *wanna* get."

"Oh yeah?" he says. "Then where is she?"

He looks down at the floor and that's when I realize, hey, this guy's never been within one foot of a broad. I call Jimmy Powell over. He's maybe forty-five years old and as skinny as a sewing needle.

We piled into my Hudson Essex Terraplane and Jimmy tells us where to go.

We ended up in Newark. It was really dark out, I remember that, and it's this neighborhood, warehouses and factories and not a soul on the street.

We get out of the car and walk into this building, like a three-story townhouse. It's a bordello. Big surprise, right? Well, it *was* a surprise because this was no rundown dingy whorehouse, this was a very, very flashy joint. Velvet all over the place, velvet curtains and rugs from Afghanistan or Persia, moldings in the wall, sconces and candelabras and gold lamps and furniture from eighteenth-century France.

There's a living room and it's wall-to-wall red velvet in there and there's about nine, ten chicks in it. Some of 'em, they're pretty—and I don't just mean pretty for Newark at four in the morning. And they had the works on: pearl necklaces, merry widows, garters, the whole kit and caboodle.

Zig says to me, "You wanna go first, Snuffy?"

I tell him I think I'll pass.

"What about you, Jimmy?" he asks, and Jimmy Powell passed too.

I say to him, "Why don't you just do the job, Zig? It's late."

So Ziggy paces up and down, gets an eyeful of these whores. And he went for the ugly duckling—he picked the ugliest one of them; this girl's flab had flab. They climbed the stairs and then me and Jimmy Powell waited on the couch and the chicks slowly filed out and went back to their knitting, working with the handicapped, and Bible study.

"Snuffy," Jimmy said, "I don't think that boy's gonna know where to poke his stick."

"Jimmy, if he can't figure it out, then you're going up there and telling him," I say.

Two minutes later the broad who's runnin' the joint is flying down the stairs. A big gutsy blonde, like Dorothy Malone in her prime plus thirty pounds. And she's runnin' down the stairs and it's some big emergency.

Jimmy Powell asks her, "Alice, what's going on?"

"He's stuck," Alice says. "The fat boy is stuck."

I'll never forget that. It's one of those things you hear and it just stays with you. The fat boy is stuck. That's what you should call *The Ziggy Bliss Story*, Ted. *The Fat Boy Is Stuck*.

Me and Jimmy run up the spiral stairs to the third floor. The pole that goes up the stairs, the newel? This thing was 100 percent pure marble and there were little carvings of naked broads with long tresses in it with serpents all around 'em, like from Greek myths. Alice is running behind us and she tells us room number seven. So me and Jimmy open the door to room number seven.

The very first thing I see is Ziggy's big ass. This big red medicine ball and it's shakin' like raspberry Jell-O in a hurricane.

"Is that you, Snuffy?" he asks me.

I tell him, Yeah it's me, and that Jimmy Powell's here too.

"I can't get out, Snuff. I'm, like, *lodged*."

"Goddamn, man," Jimmy Powell whispers to me.

Alice asks the girl underneath Zig if she can breathe, and she says, yeah, she can breathe but not really too good.

Alice tells me and Jimmy to get Zig out of there. I say to her, *"What do we do, call the fucking fire department for this?!"* I mean, Jesus Christ . . .

"We could try just givin' him the heave-ho," Jimmy says.

And that's what we did . . . I take one leg and Jimmy Powell takes the other and we tried to dislodge him. But there was no give . . . it wasn't working. And we were really trying too—we rolled up our sleeves and planted our feet and did it on the count of three. But no dice. And then Alice gets all the other girls and now you've got me and Jimmy and ten hookers and we're tugging on Ziggy's arms and feet and there's just no way to extricate him. And now, hey, the idea of calling the fire department isn't really too outlandish all of a sudden.

"I got an idea," Jimmy Powell says, and before you know it we're all tying velvet curtains and bedsheets together. Yankee ingenuity at its finest. Jimmy flings this makeshift rope of curtains and sheets out the window, and then me and him go downstairs to my Terraplane. We tie one end of the rope thing to the rear fender, and upstairs Alice and her harem tie the other end around Ziggy's waist.

We're in the car and I start it up and press down on the accelerator. We don't move. I'm really gunnin' it and the wheels are spinning and we're kickin' up dust. Finally I just floor the sonuvabitch and—my hand to God—from upstairs in that house I hear a sound like a fifty-gallon bottle of champagne being popped open. *POP!!!* And me and Jimmy Powell look back up and, Jesus Christ, my Hudson damn near pulled Ziggy Blissman straight out the window too.

We go back upstairs and the poor kid—I mean, it's his first time with a girl and there's ten people standing around him and he's naked and all red and everything—he's shaking and almost in tears. I got an eyeful of Ziggy's *shvantz*, I couldn't believe it . . . it was like a goddamn baseball bat. Which was, I guess, the problem to begin with.

So he gets dressed now and me and him and Jimmy Powell and Alice are at the front door and the sun is coming up over Newark.

And this, I'll never forget. We're about to leave and Jimmy Powell reaches into his pants and pulls out a wad of bills and hands about fifty bucks to Alice and tells her to take good care of the girl. And then he looks at me and says, "That fat boy don't ever come to this house again, you understand?!"

So I guess Jimmy Powell was runnin' the joint, which is how he had all them fine threads.

● ● ●

GUY PUGLIA: The band finked out on us too. Vic and me, we tried to round 'em all up. But it was funny how they was all "out" that day. I called the trumpeter and his wife tells me, "His brother in Omaha died. He's in Omaha." I called the trombone fella and his wife says, "Oh, *his* brother in Omaha died today too." Three dead brothers in Omaha later, we get the message. Vic had no band.

One day at a Red Sox game, Vic says to me, "So we gotta go back to Codport, huh?"

"And what are we gonna do in Codport?" I ask him.

"I guess we tote fish," he answers.

"You wanna tote fish, Vic? Is that what you wanna do?"

So that night we hopped a Greyhound to New York.

I had a cousin, Gino Puccio—he worked the desk at the old Monroe Hotel on Forty-ninth, just off Broadway. The Monroe at this time was on its way down. And it didn't have too far to go either 'cause I don't think it had ever had its way up.

KATHY PUCCIO [wife of Guy Puglia's cousin]: One night we're having dinner at our house [in Long Beach, Long Island], Gene, me, and the kids, and there's a knock at the door. My son, Paulie, gets the door—in those days you didn't have to look through the peephole—and there is this tall well-built guy in a blue suit and right next to him is this short fellow, not much bigger than Paulie, who was maybe nine at the time.

"Mom, there's a man with blue hair at the door," Paulie said. And for some reason my daughter, Theresa, runs into her bedroom and closes the door. She was sixteen.

"Gino *baby!*" Guy says.

"Is that my Cousin Gaetano?" my husband says.

"Hey, Pooch," Guy says. And they hug and pinch each other's cheeks.

And not a minute later our guests are sitting down with us, and Vic and Paulie are boxing with each other—you know, just screwing around—at the table. Vic and Guy wolfed down about ten pounds of food in thirty seconds.

GUY PUGLIA: You had all kinds staying at the Monroe. Hookers, drunks, junkies, freaks, crackpots who thought the world had five minutes to live, musicians and hepcats and vaudeville wash-ups, burlesque girls, actors on their way up, actors who'd already come down. More ambulances pulled up to that joint than taxis, that's the truth. Walking down them long hallways you saw things that'd curl your hairs quick. People injecting junk with the doors open, men dressed up as women—that wasn't even abnormal after a while. Some guy left the door open and I saw two ostriches prancing around the room. Ostriches!

The idea was to get some work. Vic didn't want to do nothing but sing. But me, I'd do anything. Gino'd been working the desk for almost fifteen years—he had to go by the name of "Eugene Purcell," by the way; that was the name on his uniform—and he knew a lot of Broadway people. He said he'd try and help Vic out. In the meantime I got a waiter job at Handelman's on Fifty-first Street. And a week or so after that, Vic got a job too, working three days a week. Doing what, you may ask? He was working at a soda fountain on Broadway and Eighty-first Street. A soda jerk again.

KATHY PUCCIO: Vic and Guy would stay with us a few days and then, when I started to complain about how much they were eating, Gene would sneak them into the hotel for a few days. Guy had gotten a job after a while but Vic would just hang around in the house. Eventually I got him to help me clean up.

My son loved Vic. They hit it off. My husband worked at night, came home at five in the morning, slept till noon, but Vic would spend time with my Paulie . . . they'd play baseball, stickball, handball, all that stuff. Theresa eventually overcame her shyness, but at first she never said a word to either Guy or Vic. I remember one dinner we were having, Theresa's best friend Betty was eating with us . . . I looked over to Theresa and noticed she was staring at Vic. I kicked her under the table and she said, "Ouch!" A minute later she's staring again. So I snatched the napkin off her lap and sort of whipped her arm with it. Then I looked over to Betty and saw she was ogling Vic too.

By that time I was having trouble functioning. I really had it pretty bad for him.

Vic was very nice to me. He'd help me clean, he'd scrub the floor like it was a marine barracks, he would even chop up vegetables. We weren't millionaires, but it was a nice house, only two houses from the beach. You opened up the door and the salt and the spray would wash over you. And with Vic working up a sweat and walking around in an undershirt . . . well . . .

He would offer to rub my back. He'd set me on the sofa and he'd sit right behind me and those strong fingers of his would just go all over my neck and shoulders and spine. I tell you, it was like dreaming, like being half-asleep and half-awake. One day he was doing this and I turned around and looked right at those gorgeous turquoise blue eyes of his. I had a pink blouse on, I can remember, with small buttons. I put my hands in his face and then I closed my eyes. I waited for him to kiss me. Silly me, I probably even puckered up my lips! I waited for about half a minute. I opened my eyes and he was still there.

"Well?" I said. "Don't you want to kiss me, Vic?"

"Can't, puddin'," he said. "Uh-uh."

"Why not?"

"I just couldn't do that to the Pooch," he said. "Wouldn't be honorable of me. He's my pal."

I looked down at a little pleat in my pink blouse . . . and the pleat was moving because my heart was going like crazy.

I was dumbfounded. I said to him, "You can call a woman 'puddin' and not kiss her?" I didn't think that was legal!

He got up and went outside to smoke a Chesterfield. I saw him through the curtains. And I stayed on the couch and felt as if someone had just robbed me.

The next time I saw my husband, to be honest with you, I wanted to wring his neck.

• • •

FREDDY BLISS [son of Ziggy Bliss]: My dad told me the story a million times. Bertie Kahn of the Bursley-Bates firm is up in the Catskills, at Marx's in White Lake. Bertie's only about thirty then but already he's a big hotshot, repping Broadway people and music people. Bertie Kahn was up there because Dad had clipped every review in *Variety,* every little mention in the Wilkes-Barre *Bugle* or the Tenafly *Times,* and sent it to him. My father arranged it that Bertie would get the best seat in the house.

The Blissmans did two weeks at Marx's; a ventriloquist with a dummy opened for the Blissmans and the headliner was the Hal Ketchum Orchestra.

Now, the way Dad told the story he had a choice: he could just do the normal act or he could really turn on the juice. But this is make or break, so he decides to crank up the juice to the max. The ventriloquist, Jerry Ochs, came on, and three minutes into his act Dad was onstage. This hadn't happened before—for a week Ochs, who feigned a thick Yiddish accent in the bit, and his aristocratic dummy Little Lord Goodwood, had been coming on and Dad left them alone. But on this night Dad was running rampant. He's going, "You're moving your lips, Jerry!" and "Goodwood's a pansy and I've got the splinters in my *tuches* to prove it!" And Jerry Ochs, he tries to keep up with Dad, but of course he can't. He's on for fifteen minutes and my father's on for twelve of them and everyone in there ate it up. Dad got the dummy out of Ochs's hands and was trying to make it talk . . . he had the little wooden doll grabbing women by their fannys.

He told me that Bertie Kahn was laughing so hard he was just paralyzed. *Bertie Kahn!* Who had lips of stone. But I bet that Jerry Ochs wasn't too pleased.

SALLY KLEIN: Bertie was very tall, a little overweight, and he dressed impeccably. Arnie said he was the spitting image of Sydney Greenstreet, and he was right. He was very imperious and smoked fancy foreign cigarettes. Also, he rarely said a sentence more than five words long. And here he was, red in the face and literally slapping his knees!

Ziggy is backstage afterward, drenched with sweat, soaking. Such a *shvitz* you've never seen. Hal Ketchum strolled up to him with a big cigar and his clarinet dangling from his neck on a strap. He said to Ziggy, "You spilled over into our time. My time is precious to me. You do that again, I got a drummer who'll fry you with onions for his breakfast."

At this second you felt really sorry for Ziggy. Hal Ketchum is a foot taller and thirty years older. But now Bertie Kahn came over and steps between them. Hal Ketchum said, "Hey, you're Bert Kahn." And Bertie said to him, "Scram, Ketchum. Chase a breeze." And Ketchum just slinks off. It was wonderful!

Ziggy asked Bertie, "Enjoy the act, Mr. Kahn?"

"Very much so. Here's my advice. Lose the midgets. They're killing you."

DANNY McGLUE [joke writer]: I was a bellhop at Marx's, the only Irish *punim* for miles, and I'd joke around in the nightclub, the Red Room. Larry Marx had a piano on the stage and I'd get up there and sing my silly nonsense songs, do some double-talk. I studied the piano growing up in Yorkville [Manhattan]—the idea was for me to become the next Horowitz or Rubinstein but here I was in the Catskills singing, "I want to marry you, I want you to have my babies, I love you more than my dog, but unlike him, you've got rabies."

The night after Bertie Kahn had introduced himself, Ziggy walked up to me in the lobby and said, "Danny? You're Danny McGlue . . ."

"I admit it," I said. "I am."

"Could I buy a few of your songs?"

I had no idea what he meant! *Songs? What* songs?

"Those little silly numbers you do, Danny," he said. "Like, 'I thought you had a nice complexion, but upon further reflection, something escaped my detection, I think I'll make another selection.' That kind of stuff."

I said to him, "Look, Ziggeleh, it's not as if I ever write down these little ditties . . ."

He scratches the freckles on his chin and then reaches into his trouser pockets and hands me a twenty. And he said, "Here. Write 'em down, Danny. I'm going places. Maybe you wanna hop along."

I hopped along. For the rest of my life.

SNUFFY DUBIN: Everyone's got an entourage. Elvis had the Country Cosa Nostra or the Memphis Mafia, Robin Hood had the Merry Men, and Jesus had his crew too. Vic had Hunny Gannett, Ernie, Guy, Ices Andy, and Chinese Joe Yung—man, even Vic's entourage had entourages!—and Ziggy had Sally and now was gathering up me and Danny and then eventually Shep Lane and Buzzy Brevetto. It was all coming together. Every big cat's gotta have his kittens around him. You need that support system, right? So if you wake up one morning and you got a baseball-sized pimple on your nose, there's some schlemiel-for-hire to tell you "You look great, boss!" An entertainer really needs that. The problems begin when you start believing them.

* * *

ARNIE LATCHKEY: The Smokestack Lounge was right near the Brooklyn Navy Yard, around Vinegar Hill. Maybe a hundred people could fit in there, depending on that day's bribe to the fire chief. Vic I think was making forty bucks a week singing there and they were literally paying him with silver. He must've sounded like Marley's ghost, boy, rattling his chains at the end of each night going home, with all those quarters.

GUY PUGLIA: The Smokestack Lounge? Stickiest floors you ever saw in your life. Nobody ever danced there because nobody *could* ever dance there. It wasn't too easy to get from one place to another . . . it'd be like jitterbugging in glue.

You know, Vic was a great mimic. So at this time—and I don't know if the bandleader, who was Mickey Ford, told him to do it or he come up with it himself—he was just imitating other singers. Dick Haymes, Devane, Perry Como, Columbo, Dick Fain . . . *he was just putting on their voices!* And I couldn't believe my ears. 'Cause now alls of a sudden his range had really stretched out. It was like someone handing him a baseball bat and saying, Here, hit the ball. And he couldn't do it. But then someone says, Okay, Vic, now imitate Ted Williams's swing . . . and *bang!* He's hitting all the notes, he's carrying the song. Everything was perfect and it wasn't like he was really even singing!

KATHY PUCCIO: I would sneak off to see him. This was pretty daring— it's not easy to get from Long Beach to that part of Brooklyn, and a girl in those days didn't go out alone. All those workers from the navy yard, it made me a little nervous. So Theresa and her friend Betty and I went out together. We looked just like three sisters. And Gene never knew because he was at the hotel.

I'd catch Vic's eye every once in a while up there. One night he was singing "Moonlight in Vermont" and he winked and smiled and I thought I was going to swoon backward, which wouldn't have been good because the floor there was so disgusting. I thought, He's doing this just for me. Nobody else sees it! And then Theresa elbows me and says, "Mom, Uncle Vic just winked at me!" And I'm sure Betty thought so too.

Uncle Vic. That's what my kids called him.

It was killing me. He was living in the house walking around in a T-shirt, a tanktop. That gorgeous, smooth olive skin. Even the hair on his shoulders . . . the hair was in these perfect tight little black coils. I used to fake backaches and charley horses just to get him to touch me.

One day I took the subway into Manhattan and just walked around. I didn't know what I was doing. I went to Macy's, Ohrbach's, and Gimbel's, walking around with my head in the clouds. I didn't buy anything. I kept thinking of Vic. I called Theresa from a phone booth and made up some cockamamie story and told her she should cook Paulie and herself dinner that night. I went to see a movie—it was *Dark Victory*. Halfway through I walked out. I got a cab and at first I thought I'd go to the Smokestack Lounge and see Vic perform . . . but I was so mixed up I didn't even know what night it was. The taxi took me home.

I walked into the house and the place was empty. Where Paulie was, I don't know. I walk into my bedroom and the very first thing I see is Betty, Theresa's friend. She's stark naked, facing me, these little sixteen-year-old breasts, like chestnuts. She had long curly auburn hair. And I see Vic's feet, the bottom of his big feet on the bed. That's all I see of him. He's flat on his back and Betty's on top of him, facing me.

Betty sees me see her and she gets off Vic and picks up her blouse and runs into the bathroom. And then I saw Theresa. She was naked too. She was—she was facing away from me . . . I don't even want to say what Vic was doing to her.

It all happened in a flash. I'll never forget it.

"Ma!" she said when she turned her head around.

I was paralyzed. I don't know how long I stood there. I tell you, it might've been for an hour.

Honorable! Wouldn't be honorable?! That's what Vic had said. But this *was?*

Two weeks later Theresa was in a convent and three years later she was a nun.

So now I hated everybody in that house. Vic I wanted to murder. That bastard. Theresa I would've strangled with my bare hands; Paulie I could've shot, and Betty I never allowed in my house again.

But the next morning when Gene came home I flung my arms around his neck and kissed his cheeks all over and must've told him thirty times how much I loved him.

GUY PUGLIA: Vic must've liked the Monroe more than me because after shuttling between Pooch and Kathy's house and the hotel, he all of a sudden decided he didn't want to stay in Long Beach no more. You know, if you didn't mind whores and hopheads, if you didn't mind some washed-up opera singer singing *La Traviata* while gargling with Hiram Walker, then it wasn't such a bad joint.

[Boxer, raconteur, saloon keeper] Hunny Gannett got booted from where he was living—some broad he was shacking up with in the East Twenties got wind he was married, not to one but to two women. So Vic told Hunny about the Monroe and now you had all three of us living there.

Gino one day walked up to Vic at the barber shop near the Monroe while he was getting a shave. Pooch says, "Vic, this is Bert Kahn." So Vic starts talking to this Kahn fella, who don't say so much when he talks. And Gino is playing Vic up, he says, "You gotta hear this guy sing, Mr. Kahn, the girls go crazy for him." And Kahn sends Pooch away with a five-spot and he promises he'll check out Vic at the Smokestack.

Bertie Kahn never showed up but *someone* sure did. Because in a week an agent from Worldwide American Talent had called him at the Monroe and a week after that he was belting out songs with the Don Leslie band at the Ambassador [Hotel]. When Vic auditioned, he just "put on" Bing Crosby's voice, like an impressionist, and Leslie fell for it. Ha! Vic said to me later, "That was like puttin' on an Einstein mask and getting a job teaching physics." He even cut a record. "My Tall Blue-Eyed, Blonde Dearie." That was the very first record he ever sung on. It was a 78 and I still have a copy somewheres. The voice is the spitting image of Sinatra's . . . I remember Vic giggling and telling me, "If Frank Sinatra ever hears this thing he's gonna think *he* sang it." Vic sent ten copies back to Codport, including one to Lulu.

We were going places, we thought.

ARNIE LATCHKEY: When I first hooked up with Vic I asked to look at paperwork, the contracts. I don't think he'd ever even heard the word "paperwork." I said to him, "You've signed some things, right?"

"Oh yeah, sure," he said. "I've signed some things."

But he didn't have any copies.

After a few phone calls to [company president] Herb Blackstone at WAT, I had the paperwork. Vic had signed some things all right. Vic would sign a shoeshine boy's rag if it had dotted lines on it. What I saw I couldn't believe. He was paying Don Leslie, he was paying Mickey Ford, he was paying Worldwide. For every dollar he made, he owed a buck twenty.

• • •

DANNY McGLUE: They played every resort in the Catskills. They'd work for peanuts, sometimes less, just the shells. (I wrote that gag for them and they used it.) Their car made the crate Jane Darwell drove in *The Grapes of*

Wrath look like a Corvette. They'd do a week at Grossinger's or Kutsher's, pack up, head down the road to Heine's Hideaway, which was the grandest joint of them all—it put the Concord and Grossinger's to shame. If there was a room, if there was a microphone and a piano, they'd play it. They'd play outdoors outside a collection of little bungalows and they would play these summer camps too, places where the kids were taught to salute pictures of Leon Trotsky and sing the Communist national anthem. Camp Hammer-and-Sickle, Ziggy called those places.

I caught up with them at Koppelman's [Resort]. I had a day off and Fred Stein [a coworker at Marx's] and I drove over to Loch Sheldrake to catch the act. See, I'd written two songs for Ziggy, two nonsense songs. "The Numb Dumb Drum That Is My Heart" and "The Itty-Bitty Ditty," which was fairly risqué for its day: "Okay, I'll let you wear my ringy if you can help me find my thingy . . ."

This was exciting to me. Someone other than me was going to sing my songs! Now, Ziggy had told me that Harry and Flo loved them too. So Fred and I were sitting toward the back and we're waiting and waiting and I say to Freddy, "They're gonna do it. You just watch!" But meanwhile Ziggy's *shpritz* is just going on and now I'm thinking, What am I doing here?

Finally Florence starts to sing a song but after a few bars Ziggy nudges her and says, "Mommy?"

And Flo—by now I guess she was used to being interrupted—says to him, "Yes, Sonny?"

"I have a little song I'd like to sing," he says.

From ten yards away I could hear Flo's mouth go dry in a flash. And I knew at that instant that Ziggy had never told his parents about my songs.

"What are you going to sing, Ziggy?" she asks him warily.

Ziggy—he'd given the pianist the charts—nods to the five-piece band and all of a sudden he's singing "The Itty-Bitty Ditty." This was to the tune of that old corny ballad "My Tall Blue-Eyed, Blonde Dearie." But we sped it up a bit. *"I left my thingy in the dinghy, help me find it if you don't mind it. Is it small? Why, not at all. If you give it a call, it will stand quite tall . . ."*

And to my delight the audience loved it. People were laughing, tapping their toes. But I tell you, you could almost smell the smoke coming out of Flo's ears.

SNUFFY DUBIN: Dolly Phipps was her name. Physically, she resembled a young Eleanor Roosevelt but with bright blond hair, a pageboy cut, pale, and with teeth like a mule. She was about nineteen years old, I'd say. Me, her, and a few others went up to see the Blissmans at Berenson's Hotel in the mountains. Dolly was kind of simpleminded. Oh yeah, she had a mild lisp too. The one word people used to describe her was "daffy." Very tall and gawky and the biggest feet you ever saw on a chick. But she was a good kid. Someone told me her parents had tried to send her to finishing school but nothing took. How can you finish something that wasn't ever started? She might not have been able to balance a book on her head but I think she could have toted the entire Library of fucking Congress on each foot.

So we're watching the act and naturally she's cracking up, everyone is, watching Zig. And now Danny McGlue had written a few songs for the act as well as some fresh gags, and I gotta tell you: Ziggy never gave Danny credit, not then, not ever. He'd say, "This is a song I wrote last night in the bathtub while fiddling with my ocarina."

After the show Ziggy comes over to our table and he and Dolly instantly had this mutual attraction thing, probably based on the fact that everyone else found them so unsightly. He's talking and being Ziggy and her face is beet red because he's just so fucking hilarious. She's not laughing though. Too self-conscious, right? She's sitting there and trembling and sweating like a hog in a sitz bath because she's keeping it all in. Then she gets up abruptly and runs away! *Runs!*

"Who's the hot tamale?" Ziggy whispers to me. "She's cute."

I said, "She is?"

"Yeah!" he said. "You don't think she's cute?"

"Yeah. She's cute, Zig," I say. "She's a doll." What the hell . . .

She came back to the table about ten minutes later. I guarantee you she's not the first person, man or woman, who Ziggy made wet their pants.

SALLY KLEIN: It was very ironic because it was as if Harry and Flo had lost their one child now that they'd incorporated him into the act. In some way, it was good for poor Harry. Ziggy *was* the act, Harry knew that. So it was less pressure on him. He was relaxing. Reading, taking walks in the woods with Flo or by himself, enjoying life.

Ziggy would corner me in a hotel lobby or backstage and say, "I'm stuck in a Ma and Pa Shtetl act!" He'd gripe about his parents all the time.

I was a pretty tough girl. I'd bait him. I said to him, "So why not just dump them like Bertie Kahn said? Go solo. If you don't need them like you say, just go solo. You're the whole act, right? *Lose the midgets, Ziggy.*"

Well, now that this was actually a possibility, it wasn't so wonderful, was it? With Harry and Flo there, he had people to play off of, he had people he could rip apart. Without them up there, it was just him.

A week after this conversation—it was at Fiedler's Inn in White Lake— he introduced me to Dolly Phipps. He said, "Dolly, this is my cousin, Sally; Sally, this is my new partner, Dolly Phipps."

New partner?! I thought I was going to die!

He told Harry and Flo he was teaming with Dolly for four weeks and that they should go home to Echo Beach. He and Dolly would take their bookings. They were flabbergasted.

Danny and Ziggy wrote some brand-new material. It was—I think Danny would agree—second-rate stuff.

DANNY McGLUE: Did Sally really say that? Hmmm. Because I thought some of the material was actually pretty good. But she [Dolly] was just so incredibly stiff. The best comedy in the world would have died crossing her lips.

This was the first tough time Ziggy ever had, performing. It went over like granite, and now he couldn't improvise his way out. If he went into the crowd to fiddle with the band or to *shpritz* with the audience, he would've looked like a scared fat kid trying to weasel himself out of a jam. There was truly a touch of the pathetic to it. And he couldn't ad-lib . . . there would be no snappy Ziggyisms at Dolly's expense. Because she was his girl. Harry and Florence he could make fun of—he could toss out an aside like, "Oh well, they'll be dead soon anyways."

But you can't do that to a girl you're seeing.

SNUFFY DUBIN: Like a goldfish with a bad cough, that act died.

You can guess the act. She's the dumb clumsy blonde and he's the little fat nebbish. Not once did it click. Burns played *against* Gracie Allen. She said crazy, spacey things but it all made sense. That was the brilliance. With these two, though, it was like two brain-damaged kids. People were cringing.

Ziggy had indicated to me he wanted to go solo. But no way he wanted to play it alone. No way. Any comedian will tell you: Being up there by yourself is like being buck naked with your hands tied behind your back and everybody's got darts. For a while he'd been trying to dump his parents and team up with me . . . but I didn't want any part of that. No thanks.

So only two weeks into the Ziggy and Dolly Era, he's on the phone again to me. "Snuffy, you gotta get this broad outta my life! You *owe* me!"

I say, "How the hell do I owe you?!"

"'Cause you got her *into* my life in the first place!"

DANNY McGLUE: Ziggy and I were never truly close friends. At first, he was a performer and I just worked at the hotel. The money he paid me for the songs and the jokes—it was in cash then, maybe $25 a week, which I needed. But we weren't close.

This was the first time he ever blew up at me. Not the last, of course. When it happened, I was stunned. I shouldn't have been—I'd heard him yell and say the cruelest things, things which really hurt, to Sally. Making fun of her hair, her nose, everything.

Backstage after a show I was in his little dressing room. He had a glass of seltzer, I remember that. And he was naked except for a towel around his neck. Naked and very sweaty. Not a pleasant sight, all those red bumps and pimples and the flab. And that *shlong* of his, like a prize-winning carrot at a state fair.

"I'm dying every single night, Danny," he said. "Sometimes two times a night."

I started to say, "Ziggy, this act with Dolly—"

"What *about* Dolly?! What about her?!" he snapped at me.

Now, I had to stand my ground. Because it *was* her fault, not mine. I said, "Zig, I'm sorry but I think she's very stiff up there."

And he said, "Did it ever occur to you it might be your jokes and your songs? Maybe *you're* very stiff?"

"She's a lovely gal," I lied. "She's really the sweetest thing. But she's just not funny." And that's when it happened. He took his glass of seltzer and smashed it into the mirror right next to him, the vanity mirror. And he yelled at me. He was yelling at the top of his lungs and every pore of his body was flushed like a strawberry. Called me every name in the book. He was humiliating me—he was as loud as his mother when she sang and everyone in that hotel could probably hear it and I was shaking with fear and shame.

It lasted ten minutes. I wiped my eyes with a handkerchief. I'm thinking to myself: I don't *need* this. Big deal. A few dollars a week. It's not worth it. I'll have a drink and tell him I'm quitting and if he screams at me for that I'll just walk away.

He pours me a scotch and I thought, Okay, one more drink and then I'll tell him I'm out. So he poured me another.

And then he went into his wallet and slapped four fifties on the vanity. And he said, "Okay, let's burn the midnight oil, Danny. Take the dough. It's yours. Jeez, just for letting me yell at you like that, you should get a grand."

And we worked until six in the morning and wrote completely new material. We played off each other: I'd be him and he'd be Dolly or he'd be Dolly and I'd be him. And we kept saying, "Socko stuff." "Mucho yuks." You know, like a *Variety* review. At one point we were cracking up so much he said, "Hey, Danny, you're doing so good as Dolly maybe I'll team up with *you!*" By the next day I'd nearly forgotten about the torrent of abuse he'd unleashed.

The new material died. Died. You know how good this stuff was, Ted? Years later we recycled it—with some touchup work, obviously—for Ziggy and Vic's TV show.

"Okay," he told me. "I'm getting rid of that blond ball and chain."

SNUFFY DUBIN: He was afraid to give Dolly the heave-ho. He actually wanted me to drive up there and, one, fire her from the act, and, two, break up with her for him! *He wanted me to do this!*

I say, "Ziggy, this is your doing. I ain't doing this for you. I just ain't." And in the back of my mind is when Jimmy Powell and me had to extricate him from that girl in Newark.

"Come on, Snuff," he says.

I tell him, "No, Zig. This is just morally and ethically wrong."

"I'll give you six hundred dollars," he says.

"Make it eight hundred plus expenses and you're on," I told him. "And I already got a plan too."

He says, "Okay. Eight hundred. And hurry your *tuches* up here."

The next day I'm in Loch Sheldrake, in Dolly's hotel room. I'm looking all solemn and everything, right? I got a black suit on, my hair is slicked back, I look like John Q. Undertaker. I sit down and I take her hand and I say, "Dolly . . ." And I'm whispering too! Talking *very* gently, *very* seriously in these hushed tones. I say, "Dolly, Harry Blissman has a contract out on your life. It would really be in your best interest to skip town, to leave the act and the state and this portion of the country and maybe just . . . just get lost for a while."

She's a got a look on that face of hers like I'm trying to explain relativity to her. *Huh?!*

"There are people," I say, "people who work for the Pompiere family in Jersey, and they're coming here to kill you. Lou Manganese is on his way as we speak, my contacts are telling me. They're going to cut you into two pieces and send one piece to your parents and the other to Harry so he knows they did the job."

And her teeth, those big buck teeth, I tell you, they were *twitching!* And she says, "But . . . but what about my *career?*"

I was almost bursting at the seams! I wanted to say, "Honey, a wax pear's got more charisma than you do." But I said instead, "Dolly, sweetheart, this is your life we're talking about." And I handed her an envelope and inside were two tickets. I said to her, still whispering solemnly, "Go to New York, Grand Central Station. And then go to Laramie, Wyoming. When you get to the Laramie depot you'll be met there by a man with an eye patch named Millard La Chance. He'll set you up there. He'll give you ten, maybe fifteen grand to start over. You'll be safe there. You have my guarantee. And when things have settled down, we'll send for you and you can return. But not until then."

She was sniffling a little.

"Dolly," I said, "you better get moving. Time is of the essence like you got no idea."

I helped her pack. And all the time I'm looking out the window as if two hit men were about to drive up with Thompson submachine guns.

We're in my car heading toward the bus station to get to New York.

She asks me, "What's the name of this fella with the eye patch again?"

"It's Millard La Grange," I said. "Right?"

She said, "No. I think it was La Chance you said."

"Oh yeah, right," I said. "La Chance. That's it. Right."

For all I know, Dolly Phipps is still wandering around Laramie, fucking Wyoming, looking for some guy with an eye patch named Millard La Chance.

• • •

RAY FONTANA: I saw the Don Leslie band at the Ambassador, sure. And you could hear 'em Fridays on the radio, brought to you by Elgin watches. One time Vic put me on the comp list and I brought my wife, who was then just some girl I was seeing.

The whole band wore white tuxedos. Don Leslie, though, he wore white tails. It was the kind of music where you expected champagne bubbles to float out of the tuba. This wasn't my kind of music and, to be honest, I felt out of place, me an Italian fisherman with all these swells and debutantes. But Vic looked like he belonged up there. He slicked back his hair so it wasn't hanging all over his face. And when that voice came out his mouth I looked around—I thought it was a joke. *This isn't Vic singing!* That's what I thought, that someone else was singing and he was just up there moving his mouth. But it was him.

I don't know if it was his idea or Don Leslie's but Vic wasn't wearing white. He was the only one. The lady singer [Ruth Whitley] wore white too. But Vic had on this powder blue tux and matching shoes. And when I saw that, *I remembered!* The choir. When he was in that choir, he'd wear a different color too.

GUY PUGLIA: Two hundred a week—this was the most dough Vic had ever made in his life by far. I remember I called 'em two hundred clams once and Vic says to me, "Please, they ain't clams." You just couldn't bring up seafood to him . . . it was like a jinx.

And he got a car too, his first car. A black Buick Century coupe. Used. But with all that dough we was still staying at the Monroe.

Don Leslie, he tried to play father to him, but that Ozzie Nelson routine didn't go too far. First thing Leslie did was change Vic's name from Fontana to Fontaine, like in Joan Fontaine. He bought Vic clothing, told him about fine food. He's trying to tell Vic that you should have this wine with this veal and Vic's stuffin' his face and saying, "Oh yeah, Don? Then what kinda beer should I have with this fuckin' hot dog?" He wanted Vic to go to church every Sunday, he wanted Vic to stop going to the track, he told Vic the booze would ruin his pipes. One time he caught Vic with his hands up a floozy's skirt in the stairway of a nightclub and he pulled Vic off the broad and tried to deliver a lecture right then and there. Started talking about disease and filth and sin. Vic told him to cram it up his trombone.

Leslie was a real straight arrow. He had that big Waspy image to protect. Ruth Whitley was his girlfriend and they stayed in separate rooms but one time I saw him sneaking to her room at 3:00 A.M. Some straight arrow, huh?

He even found Vic a nice spread on Broadway in the Seventies. "You don't want to live in that lice trap, do you, Vic?" he asked him. And Vic said, "Hey, they're *my* lice."

ROGER DILLARD [trumpeter with the Leslie band]: Don Leslie's previous singer was Phil Hardy, who was a first-class prima donna. Then Hardy met a widowed millionairess, married her, moved to Newport, and was never heard of again until the woman found him in a hammock with a yacht boy. So Vic was a breath of fresh air, he was just one of the guys.

The girls in the audience . . . they adored him. Couldn't keep their eyes off of him.

He did have trouble with the lyrics. That was Don's big complaint. When Vic couldn't remember the words, he would mumble, moan, and basically slur over the words. And with the style of relaxed, lulling singing he was doing, you almost didn't notice it. I guarantee you, he could have slurred over an entire set and not one girl at the Ambassador would have noticed. Or if they did they wouldn't particularly care.

SNUFFY DUBIN: The very first time I ever heard of Victor Fountain or Fontaine, it was at the Mosque Theater in Newark. He was billed as "the Singing Fisherman" with the Don Leslie All-Goyishe Kupf Orchestra. My first thought was, when I heard him: Devane. This guy is doing Fritz Devane. Next song: Dick Fain. After that: Como. The man wasn't using his own voice, his own style. I saw right through it like it was fucking cellophane.

GUY PUGLIA: It was like a revolving door! Girls comin' in, girls goin' out. There were times when he'd finish up with one, bring her down to the hotel lobby—'cause he had class; a lot of other guys would've just swept 'em out the door—and then the next one was in the lobby waiting for him and he'd just bring her back up.

And don't forget it was my room too! Sometimes I had no place to go, while he was busy "accommodating" these girls. So I'd wait in the lobby and read a paper. I spent a few nights sleeping in the back of the Buick, no kidding. Or I'd go to Jack Dempsey's bar on Fiftieth Street or goof around with Hunny. Or I'd hide in the closet and listen to Vic.

There were some classy girls too, girls right out of the society columns, like Elsa Maxwell's or Hilda Fleury's. I'd be reading about some rich horse owner up at Saratoga and four floors upstairs at the Monroe, Vic was putting the sausage parmigiana to the guy's daughter.

So it wasn't all bimbos. But there were a lot of bimbos too.

Hatcheck girls at the Ambassador, waitresses at the Blue Beret Cafe, a busboy's wife, a cigarette girl here and there. Or just some lonely married lady. It just went on and on.

And I was doing all right for myself too, you know? Just from being Vic's buddy and getting his rejects. But some of these girls . . . *marrone!* I think I had a better time alone in the back of the Buick.

ROGER DILLARD: Vic started to get Don very angry, and I suppose that was only a matter of time. It was the girls, it was the booze and the gambling. Vic—and you have to admire him for it, I guess—he didn't do anything to hide it. He *flaunted* it sometimes. Vic once walked over to Don while he was drinking a glass of milk and he poured a shot of Johnnie Walker into it. "Here, boss, this'll put some hair on your nipples," Vic said to him.

Don once said to Vic, "You're going to get a girl in trouble one day, you know that?"

And Vic laughed and said, "Man, I already did that! A *few* times!"

It was contagious. Vic wouldn't show Don any respect and it just followed that the band fell in with Vic. We'd be rehearsing and Vic would lay a fart into the microphone and then the drummer would cut one and we'd all pick up our horns and make fart noises with them. Don Leslie just stood there with his trombone, shaking with anger. You almost felt sorry for him.

Whenever I read nowadays how Vic Fountain was such a great song stylist, a skillful interpreter of the American songbook, a master of phrasing, the first thought in my head is of him placing the mike near his pants and ripping out a loud fart. I just don't know if Tormé, Fitzgerald, Sinatra, Bennett, or Eckstine ever did that.

RAY FONTANA: My mother would send me around Codport when the Elgin watch show was on. We were supposed to listen at the door or through the window to see which families were tuning in and which weren't.

I remember coming to Rocco Straccio's house. I'm listening in at the front door and I don't hear anything. I go to the window, I don't hear a peep. All of a sudden someone grabs me by my neck. I never was so scared in my life. It was Straccio, but you could hardly see him. I thought my heart was gonna just slip out my mouth. He asked me what I was doing and I tried to answer but no words came out.

He grabs my nose between his fingers, twists it, and says, "I got your nose." I ran back home holding my nose and I told my mother I was never doing that again.

GUY PUGLIA: Hunny Gannett—we first met him at the Smokestack Lounge—introduced Vic and me to the ponies. Vic at first couldn't really understand the *Daily Racing Form*. Now, Hunny—who knew if he could even read at all, but all them little numbers and symbols he could make out just fine. And he knew some of the jockeys too. He'd say, "Vic, stick four to win on Sugar Grove in the third" and then two minutes later Vic, who'd lost his shirt already on the daily double, now had his shirt back plus a few new pairs of pants.

You know what happened one time? Me, Hunny, and Vic was at the track, at Belmont. And someone recognized Vic! It was the first time. This guy walks right up to us and says, "Hey, you sing with Don Leslie!"

And Vic says to the guy, "Yeah, I sing with Don Leslie."

The guy says, "My fiancée really likes you."

"Oh yeah?" Vic says. "She here?"

The guy points and says, "Yeah, she's over there."

And there about fifteen seats away is this broad with curly black hair in a black cloth coat with a red scarf on, a very pretty girl, and I see Vic's face turn white. And so does hers.

"Why don't you go over and just say hello?" the guy says. "Her name's Patty. It'll make her day."

And Vic says, "Just beat it, pal. Okay?"

And this idiot just stands there—he doesn't put two and two together. And I see this girl panicking; she sees Vic and is petrified he's gonna come over with her beau. Everybody knew what was going on except that idiot. Hunny picks the guy up, walks him over, and plunks him down in his seat right next to Patty, who's still shaking with the fear of gettin' caught.

"Thanks, Hun," Vic said.

ED J. McDOWELL [former editor at *Ring* magazine]: Hunny Gannett was the prototypical club fighter of the thirties, forties, and fifties and was barely qualified to make anyone's Bum of the Month Club. After he became a saloon keeper, restaurateur, raconteur, actor, bon vivant, and game show panelist, people often forgot he'd been a prizefighter. Tracking down his record as a heavyweight is a futile enterprise as he fought under so many *noms de guerre.* Tiziano "Big Red" Vecellio, "Batsy" Patsy Conklin, "Mighty" Moses Klein, "Kaiser" Willy Mueller, et cetera. If there was an ethnic group, he carried their standard. His father was Hungarian, from just outside Miskolc, and the last name, now lost to us, was anglicized from something similar to Gannett, but with many *z*'s, *s*'s, and *k*'s in it. Hunny's real first name was Atillio and from that we get Hunny, as in Atilla the Hun. Some people make the artful leap: boxing, the sweet science, sweet, honey, Hunny. But that's a flight of fancy. Hunny comes from Hun.

[He lost] to Max Baer, he lost to Primo Carnera, he lost to Joe Louis, he lost to Tonys Galento, Zale, and Mutti, and innumerous other Tonys long forgotten. One night he lost by a third-round knockout on the undercard in Paterson, New Jersey, and then fought under a different name two fights later and was knocked out again. It should be pointed out that his father had moved from Hungary to Oakburn, Manitoba, before Hunny was born; the lad grew up in a house on 31 Queer Street. It was supposed to be Queen Street but there was a misprint on the map and the name stuck. As every fight fan knows, "Queer Street" is ring argot—as is "spaghetti legs"—for when a boxer is punched so silly, he has no idea where he is, who he is, or why. It should also be pointed out that Gannett, when his fight career was over, briefly endorsed a macaroni product called Spaghetti Legs. The box that this pasta came in featured a small picture of the retired prizefighter, with his boxing gloves on, holding up a plate of steaming leg-shaped noodles.

Hunny *won* fights too. He won them savagely, brutally, sometimes very suddenly. Sometimes not. There was no artistry, no pugilistic panache, no Fred Astaire élan—he floated more like the *Merrimac* than he did a butter-fly and on those occasions when he stung it was more like Big Bertha than a bee. More Marquis de Sade than Marquis of Queensberry.

He killed at least four people in the ring. A palooka from Evanston, Illi-nois, named Joe Pollo he dispatched to his maker with one left hook in the ninth round. It was the first and last punch Hunny Gannett threw the entire fight. By that time his own face looked like so much cold spaghetti and tomato sauce. One punch and the Evanston Assassin was dead. The Chicago *Tribune* wouldn't run the photo, not because Pollo had died, not because of how slack his body looked laid out on the canvas, but because Hunny Gan-nett's face—the face of the victor, mind you—was such a nauseating eyeful.

Grayling Greene, the columnist, once wrote that Hunny Gannett left more brain tissue, his own and others, on canvas than Reubens did paint. I told Hunny that line at his saloon and he had a clever comeback line; he said, "Did I once have brain tissue, Eddie?"

GUY PUGLIA: People think of Hunny and they see his big head with these big dark eyes and those car-tire lips and the Frankenstein forehead . . . and they think of his saloon. Or they think of him on the panel of *What Is It?* They didn't know Hunny *the man.*

One time in the fifties, Vic, [valet] Joe Yung, me, and Hun was at Santa Anita. Vic put $100 across the board on a ten-to-one horse Gerry Kent was riding. The horse wins and we all go to the winner's circle and then the barn to meet Gerry Kent. Now Kent recognized Vic of course and he recognized Hunny but he didn't know me and Chinese Joe from Eisenhower and Madame Chiang Kai-shek. So I shake Gerry Kent's hand and he says to me, "Hey, you should be a jockey."

I said to him, "I ain't no jockey."

And he says, "I think I'm taller than you. You should ride horses, pal."

I said to him again, "I ain't no jockey."

He says, "There's something wrong with being a jockey, is there, pip-squeak?"

I make a lunge for him . . . we're on the ground and I'm punching him in the face and he's trying to bite my hands, him in his lime green silks and yellow beanie with a red hoop. Gerry goddamn Cunt. He was pretty strong—the sonuvabitch rode race horses, for Christsake—but he wasn't no fighter. I'm trying to get at his face and suddenly—*whoosh*—Hunny lifts me off him by my collar, with one hand yet, lifts me right off him.

Then Hunny says to Gerry Kent—and you gotta remember that when he spoke he sounded just like a cow if a cow could talk—he says, "Okay, Gerry, now eat some slop."

"Huh?" Kent says. And there's some mixture in a big square bucket that the horses eat, it looked like mud and quicksand and oats and I-don't-know-what.

"Eat the slop."

He had no choice. So we all watched as he stuffed his face full of about five pounds of this horse meal. He couldn't race the rest of the card 'cause of the weight gain.

And that's Hunny Gannett.

You know, Vic was booted out of the Leslie band because of the Kid Burcham fight. It had nothing to do with singing.

Hunny was fighting at Sunnyside Garden. Kid Burcham—he looked like Tab Hunter but with real solid muscle—he was from Ohio and worked out at Pops Deegan's Gym on Amsterdam Avenue. Pops was a great trainer, he knew boxing inside and out and would take on raw street toughs and train them, but the word was that he was a *finocchio* and had flings with a few of the fighters in his stable.

Hunny had gotten me, Vic, Don Leslie, and Ruth Whitley tickets. Ringside. And Leslie had shown up in his white tie and tails. All immaculate-like.

When Hunny seen this Kid Burcham in the ring, his eyes lit up, and those were dark eyes he had too. People called Burcham the Akron Adonis and the Ohio Apollo. He didn't have so much as one nick on his face. And Hunny was just a big bohunk galoot, you know? He wanted to smear the Akron Adonis like jam all over Queens Boulevard.

ED J. McDOWELL: Gannett was paid a hundred bucks to lose. Al Pompiere's son-in-law, Lou Manganese, had walked into the gym where Hunny trained and said to him, "How'd you like to lose Friday night in Sunnyside?" Manganese wasn't merely being curious and it wasn't really a question, and he tendered the fighter a C-note to prove it. "And I want you to lose by a decision. No dives, Hun," Manganese said. Hunny promised him, "Okay, Lou, I'll be on my feet when the bell sounds."

It was one of the worst sanctioned beatings ever inflicted in a so-called civilized society. Kid Burcham hit Gannett with everything he had and when he ran out of the things he had, he cashiered his own future for more. Burcham walloped him, he thrashed him, he kept coming and coming. Not once did Gannett hold his fists up to defend himself. By the fifth round both of Hunny's eyes were swollen shut, and there was a paperback book-size cut running along his forehead. His lower lip had to be stapled back on. The referee had fashioned a makeshift headdress out of a towel to protect himself from the bile spraying onto him from Gannett's face. Hunny didn't move, he just stood there and took it. In the seventh round he was being hit by his own teeth; he'd lost two teeth, which were now embedded in Burcham's glove, and each time Burcham punched him it was like a mallet coming at him with two razor blades attached.

Gannett was behind on points. In between rounds when Gussie Beck, his trainer, held out a bucket and implored him, "Liquid! Spit! Spit out some liquid!" Gannett uttered to him the now-classic corner quip: "Gussie, the only liquid I got left is my checking account!"

Kid Burcham was exhausted; he'd run a marathon, he'd fought a war, he'd spent it all. Pops Deegan was about to throw in the towel for him, but this doomed blond gladiator wouldn't have it. The bell in the final round tolled—almost mournfully, some said—and Burcham staggered to the center of the ring, where Gannett strode with no small measure of gallantry to meet him, almost slipping on the five humors he'd shed. Burcham could barely lift his own arms. "Come on, Kid," Hunny said to him, "come on and lick me." He raised his gloves at this point, beckoning for Burcham's fists—the first time Hunny's hands had been lifted above his waist since he'd shaken his opponent's hand and wished him luck. But, above his own desperate wheezing, the Kid couldn't hear anything Gannett was saying.

They stood there for a minute.

"All right then," Hunny said, keenly aware of the ticking clock.

Hunny reared back with his right and swung flush into Kid Burcham's forehead. There was no whiplash, no sudden snapping. "The roof came clean off of Kid Burcham's house, as if blown off by a tornado whirling inside it," some scribe in the *Daily News* wrote, "and all the belongings came exploding out." There was a god-awful, terrible silence. A stentorian silence. Burcham fell like he'd been thrown down a garbage chute.

The bell sounded as the referee was counting him out. Kid Burcham was saved by the bell. He was dead. Hunny had killed him, had rent his head in twain, but the Kid had won on points. And Gannett got to keep his hundred dollars.

GUY PUGLIA: The Kid Burcham fight was like sitting in on spleen surgery done with tire irons. When it was over, there was no noise, no clappin' or cheers or nothin'. A few people stood around the ring to officially pronounce the Ohio Apollo dead. I looked down . . . I was gonna say a prayer. Then I saw that I was covered with blood and stuff. I elbow Vic and I say, "Get a load of this!" And Vic looks at me and then at himself. And he's got it all over him too.

There were little strands of stuff on me, like macaroni. And worse stuff, much worse stuff. I bend over in my seat and I start retching . . . Vic's vomiting too. And while we're doing that we looked over to Don Leslie and Ruth Whitley and they're covered with the same muck. They got it worse than we did—it looked like someone had tossed two gallons of Maypo on each of 'em. You couldn't see one speckle of white on Don Leslie's tuxedo. They were both passed out.

The next day when Vic showed up to rehearse he was fired.

And a week after that we was back in Codport again.

* * *

SALLY KLEIN: After Ziggy got rid of Dolly, he started to go crazy with girls. He wasn't famous yet and he wasn't good-looking—he wasn't *ever* good-looking—but with some women, if you just put a microphone in front of a man, even if he looks like three-week-old gefilte fish, he becomes Clark Gable.

There were girls in the towns in the Catskills—I don't even know if you could say they were call girls; I doubt they had phones or knew how to use them. Somehow he found them.

I called Rosie Baer in Pennsylvania . . . I really was at the end of my rope. All that tension. Harry, Flo, and Ziggy . . . such arguing like you've never heard. Rosie told me that if it was really too much for me I should quit. Then she mentioned how much the act was bringing in a week. Now, it wasn't thousands, don't get me wrong, they were not living like the Rockefellers. But it was a lot. Rosie said that Harry and Flo's old manager [Jerome Milton] was getting suspicious now; he'd ripped up all the contracts but by now he'd heard how well they were doing. And Rosie had even gotten calls from Joe Gersh from MCA and Murray Katz from Worldwide American . . . those sharks were flitting around.

So there was all this money and excitement now. But Rosie said that if I wanted to quit I should quit.

My mother told me that if I dropped out, someone else would take my place. They reminded me that this was my own family, my cousin and my aunt and uncle.

I didn't know what to do.

I was having dinner with Ziggy and I just came out with it. I told him I had no life, that my life was making sure that Harry and Flo didn't have nervous breakdowns. I didn't have a boyfriend and I wasn't in school and this wasn't really a job. He said, "Sal, when things fall into place I'll have either Joe or Murray put you on the payroll. Until then, I'll add another thirty bucks a week to your salary."

I said to him, "Joe Gersh or Murray Katz?"

And now I knew those sharks were flitting around because Ziggy had contacted them. He was trying to dump Rosie Baer.

LENNY PEARL: To me, radio was a big racket. I never felt like such a *gonif* in all my life. After vaudeville and burlesque, radio was a day at the beach! I had writers, producers, engineers, I had three or four other people on the air with me, like [announcer, singer] Billy Quinn, who was a dear man. And Viceroy [cigarettes] was paying me more money than I knew what to do with. A real racket.

My producer [Tony Freedman] comes into my dressing room one day and says, "Do you know anyone named Rosie Baer?" And I said, yeah, sure I did. And I get on the phone and Rosie and I exchange pleasantries and she tells me how good the Battling Blissmans were doing. I thought it was April Fool's Day! She might as well have been trying to tell me Hitler was good for the Jews. She tells me that it wasn't the Battling Blissmans now, she says that Harry and Flo had taken a backseat, to which I replied, "Can anybody even see them sitting back there?"

I sent one of Tony Freedman's assistants up to Marx's over the weekend to catch the act. He calls me from the hotel, tells me that the act is hilarious. I said, "Hey, are you *sure* you went to the right hotel?"

So then I sent Tony Freedman himself up and, son of a gun, he actually called me *during* the act. He said, "Lenny, we gotta put them on."

I was baffled. Because you have to understand, when I think of Harry and Flo I think of people snoring and getting up to leave. And now my producer is urging me to give them air time!

"All right," I said. "Let's put 'em on. What the hell."

GLENN PETTIBON [assistant to the producer of *The Viceroy Hour*]: Lenny Pearl didn't ever rehearse. I read something once where he said that that took away all the spontaneity—well, that's hogwash. He didn't like to rehearse because he had other things to do, such as nap and play pinochle, chase girls, and ignore his wife. So we'd take turns filling in for him at the rehearsals. A lot of time it was Billy Quinn, who detested Lenny. He'd make fun of Lenny while standing in for him . . . and it was hilarious. He did the New Yorky accent, he flubbed the lines, he'd do some off-color material—it was the funniest comedy they ever had on the show and of course nobody outside the studio ever heard a word of it.

Tony had allotted about ten minutes of airtime to the Blissmans. If you went over by one second it was considered high treason. They had eight minutes to do their material, and then Lenny would shoot the breeze with them for two, and then they broke for Viceroy advertising. So for our first rehearsal Billy Quinn—he died in North Africa in the war, by the way— "was" Lenny Pearl. Ziggy and his parents had a routine: he wanted a pet parrot and his parents were against it. So they're doing the routine and it just wasn't going anywhere. Tony calls for a break and asks them what's wrong. See, they were used to all sorts of pandemonium, to chaos and ad-libbing, but now they were in a studio and they *had* to do their act in eight minutes. (I saw Fountain and Bliss a few years later in Miami Beach and they couldn't put out a cigarette in eight minutes!)

They took it from the top and tried to play it a little looser but now it was as if they were *playing* at being looser and freer. It just wasn't natural. So Tony talked to them again and Ziggy was sweating up a monsoon. Billy Quinn came over to me and said, "Who are these pip-squeaks anyway?" And I said, "I heard they were funny," and he said, "Well, they're not."

The night before we went on the air we did the last rehearsal and I stood in for Lenny Pearl. The Blissmans had gotten no better, Ziggy was fidgety and sweaty—it was as if you'd locked a wolverine in a tight cage. He was squirming.

I said to Billy, "They're going to stink. Lenny's going to have a stroke." "Good!" Billy said. He really hated him that much.

SNUFFY DUBIN: I was at Jimmy Dooley's [bar] on Eighth Avenue with Zig an hour before he went on. He was beefing about how's he supposed to do the act in eight minutes, how's he supposed to be himself? I know exactly where he was coming from. My Vegas act was an hour, an hour and a half sometimes if I was really *on*. I go on Carson, I get five minutes. I do Merv Griffin, Mike Douglas, I get enough time for a hiccup. It's like trying to get twenty pounds of chopped liver on one fucking saltine. She ain't gonna hold.

So I say to Ziggy, "What the fuck do you care about Lenny Pearl? Just be yourself. He gives you eight minutes, take a week. He gives you a week, you take a decade. Do what you wanna do and the hell with him."

Yeah, it's all my fault. Mea fucking culpa.

GLENN PETTIBON: Tony Freedman finally told Lenny that the Blissmans, Ziggy included, was a subpar act. This wasn't easy for Tony—he was the one who suggested they put them on. And Lenny was steaming . . . he was just irate. "So it's like it was years ago!" he was yelling. "The crowd used to rise like it was the National Anthem and walk out! Except now half of America is going to leave America!" Of course, half of America wasn't listening; *The Viceroy Hour* was not a popular show. But still . . .

The show began and Billy sang a song and kidded around with Lenny, and Lenny did a few jokes and then brought out the Macy Twins, who sang a song. And now it's the Blissmans' turn. Lenny brought up how he knew the parents from his days in vaudeville and now they had "something resembling a child and they *shtuck* him into the act because no one else would have him." Then he stepped aside and they were on the air.

Ten seconds into the routine I realized: This isn't what they rehearsed! Tony Freedman was looking at the clock, praying this new material went under ten minutes. Billy Quinn had this mischievous glint in his eye. The only one there who didn't know something strange was going on was Lenny . . . *because he'd never been to one single rehearsal!* I even heard Lenny whisper to Tony, "Hey, what the hell were you worrying about? They're damn good."

Soon everything was in chaos. Ziggy was being Ziggy and the parents were rolling with it. I thought Tony Freedman was going to faint. There was no routine anymore—it was just Ziggy. Lenny whispered to Tony at one point, "Did he forget about the parents? This is the bit?"

Eight minutes passed and this was when Lenny was supposed to come back on and talk to his guests. But Ziggy doesn't let him! He's joking around and when Lenny tries to wrest the mike away, Ziggy engaged in some funny wrestling. It was going over well with everyone . . . everyone but Lenny Pearl. I remember Ziggy said to him, "Hey, my folks said they knew you when you was nothin'," and Lenny said, "That's true. That was years and years ago." And then Ziggy said, "No, they meant last week."

Tony Freedman signaled Billy Quinn to announce they were breaking for a commercial, but Ziggy wouldn't let him. He started joking around with Billy and while that was going on Lenny was trying to get a few words in edgewise. To no avail.

Lenny was furious. He wasn't in control . . . this was a nightmare for him.

Ziggy started clowning around with the Macy Twins and flirting with them. Everyone was going with it! Billy Quinn was, the Macys were . . . nobody did anything, nobody helped Lenny. There would be absolute hell to pay the next few weeks but while it was going on, seeing him shake and go red like that, well, it was kind of worth it.

LENNY PEARL: *I wasn't angry!* I loved it! I ate it up! I thought it was a little unprofessional, yeah sure. But Lenny Pearl knows funny when he sees it.

Let me tell you, though, there is a time and a place for everything. What they did, yes, it was humorous, but it was wrong. And I don't know what it was that held me back but I was going to wring that little fat bastard's neck on live radio and say, "Your real old man isn't this midget over here, it's some foreign Armenian magician your mother banged on the sly!"

Now *that* would've been something, huh? You want unprofessional, that would've been it. That fat red son of a bitch!

SALLY KLEIN: Everybody was calling and writing . . . they wanted Harry and Flo and Ziggy back on. NBC was *deluged*. But Lenny Pearl didn't want to invite them back.

ARNIE LATCHKEY: Screwing around live on Lenny Pearl's Viceroy radio show was *fantabulous* publicity! It was the first time I'd ever heard of Ziggy Blissman. I pick up a *Variety* and there's this little article about all the mayhem some kid had caused on NBC. They ran a picture of him, his eyes bulging out in ten different locations. I examined the photograph carefully and I thought, Gee, this must be some sort of misprint.

GLENN PETTIBON: I'd never seen Lenny angrier. He usually daubed about a half pound of pomade on his hair . . . this glop smelled like turpentine and peach brandy but it lasted about six hours. Well, when Tony was in Lenny's dressing room after the radio show, all the pomade was gone and Lenny's hair was just going everywhere. "He looks like a Jewish Medusa," Billy said.

But Tony Freedman wasn't dumb. He knew that there was going to be a lot of what today they would call "buzz" over this whole thing. So Tony had to do two things: keep Lenny from having a stroke, and try to convince him to get the Blissmans on again.

"Never. Never. Never ever ever," Lenny bellowed. "And if you ask me ever ever again, I will have you smoked, sliced, and eaten!"

Over the next few days, though, it was in all the papers: Ziggy Blissman had made quite an impression. It was in Bud Hatch's column and Grayling Greene's . . . it really was everywhere! And then Viceroy's people told Lenny Pearl: Put them back on or we take you off.

● ● ●

DOMINICK MANGIAPANE [Lulu Fountain's (Vic's first wife) older brother]: I never liked Vic. I didn't like Vic when he cheated at marbles in the street and I still didn't like him when he hit it big.

Yeah, I begrudge it to you that he was different with Lulu than with most other girls. See, there were two types of women with Vic Fountain: girls and broads. Lulu was for him a girl. But most of them was just broads.

[He] sent flowers to Lulu when he returned [to Codport] and got her a nice hat with a kind of a fur trim. That really bowled her over. Lulu's first boyfriend was Vic Fountain. And her last.

ARNIE LATCHKEY: People asked me for years and years what was it about Lulu that tickled Vic's fancy, and the definitive answer is: I have no idea. She wasn't a great beauty or a great cook and she wasn't particularly sweet. She wasn't great at anything except being very plain.

But they were a handsome couple. Vic was strong, very tall, and dark. And Lulu was also dark. And very thin. So maybe any person who walks around with Vic—it doesn't matter if it's Esther Williams or Ethel Waters—it's a handsome couple. You sort of bathed in that glow.

Cut to: Tenafly, New Jersey. Murray Katz calls us at a hotel in Tenafly; he knows the Lomax band's got a few dates free. He says, How'd you like to open for Fritz Devane in New Bedford? Now, Floyd *hated* Devane, the band hated Devane, I hated him. Most everyone did—he was probably the most unpopular–most popular singer of the twentieth century. But Floyd Lomax knew that old Fritz could pack 'em in. So onto the bus and up to New Bedford we go.

Devane was really one of the most repulsive characters I ever came across, and that *does* include people I've met in show business. The man must have been allergic to soap and mouthwash—you walked into a big room and you breathed in, shuddered, and said, "Hey, was Fritz Devane here within the last twenty minutes?" Linda Darnell—maybe the most beautiful woman I've ever met in person—filmed a kissing scene with him for *Dashing D'Artagnan,* and after they yelled "cut," it was right into the shower just trying to rub the Fritz off her pores. That must've been one long shower, believe you me.

I admit it, the man could sing though. *At one time.* But after 1937, say, it was all coasting. By 1955 he was a living legend but not one single person could remember why.

And you wanna talk cheap? Jack Benny had his ongoing skinflint gag going but Fritz Devane was so cheap that nobody could ever joke about it. One time he finds a parking space in New York on Broadway, pulls in and parks, puts a quarter in the meter because he didn't have any nickels on him. He goes into his tailor, gets back the socks he had mended, then gets back in the car. He waits twenty-eight minutes so he can get all his money's worth out of the parking meter. And when the needle points to zero and it clicks, *then* and only then does he proceed onward to the emergency room at Roosevelt Hospital so his grandson can receive treatment for a fractured skull.

RAY FONTANA: It was a hot ticket, Fritz Devane at the New Bedford Ritz. It was me, Tony Ferro, and my brothers Sal and Vic, who almost didn't go because he was involved in some three-day-long pool game at Kitty's Korner. Sal went into Kitty's and dragged him out by the ear. "You're going," he said.

It was a good show. The Lomax band did about forty minutes. Dick Fain sang a few tunes . . . I remember he did "Without a Song." We were all the way in the back but even from there you could tell that Fain was in some kind of pain. He had eyes and cheekbones like they'd been hollowed out with a vacuum cleaner.

Then Devane came on. Oh, how Vic used to worship him! Growing up and all. That was the voice, the style that really impressed him. Devane did "My Sunny Day Has Gone," "Broken-Hearted and Blue," and "Just One More Chance." He made a few jokes about whales that someone had written for him because it was New Bedford. But he wasn't using up much gas, he was really loafing—he was so famous, it didn't matter. The crowd was in his pocket.

TONY FERRO: We're in the parking lot outside the theater and it's nighttime and we're going to head back to Codport. "I got a pool game I could get back into," Vic says.

Sal said to him, "Just come home. Mamma don't like you staying up so late."

Vic says to him, "Hey, it's not like she's sitting up by the window till five A.M. waiting for me to come home."

"She is, Vic," Sal says.

Just then who do we see coming our way but the Grand Forks Golden Boy himself, Fritz Devane. He's next to this big fellow, like a bodyguard. Devane's got his trademark tweed racing cap on and a beige cashmere coat.

"Hey, Vic, look," Ray said. Jabbin' us with his elbow.

Vic turns around and he sees him. His boyhood idol.

"Go say hello," Sal says. He was the oldest of all of us.

"Nah," Vic says.

"C'mon. Go ahead."

Vic cleared his throat and called out, "Hey, Mr. Devane? Mr. Devane?" His voice squeaking like a thirteen-year-old boy.

Devane's bodyguard said, "Get the hell away."

"Introduce yourself to Devane," Sal said to Vic.

Me, Sal, Vic, and Ray stop Devane and his guy in their tracks. There was a big fancy Studebaker Commander with white walls . . . that's where they was headed to.

"Hey, Mr. Devane," Vic says. "I'm a big fan of yours." Vic sticks out his hand and Devane lets it die there, in the air. "I do some singing myself," Vic says, his voice still squeaking.

"Oh, really?" Devane says. "So does my Labrador."

"No, no. Really. I've sung in some bands. On the radio. In New York and Boston."

Devane says to his guy, "Billy, get this greaseball away from me. I'm going to have to wring my jacket out just from looking at him."

And now this Billy guy reaches into his jacket, like he's got a gun in there. Who knows if he had one? But he had that kind of flattened, squashed-in nose which made you think he did. So we backed off, and they got in the car and drove away.

"That skinny famous fuck," Sal says. Sal was tough. Nothing much impressed Sal.

"I can't believe it," Vic says. "That was Fritz Devane!"

Sal got really mad. He grabs Vic and says, "Yeah, that was Fritz Devane and he just called you a greaseball! You shouldn't let nobody treat you like that!"

"Goddamn *stronzo*," Ray said.

It took ten minutes to get Vic as mad as we were. But it worked. Man, did it work.

We drove to the Grand Spouter Inn, figuring that was where Devane was staying. Vic was cursing him out the whole way. Sure enough, there's his Studebaker Commander in the parking lot. What a gorgeous car! It's two in the morning, no one around. We work the front door of the car open and pile in. Except Sal. Sal's working on the engine, me and Vic and Ray are doing everything we can inside the car itself. We redid that old Stu

from the running boards up, everything but the rearview mirror. By 4:00
A.M. it wasn't worth ten bucks.

This hotel dick, an Irishman, comes up to us—out of nowhere—and
says, "And what do you think you lads are doing?"

Sal says to him, "We're from Codport . . . we work on the piers."

"Yeah?" the dick says . . . he's taking in what's left of the car.

"Our dads work on the piers too," Sal says.

"This car belonged to Fritz Devane," the dick says. *Belonged.*

Vic says to him, "Fritz Devane called me a greaseball. To my face."

"He did, did he now?" Twirling his billy club, he told us: "My wife is a
maid at this hotel. She cleaned Mr. Devane's room only this morning. Mr.
Devane took out a ten-dollar bill and asked her, 'Miss, do you like your
job?' My wife said, 'I *love* my job, Mr. Devane.' And then he said, 'Well,
then it seems you certainly won't be needing this ten dollars.'"

The dick takes his billy club and *crack!* The rearview mirror was gone
now too.

GUY PUGLIA: We're shooting nine ball at Kitty's one night and this Greek
guy I know comes waddling over and says, "You gotta check out this fella
shooting pool." Vic says, "Why? What's so special about him?" And
Georgie K. says, "Oh, nothin'. Nothin's special if you don't think having
sixteen fingers is something special."

PIP GRUNDY [guitarist]: I was once a short order cook in Council
Bluffs, where I grew up. I didn't always make the right orders and they
weren't the best eggs or sandwiches in town but I could serve ten people in
a minute. I've always, whether it be as a chef, a musician, or a sculptor,
tried to make my handicap work *for* me.

Vic said, "Hey, I recognize you. You play guitar for Floyd Lomax's outfit."

He told me he'd sung with a few bands and I pricked up my ears. He
told me that he and a few of his pals had recently given Fritz Devane's car
a real going-over.

"Admirable," I told him.

Vic told me he'd sung with the Don Leslie band. Well, I'd seen them
perform and then I realized it: I'd seen *him* too. He started telling me about
bouncing around from band to band and club to club, and I could tell that
he was still quite hungry to sing. Some people, after they've had a taste of
the limelight, it's as insidious as a narcotic. When I left I was glad. It was
like marrying off a fat daughter.

"You know," I said to him, "I've heard Johnny Nelson is looking for a
male vocal."

"The Nelson band . . . in Philly?" he asked me.

I told him who to call. I believe it was Joe Gersh at MCA.

GUY PUGLIA: When Vic called Joe Gersh, Gersh told him he'd heard him sing, he knew him from this band and that band and had seen him at the Ambassador. We borrowed Sal's car and drove down to Philly, Vic and me did. He'd sold his Buick 'cause he needed the spending money.

I took in a few of Vic's suits to be pressed before we left—nope, you know, I ironed 'em myself—and Vic did the audition and got the job.

RAY FONTANA: There it was: the Johnny Nelson Orchestra with Victor Fontaine, as he was then known, and who's opening for them? The Blissmans!

You want irony? The first couple nights, Vic never caught the opening act.

Lulu had seen them, though, and she told Vic they were ripping up the joint. "Those are three crazy Jews," she said.

SNUFFY DUBIN: I've heard a thousand stories about the first time Ziggy and Vic met. Two thousand maybe. [Columnist] Earl Wilson wrote they met at Handelman's in New York two years before they actually met! I remember Ziggy once had somebody ghostwrite something for him for *Parade* magazine, like an autobiographical thing. In that, Ziggy said he met Vic outside a church. No way that happened.

Vic once told me he had no idea where or when he first met Ziggy. I believe it.

MICKEY KNOTT [bandleader; drummer with Johnny Nelson's band]: Vic and I walked into the Hacienda [in Philadelphia] and the Blissmans were onstage. "I wanna see this, Mickey," he said. "My girl told me they was funny."

So we looked at the act. Ziggy had a trumpet in his hands and was trying to play it. His mother was matching him note for note with that voice of hers. (Shit, thirty years later he was doing the same thing. I was on *The Tonight Show* guest-drumming with Milton DeLugg and the band, and Ziggy was going note for note with Ethel Merman.)

"This is our opener, huh?" Vic said.

"The Blissmans," I told him. "The kid's a pisser but the parents are just hanging on."

Ziggy's mother then started to sing a song, some really corny number from about 1880. She's doing that and Ziggy goes into the audience, like he's trying to hide from that noise, which sounded like an air-raid siren inside your skull. And Ziggy is going under the table, standing on tables, spritzing himself with seltzer water. Then he comes over to Vic and me—we're way in the back, against the wall. And he looked up at Vic and Vic looks down at Ziggy—don't forget, Vic was one foot taller and about ten yards handsomer—and Ziggy's about to do something for a laugh, like maybe cut Vic's tie or step on his foot or jump into his arms. Vic muttered—real low so no one in the crowd could hear it—he said to him, "Don't even think about it, kid."

And Ziggy slunked [*sic*] off and went back onto the stage.

He did that thing he did at the end of his performances: he apologized and told everyone how sorry he was if he hurt anyone's feelings. Sentimental, syrupy, a total horseshit Vegas thing. But tonight he was just "off." The second after he'd seen Vic. When he was making his way back to the stage, he stopped and turned *two times* to look back at Victor Fontaine. Two times. He could barely make the syrupy speech.

He'd been thunderstruck, you could say. You know, I haven't ever thought of this until now . . . but you ever see *Ben-Hur*? You know when that mysterious shadow falls over Charlton Heston? In the boat and in the leper colony? It was really as dramatic as that.

ARNIE LATCHKEY: So how, where, and when did I first formally meet Vic Fountain? Well, it was—as so many other great things *aren't*—in Camden, New Jersey, in 1930-blah-blah-blah, Year of Our Lord. The Lomax band was playing the Duplex. I'm going over some piddling business things with this terrifying brutish gent named Lou Manganese, who just so happens to be Al Pompiere's son-in-law. Now why Al Pompiere, who could have "persuaded" Casanova himself to come back from the dead to marry his daughter, let her marry this lowlands gorilla I don't know, but then again she wasn't the prettiest primate herself. So this King Kong in spats is telling me this and that and I'm agreeing with everything he said because the inspired notion had just struck me of keeping both my testicles inside their scrotum where they belonged.

It's Lou Manganese, me, and some *shmegege* manager. There's a knock on the door and in walks this young man with turquoise blue eyes and a head of hair like a tangled ball of navy blue yarn. And he says, "Anybody see Pip Grundy?"

"We're talking business here," Lou says.

"Anybody see Pip Grundy?" Vic didn't even hear Lou.

The *shmegege* manager winked at me. Well, I knew what that meant. "Take care of this for me, would ya?" Sometimes it's a wink, sometimes it's a nod or a smirk, it could be a rolling of the eyes. CEOs give it to VPs, kings give it to dukes, baseball managers to first-base coaches.

I stood up and I ushered Vic out and now we're in a dark, narrow hallway.

"You know who that is in there, pal?" I said. Keep in mind, who this ginzo Johnny Luscious is I'm yakking with now, I've got no inkling.

"No. Who?" he says.

"That big chimp with a thirty-eight is married to Al Pompiere's daughter."

"Oh yeah?" he asks.

"Yeah."

He thinks about it a beat and says, "Big fuckin' deal. Where's Pip Grundy?" While I admired the stripling's raw bravado, I pitied his naïveté.

I told him, "You're not going to live very long in this world, you know that?"

"I'm just trying to make it to tomorrow afternoon's nap, buddy," he said.

(Man, he could've had that etched into his family crest.)

He told me he wanted to see the Pipper so he could thank him for setting him up with the Johnny Nelson band, who were playing in Trenton just then. I informed him I'd try to relay the message but I added that, in all honesty, I'd probably forget to.

Then I said, "You sing for Nelson, huh? 'Cause let me tell you, the way things are going with us, it's really very touch and go."

His eyebrows perked up visibly. "What you mean?"

"Connie Bishop just got married and bolted the band," I told him, "and our other vocalist is addicted to pain."

"Dick Fain? The baritone?"

"Yeah, him. The man pays local high school quarterbacks to throw rocks at his head and two-hundred-pound whores to put out cigarettes on his *tuches.*"

"But he can still sing good."

"What you hear is merely the dead echo of his charisma."

Vic said, "His picture's outside, on the poster . . . how old is Fain anyway?"

"Thirty-five," I said.

"Going on seventy . . ."

"I'm aware of it," I said.

"I mean, he looks like he's been through some real hell."

"I'm familiar with it. Trying to electrocute yourself for a quick pick-me-up will do that to you."

"Jeez, me, I just down a coffee."

"Let me drop by your gig tonight," I said to him. "I'll hear you chirp. Fain is either headed back to the nuthouse for his fifth sabbatical there or he's going to finally give himself one volt too many and sauté himself for good. We could use a young handsome set of pipes like you."

"Hey, for all you know, I sing like a hyena."

"Hey, this is Floyd Lomax's outfit we're talking about. We turn down hyenas for singing too good."

"Well," he says, "tell Pip I came by, would you? What's your name anyways?"

"Arnie Latchkey."

"Arnie Latchkey, huh? . . . And what do you do?"

"Usually anything anybody tells me. And what moniker do you go by?"

"I'm Vic Fontana but they've been calling me Vic Fontaine lately."

"Oh, like in Joan? Well, Floyd'll change that, mark my words."

And that was it. He walked down the hallway—slow fade to gray—and then exited and, Teddy, I knew I'd be seeing him again. I just knew it.

That goddamn kismet'll bite you in the ass every single time.

PIP GRUNDY: Cueball, Arnie, the twins [pianists Larry and Stu Morrell, Siamese twins], and I went to the Hot Spot in Trenton to hear the Nelson Orchestra. It was a frigid, windy evening.

Dick Fain's days were numbered. We had to take precautions with him. Intricately covering the sockets, removing sharp objects from hotel rooms. Arnie would get him girls occasionally but all you heard coming from the room was this ungodly pounding.

Vic sang well, was better now than when I'd first seen him. He really wooed that crowd. The Nelson band was mediocre at best, but Vic made them better.

"He's not bad," Cueball Swenson said to me. "His singing is swell."

"He's got something," Arnie said to Cue. "I just don't know what it is."

Stu Morrell, who had little interest in music, said, "I'd say it's called 'presence.'" Larry said, "His range ain't much but—"

"*Isn't* much," Stu corrected him.

"*Isn't* much. But what he does with it is good."

I added that the girls were lapping him up too.

"Like so much melting spumoni," Arnie chimed in.

We glanced around. There were forty girls there with jaws agape.

We began talking about it, how to get rid of Fain. If we didn't fire him, how could we nudge him out? We knew Floyd was dying to make a change . . . but Floyd had other things on his mind, for by then he'd already met Thalia [Boneem].

"If Fain dies, then he's out of the band," Arnie conjectured. "And that could happen any second. Jesus, one rock in the temple too hard and he's a goner."

We went over every possible scenario . . . but one thing we agreed on was that Murray Katz and Floyd had to hear Vic sing. Soon.

ARNIE LATCHKEY: I went back to the Hot Spot the next night. Real solo-like. Arnie Latchkey, the stealth bomber. After the Nelson band wound up I passed a fiver to a stagehand, in lieu of a business card. I said, "Tell Vic that Arnie Latchkey from the Lomax band is here."

Two minutes later Vic and I are in a hallway.

"I like the way you warble, Vic," I said to him. He shrugged. "Where'd you learn to sing like that?"

He said, "I had lessons."

"No. People can't teach what you got. If they did, they'd get fired. How much is Johnny Nelson paying you?"

"Not much."

"Lomax could top that. How does 'not quite enough' sound?"

"I'll take it."

I asked him, "You got a contract with Nelson, right?"

He said, "Yeah, I guess. But if I do, it's no big deal. I'll quit and he'll just get another palooka. I've broken contracts before."

He struck me as the kind of guy who didn't give a fuck about anything. And I liked that. It reminded me of me—not the way I was but the way I wished I could be.

I said, "You know, you were once so nervous about going onstage you puked on the reeds of our tenor sax man, Joe Lambeau. In Massachusetts. You still do that?"

"Sounds like me. But I ain't like that anymore."

"That's good. Although that was the best that Joe Lambeau ever played," I jested.

I told him to come by our hotel at six.

He sang "Ol' Man River" and "Always" at the audition. The first was beyond his range—only Paul Robeson and a humpback whale can really pull that off—but he nailed "Always" shut.

After the tryout we went outside into the parking lot, me, Floyd, and Vic.

"You're good, kid," Floyd said to Vic.

"I'm better than good," Vic said. "I'm decent."

"We got a problem, though, and its name is Dick Fain."

I asked Floyd if there was an insanity clause in Fain's contract and Floyd said that if there was, Fain wouldn't have signed it because Fain wasn't crazy. Floyd and Murray Katz had been trying to nudge Fain out for weeks but the only way Fain could get the boot was if he died or quit.

Then—Eureka!—I got an idea and was it ever a masterstroke. If the Nobel committee were around, I'd be sporting a gold medallion right now, my friend. Now, there are many shady, low-down things in my life that I've done that I'm not proud of, but this one I'm real proud of. We'd have Vic sing with us in rehearsals and sit in with us on gigs and radio dates. If Fain asked, "Hey, who's the Italian kid?" we'd answer, "Huh? *What* Italian kid?" If he asked, "Why's this handsome guy sitting in with the band?" we'd answer, "What handsome guy?"

It was beautiful.

GUY PUGLIA: You read the old *Look* magazine article about Vic, it says that he agonized over the decision to change bands. *Agonized* over the decision! Vic didn't agonize over anything unless it was to decide olives or a twist.

PIP GRUNDY: We played a week in Wilmington, Delaware, and Vic sat next to Dick Fain with the band. Vic never sang, he never stood up from the chair, he just sat there right next to Fain.

"Did you see that guy sitting on my right, Pip?" Dick asked me one night.

"No, I didn't. What guy?" I asked.

"The guy with the blue hair sitting immediately to my right . . . you didn't see him?"

"Nope," I told him almost too casually. "Blue hair, eh, Dick?"

I remember that on the last three nights of the Wilmington engagement, when Dick would get up to sing at the mike, Vic would slide over to Dick's chair so that when Dick sat back down he'd have to sit in what had been Vic's chair.

We'd call for rehearsals at 3:00 P.M. but tell Dick they were at 3:30. Dick would come in at 3:30 and he'd see Vic singing with the band. And Vic—he was a superb mimic—would be imitating Dick Fain; he had the phrasing, the glissandos, the tone and pauses down pat. Dick would see this, hear this, and his face would turn the color of a cigarette ash.

I was talking to Cueball Swenson one day and Dick came over and asked, "What are you guys talking about? Were you talking about how paranoid I am?"

Cue said to him, "We were talking about how you probably think you're going to be replaced."

GUY PUGLIA: The Lomax band was playing the Hippodrome in Baltimore. The furnaces were turned up full blast and big Floyd is drippin' sweat like he's Niagara Falls. He's at the mike and he says, "And now Vic Fain would like to sing for you 'Without a Song.'" And Fain stands up and then realizes as he takes his first step, Wait, my name isn't Vic Fain. And while that's occurring to him Vic has made it over to the mike and he's singing "Without a Song." Dick Fain inches back to his chair, slowly sits down, and for a week he never stood up except for when it was to leave the entertainment business for good and hightail it into a Swiss sanitarium. He must've been happy there . . . the rumor was he was gettin' shock treatments three times a day.

ARNIE LATCHKEY: Floyd asked Vic, "Where are you from anyway, kid?"

"Codport," Vic said.

"Oh yeah?" he said. "Arnie, get this kid some soap. I don't want the whole band reeking like haddock. And from now on you're Vic Fountain. I don't want anybody coming to my gigs thinking they're seeing Joan Fontaine's long lost Italian brother and then leaving disappointed."

"Who's Joan Fontaine?" Vic asked.

Floyd shrugged and said to me, "Arn, with a pretty kisser like this he's gonna steal all my cooze away from me! Ha ha!" But by then big Floyd was pretty smitten with this doll he'd met named Thalia.

They billed Vic as "the Singin', Swingin' Fisherman." He wasn't too happy about that.

•   •   •

SALLY KLEIN: Well, guess who appears out of nowhere all of a sudden? Jerome Milton! He read Grayling Greene's column and called up Rosie in the Poconos.

Rosie says to him, "Uh, Jerry darling, you did rip up the contract, didn't you?"

Jerry says to her, "I ripped them up only on *paper,* yes, de facto technically."

And Rosie says, "What do you mean, 'de facto technically'?"

Jerry explains that while, yes, he did rip up the paperwork, the contract was for ten or so more years beyond the paper it was printed on, that the paper was only the physical manifestation of the actual agreement, which was some sort of Platonic ideal. The agreement itself was immutable and eternal, the paperwork merely transitive. "One is earthly, Rosie, and material," he said to her, "and the other is ideal and is in heaven." And Rosie says, "Jerry, you book circus geeks into sideshows in Tennessee! What the hell are you talking about?!"

"I'm talking," he tells her, "that this act is getting hotter every day. I don't know if I can keep Joe Gersh or Murray Katz away anymore from my door!"

And Rosie said, "What in God's name are they doing at your door anyway?!"

It was a good question.

Ultimately, Ziggy agreed to sign with Murray Katz, and then Murray

Katz sold a portion of the contract to Joe Gersh. But Uncle Harry couldn't care less. You've got ten agents and managers dipping their hands into the pie, but the thin little slice that was left for Harry and Flo was still a lot more pie than they'd ever eaten before.

We're in the Catskills, in Loch Sheldrake, and we're driving around and Ziggy says to me, "Sal, I've got it. It occurred to me last night driving back to the hotel. I'm going solo."

I grabbed the wheel from him and pulled us over and we almost mowed down the last line of a Burma Shave ad. I said to him, "You could hardly hold a crowd when you had Dolly Phipps!"

"That was Dolly's fault, that wasn't me. And don't ever bring her up again."

"You think you've got the *baytsim* to get onstage all by yourself?"

"Sal, I've been carrying Harry and Flo on my shoulders. Imagine how good I'll be when the only thing on my back is my hair and freckles."

"I should get out and walk!" I told him.

"Go ahead then. Walk."

But we were in some hills and ten miles away from anything.

"Are you going to fire them?" I asked him.

"I'd sort of like *you* to. I mean, this is the kind of thing you're here for."

I leaned my head against the window and stared at the trees and bushes until they became blurry. I told him I wouldn't do it.

He started up the car and said, "You know, I'm doing this for Harry and Flo too, not just for me. They been working hard all their lives. They deserve a break."

He said something about them taking some time off, he'd pay for a trip to Paris for them. I was so distraught that I didn't even tell him that they couldn't go to Paris because the Nazis just so happened to be there. Although maybe that was what he had in mind.

Ziggy got Jerry Milton, that doll, to fire them.

SNUFFY DUBIN: I take some credit for this. Zig sent them to Laramie, Wyoming! For all I know, when they got off the bus there, they ran into Dolly Phipps.

I was playing a joint in Passaic, a real dive. I was putting my act together, getting the rhythm and the pace, and picking up that sense of interaction with the audience, the rapport. Ziggy calls me up real early one day and says, "Big night tonight, Snuff, big night."

I think, *Huh?* I thought he was talking about something other than himself for once and I was trying to figure out why it was a big night for *me*. So I said, "Yeah, big night."

"Snuffy, I need some gags," he said.

And I realized it, that he was talking about himself. It was his big debut as a solo . . . he was calling me from Heine's in Loch Sheldrake.

"You got Danny McGlue for that, Zig," I said. "I give you my material, people will think I swiped it from you when they see me perform."

"Just give me three jokes and I'll give you credit."

"Danny McGlue, Zig," I said.

"Snuffy, I think I made a mistake. I don't know about this solo deal. I mean, who do you play off of when you're up there?"

"Nobody," I told him. "You're naked. It's you and the walls and two hundred people who fucking hate you for raping their daughter and then burning her alive. That's what it's like."

"Christ, that don't sound too good."

I said, "Zig, you're ten times funnier than I am. You were born with it. A guy like you don't even need gags. Just get up there and *shpritz*. You'll have 'em in your hands in a minute."

"You think so?"

I could tell he was getting confident and excited. "I know so, pal," I told him.

I hung up the phone and I realized: I either just created a comedy juggernaut or the biggest dud since the Stone Age.

DANNY McGLUE: I saw Harry and Flo get on the Greyhound . . . a bellhop helped Flo with her bag, which was bigger than she was. He tried to help Harry too but Harry insisted on carrying his valises himself. He could barely do it. The bus driver loads the luggage into the bus, and Harry and Florence are about to board. 'Bye, Mommy! 'Bye, Poppy!" Ziggy calls out from outside the lobby, under the awning. He looked like a kid, like a ten-year-old. And they looked so old. Flo called out, "Good luck, Ziggy!" and Ziggy called back, "Thanks, Mom!" She told him to eat well and wear a scarf and cap at night because it got cold up there, even in the summer. Harry called out to him to not be nervous and to keep 'em laughing. "Okay, Pop!" Ziggy yelled out. They got on the bus and my heart nearly broke.

Ziggy's first performance was on a Wednesday night in late spring. It was a good crowd. There was a lot of local tub-thump . . . the posters said ZIGGY BLISSMAN, ALONE AT LAST.

You know, I've seen a lot go wrong in this business. Once I saw a tenor have a heart attack and die onstage exactly at the moment in the opera when his character was supposed to die, and the cast and the audience had no idea he'd really died. I've also seen an actor deliver one of the most breathtakingly beautiful versions of the *Hamlet* "To be or not to be" soliloquy, but unfortunately he was appearing in *Macbeth* at the time.

Ziggy's solo was the most traumatic thing I've ever seen. I don't know, to be honest, how I felt: Was I pulling for him to succeed or did I want him to fail? Well, if I wanted him to fail, I certainly didn't want him to fail this miserably.

He got onstage, adjusted the mike down to his size, way down because he was only five foot four. That was the last laugh he got. That was the last *sound* he got.

He shook his head to one side, like he was trying to shake out some words there, then he shook it to the other side. He began twitching a little . . . and sweating a lot. It was pouring off him. I was worried about him getting electrocuted by the mike, with all that perspiration. His lips were moist and he was just staring off, like he was catatonic. This was going on for five minutes. I was thinking, This is what you get for getting rid of your parents, you schnook, but, you know, it was too pathetic; he was too sad a figure to be angry about or vengeful over.

It's time for me to play the cavalry now. So I go onstage and sit down and I'm just about to play some songs that he and I had performed, when I hear this very slight whimper come out of him. He won't be able to sing, I thought. No way.

I walked over to him and whispered to him, "Are you okay?"

He said, "I'm scared."

"Let's go then, okay?"

"I can't walk, Danny. I can't move."

"Come on . . . just take my hand. I'll do the moving for us."

"Tell them to turn the lights off. Please."

I made the throat-cutting gesture and the lights went out.

He took my arm. I never felt a hand so cold in my life. It gave me goose bumps. He grabbed tighter and very, very slowly we made it off the stage.

SALLY KLEIN: I'd never seen someone so mortally terrified in all my life, and when the lights went down and I heard nothing but Danny and Ziggy's footsteps slowly creeping off, something hit me and it scared me half to death: I thought, Oh my God, I'm going to be with Ziggy Blissman until the day I die.

DANNY McGLUE: I took him to his little dressing room, closed the door, and poured him a scotch—he always kept a bottle of Dewar's or Johnnie Walker in his dressing room.

"Take some, Ziggy," I said but I don't think he heard me. He sat there and was shaking and was as white as a ghost.

"Look, this happens," I told him. "You're not the first person this has happened to." He rubbed his hands over his head, in his hair, then he put his head down in his arms on the vanity table.

I heard a knock on the door and figured it was [hotel owner] Bernie Heine. I said, "Go away, Bernie," but I heard Sally say, "It's me, Danny," and I let her in.

Ziggy started weeping softly. Sally and I sat down.

"I'm such a failure," he said. It was hard to make out what he was saying—his arms were muffling things. "I'm a failure, a failure, a failure . . ."

"You had two hundred people in that room," Sally said, "because they'd seen your act with your parents and *loved* you! You are not a failure."

He said, "I'm so ugly . . . I'm ugly. I've always been ugly. Funny *looking!* I'm funny because I'm so ugly."

Sally and I looked at each other. I couldn't think of anything to say except, "Ziggy, there are plenty of ugly people like you who *aren't* funny." But I didn't say it.

"What am I gonna do?" he said, still sniffling like crazy. "What job could I ever have? I can't do nuttin'."

Sally said, "Zig, there's plenty you can do . . ."

"I'm so lonely," he said. "I hate being me . . . I *hate* it. I'm so lonely."

I said, "When you're onstage they love you. The crowd loves you."

He said, "They love me 'cause I'm funny. Why am I funny? 'Cause I'm ugly. I can't do nuttin'." God, I think he even said he was going to die.

There was a knock on the door and I said, "Go away, Bernie." Bernie said, "The kid owes me a show, for Christsake!" Then Bernie went away.

Ziggy said, "I can't never go on alone again. Ever! And when my parents die or they quit then nobody will *ever* like me and I won't be able to get a job nowheres. I got *bubkes*."

"Ziggy, Ziggy, Ziggy . . ." I said.

(And you have to remember: Me and Ziggy, we're not really friends yet. We're not that close. And I kept getting in these emotional scenes with him, for years!)

"Do you want to take a walk?" Sally asked.

"No, Sal. Just leave me in here," Ziggy said.

So she and I stood up. I remember that on the way out I accidentally touched Ziggy's neck and his skin was still ice cold.

We walked out and I gently closed the door.

"You think he's gonna be all right?" I asked Sally, and she said she didn't know.

We heard him from behind the door . . . he was sobbing now.

Sally grabbed a chair from down the hallway and set it up right outside his dressing room. She sat down and said, "Danny, go to sleep. Don't worry—I'll make sure he's okay."

"Now I'm worried about *you*," I said.

She rolled her eyes like I was an idiot to care and I left her there. The next morning at seven she was still in the chair, fast asleep, and Ziggy was still inside.

When I saw her then—I think it was that moment. I had a serious case on her.

SALLY KLEIN: Ziggy was booked at Heine's for a week. And for a week people showed up. But he couldn't get himself onstage. He would go to his dressing room and then not move. Bernie was furious. We canceled the other engagements he had . . . Joe Gersh and Murray Katz had lined up three or four weeks' worth.

He was like a zombie. He wouldn't eat. Finally, after a few days, I convinced him to walk outside and take a few steps . . . but he would just stare at the ground. He got tired very easily and slept a lot.

One day—it was June and very beautiful out—Ziggy, Danny, and I drove out to a lake and went swimming. There were lots of children around with their parents, dozens of kids running around. It was a very happy scene . . . that wonderful noise that kids make on the beach or near swimming pools, like happy birds. Kids would run up to Ziggy and he would make faces at them and they would make faces back and he'd make a more funny face and they'd start giggling and then run away to bring back their friends.

It was late in the afternoon—his shoulders and stomach were red from the sun—and he started talking about new routines and performing and also the contract with his parents and how he'd like to get out of it.

I looked over at Danny because I thought this was a good sign.

DANNY McGLUE: I remember thinking, Hey, good! Ziggy's being Ziggy again! But then I thought, Oh no, Ziggy's being Ziggy again.

● ● ●

PIP GRUNDY: I have no idea if Thalia Boneem was her real name. She was dark-skinned and had luxurious raven black hair, but the thing that struck you right away was her eyes. They were big and dark—like Turkish coffee—and melancholy, and she spoke with just a hint of an accent.

There were always women around—it's that way with musicians. They were in the lobbies of the hotels, they were waiting outside the clubs, they were in the bars. I married my high school sweetheart and I remained true to her. I cannot tell you how rare that was. Cueball Swenson was married and had three kids but he was known to take the occasional dip. Harry Bacon, who was really Harriet Bacon, had a wife but Harry played around too, though how and with whom and with what I do not know.

"I can't get enough," [Floyd] told me once. "I can't never get enough. The more I get, the more I want. And the more I want . . ."

But all that ended with Thalia Boneem.

ARNIE LATCHKEY: He met her in an elevator at the Hotel Casey in Scranton . . . we were there for a weekend in the spring. The way I heard it, he didn't say a word to her, she didn't say a word to him. There was electricity between them, bolts of it, like in Frankenstein's laboratory. It just lit up and cackled.

She was about twenty-four or twenty-five years old and she was a virgin. I'll take his word for it.

I have never seen such a change in a human being in all my life. "This is the one, Arn," he said to me once before a gig, when everybody was setting up. "My whoring days are through."

I looked over to her; she was standing in a corner, dressed all in black. Looks-wise, was she something to write home about, you wonder? Well, I might have written home about her, sure, but I don't think that the letter would've been very long.

"Latch," Floyd told me once, blushing like a tomato, "she just turns me into a big baby all over again."

PIP GRUNDY: Despite the unprofessionalism of our orchestra, we'd always been consistent. We always showed up twenty-five minutes late to play . . . but still, it was *always* twenty-five minutes. We were known to play the wrong notes here and there . . . but they were always the same ones in the same songs at the same times. Vic had been with us for a few months now and we were much more energetic with him than we'd been with Fain. The energy was really bouncing back at us from the crowd, particularly from the women.

I remember in a parking lot in Cleveland; Vic emerged—it was after a show—and he had a woman under each arm, two blondes with sunny smiles, fresh wind-pinched faces, bright lipstick, blue eyes.

Floyd was getting into a car and Thalia Boneem was in the front and Vic winked at Floyd. Floyd walked over to Vic and said, "What was that about?"

"I was just remembering how you said I was going to steal all your cooze away, that's all," Vic said.

"You can have it, Vic. And you know, you shouldn't talk like that," Floyd said. He got into the car and drove away.

ARNIE LATCHKEY: Stu and Larry Morrell was the closest to Floyd personally, but because they were Siamese twins, you couldn't keep too many secrets. You want to talk about in one ear and out the other?!

So Stu told me what it was all about. It was the fit. That's all it was. The fit. Floyd must have oozed into her like a hand into a glove with a quicksand lining. It was that simple. He called her his little bear trap.

You could hear them down the hallway and four flights up. He sounded like an elephant getting its trunk amputated without any anesthesia, and she made these squeaky noises, like a manual pencil sharpener handle that needs oiling going around slowly.

But he eventually became this whimpering bowl of jelly. Thalia once told him that she kissed a boy when she was fifteen back in the old country and he started blubbering for three hours straight. The gig was canceled that night. In a hotel in White Plains, Thalia told him when she came to America she'd worked for some guy sewing buttons onto *schmattes* on Essex Street and that he'd once put his hand on her tush, and Floyd destroyed the hotel room . . . the furniture and the floorboards were splinters. She would bring up a man that she knew only casually and Floyd would grill her for hours and hours . . . it was like a personal Spanish Inquisition.

I think about fifteen gigs were canceled on account of this behavior.

She had him under her thumb, this little dark Gypsy-ish girl and this massive bald Humpty Dumpty-like trumpeter. For hours she would sit in the bed and he'd just bawl his eyes out, in boxer shorts that Moby Dick couldn't fit into . . . all because some fella had once asked her for her phone number.

Don't forget: she was a virgin. And she was exotic. And . . . well, let's not mince words here, my friend: She must have been like a goddamn cyclone between the sheets.

PIP GRUNDY: We got off the bus and filed slowly into the lobby of the Eliot [Hotel] in Boston. We got the feeling back in our legs—it had been a very long bus ride. Floyd was talking to Arnie, going over room arrangements and rehearsal times, and Cueball poked an elbow in my ribs. One of the bellhops—this boy could not have been older than eighteen—was talking to Thalia; she was looking at him with those dark mystical eyes. Floyd then espied them talking to each other—it really was quite innocent—and he abruptly stopped the conversation with Arnie. He watched the two of them talk, his face getting more flushed by the second, and we watched Floyd watch the two of them. The bellhop walked away and everybody turned to Floyd. He sat down in a chair in the lobby and buried his head in his hands. A minute later he beckoned for Arnie, and he and Arnie whispered to each other.

Arnie then gathered us in a circle and said, "Uh, guys, the gig is off."

We groaned and Floyd lifted his head out from his hands and shot us a very nasty look.

"Okay, everybody back on the bus," Arnie said.

GUY PUGLIA: I'd seen Vic with every band he'd been with, from that crew of Boston blue bloods and that dive in Brooklyn with the sticky floor, and this was him at his best, so far. They even recorded a few songs, including "What Would I Do Without You?" and "Good-bye, Sweetheart, Farewell."

He'd send stuff to Lulu, he'd send her earrings and stockings and chocolates and stuff. But he wasn't too big on writing letters. One time me, Hunny, and Vic were in Jimmy Dooley's bar in New York and I says to Vic, "Hey, how come you don't write Lu a letter?" Hunny says, "Yeah, Vic, write that nice girl a letter." So Vic grabs a piece of paper from the hatcheck girl and a pen, and he shoves it over to me and says, "Gaetano, write something nice for me, would you?" I said, "Me? I don't wanna marry her!" I shoved it to Hunny and Hunny said he didn't want to marry her either and he wasn't too big on writin' nothing. "Just write something nice for me, okay, Guy?" Vic said to me.

So I wrote this really drippy sweet letter to her, like "Vic is really, really missing you and he really wishes he could be with you. You mean so much to Vic, you're the thing that keeps him going, the first thing he thinks of in the morning and the last thing he thinks of at night. He's just no good without you." And it went on. It was really very emotional . . . I was gettin' all choked up writing it! I slid the page over to him and he didn't even read it! He just said, "Thanks . . . send it tomorrow morning first thing."

PIP GRUNDY: The buses we traveled in . . . I never did enjoy them. Too cramped, too smoky, all those nasty smells coming from twenty men. You can imagine. The trains were fun though. We were based in Camden but went as far north as Maine, as far south as Florida, and as far west as Kansas. In the trains you could spread out and unwind.

Floyd and Thalia shared a sleeper, all very hush-hush because it was 1940. But perhaps not *so* hush-hush, for at three in the morning I'd wake up to what I thought was a long freight train going in the opposite direction, but it was just Floyd and Thalia attaining their climaxes.

But the dining cars, we used to take them over . . . that's where the card games were, the dice games too. We'd be tending to our instruments or just fiddling around. Some of the boys were serious about music and knew all about Lester Young, Basie, Coleman Hawkins, Ben Webster, Django, and Roy Eldridge. It's a pity that Floyd insisted on that middling "society" sound.

ARNIE LATCHKEY: Vic arranged it, he set the whole damn thing up . . . I had nothing to do with it except I went along with it.

Who was in that card game? . . . let's see . . . it was Harry Bacon, Cueball, Sid Gibson, and Floyd. Cueball lost all his dough and then Roy Lindell hopped in and he got cleaned out quick. When Roy dropped out, Vic came in to the dining car and took his seat. I remember distinctly he rubbed his nose with his forefinger when he sat down. He asked for a drink and Sid passed him a flask. It was Floyd's deal and he was shuffling, and Vic asked the porter for a hot towel.

Floyd dealt and I was pretending to read the paper but I had my eyes on Floyd's hand. I could see the whole thing. They were playing five-card draw mostly. I could see Floyd's hand and Harry's and Sid's . . . best seat in the house. Vic and I had worked out the system: I scratch my nose this way it means this; I scratch my ear that way it means that. It was perfect.

Vic won the first hand and Harry gets the deck. We're all making small talk, farting and smoking and what have you. Vic gets the hot towel, wipes his hands and his forehead. He won this hand too, thanks in great part to me scratching and twitching and rubbing. Now the deck went to Vic. I remember Floyd had nothing, just ace high, and Harry had even worse. I licked my lips and Vic bet low so as to keep them in the game. They drew and Vic suckered them in and he beat them, three hands in a row.

Floyd is now shuffling. He changes the game to seven-card stud. No, what he did was, he put his head in his hand and thought about it for a while and *then* changed the game. He'd dealt them two cards and he said, "Hey, Vic, where you been?"

"Just getting some shut-eye, Floyd."

"This card smells like cooze," Floyd said.

"I don't know about that," Vic said.

"Harry, smell this card," Floyd said and he passed the card—which was a queen of diamonds—over to Harry. He said, "I don't know . . . it smells like a card to me."

"Yeah, like you know the smell of cooze!" Floyd said and he dealt the card. He's still dealing and he gets another whiff and says, "You sure you were just getting some shut-eye, Vic?"

"Sure am," Vic said. But I started to get uneasy . . . because Vic was looking uneasy.

Vic wipes his hands with another hot towel and Floyd continues dealing and then he comes to a card—it was the ace of spades that Vic had won with the game before—and he draws in a huge, huge breath. Vic looks over to me. He looked very scared . . . the color drained out of his face like it was sucked out.

I heard this noise, this strange noise. It came from Floyd's gut, his huge stomach . . . it was this inner yowl, like a lonely dog baying miles away. Floyd cleared the card table with his hands, he just swept the cards and the ashtrays and the money off the table. His face is all red and he's quaking.

Well, Arnold Latchkey felt the fear of the Almighty shoot right through him . . . because well I knew that big Floyd Lomax kept a pearl-handled Colt with him, in his trumpet case. And there was his trumpet case, right next to him. I stood up and said to him, "Okay, look, I can explain . . . yeah, we was cheatin' but it was all Vic's idea . . ." but he wasn't even listening to me. He yelled at the top of his lungs, "THALIA! THALIA! THALIA!" It was deafening, no exaggeration. "THALIA! THALIA! THALIA!" Imagine being inside the belly of a timpani for Beethoven's Ninth. That's what this was like.

He reaches for his trumpet case and Vic is standing up and backing away and saying, "Floyd . . . I can explain . . . it wasn't me . . . I swear . . ." Floyd is struggling to open the case but is quaking so much he can't get a purchase on it, and Vic says, "She came to me, Floyd, my hand to God! She started just rubbing herself against me real nice and—".

"THALIA!!!" he yelled.

Floyd snapped open the case and I thought, Okay, he knows now I cheat at cards, what do I do here? Do I stay? Do I go? If I go, where do I go? What do I do for the rest of my life? All these questions in a hundredth of a second but no answers.

"Arnie, let's go!" Vic yelled to me and that seemed like the only answer there was. I made my way around Floyd—no small feat, that—and me and Vic ran out of the dining car. Behind me I hear a gunshot and then the train whistle and I heard these big pounding footsteps of Floyd coming at us, like Sasquatch himself. We made it through one sleeping car and there was another gunshot. The next thing I know, Vic and me—his hair was blowing all over in the wind—are standing between two train cars and we see and hear Floyd stomping toward us.

"I can't believe you, you dumb guinea," I said to him. "You gotta wise up in life, you know that?"

"Maybe so," he said. He told me he'd been trying to wipe the scent off with the hot towels.

"So by the way," I asked, "how was she?"

He told me she was only so-so and then said, "I guess we jump, Arn."

"Yeah, I guess so."

The ground hurt when we hit it and we rolled for a few yards. I felt dirt kick up around my foot—Floyd was shooting at us. I stood up and looked at the train and it looked like the whole goddamn train was big Floyd's bald egg-shaped head streaking away . . . I heard the train whistle and the words "THALIA! THALIA! THALIA!"

I helped Vic up and he picked a twig out of his hair, wiped the dirt off himself, and straightened out a stray pleat in his pants.

We walked for a while. We didn't say a word. At first it was pitch-black out but then the clouds cleared away from the moon and things were starting to look very familiar from my old *tummling* days. The air smelled sweet and the wind was rustling the leaves. It was summer.

After about an hour Vic asks me, "Hey, Latch . . . you got any idea where the hell we are?"

"We're in the Catskills, Vic. Loch Sheldrake."

"What the hell are we gonna do now?"

I told him, "I got an older brother named Marvin owes me a favor. Big time."

* * *

DANNY McGLUE: It was the lowest, coldest thing I think I've ever heard of.

I knocked on his door . . . by this time Ziggy had his own bungalow at Heine's. It wasn't much; there was a radio and a Victrola, a bed and copies of *Variety* and *Billboard* and *Metronome* all over the floor.

I walked in and there are two people sitting there, a man and a woman in their fifties, as Irish-looking as a four-leaf clover. Ziggy had a sheepish, guilty look on, as if I'd caught him at something. He was standing and they were sitting.

Ziggy directed me to a corner and told me, "They're auditioning to become my folks."

All I could say was "*Wha—?*" I mean, I was dumbstruck!

"Danny," he said, "I'm really very miserable with the present arrangement."

He stared talking about how his contracts were with "Sigmund Blissman and Parents" but that they never did say Harry Blissman or Flo Blissman. He's telling me all this and I'm taking in the man and the woman sitting there—I felt sorry for them. They needed work. I had 'em figured for vaudeville hoofers right away. I have no idea how Ziggy found them.

"So you're replacing your parents with these two?" I asked him.

"If they're good enough."

"Harry and Flo have no idea about this, do they?"

To everyone he suddenly said, "Alas, I am being rude!" He introduced me. Their names were Jimmy and Kathleen O'Hare. They'd been in the Gus Edwards and Considine and Sullivan circuits; they'd worked with the Marx Brothers way back when, but were small potatoes. And they weren't even husband and wife—they were brother and sister! A pauper's Fred and Adele.

"You gotta hear this broad sing," Ziggy says to me. "What pipes."

I whispered to him, "You know, your own mother has pipes from God."

"This one don't bust eyeglasses, Danny." And then he pulled me back into the corner and said, "I really think this is going to work out for the best."

What could I do? I felt terrible. Harry and Flo had always been won-derful to me. They'd sung songs by Kern, Foster, Arlen, the Gershwins, and Berlin, and then along comes Danny McGlue and I'm giving them non-sense like "Ol' Man's Liver" and they never once raised a fuss.

I went along with it and I'll probably burn in hell.

SALLY KLEIN: They came back from Laramie in June. They looked won-derful—vigorous and tan and refreshed. Harry especially—he looked five years younger.

Ziggy hadn't played a date since he froze up onstage. Bernie Heine and the owners of Marx's and Berenson's and Kutsher's—they weren't exactly thrilled with him. He told me to tell them—which I did—that his parents were coming back any day now.

Harry and Flo knocked at my room at Berenson's resort and we all hugged and kissed and I let them in. They told me what a wonderful time they'd had and after ten minutes we got down to business.

"So is there anything lined up?" Harry asked.

"You're booked here this Thursday through Sunday. And you've got the White Lake Lodge the following weekend."

Harry asked, "So did Ziggy's solo act go over like gangbusters?"

"Oh no!" I told them. "He hasn't worked in a while. He knew you were coming back and he had Joe Gersh book these dates."

I told them about how he'd failed miserably, how he was practically comatose afterward. It really got to Flo. You know, they hadn't treated him well when he was a boy and by now he'd exacted his revenge. I think that now, in their hearts, it was time to call the war off. The hatchets were buried.

I had no idea whatsoever what was going to happen.

ARNIE LATCHKEY: Freud would have had a field day with this. *This is classic stuff!* Biblical stuff! Ziggy was once the loneliest kid in Brooklyn, practically abandoned. He rises up and wreaks his revenge on his parents. What's the word that comics use when they have an audience in hysterics? They *slay* them. And now here you've got Ziggy slaying his parents. I mean, this is like Greek mythology. Just classic stuff.

SALLY KLEIN: Every show that Harry, Flo, and Ziggy did, the O'Hares were there . . . with the very best seats in the house, courtesy of Ziggy. You've seen *Strangers on a Train*, when Robert Walker is at the tennis match and all the heads are going back and forth, following the ball? Except Robert Walker, he's fixed on Farley Granger? Well, that's just what was happening here. These two were *glued*.

"Who are those two people following you around?" I asked Ziggy one day.

He came out and told me he was replacing Harry and Flo with the O'Hares.

"This will kill your parents!" I said. I was incensed. "This will kill them!"

He didn't say anything.

"You're really going through with this?" I asked him.

"Sally, I'd like you to be the one who fires them."

"You don't have the guts to do it?" I hissed at him. "You dream up this cockamamie scheme and you don't have the guts to do it?"

"Sally, you do this, I swear . . . I'll buy you anything you want. You want a fur? I'll get you one. Chinchilla, mink, sable, whatever you want, it's yours."

"You could get me every fur in the world," I told him, "I won't do it, you weasel."

"I'll remember this," he said.

I have to admit: That frightened me. I didn't want to work in my father's girdle factory. I loved being in show business. It was fun and I didn't want to leave.

I told him I wouldn't do it and I don't think he ever forgave me.

DANNY McGLUE: He did the engagements with Harry and Flo at night and then in the daytime he rehearsed with the O'Hares in his bungalow.

It was the most nefarious thing.

One day I ran into Harry in the lobby at Berenson's. We sat down in those big plush chairs they had and he said, "You know, everything is wonderful for us right now."

I thought, Hey, okay, maybe Ziggy's told them about the O'Hares and they're fine with it. So I said to Harry, "That's good, that's good."

Harry told me about how there's been some sort of unspoken *rapprochement* between him and Ziggy. He said that from now on it was all business, that they worked for their son. They were resigned to that.

"We never thought we'd ever be this successful. You should've seen some of the places we played, Danny. Black holes of Calcutta they were."

The O'Hares suddenly walked by, about twenty feet away.

"Hey, those two are our biggest fans!" Harry said to me. "They're at every show!"

I looked at him—he was still looking at the O'Hares and smiling—and I nodded and said, "Uh-huh."

SALLY KLEIN: One day Ziggy came to me and said, "Would you do me a favor, Sal?" And he asked me to take Harry and Flo out to dinner, to

Tremolo's restaurant in Loch Sheldrake, on a Tuesday night. I asked him why and he just said he had to go to New York and it was their anniversary and he wanted them to have a good time.

That Tuesday night, Harry, Flo, and I are having this sumptuous feast and I said to them, "Happy anniversary!" They looked at me like I was crazy! I said, "This isn't your anniversary?" And they said no, it wasn't.

Snuffy Dubin told me, a week or so later, what it was all about.

Ziggy had gone on Lenny Pearl's Viceroy radio show that night. With the O'Hares playing the "parts" of Harry and Flo. Tremolo's was just to keep the real Harry and Flo from knowing about it. I was a diversion and I didn't even know it.

LENNY PEARL: I dreaded Ziggy being on my show! To me, he was the black plague of Echo Beach. I told those Viceroy big shots, "Okay, once a month. I'll have 'em on once a month. But no more. Because I don't think I can take any more than that." Ziggy's shtick . . . it was unprofessional. My staff and I, we worked all hours into the night, every night, honing and finely polishing and crafting that show. And then Ziggy comes on and it's all shot to hell.

So now Ziggy shows up with these two people and he's telling everybody they're his parents! The sheer chutzpah! See, I had no idea he was going to do this—due to prior commitments I hadn't been able to make it to one single rehearsal that week.

These two people, his new mother and father—who they were, I don't know, they just played right along. As a matter of fact, I thought they had more polish than Harry and Flo ever did, may all parties involved rest in peace.

SNUFFY DUBIN: I'm working the Colonial Inn in Signac [New Jersey] and there are more people backstage than in the crowd that night. I'm washing my face in the john and I hear Ziggy on the radio—some stage-hand is listening to Lenny Pearl's Viceroy show. Then I hear this woman start to sing, I don't know her voice from Minnie fucking Mouse. And Ziggy's calling her Mommy and then I hear this other voice I don't know and Ziggy's calling him Poppy.

I may have been flabbergasted but I wasn't surprised.

ARNIE LATCHKEY: Marvin was older than Vic and myself, he was about thirty at this time. He didn't have too much going for him, he wasn't born with my savoir faire for deals or anything. But he was still my flesh and blood and he sure owed me one.

He took me and Vic in at Heine's and I told him every single thing that had happened, leaving out a few details here and there. I said, "Marvin, this Italian kid, the girls soak him up like a sponge does spilt coffee."

Vic was in a corner smoking and brushing up on Skeezix in *Gasoline Alley*.

"Can he sing, Arnie?" Marvin asked me.

"The answer is yes. And besides, it don't matter."

I asked him if the small house band was good enough to back a crooner like Vic Fountain, and he said they were better than the Lomax band. I asked him if he could put Vic on the bill and he started hedging. That's when I played the ace: "You knocked up a Wall Street banker's daughter and it was me who got a Bellevue janitor to do the dirty work on her!" He said he'd do it on one condition. "The name's gotta change," he said. I told him that this was my guy, this was my talent, and who's he to go around changing names? He said people hear the name Fountain, they're gonna think Fontana or Montana. Change the name, Arnie, he said, and we'll put him on. I quickly acquiesced.

Vic rehearsed with the house band the next day—they *were* better than the Lomax band—and in three days he was an opening act.

We're in the lobby at Heine's and they're putting the poster up. On top in small print is VICTOR FELDBAUM, FORMERLY WITH THE FLOYD LOMAX ORCHESTRA. Underneath that and in much bigger letters was a picture of Ziggy, and it just said THE BLISSMANS! LAFF RIOTS! And, to my surprise, underneath that in the biggest letters on the sign, it said SPECIAL GUEST: LENNY PEARL!

What had happened was, on the Viceroy show on NBC, Ziggy had lured Lenny Pearl to come to Heine's. He baited him into it, he challenged him. He said things like, "Too scared of the altitude, Lenny?" and "Oh, it's safe inside a studio with a sound-effects man doing all the laughing for the audience . . ." And Lenny, just to shut the kid up and save face, agreed to play the place.

Classic, *classic* show business boner. One for the books.

The morning before he's going to open, Vic and me were having blintzes at some roadside dive. He said to me, "You know, I've seen the Blissmans before. When I was with Johnny Nelson's outfit."

"And?"

"And I'm glad I'm opening for them and not the other way around."

"Why's that?" I inquired.

"'Cause the kid is insane. He's loony. He goes into the crowd, he spills things on himself, he does a pansy act and double-talk. They go over by an hour sometimes."

And then I remembered: I'd read about Ziggy in *Variety*. He'd screwed up Lenny Pearl's whole show on the radio.

I said, "You're right . . . this kid is a freak. You better hope he don't come on during your act, Feldbaum."

Vic said, "He does, I'll rip that red mop right off his head."

SALLY KLEIN: Ziggy knocked on my hotel room door at about noon. I was on the phone to my mother, I remember that. He said, "Sal, tonight is the big night."

I'd been living in fear for two weeks. When were Harry and Flo going to get the ax? Who would tell them? How were they going to react? I could hardly eat . . . I would just stay in my bed and curl up and try not to think about it. But it didn't work.

"Have you told them yet, Ziggy?"

"I asked Jerry Milton to do it."

"So he told them?"

"He won't do it."

"So *you* told them?"

"Then I called Rosie Baer."

"And?"

"She wouldn't do it either."

I asked him, "*Has anyone told them yet?*"

"Then I tried Murray Katz."

"And?"

"No dice. He said, 'I may be a theatrical agent and I may be loathsome and dishonorable but somehow you've found something which is beneath me.'"

I said to him, "So nobody has told them yet? This is what you're telling me now?"

"You sure you don't want to do it?"

"I can't, I can't," I told him. Tears were running down my cheeks. He said, "Poor Cousin Sally." He tried to hug me and I let him but then I broke away.

"This is for the best," he told me.

I shook my head and no words came out.

Nobody ever told them. Nobody had the nerve.

ARNIE LATCHKEY: Vic and I are backstage and there was this great buzz around, this murmuring in the crowd we heard. It's maybe the second week of June, the place is packed. *Packed.* Because of Lenny Pearl. Wall-to-wall Christ killers, Vic said to me, but he was only kidding . . . we could do that. I could call him dago or guinea, he could call me *mazza Cristo*. No harm, no foul.

The emcee comes on and says, "Ladies and gentleman, please give a warm Loch Sheldrake welcome to a new performer making his very first appearance at Heine's tonight . . . from Boston, Massachusetts: Vic Feldbaum!"

I pushed Vic onto the stage and the piano starts up. I'm watching all this through the curtains. First thing I do, I key on all the women in the crowd. The girls, they're oohing, aahing, and ogling. Vic sang "It Was You," a very up-tempo number, and they were eating him up, male and female alike. He was swinging and they were swinging along with him.

He went into his second song, a more adagio-type number, and I turned around and saw—for the very first time in the flesh—Mr. Ziggy Blissman of Echo Beach, Brooklyn. The hair, up in what was called an Afro later. And the body . . . the Human Basketball, that's what he was. And the eyes . . . he could really pop them out every which way.

He sidles over to me and says, "Who's this?"

I said, "His name's Victor Feldbaum."

And he said, "Yeah, and I'm Benito Mussolini."

I laughed at that. My type of joke.

"Who is he really?"

I told him he was Vic Fountain. Ziggy remembered he'd met him once, at the Hacienda, and—this really shocked me—Ziggy rattled off every single band that Vic had ever played with. Every single one. He mentioned Don Leslie, he mentioned Lomax, he mentioned Mickey Ford at that joint in Brooklyn near the navy yard. For Christsake, *he even mentioned that barbershop quartet up in Massachusetts!* He pointed to his forehead and said, "It's all up here. Einstein's got nuttin' on me except the mustache." Well, I found out later that Ziggy read every single show business trade newspaper, every gossip column, and he locked it up there in his gray matter or whatever color Ziggy's cerebellum happened to be.

We're still watching Vic sing and I said to Ziggy, "He's good, don't you think?"

"He'll do," Ziggy said.

Then he asked me if Vic would mind it if he ran onstage right now and started goofin' around. I said, "You wanna wake up without your balls tomorrow?"

He said, "No, I got a tendency to need those."

He asked me who I was and I said Arnie Latchkey. "I'm managing Vic," I told him.

"My condolences, Arnie," he said.

SALLY KLEIN: Before every show Harry and Flo would drink tea, especially Aunt Flo. She would always put a lot of honey in it for her voice. So we were in their room and I kept looking at the clock. Harry was talking to

Flo and to me but I didn't hear a word. Because my own thoughts were blaring so loud: Tell them, Sally, *tell them.* You have to tell them. You *have* to!

Every time I tried, the words wouldn't come out. One time I even got as far as "There's something I have to tell you." Flo said, "What is it?" and I said, "Nothing."

I went to the bathroom and vomited with the water running so they wouldn't hear it. I stayed in there for five minutes. The phone rang . . . it was time to go to the dressing room to get ready.

Ziggy purposely had them called ten minutes too late.

ARNIE LATCHKEY: Vic had really mastered his stage persona. I was surprised. At the end of the five songs he did, he said straight out of nowhere, "Thank you, ladies, thank you, gentlemen. It has really given me such unbelievable *naches* to come up and sing for you tonight! You're a great crowd and you couldn't make me feel more accepted. And—for all you lovely Sadies, Selmas, and Shirleys—I'm in room four-thirteen."

Now where did *this* come from?! Where did *naches* come from? I knew he was *shtupping* girls and I guess maybe he'd asked them for a few words of the local argot. I don't know. And the joke at the end? Room 413? He'd never said one word onstage before this night—he just warbled.

There truly was something magical in the air that night.

SALLY KLEIN: I walked with Harry and Flo down those long halls. They seemed endlessly long, a mile long. They were holding hands. God, they were so tiny.

I remember the elevator didn't work. We waited for two minutes and then we decided to use the stairs.

Going down the stairs we passed this man coming up. He was dressed in a tuxedo, he had his hair parted in the middle and it was very shiny. And he had a very long, thin handlebar mustache. I remember that he smelled of paprika.

"Oh my God," Harry said.

Flo gasped and covered her mouth, like she was in shock.

I don't know who it was.

I took them downstairs and into their dressing room and closed the door. I started crying again.

ARNIE LATCHKEY: "Ladies and gentlemen, the Blissmans!" the emcee said and then the O'Hares and Ziggy went onstage. Now, I'd never seen the act before but it didn't take Watson and Crick to see that the O'Hares weren't related to Ziggy Blissman. The crowd, though, they were confused: most of them had seen Ziggy with Harry and Flo. And they're asking themselves and one another, "What's Father Flannigan and Mother McCree doing onstage with Ziggy?"

Ziggy never broke stride. The routine began and Ziggy just flowed with it. He had the knack, that gift all funnymen have, to glide through troubled air.

Behind me I hear a commotion, a little one. I turned around and there are these two tiny people and they got the Max Factor Pan-Cake makeup on. It's Harry and Flo.

They inch up to where I am, backstage, and peer though the curtains. They see the act, they see the O'Hares and Ziggy. And Ziggy's hugging Kathleen O'Hare and calling her Mommy and he's calling Jimmy O'Hare, who was the spittin' image of Bishop Fulton J. Sheen, Poppy.

Flo, who is aghast, turned around and Sally was right behind her and Flo said, *"Who is that?!"* And Sally said, "That . . . that's you. That's you and Harry. Ziggy replaced you." I could tell . . . she wanted to say something like "I'm sorry" but she just couldn't get the words out.

I looked at Harry, I looked down at him . . . he was shaking violently, like an electric toothbrush. The man was *humming!* Sally went over to him and wrapped her arms around him and then Flo collapsed . . . she was about ten yards behind us. *Thud!*

Two stagehands lifted her up and propped her on a chair, and Harry tries to walk over to her but then he collapses too. They dragged both of them, Harry and Flo, very slowly, very delicately, into their small dressing room. And that's where they died.

The lights came down quick. Just when the O'Hares and Ziggy began clicking. The emcee took the mike and said that due to some problems the show would be temporarily halted.

SALLY KLEIN: The next thing I know we're in Ziggy's bungalow, me, Ziggy, and Dr. Schwartzman, the house doctor at Heine's.

"They're dead, Ziggy," the doctor said.

Ziggy was sitting on his bed. He put his face in his hands. He started sniffling and blew his nose.

Dr. Schwartzman said, "I didn't know it was possible but my guess is they had a sort of mutual stroke. She had one. Then he had one."

Ziggy was crying now.

There's a knock on the door and I said, "Go away, Bernie," but Bernie Heine walked in. He used the key.

"Ziggy, I'm so sorry," he said.

"Thanks, Bern," Ziggy said. His face was very red and puffy.

"But we got four hundred people out there," Bernie said, "and they want a show."

"Can't the O'Haras do some soft-shoe for 'em? Till Lenny Pearl comes on?"

"It's the O'Hares, and they walked. And Lenny can't go on . . . he's not even here yet. Ziggy, you can't screw me over again!"

"Bernie, there's just no show left in me," Ziggy told him. "Just have that Vic Feldbaum do a few more numbers."

ARNIE LATCHKEY: My brother Marvin finds me in the lobby, tells me I gotta find Vic and I gotta do it PDQ. I ask why and he says, "'Cause now we're even favor-wise and this is starting a whole new go-around." So I run up the stairs to room 413 and I bang on the door and sure enough Vic is with some doll named Selma.

"It's me, Latch," I told him. "You gotta finish up soon, Vic, this is crucial!"

"Okay, hold on," I heard from behind the door. Then three seconds later I heard him say, "Okay . . . done."

We ran down the stairs, he's zipping up, and I told him he had to go back on. He said, "Are they gonna pay me double for this?" and I said, "Pal, we ain't even received one cent so far for this gig, and if you don't go on now we never will."

So the emcee is back on, the lights come up, and he says into the mike, "Ladies and gentleman, please give a warm Loch Sheldrake welcome to a new performer making his very second appearance at Heine's tonight . . . from Boston, Massachusetts: Vic Feldbaum!"

Well, this time the welcome was something less than warm, let me tell you.

The band starts up again and the audience lets out a sporadic groan here and there. And Vic is singing "It Was You" because, you got to remember, he'd only rehearsed with this band for a few days! They had no repertoire. And in the middle of the song, people begin to cough and hiss, so Vic stops singing and says, "Okay then, maybe it *wasn't* you!"

SALLY KLEIN: "I can't go on solo, I just can't," Ziggy is saying.

Bernie told him, "You got no choice. You go onstage and you piss in your pants and then you go off, but you go onstage and you do it now!"

"What would your parents want you to do, Ziggy?" I asked him.

"That's really a moot point now," he answered.

ARNIE LATCHKEY: Vic's dying up there, he's dying. The band lost interest . . . the drummer even left to take a leak. And Vic is just trading insults with the audience. The Codport is really coming out. He was telling one guy to stick the mike up his you-know-what and he told another one to pull it back out.

All of a sudden the spotlight drifts over to the audience. There's Ziggy. And then there's another spotlight on Vic. The rest of the place is absolutely black.

"Where you been?" Vic said.

"I been in my bungalow," Ziggy said.

"It's been lonely up here, you know that?"

"I wasn't exactly livin' it up in my bungalow either, Feldbaumelli."

"Where's your folks?"

"Which ones?" Ziggy says.

That got a big laugh . . . 'cause everyone knew the O'Hares weren't Harry and Flo.

"The ones you were supposed to be onstage with," Vic said.

"They died."

"Oh, they died, did they?" Vic said.

"Yeah, Vic, almost as bad as you just was."

And with that, it was like a great wave of laughter hit.

Waving his fist, Vic said, "You think this is dead, wait till—"

"Wait till tomorrow when you got to sing the same five lousy songs you know again."

Vic laughed for a second and said, "Hey, you know, you're right about that."

Teddy, let me tell you . . . it kept going. And going. The chemistry, the timing, the *music*, it was all there. It was filet mignon and Dom Pérignon and caviar and crème brûlée.

"You know, you keep foolin' 'round with these Jewish girls up here, Feldbaumino," Ziggy said, "and you're going to wind up paying for it."

"Nah, Ziggy, I heard *you* was the one who had to pay for it."

And once again, it was like this massive tumult from the sky rolling over the place, an explosion of laughter. The floor was shaking, I swear to God.

"You don't look like no 'Feldbaum' to me, Vic," Ziggy said.

"And what does a Feldbaum look like, I'd like to know."

"Like me."

"Like a basketball with three hundred carrots springing right out of it, you mean?"

Zig said, "Hey, look, Vic, the people in here could use a nap, why don't you sing a few songs?"

And Vic started to sing "Just One of Those Things" and Ziggy is jumping and skipping and hopping and he jumps in Vic's arms and the whole joint was on goddamn fire! I have never ever seen anything like this! So raw, so new, so fresh, so spontaneous, so absolutely godddam hysterical! Every molecule in the air that night was charged. Westbrook Pegler once called their act "table tennis with a comet."

Magic. Absolute, pure, unadulterated magic. They had it. Thunder and lightning.

They did two hours. Two whole hours, I do not exaggerate. Playing off each other. The crowd was hoarse; by the end, their hands hurt so much that they couldn't clap anymore.

Lenny Pearl never got on. He finally showed up but by then the audience had been wrung dry to the bones. The only people left were the busboys mopping up. Lenny turned purple, cursed Ziggy and Vic for ten minutes straight, and left the mountains.

Oh yeah. There was one other thing. Two women were laughing so much they had to be rushed to the hospital because of stomach pains. And some man in his fifties had laughed so much that he had a massive coronary arrest and died.

When I heard that, boy, that's when I knew we'd really hit it big.

ARNIE LATCHKEY: Bernie Heine came to my hotel room at midnight, after that first show, his face still borscht pink from laughing. He said, "Arnie, that was the most sensational, scintillating thing I've ever witnessed in this hotel or in any other."

Now, I didn't go to the Wharton School of Business. I have no business degree in anything other than swingin' deals off the seat of my pants. But I knew to play this thing so nonchalant that a nurse, had there been one on the premises, would've checked my body for vital signs and not found a single one. I said to Bernie, who'd already played his hand, "Oh really, Bernie? I suppose it *was* rather funny, wasn't it?" I added a yawn at the end for good measure.

He said, "Vic is booked through the week, you know. So is Ziggy Blissman."

"And Vic is ready to fulfill that. But what that Blissman kid does, that's his business." I don't let on for one second that I realize Bernie is famished like a third-world country for more Ziggy and Vic.

"You've got to talk to them, Arnie! You've got to get them to do this again. And again." The man is on the verge of drooling on one of his own oriental rugs.

"Bernie, could you help me get this shoe off?" I said, and sure enough the man who'd once fired me because my *tummling* act was like a graceful lemming dive into a vat of boiling tar is now kneeling down before me and wriggling the shoe off my foot, his nostrils crinkling and blanching. I'm eating this thing up, I don't mind telling you.

"Perhaps I'll talk to this Blissman kid and see what I can do," I told Bernie. "But, you know, he's all bereaved right now."

SALLY KLEIN: Ziggy, who was shaking terribly, and I were in his bungalow, just after his parents died. "We have to make some arrangements now," I told him solemnly. "The sooner the better." He had on what he always had on after a show: a cold towel with ice draped over his head.

"I know, Sal, I know," he said.

I was thinking, Did Harry and Flo ever tell him how they wanted to be buried? Did they ever talk of cremation? Would they want to be buried in Brooklyn?

"I never thought it would end like this," I said. I gave him another minute. He was flushed all over, still sweaty and shaking, and the ice was melting over his forehead. "Well?" I asked him. "What should I do?"

"This is what you do, Sal. Find out what room an Arnie Latchkey is staying in . . ."

I thought: *Who?* I'd never heard Arnie's name before! I'm thinking that Arnie Latchkey is a funeral director or an undertaker or maybe he's a rabbi staying at the hotel.

"Tell him to come down here right away," Ziggy said. "Tell him the sooner we get this done, the better for all parties involved."

I went to the front desk and found out what room this Arnie Latchkey person was staying in. It occurred to me in the elevator that Ziggy had said "all parties involved." I couldn't figure that one out. Two of the parties involved were dead.

I knock on the door and Arnie answers in his plaid bathrobe, which was sort of ratty. He looks at me—I'm five foot three, I've got cat's-eye eyeglasses on, I'm eighteen years old but look sixteen—and he says, "Honey, Vic ain't here and besides, you don't look like you even had your bas mitzvah yet," and starts to close the door. I put my foot in the door so it didn't close and said, "Ziggy Blissman needs to see you in his bungalow. Now."

"Tell him," he said very seriously, "I know what he wants. I understand. I'll be down in five minutes."

So I take the elevator back down to Ziggy, convinced that Arnie Latchkey is an undertaker!

I told Ziggy that Arnie would be down any minute. By now he's stopped shaking. I imagine he might have had two belts of Dewar's by then. Beneath the chair he sat on there was a big puddle—it was the ice melting, mixed in with his own natural *shvitz*.

"I'd like you to be here when this Latchkey guy comes," Ziggy said.

"I'll be here for you, Ziggy," I said.

"These things can get ugly. If he asks for too much, we'll forget about them."

While I was wondering what he meant by this, there was a knock. I was expecting Arnie to be dressed in black or at least dark gray, but he was decked out in his usual powder blue.

"Ziggy," he said.

Ziggy said, "You've met my cousin Sally." Arnie and I nodded to each other. "Isn't she pretty?" Ziggy said. He was always doing that, always trying to fix me up with the wrong *shlub*. Well, I wanted a boyfriend and eventually a husband, yes, but not a funeral director.

"Look, let's make this short but sweet. I've had a rough day," Ziggy said.

"I should say so!" Arnie chimed in.

"Vic's signed for the rest of the week and so am I."

"I'm familiar with it."

"But I lost two sets of parents tonight . . . my stage ones and my real ones."

"I'm aware of it. My condolences, by the way, as regards both sets."

"Yeah, sure," Ziggy said. "What's this Vic Feldbaum's future look like right now?"

"I'll be honest with you, Ziggy," Arnie said, sitting down. "If it's not dark, then it's indeed quite dim."

"That's what I was hoping."

Arnie undid a button on his shirt and said, "And *your* future, might I be so impertinent enough to ask? What's the forecast there, in terms of light?"

"Murky at best, gloomy at worst."

Ziggy poured Arnie a Dewar's . . . that's when I got my first taste of the table manners of Arnie Latchkey. The loudest drinker, chewer, and swallower in the history of the Catskills, which really is saying an awful lot.

"You know what I'm aiming at, don't you, Arn? You know what I'm talkin' about over here?" Ziggy said.

"I believe I do."

"How do you think Vic's gonna feel about it?"

"On behalf of my sole client, my opinion is that, as he probably doesn't really give a shit, I'm sure he'll see things your way—*our way*—as to this one regard."

"Are you going to ask him tonight or—" Ziggy began.

"I've already interrupted him with one girl tonight, Ziggy. Two times, I think he might go for my carotid artery. This can wait."

"Let me know first thing tomorrow, wouldja?"

"Will do, Zig."

Arnie got up and walked to the door, and Ziggy—he's still got the turban on even though the ice has melted—walks over to him.

"There's the little matter of percentages, you know?" Arnie said.

By this time, of course, I realized that Arnie was not a rabbi or a funeral director. So I was expecting Ziggy to throw out something like 70/30 or maybe 60/40, in his own favor. What I heard, though, staggered me, considering that this was Ziggy Blissman, who could never be moved to give even his parents a fair deal.

"Arnie, we split things fifty/fifty down the line, all the way. I hope your sole client is amiable to that."

"Fan*tab*ulous," Arnie said. "And you mean 'amenable,' I believe."

"As for your and Sally's cut, I'd like—"

Arnie waved his hand—that discussion would wait until a better time. They shook hands and Arnie walked out, then Ziggy sat down and let go a big sigh.

"There's the little matter now," I reminded him, "of burying your parents . . ."

"Oh yeah . . . them," he said.

They were buried side by side not too far from Grossinger's. I had to arrange "kiddie coffins" for them because they were so small. There was one tombstone; it said "The Blissmans" and the years of their births and deaths. Seeing their names that way reminded me of when they were in vaudeville and their names were up on a marquee. But then I remembered that their names never did make it to a marquee.

Years later, Ziggy had them moved to Home of Peace [Cemetery in Los Angeles], to a very grand mausoleum, something fit for royalty. Whether he ever visited it or not, I don't know.

SNUFFY DUBIN: I get a telegram the next day from Ziggy. Something to the effect of: "Snuffles STOP Have struck Italian gold STOP Remember our nonexistent plans to double STOP Well, plans are off STOP Who needs you anyways, you big putz STOP Ever heard of Vic Fountain from Floyd Lomax band STOP We're a duo now STOP Can you come to Heine's PDQ STOP PS On sad note, parents dead."

I was playing the Shea Theater in Buffalo and I told the manager I couldn't make the next show due to a death in the family. I used that excuse a lot—man, I think I must've killed off about eighty aunts and uncles that way.

I drove to Heine's and caught the act. I'd seen Vic sing before and by now his voice and his style had gotten a lot better. He was talking to the crowd now too, relating to them. In the fourth song Ziggy came onstage and that's where it began. They didn't do jokes, they didn't do gags. There were no punch lines. It wasn't the Ritz Brothers, it wasn't Burns and Allen, it wasn't Groucho and Chico. It wasn't like anything I'd ever seen before.

ARNIE LATCHKEY: I called Vic at ten in the morning and to my surprise he was awake. Probably, though, he hadn't fallen asleep that night. I told him to meet me right away in the coffee shop right off the lobby. He said, "Latch, do I have to?" And I told him, yeah, he really did.

Ten minutes later we're sitting at a table and having coffee. There are about thirty other people there and as Vic and I confab, they're all looking at us. This was my very first taste of this. They're looking and leaning toward each other to whisper and sort of pointing at us. What they were saying was: *"That's Vic! The guy who was so funny last night!"*

"Ziggy Blissman wants to do a double with you," I told him.

"Oh yeah?" Vic said.

"Yeah, like a song and comedy thing. Mostly comedy."

"What did you tell him?"

"I told him I would talk to you."

"Well, tell the kid sure. Sure," Vic said. He was thinking it over as he was talking. Or maybe it was like he heard his own voice coming out his maw and he happened to agree with it. "It's a really good idea. I think it'd work out. Sure."

"There's all kinds of stuff to go over," I said to him. "There's stuff with Murray Katz and Joe Gersh and all kinds of people."

"I don't wanna know about that," he said. "I'll sing. I'll play with the kid. I'll do whatever. The only paperwork I want you to give me has George Washington on it."

"Gotcha, Vic."

You know, I never had any kind of deal with Fountain and Bliss. There was a handshake but I'm not even certain we shook hands all around; I shook Vic's hand and Ziggy's too, but I'm not too sure if they ever shook each other's. If you're picturing *The Oath of the Horatii* or the Three Musketeers hoisting up one big "all for one and one for all," boy, you got it all wrong.

Let's say Ziggy and Vic were booked into Ciro's or the Blue Beret. Or the Copa. I get off the phone with Jules Podell and tell the boys, "Okay, guys, you're booked into the Copa for a week and you're making twenty grand." And Ziggy would say, "How's three thousound, Latch?" And I'd look over to Vic and he'd shrug. I'd say, "Sounds good." Vic didn't really care how much I made—sometimes I don't think he even cared how much *he* made—but I always made certain the figures were square with Ziggy. He knew the numbers like most people know their own birthdays.

SALLY KLEIN: That whole week it was standing room only at Heine's. The same people were coming back too, night after night! We had to turn people away.

I met with Arnie in his hotel room. We had to talk to Rosie, Jerry Milton, and the rest. And we had to do it before they read about Ziggy and Vic in *Variety*, *Metronome*, or *Billboard*. The plan was to play it down. Think about it: You had Ziggy, who'd once frozen like a Popsicle onstage alone, and you had Vic, who bounced from lousy band to lousy band and had never struck it big. It was, on paper, a disaster. This was like me calling up and saying, "Guess what?! Lizzie Borden and Rasputin are teaming up to do a tap dance act!" Arnie and I hoped that everybody would run for cover when they heard that.

It worked. They ran.

Rosie told me, "They're yours!" I reminded her of Jerry Milton, how he'd pulled that Platonic ideal contractual thing, and she said, "I don't know about that and I don't know who this Vic Fountain fella is. Sally, they're all yours! Take 'em."

I called Jerry in New York and then Joe Gersh and Murray Katz. Joe and Murray knew all about Vic and weren't too sad to see us take him off their hands. Arnie then called a lawyer he knew in New York and all of them—Rosie, Jerry Milton, Gersh and Katz, even Don Leslie!—gladly washed their hands of the matter. It was like we were trying to borrow a car and they thought it was a Corvair and said, "Here. Please. Don't bother returning it." But it turned out to be a solid gold Rolls.

ARNIE LATCHKEY: It all happened quickly, like surgery. Sally handled Ziggy's people, I handled Vic's. Sally had quite the business acumen for such a young girl. Her old man manufactured girdles, so maybe that was it. And I was no slouch either. She'd make a call and she'd write things down that the person on the line was saying and I'd write down things to her, and then she'd do that to me when I was on the phone. It was very symbiotic, let me tell you.

My one worry was that one of these people was going to say, "You can have Vic in his entirety in perpetuity forever but you'll have to pay me ten grand." Now, well I knew that the act I was sitting on—Fountain and Bliss—was going to make ten grand easy. *Easy!* But we didn't have that kind of money just then. As a matter of fact I didn't even have any kind of money just then. So when I'm on the phone and talking to these people, in the back of my mind is: Where am I gonna get this dough so quick? There's my brother, but he don't have that kind of cake and we're even—he don't owe me any favors anymore. There's my old man, but he don't have that kind of cake either and besides we barely talked. I can't call him up and say, "Hey, so how is everything? Lend me ten grand to buy out Ziggy Blissman and Vic Fountain." Even I had some sense of decorum.

Sally and I agreed that, in toto, the ceiling would be ten grand all around. That's the most we could go, was buy out Vic Fountain and Ziggy Blissman for ten grand.

So now Don Leslie and I are on the phone and he says, "There is the subject of money, of course, Mr. Latchland." The man called me Latchland, Lapland, Bletchley—everything but Latchkey, that *momzer!* And I said, "Yes, Mr. *Wesley,* there is that touchiest of all subjects known to men." And he says, "I should hope that negotiations between us are conducted in a cordial yet frank manner, Mr. Lakeland." And he's probably thinking, I'm not letting you rob me blind, you dirty stinking Jew! So I say to him, "Why, naturally, Mr. Westfield. We are both gentlemen of the old school, are we not?" I'm getting ready to throw out a dollar amount, how much I am willing to pay to own, if you will, Vic outright. He says, while all these numbers are swirling around in my head like so much confetti, "How does two thousand dollars sound, Leakey?" And I say, "Capital!" And exactly while I'm thinkin', Now where can I rustle up two grand? Don Leslie says, "I'll wire the money to you at Heine's first thing."

Sally got a grand and a half from Rosie Baer too. So, not only did we not have to part with $10,000 that we never did have, we actually wound up *making* $12,000 from everyone!

• • •

TONY FERRO: The first time I ever in my life heard of Ziggy Bliss was when Ray Fontana tells me that Vic is now partners with him. The name meant *niente* to me. I say to Ray, "How long do you think this relationship is gonna work out?" and Ray says, 'cause he knew Vic's track record, "I give it a maybe a week, tops."

CATHERINE RICCI: I'd just gotten engaged to Carmine [Ricci] when Vic told me the news. He called home to tell Mamma first but she was working at her fortune-telling parlor. Vic told me he was no longer a singer and I asked if he wasn't that, then what was he doing, playing pool? And he said he was "entertaining." I said to him, "You're entertaining but you're not a singer? What are you doing, *juggling* pool balls then?" He said, "I'm kind of in a comedy deal, you could say, with this other fella, this Jewish guy." I said to him, "You want me to tell Mamma this? 'Cause I'm not doing it."

I dropped in on Carmine at his bakery and told him what Vic had told me. Carmine had heard of Ziggy Bliss because he'd heard him and his parents on Lenny Pearl's old radio show. "I didn't know Vic was funny at all, Cathy," he said to me.

"I guess he's going to be the one that's not funny," I said to him.

But it occurred to me: Vic was always a really funny kid. He was sometimes better at being funny than he was at singing, as a matter of fact. People were always calling him a wiseass.

RAY FONTANA: Somehow it became my duty to tell my mother. Probably 'cause everyone else was afraid to.

I went to Haddock Street where the Madame Violet fortune-telling parlor was. This wasn't goin' to be easy—imagine you want your kid to go to medical school and now you hear he's waiting tables. I climb the stairs—this place had beads, pictures of the Virgin Mary, candles all 'round—and there's Lulu working the till and three old ladies sitting on a couch waiting to see Mamma.

"What's going on, Ray?" Lu asks me. Jesus, I was so worked up about how was I gonna break the news to my mother I'd forgotten that Lulu was going to be there too.

"Lu," I say, "it's about Vic but don't worry. He's okay. He's giving up the singing a little and he's gonna be in a comedy act."

Lulu said to me, "But I thought you said Vic was okay."

She brought me in to see my mother and it was just me sitting between the two of them on a couch. Not a position anybody'd ever wanna find himself in, believe me . . . I'd have rather been gutting scrod at that second.

When I broke the news Mom picked up her crystal ball and tossed it across the room. If the women on the couch hadn't ducked in time, I'd still be pluckin' the glass out of their cheeks.

CATHERINE RICCI: Me and Ray borrowed Sal's car and we drove to the Catskills. From how Carmine had described it, I was envisioning Ziggy like an adult wearing diapers and with a pacifier. I was picturing all kinds of things. I imagined Vic dressed in a clown suit, I imagined Vic and Ziggy looking like Laurel and Hardy but *both* in diapers. Everything ran through my mind.

I'd never been to Heine's before, or to any of those places . . . Grossinger's, the Concord, Marx's, Kutsher's. This was a whole new world for me. I got out that car and people were looking at us like we just stepped out of a flying saucer.

RAY FONTANA: Pop would've said something like, "*Mazzi Cristo,* wall-to-wall." Christ killers all over.

[Cathy and I] checked in and we were tired . . . it's a very long drive from Codport to the Catskills. We get our rooms and then this guy in the lobby, he was wearing a Heine's uniform, tries to joke around with me. But I wasn't up for no jokin' around, right? . . . I wanted to go to my room and wash up and then see Vic. This guy's doing all sorts of jokes and stuff but I'm not playing along. Jesus Christ, I can't tell you how out of place I felt. I say to this guy, I whisper to him right in his ear, "Leave me the fuck alone or I'll mash your fuckin' nose down into your throat." And he decided to leave.

Cathy and I are walking through the lobby and we see this poster; it said on it something like HILARIOUS SENSATION or SENSATIONAL HILARITY or something. There was a photo of Vic and one of Ziggy Bliss, except he was still Ziggy Blissman then. I gotta admit: Alls I did was take one look at that picture and I started giggling.

ARNIE LATCHKEY: "Fountain and Blissman," it occurred to me right away, not only did not have a ring to it, it had a built-in thud. It dies on the tongue like ten-year-old cottage cheese, am I right? Now, the straight man usually comes first: Burns and Allen, Martin and Lewis, Abbott and Costello. Of course, you've got Laurel and Hardy but Laurel was British and they also drive on the wrong side of the road. Rowan and Martin. Rossi and Allen [*sic*]. I did try Blissman and Fountain and, you know, that sounded better . . . but still, the funny guy comes second.

I called up Ziggy's bungalow and said, "Hey, how'd you like to change your last name?" I stated my case and, as I did so, in the back of my mind is: Uh-oh, this is going to be our first quarrel and the kid is going to throw a fit and then it's all over. (That day, Sally had warned me about his temper and his fits.) But he said, "Arnie, I think that's a real good idear. Ziggy Bliss it is. I'll have Sally handle the legal stuff on that real pronto-like." End of phone call.

I thought, Jesus, this road is really going to be smooth. It ain't even gonna be a road, it's gonna be more like a path.

SALLY KLEIN: For the first year they were together, I remember hearing people mistakenly refer to the act as "Fountain of Bliss."

• • •

DANNY McGLUE: It was the most sensational act I'd seen up to then. I'd seen Berle, [Phil] Silvers, Jimmy Durante, Cubby Cavanaugh, Burns and Allen, Benny . . . but even they after five minutes could get so predictable. The first time I saw Ziggy and Vic together—it was at Heine's—I had no idea where it was going. You ever been dreaming and you *know* you're dreaming and you're thinking, Okay, where is this going to end? Do I let it end or should I wake up? That's what the act was like.

It wasn't easy for me to get backstage . . . it was so crowded. Oh, you know who was there? Bud Hatch from the *Globe*. And there were all kinds of people, it was bustling, like the stateroom scene in *A Night at the Opera*. So I shouted over to Bernie Heine, "Bernie, tell Zig that Danny McGlue's here!" He shouted back, "Okay, Danny, but there's lots going on back there!" That SOB waited a good ten minutes before he went in to Ziggy's dressing room. And you know, they'd used some of my gags and songs, Vic and Ziggy had.

Finally this tall guy in powder blue with Coke-bottle eyeglasses, a long face, and rubbery lips comes out and says, "You're Danny McGlue?"

I tell him I am and I ask who's he and he says he's Arnie Latchkey.

"Look," he says, "I know we used some of your material and we're willing to remunerate you for this. If you contact a Miss Sally Klein at—"

"Look, I'm not here for remuneration," I said to Arnie—I didn't even know what the word meant, I just knew that I wasn't there for it.

A minute later I'm in Ziggy's dressing room. He's got the white towel over him and the ice is dripping down. And instead of a bottle of scotch, there are two bottles of champagne in two buckets.

"Danny, this is Vic Fountain," Ziggy says. "Vic, all those jokes that didn't get no laughs—Danny wrote those."

Vic and I shook hands and I told him I thought the act was socko. Someone pours me a glass of champagne and I start to tell Vic the whole Danny McGlue and Ziggy Blissman saga. I'm halfway through and he says, "Uh-huh," then veers away and starts talking to a blonde. I don't know if he caught a word of what I was saying. If he did, he sure didn't seem to care.

GUY PUGLIA: I was back in New York, sparring for a few bucks a day at Gleason's Gym and at Pops Deegan's and waiting tables some nights. I'd spar with Hunny, who had fifty pounds on me, which was a joke. He'd go thirty seconds and then want to take a break to throw back ten hamburgers.

One day at the Monroe, my cousin Pooch hands me a telegram, it's from Vic. It says that I was to go up to the Catskills as soon as I finished reading the wire . . . Vic would pay me back for the bus fare, it says. And the last line, I swear, is *"Goomba, we're going to be rich real soon."* With that in mind, I was on a Greyhound within ten minutes.

SALLY KLEIN: Look at this wonderful old picture of the dining room at Heine's. Arnie must've taken it. You see how there's Vic's side of the table and Ziggy's? Cathy's there, with her brother Ray. They'd never had Jewish food before. I really think they were looking to pour some marinara sauce on the noodle pudding. That's Guy Puglia sitting next to Ray. This must be one of the last photographs of Guy before that horrible thing happened to him. So sad. Bud Hatch, the columnist, is next to Guy, and that's Jean Hatch, his wife. In his column he always referred to Jean as "the SL," as in Scintillating Lady. Far from it, you can see. She used to drink a tub of gin for breakfast, it was said, but Bud was the very first reporter to cover us. I don't know who these two girls are, on Jeanie Hatch's right. In every group picture taken at Heine's or Grossinger's, there are always two people and you have no idea at all who they are, and these must be them.

That's Danny on Ziggy's left and that's me sitting next to Danny. He was quite handsome then, don't you think? A few weeks after this picture was taken, Danny and I were very deeply in love. I'd already had a crush on him for a few weeks but nobody had any idea. *Who could I tell?* On my left is Snuffy Dubin, who looked very dashing and dapper back then . . . he's sure put on a few pounds since then, but who hasn't? The woman next to him is Gertrude Heine, Bernie's wife, and that's Bernie Heine next to her. Bernie passed away on the same day they dynamited his hotel to smithereens in 1967, which is not as coincidental as it may sound considering that Bernie made sure to be in the hotel when they pushed the plunger. He wanted to go down with the ship, he said, but wound up going all over it instead.

If you notice, everyone at the table is looking at the camera. Except Ziggy, because he's mugging with his eyes. But look at Vic. He's the only one who's looking away. And I can tell you why. Because there was a very hot redhead at the table to our right, the next table over. I remember that distinctly.

ARNIE LATCHKEY: Bud Hatch wrote it up in the old *Globe*. He used adjectives and adverbs you usually reserve for the ceiling on the Sistine Chapel. Ostensibly he said that if you had the chance, you should head for the hills and check out this new dynamic dynamite daffy duo. He promised a gargantuan gaggle of guffaws.

Now, you must understand that the Catskills was a very select area, not select as in some elite Wasp country club, oh no, *au contraire*. Fountain and Bliss may have been playing to a packed house, but it was as far in mental mileage from the Big Time as the Wailing Wall is from the Royal Albert Hall. This was not the Copa, El Morocco, the Blue Beret, the Roxy, or the Chez Paree.

Which meant we had work to do.

With the twelve grand windfall, I opened up an office in New York, in the Brill Building. The rent was staggeringly low by today's standards. I named our little operation Vigorish Productions, Inc. Combination Vic and Zig.

Sally had an office and I had an office and there was the "living room." We needed a secretary so Murray Katz sent us his niece, Estelle Fein, who'd been sewing size labels onto blouses on Thirty-seventh Street. She was about eighteen then and was a lovely girl, tall and long-legged with a mane of auburn hair that Rita Hayworth would've killed for. How do I know this? Because Rita Hayworth a few years later said directly to Estelle—and by then, may I add, the latter had become Mrs. Arnold Latchkey—"I would *kill* for your hair!" But Rita had a low hairline—she had long boun-teous tresses coming out the bridge of her nose—so she might have even killed for Yul Brynner's hairline too.

I remember dropping off at Bertie Kahn's office a clipping of the Bud Hatch review as well as a write-up from a rag up in the mountains, the Loch Sheldrake *Picayune* or some such thing. Bertie sent me a telegram the next day; typical behavior for him even though his office was only two blocks away. As long as I live I'll never forget the wording: "Oil plus water = TNT. Or poison." You didn't get too many words out of him.

Bertie, though, was willing to work for us. *With* us. He was the best PR man in New York at the time. And his cousin was Gus Kahn (not Gus Kahn the songwriter), who everybody referred to as Genghis and was the head of Galaxy Pictures. And if you think for one second that that incredibly precious little tidbit escaped Arnie Latchkey's purview, then brother, are you sorely mistaken.

DANNY McGLUE: Every morning we'd meet at the Vigorish office on Broadway at the exact same time, 10:00 A.M. Vic wanted it to be later; he used to joke, "Hey, I fall *asleep* at eight A.M." It was Sally, Arnie, me, Vic, and Ziggy at first, but after a while Norman White and Sidney Stone would be at the meetings too; they were gag writers who were with us many, many years. Vic sometimes did look like he'd only slept two hours when he came in, but after a Chesterfield, a dose of *Terry and the Pirates,* and some Chase & Sanborn, he'd perk up real quick. We had a piano in there too, and we'd send out for food from Bratz's on Broadway and Fiftieth or sometimes we'd all go to Handelman's or Lindy's.

I wish there were tapes of those meetings. As funny as Ziggy was, and Vic too, Norman and Sidney were more *clever,* in terms of jokes and one-liners. Norman had worked on a few radio shows in New York—*Allen's Alley* and *The Joe Penner Show*—and then done some punch-up script work for MGM, where he'd met F. Scott Fitzgerald. Sid had done some gag work for the Marx Brothers at Paramount. But they hated California, just hated it.

That room was jumping sometimes.

Now, it wasn't *all* productive. I mean, I think that a quarter of the time we were just making fun of how loud Arnie chewed. But you know, now that I think about it, we even developed a routine out of that.

ERNIE BEASLEY [songwriter]: I met Vic and Ziggy because my rehearsal studio was two doors down the hallway from the Vigorish office. I was writing jingles then with Max Marcus, stuff for Texaco, L&M cigarettes, and Gillette razors . . . or for anybody really. This was not the road I'd chosen in my life, having studied with Otto Korda at Juilliard. But the pay was good and I was living in Greenwich Village and, besides, that "road" was really chosen for me by my family. They would listen to the NBC Symphony Orchestra on our farm and—this is to their credit, I suppose—they would not let me work the farm. They were too afraid of me bruising or hurting my fingers.

Ted, I would be playing the piano in the studio and Max Marcus would be singing along and we'd be playing at fairly high volume too—and you could hear, even through those thick prewar walls in the Brill Building, even *two offices down*—the absolutely raucous laughter ringing out from the Vigorish office.

A few times I'd gather enough nerve up to knock on the door. Estelle would answer and even as I was saying something as mundane as "Could you *please* try to keep it down in there?" I'd be looking over her shoulder and I couldn't believe what I saw! You had grown men lying on the floor, standing on their heads or on furniture, sometimes with their pants at their ankles or wearing outrageous wigs. One time I went in there and Vic was playing Arnie and Sally and Norman's heads like they were conga drums! There was always food all around and always there were faces as red as roses with laughter. And it was infectious. About the third or fourth time Ziggy grabbed my hand and dragged me in. They had a small piano in there and I started to play and within a few bars I became part of that wonderful, delirious mayhem.

After that, I didn't want to go back to my studio, where Max Marcus was waiting for me. I ask you: Who in his right mind would want to write a song about Silver Crest socks or Wilson's Miracle Shaving Powder after a taste of all that?

ARNIE LATCHKEY: It was a fecund breeding ground. The ideas, the jokes, the *everything* that was born in those rooms . . . many years later we were still using the material. I once saw Ziggy and [second wife] Pernilla on that Bert Convy game show *Tattletales* and Ziggy used some joke that he and Sid Stone had written! Three decades earlier!

SALLY KLEIN: Arnie and I could only do so much. Ziggy and his parents had been booked for a few more engagements that summer in the Catskills. But now Harry and Florence were dead. I made some calls and got Fountain and Bliss in for those dates . . . I think it was Fiedler's, Grossinger's, and the White Lake Lodge for a week at each place. But after that, the calendar was clear. Which is very frightening for entertainers.

"Estelle darling, call Murray Katz at Worldwide, would you," I remember hearing Arnie say one day.

I went in to his little office and said, "Why are we calling *them?*"

"Because as Bert Kahn says, this act could be TNT . . . but as long as we're only in the mountains, it won't amount to more than a moist firecracker."

"We could call places," I said naively. "We could call other people. I have a friend who knows Julie Podell at the Copa."

"And, Sally, the man who shines my shoes also shines the shoes of the man who does manicures for the man who cuts Sherman Billingsley at the Stork Club's hair!"

In my heart I felt that calling Murray or any of Herb Blackstone's people at WAT was a betrayal . . . it was going outside our little *mishpocheh*. But Arnie tried to make me see—frankly, he wasn't very convincing—and then Bert Kahn in six words convinced me that for big-time talent you had to use big-time people.

Still, when Murray Katz showed up one day for a meeting of prospective venues I had a very bad taste in my mouth. Until he started rattling off dollar amounts. I must admit, the bad taste vanished very quickly.

DANNY McGLUE: I was living in a dumpy studio apartment off Columbus Avenue on Seventy-fourth Street. Sally was living in the Eighties on West End Avenue. I'd see her every day at the office and we'd talk and joke around for hours at a stretch. In the evenings, I would want to phone her or take her out to dinner but I never could summon up the nerve.

I didn't have the dough or the space for a piano so sometimes at night I would go back to the office to play and write my silly songs. One night I'm there writing some little ditty and what happens? Sally Klein walks in, looking very surprised to see me there. She told me she'd forgotten some paperwork and that's why she'd shown up. I continued playing and then I stopped and, well, before you know it, I was kissing her all over.

SALLY KLEIN: The first boy I kissed was in Philadelphia and that was like being with a camel, frankly. Well, Danny knows this now but I returned to the office that night not because I'd forgotten anything, but because Arnie had told me that Danny sometimes would tickle the ivories at night. So I was hoping that he'd be there. And he was.

Even as Danny and I were kissing, it occurred to me: Ziggy is not going to like this.

● ● ●

RAY FONTANA: After they went back to the Catskills for a few more weeks and Vic had some more dough, he got his first real spread, right near the Ansonia. I drove Lulu, Mom, and Pop down to New York one weekend—it was their first time there. Lu and Vic hadn't seen each other for a while, but I got to tell you, I've seen couples who've been apart for a while and this wasn't like that really. It was more like two cousins. He did give her some gifts though—earrings and a coat. He got Mom some stuff too, but she wasn't too big on clothing or jewelry. Pop refused to accept anything from Vic; he wouldn't even let Vic buy him the *Daily News*. We went to Antonio's, an Italian restaurant, and Vic paid, but even after that Pop slipped him the dough for his and for Mamma's meals.

Vic showed us all these newspaper clippings, stuff from the *Post* and the *News* and *Variety*. It was really very impressive. And my parents met Ziggy for the first time. He tried to make 'em laugh, he was really cranking it up . . . he even got my mom goin' a few times. But Pop didn't crack a grin, not at all.

I remember that while Ziggy was entertaining everyone in the main room of the Vigorish office, Vic excused himself to make a call. Ten minutes go by and then I go into Sally Klein's office where Vic was, alone. And Vic is whispering into the phone and his back is turned. I heard him say something like, "Baby, they're all leaving today, I'll meet you at Jimmy Dooley's joint at ten sharp."

Jesus, Lulu was in the next room!

* * *

SNUFFY DUBIN: I now had Leo Silver at WAT as my agent. Finally having an agent was a very big deal for me, but nothing was lined up. Leo also handled the Louis Bingham Orchestra, who had a radio show on the old Mutual Network, sponsored by Brylcreem. Billy Ross was their pianist, by the way. So I'm having lunch with Leo Silver at Lindy's one day and at the next booth are Arnie, Ziggy, and Vic, who Leo had seen a few weeks before at the White Lake Lodge. Enter through the door: Lou Bingham and the show's producer, Marty Miller. Lou and Marty sit at our booth and before you know it, Ziggy and Vic are going to audition for the Bingham radio show. Which was a fucking *lock*: you just knew they'd get the job. This happened in the blink of an eye! I hadn't even taken one bite out of my cheesecake yet! So they're standing and shaking hands all around and I'm sitting there like a lonely dill pickle, thinking, Hey, what ever happened to *me*?

ARNIE LATCHKEY: *The Shadow* and *The Falcon* were on Mutual, and the Macy Twins, from Lenny Pearl's show, had a program on Mutual too. Those two made the Andrews Sisters look like ravishing beauties. Years later, the Macys got an offer to do television, but they wisely retired instead. Cheated the hangman, you could call it.

Lou Bingham came up to the White Lake Lodge with Marty Miller and a few Brylcreem execs and two days later we're signing the paperwork in Herb Blackstone's office. We were signed for about twenty shows; Ziggy and Vic were guaranteed $250 each a week. Worldwide American took out their usual 12 ½ percent, those *gonifs*. Sally and I were coproducers of the show, but, to be honest, we were only responsible for the fifteen-minute segment that Ziggy and Vic did midway through the show, which was an hour long. What Lou Bingham did, played, or said had nothing to do with me. I didn't even listen to the show, other than to Fountain and Bliss, and I was getting paid a hundred a week.

Lou would play a few tunes, interview a few people who were usually plugging something. Lou was a little bit of an Arthur Godfrey type, except he played the clarinet and not the ukulele, thank God almighty. About half an hour into the program he'd turn the mikes over to Ziggy and Vic. Vic would sing a number with the band too. Sometimes Ziggy would interrupt the song but more often than not it was sketch comedy.

Now, this is what separated Fountain and Bliss from Abbott and Costello, who hadn't yet appeared on fat Kate Smith's radio program, and Martin and Lewis. The sheer *range*. Costello was always Costello, the dumb sap. Lewis was always the Melvin character, the pansy. Groucho and Chico had a radio show—it went straight into the toilet—and Chico was always stuck, like the Dutch boy's finger in the dike, doing the Italian thing. But Ziggy could do it all. It was like Gleason later on, who did Reggie Van Gleason, the Poor Soul, Ralph Kramden. Ziggy could do the German cook, the Hungarian scientist, the Japanese gardener, the Yiddish tailor, he could do the pansy, a Li'l Abner rube. They had this one slow-burn routine where Vic has just married this girl, played by Zig, and now they're having their very first meal as a couple and Vic realizes, *Oy vey iz mir,* my bride chews really, really loud! (Where they got this idea, I don't know.) And every sketch was so, so smooth. Vic's timing—nobody was better. Every single pause and note he'd hit on a dime. *On a dime!* You could practically hear him doing double takes on the radio! It was a revelation.

DOMINICK MANGIAPANE: We could hear the Bingham Brylcreem show in Codport . . . there was a local Mutual affiliate in New Bedford. It came on after *The Lone Ranger*. It was very funny stuff, very out-of-control-type material.

Every week now, something would come in the mail from New York. From Vic. My sister [Lulu] and I would get in screaming fights . . . you think just 'cause she was five foot two and slim she couldn't scream? The voice she had on her! Still does.

I would tell her, "Lu, I don't trust Vic. I don't like him and I don't trust him."

And she'd hold up a pair of shiny leather gloves and see, "Look at these! How can you not trust him?!"

"Just because he sends you gloves from Wanamaker's he should be trusted? He used to cheat at cards, he used to cheat at pool, he even cheated at Go Fish!"

"Yeah, but he don't ever cheat me, Dommy!"

"Oh yeah? How do you know? How do you know he don't cheat you? You're here, he's maybe wining and dining all kinds of girls on Broadway."

"Vic ain't like that," she said.

But I couldn't tell her what I knew. I couldn't tell her that Vic had banged Joe Ravelli's wife and Virgillio Marchi's wife and Angie Crosetti's mom and he'd banged big Patsy Jones with five other guys one night under the gazebo or that he'd probably bang a dead trout if it was wet enough. I didn't want to break her heart.

"All right, Lu," I'd say. "Whatever you say."

When she told me that she was going to marry him, I couldn't bring myself to congratulate her. She was telling me how happy she was gonna be, and all I could remember was him going at Fatsy Patsy under the gazebo, that look on his face.

DANNY McGLUE: Snuffy really was Ziggy's only pal around the time of the Bingham show. Hunny and Vic would go out together, Guy Puglia too. Ziggy wasn't invited and I don't know if he'd have gone out if he was. See, Vic and Ziggy didn't have common interests. Vic loved boxing, baseball, and the track but Ziggy just liked the theater and comedy and movies. He'd try to get Vic to go to Barney Arundel's Blue Beret Cafe with him to see so-and-so or such-and-such but Vic would rather go to the fights. Also, Vic had started "seeing" Constance Tuttle, who was on the Consolidated [radio] Network, on *The Murphy's Oil Soap's Edmund Sligh's Peerless Radio Theater* show.

GRACE WHEELWRIGHT [actress; friend of Constance Tuttle]: I was Connie's roommate for many years, until she married [Broadway producer] Jake Nealy. Connie was a classically trained actress, had been educated as a girl in Switzerland, and then studied drama in London in her late teens. Well, that's what she told everybody. She told me that a few of her British pursuers had included Ivor Novello, Michael Redgrave, and Charlie Chaplin. And Robert Donat too. He had terrible, terrible asthma and Constance said that when he made love to her he always made sure to have three tanks of oxygen near the bed. By four in the morning, supposedly, the tanks were emptied and Robert Donat's valet had to deliver three more.

Connie, did you know, almost landed a big part in Alfred Hitchcock's *Lifeboat,* a part which was simply perfect for her. But Tallulah Bankhead edged her out. "Oh well," Connie said to me, "at least I don't have to kiss William Bendix."

She was a bit of a prima donna. She lied about her age and used to dress in ridiculously opulent furs and jewels, most of which were borrowed. Edmund Sligh, who wrote, produced, directed, and acted in the Murphy's oil soap show, did not pay Constance what she thought was even half her due, but I suppose the Rockefellers and the Rothschilds combined would not have been able to do that either. She really did think she was the cat's meow. For someone who spent the first twelve years of her life in Columbus, Ohio, Connie did sound veddy, veddy British. I mean, she'd only studied at RADA for a year! (If that.) But you would have thought she was Dame May Whitty the way she rolled her *r*'s.

When Vic entered her life she was about forty years old. It's hard to say. When she died, even the *Times* was unsure about her age, something Connie would have loved. (Although she would have preferred getting more than two paragraphs on the obituary page.)

"I've just met the *most* delicious young boy!" she told me one night.

"Oh really, have you, Connie?" I asked, actually imagining an eight-year-old.

"He's on the Louis Bingham program, darling. Have you ever heard it?"

I told her I did not listen to such fare, something which she was already aware of.

"Tell me, Gracie," she asked me, "have you ever been kissed by a dago?"

The veal I was eating nearly slipped into my lungs.

"I beg your pardon, Connie?"

"This boy is as Italian as zucchini and just as delectable," she told me. "He can't be more than twenty-two or twenty-three years old. Has the blackest hair you've ever seen. Why, it's almost *blue*! Like an eggplant! And such shoulders. *Mmm-mmmm!*"

She told me that she'd recently met him at Schrafft's. They'd chatted very briefly after being introduced and then he asked for her phone number.

"I find this very intriguing, Grace," she said with a long, deep puff. She used an incredibly ornate and long cigarette holder.

That night in our apartment, she turned on the Bingham show, and while I heard the audience laughing at Fountain and Bliss, I stumbled on a small crumpled piece of paper. Written on it was a phone number. It was Watson 349 or something or other. And written over the number were the words "Big tasty Vic."

So I knew right away that she'd actually asked *him* for *his* phone number!

GUY PUGLIA: Sure, I met Constance Tuttle a few times. You remember that *Three Faces of Eve* movie, with Joanne Woodward? Well, this was

Two Faces of Connie. She'd come on all prim and proper and regal-like but by her fifth old-fashioned at the Colony [restaurant], she'd be saying something like, "Vic, let's go into the bathroom now so I get in just one lick of your exquisite cock." I heard that! In five minutes she went from sounding like the Duchess of Kent to a whore working the London docks.

ARNIE LATCHKEY: That nutty broad would've worn a sable coat, a silver fox stole, and chinchilla panties on a dune in the Sahara during a heat wave camped near a large space heater. And I thought she was going to pry my pupils out with that épée of a cigarette holder she wielded.

[Vic was] missing our usual 10:00 A.M. meetings at Vigorish. He'd either show up an hour late or he'd call in hungover and sometimes he didn't even bother to call.

"Latch, where's my better half?" Ziggy said to me one morning in my office.

"I have no idea," I said to him.

"This is approachin' three days in a row," he says.

"I'm aware of it," I said.

"I ain't ever missed one meetin', Latch. You know that. Not one."

"I'm familiar with it."

"I mean, if Vic wants to keep standin' me up at the altar, that's okay. I really don't mind. But Norman and Sidney, they're kinda fed up to their pharynxes about it. They're saying it's really unprofessional, Arn."

"I'll talk to Vic about it."

"It's this Tuttle dame. A guy fucks a broad in a fur, he forgets about all his friends and responsibilities. That ain't right."

"True, true," I said. And it *was* true and still is.

Now, this was the first time Ziggy had ever talked about Vic to me, either good or bad. The thing is, I'd been thinking that Ziggy had *enjoyed* it without Vic at the meetings! Because you had about seven people and now Ziggy was the main center of attention.

Not five minutes later Sid Stone is in my office. With Norman White.

"What's up, guys?" I said.

"Vic is missing a lot of meetings lately, you know," Sid says.

"I'm aware of it."

"He seems to have lost interest."

"I'm familiar with it."

"Good," Sid said. "'Cause I don't know how you're dealing with Ziggy."

"With Ziggy?"

Norman broke in and said, "Ziggy said that you were fed up to your pharynx with this sort of behavior."

"Hmm. I see, I see."

They strode out of my office. For some reason I picked up the phone . . . but then I realized: I got nobody to call about this. *Who do you call?!* Oh, the forlorn, lonely life of a manager! So I hung up and probably put my hands through my hair, which, not coincidentally, was at that precise second just beginning its long, irrevocable journey into disappearing.

SALLY KLEIN: Ziggy would call me up for a movie, a show, or dinner. He was very lonely. Often he'd call me up and ask me, "Hey, you seen Danny around?" and I'd tell him I had no idea where Danny was. Which was a lie, since Danny was on my couch, either with his typewriter or with me. Ziggy would ask me, "You wanna go out to Lindy's? You wanna see a picture?" And I'd tell him I was too tired.

He was jealous of Vic. Vic was the "good-looking" one, of course. That eventually became a big part of the act and Ziggy played along with it. But if you ever saw his face while he's in the corner and Vic is being fawned over by two or three girls—it was a pout you could've used in a diaper ad.

GRACE WHEELWRIGHT: I remember coming home from a rehearsal one night . . . the first thing I saw was one of Connie's chinchilla coats on the floor. I went into the bathroom and . . . there they were in the tub. He was standing and she was on her knees, all covered with soap. She was actually pouring champagne onto his private parts!

"Oh please, Gracie dahhhrling," she said to me, "do jump in and enjoy some of this scrumptious bubbly."

I hope you'll mention that I closed the door and went to my room!

GUY PUGLIA: Vic would tell me everything about Connie Tuttle. I'd never seen this broad naked but if they blindfolded me I could put my finger on a freckle or a mole, I knew her that well. Hey, it's kind of ironic, I guess, that Murphy's oil soap was the sponsor of that radio show 'cause you'd need twenty gallons of that stuff to wash out that filthy mouth of hers.

"She uses words I ain't even heard of for it, Guy," Vic told me once. "For what?" I ask him, and he says, "For everything. She's got pet names for my nuts, for my sac, even for my veins down there. She calls one of the veins spaghetti and another linguini. My nuts she calls watermelon and cantaloupe." I says to him, "Vic, I don't know if I wanna hear all this." He tells me, "She calls me up at the Vigorish office or at the radio studio and says, 'I want to devour you whole, you succulent slab of mortadella, you.' And you gotta see what she does with food!" "With food? Most people just eat it, you know," I says to him. He says, "Oh, she eats it all right. She eats it off me. You ever had caviar, Guy?" I tell him I've never even seen it, and he tells me she put caviar on him, in a very, very specific place. And then sucked it out.

"Hey, Vic," I says to him. "Caviar is fish, did you know that?"

"Huh?"

"Yeah. Caviar is fish. It's the eggs of a fish."

"Aw, shit."

He told me that one thing she wanted to do was pour some rum on him down there and then take a match to it. And while he was on fire she would lap it all up. But he said no to that.

ARNIE LATCHKEY: We had a radio show to do and Vic had only made it to one meeting and one rehearsal that week. But I gotta tell ya: He had a mind like Fort Knox. You give him a script, he rehearses it one time, it's *sealed* in there. My big problem was not him not being there—it was Ziggy manipulating, instigating, and provoking. He'd tell Sally something that I'd said, which I'd never said at all, and then he'd tell me something that Sally had said, which *she'd* never ever said. Of course, Sally and I would talk about it and put two and two together. It's one thing to lie, but to be so reckless about it—it just doesn't reflect well.

"Vic, you gotta start showing up on time," I said to him one day.

"Why's that?"

"Because everybody else does. It looks bad."

"Who's mad at me? Is Sid mad? Norman?"

I shrugged.

"Is it Danny? Is Sally mad at me? Is it Ziggy?"

I cast my gaze down at my mushroom and barley soup.

"It's Ziggy," he said.

"Look, it's maybe no one in particular or maybe it's everyone as a whole."

He lit up a Chesterfield and leaned back in the booth.

I told him, "You look like shit, you know that? How many hours sleep you get?"

"Who sleeps, Latch?"

"Is it Constance Tuttle? Is that it? She's old enough to be your mother, you know." I noticed something strange just then. "Hey, do you smell rum?"

"Rum?"

"Yeah. Rum."

"Nah, Arn," he said. "I don't smell rum. This is Bratz's deli. They don't serve rum at Bratz's."

GRACE WHEELWRIGHT: She called him all sorts of pet names, right in front of me. "Marshmallow" was one. "Big Beluga," too. He called her things like "Puddin'" and "Hot Tomato." He'd be reading *Gasoline Alley* on our couch and she'd be looking at a script, with her head resting on his lap. And I couldn't help but notice that she'd be moving her head there, sort of grinding it against him. A minute later he'd stand up and swagger into Connie's room. She'd head for the refrigerator, find something, and then bring it into her room and close the door.

I did start noticing the strangest delicacies in the house. Suddenly there were many jars of capers. There would be tubs of Horn & Hardardt applesauce and different kinds of honey—oh yes!—and maple syrup from Vermont and all sorts of exotic jellies and preserves. I remember leaving the house for the theater one night and seeing a jar of molasses in the cupboard; when I returned hours later, the empty jar was in the trash. I heard Vic in the shower yelling out to Connie, "This stuff ain't comin' off too easy, baby."

SNUFFY DUBIN: When he wasn't complaining about Vic to me, Ziggy was going to whores, to hookers. A few of the cats in the Bingham band had some phone numbers. There was this place on Eighth Avenue in the Fifties, near Roseland, an apartment building. The fifth floor of that building, man, every chick was working some kind of operation. With that *shvantz* of his, I didn't know how he managed. But he did mention something once about Crisco vegetable shortening.

DANNY McGLUE: Fountain and Bliss had a contract for so many weeks, maybe fifteen or sixteen weeks, with Lou Bingham. The show went on hiatus for a few weeks and it was just a given that the deal would be renewed for more money. Despite the time slot being opposite Burns and Allen, it was a success, and Bert Kahn was getting the act some ink. He'd brought them over to Westbrook Pegler's table at the Stork Club and they had him in stitches—Pegler gave them about two paragraphs the following day—and Winchell gave them some airtime too. Winchell knew that Vic was involved with Connie Tuttle and hinted at it.

The final week in the radio contract Vic was showing up again. He'd be there on time and he was participating. Everything was copacetic and he and Ziggy were gelling.

The first truly big crisis the act ever had was on the final night. They were going on in two hours and nobody had any idea where Vic was.

ARNIE LATCHKEY: I called Vic at home—he was living at the Dorilton on Seventieth near Broadway—and there was no answer. I called Hunny and Guy; they didn't know where he was. Guy said to call Constance Tuttle's spread. Meanwhile, I'm sweating like Niagara Falls—I've got to be at the studio any minute! I called Connie Tuttle and she ain't home but her roommate says she's positive that Connie and Vic are at Vic's pad.

"Sally, you gotta go up to the Dorilton and round up Vic," I say. "Take Danny."

"What if he's not there?"

"If he's not there, then we're sunk! Hurry."

She leaves with Danny, and Ziggy, who's already so *shvitzy* he's making me look like a fresh sheet of sandpaper, sidles up to me and asks, "Where the hell is he, Arn?"

"We're gonna find him, Zig. I swear to God. I hope. Danny and Sally are going up to the Dorilton right now as we sweat."

"Danny and Sally?"

"Uh, yeah. Why?"

He's patting himself on the forehead with a hanky and he says, "They seem awful chummy sometimes around here, don't they?"

"Well, we all do. I mean, I'm chummy with you, right? And Sid Stone is chummy with me."

"Yeah, but you and Sid don't have tits."

SALLY KLEIN: Danny and I took a taxi and told the driver to step on it . . . we were on Seventieth Street in no time. The doorman buzzed up and there was no response, but Danny told me that a lot of times Vic never answered the door or the phone anyways. The doorman says we cannot go upstairs under any means whatsoever, so Danny gave him a five-dollar bill and he let us up.

We ring and we knock and we shout through the door but there's no answer. Danny goes back down to the doorman and gives him another five dollars and now we've got the house keys.

Danny and I walk in and the first thing I saw made me jump almost to the ceiling! I thought it was a dead rat, but it was just a chinchilla stole lying on the floor. I thought I was going to die.

"Vic? Vic? You in here?" Danny says. We're holding each other's hands.

There's no answer. This was only the second time I'd been in Vic's apartment. It was furnished in a sort of garish, swank style of the time. There were two empty champagne bottles on the couch, and Vic's clothes, including the tuxedo that he wore for the Bingham show, were on the floor.

"At least he *tried* to get dressed," Danny said when he saw the tux.

We tiptoe to the bedroom, which is dark. Danny flips on the light and we saw that the whole bedroom was in a shambles. I saw this bundled-up mink coat on the bed. And it was moving slightly up and down, like breathing.

"Constance?" Danny says. "Miss Constance Tuttle?"

I noticed that there was not only a mink coat on the bed but two smaller things, two more swatches of fur where the feet were.

"Miss Tuttle? Do you know where Vic Fountain is?" Danny asked.

Just then we heard this deep baritone snore. Danny and I knew that instant that it was Vic. Sometimes when he sang, in that sleepy Perry Como style, it could sound like snoring. We recognized the noise.

Danny and I are at the bed and we turn Vic over. He's out cold and has nothing on but the fur coat and the two pieces on his feet. Danny sits him up, against the headboard, and I went to the bathroom and got some cold water and threw it on his face. We're imploring him to wake up. There's still time to get him dressed and get to the studio.

Finally he begins to regain consciousness. "Jesus Christ," he muttered.

"Vic, you've got a show to do . . . you're on in a half hour," Danny told him.

"A show?" Vic said. "Oh yeah."

I went into the living room and picked up Vic's tuxedo and cummerbund. But when I went back into the bedroom Vic was whiter than the sheets on the bed and Danny looked sick too. They were both frozen . . . frozen stiff. They were staring at Vic's feet.

Danny had lifted the two pieces of fur off. Two of Vic's toes were missing! They were gone. There was blood on his feet and on the bed. It was the pinkie toe on the right and left feet. Gone.

"Vic . . . what happened to your feet?" Danny finally asked him.

"Aw fuck," he said. "That crazy broad."

I went into the kitchen to get some water and wet some towels . . . to keep around Vic's feet until we could get him to the hospital. So I'm wetting these dish towels in the sink and I hear this faint little noise. It was like a sizzling sound. And I smell garlic. I looked over to my right and there in a frying pan were Vic's toes! His two pinkie toes.

I got sick into the sink. That's the last thing I remember.

Danny had to not only revive me, he had to take Vic to the hospital too.

ARNIE LATCHKEY: He missed the show. I told [producer] Marty Miller that Vic had to be rushed to the hospital, and Marty asked me if Ziggy could go on for fifteen minutes solo.

So I go to the greenroom and say to Ziggy, "Vic can't make it."

He's trying to wedge himself into his tux. It wasn't easy to get even a master tailor to make clothing for him . . . his measurements defied common sense.

"I think we got to fire him, Latch."

"And replace him with who? The goddamn *O'Hares*? Forget about firing Vic. What are you gonna do *tonight*? Can you give Lou fifteen minutes?"

"A solo?"

"Yeah. Solo."

He sat there, started twitching a bit.

"You okay, Ziggy?"

"Fifteen minutes, solo?"

"That's what I need. That's what *you* need, Ziggeleh."

"I got no solo material. The only material I got is me and Vic."

There was a knock on the door. A stagehand yelled out, "Ten minutes, Mr. Bliss."

I sat down and pulled my seat up next to him and I said, "How about if *I* do your part tonight and you do Vic's?"

"You could do that, Latch?"

"Could you do Vic's part?"

"What? The straight man? Ha! That cigar you're smokin' could do that!"

"Good. Now how about this: You do *both* parts. You do Ziggy and you do Vic. Can you do that?"

"Gee, I don't know . . ." he started hedging.

"Ziggy baby, come on. I know you can do it. You know you can. This is for the sake of the act. One time, pal, one time."

"This is tough, Arn," he said.

I wanted to throttle him! I knew he could do it and he knew it too! He just wanted me to beg him . . . he wanted me to get down on my goddamn knees and plead with him!

So I did.

I'm on my knees and my hands are clasped like I'm praying to God that the plummeting aircraft which is my life don't crash into the drink. I'm begging, I'm pleading, I'm beseeching, I'm making entreaties.

"Okay, I'll do it," he says finally.

He went on the air and he was fan*tab*ulous. He was perfect, he was wonderful. He was Joe DiMaggio, Joe Louis, Sid Luckman, Eddie Arcaro all rolled into one.

Bertie Kahn got it into the papers what Ziggy had done, how marvelous the performance was. He'd called Grayling Greene up during the show and made sure Greene was listening. It was a combination of damage control and an ink extravaganza all in one shot. Bertie told everyone that Vic was suffering from nervous exhaustion due to the rigorous rehearsal schedule, the radio show, playing the Catskills on the weekends and whatnot. Hatch, Greene, Pegler, Winchell, Fleury, Sullivan . . . they all made mention of it.

And the beauty part is this: Vic never had to enter the army. Why? *Because that lucky bastard was missing two of his goddamn toes!*

We should've sent a check for a million bucks to Constance Tuttle for that.

Okay. Now . . . *dissolve.* It's about fifteen years later, I'm at Al Roon's Health Club on Broadway, right near the Ansonia, in one of those big old sweatboxes. You sit in there, they close the door on you, you lose fifty pounds of perspiration in ten minutes, and you come out looking like a bleached raisin. For this I had to pay Al Roon five bucks a month? I could've just had myself dry-cleaned.

I look over to my left and there in the next box is none other than Edmund Sligh. That guy was *married* to the theater—ancestors of his were in the theater when Shakespeare was just a lad making wee wee into the Avon. I'd read that morning in Ed Sullivan's *Daily News* column that Sligh's theater show was about to bite the dust and I offered my condolences. He didn't look too happy, I gotta tell you, but then again he was sitting in a crate of molten lava at the time.

The conversation got around to Constance Tuttle, who'd left the show a few years before and was now playing some eccentric matriarch on *The Edge of Night.*

The heat and the sweat must have gotten to me because I related the story to Sligh, about how Constance Tuttle had gotten Vic stewed to the gills one night and then sliced off two of his toes and tried to cook them in a white wine and shallot sauce. I said to him, "It's a good thing she was a lousy cook 'cause she probably would've gone for the fingers next, Eddie."

"Oh, would she have?" he said.

A few minutes later, he gets out of his box. He's buck naked and drying himself with a towel and I get an eyeful of the man's physique. It was a little bit hard to see in there because of all the steam, but I know what I saw: Edmund Sligh had just a tiny thimble-size stump where his *shlong* should be.

So maybe Constance Tuttle wouldn't have gone for the fingers next.

* * *

SNUFFY DUBIN: That was the first big dose of press they ever got. And what was it about? It was about Vic collapsing and Ziggy being the trouper. About Vic being "nervous" and exhausted and Ziggy being strong. Vic was the goat and Ziggy ate it up like it was a plate of *kasha* fucking *varnishkes* during the worst famine ever. Cutting articles out, pasting them into a book, talking to Bud Hatch and even Hilda Fleury, the society columnist. I remember him telling me, "Somewheres my parents are proud of me somewheres, Snuffles." He didn't talk about his parents that much—this might've been the first time since they died.

Yeah, things had changed. Vic knew he'd let down a lot of people. Lou Bingham, Arnie, Sally, Sid Stone and Norman White, and the Brylcreem sponsors. And Ziggy too. But I don't think he felt too bad about that.

DANNY McGLUE: Ziggy was really lording it over everybody. It was a big Hail-the-Conquering-Hero thing. But sometimes, I guess, you want to hail the conquering hero, grab him by his throat, and then strangle him.

Lou Bingham and the Brylcreem people were not happy with Vic's stunt, even though it had brought the show a lot of tub-thump. Arnie worked it out with Lou and with the Mutual radio people that Fountain and Bliss would be off the show but that they would get a fifteen-minute radio spot *before* the Bingham show came on. Fountain and Bliss would lead into the Brylcreem show. Arnie and Marty Miller scrambled around and got Lifebuoy soap to sponsor the new show.

Things fell into place quickly. Billy Ross left the Bingham band and led a small band for the new Fountain and Bliss Lifebuoy show. Ernie Beasley now began writing serious songs for Vic . . . when he wasn't soused, I might say. A lot of people think I got jealous or upset when Ernie became our unofficial cleffer [composer] but I didn't, because I knew that my music wasn't really music and that it was silly. I was more than content being just a joke man. And—Ernie will tell you this is true—once in a while if he was stuck for a nice turn of a phrase or a rhyme, I was always there to throw my two pesos in.

During the hiatus, I remember, Arnie had approached Lee Sperling from the Schuberts about putting Fountain and Bliss in a Broadway show. It was a sort of Busby Berkeley meets Flo Ziegfeld meets *Dames at Sea* thing called *Aweigh They Go*. Dancers, songs, comedy, some drama. Arnie was all for it but when he told Ziggy and Vic about it, there was a rift. Vic wanted to do it—it would give him a really good chance to use his pipes, he said—but Ziggy threw a fit. He refused to even consider it. They'd be saying someone else's lines, he screamed. The material wouldn't be from him or Sid or me or Norman, he shrieked. It wasn't really their act, he hollered. All that yelling—I thought I was listening to Flo Blissman singing again! He was throwing stuff around and his face was red—ever see *White Heat* with Jimmy Cagney? That's what it was like. Now, I'd seen this sort of behavior before and so had Sally, but this was the first time that the others had. God, you should have seen Sid Stone and Norman that day. They both had these incredible "What-are-we-doing-here?" looks on. After this ten-minute explosion, Arnie defused it by saying, "Okay, I'll tell Lee Sperling the answer is no." (Sperling eventually got Cubby Cavanaugh and Jack Haley and it did whammo box office.)

In a small way, this was good for Vic, for his ego. Because the whole toe incident had really cut him down to size. He'd been acting sheepish and been quiet because of what he'd done. Now with this fit, this *White Heat* attack of Ziggy's, Vic got a little more credibility. It was like he was saying to everyone, "Okay, I was so in my cups that this woman cut my toes off but look at this little red gorilla having a seizure now!"

ARNIE LATCHKEY: To be honest, Lee Sperling's heart wasn't broken when I told them my clients had pooh-poohed the deal. It was one of the shortest conversations I ever had with a producer in any medium, as a matter of fact. Ten seconds, tops.

One day we're at the office and Sidney Stone says that he and Norman could dig out a play and blow the dust off it—a play they'd both written when they were in Hollywood—and that maybe Ernie Beasley could write songs for it. Sid Stone had balls the size of the Statue of Liberty's because he did this only days after Ziggy went nutsy over the Schubert thing.

Ziggy said to Sid, "You wrote it, Sid? Honest?"

Sid said, "Me and Norman did, yeah, Ziggy. On the Paramount lot."

You heard about ten hearts pounding in that room and two of them were mine, Teddy! Who knew if Ziggy was gonna pull another Mount Vesuvius act?

"Is it any good, Norman?"

"Ziggy, it ain't *Mourning Becomes Electra,*" Norman said, "but it's good enough."

"I'll take a look at it, guys. Okay?"

Everyone in that room had muscles so tight that if a slight breeze blew in we would've all fallen apart, but now we all sort of exhaled and relaxed.

"Vic," Ziggy said, "you wanna look at the script?"

Vic said, "Nah, you look at it, Zig."

Ziggy said, "You still anxious to get your toes wet on Broadway still?"

Vic looked down . . . at his toes. Had Ziggy purposely meant this as a cruel, cutting *jeu d'esprit*? To antagonize him? To get his goat? No man will ever know.

Vic looked back up and said, "Just read the damn thing, okay?"

It was called *Three of a Kind* . . . it was typical Broadway fare of the day. It was a version of the old Noël Coward play *Design for Living,* but set in Hollywood. Ernie already had three wonderful songs that would have been just swell with the play. Sid and Norman adapted and tinkered with the thing and changed it around to suit Ziggy and Vic more. We got it to Murray Katz at WAT and he said it'd be a difficult sell. He tried Lee Sperling but Sperling passed. We got it to Morgan Talvert and Norman Barasch but they passed too. Murray's heart wasn't in it and now neither was Sid Stone's or Norman's. Ernie Beasley came in one day and played "Malibu Moonlight" for us, which he'd just written for the show. We knew that song, whether it got into this play or not, would be a hit one day and it was . . . it was perfect for Vic's style.

Three of a Kind never got off the ground. It was a huge setback. Our first. The office was not the usual fun house it was, unless you consider a morgue a fun house. We'd meet at ten and we had these shell-shocked looks on our faces, like all our mothers had just died in one bus accident.

The Lifebuoy show was about to start and we had little or no material. Things were very bleak indeed.

The phone rings one day and Estelle picks up and hands it to Sally Klein. Sally takes the call in her office and meanwhile in the living room you've got about six men swallowing, coughing, excavating their noses, and scratching their privates.

Sally comes out with one of the arms of her eyeglasses in her mouth and says, "That was Barney Arundel. Charlotte Charlot, 'the *Charmant* Chanteuse from Chantilly,' isn't going to play her Blue Beret Cafe engagement. Turns out she's a Nazi sympathizer and can't get a cabaret license. Barney wants to know if Fountain and Bliss can give him two weeks."

I said, "It sounds like a good idea to me, Sal. Call Barney back. Tell him the answer is *oui, oui*. Tell him we'll do it."

"I don't have to call him back," she said cockily. "Because I already told him we'd do it."

Boom! Back in business. Just like that.

III

GUY PUGLIA: Whenever there was an open date, Ziggy used to like to line up a girl—who usually had tits just like Jayne Mansfield's—for exactly 10:45 at night. Now, Hunny had a friend who was a New York cop and he borrowed this cop's uniform and badge. Vic was setting this whole caper up—at this point Hunny and Ziggy have never met. Hunny goes upstairs to this hooker's spread and puts his big ear to the door and hears all this groanin' and gruntin' and he knocks. "Open up!" he says. "Vice squad." The girl opens the door in a red kimono that she's droopin' right out of and says, "Hey, I paid you guys off last week!" and Hunny sweeps past her and looks for Ziggy, who's now thinkin', My career's over, my career's over. Officer Hunny's in the bedroom now and there's no sign of Ziggy, but he peeks under the bed and there he is, hiding. Somehow Ziggy had managed to squeeze his body underneath there, I don't know how.

Hunny plucks him out and Ziggy says, "Hey, Officer, how does a week free at Heine's resort in the governor's suite sound to you?" Hunny says he's now got him on bribery charges.

He asks Hun if he can make a call and he calls Sally Klein at home. Ziggy is bawlin' and tellin' Sally that this girl is his girlfriend, that he had no idea she was a whore, but Sally was tough and the next thing Ziggy's doing is saying, yeah, she's not his girl and she is a whore but he wasn't really paying for it. Hunny takes the phone away and hangs it up and cuffs Ziggy. "What's gonna happen to me, Officer?" Ziggy asks, and Hunny says, "We're taking you to the Tombs." Ziggy says, "The Tombs! What's gonna happen to me there?" and Hunny says, "The other prisoners'll probably put you through the grease line." And Ziggy nearly craps his pants.

There was no such thing as a grease line. Vic had made that one up.

So Hunny hauls Ziggy into the living room and what's the first thing the two of 'em see? Vic's on top of the girl and he's goin' to town with her. That's when Ziggy realized it was all a gag. Hunny told me that Ziggy was crackin' up. And maybe he was, but whether it was real laughter or just laughing to hide the fact that he'd been taken for a sap, I don't know.

• • •

SNUFFY DUBIN: Before they began their gig at the Blue Beret, they did a tune-up at a much smaller place called Club 18. The pay there was nothing compared to what they could pull in at a Catskills gig. Now, I played Club 18 a few weeks after Fountain and Bliss but for *me* the pay was good. Ziggy got me that engagement—maybe the only favor he ever did me. Must have been an oversight on his part.

Club 18 was in a basement in midtown. This place drew all kinds of celebrities and high society and so forth. The atmosphere was dark, the drinks and service were second-rate . . . so why did they go? *To be put in their place.* These VIPs would go to this club to get insulted by comics, all for a laugh. The week I worked there Clark Gable comes in with Carole Lombard. I see that and my heart starts racing like Man o'fucking War. *Jesus Christ, Clark Gable is coming to see Samuel Dubinsky from Harrison Street in Chicago tell jokes?!* Absolutely unbelievable shit to me, right? But I gotta do the Club 18 thing now, I've gotta insult them and tell jokes at their expense. "Hey, Carole, I hear you walk around the house naked," I said to her, which was a rumor everyone knew. "Is it true Clark opens the blinds and charges the neighbors a buck a peep?" Okay, not the best gag in the world, but, man, was I scared! The week Fountain and Bliss appeared, Humphrey Bogart and his wife were there and Vic started imitating Bogart—had him down to a T—and Ziggy is being Mrs. Bogart and then they start punching each other . . . because everyone knew that Bogart had this very rough relationship with her. Bogart was on the floor. Jack Dempsey came in, the George Gershwins, Hester Warnocke, Felix Frankfurter, Eddie Duchin, a Whitney or two. Howard Hughes comes in with a doll who's stacked like the New York Public Library and Vic is coming on to her and Ziggy is coming on to him, and Hughes's face is on the table, he's laughing so much. Spencer Tracy and Katharine Hepburn came in one night, and the next night Tracy showed up with his wife; his *Dr. Jekyll and Mr. Hyde* had just come out and he got a standing ovation on both nights. Gus Kahn of Galaxy Pictures was in New York and went to Club 18, and Ziggy and Vic were just relentless, making fun of his pictures, how much money he had and his gambling. Two weeks later Gus Kahn is in New York again and now I'm at Club 18. I'm doing the same kind of stuff and he gives me a look like I'm Hermann fucking Goering about to bomb his Beverly Hills estate in my Messerschmidt. The maitre d' at the club would take Arnie aside and point out some of the socialites and debs and blue bloods, 'cause Vittorio Fontana and Sigmund Blissman didn't really move within that smart Newport horsey set. So you had Warnockes, Rockefellers, Mellons, and Standishes and all this upper-crust Four fucking Hundred crowd, and Ziggy and Vic have got 'em in their pockets. They *own* them!

CHARLES FRAME [stage manager at the Blue Beret Cafe]: The club was originally called the Red Beret Cafe, did you know that? That was the name when Barney Arundel opened it. But one evening in, say, 1938, J. Edgar Hoover and his intimate companion Clyde Tolson came in and asked Barney why the *Red* Beret . . . why *red*? Why are the tablecloths and the napkins and the menus *red*? Why are the strawberries red? Barney was not a political man and he'd chosen the name of the cafe simply because his daughter wore a red beret. That simple. Barney walked away and overheard Mr. Tolson saying to Mr. Hoover, "Well, you didn't have to be such a bitch about it, Edwina!" The next week the place was renamed the Blue Beret—and so it remained until it closed in the 1950s—with blue tablecloths, blue menus, blue napkins, and, yes, blueberries.

Pete Conifer was in charge of the entertainment. Yes, *that* Pete Conifer, who was later the head of the Oceanfront [Hotel and Resort] in Las Vegas. He was only in his twenties at the time but was going places, you could tell, and he really knew how to kiss up to the important patrons. One night Jack Warner came in with his wife, and Pete sent over flowers to the table. Everything was free for them, and Pete even sent flowers and champagne to their hotel suite too. Franchot Tone and Joan Crawford (but not together), the Luces, the Cagneys, Fiorello La Guardia, Myrna Loy, Louis B. Mayer, the Fritz Devanes—he did the same for them. Meanwhile, though, there were the hatcheck girls and *les* Blue Beret *danseurs*, and Pete couldn't keep his hands off them, he was like a hungry dog. Some of them were truly terrified of him, so terrified that they even quit to work at the Copacabana, the Riobamba, or at El Morocco.

We were excited to get Fountain and Bliss for two weeks—we'd never had comedians perform there; it had always been music. There would be a cabaret singer, like Jeanne Courbet or Paul DeMarche, or we'd get the Ben Bentley Orchestra with Virginia Carstairs. But Barney had found out that Charlotte Charlot was not only a Nazi sympathizer, she sympathized *rabidly*. She'd done some fund-raisers around the Yorkville area, also known as Germantown, for the German-American Bundt. She'd sung at an America First rally and palled around with Father Coughlin. Even Neville Chamberlain, believe it or not, had banned her from performing in England.

When Fountain and Bliss were at the Blue Beret, material kept being delivered to their dressing room that had been intended for Charlotte Charlot. There were Nazi leaflets, Nazi newspapers with these horrid cartoons with salivating vermin in skullcaps raping Aryan women. Shady-looking men in trench coats stopped by and wanted to meet Charlotte.

One such fellow handed our maitre d', Michel Perpignan—real name: Mickey Peters—a bundle of something and said it was for Frau Charlot. We looked inside and it was about a pound of German sausage. Barney may have done what Hoover and Tolson told them to do when he changed the cafe's name, but he was not about to let the club become a beachhead for Hitler on Fifty-third Street!

SALLY KLEIN: After Club 18, the boys were ready for the big time on the nightclub scene. You paw Howard Hughes's girlfriend, you make fun of the size of Clark Gable's you-know-what, you're ready for anything. The Blue Beret seated about five hundred people. Billy Ross, Vic's bandleader for many years, led a small band, and Vic sang a few numbers before Ziggy would "interrupt" him. Ernie Beasley wrote two songs specifically for this engagement, "Back on the Boulevard Again" and "My Sweet Cheri," and Vic also sang Cole Porter's "Do You Want to See Paris?" from his *Fifty Million Frenchmen*, which I'd seen as a young girl with my mother.

Not only were the gossip columnists there, but music critics too. Danny Richman from the *Post,* Robert Schappell from the *Globe.* And so on. Bertie Kahn asked for a few tables from Barney Arundel and planted a bunch of people there to laugh and applaud. He hired a few top-notch "ladies of the evening," got them dolled up in very fancy evening clothing and hairdos, and told them to pour it on and applaud their hearts out for Vic's singing. Nobody had any idea what these women really did for a living.

But, you know, we didn't even need those gimmicks. The boys were supposed to do a hour and a half, they did twice that. They ad-libbed, they danced and did impressions; they'd toss that invisible, imaginary fireball of theirs back and forth. There were times when Ziggy would be so funny that Vic was on the verge of cracking up, and when that happened it was infectious and the audience was laughing too. The third night, Ziggy—Vic had no idea he was going to do it—dressed up as Charlotte Charlot: the tight black sequined gown, twenty pounds of rouge, the red feather boa, the cigarette holder and guitar. He adjusted the boa halfway through a song that Danny had written and then you saw he also had on a swastika armband. After the song—Billy Ross was accompanying him on the accordion—Vic "interviewed" her. And they were just *on*. Vic knew what to ask, Ziggy knew what to answer. It was absolute magic! They kept the routine, not only for the rest of the engagement, but for the rest of the war. It really helped destroy Charlotte Charlot's career, thank God.

TONY FERRO: My late wife, Maria, may God rest her soul, was living in Brooklyn with her Aunt Nancy, in Flatbush. We weren't married yet—that was a few months away. I took a train to New York and Vic got us a table

at the Blue Beret. Here I am, I'm a butcher now and the son of an immi-
grant fisherman, and I'm with this lovely girl and we're at this swank
nightclub. I'll never forget it. Never.

After that, though, I don't know . . . Vic and me, we drifted apart. I
didn't hear from him again. Hell, we worked at Jiggs's together. But he
went his way, I went mine.

ARNIE LATCHKEY: It happened again. At the Blue Beret. Some man in
his late sixties was laughing so much he burst a blood vessel in his brain
and bought the farm. This happened in week one, maybe the fifth night.
The Edward G. Robinsons were in the audience that night, and Ziggy is at
their table and he and Vic are doing a bit about ordering Robinson a "little
Caesar salad." Get it? *Little Caesar?* So this poor man in the audience dies.
I saw him too . . . you ever see a corpse frozen stiff with a smile as big as
Florida? We should all be so lucky to go out like this!

The next day I'm on the phone with Bertie Kahn, which was almost like
being on the phone with dead air, he was so damn terse. We were talking
about the guy who'd died laughing and I said, "What do we do about this,
Bertie? Do you want to call up Winchell and Pegler and Greene and have
them bury this?"

"Bury this?" he said.

"This is two people who've died now," I reminded him. "And that's just
the ones we know of. We don't want people to be afraid to see the act!"

"We don't?" he said, debonairly puffing a Gitane probably.

And it struck me like lightning, right in that office—in my chair this
jagged bolt struck me! *Of course* we wanted people to be afraid to see the
act!

Bertie made some calls and not only was it in the gossip columns, it was
in the news sections too. The *Daily News* ran it on the second page and all
the Hearst papers carried it too. It was absolutely terri*f*ulous press!

DANNY McGLUE: I went to every show. They did two shows a night;
they didn't get off until two in the morning, sometimes three. The best
shows were always the second ones because there was no time constraint.
Barney and Pete Conifer had to get five hundred people out of the club at
ten and get five hundred new people in at eleven. The second shows were
always outrageous, very free-form, almost stream of consciousness.

About three women each night thought they were having appendicitis
attacks and had to be escorted out. I remember this one gent getting up
with his wife—he had to take her to the hospital. They stood up, he's helping her walk while she's doubled over in agony, and he's taking her to get
their coats. But meanwhile, he doesn't take his eyes off the stage. They

were at the coatcheck and his wife's got her coat on but now the husband isn't even aware his wife has to go to the hospital anymore! She elbowed him, as if to say, "Remember, Harold? You were taking me to Mount Sinai?" And he said to her, "Beverly dear, can't you make it there alone?"

After the engagement, I had lunch with Pete. He told me he wanted to leave the Blue Beret, maybe start a club in Los Angeles. If he did, he wanted to know, would Ziggy and Vic play there? We didn't have any plans like that, I told him, we were locked in for the radio show and that was in New York. When was this club going to happen, I asked him. He said it could take years to set up such a venture. Do you think Fountain and Bliss will still be together in two years, he asked me. I saw no reason why they wouldn't be together forever, I told him.

CATHERINE RICCI: When Sal [Fontana], Carmine, and I went to New York to catch a show, Carmine's sides were splitting in agony, he was in so much hysterics! The act had something for everyone . . . Vic would slip in an Italian word here and there and once in a while Ziggy would do some Yiddish. They made fun of Germans and did a thing about Japanese and even British people too. (They never made fun of colored people, though, you have to give them that.) Sal was a lot like Papa, he didn't laugh too much ever, but now I saw him using the handkerchief to wipe the sweat off his forehead from all that giggling.

I asked Vic how much he was making from this nightclub and when he told me I thought he was pulling my leg. A few weeks later Guy Puglia drives up to the house in Codport with a brand-new turquoise blue Studebaker Business coupé and says it's a present from Vic for Mamma and Papa. This car was stunning . . . it would've been the flashiest car in town. Mamma wanted it—she was almost salivating—but Papa stared at Guy with his icy eyes and slowly shook his head . . . then Guy drove it away.

"He's just drivin' it back to New York, huh?" Carmine said to me.

"Yeah, I guess so."

"Hey, maybe that younger brother of yours'll buy us a fancy car one day, Cathy."

"Don't get too pushy now," I said to him.

"I mean, if he's so generous, why not—"

"Carmine, please!"

The next day, I'm at the bakery with Carmine and we see the turquoise Studebaker go by. We both run out and who's at the wheel? Dominick Mangiapane! With his sister Lulu by his side. Both of 'em just tooling around like a couple of sports.

"That could've been ours," Carmine muttered to me while we both waved like morons at those two.

* * *

ARNIE LATCHKEY: "I wanna put Guy on the payroll," Vic tells me one day in the Vigorish office.

I knew something was up when he came into my office and closed the door behind him. That foreboding click of the door, like a pistol to my head being cocked.

"Guy Puglia?" I said, stubbing out my cigar and clearing my throat.

He says, "Ziggy's got Sally and Danny on the payroll."

"Sally and Danny actually work for us, though, Vic. You know that."

He lights up a Chesterfield, fixes a pleat in his pants. The Blue Beret dates were finished, the Lifebuoy show was doing well, he'd bought some new duds. Very fancy ones. Gilbert Perreault suits, Rene Robert ties, Richard Martin shirts. Lots of 'em.

"Yeah, I know that. But they're his family, Latch."

"Sally is his family but Danny isn't," I reminded him.

"Yeah, but they're bangin' each other."

The man didn't pull any punches, let me tell you, if he wanted to land one.

I cleared my throat. "That's classified dope," I told him. "Okay?"

"Look, Guy and me, we go back a long ways. He's like blood to me. He was with me when I was singin' 'Ain't She Sweet' for pennies in Boston. We bunked at the Monroe together. And he does stuff for me now. And I feel that he should be paid for it."

I cleared my throat and asked, "What kinds of stuff does Guy do?" Now, I liked Guy Puglia. I still do. I had *wonderful* times at the Hunny Pot [Hunny Gannett's saloon] and at Guy's restaurant in Los Angeles. I adore Guy. But, really, I had no damn idea what he did!

"He just does stuff, Arn," Vic said.

"Can you give me one example? One thing?"

"Well, you know, he takes my suits in to be cleaned, gets my shoes shined. He makes reservations for me at restaurants. I see a girl I like in the crowd, he gets her backstage."

"I see. I get the idea," I said. "You know, Vic, these are things that I could do." It killed me to say that. I didn't want to take Vic's clothing in— it was so much clothing already I think I'd have gotten a hernia from it. And besides, those days were behind me.

"Nah, this is what Guy's for. But if you're really willing to get my shoes sh—"

"I think this thing can be arranged."

"Good. Because I was also thinking of gettin' Hunny on the payroll too."

SALLY KLEIN: Hunny started coming to the office every Friday at about noon to pick up his checks. Estelle would hand the check to him—it was only for about fifty bucks—and he'd say, "Thanks, 'Stelle." He'd make small talk for a while, then he'd go.

After a while we realized that Hunny never cashed or deposited the checks. We found out many years later that he'd never once even owned a checking account in his life. There were a thousand checks—not just from us, but from all over—in a drawer somewhere.

ESTELLE LATCHKEY: I didn't have too many brainstorms—I was just a secretary, don't forget, and then I married Arnie—but one thing I did come up with was, why not get Ziggy a girlfriend? I said this to Sally one day at lunch at Schrafft's. It was just us girls. Sally and I were the same age and she was such a doll, really, a wonderful person. I knew about her and Danny. Everybody did. Except Ziggy.

"And who do you propose for this girlfriend, Estelle?" she said to me.

"I can't think of anyone," I said. "My Aunt Dora in Coney Island does matchmaking though."

"I don't know about a *shiddach* for Ziggy," Sally said. "It's not like this is Tyrone Power we're talking about."

"Surely there must be someone," I said.

"He *is* in show business," she said. "That helps."

"That's right, Sally. It almost doesn't matter what he looks or acts like."

Well, Jane White was the daughter of Joseph Weissblau, whose firm did the books for the Blue Beret and for many other entertainment venues and corporations. She'd been raised in New York, grew up on Fifth Avenue, and attended all the proper schools. She was a pretty girl but not striking—there was something a little bit "off" about her. Jane had auditioned to become a Blue Beret dancer but she just didn't have it, although she'll tell you she did. So Barney Arundel, as a favor to her father, employed her as a cigarette girl for two weeks. Jane had a very bright, very big smile. Pete Conifer was after her, but he was after the house cat too.

JANE WHITE [Ziggy Bliss's first wife]: Yes, it's true that my father was Jewish. But he was only, as far as I know, half-Jewish. My mother was, I believe, a quarter Jewish and, according to Jewish law, I believe, this only makes me one-third Jewish. When she and Dad divorced, she changed her last name to White. My given name was Judith Weissblau. *Yeech.* I mean, I could hardly *spell* Weissblau! And it makes no sense—it means "white blue."

I was an attractive, active, very happy-go-lucky girl. I learned how to ride a horse and I studied ballet and art. My mother sent me to the Brearley School, where my best friends were Custis Warnocke, Grace Anne Payton, and Lanie Danforth. They didn't mind having a friend named Jane White, but Judith Weissblau they would have had trouble with.

I met Ziggy when I was a dancer at the Blue Beret. Those were really marvelous days, before the war. I met incredible people, celebrities and socialites, all sorts of wonderful people. I had seen Ziggy perform with Vic and it was the funniest thing. New York "ethnic" humor was not to my liking, but Fountain and Bliss was so much more universal.

I will not lie to you and say that I was physically attracted to Ziggy at first. He was hysterical, it's true, but he had such red, craggy skin. And that hair! Anyway, Sally and Estelle asked me out to Schrafft's one day and they began talking to each other about how funny and talented Ziggy was and how rich he was going to be. I finished my ham and mayonnaise on white bread and as we were leaving, Sally said to me, "So, Janie, are you seeing anybody?"

"I have a few beaus, Sally," I said. I began to rattle off the names of my admirers: Keenan Maynard, Jimmy Hetfield, Mitchell George (of the Connecticut Georges).

"Why don't you and Ziggy maybe go out on a date? Have dinner maybe? See a show?" Estelle said.

"You're kidding me? Ziggy Bliss?"

"Yes! Ziggy Bliss!"

"Okay," I said with a chuckle. Life was short, right? I may as well give it a try.

● ● ●

ARNIE LATCHKEY: Everything was smooth sailing on our little raft, the USS *Fountain & Bliss,* which I soon learned was usually a bad sign. That eerie calm in the fan a second before the excrement wallops it head-on. The new radio show was making some noise, they're playing the Riviera in Jersey, the Copa, El Mo. We had them lined up to open a picture at the old Capitol Theater on Broadway the second week of December. And then one day Vic comes to me and says, "I need some help."

"What is it?"

"I knocked up a broad, Arn."

"This doesn't surprise me. The way you run around all the time."

"Hey, what me and Mr. Baciagaloop"—that was his name for his *shlong*—"do in our spare time is my own business."

"But you're about to make it my business too, aren't you?" I said to him. "So what do you want me to do? *No!* Let me guess . . . you're going to marry this woman and be a father to this child and you want me to see to all the wedding arrangements. Is that it? And to arrange for college for this little stripling? Well, where shall we send this promising youth? Drake? Bowling Green? Where?"

"Not quite, Latch."

"I didn't think so."

"There are these doctors, you know . . ." he began.

"I'm aware of it."

" . . . and they can . . . well, you know. And sometimes, some of 'em ain't even real doctors."

"I'm familiar with it. Who's the girl?"

"Just some girl. Why? You want a name?"

"Nah. I don't want a name. A nice girl? Intelligent?"

"Not really, no."

"Pretty girl, is she then?"

"Not particularly, no."

"I'll make a call, Vic. Okay? We'll get this done. Can you make sure she doesn't go blabbing this around town?"

"She won't do that, don't worry. After she told me the news, I introduced her to Hunny."

"Gotchya."

"See!" he says. "It's a good thing we're payin' him, ain't it?"

"Yeah, it's terriff," I said.

I asked him how Lulu was doing and when he was gonna make an honest woman out of her, and he joked, "Who's Lulu?"

I made a few calls and this little problem was taken care of. And it wasn't some seedy back alley job either, done by some creep with a coat hanger; no, this was done by a Park Avenue surgeon who did the thing on his coffee table in his West End Avenue apartment.

Vic thanked me profusely, said it wouldn't ever happen again, although he added that he wasn't completely sure about that.

SALLY KLEIN: "You hear what Vic did?" Ziggy asked me one day. "He got some broad in a family way."

"Really . . ."

"He should be more careful, don't ya think?"

He was trying to create trouble. He was trying to manipulate. Always.

"Wanna know who the girl is, Sal?" he asked me.

"Honestly? No. I don't."

We were supposed to be talking about the radio show. Bormann beer was about to become the new sponsor. We were expanding to a half-hour, getting a new time slot. But we'd been coming on after *The Dr. Jones Liver Elixir–Enzo Bugatti Piano Hour* and this was like poison for us. We talked about that for three minutes, then . . .

"You ever meet any of Vic's friends? From Lobstertown or wherever he's from?"

"It's Codport. Yes, I've met a few," I told him.

"What do you think of Guy Puglia?"

"I like Guy. He's a little rough but he has a really sweet heart. Why?"

"What do you think of Tony Ferro? You met Tony ever?"

"I've met Tony. And his fiancée, Maria," I said. "She lives in Flatb—"

"Hey, *that's* the girl Vic got in trouble!"

I said nothing for a few seconds, then said, "That's very bad. Does Tony know?"

"Nah. No idear."

"Okay, Ziggy," I said. "I've got work to do."

ARNIE LATCHKEY: An engagement at the Capitol Theater would have been *massive* for us. Three or four shows a day, a band, Ziggy and Vic opening for a movie, which if my memory serves me well was *Sergeant York* with Gary Cooper. Bertie had some stunts arranged; he had arranged for a hundred screaming bobby-soxers, he organized for there to be a hundred nurses on call in case anyone laughed so much they'd have a heart attack, there were going to be a dozen ambulances parked outside. This would've been *the* big push, the thing that put us over the top, into the cream of the crop, the elite. And what happens? The Japs somehow have the chutzpah to ruin this shindig by bombing Pearl Harbor. It's like Emperor Hirohito himself didn't want Fountain and Bliss to strike it big!

The guy who booked the Capitol calls me up on December 8th and says, "Arnie, the boys can't go on."

I said, "Look, that's Hawaii. That's fifty thousand miles away. This is Broadway."

"We can't do it. It's off."

"But life's gotta go on," I told this idiot. "Look at England. They got pummeled, pelted, and pounded in the Blitz . . . you think the London theaters canceled their shows?"

"I don't know."

Neither did I.

"Arnie, when this whole thing is over," this moron said, "we'd love to have Fountain and Bliss. We won't forget you."

"Yeah, bub, and I won't forget you either!"

I bid the imbecile a sweet adieu and thought to myself, Okay, the hell with this schlemiel. We'll play the Paramount then, if they want us.

DANNY McGLUE: I couldn't stand [Ziggy] nosing around, always asking Arnie, asking Vic, asking Estelle about us. Sid Stone would tell me, "He's asking questions about you and Sally again." I also didn't like it when he tried to get me to go to the hookers he frequented. "They really know how to treat a guy," Ziggy said. "No thanks," I told him. "Well," he asked me, "where else are you gettin' it from, Danny boy?"

He kept trying to fix Sally up with men who really had nothing going for them. Waiters and ushers and lawyers. Sid would say to me, "You're gonna have to tell him one day, Danny."

"How can he object to us?" I asked Sally.

"Well, you're not Jewish."

Now, I'd worked at the Catskills for several summers. That was my life. I grew up with Jewish kids. I worked in an office with Arnie and Sid and Norman. "I'm more Jewish than he is sometimes!" I told her. "Give me another reason."

"He's meshuga. That's another. I don't think he wants me to get married before he gets married. He's lonely, he wants me to be lonely too."

Sally and I realized that Ziggy had no leverage here. Everybody knew that he had his 10:45 call girls and he knew everybody knew. So how is he going to tell Sally who she was allowed to see?

ARNIE LATCHKEY: Danny came to me one morning and told me he was going to tell Ziggy about him and Sally. I told him that, not only did I understand, not only was I behind the move a hundred percent, not only did I think it was the the ethical, intelligent thing to do, but that I didn't want to be within a radius of thirty miles when it happened.

So they told him in his apartment, a few days after Pearl Harbor. Sally went over there with Danny. The second he opened the door and saw those two lovebirds, he knew. Ziggy didn't erupt, there was no Mount Vesuvius. No yelling, no throwing chairs around, none of that.

Dissolve. Next day. My office. Ominous Smith-&-Wesson-like click sound is heard from door. Ziggy says to me, "Danny gets the ax or I walk."

"I think we should talk about this."

"No talking. He's out."

Danny was so important to us, you got no idea. I'll tell you how important. When I went to Vic and told him about all this, Vic made a pun. He urgently wanted to keep Danny. He knew he was crucial to the outfit. Vic said, "But Latch, Danny's really McGlue that holds us together!" *I mean, Vic had made this stupid pun!*

I asked Ziggy—I tried to be reasonable, which can be a real disaster when you're dealing with entertainers—"Why is this so important to you? What does it matter?"

And he said that what we had was a business. It was radio, it was the

Catskills, it was the nightclubs, maybe one day, God willing, it'd even be movies. And we couldn't have people messing with business.

Now this made sense to me except for two things. One: most of the time we were all together, it hardly seemed like a business. We'd be just screwing around, trying new material, goofing off. This was not a board meeting at General Motors, you have my utmost assurance. And the second thing was, I had begun seeing Estelle, my own secretary, by then.

Danny nipped it all in the bud. He offered me his resignation. I accepted it. I wished him luck and told him I'd do anything to help him get a new job. He wants me to call up Murray Katz at Worldwide, he wants me to call Fred Allen or Jack Benny or Lenny Pearl, I'll do it. I'll call up John Perona at El Morocco or Sherman Billingsley, I'll call up anybody with a telephone or who lives within a mile of a phone booth, I told him. But instead the next day that patriotic *shmendrick* enlists in the navy.

CATHERINE RICCI: [My brothers] Sal and Ray enlisted, Ray into the army and Sal the marines. Pop was against it, but they would have been drafted anyway. My father didn't want them killing Italians, he didn't want them getting killed by Italians. He gave them both addresses and names of relatives to look up in Messina, Palermo, or around Calabria, just in case they found themselves there and wanted to desert. "You need help," he said, "you find these people." It didn't happen though. Ray wound up in France, although he didn't see much action, despite what he may tell you. And Sal fought in the Pacific.

They wouldn't take Vic on account of his feet. I have no idea how he lost those two toes . . . it was in the news that it happened while he was picking up some lobster traps as a kid, but Vic wouldn't go within an inch of a lobster, dead or alive, Newburg or thermidor. There were rumors he'd shot his toes off to avoid military service, but that's just not true. My other brothers went, so why wouldn't Vic?

SALLY KLEIN: Do you think Ziggy would've lasted one day in a training camp?! To do one push-up would've taken him all day and even then he probably couldn't finish it. Arnie had him go to two or three doctors—they were going to tell him what his status would be. They took one look at him and said, "Kid, don't worry. They won't take you." And they were right. Ziggy said that for him they invented some new category. He wasn't too short, he wasn't too fat, he wasn't too crazy . . . he was just too *round*.

They did this routine on the tours they did to sell war bonds. Vic is "interviewing" Ziggy.

Vic asks him: "So how come you ain't in the army, Zig?"

Ziggy said, "I'm Three-F."

Vic said after a perfect pause, "*Three*-F?"

Ziggy said, "Yeah, Three-F."

"Well, I've heard of Four-F before but—"

"Three-F, Vic. Three-F."

"Well, I've gotta ask ya," Vic says. "What's that stand for anyway?"

And Ziggy said, "Fat . . . funny . . . and *'fraid!*"

When they did that routine in the Catskills, though, they made some changes. The third *f* was for *faygeleh*.

Oh, did you know that Bormann beer was dropped as the sponsor after a season? It turned out that the family who owned the brewery was related to Martin Bormann, who was a bigwig in Hitler's crowd. So we got rid of them—they weren't the nicest people in the world anyway—and Dickinson's witch hazel sponsored the show.

GUY PUGLIA: Can you see Vic in a foxhole? Fixing his hair after a kraut bullet whistled over it and mussed it up? Or on a battleship? Like he'd ever get close to the fuckin' ocean?

I tried the army, I tried the marines, and they both turned me down. Too short, they said. Like being short has anything to do with not being tough? I really wanted to go. Someone told me to apply for the navy, tell 'em I'm from Codport and that I've been on many boats in my life, fishin'. And that I should do it in New Bedford, not New York. And this fella told me to put these lifts in my shoes. I did it . . . it added a few inches and I was in.

And then . . . well, I guess you wanna know how this thing happened to me.

I don't like tellin' this story, not one bit. But I will.

I'm two days from going to Virginia to report. I'm in Codport and I'm hangin' around with the old crowd and my old man too, who's now got cancer. I'm going to the pool hall, and I'm eatin' hot dogs and gettin' ices from Joe Ravelli on the boardwalk and seeing Lulu and Dominick and Tony [Ferro], who was now married. I'm in a bar and in walks Rocco Straccio. Tells me he wants to have a little powwow with me. Those goddamn black gums and teeth of his. Well, that scumbag didn't scare me no more. He was just a fuckin' hood. I've lived in New York, right? I know Hunny and I've met Al Pompiere, Frank Costello, Angelo Galvanese, and Louis Lepke. I've even met Bette Davis, for Christsake! What do I need this goddamn hood for?

He tells me he wants a cut of Vittorio Fontana's pie. I tell him I don't know anybody by that name. He says Vic Fountain is Codport's leading export now, other than cod. I tell him Vic ain't interested in small-town hoods like him. It's dark in this bar, the only light is coming from the clock, I'm just trying to enjoy my beer. Straccio says he wants me to talk to Vic, if not he can make a phone call to some people in New York—he tells me [gangster] Joe Adonis owes him a big favor. He says it isn't fair that this guy comes from this town and doesn't put anything back in it. Straccio wanted his tribute, that's what he wanted. "Must be a lot of dough in those big fancy New York clubs," he says. I said, "You want a piece of Vic's pie, you can have a piece of me first, scumbag." That's just what I said. Then he put his hand on my nose and laughed like he used to when I was a kid. He says, "I got your nose," and laughs. Ha ha ha, he goes. He pulls his hand away and there's blood squirting all over the place, it's squirting like it's comin' out a kid's water pistol. It took me a few seconds before I felt it—I just saw the squirts first. I looked at his hand and he's got all the flesh of my nose—it looked like a thumb—in his hands. And a razor blade too. That fuckin' sonuvabitch fuck had sliced my nose off. And on account of that, I never got to serve my goddamn country.

ARNIE LATCHKEY: The negative flack we got from Vic not going in was incredible. Here's a guy in his early twenties, he's big, he's strong, he's healthy. Every Tom, Dick, and Harry is being inducted, but not Vic Fountain. And to make things worse, you had all kinds of celebrities going into the armed forces. And they always made a big hullabaloo about it too, to boost morale and get everybody gung-ho. I pick up the paper and there's a picture of Jimmy Stewart getting his physical. *Oy vey*. I see that, I get a duodenal ulcer. Here's a photo of Clark Gable enlisting. Now I got the angina. Hank Fonda goes into the navy. I can feel my lungs starting to collapse. Tyrone Power into the marines! My prostate is the size and temperature of the *Hindenburg*. Thank God for Frank Sinatra and Duke Wayne.

We did damage control. As best we could. They played some army and navy bases in the South, they raised thousands and thousands for war bonds. They toured with Georgie Jessel and opened up for Glenn Miller in Boston to raise money. They even did a USO show with Lenny Pearl. Once in a while you heard booing. These guys in uniform—hey, next week they might be on Okinawa or in Tobruk, so who could blame them?—they'd yell things at Vic. Coward, sissy, candy ass, and some ethnic things too. Nobody ever called Ziggy a coward though . . . I guess with him it was quite evident why he wasn't serving his country.

Bertie concocted the whole lobster-trap tale. When Vic was a kid, this saga went, he was picking up a lobster trap one morning in the bay. The trap is empty, to his abject shock. Vic's looking inside it and as he's doing so two lobsters clamp down real tight on his feet. They each one take a little toe off. Vic staggers back to the shore and *just* makes it to a doctor, who manages to save his life. Real Herman Melville, Joe Conrad-type material, right?

It was perfect. But some people weren't buying it.

I'm at the Stork with Grayling Greene and he just doesn't purchase this bill of goods. He even doubted that Vic was missing any toes to begin with. I call Vic from the phone at the table and twenty minutes later Vic is at the table too. I say to him, Let Mr. Greene get an eyeful of those tootsies. Vic whips off his socks and shoes and, voila, there they aren't: not even stubs where the little toes were. Grayling looks at 'em, nods, jots down a few words, Vic leaves, goes back home to finish the job on who-knows-which broad he was with at the time.

"How do I know that he didn't shoot them off, Arnie?" Greene says to me.

"Shoot his toes off? That ain't Vic."

"Why not?"

"Vic don't like guns."

"Which is why he doesn't want to join the army. So he shoots his own toes off—men are doing that, they say. Or Vic pays a surgeon to amputate them."

"It was the lobsters. I swear it was. On the grave of my mother." Who, at that time, was still alive and kickin'.

Grayling Greene snorts, jots down a few more notations. I'm getting up to go and I'm thinking: This guy is plugged in to everybody. Gary Cooper jerks off in Beverly Hills, Grayling Greene knows about it on Fifty-eighth Street. He maybe knows that that cannibal Constance Tuttle sautéed Vic's little piggies. Hey, Sinatra had a bum eardrum, right? That's what kept him out of the war? For all I know, Connie Tuttle plucked it out and deep-fried it while Frank had a bun on.

As I'm walking out, I pass by Winchell's table. He says to me, "Two lobsters, huh, Arn?"

Vic did an interview with *Life* and addressed the subject. He said these words exactly—I know, because I rehearsed him over and over again: "It's one of the lousiest breaks I ever got, this toe deal. I would love to be over there killing Japs. I really would. This country has been great to me and my family. I sure owe it one. Heck, my older brother Sal is in the Marianas right now . . . I'd give anything to be there with him, giving him some cover." "Oh really?" the smart alecky, pain-in-the-ass interviewer said. "Would you even give your toes?" (*Life* didn't publish that clever rejoinder, fortunately for us.)

SNUFFY DUBIN: I was just about to head to Parris Island for my basic training. Okay, one thing I don't do is, I don't talk about what happened to me in the war. I could've come back and gotten a hundred hours' worth of material out of it. The characters I met, the stupid stuff I had to do—some of it was funny. But you get a guy's brains blown onto your lap, you forget the funny stuff real quick. Shit, after I made it as a comic, they offered me parts in *The Dirty Dozen, The Longest Day,* and *Kelly's Heroes.* Turned 'em all the fuck down.

This socialite columnist Hilda Fleury ran an item a week before I reported, it was about Fountain and Bliss. It was a blind item but anybody in the know could tell who it was. Someone had told her that Vic had had his toes amputated by a surgeon, to avoid the army, that this lobster thing was a lie. She doctored the item up and ran it really small. Vic saw it, he hit the roof. To him it was one thing if you get sozzled and some broad lops your toes off after you give her the high hard one, it's another thing to *pay* some doctor to do it to avoid serving your country. And besides, after a while, Vic had probably convinced himself that he could've been some kinda big war hero. So Vic sends Hunny over to Hilda's house, on Park Avenue. The doorman tries to stop Hunny, Hunny nails him with a left hook. Hunny rings the buzzer, Hilda's butler answers the door, starts asking who wishes to see *madame.* Hilda comes to the foyer and Hunny is pounding the butler . . . *Bam! Bam!* Hilda gets the phone to call the cops, and maybe Hunny Gannett ain't Albert fucking Einstein but he ain't brain-dead either. Not yet. He rips the phone out, tears this poor butler's shoe off, then breaks the butler's little toe. *Madame* gets *le message.*

The upshot of this story is this: Who do you think it was that went to Hilda Fleury and told her the story? Who told her that the lobster trap thing was a lie? Of course. It was Ziggy. Who the fuck else?

• • •

JANE WHITE: Ziggy and I went to "21" on our first date. I thought we'd be there for an hour but we wound up being there for three. I'd really had myself done over for the date. My hair was naturally brown but I had it colored sunny blond, and I bought a new dress at Lord & Taylor. I remember being all scared because that day at Lord & Taylor, they thought I had stolen a gold silk scarf. They brought over a security person and I explained to him that it was all some mistake. I showed him that I had about $30 in my purse and that if I really wanted the scarf I could afford it. It was an accident, I explained. He didn't know what to believe and when I began to cry, he escorted me to the door and let me out on Fifth Avenue. I told Ziggy all about that and he made me feel better about what happened, joking about it and everything.

Ziggy could not believe the way I was brought up. He said he never heard of a Jewess being on a yacht and I told him that I really could not be considered a Jewess. He told me about his childhood and I'd never heard of anything so sad in my life. It was almost as though he'd been an orphan. During dessert the maitre d' brought the phone over and Ziggy got on and said that he'd be over at 10:45 that night. When he hung up he told me it was Vic Fountain. I asked him if he got along with Vic, and he told me they never socialized. I said, "But you're seeing him at ten forty-five tonight." And he said, "Oh yeah. Right. Well, there's a first time for everything."

He actually wanted to take me home in a horse and buggy! I said that was embarrassing so we took a cab. He walked me to the front door of my apartment . . . I was so tired from laughing at this point, I really was. He didn't try to kiss me. I told him that I'd had my hair done especially for him, for this date, and it made him happy.

"So do you think you'd maybe want to ever do this again with me ever?" he said.

"I had a wonderful time tonight," I told him.

"But not wonderful enough, izzat it?" he said.

"Do you want to see me again?" I asked him.

"Would that be something that you would consider doin'?" he asked me.

I told him that, yes, I would consider that. I'd had such a great time at the "21" Club. Tommy Dorsey had said hello to Ziggy, and Cary Grant had come over and introduced himself! And two people came over to our booth and asked Ziggy for his autograph. It was quite exciting.

The next day the doorman buzzed me and said there was something for me in the lobby. I went down there and there was a box from Lord & Taylor. Ziggy had sent me twenty gold silk scarves.

FREDDY BLISS: My mother's hair when she was young was jet black. She had very curly black hair, a little bit like Hedy Lamarr's, and had to iron it to get the kinks out. She used to dye it blond all the time. Any time a root reared its ugly head, it was off to Mr. Paolo.

After she and Dad moved to Los Angeles, Mom had her nose fixed. The plastic surgeon, the best there was, did a wonderful job. No bumps or ridges or anything. It was perfect. And then she had it redone. Why? Because it was *too* perfect. It made her look like a Jewish woman who'd gotten a nose job trying to disguise the fact that she was Jewish. Which is what she was. So she went back and the same doctor put in just the slightest, slightest ridge. And that was Mom.

I've been told that when Dad wanted to get me circumcised, she really raised the roof.

• • •

ARNIE LATCHKEY: You want to talk termites crawling headfirst out of the woodwork? Guess who phones me one day? Estelle calls out, "I have a Floyd Lomax on the phone for you."

My first reaction: It's Ziggy playing a hoax on me. They were always doing that.

I pick up the phone and I say, "Hey, Floyd darling, long time no speak."

"Yeah, Arnie, too long. How's tricks?"

"Tricks is good. How's by you?" I'm just looking for some sign that this is Ziggy, feeling him out like we're two prizefighters stalking each other in round one.

"My life is hell."

I was pretty sure it was Floyd Lomax now. But I had to make completely sure.

"Hey, Floyd," I said, "what was it again that you had written on all your boxer shorts? I was musing over this the other day and it somehow escaped my mind."

"It was ''Tis all pink on the inside,' Arn. In gold stitching."

"Floyd, how are ya?!"

"My life is in the toilet."

I'm not a hard-hearted man, Teddy. I'm not made of stone. I watch *Mrs. Miniver,* which I've seen a hundred times, I break down like a baby. Floyd Lomax's band—that's how I made my bones in this business. But the last time I saw him, he was shooting a pearl-handled Colt at me because we'd cheated him at cards. So naturally I feel that maybe there's some atoning to do.

"The toilet ain't such a terrific place to be, Floyd," I said.

"I don't even have a band anymore. I get a recording date now and then or I sit in with Jimmy Babcock's band."

Is this some sort of touch? . . . that's what I'm thinking, that he's gonna hit me up for cash. Christ, I'd wire the sonuvabitch two grand if it'd get him out of my hair for ten years.

I tell him I'm sorry about his career. And then he says the words I dread.

"I blame Vic for this."

"Vic? What did Vic do?"

"Thalia Boneem. The only girl I ever—"

"Oh yeah. That. Sure, sure. Look, Floyd, I'm a busy man nowadays."

"So I've heard, Latch. Jesus, the Copacabana, all sorts of swell joints, huh?"

"Yeah, well, such are the haphazard spins of Dame Fortune's wheel, Floyd. I gotta go—"

"Tell Vic I said hello, okay? Tell him one day I'll catch up with him."

And then he hangs up.

I did not relay this message.

• • •

ESTELLE LATCHKEY: Before I married Arnie, I lived with a girlfriend named Shirley Klein in Greenwich Village. Only about three blocks away from Ernie Beasley, as a matter of fact. One night Shirley and I were home . . . the bell rang and two men came to the door, two very serious-looking, no-nonsense men. They were dressed in identical gray pin-striped suits and gray fedoras. The shorter one of the two showed me some identification that said he was from the FBI.

They came in and politely asked Shirley to go to the other room.

The shorter man did all the talking. He asked me lots of questions, about where I'd gone to school, who my parents were, and what they did. Then he began asking questions about Fountain and Bliss and about Arnie too—oh, it was a whole third degree. He seemed to be already familiar with a lot of information about them; he knew, for instance, that Ziggy had been to two doctors to talk about the draft and that Vic had changed his last name a few times. The agent also knew that Ziggy and his parents had performed in the Catskills at some places where they sang the Communist theme song. I kept asking what this was all about and he said that eventually I would find out. I was not to tell anybody about the visit, not even Arnie, who, somehow, he knew I was going out with. And this my mother didn't even know yet!

The two men made me promise that I would never tell anyone about the visit. I told them that I loved my country, that loose lips sank ships, and it was between me and God.

When I told Arnie ten minutes later, he told me that the same two men had visited him.

ARNIE LATCHKEY: Those two G-men scared the bejesus out of me! Now, I didn't go into the army because of my eyesight—I'm legally blind ten times over—and after they made it abundantly clear they weren't going to execute me for treason and cowardice I started to worry they may really have been Nazi spies, like Peter Lorre in *All Through the Night*. Maybe it was something to do with Charlotte Charlot or some routines that Ziggy and Vic were doing. I'm thinking, Oh no, tomorrow Arnold Latchkey is gonna be found ground into 180 pounds of bratwurst and they'll be serving me up at the Kleine Konditorei on Eighty-sixth and Lexington.

A week after that first visit we had an engagement at the Chez Paree in Chicago. Fountain and Bliss are doing their thing, absolutely ripping up the place, and I'm surveying the crowd. And who do I see out there, sitting in the back? Heckle and Jeckle in gray pin-striped suits, fedoras on the table. Only people in the entire joint who didn't have a drink.

Cut to a week later. Fountain and Bliss are playing the Vogue Room in Cleveland and then, after that, the Beachcomber in Florida. Who's in the crowd? The same two suits and fedoras, the same monotone expressions, the same lack of drinks on the table.

A week or so later I'm leaving my apartment building about to go to work and there they are, waiting for me. They ask me to get into their car. I get in and I'm thinking, Okay, this is my last minute alive. At least I'm going to get garroted in a nice big Cadillac. I've truly come a long way in life.

They had a driver and he was taking us toward midtown.

"We want Fountain and Bliss to perform a significant service for their country, Mr. Latchkey," the short one said. "I'm sure that they'll come through for us. Won't they?"

"Can you give me an inkling as to what they have to do?" I said.

"Just keep the week of July tenth free on their calendar. We know they're booked at the Riverside Club in Detroit the week before that, which is fine. But just keep that week free. It is absolutely *imperative*. Do you understand this?"

"But we haven't talked dollars and cents yet, guys."

They looked at each other and, for the first time since I'd been observing them observing me, they changed their expressions.

"That will be taken care of, Mr. Latchkey."

We pulled up to Fifty-first and Broadway and the tall one opened the door and I got out. The car drove off.

"Sons of bitches didn't even drop me off at the office," I muttered under my breath.

* * *

SALLY KLEIN: I remember seeing Ziggy on *Merv Griffin* in the sixties—he told Merv that Fountain and Bliss had never truly felt comfortable on the radio. He said that radio was too small for them. A lot of what Ziggy said to interviewers and reporters never came close to smacking of the truth, but in this case I think he was right.

Fountain and Bliss was all about craziness, about anarchy almost. It was about not knowing what would be next. On the radio, though, it was like they were locked in a small closet sometimes. They could do a two-hour show in a nightclub and do whatever they wanted to, but then every Sunday they have thirty minutes and five of those are for commercials for Dickinson's witch hazel or BiSoDol antacid mints, which became their sponsor right before the war ended.

When Danny left us, it had a big effect. I know that Vic tried to reason with Ziggy, but Ziggy wouldn't listen. They had even gone out to lunch and Vic tried, in his own mild Vic Fountain way, to get Ziggy to change his mind. But he may as well have been trying to get Ziggy to give up show business for the priesthood. "No dice, Sal," he said to me when he got back from Sardi's that day. Me, I was so incensed that I couldn't even talk to Ziggy about it. Who was he to interfere with my life like this! I had schlepped from town to town in the Catskills and baby-sat his parents for him and meanwhile what life did I have of my own?! None. *None*.

We had very bad time spots on the Mutual Network. They put us on Sunday nights at seven opposite *The Jack Benny Show*. This was like running against Roosevelt. Murray Katz raised a big ruckus and so what did they do? They moved the show to 10:30, opposite Fred Allen. That was the last straw. Norman White left to write for Bob Hope, and Sid Stone did some more script work for Paramount. Fountain and Bliss then moved to the Consolidated Network, which had fewer affiliates than Mutual. Hiram F. Beckwith, who started Standard Lanolin and owned a few newspapers in Texas, kept gobbling up radio stations and tried to take on CBS and NBC and Mutual. He swore to Murray and Arnie he'd get us a good spot. He offered us Fridays at eight, opposite Kate Smith's show, which she did for Jell-O. Arnie hit the ceiling! "We do Fridays at eight, the show can't be live then!" he yelled. See, that time was atrocious for us . . . it would've cut into many, many club dates. Beckwith said, Okay, tape the show, then do your nightclubs.

Taping the show was a godsend. It really was. But still, the show was losing its zest. "When Danny gets back from the navy," Vic said to me, "he better come back with us. He writes for Benny or Hope, I'm gonna pick up my fishing net and make an honest living again."

ARNIE LATCHKEY: "You guys may get a script you've got to stick to on your *own* show," I hinted to Ziggy and Vic one day at Lindy's, "but, you know, there's no law that says you gotta stick to a script on somebody else's."

Ziggy got it right away . . . he got that impish sparkle in his eyes. But Vic said to me, "I don't savvy."

I tried to do it like Socrates would. I said, "I hand you a script. The show begins with Vic singing 'God Bless America' and then Ziggy interrupts it. Is that going to make any waves?"

"Probably barely a ripple, Latch," Vic says.

"Or Ziggy breaks into 'God Bless America' and you interrupt it as per the script. Is this going to change the field of human endeavor any?"

"I doubt it."

"But Kate Smith is singin' it on her strawberry Jell-O show and all of a sudden who's in the studio but Ziggy and Vic and they're singing along and doing this and doing that, is that going to create a ripple?"

Vic pulled his Chesterfield and said, "A fuckin' tidal wave, Latch."

So this was our "assault plan," you could call it. You know what had happened? We'd lost the *juice*. The juice. George Patton had it right: *Tou-*

jours, l'audace! We needed a shot of something, something new and big and bold. *We needed to be audacious!*

So we began doing these surprise "walk-ons" as soon as we moved to Consolidated. Let's face it: CBS was known as the Tiffany Network but do you know what they used to call Consolidated? The Dead Lamb Network, because the money behind it came from lanolin, from sheep. We would crash these big shows, invade them. *Kay Kyser's Kollege of Musical Knowledge?* Oh, we were all over that one! Kyser was doing "Praise the Lord and Pass the Ammunition" and in storm Fountain and Bliss and they're singing "Praise the Broads and Pass the Gin Martinis." They stormed onto Kate Smith's show—they threw some strawberry Jell-O around—and Vic was coming on to her and she was actually playing along! *Kate Smith is flirting!* This is bordering on bestiality, I tell you! It was all wonderful publicity, fan*tab*ulous for us. The picture of fat Kate and Vic making goo-goo eyes at each other while Ziggy was pouting and sucking his thumb—that must've run in fifty papers the next day.

There was a big boxing match, I think it was 1944, a middleweight title fight, Tony Zale versus Tony Mutti. Don Dunphy, a dear man, is calling the fight and sure enough Ziggy and Vic wrest the mike away from him and they proceed to announce the rest of the bout. Zale knocked out Mutti in the fifth round but nobody listening to the radio had any idea what the hell was going on, no idea at all. I listened to the thing at home and I was doubled over. Ziggy was imitating Dunphy and said that Jimmy Cagney was stopping by and then Vic did his Cagney impression. And Vic was a great, great apist, let me tell you that. Then Vic said Eleanor Roosevelt was now in the ring taking a savage beating from Zale, and then Ziggy pretended to be Mrs. Roosevelt. You could hear Dunphy saying to them, "Okay, guys. Can I get the mike back? Please?" But he couldn't get the thing back.

It was marvelous publicity.

DANNY McGLUE: I came back in '44 and I didn't know what to do with my life. I'd had it pretty easy in the navy . . . very few times did I ever think my life was in jeopardy. The worst problems I had were boredom and seasickness. And missing Sally. I would write her letters all the time. But I never sent them.

I was listening to Devane's radio show on CBS one night. Don't ask me why. And I hear [announcer] Bob Williams going through the *shpiel* about De Soto automobiles, which used to sponsor the show. But Williams is saying that the car is made out of balsa wood and that it won't last three miles and the steering wheel will come off in your hands. Now what the heck is *this*? Has Devane lost it? Williams turns it over to the Grand Forks Golden Boy and Fritz starts singing his theme song, "Believe in Me." But he's singing instead "Believe in Flea," about a dog who's got fleas! And then it dawns upon me: This cockamamie ditty rings a bell . . . *'cause I wrote it!* This isn't Fritz Devane singing! It's Vic Fountain! That wasn't Bob Williams. That was Ziggy Bliss!

As far as I know, that was the one time that it didn't go over well. Vic told me that while they were in Devane's studio, he thought that if Fritz had a gun he would've shot them both. But the show was live, mind you. Devane did the smart thing: he let the two of them wreak their havoc and then leave. (Well, not before they plugged their upcoming appearance at the Riviera.) And when they were finally gone, Devane let them have it. He called them amateurs and idiots, he used the words "ne'er-do-wells" and "rapscallions"! He started going on about how sacred airtime is, as though he was John the Baptist talking about holy water. He started playing the patriotism angle too somehow—he said that our men were fighting and dying overseas to protect freedom of speech and now these two nincompoops had exploited the airwaves. As if I'd served two years on a destroyer so that Fritz Devane could croon "Believe in Me" and sell De Sotos!

The next day I pick up my *Post* and there on the third page is a photo of Fritz Devane standing between Ziggy and Vic. Fritz's tweed hat is in shreds, like confetti, and his golf club is twisted around Ziggy's neck. Great, funny photo. Tons of free publicity.

RAY FONTANA: Vic grew up listening to Devane and idolizing him and now there was this big feud between them. If you ask me, it started in that parking lot in New Bedford. Someone calls you a greaseball, someone treats you like dirt, you take it to your grave.

• • •

SALLY KLEIN: Ziggy was starting to see Jane more and more, but it was taking a while. Jane felt that Ziggy was "beneath" her. Sometimes she tended to forget that—despite the education, the nose jobs, despite her rich friends letting her aboard their yachts—her father was just Joe Weissblau, a bookkeeper.

I was with Ziggy and Vic one night at Bratz's and Ziggy, out of nowhere, said, "Do you think there's any way to track someone down? Like, if you hadn't seen a person for years and they may have gone a long, long way, could a private dick find this person?"

"Why not give Mr. Keen, Tracer of Lost Persons, a call, Zig?" Vic joked while slapping Ziggy on the back. "Maybe he can find the O'Hares for you."

"Nah, it ain't like that, Vic," Ziggy said.

"Who are you looking for?" I asked him.

"Ah, no one. I was just curious."

The next day he came into my office and said to me two words: Dolly Phipps.

"You want a private investigator to find Dolly?" I said.

"Yeah. I been thinkin' about it."

"Why?"

"'Cause, you know, she didn't like Ziggy Bliss of Fountain and Bliss and of El Mo and the Chez Paree. She liked *me*, Harry and Flo's kid."

"But what about Jane White? She likes you!"

"Ah, I dunno about that."

"Oh come on. I've see her face light up when you're around."

"It's prolly just still lit up 'cause I got her into the Copa. Or 'cause I bought her some shoes. Dolly wasn't like that."

I told him that I didn't know anything about tracking her down and that I also didn't think it was a wise thing. From that day on, though, he always told me before he did a show in a club or a theater to keep an eye out on the crowd, to see if maybe Dolly Phipps was out there somewhere.

Out of nowhere he said now, "I miss my parents sometimes, you know that?"

I told him that I missed them too.

"I think they'd be really proud of their sonny boy," he said.

"Of course they would!"

"I just wish I could talk to 'em sometimes. I wish I could help them out. I could put 'em up in a really great spread now, Sal, with a great car. Remember that old jalopy we used to bounce around in in the mountains? I could get 'em a Cadillac today. They could live on Fifth Avenue and Flo could be wearing chinchillas and diamonds."

"I don't know if that would've made them happy," I said. "Just seeing you happy would have done that."

"Who says I'm happy?"

ARNIE LATCHKEY: The war is almost over. The Russians are politely tapping on the door to Hitler's bunker, the Americans are in France and Germany, and Mussolini and his lady friend have already been hung up on a meat hook. It's the bottom of the ninth and the Triple Axis powers are down ten–zip.

The two gray pinstripes and fedoras are in my living room.

"Have you ever been to New Mexico, Mr. Latchkey?" the shorter G-man said.

"Nope," I told them.

"Are you at all familiar with the terrain or the climate?"

"Can't say as I am, my friend. Why? What gives?"

"We want Fountain and Bliss to perform for the men there."

"The *men*? Soldiers, you mean? What, after we get through with Hitler we're invading Arizona?"

"Not quite."

I couldn't get anything else out of him. He told me he wanted Fountain and Bliss to travel to New Mexico after our Detroit engagement—the boys were to put on one show. And then the kicker: he offered twelve grand.

When someone makes an offer, you ask for more. This has been going on since before Adam. Even if you don't need the dough, even if you only go one measly cent over what they offer, you ask for more. So I'm gonna toss out an asking price of twenty grand and hope I can get him up to fifteen before I shake that gray pin-striped hand of his. So I say twenty grand and brace myself. But he says, "Okay, twenty grand, it's yours." I immediately wished I'd said twenty-five.

"Look, guys," I said, "when all this is over, can this be told to the public? Can Joe Doakes and Jane Doe find out about all this?"

"Yes," the short one said. "When it's all over and only we tell you the time is right."

They go to the door and tell me transportation will all be arranged from Detroit. I ask him, "Why us? Why not Abbott and Costello or the Marx Brothers or Hope and Crosby?"

"Mr. Clyde Tolson adores the act. And so does Mr. Hoover."

I say to him, "Where in New Mexico is this joint anyways?"

"It's in a place called Los Alamos, Mr. Latchkey."

• • •

CATHERINE RICCI: My brother Sal died at Tarawa. A shell got him. It's so sad. In his hand they found the crumpled-up piece of paper with all those addresses on it, the list Papa had given him. Even though those people were half a world away, Sal was holding it. He must have been terrified before he got hit.

[Carmine] was back from the war. He was an army cook in the south of England. The only fighting he ever saw was when a few GIs were mad at him for burning their flapjacks, he said. We'd moved to New York City, to Brooklyn, and Carmine and another guy had opened up a bakery on Bleecker Street in Manhattan.

I used to read all the papers, the *Post*, the *Herald Tribune* and the *Daily News* and the *Globe*. I was up on all the latest gossip. So I should've been warned when a neighbor told me one day that Ed Sullivan, on his radio show, had made a reference to Vic, about his avoiding the war. The next day Walter Winchell, who hated Ed Sullivan and vice versa, picked up the baton.

He was writing all sorts of garbage about a certain sleepy Italian crooner who'd paid a surgeon to have his toes amputated because he was too much of a pantywaist to serve his country. He never mentioned Vic's name but *anyone* could tell who it was! He said this singer can stand up on his own eight toes and entertain with his round partner at such nifty niteries as El Morocco and the Copacabana, but when it comes to standing up for his country, he suddenly loses his balance.

It was outrageous!

Lulu had heard it too because [Winchell] had said the same thing on his radio show. She was furious. We were on the phone for ten minutes. She was saying that Vic should get Hunny Gannett to work Walter Winchell over, to bash all his teeth in.

Carmine walked in and I said to Lu, "Look, I've gotta go."

"Cathy?" Lu said in that husky, raspy voice of hers.

"Yeah?"

"How *did* Vic lose them toes anyway? Do you know?"

I told her I had no idea and said good-bye.

．　．　．

GUY PUGLIA: Straccio had sliced the whole thing off. The skin, the cartilage. Gone. So now the rest of my life I gotta walk around with a bandage over the thing.

I was in St. Vincent's Hospital recovering from an infection—Hunny was there every single night, he'd spend hours with me, and Ernie Beasley visited a few times, so did Arnie and Estelle. Vic come once. Once. He brought me a bottle of scotch. We talked bullshit for a while, then he says, "Maybe it'll grow back, Gaetano."

I told him, "It ain't growin' back."

He said, "But I cut the skin on my finger, the skin always grows back."

"It ain't growin' back, Vic."

I didn't tell him that the reason it was cut off was 'cause Straccio was asking for a piece of Vic Fountain. I didn't tell him that.

The papers and magazines . . . they was all talking about how Vic got out of the draft. The Hotel Astor and another joint even canceled their shows. You had lots of soldiers comin' back from overseas, some of 'em in real bad shape. When Winchell was hinting that Vic paid a doctor to amputate his toes, that didn't go over too good.

ARNIE LATCHKEY: Vic told me he wanted to get Hunny to work Winchell over. I said, Hey, what you do to Hilda Fleury's butler, that's fine.

Hunny can work Hilda over too, for all I care, that anti-Semite old bag. But not Winchell. That won't wash.

"You think you're gonna solve every single problem," I asked him, "by working someone over?"

"If not solve them," Vic said, "then come real close."

"Look, I got something better for you. After the Detroit trip, you're gonna perform a service for your country like you don't know what. They'll be so much positive ink on this, it'll be like both your missing toes won Congressional Medals of Honor."

But I couldn't tell him exactly what it was because I didn't know.

JANE WHITE: Ziggy and I went to Le Pavillon for dinner. I'd bought a new pair of shoes at Saks and had my hair done. He kept me laughing the entire time—I almost couldn't eat. He walked me home and, yes, we kissed for the first time. But he was a gentleman . . . he didn't try anything further than that. I knew he was going to the Midwest to perform and I said to him, "Well, I guess I'll see you in a week or so." But he said it would be two weeks. He had someplace else to go, he told me. "Oh, golly!" I said. "Where?" He shook his head and said it was classified. "Is it Hollywood? Are you going to Los Angeles?" He pinched my cheek and said some words of endearment in Yiddish, something like "such a *goyishe shayne punim* you got on you." I told him I didn't like him talking like that. We kissed again and then he left.

* * *

REYNOLDS CATLEDGE IV [soldier, employee of Vigorish, Inc.]: I was General Emmet "Woody" Woodling's adjutant in Washington, D.C., and also at Los Alamos, New Mexico. General Woodling served as a liaison between the Trinity group in New Mexico, the Manhattan Project in Chicago, and General George Marshall in D.C. My father, I should mention, was General Reynolds Catledge III, who served in Patton's Third Army and who'd graduated second in his class at West Point and served under General Pershing in World War I. His father and grandfather had both attended West Point and I too had attended—I did not fare well there—and, though I urgently requested an appointment in the European Theater, I was instead assigned to General Woodling in Washington. I dearly wanted to see combat, to test my mettle, but my father used his position and connections to keep me stateside, and I was relegated to a degrading, humiliating desk assignment.

To my dismay, I was little more than a secretary at times, or a valet. Occasionally I would have to get the general's shoes shined or bring in his pants to be pressed, and I found myself sewing buttons onto his shirts. The general was married to Lucinda Hodge, whose father was Elihu J. Hodge, the department store magnate, but General Woodling was carrying on a rather indiscreet affair with a woman named Betsy Cunningham, whose father worked in a Rexall drugstore as a stock clerk. One of my duties, on the evenings when the general would be occupied with Miss Cunningham (which was practically every evening), was to keep Mrs. Woodling company. A dowdy, tedious woman in her late forties, she and I would dine and attend the theater together or have tea in her living room. To this day I thank God that it was tea I was drinking and not liquor—otherwise I would have fallen asleep in her company. On the other hand Betsy Cunningham had once—or so she'd informed the general—won a beauty contest in North Dakota; now she was twenty-three years old, twenty-seven years the general's junior, and was a shapely blond tart with wavy golden hair and succulent Cupid's-bow lips. And here I was, twenty-four years old, spending World War II, not leading a group of men at Monte Cassino or on the Rhine, but playing canasta and gin rummy with this dull, white-haired dowager in frumpy flower-print dresses and a pearl necklace.

None of my requests to be transferred were granted. I tried everything but was stymied by my father every single time. "The lad will not last a day in combat," he told my mother.

I made numerous arrangements to fly the general into and out of Chicago and New Mexico, always on army air force planes, but was never told precisely why he was going there. He would receive phone calls from Dr. J. Robert Oppenheimer and even from physicists Neils Bohr, Emilio Segré, and Ernest Rutherford, and I would have to put them through, but I had not the vaguest notion as to why they were calling. General [Leslie R.] Groves, who supervised the Trinity program for the army, was a frequent caller. One afternoon Betsy Cunningham was in the general's office, which adjoined mine, and the door was locked. One can only imagine—which I did, often—what was going on in there. Dr. Oppenheimer phoned and informed me it was urgent. I buzzed the general and relayed that to him but was brusquely instructed to tell Dr. Oppenheimer that the general would call him back in a half hour. I did as I was told. Through the door I heard the sounds of Miss Cunningham and the general arguing. And then not arguing.

Early in 1944 I, for the first time, accompanied General Woodling to New Mexico. Miss Cunningham was also on the plane, which was a violation of protocol . . . I'd had to refer to her as "Army Nurse Cunningham" in order to procure her passage. I sat by myself on the transport plane and the two of them sat in front of me, alternating between infantile giggling and stern silences. It was just we three. At one point in the flight, General Woodling fell asleep and I noticed that Miss Cunningham began looking through his kit bag, but he awoke and admonished her. She nibbled on his ear and the matter was quickly settled. He fell asleep again and she turned around to me and made a flirtatious "kissy gesture" to me, not the first time she had done so. At another juncture in the flight, the general came over to me and, his breath reeking of bourbon, said, "Reynolds, I know that the past two years haven't been easy for you, that you haven't appreciated being kept in the dark. But very soon you're going to learn what this is all about and why it had to be that way." As I was telling him that I understood the need for complete confidentiality, I espied Betsy Cunningham applying a glistening red lipstick and looking back at the two of us. "How's Mrs. Woodling doing?" the general asked me. "I spend far too little time with Lucinda nowadays." I told the general that she was doing well, that her teas, social functions, and canasta games kept her busy. Miss Cunningham at this juncture crossed her legs and tugged at her skirt slightly. There was a brief flash of skin, the skin between the upper rim of her stocking and the hem of the skirt. Unbeknownst to General Woodling, she saw me see this flash of skin and then made a crude yet alluring tongue gesture.

Los Alamos, which General Groves and Dr. Oppenheimer had selected as the laboratory and test site, was the ideal location. It is unimaginable that any other place would have sufficed. The scenery was awe-inspiring. The sky stretched out forever in all directions; hills and mountains rose and fell with unbearable majesty, and the play of colors was almost unendurable: umbers, ochres, puces, and the pale blue sky arcing overhead . . . truly an awesome vista. Miles and miles of desolation, of isolation, an endless, broken terrain of terrible emptiness. It was as harrowingly lonely a place as I have ever been to in my life.

And that was the problem.

ARNIE LATCHKEY: See, you had all these highbrow $E=MC^2$ types, these chemists and engineers and physicists, and you had some army guys, and some of the wives there too . . . *but there wasn't anything to do!* Take the most exciting two hundred people in the world and plop them down right smack in the middle of Death Valley. Things would get pretty dead pretty quick, wouldn't it? But this was worse. Because these people were not exciting. A scintillating time for them was getting a new piece of chalk to write a formula with.

That's why we were there. Sure, they had their chess games and their little parties before Fountain and Bliss arrived. There were square dances and Enrico Fermi used to play the piano and I think Edward Teller used to even play the fiddle. But, you know, even a physicist who's designing the most powerful weapon in the history of mankind at the most crucial moment in history wants to get up and swing once in a while! That's what General Woodling told us: This was for morale. We were to play one show and then get the hell out of here. I had no idea, Vic and Ziggy had no idea, that they were working on an atomic bomb.

On our first day there we were taken to a small dusty barracks to meet Woody and Oppenheimer, who was as skinny as a lollipop stick. I said to him, "Oppie, *bubeleh,* eat something!!!" I don't care how much a guy knows about the cosmos and uranium and neutrons, I don't care if he *has* become Death, shatterer of worlds, just *eat something!* Ziggy even said he was going to call Sally and have her send him ten pounds of *rugelach* . . . but Oppenheimer reminded Ziggy that we were not allowed to use the phones. Vic said, "No phones? Doc, this place is deader than last week's beer!" "Yes, it is," Oppie said. Boy, you couldn't get a giggle or a smile out of that guy.

"You're going to perform one show," Woody told us. "It will be the night of July fifteenth. It will be at an undisclosed location on the base . . . you'll be informed hours before the show."

"Jesus, I hope we're flying Billy Ross in," Vic said.

"Who's Billy Ross?" Oppie asked.

"My arranger and bandleader. I ain't going on with some nickel-and-dime army band."

While Oppie and Woody now confabbed in a corner for a second, Ziggy, Vic, and I took the opportunity to similarly huddle together.

"This place is death," Vic said. "I want out."

"This is important, guys," I said.

"Vic's right, Latch," Ziggy chimed in. "I'd rather play a prison full of condemned deaf mutes than this joint."

"Look, we do one show, we do two hours, then we get going. The Astor canceled on us because of Vic's toes. The Hippodrome dropped us in Baltimore too. I promise you, I give you my word, that this thing is going to fix that. *We need this!*"

"And I need a drink," Vic said.

General Woodling and Oppenheimer came back and Woody said, "We're not flying Billy Ross in. I'm sorry. We have several people here who play musical instruments. I'm sure that they would love to provide accompaniment for you."

"Hey, who's the dish?" Vic said. Out the barracks window we saw some blond doll in a jeep with a figure like Linda Darnell's. She was looking in the rearview mirror, fixing her hair.

"Back to this music problem," Woody said. "Do you have any—"

"Yeah!" I said. "I got the charts!" I opened up my suitcase, which those Army security *momzers* at the gate had thoroughly searched—Vic and Ziggy were chuckling to no end about my polka-dot boxers—and I handed Woody the charts.

"What are you guys working on here, Doc, " Vic asked Oppenheimer, "some sort of super-deluxe martini shaker to get the Nips so bagged we can just waltz into Tokyo?"

"Perhaps we should devote ourselves to that, Mr. Fountain," Oppie said to him.

"Lieutenant Catledge will show you to your quarters," Woody said.

"Is there any booze in this operation?" Vic asked. "I'm parched."

General Woodling told us that there was alcohol and that he would have some sent over to our quarters after Catledge filled out the proper requisition papers.

"Jeez, I go to Jack Dempsey's bar, I don't have to fill out any requisition papers," Vic said.

We walked out and Lieutenant Catledge walked us over to a little Quonset hut setup, about a mile's walk. Ziggy was huffing and puffing as we walked and Vic kept saying, "Where's our hotel room in? Fuckin' Brazil?"

The hut was so bare I almost blushed out of embarrassment. Three cots and a toilet. And a window with a breathtaking view of absolutely nothing.

"What kinda design style is this? Early igloo?" Ziggy said.

"No phone, huh?" Vic chimed in. "How'm I supposed to call my bookie?"

Catledge told us that there were phones but that we did not have clearance to use them. Vic said, "Look, pal, if *you've* got clearance, do me a favor. Put a fin on the Red Sox today."

"I wouldn't know who to call for that, Mr. Fountain," Cat said.

"I was only kiddin' ya," Vic said. "And it's Vic, not Mr. Fountain."

Catledge left and we *plotzed* as one on our respective cots.

"Where the hell's our next show after this, Latch? We playing for some bedouins at the Club Sahara?" Ziggy said.

"Yeah, Zig," I said. "I'll try to line that one up for us."

REYNOLDS CATLEDGE IV: I'd been at the base a few weeks before Fountain and Bliss arrived and was on the verge of losing my sanity. There were square dances on weekends and there was even a low-watt radio station, but I really did feel as though I was at the very edge of the world. The food was not bad—Edward Teller's veal *paprikosh* was splendid. But the place needed a jolt, a shot in the arm.

My only source of diversion was Betsy Cunningham. One day she came into General Woodling's office. She wanted to use the phone, she told me, and I told her this was impossible. She sat on my desk, crossed her legs. She ran her fingers through my hair, told me what a handsome boy I was. "Poor wittle Reynolds," she said, pinching my lips together with her hands, "wittle, wittle baby boy who works for big, big strong general but wants to fuck the general's girl and who's got this wittle, wittle hard-on right now."

She told me that I should wait up for her that night, that she would tap on my window at three in the morning and, like a fool, I did.

ARNIE LATCHKEY: They wouldn't let us do anything! We wanted to walk around, get the feel of the place, but everywhere we went, someone told us we couldn't go here, we couldn't go there. Ziggy was sweating up a storm . . . the place was like being inside an oven. I said to Catledge, "You gotta give us a jeep, Cat," and he said he'd do what he could. We got the jeep. Vic went to the mess hall on our second day and "liberated" some gin and vermouth and some bourbon and seltzer. Meanwhile Ziggy's clothes are sopping wet with his constant *shvitz*. "Can you get this guy some new duds?" I say to Catledge and boom, ten minutes later Ziggy, me, and Vic are all decked out in army fatigues. (Boy, did Vic ever get a big kick out of walking around in an army uniform for a few days!)

That night we're back in our hut and just shooting the shit. Tellin' stories, reliving some of the good times we've had. You know, Vic and Ziggy were now sort of becoming pals. The Detroit shows had gone really well. We'd gone out to dinner and lunch there every night, all of us together. Their rapport was improving. They had all that chemistry on the stage and now they were getting it offstage too. And that was the first time we ever started insisting on things. And we did it just for the hell of it. In the hotel in Chi, Ziggy called down to the front desk and said he wanted ruby red sheets and pillow cases, to match his hair. *Ruby* he wants! And they did it. Then he calls Vic's room to crow about that, and Vic now one-ups him . . . he says he wants turquoise, to match his eyes. And they did that too.

So we're in the hut drinking martinis and Catledge comes in, just to check on us.

"Any broads around here, Cat?" Vic says to him.

"There are indeed," Catledge told us. There were the wives, there were some lady scientists, and so on, he told us.

"Nah, you know what I mean," Vic said. "Where can a fella get some action in this one-ghost town? Mr. Baciagaloop needs to whet his whistle."

After we assured Cat that we hadn't snuck [*sic*] anyone named Mr. Baciagaloop onto the grounds, he said to us, "There are some girls if you're really interested."

Vic perked up, offered Catledge a drink. Vic said, "I'm a two-a-day man and I ain't even had my first yet. You and me, Cat, whattaya say?"

Catledge—he was a small, serious crewcut guy who wouldn't smile if you stretched his lips with pliers—blushed, and Vic looked over to me and Ziggy. Ziggy said, "I'm game for some broad action—you know me." Vic said, "You stay here and keep Latch company, Zig. Me and the lootie have some reconnoitering to do, ain't that, right, Lieutenant Catledge?" Vic slapped Cat on the back and then he and this bashful lieutenant go driving off into the darkness.

Two days later who shows up? Hunny Gannett!

Vic said that he would not go on, would not do the show, would in fact leave the whole area, if Hunny was not on the premises. He made this abundantly clear to Catledge, who in turn made that known to the top pooh-bahs at Los Alamos. Turns out that the two pin-striped FBI guys had already cleared Hunny. Too dumb to be a spy, I guess. They flew Hunny in, dragged in another cot, and now it was the four of us, swilling martinis, goofing off and swapping stories.

Boxers back then would do exhibitions. You go from this base to that, you strip to your trunks and strap on the Everlasts and shuffle and jab, and you've done your duty. Keep the boys entertained, keep your *tuches* in one piece. Vic's idea was to have Hunny maybe take on some of the army guys on the base. "It'd really loosen up the place, Arn," he said. The army bought it.

REYNOLDS CATLEDGE IV: There was a makeshift three-hole golf course on the base, and when Vic Fountain found out about that he was very pleased. He would spend hours at the course, driving and putting. Dr. Ursula Fischer, an Austrian physicist, came to the course one day to relax and get a few holes in. Dr. Fischer was an integral part of the Manhattan Project, whose work in radioactive isotopes has never been fully appreciated; she was twenty-seven years old and had studied under Dr. Heisenberg in Germany. She was pretty, fair-skinned, tall with hazel eyes. Vic saw her driving some balls and he sidled up to her. Within a few minutes she was giggling like a Viennese schoolgirl and Vic was helping her with her stroke. He asked her if he could take her out to dinner that night but she reminded him that there was no place to go. He asked her where he might find her, and she, in between giggles, told him which dormitory she was living in. He said he would swing by and they could, in his words, "talk physics."

ARNIE LATCHKEY: Yeah, Vic had something going with one of the local brains. He came stumbling into the hut one morning and I asked him where he'd been all night. He said he'd been with a girl. I asked him, "Which girl? Humor me. I'm lonely. I miss Estelle." I asked him, "Was it the physicist Austrian broad from yesterday?" He said, "Who? Madame Curie with tits? Yeah, it was her."

Ziggy would do his thing in the mess hall and he had all the army boys and the brass and even the science guys in stitches. There was a food fight that he instigated one day between the chemists and the other guys . . . the chemists *killed* 'em! It was no contest. (I guess if you know the correct properties of baked beans you can hurl them at a better angle or something.) One night Catledge took us to the little radio station—they were playing Brahms's Fourth Symphony at the time—and Ziggy and Vic grabbed the mike and started doing their celebrity shtick, imitating Cagney, Gable, [Bette] Davis, Cooper, Bogie, Nelson Eddy and Jeanette MacDonald, everybody. When they were doing that I looked out the little window of this shack we were in . . . I looked from barracks to barracks and I could see silhouettes in the windows. People were laughing.

Slow dissolve. Outdoors, a field. Day before the big show. Hunny had his exhibition. In the middle of nowhere these army engineer guys set up this jerry-built boxing ring. Hunny had brought a couple pair of Everlasts and was ready to take on all comers. Believe me, they came. Soldier boy after soldier boy got in the ring—these poor kids had been cooped up in the desert all this time, with nothing to do, with no war to fight. Hunny would toy with each kid, circle and circle, and if the solider hit him he'd pretend to be hurt. But after a few minutes he'd just rear back and let loose a haymaker. Even "Steady" Eddie Teller got in the ring but General Woodling told Hunny to not hurt this guy, he was important, so Hunny played nice. (Not the first time he took a dive.) Woodling was sitting with this blond dish, the same broad we'd seen in the jeep a few days before. This girl could've been a movie star, all the bits and pieces were in the right place. But she wasn't having such a great time right now. You know how you take a girl somewhere and she gets in a bad mood and so she tries to make it a miserable a time for you too? That's what she was doing. She and the general left before the thing was over.

That night in the hut, before Vic snuck [sic] out, he and Ziggy went over which routines to do. We agreed that the joint was looser than when we'd first arrived. When we got there, it was like granite; now it was like any old Wednesday night at a club in Toledo, Ohio. A little tight but some grease would loosen it up quick. Fountain and Bliss could play the goddamn Reichstag, we all agreed, and have the place jumping.

"Hey, I met the guy who invented the radio today!" Vic said suddenly. "He's an Italian just like me! He's gonna be leading our band tomorrow too."

"What the hell are you talking about, the guy who invented the radio?" I said.

"Enrico Fermi. Yeah, I met him today."

I said, "Marconi invented the radio, not Fermi!" and I threw a pillow at him.

"All right, I better get going," Vic said, looking at his watch and grabbing a bottle of Gordon's.

"Where you goin', Vic? Huh? Take me along," Ziggy said.

Hunny grunted. "Betchya it's that isotopes broad."

The next morning I'm in the mess hall alone when two gray pin-striped shadows with fedoras slowly descend over my bowl of oatmeal.

"Hey, guys, hop in," I said, indicating the gruel.

They asked me how everything was going and I told them it was all hunky-dory, considering our current locale. They started to walk away and I grabbed the shorter G-man by his jacket tail and tugged him back to me. I said to him, "Me, Vic, and Ziggy, we're outta here in a few days, my friend. And we ain't coming back, not if you offer us forty grand. Hey, for fifty, maybe we do it. But I need—the act needs—some proof that we were here. You get me? Remember? You promised me that Joe Doakes and Jane Doe would find out about this gig!"

So at about three o'clock that day, Oppie drives up to the small golf course, and me, Ziggy, Vic, and Hunny pile into the jeep. We keep driving. Off in the distance—and, believe me, there was enough distance to go around—I see a tall metal tower. The jeep pulls up at the tower, there's a bunch of guys standing there. It's all the hotshots . . . Fermi, Ken Bainbridge, Segré, Bohr, "Steady" Eddie Teller, General Groves, Rutherford, a bunch of other fellas. The two gray pin-striped guys are there. And there's an official army shutterbug too. It's Joe Doakes time.

The scientists, including Oppenheimer, gather around Ziggy and Vic. They're all standing right underneath this big tower. The sun is blazing hot. Vic puts on his romantic crooner look and Zig bugs out his eyes northeast and southwest. *Snap!* The picture is taken.

The G-men are standing next to me, behind the fotog, when everybody says cheese. I mutter to the short one, "I'd like three hundred and fifty of those, if you don't mind."

REYNOLDS CATLEDGE IV: When Arnie said he couldn't guarantee a great show because Victor Fountain was very hung over, I got some aspirins over to their hut right away. He also said that Ziggy was in a rotten frame of mind. I inquired as to why, and Arnie said that I would not understand. He then asked me where I'd taken Vic on the first night, when Vic wanted a woman. I said there was a barracks where some women who "serviced" the community were kept. "Can you take Ziggy there, Cat?" he asked me. I said I would do so. He said, "I don't think you get me, soldier boy. Can you get him there *now?*" I said I would do so immediately.

Unfortunately, there was a problem. The woman that Ziggy Bliss had selected refused to service him, once he'd removed his clothes. Ziggy said he would pay her three times what she usually made for such an endeavor but she held firm. A rather large woman who worked there said that she could handle him but insisted on four times the usual rate. They went upstairs. A minute later, Baldwyn Sloate, a short man who worked for the FBI and who always wore a gray pin-striped suit and a fedora, as did his partner, Timothy Jones, walked in and told me that the entire place had to be evacuated. I foolishly asked, "Can we possibly wait four more minutes?" but Sloate said we could not. There were several army trucks parked outside. The women were not even allowed to gather their personal effects—they were led into the trucks by several soldiers, some of whom they'd no doubt pleasured. The woman who was with Ziggy was fetched by Agent Jones, and Ziggy appeared at the top of the stairs with nothing on but a towel. "Hey, I was just about to unload my buckets!" he said. He was very angry. He put his army fatigues back on and I drove him back to the hut.

A few hours later I was in General Woodling's headquarters—he was not in at the time nor had be been in all that day—going over some paperwork when Agents Sloate and Jones walked in and closed the door.

"What do you know about Betsy Cunningham?" Sloate asked me.

"What do you want to know?" I asked.

"Every single thing, Lieutenant."

In the space of a second, I weighed several things over in my mind. By this time I had come to detest the general; I loathed how he'd forced me to spend evenings with his wife, how I had to cover up for his assignations with Betsy Cunningham. I'd even had to go to department stores in Washington and in Virginia and buy her lingerie! Miss Cunningham would taunt me publicly. Three times she had pinched my buttocks and started giggling while General Marshall was addressing the staff in Washington. On one occasion in Washington while General Woodling was in his office with the door closed, she paced back and forth, waiting for him to let her in. I could not concentrate on the work at hand. The sound of her heels, the saliva clacking in her mouth. She said, "Two more minutes and I'm never talking to that fat old jackass again." She opened a file drawer and I told her that she had to close it, the information in there was classified. "This is really important!" she said to me. I asked her, "May I inquire as to the nature of the business at hand?" And she said, "Yeah, this is the business," whereupon she stood before me, shifted all her comely weight to one side, and lifted up her skirt. She was not wearing panties. I swallowed . . . I got dizzy very quickly. "You want it, don't you?" she asked me. "Like the way it's shaved?" I could not contain myself any longer—months of frustration and bitterness seemed to overwhelm me—and I foolishly reached for her. She brought her skirt down quickly and said, "Ha! Take a long walk on a short pier, sissy." The door then opened and she ran giggling into the general's office. The door was shut but I was able to listen to their coupling over the intercom.

I told agents Sloate and Jones that Betsy Cunningham was the general's mistress. They'd been having an affair for three years and had first met at a lunch counter in Arlington. I named every hotel in Virginia and Washington where they had their trysts, and added that I myself had had to book their rooms. I related the incident about her looking through the general's effects and opening the file drawers. I even told them what size bra she wore—34DD—I knew as I'd had to purchase several of them. I told them that her father worked at a Rexall in Virginia, and they looked at each other.

Baldwyn Sloate asked me how I'd come about the information regarding Miss Cunningham's father and I told them that she had told me. They asked me if I'd ever met her father and I told them no, I had not. They asked me if I had ever had any sexual relations with Miss Cunningham and I told them that although I had not I was dying to. They told me they understood.

I never saw Miss Cunningham again, not in the flesh. Nor did I ever see General Woodling.

The general had already been relieved of his duty earlier that day, I later discovered, and eventually he vanished into obscurity. Sloate and Jones had him ushered off the base and flown to an undisclosed location for interrogation. An innocent, gullible man, he was exonerated from any wrongdoing other than being a bored fifty-year-old man married to a frumpy, white-haired, canasta-playing wife. But Miss Betsy Cunningham, whose real name was Ludmilla Danilova, was deported to the Soviet Union in 1963.

ARNIE LATCHKEY: I don't know what Enrico Fermi did when it comes to atoms or molecules or radiation, but it's a good thing he stuck to that and not the piano. *Ouch!* Talk about matter being transformed! Here's a perfectly fine in-tune Steinway and he's making it sound like a kazoo. There was a ten-piece band and this combo was about as off-key as a second-grade music class. Vic was trying to sing a few numbers and he actually did make it through, but you think the A-bomb made a racket? You should have heard Fermi mangle "Night and Day."

The show was in the mess hall. Hunny was tending bar and, boy, were the drinks flowing that night. The chemical boys had some grain alcohol and Hunny had gotten some lime or lemon flavoring and he made this big vat of punch. Some army cutup had taken some paint and drawn a picture of a uranium atom on the thing, that's how powerful this joy juice was! And they were lining up to guzzle it, all the highbrows and the soldiers and the wives.

Ziggy and Vic were on for about three hours. At the end, nobody could even laugh anymore. Too hoarse, too wrung out, too smashed. That was the night Fountain and Bliss originated their Dr. Louie Kablooie bit, where Ziggy puts on an Einstein wig and mustache and Yiddish accent and Vic interviews him. Now keep in mind, we still had no idea what the hell all these science guys were working on but we figured that to put everyone out here in the middle of nowhere and to have a fence around the joint and to send those agents to talk to Estelle, it's gotta be something powerful. So Ziggy and Vic had guessed it had to be a bomb, right? But the fact that this bomb had some atom splitting inside of it—well, we were in the dark about that. This Louie Kablooie bit really had 'em on the floor. And for the very first time in the week we were there, Oppie was even smiling. When the show was over he came over to me and said, "Your act has done us a great service." To which I, ever the astute manager, replied, "Great. Where's our dough?"

Sure enough when we get back to our hut, there's twenty grand in cash in a GI duffel bag waiting for us. Right on my pillow. Vic and Zig took fourteen, gave me and Hunny three each. All in all, not bad for a day's work.

Cat woke the four of us up at 3:00 in the A.M. that night. "Everyone has to go," he said. "Right now. Orders from the top." We piled into a jeep and drove off into the blackness.

We slept in the jeep most of the way, with Cat driving . . . I remember there not being a cloud in the sky . . . there was nothing but white and blue stars, big, close, and twinkling. The next morning we were in Albuquerque, billeted to some small cheap hotel that was as hot as a goddamn steambath. We slept some more. That was the day, it turned out, that the first atom bomb was tested. We weren't allowed to see it. Years later, Vic and Ziggy were still griping about that. The nerve of the army, right?

After a day in Albuquerque, Cat drove us to Las Vegas, our first time there. We stayed at the Last Frontier. I said to Cat, Hey, if you ever get out of the army, look me up. And I offered him a grand. "I'm not permitted to accept this," he said, so I said, "Are you permitted to accept two grand?" Apparently that fell within the regulations of army conduct, and the next day we were on a train to Chicago and then we were back in New York.

I get a *Post* one day and the first thing I read is Bud Hatch, who'd always been a friend to the act, weighing in on Vic's toes. Bud was on our side but, still, it was annoying that this thing was still being bandied about. (It was probably his wife, the so-called Scintillating Lady; she got half of the scoops, wrote half the column, bore half the grudges, and drank all the gin.) A day later, the short gray pin-striped guy called me on the phone at the office and I asked him, "Hey, you promised me publicity! When can we break this thing to the press?!" He said that soon I could tell everybody everything. Where are the pictures of my boys with all the science guys? I asked him, and he told me that in good time I'd get the pictures. "I get my talent out there in the middle of that desert to play a show for a bunch of stiffs and I can't even tell the press!" I barked out to him. "That's absurd!" He said, "You *were* paid twenty thousand for it." And that shut me up good.

Weeks passed. More negative press. More canceled engagements. John Perona at El Morocco is even starting to come on all queasy-like. Vic comes in one day and he's fuming; he reminds me that I'd so much as promised him he'd come out on top with this thing. I said to him, "I *so much as* promised you, but I didn't promise you." I told him to hold tight. But frankly, Teddy, I was starting to get antsy about it too. That maybe we'd been had by Uncle Sam.

"Lulu and I are getting married," Vic then told me.

"When?"

"We ain't set a date yet."

"So Vic Fountain is finally going to settle down, huh?"

"Probably not."

Snuffy Dubin comes back stateside and he's *begging* Ziggy for a spot on the radio show. Snuffy was broke; he really hadn't made *bubkes* as a comic yet, don't forget that. He said to Ziggy and me, "Just give me two minutes a week, come on." Ziggy wouldn't budge. He said that it wouldn't blend in with the rest of the show. I felt for Snuffles, I really did—he'd had a tough time in the marines—but I just couldn't alienate my talent. And Vic, he didn't care, so he weighed in with Ziggy.

Then I pick up a *Daily News* one morning and there it was. We'd dropped the big one on the Japs. A super-deluxe martini shaker, all right, that's what it was. The second I read that I knew this was what they'd been cooking up out there in the desert. Ha! Arnold Latchkey from the Bronx— a guy who'd been reaming spit valves just a few years before—eyewitness to history.

So I go into my office in the Brill Building and what's on my chair? An envelope with 350 eight-by-tens of Fountain and Bliss with Oppie and Fermi and "Steady" Eddie Teller. And the tower in the background. The tower, my friend, that they dropped the first bomb off of! The short gray pin-striped guy calls me and says to me, "Okay, Mr. Latchkey. You can let her rip."

The next three days Bertie Kahn and I called up every newspaper, every magazine, every single sonuvabitch with a pencil and a piece of paper. We sent out the photos. It was all over the place, it was everywhere. They started referring to the act as the Atomix Comix!

That schlemiel at the Capitol Theater calls me up one day and says, "So, Arnie, can we get the boys to open up a movie for us now?" And I said to him, "Oh yeah, sure we can. They'll open up a movie. *At the Paramount they'll open up!*" And I hung up on that schnorrer.

Then one day Murray Katz at WAT phones me and says the words I've been having wet dreams of hearing for years.

"How would Ziggy and Vic," he asks me, "feel about taking a little trip to Hollywood?"

IV

ARNIE LATCHKEY: We played the A-bomb card for all it was worth. Talk about nuclear fallout! This was radioactive manna from heaven, the way it fell right into our laps. Ziggy and Vic did a weekend at the Riviera in New Jersey and posed with Albert Einstein for an Associated Press fotog; the *Daily Mirror* ran the picture and captioned it "Nuclear Nuts." Bud Hatch mentioned an upcoming engagement in Philly at the Earl Theater and said something like "Do not miss this atom-splitting, sidesplitting act." *Variety* called the act "radioactive ridiculousness."

Lulu came up to New York one weekend and she, Vic, Estelle, and I had dinner at Delmonico's. Lu had her engagement ring on—the thing was bigger than her head. Now, Estelle knew all about Vic's reputation with the girls—as our receptionist, she often had to juggle three girls at once for him—and she and I had talked about their upcoming nups. "It's just not going to work, honey," she'd warned me, and I said to her, "Some of these shiksa wives, though, they know something's going on with their husbands and another woman, so they just look the other way." And Estelle said, "But Vic's with so many girls, she'll run out of other ways to look."

Vic says to me at Delmonico's now, "So this Hollywood trip, does this mean we don't have to do the radio show no more?"

"You got meetings at Columbia, MGM, Galaxy, and Paramount," I told him, "but for all we know Harry Cohn, Louis Mayer, and the rest of 'em will toss you headfirst out their offices and into the raging Pacific surf. I wouldn't count any chickens before they're hatched."

"I tell ya, movies seem like a swell racket, Latch. You do two pictures a year, the rest of the time you're just playing golf or taking it easy."

"There's some difference between playing golf and taking it easy?" my darling, clever, beautiful wife-to-be cracked wise.

Now, I'd sort of picked up that Vic wasn't thrilled with the radio show. He was still showing up late for rehearsal. When the ON AIR sign lit up, he'd go great guns, full speed ahead—that was the professional in Vic. But to get to the professional in Vic, you sometimes had to peel away about twenty layers of unprofessional, like an onion. He once said to me that the radio show was like having a real job and he didn't get into show business so he could have a real job.

"You know, Ziggy *is* the other half of the act," I told him. "He likes the radio show."

"Yeah, he would," Vic said with a sneering curl of the lip, upper right side.

When I told Ziggy about the Hollywood trip, you know what the first thing he said was? "Uh-oh, I hope this don't mean we have to give up the radio show."

• • •

GUY PUGLIA: I was embarrassed. It never bothered me being a short guy 'cause I knew that even though I was a half-pint I was the toughest guy wherever I went. Hunny and I would go at each other sometimes, just goofin' on each other, and he had a foot and fifty pounds on me and I could lick him sometimes, he was so slow. At Barney's Beanery [in Los Angeles] one night I got into a scrap with a big, strong Hollywood stunt guy and they had to pull me offa him so I wouldn't kill him. But what embarrassed me now was the nose. I stayed in St. Vincent's a week longer than I really needed to, 'cause I just didn't want to go outside with the little bandage over my face. Here I am, this little piece of scrap iron, and I'm worried about how fuckin' pretty I look.

The day I went home I even made sure to have a cab waiting right outside the hospital. So I'd only be outdoors for a second.

When I was in the lobby about to run for that taxi, who do I see but Hunny Gannett. He gives me a big bear hug and we pile in and head home. He's got a bottle of champagne and by the time we made it to our spread on Fifty-sixth Street we were smashed.

"Everything's gonna be all right, Gaetano," he says to me in the car. "You'll see."

"I don't know, Hun," I said. I didn't tell him I was embarrassed. I didn't talk about them type things.

"You're gonna be okay," Hunny says. "Nobody's gonna pick on you. Anybody does, the Hun'll pulverize 'em."

He took a long swig of the bubbly and I says to him, "Hun, you got a fight tonight, don't forget."

He opens the door to the apartment and the first thing I see on the couch is Vic Fountain, my *paisan*. He's got two naked broads with him, one on each side and both of them with red ribbons around their necks like they was gifts, and there's a bottle of champagne on the coffee table. "Take your pick, you little sawed-off sonuvabitch," he says to me. "Or take both. It's on me."

I figure, what the hell. Why not? I didn't have a girl. I didn't ever have a girl. I picked the shorter one, the brunette, and we went into the next room.

About the only time Vic and I ever talked about this whole nose thing was a few days later. We was at Hunny's saloon. He says to me, "Guy, I know some serious people. Connected guys. People who can take care of Straccio."

Now this was something that I had no problem with. I says to him, "Take care of him? Like how?" I wanted to make sure we were on the same wavelength here.

"Like, he don't ever bother nobody ever again. Like, he don't even breathe another breath of Codport air. These guys, they do something, it's clean. No dirt ever sticks to you or me. They're professionals about it."

I ask him who he would go to and he says either Joe Adonis or Al Pompiere. Now, I didn't want to tell him that Straccio had told me that Joe Adonis owed him a favor, 'cause I didn't want Vic to ever know that I'd lost my schnoz 'cause Straccio was threatening to lean on Vic. Right? So Joe Adonis is out. I says, "Awright, see what Al Pompiere can do."

A day before he and Ziggy hop on the train to Hollywood, I'm at the same table with Al Pompiere and Vic. Big Al says we need another chair because his son-in-law is coming any second to join this get-together.

"Big movie star, huh, Vittorio?" Pompiere says. "Once you get an eyeful of all them juicy Hollywood actresses you'll never come back east."

"It can't happen a minute too soon, Al," Vic says.

"And I want to hear all about when it does. That Lana Turner . . ."

Vic then puts his arm around my shoulder and says, "Look what that fuckin' *stronzo* did to my buddy, Al. Look at this. Fuckin' guy rips his nose off with a blade. Someone does that to a buddy of yours, what do you do to him?"

Al Pompiere says, "He rips my buddy's nose off, he loses his *coglioni*. Case closed."

"That's what I'm saying. Al, can you take care of this guy for me?"

Big Al is mulling this over and I'm starting to think, What the fuck is this powwow about? Vic doesn't really want to get anything done.

Al says, "Vic, you asked me what I would do and I told you. But now you want me to take care of your business? Why don't *you* rip this guy's nuts out like I would? I mean, why did you bother even asking me? Where does Al Pompiere fit in?"

Vic got all red in the face. He liked to come on like a tough guy, but he was no tough guy. He just liked to hang around with 'em sometimes.

"What do I get out of this?" Al says. "The thrill of knowing that I had some small-town rodent hit three hundred miles away? I need these jollies? I'm a businessman, Vic."

The door swings open and this big shadow approaches. It's Lou Manganese, Big Al's son-in-law. Lou the Ape. He sits down and joins us and Big Al introduces us.

"You and I met once but you maybe don't remember, Vic," Lou says to Vic.

"I meet a lot of people I don't remember, Lou," Vic says. "I'm an entertainer."

"Nah, but you hardly was one when we met. It was at this shithole dive in Camden. Herbie's Duplex. You pretty much told me to get the fuck lost."

"Vic," Big Al said, "you're not so stupid you'd do a thing like that, would you?"

"At that time I might have been," Vic said.

"Vic wants us to kill someone, Lou. Like we got nothing else to do?"

They both break up laughing and Vic begins to melt quicker than the ice in his scotch. They recover from their laughs and Big Al says to me, "Hey, did anybody in your first grade class call you a sissy or maybe steal your Spaldeen? Maybe Vic wants me to cut that kid's head off." And he and Lou are breaking up again.

"Ain't you guys ever heard about sticks and stones?" Lou the Ape said.

We walked out of there and Vic was in a rotten mood. "If I was Errol Flynn they'd have done it for me," he's fuming.

I felt like an idiot. Al Pompiere was right.

"I'm gonna take care of this thing for you, pal," Vic said to me.

It would've been nice if every once in a while, instead of getting me a whore or trying to have someone knocked off, he asked me how I was doing.

●　　●　　●

ARNIE LATCHKEY: We took a train to Chicago and did a week at the Rio Cabana there. Packed every night. Tons of ink. Billy Ross was now the official arranger and bandleader. From there it was down to Ohio, they played Cleveland and Cinci, then the Statler in St. Loo. Did a walk-on at the old Tunetown Ballroom. Killed 'em. Ovations, laurels, moolah galore. We were moving like a steamroller, like the Green Bay Packers in their prime. Then on to Kansas City to do a few dates there. The Fountain and Bliss Express is rolling like thunder. This is the farthest west the act's ever been and we're a combination of Lewis and Clark and Napoleon and we're taking over the world. The best thing: In Chi, Lenny Pearl was playing the old Palace Theater a few nights while we were there and he couldn't even half fill the place. That thrilled Ziggy to no end.

From K.C. it was all aboard the *Santa Fe Chief*. Hollywood or bust.

Bertie Kahn told me that Morty Geist at Bursley-Bates in Los Angeles would be doing the publicity. This guy was a kid, he was twenty-two years old *tops*, but he was a prodigy, like Mozart with a telephone. The kid had handled Rin Tin Tin and look at all the fuss he created out of a German shepherd and, from what I hear, not a particularly intelligent one either. What Bertie failed to mention to me about Morty Geist was that the kid was a nervous wreck. You remember *What Makes Sammy Run?* Well, this was *What Makes Morty Tremble?* But he was a whiz kid and he knew his business . . . it just pained people to see him working, that's all.

The train pulls into Union Station in Los Angeles and the only thing we're expecting is maybe a redcap to help us with our trunks. We're ready to step off the train when I hear this racket—it was a roar, like the ocean at high tide. Ziggy even said to me, "What the hell's goin' on, Arn?" And Vic says, "Maybe some big celebrity is here or something."

But it was for us! Well, not really. Morty Geist had rigged it all up. He'd gone to UCLA and USC and told every coed there that Hank Fonda, Cary Grant, and David Selznick would be casting a movie at the station and they needed young kids who screamed very loud for an upcoming motion picture. There were a thousand kids there and to this day I don't know if my eardrums have recovered. Meanwhile Morty had told the press that the hubbub would be for Fountain and Bliss! So you had fotogs from the *Examiner* and the [Los Angeles] *Daily News* and people from the *Hollywood Reporter* and *Variety* and they all reported this hysteria was for Fountain and Bliss, who simply forged their way unmolested through this screaming mob. And then we got in our taxis and headed for the Hollywood Plaza Hotel.

Morty met us there, in the lobby. This kid was just on a different plane. His mind raced a million miles a second and I think so did his pulse too. "It went off good, didn't it, at the station?" he said. And I told him it sure did. Even with that good news, he's biting his nails down to the knuckles.

SALLY KLEIN: When I first met Morty, at the Plaza, I just knew that this was a doomed person. I didn't think this kid would make it past thirty. I used to tell him, "Calm down, Morty," and he would say, "Sally, this is me being calm."

Estelle's roommate, Shirley Klein, had told me in New York to look up her older brother Jack in California. He was a recent widower and was a real-estate lawyer. I said, "Why should I look him up?" and Shirl said, "Because, Sally, he's a really nice man."

And he was. So I married him.

DANNY McGLUE: It wasn't a good time for me. I got out of the navy and I hopped from apartment to apartment, radio show to radio show. Murray Katz at WAT told me he couldn't represent me, and there was no doubt in my mind that that was on Ziggy's instructions. Why else would Murray drop me like I was a hot potato schmeared with cyanide? But Murray passed me over to Joe Gersh, and he would get me these radio jobs. But they weren't any fun. I wrote for Dinah Shore, for Arthur Godfrey, for Len Coles. The pay was okay but it wasn't like the old days with Ziggy, Vic, Arnie, Sid, and Norman. That was home for me.

Snuffy told me that Zig and Vic were in Los Angeles meeting producers and directors and, well, you know how you can get really happy and really miserable at the same time? That's how I felt. I was happy for them—for Sally too, of course. But I really wanted to be with them.

ARNIE LATCHKEY: Hank Stanco, our man at WAT in L.A., set up the whole agenda. The first meeting was with Harry Cohn at Columbia. Now, I was under the impression we'd be meeting with one of Harry's underlings. But Morty Geist calls me in the morning and he's a nervous wreck and he says, "The meeting is now with Harry! His brother Jack has seen the act at the Copa and Harry wants to meet the boys personally." That's when I got scared. *Harry Cohn? Personally?* This guy was vicious like Gandhi was peaceful! I say to Morty, "Are you sure we should do this?" and he says, "Sure I'm sure." I say, "Morty, what's that knocking noise I'm hearing now?" and he says, "Those are my knees, Arnie."

Columbia sends a car for us, and let me tell you, for the first time ever, the boys are nervous. They're both fidgeting. "What's gonna happen here, Latch?" Vic asked me while we waited for the limo. I tell him I have no idea. A minute later Ziggy asks me, "So what do you think is going to happen?" I say to them both, "If I knew the answer, I could cancel the meeting and we could all go on as if it had already happened." "How big a deal is this Cohn fella?" Vic asks me and I told him he was the cat's meow. "So Harry Cohn is a real big deal, ain't he?" Ziggy asks me two minutes later, and I said, "You two guys are making *me* nervous now!" But I was already nervous by then.

We're ushered into Cohn's office—I don't think Mussolini's executive chambers could have been more imperial—and what is Il Duce of Poverty Row doing when we walk in? Yelling. *Of course!* I mean, this is a given. He's yelling his lungs dry, standing and shouting, and I could count the capillaries on his temple from twenty yards away. He's on the phone to his brother Jack, who ran Columbia in New York, and Harry's screaming, "You fucking son of a bitch, how could you be such an idiot?! . . . I'll destroy you, you fucking bastard! . . . You goddamn idiot, I'll kill you and eat you and spit you out into the toilet where you belong, you fucking piece of dirt!" Then there's a space where Jack is speaking to him and all of a sudden Harry calms down, sits down, and now they're brothers again and not talking business and this serene air settles over him. "And how are the kids, Jack? . . . really? . . . wonderful . . . How's Jeanette? . . . Wonderful . . . give the kids a big kiss from their Uncle Harry . . . okay, I'll call you tomorrow and yell at you some more. Toodle-oo." This guy could separate business from pleasure with a feather.

We're only in Harry Cohn's office for ten minutes, tops. The upshot is he's got a script that's been knocking around the industry since the Lumière brothers. It's called *Shall We Dunce?* It was first intended for Astaire and Rogers, then for Kelly and Grable at MGM, then for Leslie Howard and Rita Hayworth, but then Leslie Howard died in the war. Ten producers, a hundred writers, and two title changes later it's a short and nobody can remember what the original idea was or who the writers were. They were now leaning it more in the direction of Abbott and Costello. Cohn said there was once the germ of an idea here and then the germ became a virus, but now the epidemic was under control and he wanted this thing filmed. It would be a fantastic vehicle to launch a comedy team, he said. He told us the premise—two guys run a dance school and start romancing their female students, blah blah blah.

"And the beauty part," Cohn says, "is that Clarence L. Gilbert, who's been here since the silent pictures, would kill to direct this."

Me, Zig, and Vic all looked at each other and nodded very impressed nods. I said, "Wow, Clarence L. Gilbert!"

"Oh yeah," Cohn says. "Ned is literally droolin' to do this picture. Look at the script. See these three spots? That's his spittle." Ned was Clarence Gilbert's nickname.

We took the script back to the Plaza and I said he'd hear from us soon. He threw out a figure to us and I almost got blown off my feet. He said, "Latchkey, this movie the boys could do in a week. There's only two sets. You turn this down, you're mentally ill."

Sally read it and said, "It might work if Sid Stone and Norman took a whack at it. Or forty." We couldn't tell if the script was for Moe Howard or Leslie Howard. I knock on Ziggy's door and hand it to him and twenty minutes later he knocks on my door and says, "It'd need a lot of work." We knock on Vic's door and he's not even in. Turns out he was at Barney's Beanery shooting eight ball. I called Murray at WAT in New York the next day and he says that Harry really wanted us for this picture. He says he can squeeze Columbia for twenty grand and it's less than a week's work. He says, "I don't know if there's anything to lose here, Arn," and I said, "Yeah, but you ain't read the thing. It's so all over the place that it's nowhere."

Dissolve. Next day. We're at MGM, in L. B. Mayer's office, which is as big as the left side of Canada, and we meet the old man. This time Ziggy and Vic are a little looser because, one, there's no threat that Mayer is going to decapitate us—he's like everybody's uncle who falls asleep after a big Thanksgiving meal—and, two, we'd already heard Harry Cohn screaming. Why would you be scared of a furry puppy after being in a cage with a rabid python? But Mayer just isn't paying attention to us . . . Ziggy is trying to yuk it up and L. B. ain't buying it. After taking calls from Tracy, Fleming, Cukor, and Garland and leaving us twiddling our thumbs, he said to us, "Now, why did you fellows want to meet me again?" And I said, "We thought you wanted to meet *us*!" And he said, "Apparently a grave error has been committed." Like the *Bismarck* we sank into the plush leather furniture.

It's time to go and Mayer gets up and walks us to the door. He asks, "Did you two fellows once play a place called Club 18 in New York?" And Ziggy and Vic's faces light up! We thought here's our chance to get in good with the old man. And Vic says, "Yeah, we did!" And Louis B. says, "Yes, I saw you perform . . . you said some very insulting things about me and my company." Teddy, I wanted to grab this guy by his collar and say, "That's what was *supposed* to happen at Club 18, you old bastard! This is like buying tickets for an airplane and then complaining afterward that it left the ground and flew!" Ziggy said to him, "We saw you laughing, though, Mr. Mayer. You can't deny that." And he said, "I can afford to laugh."

We left there with the taste of rust in our mouths.

That night we tried to get Vic to read the script and he said he would. The next morning he and I ate breakfast together and I asked him, "So whatchya think?" and he answered, "I thought the flapjacks were real good."

"Not that. Are you gonna ever read this thing, Vic?"

"Can't you and Ziggy make the decision? I'll do the acting and singing."

"You trust Ziggy with a decision this important?"

"I'll do whatever you want me to do, Latch."

"I want you to read the damn thing is what I want!"

"All right, give me the script then."

"I already did! You've still got it!"

He said to me, "Look, don't get all worked up. We do this movie, we get a sweet payday, we go home. I mean, what's the big deal here? Whaddaya think?"

I was so exasperated that all I could respond was, "I thought the flapjacks were real good, Vic."

The next day a driver from Gus Kahn's office picks us up. Now, I've heard that Gussie Kahn can make Harry Cohn look like a goddamn saint.

He's louder, he's meaner, he's ruder, he's cruder, and, unlike Harry, he don't even like his own relatives. The driver takes us on the scenic route to Galaxy Pictures because, he tells us, Gussie is going to be a little late that day. So we're driving around and the mood in that car was not good. Ziggy is now wanting to get back to New York, and Vic knew that we knew he hadn't read the script. We'd been on trains together, in hotels together since Chicago, we urgently needed to be apart.

"I got a new idear for the radio show, guys. A new bit," Ziggy said. We were all three of us tightly crunched together in the back of that car.

"I got an idea for the radio show too, Zig," Vic said. "We cancel it."

"Why you wanna cancel it for?"

"'Cause I got better things to do at night than that."

"Like what, Vic? Bang as many broads as you can before you marry Lu?"

"Yeah, Zig, that *is* what I'm doing. It's a plan. I figure, I get that out of my system before I'm a married man, then maybe I won't want to do it so much when I am one. And at least, partner, I don't have to pay for it."

Ziggy elides over the latter part of that statement and says, "And we should cancel the radio show on account of this ten-point Marshall Plan of yours?"

"Guys, please," I said.

Vic says to the driver, "Where the hell are we, buddy?"

"I thought I'd show you some of California's beautiful shoreline, Mr. Fountain."

We were in Santa Monica. Right near the pier.

"Did I say I wanted to see the goddamn shoreline, you fuckin' punk?!" Vic barks at the poor kid. "Did I ask to see that?!"

"S-s-sorry," the poor kid simpers.

"I grew up near the goddamn shoreline! I need to see the same goddamn thing here?!"

"But this ain't the same ocean, Vic," Ziggy butts in. "This is the Pacific."

Vic gets out of the car, he's in a rage. He opens the driver-side door and pulls the driver out by his collar. He grabs the cap off the kid and stomps on it a few times. Vic gets back in, into the driver's seat, while me and Ziggy just sit there with our jaws slung open to New Zealand. "I'll fuckin' drive us where we wanna fuckin' go!!!" Vic yells.

Five minutes later Vic says, "Where were we going again?"

"To Galaxy Pictures," I told him. "Do you have any idea where that might be?"

So Vic pulls a U-turn and drives back to the pier . . . Vic gets out and grabs the kid again by the collar and pushes him back into the driver's seat.

"Take us to Galaxy, kid," Vic says. "Here." And he hands him $300.

"Gee, thanks, Mr. Fountain," the driver says.

So we arrive at this meeting not in such a fantastic mood. And Gus Kahn ain't even there. The secretary tells us that and Vic mutters to me, "Let's just do the *Dunce With Me* flick, Latch, okay?" I reminded him the name of the vehicle was *Shall We Dunce?* The secretary says that Gus Kahn is at the track today and he'd like to meet us there—the driver will take us to Santa Anita right away. This seemed to ameliorate Vic's mood somewhat, but Ziggy quickly soured. "We gotta go to the track, Arn?" he asked me in a sort of annoying whine. "Maybe we should just do the dunce flick for Columbia."

An hour later we're at the track sitting next to Genghis Kahn himself. The man is five foot three and dresses like a millionaire, which he was, of course, and he's got these solid gold binoculars around his neck. He barely looks at us the entire day. He's got a flunky there, maybe an assistant producer or something . . . Gus studies the racing form, tells this flunky to go bet so much on so-and-so, and then off goes the guy. Well, Gus is blowing hot and cold today, winning and losing. Me and Vic start betting but we cannot believe the sums that Kahn is wagering. "A thousand on the three horse, Bill," he says. "Put two grand on the nine horse," he says. Every time he does this, me, Ziggy, and Vic turn to each other in awe. But Gus don't see this, because the man is just glued to those binoculars. At one point he says to us, "I hear you guys are hilarious. Is it true?" Ziggy says, "Yeah, we can be pretty funny." "I saw you at Club 18 a few years ago," Gus says, "and I did notice that you were of a humorous bent. Bill, let's get serious now. Eight grand on Wayfarer to win. The five horse, that big roan colt." And off goes Bill the flunky while me, Zig, and Vic are cowering in our seats at the quantity of brass in this guy's balls. "Are you going to do that dunce picture for Columbia?" Kahn asks us. I told him we didn't know yet. Kahn tells us it had been a Galaxy property at one point. He said a short comedy about two dance teachers was a nifty premise for a picture; a few songs, some clownin' around and romance, a pretty girl . . . it could launch a movie career like you were shot out of a howitzer. He said he wished he still had it. If Cohn was willing to sell him back the property, he said, he'd buy it for top dollar and turn it into a full-length picture. Maybe get Gene Kelly and Betty Grable. I asked him if Clarence L. Gilbert was reliable and he said, "Oh, there's no one better than Ned. No one. He'll make the boys look like a million bucks."

Bill the flunky comes back and says the bet's been placed. The horse finishes dead last.

Gus says to Bill the flunky, "Bill, this is what we're doing . . . I'm buyin' this horse. Today. Buy it for three grand. And the minute he's mine, I want him destroyed."

Still shuddering from that, that night I canceled the meeting at Paramount.

"We'll do the picture," I told Harry Cohn the next day. "When can we get started?"

SALLY KLEIN: It was the first real argument I had with Arnie. He was blinded by the easy money, I'm sure he'll admit that. I read the script and I could just tell this thing was a stinker.

"The only way the boys should do this," I told him, "is if Sid and Norman can work some of their magic with it. Although I doubt anyone's wand is that big."

"Why them? Columbia has a hundred writers on their staff," he said.

"That's the problem. This thing has been through the mill already."

"You want Danny to look at this, don't you?"

"I think," I said slowly, "that he could help too. Arnie, they know Ziggy and Vic better than anyone. This script is not Fountain and Bliss."

"How do I know you just don't want Danny back in the fold?"

"Don't you too?"

He nodded. "Look," he said, "it's a short picture, it's an easy twenty grand. I say we cancel our engagement at the Blue Beret and just have the boys do this thing."

"Can you at least *send* it to Sidney and Norman? Please?"

I got that out of him. They got the script the same day. And we got it back that night at the hotel. Sid Stone had written on a note: "I work with a typewriter, not gasoline and matches. That's what this screenplay needs. All the very best, Sid."

LULU FOUNTAIN: I was all set to come in to New York to see Vic at the Blue Beret. But Estelle calls me and says that they've canceled so that they could make a movie. I was pretty angry. Estelle has to call me? Vic can't? For three days I walked around and I could've killed Vic if he was around. Then Dominick says to me, "Vic's making movies now, Lu. That's very serious business." And I realized that I was now engaged to a movie star.

FRANK LUDLAM [assistant director of *Shall We Dunce?*]: It was not the worst piece of garbage I was ever involved in, but it was certainly in the same heap. The behind-the-scenes people were either very new, such as myself, or were old veterans on the way out. The director was Clarence Gilbert; Ned had never directed a movie before. He was about fifty-five years old then and was Columbia's second-string makeup and wardrobe test director. You want to see how Rhonda Fleming or George Montgomery looks with a new coat, a new hairdo, or different makeup, you shoot twenty seconds of it with different lighting. That's what Ned Gilbert did.

Vic Fountain and Ziggy Bliss were never anything less than professional. I think they were too scared to "act up." When the hairdresser poured a ton of Vitalis on Ziggy's hair, he did not protest. There were a few of us, myself included, who knew right then that this little movie would die . . . to do that to Ziggy Bliss's hair would be like shaving Charlie Chaplin's mustache.

The lead actress was Frances Alcott, who was our model for wardrobe and hairstyle test shoots, filling in when the actual stars couldn't make it. I had coffee with her one day and she said to me, "Where the hell did Harry find these two?" When I told her they were big on the nightclub circuit, Frances rolled her eyes—she merely wanted to finish this job.

There were two songs in the movie; both were written by Ernie Beasley. Vic Fountain was already quite adept when it came to lip-synching. He did have some trouble memorizing his lines though. One very brief scene required about ten takes; I remember Vic Fountain saying to Ned, "Hey, I only read this thing this morning, buddy!" But there was never any fooling around or destructive behavior on the set, as characterized their later films.

When the filming was over, their manager, Arnold Latchkey, walked up to Ned and asked him how he thought it went. Ned said they were very good to work with and it'd be interesting to see how they'd look with the makeup and wardrobe.

DANNY McGLUE: They looked utterly lost up there. It was about twenty minutes too long and it was only a twenty-two minute film. I'm not saying this out of sour grapes, but the screenplay was a mess. It was a little Three Stooges, a little Ritz Brothers, a little Abbott and Costello. It was like cooking with all your leftovers: chicken chow mein, lasagna, a burrito—it's going to end up one stinkorama of a meal. The only thing this movie is memorable for is that Vic got to sing Ernie Beasley's "The Hang of It." [*Singing:*] "*Now, I've got the hang of it, I've got that Sturm and Drang of it, I've got the yin and yang of it . . .*"

Ziggy looked like a gibbon up there. They didn't know what to do with him—the director, the screenwriter, the makeup and wardrobe departments. They tried to tame his hair, but once in a while a strand or two would spring up, which made him look like he had horns.

"I thought these two were supposed to be funny," a guy sitting behind me in the theater said to his date.

Snuffy said to me, "Danny boy, if Zig and Vic wanted to kill any chance they ever had at a successful movie career, man, did they ever choose the right vehicle."

• • •

ARNIE LATCHKEY: Now, Hunny Gannett knew Max Rosenbloom, the prizefighter who opened up Slapsie Maxie's in L.A. (When he was just a light heavyweight, Hunny had gotten pummeled by Max.) Maxie and the club bumped an act and let Fountain and Bliss do a week. We had to cancel a week at the Blue Beret, which did not go over well. "This is very, very unprofessional!" Pete Conifer said over the phone. "Oh, I realize that, Pete," I said. What was I going to do—deny it? I told him that the opportunity to do a movie had come up. Pete said, "Well, it better be good." And I forewarned him that, no, it would not be. Pete had to scramble to get a replacement. He wanted a comic. Vic said to me, "Pete could get Snuff for the week . . . he'd do it." Ziggy said, "No. Snuffy can't work a room that size." I said to Ziggy I thought Snuffy could handle it. Ziggy said, "No. I know Snuffy, I know his limitations. If Pete signs him, it's his own funeral." So Pete got a singer instead, I think it was Tony Martin or Al Martino.

SALLY KLEIN: My third date with Jack, we went to see Fountain and Bliss at Maxie's. The first two dates, Jack had taken me to the Brown Derby and House of Murphy. He was fifteen years older than me, was thin and bald, and his wife had died two years earlier. He'd already had one heart attack. When we sat down at our table at Slapsie Maxie's a terrible thought occurred to me: Oh my God, what if this Jack Klein laughs so much he has a heart attack and dies? Well, he *was* laughing his head off, the whole audience was, but fortunately he survived the show.

Jack was very polite, very quiet. When I took him backstage to meet the boys, Vic was effusive and polite and doing the Vic thing, joking around and pinching Jack's cheeks, but Ziggy was aloof and sort of wary. I wanted to say to him, So if this Jack Klein fella isn't good enough for you, then I might as well go back to Danny McGlue!

The engagement got some wonderful press . . . Bobby Hale of the *Examiner* went a few times and gave it raves, and Billy Wilkerson of *The Hollywood Reporter* was a big fan. Many celebrities turned out. Orson Welles, Ava Gardner, who was just so gorgeous, Cary Grant, the Gary Coopers. You should have seen Vic imitating Gary Cooper. It was really priceless. You know that an act is doing very well when the waiters, busboys, and hatcheck girls are cracking up. On the final night, Clark Gable came backstage and said, "I heard you guys did a picture for Columbia. Congratulations." Ziggy said, "Yeah, Ned Gilbert directed it." "Gee, sorry, guys," Gable said and then slunked out with a queasy look on his face.

SNUFFY DUBIN: [Agent] Leo Silver calls me and says he hears the Blue Beret needs a comic for five nights. My life is at a new low now—I'm drinking too much, I'm playing dives, I'm picking up junkie chicks and taking them home with me and they're getting sick in my bed. But out of all this misery, pain, and loneliness, I'm slowly finding a new voice in my act. Before, when I was just a raw comic, I did *jokes*. Myron Cohen, Henny Youngman stuff. My room was so small, my wife is so ugly, my taxi driver was so bad, man walks into a psychiatrist's office, horse walks into a bar. What I'm trying to do now, though, is tell *stories*. The story itself is the funny thing; the way I tell it is funny. The problem is, though, the places I'm playing, nobody is liking it. I play the China Doll on Broadway or the Town and Country Club in Brooklyn, I get booed out the door. They're too drunk, they're too stupid, they got their hands up their secretary's skirt at their table. They want the dumb psychiatrist-walks-into-a-horse jokes. The only good thing about the China Doll was that Charlie the bartender had a good pill connection, some quiff-fiend pharmacist from Jackson Heights he used to set up with the girls working the bar.

I call Pete Conifer and told him word had gotten to me that the Blue Beret needed someone. But that pervert iced me. He said they got a singer in to replace Ziggy and Vic. I said, I'll open for the singer. He said, Snuff, I can't do this. I said, Pete, I'm on my knees in my apartment right now, listen to me, I'm fucking begging. I'll work the club, you just give me ten bucks a night. He said, Snuffy, I can't do this. I say, I'll do it for free, Pete, for free. He says, Snuffy, I can't do it. I ask him, Pete, is this Pete Conifer talking to me or is this Fountain and Bliss talking through you? And he says, I can't do this, Snuffy.

I got off the phone and I popped a pill, poured myself a scotch, and fell asleep.

●　●　●

LULU FOUNTAIN: I'm not gonna lie. I got lucky marrying Vic. If it wasn't for him, I might've married some guy who fishes for cod or maybe even not got married at all. I wasn't the prettiest girl on Buzzard's Bay . . . but somehow I wound up living in Beverly Hills, going to fancy restaurants, and meeting all these big stars.

I know the things people used to say when they'd see me with Vic. I know 'cause I heard it sometimes. I was at Serge's [Beauty Parlor] one day and some lady under a dryer is looking at *Photoplay,* which had a picture of me, Vic, and Vic's mom. This woman says to her friend, "I can't tell which one's the mother and which one's the wife." Everyone always wondered why he married me.

[Vic and I] were married at the Church of Saint Vincent Ferrer on Lexington Avenue. Vic picked the place and when he told me the name, I thought Vincent Ferrer was some actor or singer buddy of his with a church named after him. Vic's mom picked out the gown for me but when I tried it on in New York, Jane White and Sally told me I couldn't wear it. I said to 'em, I can't not wear it, Violetta Fontana picked it out! She's going to be my mother-in-law! You can't wear black wool, they told me. I said to 'em, Look, I come from Codport, I'm not from New York. I don't read *Harper's Bazaar*. Estelle says to me, But, Lu, you're going to be living in New York, there will be photographers there, this will be in the papers, Vic is a big deal. They offered to take me to Saks and Lord & Taylor's, said they would get me something suitable. I didn't like the way they was talking to me, especially Jane. She spent more on clothes in a day than most families do on food in a year. I just wanted to get married, move into my new home, and start a big family.

JANE WHITE: Being a wife and a mother is not easy. Being a celebrity's wife is particularly hard. There is so much temptation for a young entertainer, or even an older one—the girls, the late nights, the booze, the long trips away from home. I thought Ziggy and I would last forever. I thought Fountain and Bliss would last forever.

Lulu and I were not the best of friends. Whenever we had to do publicity shoots for Ziggy and Vic, we put on a little show, but we really had nothing in common but our husbands. I thought in many ways she was low class, frankly. A friend of mine once said she was about as refined as tar. Well, actually, I said that. But Vic was not too refined either. With him it was charming but on Lulu it did not work. I used to try to get her to improve her look. We'd go to Bullock's and I. Magnin and try on Chanel, Balenciaga, Pucci, Dior, Bill Blass, Yves Saint Laurent; we went to Elizabeth Arden in Beverly Hills. She had a nice little figure. But her taste in clothing was somewhere between drab and none at all. When we'd leave the store, it was always me holding ten shopping bags and her holding the door.

But to this day I respect Lulu. Vic put her through hell. All the girls, hundreds of them, all the late nights, the gambling and carousing. Some people would say that Lulu was a sucker for staying with Vic as long as she did. But she had a strong sense of family. She did what she did for her kids. Her marriage was a shambles but still, she stuck it out.

But sometimes, yes, I do think she really was a sucker.

SALLY KLEIN: Janie and Lulu—forget Fountain and Bliss, Ted, you could write a book just about those two! Before the wedding, Jane was really annoying poor Lu, really getting on her case. And that was to her face. But behind Lulu's back she was saying the most horrendous things. Now, I knew about Vic and all his girlfriends. Well, Jane kept saying things like, "How is that little twig going to keep Vic happy? The marriage won't last to the reception! She's nothing but a piece of salami." I said to Estelle, "I can't believe the things that Jane is saying!" And she said, "Neither can I . . . but a lot of it is true!"

ARNIE LATCHKEY: Morty Geist came up with the idea and it was pure genius. Vic's got a guest list for the wedding, it's maybe a hundred people. So what do we do? We send out about eight hundred invitations. We sent them to everybody and to anybody. We sent invites to Dr. Oppenheimer from the Manhattan Project, to Teller and to Einstein too. We sent them to actors and actresses and socialites that Fountain and Bliss had never met. What we were looking for—and, boy, what we got!—was an overflow crowd, maybe even if things went right, a slightly hysterical, out-of-control crowd. Bertie alerted the press the day before the wedding that he'd heard from the police there was going to be a mob scene, and then he called the police and told them he'd heard from the press there was going to be a mob scene. Everybody picks it up. It's in Winchell, it's in Sullivan, it's in [Leonard] Lyons and Earl Wilson and Hilda Fleury, it's like it's in skywriting! The final result? You've got this wedding of Vic Fountain to this little Italian girl from Codport at the Church of José Ferrer [sic] and there are two hundred cops, thirty fotogs, and about a thousand people screaming their *kishkes* off and they got no reason why.

It was beautiful!

ESTELLE LATCHKEY: It was one of the most miserable moods I've ever seen Ziggy in. Nobody knew the term "manic-depressive" back then . . . I don't even know if there was such a term. I know he could go from being very, very zany to being very, very miserable in the space of a second. The week of the wedding he tried to make everyone as miserable as he was—is there a word for *that* condition, I wonder?—and succeeded.

SALLY KLEIN: Vic was getting married but you'd have thought that it was Ziggy marrying the Bitch of Belsen. He'd come in sulking and in a lousy, hostile mood. We had two kids writing for us now, two brothers named Barry and Manny Singer. This was their first week, as a matter of fact. They'd done some comedy at Grossinger's and the Concord and then some radio. They'd hand Ziggy a radio script and he would read it for a minute or pretend to read it and then he would lace into these two. "You two are ignorant! How dumb are you two? This isn't funny! Are we paying you to write tragedy? This is *Oedipus Rex* you're handing me! Who the hell ever told you you were funny!" I think the first time this happened,

Barry Singer (who later wrote for Jack Paar, by the way) thought it was a prank; he kept waiting for Ziggy to stop his tirade and then start laughing. But it didn't happen. Manny I thought was going to die. He was very sensitive and after a few of these attacks he went into the bathroom and Vic heard him crying.

"What the hell's got into Zig?" Vic asked me that week.

"You're marrying Lulu," I told him. "He's jealous."

"Wha—? He wants me to marry *him* instead?"

"He's jealous of any shred of attention that anybody but him gets."

That week the act was performing at El Morocco—I think they were getting about $20,000 for sixteen shows a week then—and this young pretty British singer Julie Mansell was opening for them. They called her "the Nightingale of Berkeley Square." She was [British comedian] Eddie Bramshill's girl then. She was maybe twenty-two years old, just a little darling. And Ziggy wanted her off the bill. He called her into his dressing room and he was yelling at her so loud that the stagehands had to go in there and restrain him. "You look like a piece of spaghetti!" he was yelling. "You sing like a sparrow with a whistle caught in its throat!" This poor dear broke down crying, she had no idea what she'd done wrong.

"I'm not going to quit, Mr. Bliss. I'm simply not going to," she told him. You know, that whole stiff upper British lip.

"I didn't expect you to, you goddamn piece of string!" he spat back at her. "I can get rid of you!"

"You can't go around doing stuff like that, Zig," Vic told him when he found out about this explosion.

Ziggy said, "Oh no? They paid her off for the week and fired her."

JANE WHITE: Oh, I remember it quite well. The columnists caught wind of what Ziggy did to her. Hilda Fleury was calling Ziggy all sorts of names in her column. I asked Ziggy about it, if he had really yelled all those nasty things at her, and he said that I should never believe anything I read about him in the papers unless it was something good.

DOMINICK MANGIAPANE: It was some ceremony—all those people yelling outside the church, the fans and the cops. The police would be pushing people back and the fans would push the cops the other way. The headline in the paper was "A REAL COMEDY RIOT!"

Look, I didn't approve of the marriage . . . I thought Vic was a bum and a cheat, but still it was a very nice wedding.

Vic's sister Cathy was the maid of honor. Bruno looked very big and very quiet in his black suit, and Vic's mother was arguing with the priest. I kept looking for Tony Ferro and his wife but I found out they weren't invited.

CATHERINE RICCI: One minute before they're going to exchange vows, who stands up and walks out? Ziggy Bliss! *Who does this?! What kind of human being or animal does this?!* Not even a ferret would scamper out at that time. Maybe Ziggy was upset that he wasn't Vic's best man—Hunny Gannett did the honors and it took him a few seconds to find the ring—but still, you don't create such a commotion at another person's wedding! He told people he wasn't feeling well and had to go home, but I don't believe it.

The reception was at the Waldorf. Vic pulled out all the stops. Mayor La Guardia was even there. I was crying all day; my little brother a big star, marrying a hometown girl. His suit must have cost a thousand dollars. All sorts of celebrities were there and it was in every paper. There was dancing and Billy Ross's band and so much champagne. Snuffy Dubin made a nice, long funny toast that had everybody in stitches. And I saw Sally, who hadn't married Jack yet, dancing with Danny McGlue.

Late in the evening, Lulu came up to me and asked me if I'd seen Vic. I realized I hadn't. I asked Carmine if he'd seen him. He hadn't. Ray and Mamma hadn't seen him since the church.

GUY PUGLIA: I didn't go to the ceremony or the reception and I'll tell you why. Hunny had the idea to put the bandage on my face and then put some putty underneath to make it look like I still had my nose. But every person in that church would know I didn't. So I sat home and listened to a ball game and drank a couple of beers. It was a hot day and I had the window open and the fan going. Alls of a sudden there's a knock on the door and who is it? It's Vic. In his slick wedding getup.

"Hey, wasn't you getting married today?" I say to him. He says, "Oh yeah, I took care of that. Gimme a Ballantine." I get him a beer and he undoes his tie and says, "Now why the fuck did I go and do that? Huh? Tell me?" I ask, "Do what?" and he says, "Marry Lulu? I could be with Lana Turner maybe or Linda Darnell or Rita Hayworth." "Lulu's a good gal. Jesus," I tell him, "I'd like to get married someday. But I guess I never will now." "What's the score here, pal?" he asks me, and I tell him, "Yankees are up six to one."

He pulled up a chair to the radio and we sat in front of the window, where the fan was. We drank beer after beer and then we both conked out. When we woke up it was about ten. I said to him, "You better go home, pal."

"Nah, why don't you come out? Let's you, me, and Hunny go out and have a blast."

I reminded him it was his honeymoon night and he said he knew that.

He said, "I'm gonna have the rest of my life with her, so what's one night?" He reaches Hunny at the Waldorf and they decide they're going to go to the Latin Quarter and get blasted. He grabs his coat and heads for the door and says, "See ya, Guy."

I told him to hold up and wait for me.

SALLY KLEIN: Lulu wanted to go to Miami Beach for their honeymoon, but Vic hated the water, absolutely hated it. She also thought of a cruise to France but Vic refused to go on a boat; he said he'd only go if there were indoor shuffleboard courts where he could hustle the other passengers. Then Murray Katz cinched a big deal for Fountain and Bliss that was too good to pass up: a cross-country tour, opening up movies in large theaters, playing the very biggest clubs. And it was going to end at the old Venetian Theater in New York. So there was no honeymoon.

The Monday after the wedding Ziggy gets a call at the office. It's from Jane White. She'd been arrested at Gimbel's for stealing a patent-leather belt. She said that she'd been buying a few accessories and trying on some things and had accidentally walked out of the store with the belt on. When the security man was questioning her, she tried to explain what had happened and showed him how much money was in her purse . . . then the man noticed that the purse had a price tag on it from Saks. She said her boyfriend was Ziggy Bliss, and the man asked her which department store she stole *him* from. So right away Ziggy called [money manager] Shep Lane and they had her out of jail in only a few hours.

"You don't have to go around stealing belts, honey," Ziggy said to her.

"I wasn't stealing! It was an honest mistake," she insisted.

"Anyways, if you want a belt just tell me and I'll get you twenty of 'em."

"You will?" she said. And he gave that babyish expression, like his aunt had just bought him a jelly apple. "My hero Ziggy!" she said.

Do you know what Shep and Arnie eventually did? They brought a thousand dollars to all the big stores: Macy's, Bloomingdale's, B. Altman, Ohrbach's, Wanamaker's. A thousand dollars to each place! They gave it to them and said that when they saw Jane White take something, just let her go. Let her leave the store and write down what she'd taken and then take that out of the thousand. Janie must have thought she was a master thief, that loony girl.

We'd get a call a week. Arnie would yell out, "Saks! Four hundred and ten dollars!" Which meant that she only had that much left on her Saks "account." Shep and Arnie had a little side wager going, which place she'd drain first. Evidently Jane liked Lord & Taylor a lot.

• • •

ARNIE LATCHKEY: What scant attention the dunce flick got was highly negative. Bosley Crowther of the *Times* massacred it. He'd seen the act live and he said that this was not the Fountain and Bliss he knew. "Someone slipped them a Mickey Finn," he wrote. The *Herald Tribune* skinned it alive. So did the *Globe*, the *Post,* and the *News*. Archer Winsten butchered it. We had all the newspapers on the floor at the office and it was like the room was a slaughterhouse, there was so much blood and gore on them.

But one thing about show business, it's not all "What have you done for me lately?"—it's also "What can you do for me in the next twenty seconds?" You get knocked off your high wire, you dust off the powder that once was your spine, and you hop back on.

Murray, Sally, and I had a tour booked that would obliterate all the bad news in one fell swoop. Boston, Hartford, Atlantic City, Philly, Baltimore, Chicago, Detroit. Also, Miami and Atlanta and finally out west to L.A. at the Pantages Theater. And then back to play the Venetian. It was going to be a monster of merriment, a leviathan of laughter, a Goliath of guffaws. The Venetian sat over thirty-five hundred people . . . did you know the aisles were canals and the ushers dressed as gondoliers and poled you to your seats? It's true. (But Vic refused to go in the gondolas.) We made sure that in every town we went to, we'd be playing the biggest place, open for the best movie. This was take-no-prisoners, brook-no-quarter, no-holds-barred time. We were out to scorch the earth, my friend, and scorch it we did.

We got off to a flying stop. We test-drove the act at Bill Lee's joint in Fort Lee [New Jersey], the Riviera. We did five nights there and it went over like lead. We'd been coasting on the old stuff for a while now, on Danny, Sid, and Norman's stuff, but now that rolling stone had gathered a touch of moss. Don't get me wrong: The act was never in grave or critical condition, but was, at best, only slightly stable. And there was some friction.

Vic would sing "The Hang of It" for an opener before Ziggy came on. It was really a swinging number and the audience lapped it up. When Vic warbled this tune, you should've seen Ziggy's face when he realized the crowd loved it. One by one the freckles on his skin turned purple. After two nights, Ziggy says to me, "Vic's killing the act with that song. It's gotta go."

"How is he killing it?" I asked. "You've got five hundred people out there snapping their fingers and tapping their feet. The number really gets the juice flowing, Zig."

"He's killing it because he's killing *me*. We can't have this song in the act."

Sally had warned me this might happen. Hey, you think [comedian] Milt Kamen wants to come on right after Sinatra sings "I've Got You Under My Skin"? How'd you like to be a lousy ventriloquist comin' on right after Lincoln does the Gettysburg Address? So, yeah, I sympathized with Ziggy. But I bravely held my ground and said, "You really should talk to Vic about this."

After a few shows—we did two a night—we're back in the Brill Building and Ziggy says, "This old stuff was once lightning in a bottle but what we got now is just the bottle."

Barry Singer said that there was still time to change stuff, that he and Manny could tinker. I felt bad for those two. They were good kids.

"What if we end with that 'Hang of It' number?" Ziggy said. "Let's put that at the end, after all the routines."

Vic said, "That song gets the crowd in the mood, man. We put that at the end, we—"

"Can we at least try it?" Ziggy said. "Why don't we start with Vic singin' 'Mamselle'?"

I was worried he'd suggest that. That song, which Art Lund had a big hit with, Vic almost fell asleep while he was singing.

So we gave it a shot . . . and it didn't work. Vic and I were right. This song got the juice surging, the toes tapping, the drinks flowing. So between sets we told Billy Ross that the number was back in the beginning.

So what happens in our final set? Vic is chirping this tune and all of a sudden one of the trumpets is sounding a little diseased. Up from the pit stands Ziggy holding the horn. And Ziggy begins to engage in some comedic repartee with Vic. But Vic is a little stunned, like he'd been caught in the jaw with a jab, and he's a little ticked off here. But Vic braved this storm. You could tell though—perhaps by how tightly he was clenching his fists, perhaps by how hard he was biting his lips, or perhaps more so by the fact that he later said to me, "One day I'm going to carve that fat sonuvabitch into little pieces"—that Vic was not enjoying this. After that show, he pulled Ziggy aside and it was just the two of them in a dark corner . . . I couldn't hear what Vic was saying to him—it sounded more like hissing than anything—but Ziggy looked pale afterward.

We tried everything at the Riviera. We jiggled things, we juggled it, we tinkered and toyed. The problem was that every single person at the Riviera had already seen the act. Look, I can listen to Sinatra doing "I'm a Fool to Want You" a thousand times, but how many times can I listen to Shelley Berman doing the exact same bit on the imaginary phone with his mother?

We took a few weeks off after the Fort Lee engagement. In that time Jane White discovered Tiffany, and—perhaps more important—Tiffany discovered Jane White. Shep Lane and I brought two grand over there to begin an account for her. That's when Shep told me that Vic was keeping two apartments. He and Lu had moved into this massive place on Central Park South but he also now kept a swank suite at the St. Regis.

"That don't bode too good," I said to Shep.

SNUFFY DUBIN: Ziggy came to see my act at Jimmy Geary's Sapphire Lounge one night. This place was a dive so deep you got the bends just walking through the front door, and Ziggy had bigger tits than the waitresses, depending on what he'd eaten for breakfast. When he told me I needed to go back to the old one-liner stuff, I told him to shove it. But, you know, I had to be careful now . . . 'cause I'm working joints like this black hole of Calcutta and 'cause his name is in Ed fucking Sullivan's column every day.

There was this one blonde there named Bubbles Van Boven at the Sapphire; this girl used to balance a tray full of martinis on her chest. One night, while Ziggy and I are talking and while I'm pretending to listen to him complain about Vic, I can see he's got the hot nuts for her. You gotta picture it: It's four in the morning now, the amphetamines I've taken have worn off, and I just wanna go to the Belmore Cafeteria, get some eggs, and then go back to my pad and watch the sun rise over the Queensborough Bridge and over my miserable fucking life. "Vic thinks he's the whole act," Ziggy says. "It's a good thing Bertie Kahn plants screaming girls in the crowd, it covers up his lousy singing," he says. "I could make any ginzo singer four hundred thou a year." "Hey," I tell him, "Vic's got great comic timing. He sets you up like he's throwing batting practice." "My shoe can do that, Snuff," he says. I doze off in my chair and when I wake up, there's only one guy in there, some old shine with a mop. I say to this cat, "Where'd the guy I was with go?" And he says, "That little round man with that Brillo head? He in the back with Miss Bubbles."

I go to my dressing room and everything's all blurry like it's underwater, you know? I open the door and there's Bubbles Van Boven, naked and on her knees, and Ziggy is bending over her and rubbing his head in her cleavage. In one hand she's got fifty bucks and with the other she's pumping that rhino prick of his and, Jesus, did I walk in at the wrong second! *Thwack!* All over my brand-new houndstooth jacket hanging on the coatrack.

The next thing I know I'm sitting in the Belmore at a long table and I'm nodding off into my two eggs over easy, and what's the first thing I hear? " . . . And another lousy thing about Vic. He don't even get the jokes . . ." I perk my head up out of the gray ooze it's in and there he is, rattling away, complaining about his partner, and I've got on the houndstooth-check jacket with a jizz stain the size and shape of fucking Greenland.

SALLY KLEIN: The tour began in New York at the Luxor . . . the boys were opening a Fritz Devane movie called *Such a Wonderful Time.* We had a choice, we could've opened either that or *The Treasure of the Sierra Madre* or *Red River.* But when we were presented with this by Murray Katz, Vic's eyes lit up. "We gotta open up the Fritz movie, we've got to," he said.

The Singer brothers had sort of given up, they weren't giving it their all. We tried to get some of the old craziness going, putting on wigs and hats and stuff, and Barry and Manny were funny but not our kind of funny. Manny came to me and said, "Sal, it's not working out and we want to do what's best for the act. So what should we do?"

I had dinner with Estelle and Arnie at the Colony and we knew what we had to do. "I'll call Danny McGlue tomorrow," Arnie said. "His wilderness years are over. Sally, you call Norman and Sid." I said, "What happens if Ziggy has a fit about Danny?" and Arnie said, "We'll buy some new furniture first thing tomorrow just to keep in reserve."

But Ziggy didn't have a fit. He took me aside and said, "Look, when I busted up you and Danny I did it for you. I didn't think he was good enough for you." He said, "It didn't have nuttin' to do with the religion thing . . . I don't care about that. I mean, look at me and Janie, right?"

"Jane White is really Judith Weissblau or have you forgotten?" I reminded him.

"She's the one who forgot that," he said, "not me."

DANNY McGLUE: I'd just left the *Ex-Lax Modern Romances* show at ABC and was writing for *A Date With Judy* for NBC. That show was cornier than Iowa and Nebraska combined. Betsy Cantwell was in the cast, she was a pretty brunette from York, Pennsylvania—she played Penny Jones on the show—and we'd begun seeing each other. I was in my little dust closet of an office trying to come up with some dialogue one day and the phone rang. "Danny *bubeleh*, how are ya?!" Arnie's voice booms over the line. "How am I?" I say. "I'm writing for *A Date With Judy*, that's how I am. How are you?" And he cuts right to the chase and says, "How quick can you get to the Brill Building?" And I say to him, "I've got to finish this show, Arn, I can't just—" and he said, "Oh, yes you can. Barry and Manny Singer'll finish it . . . get your *tuches* over here pronto. And make sure you don't run the Singers over when you pass one another in the street."

And that was it. Back in the fold.

ARNIE LATCHKEY: When I had enough free time to pop the question to Estelle, she popped the answer "yes" right back to me. "Do you think it's smart," she sagely inquired of me, "that we'd be married and I'd still be your receptionist?" to which I lovingly replied, "You're not only right, *you're fired!*" So when we hitched up, I let her go and we hired Millie Roth, who, like Estelle, also had been working in *shmattes*.

MILLIE ROTH [assistant at Vigorish, Inc.]: My first few weeks on the job were very active. The Singer brothers had just left and Danny McGlue signed back on, Sidney Stone and Norman White flew in from California and we put them up at the Woodstock Hotel, and Lulu Fountain was pregnant. Ernie Beasley came in with three or four new songs and Billy Ross worked out the arrangements. The office was what you would call a beehive of activity. I remember that Ziggy was very friendly to me—not in *that* way, no—and he took me out to lunch at Lindy's a few times and I met all sorts of famous Broadway people.

That was also the time that people realized that Ernie Beasley was not attracted to women. Vic and Ziggy were getting on his case about not ever having a girlfriend—Ziggy said to him, "What are you, some kinda *faygeleh?*"—and his face turned as red as a beet. We realized it in an instant. Vic said to him, "Ernie, I don't care if you like boys, girls, black, white, purple, or sheep or cats. You just keep cranking out them songs. Oh yeah. And just keep your paws offa me." Which got a big laugh all around.

There was an unflattering comment in Grayling Greene's column about Vic, I remember that. It hinted that Vic—it never mentioned his name—could learn a thing or two about being faithful to his not-so-long-suffering bride. Vic read that and hit the ceiling. He called Grayling Greene scum, lower than scum, and then he finally settled on "not even scum." Arnie had Bertie call Mr. Greene, but the damage had been done. Now, I've never told anyone this, but I am dead certain that Ziggy had planted this item with Grayling Greene.

When Vic calmed down they got back to the business of writing and rehearsing. I'd never met Sidney Stone or Norman White before. If you saw them, you would not think these two men were funny. They both dressed very conservatively and looked like businessmen. Sid Stone always wore dark Brooks Brothers suits. But two hours into a meeting, his tie was undone, his jacket and vest were on the floor, and he's standing on his head talking gobbledygook! I kept notes and sometimes I was laughing so much I couldn't write a thing. But Danny McGlue was the person who kept things going; he was the motor and organizer. He would suggest this or that if something wasn't going right, and then it did go right.

Ziggy had told me that Danny and Sally had once been very serious about each other, but you wouldn't have known it; although once in a while I would catch Danny sneaking a peek at her and at other times her sneaking one at him. Come to think of it, that happened a lot, so maybe you would have known it.

ARNIE LATCHKEY: Oh, we were clicking again! That fan*tab*ulous, *fun*-derful magic and manic energy was back. We had a map up on the wall of the United States and Sally had put pins in at all our upcoming stops. Bertie called one day and asked us how we'd like it if Morty Geist from L.A. went along on the tour and I said to him, "Has he calmed down yet?" I mean, you could hear Morty sweating over the phone.

The thing began at the Luxor. On the marquee above the title of the movie—which was your typical Devane snoozefest that did decent box office—it said FISSION FUNNYMEN FOUNTAIN & BLISS. Four shows a day they did. Morty and Bertie really played up the "dare angle," that's what they called it. The ads said something like "In the last five years, over fifty people have had to be taken to the hospital during a Fountain and Bliss show. Can *you* handle it?" They had ten ambulances outside, they had a hundred tanks of oxygen inside as well as real doctors and nurses (supposedly). But the coup was they had about ten plants there, people to fake being taken ill. One woman—this was Morty's brainstorm—had a little thermos of water . . . at some point during the show, she would pour the water over herself and then go running out. She had just tinkled herself from laughing, it looked like! After two nights, though, we didn't need her because there were about five or so people every show who really would wet themselves with laughter.

Before we left town Fritz Devane showed up and came out for a bow and said a few words. Nobody knew this was going to happen. Devane is talking to about two thousand people and the boys are backstage and Vic said to Ziggy, "Hey, partner, remember what we did to that magician at the Circle Theater in Indy? Well, let's do it again with this son of a bitch." And they were on the stage behind Fritzy and he had no goddamn idea. They were doing this pantomime thing, making funny gestures and moves, and Fritz was getting laughs and had no idea why. His motion picture was like *The Best Years of Our Lives* but with music, and Devane was going on about how we should remember our nation's veterans and war dead and their sacrifices and how *he* should be remembered come Oscar time, but people are rolling in the aisles! Fritz couldn't figure out why—he even checked to see if his fly was zipped! Then he turns around and sees the boys doing their shtick and storms off.

• • •

CATHERINE RICCI: I remember we had Vic and Lulu over for dinner one night. Vic was a little fidgety . . . he'd get up and make a few phone calls now and then. Carmine told me he thought Vic was being rude but I said, "He's my little brother and he's famous, he's not rude."

When we were at the table I was going on and on about our son Paul, about how smart he was. And Lulu was talking about her plans for her kid, once he was born. (Of course, it turned out to be a she; it was Vicki.) I asked Lulu which hospital she was going to give birth in and just then, Vic came back to the table, told us all that he'd just won three hundred bucks on a race in Hialeah, and sat down. Lulu said, "French Hospital. Dr. Williams there promises me they're very good." Vic says, "French Hospital? Huh?" And Lu said, "Right, that's where we're having the baby." And Vic said, "Who is? Huh? Oh yeah. That."

JANE WHITE: Every day before that big tour I would get presents from Ziggy. It became almost a joke with me and my doormen. Ziggy and I had tea one day on Fifty-seventh Street and I told him how much I loved the china there and—lo and behold—the next day I get the very same china. One time I complained about a blister on my foot and wouldn't you know it, every day for a week there were new shoes waiting downstairs for me.

We'd be in the paper every now and then, as a gossip item. The pictures were not always so flattering, but it wasn't my fault. I was three inches taller than him, I was skinny and perky, and I had the brightest smile in Manhattan, and he . . . well, he was Ziggy. My father talked to me about going out with him, and my mom told me that Mitch George had called asking about me. But I told them that just being with Ziggy and meeting all these famous people—he introduced me to Joe DiMaggio once!—just about beat anything that boring old Mitch George could come up with. My mother warned me . . . she said to be careful with Ziggy.

Ziggy and I had not yet consummated. Now, I was a virgin, I hope you'll mention that . . . and it wasn't easy. (Both Jimmy Hetfield and Mitch George had put much, much pressure on me, not only separately but together.) We had tried to consummate. But there were problems. Physical problems. It was frustrating for him and it hurt me too. I would cry like a sorry duck. I wanted to make him happy. But you cannot put a square peg in a round hole, especially when the square peg is a baseball bat and the round hole was the eye of a needle.

Before he left on the big tour, he gave me the phone number of a doctor on Park Avenue. "It's Howie Baer, I've known this guy since I was just a little runt in the Poconos," Ziggy told me. "He'll take care of you good."

SALLY KLEIN: Jack was in New York a few days before we set off. He and I and Jane and Ziggy were going to eat at "21" for dinner. Ziggy had moved to Fifth Avenue and Sixty-second Street now; he had a ten-room apartment with a lovely view of the park. Jack and I waited ten minutes downstairs but Ziggy didn't show, which was unusual. The doorman let me up and I rang Ziggy's door. His maid Ruth let me in and I saw Ziggy and Jane sitting with a girl who I recognized. It was Julie Mansell, the Nightingale of Berkeley Square. There were a few tears running down her cheeks and she was holding some tissue. Jane was holding her hand when I walked in. Jane walked up to me and I asked her what was going on.

"Your cousin has the sweetest heart there ever was, Sally," Jane said to me.

"Huh? Which cousin? My cousin Julius in Miami Beach?"

"You know which one. That's Julie Mansell and—"

"Yes, I know who it is."

"Ziggy felt so bad about what he did to her. It's been costing him so much sleep just thinking about it and regretting it."

I braced myself. What had he done?

"He got her signed with MCA," she told me, "and she has a record deal now. And Joe Gersh has her booked at El Morocco and at Mocambo in Los Angeles and so, so many other wonderful places!"

I looked at the Nightingale. She was a very talented singer and seemed like a nice girl. But I couldn't tell if she was crying out of real gratitude or because she was simply disgusted at herself for accepting all this.

"And wait till you see the sable coat he got her," Jane said. "Isn't he just wonderful, Sally?"

"We're going to be late for dinner."

RAY FONTANA: Look, I never asked Vic for nothing. Not one time. But I knew that Vic had bought Cathy and Carmine a new turquoise blue Chevy Styleline Deluxe, and when I heard that, well, you know, I got a little envious, sure. And he'd gotten Guy Puglia a car too, a big blue Cadillac Fleetwood. Beautiful car. And Guy wasn't even Vic's own blood. But I never asked Vic for nothing. So one Saturday morning my wife goes outside to pick up the milk and she calls out to me, "Ray, why's there a brand-new blue Coupe de Ville in our driveway?" And right away I knew . . . my little brother had come through.

He couldn't give Pop anything though—Pop was too proud to take it. So he'd just send cash to my mother. She'd get envelopes with thousands in it sometimes. It was one thing if Vic drove up in a new Caddy and said, Here, it's yours. That wouldn't fly. But if all of a sudden Mom goes to a dealership in New Bedford and plunks down a few grand for one, then it's okay.

•   •   •

MICKEY KNOTT: Before I got my own band, the last band I toured with was Billy Ross's. Yeah, the Fountain and Bliss Express. It was the lush life all right, lush and luxurious. We stayed at the best hotels, ate the best food, smoked the best tea, played the best joints, and the chicks were superb. I knew Vic from bumming around band to band from years before, and he gave me a call when Billy needed a new skins man.

We started out in A.C. [Atlantic City] at Skinny D'Amato's 500 Club and Vic and Ziggy blew everyone away, man. They smoked. The musicians and Vic and Ziggy and Arnie Latchkey and everyone stayed on the same floor . . . there was so much craziness going on there, though, that they didn't make that mistake again. I mean, you know how these rock stars and rap stars trash hotel rooms? They had us all on the tenth floor but the next morning there wasn't a tenth floor left. Anybody who wanted to get a night's sleep in that hotel, it just wasn't gonna happen. You know, maybe that wasn't A.C., it may have been Boston.

I turned Vic on to pot then, in Philly after the Earl Theater shows. It's three in the morning and we're bullshitting about the grand old days and how they really stank and I whip out this monster reefer. Wait, maybe this was in Baltimore. "You're not going to do that in here, are you, Mick?" he asks me and I said, "Why, you wanna step out on the terrace with me and do it?" Before I knew it he was puffing on this bone and his head was lost in a cloud of smoke. "Hey, this stuff ain't half bad," he told me.

ARNIE LATCHKEY: We would often send Morty Geist to the next city we were going to a week ahead of time, to get the feel for the place and create some ballyhoo. He always made sure to have doctors and nurses and ambulances around. We traveled around with stretchers and tanks of oxygen (the tanks *said* oxygen but they were probably empty). He'd always hire plants for the crowd, screamers and laughers and people to run out because they were in so much pain supposedly. He got the idea for the Boston engagement to plant the rumor that the whole tour was like a wrecking ball, that hotel owners and restaurateurs were complaining the whole operation was out of control. You know, create this air of danger. Morty made up things . . . he told a columnist in the *Boston Herald* that in Philly Vic didn't like the hotel bed so he threw the whole thing—frame and mattress—out the window, fifteen flights down. He told them that when Ziggy heard that, he dragged the dresser to the window and tossed that out too. What happens? The Boston hotel we're supposed to be staying at, they cancel our reservations. Which gave us even more publicity. Morty was counting on that happening, so much so that we were already booked into another joint.

You know what happened? We were opening a motion picture in Miami, it was *She Wore a Yellow Ribbon*. And the distributor withdrew the picture! Because the word had gotten out that after sitting through Fountain and Bliss, nobody had any interest in the movie. We had a week in Florida and every night Vic and some of the boys in the band would go to Frank Costello's Colonial Inn in Hallandale to gamble and chase skirts. I went there once and what a sight it was, Vic throwin' dice with a girl and a grand in each hand. "Fifty the hard way!" he'd yell out. "A hundred on all the tough guys!" This was a big step up from the dice games he would have with the Lomax band in the parking lots of some of the joints we played. I couldn't believe the bets he was making! A hundred on hard six! This is insane asylum stuff. And the tips?! A cocktail waitress could make more in one minute from Vic than she did the rest of the month.

DANNY McGLUE: It was on this tour that Vic discovered what would become the passion of his life. Fishing, stamp collecting, Impressionist art? No, it was being with more than one girl at a time—what he called the Vic Fountain Double-Decker Sandwich. Mickey Knott, who was a wild man all to himself, told me about it in a coffee shop near the Chez Paree in Chicago. He'd just walked in on Vic with two girls in his hotel bed, in *Mickey's* bed! I said to him, "Mick, what can a fella do with two girls? I mean, there's only so much he can do, right?" And he said, "Maybe Vic gets creative. All I know is I walked in and I thought I was looking at a big pretzel on my bed, man, and then it started to move. It was Vic, a blonde, and a high-yellow broad."

It was a difficult tour for me sometimes. Sally was always staying at the same hotel that I was. In every city. We'd eat with Arnie a lot, sometimes with Ziggy too, and Ernie Beasley, who was having a little fling with Mike Boley, the guitarist. Many times Sally and I would wind up alone together . . . after dinner, after a show, in the elevator. But I was seeing Betsy [Cantwell] now and Sally was going with Jack. So many times I'd be opening my hotel room door to get some coffee or get a paper and she'd be coming out of her room too. Every time that happened, I felt my heart skip a beat.

I admit it . . . sometimes I'd hear a door open and know it was her, so I left my room too, just to run into her.

SALLY KLEIN: Every road has its bumps. Vic had run into Walter Winchell in Florida, gambling at the Colonial Inn. Winchell figures, I guess, while I've got Vic here I may as well get an item or two. Now, it was very late and Vic was in his cups. And he said something like "We really want to do movies and get out of radio. Movies seems like just the right racket for us." *We* being Ziggy and Vic, Fountain and Bliss. Now, this was all innocent enough; it's a stretch to think that Vic was innocent—shooting craps and playing blackjack and running around with girls—but he really didn't mean anything bad.

Winchell was down there on a little vacation so there was a delay until it hit the press. We were in Chicago opening a movie at the Thalia for five nights, and Ziggy read it in the *Herald-American*. He knocked on my door at eight in the morning, I wasn't even awake. "Look at this! Look at this, Sally! What is this?! How can he do this?!" I read it a few times and it didn't seem like anything incendiary to me. He yells, "What is this *we* thing? Who is *we*? *We* want to get out of radio and do movies?! *We* do???"

"Ziggy, Vic was probably stewed, I'm sure he meant nothing by it," I told him. "And you know that when you tell a reporter something, they twist it around."

"Oh, I'll twist it around, Sal! I'll twist it around his neck!"

He was yelling and waking up people at the hotel. Danny came out into the hallway, then Arnie. Ziggy ripped the newspaper up and kept ripping up the pieces he'd already ripped.

"You gotta punish him, Arnie," he said.

"I'm gonna do that?! He's an adult! Occasionally."

"This is bad for the act."

"We'll survive. Can I finish shaving now?"

"We got a show tonight, Latch."

"I'm aware of it."

"We got two sets to do."

"I'm familiar with it."

"Well, I ain't doin' it. Get someone else. *We!* Who's *we?* We don't do that, Arn, it's wrong. We don't go around and say 'we.' "

You know, we were only four doors down from Vic's room, but there was only a one-in-three chance that Vic was in there. Maybe he heard the whole thing, maybe he was fast asleep, maybe he was with a girl—or two of them—someplace else.

Ziggy was true to his word. He didn't go on. We had to cancel the shows.

Morty Geist spun it around masterfully though. Arnie's idea was to tell the press that Ziggy merely had a cold, but Morty said, talking a mile a minute, "A cold?! A cold?! Who cares about a cold? Who's going to care he gets a cold?! Let's tell 'em that Ziggy and Vic are fighting. Let's say they don't get along. Through a stooge we'll tell the *Tribune* and the *Sun* that they don't even talk to each other or when they do, it's either through lawyers or they yell; they hate each other and it's World War Three! This stooge will tell 'em, yeah, Ziggy's *saying* he's got a cold but it isn't a real cold at all."

"And what is the actual bone of contention here between them? We should get our story straight, don't you think?" Arnie said.

Morty said, "They don't get along because . . . because . . ."

"Yeah?"

"Because Vic planted a story in the press that they want to drop the radio show and do movies! I'll call Winchell now and downplay it, tell him what Vic said to him wasn't really true. Nah, better yet. I'll fly to New York, wine and dine him at Le Pavillon."

The next day in the *Sun* there was a story with the headline "WILD WAR III." It was about Fountain and Bliss. Our stooge—he played saxophone in Billy Ross's band—had done his work, not just in Chicago but also Kansas City, St. Louis, and Minneapolis, all the places where we were headed next. So for a day we let these murmurs of war simmer about, and then Morty talked to all the people the stooge had planted the stories with and told them that the story was false, that it was just rumors and that the boys were best friends and got along fine. A *Herald-American* reporter got Vic at the hotel and Vic scoffed at all the reports of fighting, which, don't forget, he had never even heard of because he didn't read the news. He told the reporter, "Ziggy's gonna be godfather to my kid when he's born." (Morty told him to tell that to everyone.) "And when will that be, Mr. Fountain?" the reporter asked him. "Gee, uh . . . Morty Geist'll call you back with that info," Vic said.

ARNIE LATCHKEY: Now, Teddy, I knew what I had to do when Vic found out that Ziggy wasn't going on at the Thalia. I had to tell Vic that Zig was very, very upset and hurt emotionally that he—Vic—had made these statements to Winchell. I had to make Vic fully understand why and how much he'd hurt Ziggy, and I had to remind him that this was a team. It was all about the team. We work together, we move together, we're like a three-headed hydrant [*sic*] here, and we live and breathe and joke as one. Then I had to sit Ziggy down with Vic and we had to air everything out and come to an understanding. This is what I knew I had to do and therefore this is exactly what I did not do.

"Why'd Zig cancel tonight, Latch?" Vic asked me. He called me in my room at the Blackstone [Hotel], from where I do not know.

"He's got a cold, I think it is," I said.

DANNY McGLUE: It took a few days to get all the steam coming out of Ziggy's ears to settle down. Sally and I had to baby-sit him. In the hotel, at restaurants, backstage. He'd rant for twenty minutes, pout and sulk and stare at the wall for an hour. He'd snap out of it, grab the phone, and call Millie Roth in New York and have flowers sent to Janie's apartment or he'd call Jane sometimes and they'd talk baby talk to each other for a few minutes . . . or maybe it was just him baby talking to her. One thing he'd do was pace around like he was an expectant father. He'd walk around and around and say, "I got to get back at him. Vic can't do this, he can't do this." Sally would say to him, "He didn't do anything in the first place! You've got nothing to get back at him for." And Ziggy would say, "That's beside the point, Sal."

In St. Louis, Ziggy returned fire. He did a walk-on on a local radio show on KMOX. Didn't tell anybody he was doing it, not me or Sally or Arnie. I wouldn't have known about it except it got some ink in the papers. Morty Geist went berserk—I thought he was going to have a stroke. By this time, Morty had spread it around that the rumor he'd originally spread around about there being rumors about Fountain and Bliss being at war was just a rumor. So now here's Ziggy on the radio and he's saying that the rumors were all true. The announcer talking to him says, "Wait . . . *which* rumors? The rumor that you don't get along with Vic or the rumor that you do?" And Ziggy said, "Yeah! Those!"

Mickey Knott sees this in the newspapers and goes to Vic, and this is really the first wind that Vic had gotten of all this *mishegoss*.

MICKEY KNOTT: I say to Vic in his room, "Buddy, did you read this stuff that Ziggy's saying about you?" And he said to me, "What kinda stuff?" And for the fifth or sixth time I looked at this article and I said, "I can't really tell, man. It's confusing." He grabbed the paper from me and read it a few times . . . each time he read it he tilted it a different way, hoping maybe that it'd make more sense that way.

"The nerve of that fuck!" he said.

"Yeah, I know," I told him. "But what exactly is he saying?"

"All kinds of things, Mick! He says that I thought it was unprofessional that he didn't go on when he had a cold!"

"But didn't you think it was?" I asked him.

"But it turns out he never had a cold! He even says that here. I would've thought it was unprofessional if he said he had a cold and he didn't have one, but I didn't know that till now. He says there was a rumor that I had someone plant rumors that he'd told the press that I planted a rumor about us not getting along. And he says it isn't true what Winchell printed about it not being true. I got no idea what Winchell printed, Mick! So how don't I know that it isn't not true?"

"Talk to Ziggy. I can't keep track of this stuff."

"Nah, you know what? You go into Latch's room and tell him I ain't going on tonight! I got a cold suddenly."

So we didn't play that night in St. Loo.

MILLIE ROTH: Shep Lane had to fly to St. Louis to talk to Ziggy because Jane White had gone to a car dealership in Manhattan to test-drive a Buick. It was in the *Post* and the *Globe*. She inadvertently, so she said, drove the car home from the dealership rather than around the block. Shep had given the car salesman $500 to hush him up—and he returned the car, which Jane swore to God she'd only taken home by accident—but the real problem was that she did not have a license yet. She'd driven the car onto Fifty-seventh Street and right into a doorway, not too far from the Russian Tea Room. So the police only took her in for that.

DANNY McGLUE: There was another incident in Detroit. They opened a movie at a large theater there and they got a scathing review in the paper. It said that Vic's singing was like a sleeping pill and that Ziggy's antics were juvenile. "Ziggy Bliss manages to offend everybody and is not even funny when he does so," the man wrote. It admitted that the two of them did have good chemistry but that two chemicals when mixed together right could create a toxic odor. The reviewer had recently seen Phil Silvers and Jimmy Durante and said that Fountain and Bliss were rank amateurs in comparison.

Ziggy came onstage and read the review aloud. Vic didn't even open up with a few songs, it began with Ziggy and the paper. Ziggy began this long *shpritz* against the press . . . he called the writer a coward who hid behind his typewriter. He said that two thousand people had been rolling in the aisles the night before but obviously one idiot was too stupid or too self-important to know how to laugh. I was watching this . . . I thought it was going to end any second—I kept thinking it would—and it didn't. Ziggy said that any person who questioned Vic's singing talent had to be stone-cold deaf. Then Vic started in and urged the people in the audience that night to write the editor of this paper and demand that the reviewer be fired. "This guy is a rodent, this guy is a rat, and you know what you do with rats? You kill 'em," Vic said. "But this is America and so you can't just kill a guy." If the newspaper got two thousand letters maybe that would do it, Vic said. Then the both of them went offstage and they showed the movie, which I believe was *On the Town*.

I don't think anybody sent a letter. Because you had two thousand people leaving the theater that night who thought Fountain and Bliss were even less funny than the reviewer had said.

ERNIE BEASLEY: I became Vic's confidant on the tour then. Before he began his nightly carousing after a show, he'd like to have a few drinks in the hotel bar. Some quiet time. He was lonely. Right around the time he got married, he'd met a lovely, vivacious southern gal named Ginger Bacon. She was a dancer at the Latin Quarter, had gorgeous blue eyes and strawberry blond hair and just the longest legs. He was crazy about her. So he was seeing her and he missed her terribly, and Hunny and Guy were his best pals but they were three thousand miles away. Guy was now managing the Hunny Pot, and Vic would call there and make prank calls. He'd put on an accent and say, "I've got Harry Truman and a party of twenty coming in . . . can you get a table ready in five minutes?" And Guy and Hunny'd scramble around, throw a few people out, and of course Harry Truman never showed up.

At the hotel bar, Vic told me he thought he was ready to record a few songs. He said, "When I do 'The Hang of It' and 'Someone Such as You' and 'Moonlight in Vermont,' you've seen what happens; they eat it up, man."

I told him that when we made it to Los Angeles I could call a few people I knew and that he could call Murray Katz and maybe set something up.

"This comedy thing, sometimes it drags me down," he said.

"You're great at it though," I told him.

"Ah, you know, I just hit my marks and let the little rhino take over."

"You're one half of this show."

"Who knows, maybe one day I'll get a show of my own and I'll be both halves of it."

I said that it might not be legally possible for him to make a record if Ziggy somehow was not involved. He said, "What? I'm *glued* to this guy, Bease? And when the fuck did I ever care what some contract said?"

He asked me if I had some more songs and I told him that if he made a record he didn't have to use just my songs. He did marvelous versions of "Begin the Beguine" and "Always." I told him the way he sang *under* or *behind* the music, the way he shaded the song *beneath* the beat, was really unique as was the way he got *inside* the lyric. "Oh yeah? I really do that?" he said. And I said, "Yeah, you do." And then he said, "Hmmm, how about that. Maybe I'm a singer after all if I can really do all that shadin' stuff."

He got back to the subject of comedy. He said he felt he didn't get the respect that Ziggy got. "I'm like that lion tamer guy Clyde Beatty and he's the lion. The guy with the whip gets no credit."

"In the long run," I told him, "everybody remembers Clyde Beatty and nobody cares about the lion."

"Maybe so," he said, draining his glass. "All right, baby, off into the jungle." And then he went out on his nightly revel, gambling, womanizing, drinking, and who knows what else.

ARNIE LATCHKEY: Vic and Ziggy were talking to each other onstage and also backstage but not elsewhere, on those rare occasions when their paths crossed. It's my fault, mea culpa all the way. So hang me for it, why don't you? I should've gotten them together as soon as the first turd hit the fan. I should've pooh-poohed all the negative positive publicity that Morty was spreading. But this publicity . . . *it was working*! We were playing towns we'd never been to, places that the radio show never aired in, and we were drawing hundreds and hundreds, if not thousands, of people. We killed them in Des Moines, absolutely killed them. Davenport, Iowa? Slew 'em. Council Bluffs? Assassinated. In Davenport, another man had a heart attack the first night and it was like an epidemic: the next night another guy has another one. It got into the papers too. Morty made sure of it. The way he spun things—he was the second coming of Arachne.

We're on a train to Nebraska now, the whole outfit, the boys and Billy's band and everyone. It was early, barely even sunrise. And I'm in the dining car with just Sally and we're going over arrangements in Omaha, and Vic walks in with that glazed look he sometimes had in the morning. He sits down and the steam from his coffee is rising up into his half-closed eyes and then a minute later Ziggy walks in too.

"What are you guys doin'?" Ziggy says right away.

"Not much," I said.

"Nah, come on, what's goin' on here?"

Sally said, "Ziggy, Arnie and I were looking at some figures and Vic just walked in and—"

"You doin' business without me?"

Vic said, "Pipe down, Zig, it ain't even sunup."

Ziggy said, "I can't believe you would do this to me. When did I become the Invisible Man of the act? What, I got tape all over my body and a hat and sunglasses on?"

Sally said, "Ziggy, we all just woke up and—"

Vic said, "To be honest, I ain't even been to sleep yet . . ."

Ziggy, that *nut*, thought we were having some Potsdam-like Big Three summit meeting without him! He said, "Nah, nah . . . I want the truth once for a change, please!"

"Zig, I just come in for a cup of joe," Vic said. "I didn't know Arn and Sal was gonna—"

"Oh, you didn't *know!*"

"No, I didn't! And I also don't care either. Jesus!"

I told Ziggy to sit down. It was just the four of us. I began my *shpiel*.

"Look, we been together a long time now. This is like a marriage, a marriage with four people. Now in my real marriage if there's a problem, we'll talk. I think her rib roast tastes like an old Goodyear tire, I tell her. She thinks I chew my food loud, she tells me. And maybe we compromise . . . she either improves on the rib roast or maybe she don't cook it anymore, and I try to maybe close my mouth when I eat. And then we got one happy family. You see where this is going?"

Vic puffs his Chesterfield, sips his coffee. Ziggy pouts.

I resume this sermon, which, I admit to you, I didn't know where it's going other than to Omaha. "Now what we got goin' here is a dynamo. We're a Sherman tank, we're Murderer's Row. Nobody draws like us. Nobody. We've got women coming to see the act and they bring a change of clothes because they know they're gonna tinkle in their bloomers. What other act in the solar system can claim this? So what I am asking you is, what the hell is the matter?!"

"Latch, I just think that, well, you know," Vic said, "just 'cause we got all that chemistry and whatever up there onstage, it don't necessarily follow that we gotta be best friends off of it."

Those really were not the words I wanted to hear.

Ziggy said, "I don't like the way he takes me for granted. Ziggy . . . the funny guy, the Jew, the human basketball who don't sing, he's a goddamn piece of garbage. I don't like the way he goes to all these reporters and tells 'em stuff, even if he don't even realize he's doin' it at the time. I don't even know if I like the fact that he doesn't like me. He does all this carousing into the wee hours, and where am I? I don't even know if I like *him*."

Let me repeat myself: Those really were not the words I wanted to hear. So I said, "Sally? Can you throw in your two cents worth here 'cause I'm broke."

Sally said, "Do you two remember where you were before you met? Do you have any recollection whatsoever? Vic, if your career was even in the dumps then that would've been a tremendous accomplishment, because you barely had one! You had no future or present and your past wasn't much to crow about either, young man!"

"Yeah, really," Ziggy said with a smile. "Victor Feldbaum. Hee hee hee."

"Shut up!" Sally said. "Ziggy, you were a zombie. You couldn't perform alone. You were a zombie! Did you think you were going to go places with the O'Hares? *Ha!* If they didn't work out, how many different parents would you have hired? Would you be forty or fifty or sixty years old and you would still be performing a pansy-and-parent routine?"

I thought I would chime in. So I said, "Now, Sally's right. So—"

"Arnie, shut up," she said. "Have we forgotten that Arnie was nowhere too, was not even nowhere? Before he got you two together, he was cleaning spit valves! Big, big entertainment manager and he's covering up the wall sockets in hotel rooms so the vocalist doesn't electrocute himself!" She took in a deep breath. "As for me, where was I going? What was I doing? Getting Ziggy his ice, getting tea for his parents? I didn't finish high school, I had no fella, I never even had a real job. Vic, would you stop blowing that smoke at Ziggy! And now here we are. I live at the Bel-Nord, Vic keeps two residences, owns two cars, a thousand suits and shoes. Ziggy, you've got a ten-room apartment on Fifth Avenue and everything you ever wanted! Arnie has more money than he knows what to do with! We eat well, sleep well, live well, we're healthy, we have fun, we have fine families. People love us, they travel miles and pay top dollar to see us. *Why the hell are we so miserable?* Why? Will someone please answer me this?"

I cleared my throat. I looked at Vic. He was blushing . . . I don't think he'd ever been involved in such a talk like this. Maybe he was embarrassed, getting involved in some boy/boy spat. I looked at Sally . . . she's five foot three, she's got these big cat's-eye glasses on. She was sort of quivering—I don't think she knew she had the *baytsim* to pull off this speech. But she did. And then I looked over to Ziggy and there were tears pouring from his eyes. He starts whimpering. He's shaking his head and I never saw so many tears in my life, and the mucous is popping out his nostrils like someone is blowing bubbles up there. I handed him a napkin and he blew his nose and dabbed his eyes. He was trying to say "I'm sorry," but it wouldn't come out. Sally stood up and walked up to him and put an arm around his shoulder and he hugged her waist.

Outside the train, the sun rose over the vast, flat, desolate Nebraska countryside, which whizzed by incredibly unimpressively. Sally then walked out of the dining car. I got the idea: Let's leave them alone. Let's let them talk. For the first time ever, let the two of 'em just talk to each other! So I got up and left too.

Hours later I saw Vic at the hotel lobby in Omaha and I asked him, "So did you two iron out your problems?"

He told me that after Sally and I had left, a few people started coming into the car, some waiters and one couple and then another and some people eating alone. He and Ziggy looked at them, then at each other. Then they just started goofing on everybody.

• • •

REYNOLDS CATLEDGE IV: When Fountain and Bliss came to Omaha, I bought a ticket to the show. The nightclub, a modern but unspectacular place, was called the Stalk Club and had a corn motif. I gave the maitre d' a note to pass to Vic and Ziggy backstage but when I espied other people doing the same thing—most of them females—I realized that my own note might not make it to its intended targets. This feeling was further exacerbated when, several minutes later, I inquired of the maitre d' as to the status of my note, whereupon he informed me that he'd thrown it out. "I know these people," I informed him, "and they know me. Please tell them that Reynolds Catledge is here." This seemed to shake the man, and after the show he ushered me backstage.

Vic was in a friendly mood and good-naturedly mocked my appearance and demeanor. "You ain't in the army anymore, Cat," he told me. "You need to loosen up some."

The next day was a Saturday and I was roused from sleep very early when my doorbell rang. I was stunned to see Ziggy Bliss . . . I asked him to come in and I put up a pot of coffee for the two of us. (By way of a personal note, I should add that after three years of marriage, my wife, Linda, whom I'd met and married in 1945, had recently left me and taken our son, whom I did not name Reynolds V. I was leading a boring and incredibly solitary, worthless life.)

Ziggy seemed agitated. At first he spoke only about trivial matters but then he got to the point. He had three days free and wanted me to help him track someone down. I tried to tell him that I had no interest in such a project—I even thought about making up some phony matter I had to attend to, but after a moment's reflection I realized that a long drive with one of America's top comics through the middle of nowhere might be just the proper tonic I needed, and soon we piled into my Ford woody and we were on our way to Laramie, Wyoming.

The drive was about five hundred miles long and, given the nature of the American automobile at that time, it took quite a while—long stretches of silence were broken by longer stretches of Ziggy complaining about Vic. "The guy don't even go home on his own honeymoon night!" he told me. He complained that Vic's singing style was so sleepy that he could perform at an insomniac ward and have everyone dozing within the first few bars. He said, "If we ever get some big movie deal, you watch—Vic'll get all the credit and all the girls, I'll do all the work and get nuttin'." At many points during this screed it seemed he was treating imaginary things as if they had already in fact transpired; he would say, "He's banging the daylights out of Lana Turner at the Bel-Air Hotel and here I am, working on new material in the mirror at my puny ranch house."

We pulled into Laramie that evening and procured lodging at a modest motel. We shared a room with two beds . . . there was an incredible view of the mountains but Ziggy took no notice. I said, "That's the Medicine Bow range, I imagine," and he said, "Yeah, big deal."

The first thing he did when we checked in was ask the hotel proprietor for a phone book. Ziggy looked up someone named Dolly Phipps. There were two D. Phippses in the directory and he phoned both of them; neither one of them turned out to be a Dolly. "Do you *know* Dolly Phipps?" he asked them. "Are you maybe related to her maybe?" They were not. He ripped the Laramie phone book in two and gave me the latter half of the alphabet. I was to look at every listing there was and keep an eye out for anyone going by the first name of Dolly. I did find a Dolly Marshall but he found none. It was three in the morning and he phoned the Dolly in question. A man answered, obviously annoyed at being awoken, and informed Ziggy that not only was his wife Dolly not now or ever a Dolly Phipps, but that she had passed away only two weeks before. "My most sincerest condolences," Ziggy said. "'Bye."

The next day we drove around the city. The scenery in the distance was breathtaking, the air was fresh and the sky pale blue, but Ziggy took no notice. He was driving now and we spent upward of eight hours weaving in and out of the same streets over and over again. He would drive up one street, then drive back down, over and over again. Giving up on this street, he would then drive to an intersecting one and spend a half hour traversing it. Several policemen noticed this suspicious behavior, and we were stopped on several occasions. "I'm Ziggy," he would tell them, "from Fountain and Bliss. Here's a hundred bucks."

Ziggy had two old, somewhat faded photographs of his old flame, taken from newspapers in the Catskills. He gave me one of the pictures as well as $1,000 in twenties and tens, and he took the other. We were to stop passers-by and go into every store, shop, restaurant and ask for information. It's a good thing Laramie was not a teeming metropolis.

I had not attained anything close to a lead and had handed out about three hundred dollars to a few shrewd citizens when I heard Ziggy yell: "CAT! PAY DIRT!" I ran across the street, where Ziggy stood outside a "feed store." There was an old man, approximately seventy-five years old, in a cowboy hat. This individual had a weathered, wrinkled face and sparse snowy white hair. "He remembers her, Cat!" Ziggy, quite excited, said to me.

We took the man—he said his name was "Ol' Zeke"—back to the motel and began a frustrating two-hour interrogation. He insisted that we ply him with liquor and he must have emptied a quart of Jack Daniel's. The more he drank, the more colorful his "memory" became. For example, he initially said, "Yeah, I 'member this girl come to town 'bout ten years ago," but then, after having drained half the bottle, he said, "Yeah, this gal was really sumpin', she showed some of the boys at the Golden Spur a real good time." By the time the bottle was empty, "Miss Phipps" had become the proprietor of a brothel known as Dolly's Lollies, the wife of the richest cattleman in the state—whom, rumor had it, she'd murdered—and eventually had died of an overdose of laudanum.

After we deposited, face-down, Ol' Zeke back at the feed store—it was now about two in the morning—Ziggy's mood alternated between one of sky-high elation and dark despondency.

"She was here, Cat! The old man remembers her!" he said.

"But what about the rest of his story?" I asked.

"The way I see it is, she came here, maybe she stayed here for a while.

Dolly was very shy, see, so maybe she just disappeared and moved on. But she was here!"

"What about the brothel? The murdered cattleman? The laudanum?"

"That was Jack Daniel's talking. He was just putting the touch on us for an extra grand, that sharp coot."

The next day, a Sunday, Ziggy and I split up. He was repeating his drive of the previous day while I made several inquiries of the local constabulary as well as a judge; the startling episode of a cattleman's wife murdering her husband and then suffering an overdose of laudanum rang only one bell. But this incident had occurred in the late 1890s. For $200 one of the town's clerks briefly combed through some property records but the name of Dolly Phipps did not surface.

Ziggy and I reconvened at the motel. "Zilch!" he said to me. I told him that I too had hit a dead end.

"See if the guy here's got any ice, would you, Cat?"

I returned from the proprietor's cabin with a bucket of ice. Ziggy, nude now, dumped the cubes into a towel and formed it into a turban and wrapped it around his head.

"I have to get back to Omaha," I told him. I was running a beer-distribution business then, which was not doing well.

There was a small table with a lamp on it between our beds. Wearing nothing but the towel on his head, Ziggy picked up the table and threw it against the opposite wall. He lifted up the chair and threw it through the window. His naked body took on the aspect of one large palpitating tomato, and as he raved and ranted around the room his penis swung about like the trunk of an epileptic elephant. There was a dresser in the room and that soon was being hurled to and fro. I tried to restrain him, I tried holding him back . . . but I could not. He was incredibly strong; the flab on his arms belied the muscle underneath. Within three minutes the room was destroyed . . . it was splinters, shredded curtains and sheets, tiny chips of plaster, and shards of glass.

Ziggy wrote a check for $2,000 dollars to the proprietor, who said upon receipt of this largesse, "Hey, any ol' time you wanna destroy any other rooms I got, you jus' go right ahead, sir."

Ziggy uttered not one single word on the long drive back to Omaha.

A week later in the mail a check came to me from California. It was from Ziggy Bliss and was for the sum of $5,000. There was no note attached.

● ● ●

MICKEY KNOTT: For a cat who could carry a tune, Vic didn't have too much interest in music. He did a souped-up version of "Night and Day";

everyone snapped their fingers and swayed in their seats. He'd flick the sleepy Perry Como switch and croon "Malibu Moon" and it's like a lullaby. But when we were in Kansas City some of the boys [in the band] were going to check out Dizzy and Bird, and I asked Vic if he wanted to come along. He thought I was talking about two circus clowns. I thought he was joking. I say to him, "Come on, man, Charlie Parker and Dizzy Gillespie and Max Roach!" I said to him, "You ever heard of Lester Young or Billie Holiday?" He said, "Oh sure. Wasn't she the blonde in *Born Yesterday*?" And then he asked for another dose of weed—he called it "loony tea"— which I served right up.

SALLY KLEIN: By the time we made it to California, we were starting to fray at the edges. Personally, it was very tough on me, Danny being everywhere. I still carried a torch for him. If he was staying on the same floor as I was, sometimes I'd hear his door opening—maybe he was going to get a coffee or a paper—and I would then emerge from my room and we'd just pass a few minutes together in the hallway or elevator.

Ziggy had disappeared for a few days after we played Nebraska—to this day nobody knows where he went—and he was sullen and not very communicative when he rejoined us. Arnie tried everything, Ernie and Billy Ross tried, I tried. I would ask him what's wrong and he'd just say, "Nuttin'! Leave me alone." I said, "But you seem lonely," and he'd say, "I am! That's the problem! So please let me be by myself."

Vic was pretty angry, because Ziggy had given one or two interviews on the phone to columnists in New York and to some local reporters in Seattle and San Francisco. "He gets on me," Vic said to me, "'cause I accidentally said something to Winchell when I was bagged one night, and now he's yapping to every clown with a Remington [typewriter]." Ziggy was pretty sly in these interviews; people would ask him, "Why are Fountain and Bliss so funny?" and in the answers he would always say something like, "I've been doing comedy since I was a kid. My parents, God bless their souls, were comedians. They taught me everything I know." Or he might answer, "Me and Danny McGlue spend hours and hours and weeks perfecting this stuff. It's like Michelangelo with a chisel." But he never would mention Vic.

There was some trouble in Seattle. The band and the rest of us were waiting outside our hotel, about to board a bus to San Francisco . . . it was drizzling and we had no idea where Vic was. Ziggy said, "Oh, let's just go without him!" Mickey Knott took Arnie aside and they spoke for a minute. Then Arnie told me, "Mickey and Vic picked up a few girls last night after the show. Mick thinks Vic's probably still with 'em." But Mickey, Arnie told me, was so tight the night before he didn't remember where they'd gone. It was a roadside joint somewhere, he remembered.

ARNIE LATCHKEY: Mickey and I "commandeered" a car very quickly. That is, I slipped the *faygeleh* concierge two C-notes and in five minutes I'm behind the steering wheel of God knows whose Packard. Mickey had sort of a vague idea where this place was but the previous night was mostly one smoky fog for him (and you can guess what kind of smoke that was). After a futile search for an hour, I'm ready to give up and head back to the hotel and take Ziggy up on his offer to forget Vic, when Mickey pops up like he's got springs in his *tuches* and yells, "There it is!"

It was a two-story juke joint called Spike's Bed of Nails. The place smelled like beer and urine twenty yards away, even with our windows closed. I pulled up, got out, and knocked on the door but the place was closed. "A place like this doesn't even open till midnight, man," Mickey told me.

"Vic! Vic! Are you up there?" Mickey is yelling up to the second floor.

I hear Vic yell back, "Mickey baby, is that you? You gotta help me!"

"Latch is here too!" Mickey yells up to him.

"Guys, can you get in?" Vic calls out. "I can't get loose!"

It's pouring out now, Teddy, and we're practically in the woods and any second some two-ton grizzly might pop out of a tree and maul our heads off. Mickey kicks to pieces a closed window and we climbed inside this joint. Typical late-forties, early-fifties roadhouse—sticky floors, splintered furniture, a cracked mirror, discarded bric-a-brac, a wobbly staircase, which the great drummer and I were soon ascending. On the wall going up the stairs were about twenty photographs; it was their "Tart of the Month Club." But the girls looked like Ethel Rosenberg, Rosa Luxemburg, and Dillinger's Lady in Red. No great beauties, any of 'em.

We found Vic in a room on the second floor with nothing in it save a warped, disheveled four-poster bed. Vic, buck naked, was in this bed, each hand and each foot handcuffed to a post. And, may I add, there was not one stitch of his expensive threads inside this entire hostelry?

"It's a long story," he said. "Can you get me outta here?"

"You think I got the keys to your handcuffs, Vic?" I snapped.

Mickey went downstairs and found a rusty old hacksaw . . . this thing had tetanus written all over it. He's sawing the bed while Vic is stretched out on it like it's a torture gizmo right out of the Marquis de Sade. He tells me the two girls he picked up—*two of them!*—the night previous had taken him to this roadhouse operation and how they'd all emptied a gallon of scotch. "A gallon?" I said. "You stretch the limits of credulity." He admitted, "Well, it was a lot."

Mickey is sawing away and the dust is going all over the place and the smell of booze, urine, cigarettes, sweat, and other testimony of summer nights is unbearable. Vic is telling us that he's in the sack with the two girls and they're putting on quite a show, boy; they're shakin' and shimmyin' and flickin' their tongues like they're cobras, when all of a sudden two sheriffs bust in. These two lawmen come across as real no-nonsense . . . the fact that Vic is one half of Fountain and Bliss, that means as little to them as "I was Martin Van Buren's vice president."

The girls, it turns out, are both sixteen years old.

"These sheriffs said I was looking at ruin, scandal, and damnation," Vic told us, "which didn't really bother me, but also at maybe twenty years in stir, which did. I told 'em I could make it worth their while to let me go. I said how did five grand sound and they Jewed it up—no offense, Latch— to ten." So Vic called and woke up Morty Geist, who was in Frisco now, and Morty was going to, first thing, call Shep Lane in New York and have Shep wire ten grand to the two corrupt John Laws. Morty also had to make sure this thing was kept buried press-wise. The sheriffs then left Vic cuffed to the bed and told him if they didn't receive the dough by noon the next day, they'd either haul him in or burn the roadhouse down with him in it. Which was doubtful as it seemed they most likely ran the joint. As a matter of fact, Vic said to me and Mickey, "The two girls were probably their daughters, those fuckin' *figlie di puttane*."

By now we've got Vic free but he's still got the cuffs around his wrists and ankles. Mickey swathed him in these musty sheets and the three of us piled into the Packard and made it back to the hotel. Just in the nick of time too because as we were heading back the way we'd come, Vic espied the two shakedown guys in an unmarked Ford heading toward the roadhouse.

Back at the hotel, the concierge called a locksmith and we got Vic unbound and back into his threads, $10,000 the poorer but probably not one IQ point the wiser.

*   *   *

ERNIE BEASLEY: I called Hank Stanco at the Worldwide American Talent offices on Wilshire. Hank was Fountain and Bliss's man on the West Coast. I told him that Vic was looking into cutting a record. (Don't forget: Everything was 78s then.) Hank was up for the idea and knew that Fountain and Bliss would be in Los Angeles at the Pantages Theater and Ciro's. He said that he'd make some calls. He was meeting that day, as a matter of fact, with Bobby Bishop, who was doing A & R with the Pacific Coast label then. Hank said he might be able to get Vic some studio time and I told him that Billy Ross and the boys would love to record. He asked me what song, and I said that Vic could do either "Malibu Moon" or "The Hang of It." Hank had seen the act many times and was familiar with both numbers. He said, "Of course, I'd have to look at some of the paperwork about this, contractually . . . to see if it's okay that Vic can do this without Ziggy." I told Hank that I certainly did not wish to be the one to tell Vic that he could *not* record, nor did I wish to be the one to tell Ziggy that Vic *could*. "Well, I guess that's what Arnie and Sally are for, huh?" Hank said to me.

DANNY McGLUE: Fountain and Bliss did a week at El Matador in San Francisco. It was the second-to-last stop on this whirlwind tour. We were all tired. Lulu was about to give birth to Vicki in New York, Estelle and Arnie were married but had been apart for months. We couldn't wait to get everything over and done with and then knock off for a while.

So we're in Arnie's room at the Mark Hopkins and Vic says, "Guys, listen, I don't mean to drop a big one on you, but is there any law that says we gotta still do this radio show when we get back to New York?"

Arnie said that there wasn't a law but there was a contract with the Consolidated Network.

"Contracts, Jesus," Vic said. "Why does everything have to have a contract?! Whatever happened to just doin' something or not doin' it?"

"The radio show is tremendous publicity," Sally said.

"It's also a tremendous amount of work."

I said, "What about television? That little box is going to be socko, guys. Lenny Pearl's got a show. And Berle's very hot."

Arnie asked Ziggy how he felt about continuing the radio show and Ziggy said, "I agree with Sally. Radio puts us into people's homes and into their heads."

"We can do one more season for the Dickinson witch hazel people," Arnie said, "and then we call it quits. How's that sound?"

"Only one more . . . ?" Ziggy said with a slightly sick look on his face.

Vic said, "I don't know if I can do one more show, Latch. The thought of getting in that studio is makin' me sick. I got a kid on the way any day now! I'd like to maybe spend some time bein' a father, you know?"

Ziggy said, "Oh, get a load of Judge Hardy with blue hair over here!"

"Shut up, Ziggy! At least I got a wife!"

"A wife? You didn't even make it to your own honeymoon night, you were so busy gassing it up at El Mo!"

"It was the Latin Quarter and besides, I eventually did make it home."

"Guys, guys . . . please," Arnie said. "Are we a team or aren't we?"

But neither Ziggy or Vic responded to that.

GUY PUGLIA: I really liked managing the Hunny Pot. I liked meetin' all the people who went there . . . Joe DiMaggio, Leo Durocher and Laraine Day, Ernest Hemingway, Rocky Marciano, Sinatra, Jimmy Cannon, Gleason, people like that. Anytime a famous person come in, I was supposed to call Bud Hatch or his wife. Bud had a list of jokes that a few gag writers had written. It went like this: Cary Grant comes into Hunny's joint one night, I call Bud, Bud gets a joke from this list, writes it in the column that Hunny was "overheard" cracking a gag to Cary Grant last night at the Hunny Pot. It was great publicity.

These men in black suits come in one afternoon and tell us they're from the Health Department. They start inspecting the joint with white gloves on, like it's a marine barracks. One of 'em says to Hunny, "We understand that some cockroaches have been seen on the premises," and Hunny says, "Yeah, they're my best customers." "Okay, we're closing the place down," one guy says and I go after this gent but Hunny holds me back. So Hunny locks the door, pulls the gate down, and closes up, and I says to him, "Okay, now what do we do?" He says, "We gotta get a [sic] attorney most likely, Gaetano."

We went back to the place we was sharing—most of the time he was shacked up with this broad named Maria G. that Vic had introduced him to—and an envelope that said FROM THE HEALTH DEPT was slipped under the door. Hunny rips it open and what's inside? Two airline tickets to Los Angeles. A typed note said: "Get your asses over here, you two dumb fairies. Vic."

"Let's pack," I says to the Hun, and Hunny says, "But I still need to call a [sic] attorney first." He couldn't put one and one together, I guess.

SALLY KLEIN: Jack had sent two dozen pink and white roses to my room at the Beverly Hills Hotel. That was so sweet of him. He also took a week off so he could spend some time with me. I was a little wary of introducing him to Danny . . . you know how that's always a sticky situation. I didn't tell Jack that I once had been Danny's girl. Eventually he figured it out.

The first bad thing that happened in Los Angeles was that Ziggy once again started granting interviews. He was on the phone day and night or meeting columnists at Chasen's, the Villa Capri, and the Trocadero. Louella Parsons he met at Chasen's. He wasn't saying anything completely inflammatory but he wasn't exactly being very charitable to Vic either. Bobby Hale did a long interview with him, and Ziggy barely mentioned Vic. He talked a lot about Harry and Flo though . . . [he said] every single thing he learned about show business he learned on the lap of his parents. He called them "titans." The *Examiner* was going to run the story and wanted photos of Harry and Flo to run on the page, but Ziggy told them he didn't have any. They ran the story anyway.

Meanwhile, Danny told me that Ziggy had started a thing with a model named Myrna, who lived in El Monte. She wasn't really a model—she made what they called "blue movies" back then. She was the typical Ziggy girlfriend . . . a dizzy bottle blonde with an immense bust. Danny told me that Ziggy had bought this Myrna girl diamond earrings and about three fur coats. "I guess it must get real cold in El Monte," Danny said.

Guy and Hunny were in Los Angeles now. We hardly saw Vic at all—he was off with Hunny, Ernie, and Guy most of the time. Or Ginger Bacon, who'd also flown out. Arnie was left to baby-sit Ziggy alone.

ERNIE BEASLEY: Vic, Hunny, Guy, and I went to the track one day and Vic saw Gus Kahn in his usual seats. He introduced us to Mr. Kahn, who was sitting next to a perky little blonde. It was Veda Lankford, who had done two movies for Galaxy, *The Big Kill* and *Here We Go Again* with Glenn Ford. Kahn had seen Hunny box, he told us, and had won five grand on him. "You bet on me, Mr. Kahn?" Hunny asked him. "Hell no!" Kahn said. "I bet against you!"

It was a Saturday and we stayed for only half the card. I've never placed a bet in my life but I liked being around a racetrack; I liked the wonderful characters and the electricity. Also, I had once had an affair with a jockey in Saratoga. (There's just something about a boy with taut muscles in green, gold, and lemon yellow silks with a whip!) Vic was flirting with Veda—she was billed as "the next Veronica Lake"—the entire day, right in front of Gus Kahn, who had quite a reputation with the girls. Was it Selznick who had a "four o'clock girl"? Every day at four some girl would be ushered into his office to "service his needs." Well, I've heard that Gus Kahn had a four o'clock girl as well as one for 4:15, too.

After the fourth race Gus Kahn asked Vic what he was doing.

"I got a show tonight at that big theater, the Pantages," Vic said.

"You're opening *The End of Mrs. Smith*? That's a Galaxy picture. Hey, it's too bad 'cause me and Veda are going down to Agua Caliente, down Mexico way. Fifteen roulette wheels, ten dice tables, a hot band, and more blackjack tables than you can count."

"How far's that from here, Mr. Kahn?"

"By car it's six hours."

Vic said, "But I got this show tonight, see."

"Well, there's always my plane."

A half an hour later we were on Gus Kahn's plane. This craft was very swank—there was a bartender and a chef as well as a movie projector and screen. And a piano too. I played a few songs for Mr. Kahn and he was very impressed. The tequila was flowing freely and I had a few. Everyone did. Veda was having a good time playing with the scars on Hunny's face, and Kahn asked Guy what had happened to his nose but Guy didn't want to talk about it.

The Agua Caliente resort was just outside Tijuana and, boy, it was a wild, woolly scene. Mickey Cohen and the Fratelli brothers were running it then. You think the *Federales* cared a jot that none of us had a passport? They saw Gus Kahn and everything was immediately okay. The Dick Stabile band was playing and the house was packed.

Gus Kahn went to the five-hundred-dollar-minimum blackjack tables but Vic admitted, "This is too rich for my Codport blood." He went to the craps table with Veda Lankford and I could just not believe how truly star-studded the place was—when I was walking in, Barbara Stanwyck was walking out. Ava Gardner was there that day, so were Frank Sinatra and Jack Warner and William Wyler and the screenwriter Jess Auerbach. Vic lost about two grand that day and it didn't take long before Veda Lankford and he wandered off someplace together.

I looked at my watch and saw that Vic had to be at the Pantages in about two hours. Then Mr. Kahn walked up to me, Hunny, and Guy and told us he'd lost $13,000. "Well, easy come, easy go," he said.

"Sounds more like easy go to me, Mr. Kahn," Hunny said.

"Anyone see Veda? We gotta get back to Los Angeles."

I looked at Hunny and Guy and we all shook our heads.

"Where's Vic Fountain?" Gus Kahn asked us, and we shook our heads again.

"Hey, Gussie!" Jess Auerbach said, sticking a cigar as big as a loaf of bread into his mouth. "You can take twenty grand off the price of my next script!" Apparently he had won twenty thousand at the same table that Gus Kahn had lost his thirteen.

"Go to goddamn hell, Jessie! Tell ya what, I won't even buy any more scripts from you, how's that sound, you sonuvabitch?"

"I saw that new blonde ingenue of yours sneak off with that big blue-haired dago, Gus."

"Oh yeah? Where'd they go?"

"Where do *you* go when you're here?" Jess Auerbach said to him.

"Jesus goddamn Christ," Mr. Kahn said, his eyes drifting upward toward the second floor. But, you know, he didn't look too upset or angry. "Well," he said, "I gotta get back to civilization. Nice meeting you gents."

"Mr. Kahn," Hunny said, "we gotta get back too. To see Vic's show."

Guy reminded Hunny that, as Vic was upstairs right now, there really wasn't much of a rush, and then Gus Kahn just slipped off.

Ten minutes later I saw Vic and the next Veronica Lake at a craps table. He was smashed—his hair was falling all over his face—and looked a mess. I pulled him away from Veda and I said to him, "Gus Kahn just left, Vic."

"Oh yeah? How'd he do at the blackjack?"

"Somehow we have to get back to Los Angeles."

"Guess what I did, Bease? I fucked a movie star! *Me!* Vic Fountain! I just fucked a movie star!"

"That's great, but you have a show to do in Los Angeles and we're in Mexico."

"What a hot piece of ass too. Oh yeah, I forgot . . . that don't mean nothin' to you."

I found a phone and called Arnie in L.A. at the Beverly Hills Hotel. He was fuming. "How can he do this to me?!" he was barking out. "I got enough troubles with Ziggy and now Vic pulls this?! I thought Vic was the reliable one! Now it turns out I *got* no reliable one!"

From behind Vic grabs the phone from me and I hear him say, "Who's this? . . . Latch? . . . Hey, Latch, guess what I did? . . . I banged a movie star! . . . Aw, come on, give me some congrats! . . . So I miss one show! Big deal . . . huh? . . . huh? . . . Oh, it was Veda Lankford from *The Big Kill* . . . huh? . . . Yeah, she was pretty good." And he hung up.

Guy came over and said he'd found someone who could fly us into Los Angeles right away, that that's what this person did, it was his own private shuttle service. "But this pilot," Guy said, "I don't know if I'd trust him with a paper airplane." The pilot was about fifty-five years old and had been a silent movie stunt pilot—he'd been in *Wings* even. But he had seen better days and, frankly, I did not feel so comfortable getting into that old flying jalopy of his.

"I'll have you there in no time, guys," the pilot said. "Where to?"

"Los Angeles," I told him.

The plane was from 1930 or so. There were no numbers on it and there was hardly even a cockpit—the pilot was just sitting right in front of us.

"Where you guys going?" he asked us when we'd been aloft for a few minutes.

"Los Angeles," I told him. "I told you that already!"

"Oh yeah."

"Arnie and Ziggy are going to be mad at you, Vic," I warned Vic.

"Why? 'Cause I didn't let 'em watch me with Vera Langley?"

"It's Veda Lankford," I reminded him.

"Can you believe it, Gaetano? I used to cop a feel with Angela Crosetti in Codport at the gazebo and now I got Veda Lankford's *sticchio* all over my finger."

The plane was bouncing up and down and the pilot told us it was just an air pocket. "You sure you know how to fly this thing?" Hunny asked the pilot, and the pilot said, turning around to us (which I most certainly did *not* appreciate), "Oh sure . . . I was shot down three times in the First World War." As though that was reassuring.

The plane kept bouncing and everyone except the pilot and Vic was terrorized.

"Shouldn't we have brought Veda back with us?" I asked. "Gus Kahn is going to wonder what we did with her."

"Well, first I started kissin' her, right? And then I lifted up her skirt and—"

"Gee, I hope we don't have to ditch this thing," the pilot said.

"Aw, fuck, I'm gonna die," Hunny said. His huge head was turning a greenish white.

"What decides whether you have to ditch the thing or not?" I asked the pilot.

"All sorts of factors," he said. "But I don't remember what they are."

"Got any tequila in there, Smilin' Jack?" Vic asked him. And sure enough, he passed Vic back a bottle. "If you gotta go, you gotta go, ain't that right, Hun? At least I got to bang a movie star first."

"But I didn't!" Hunny told him.

The pilot said to me, "Could you open that little drawer down there and see what's inside?" I opened a drawer and there was a parachute bag. I passed it to the pilot, who strapped it on.

"Only one?" I asked him.

"We'll make it . . . I've made it before in bad weather," the pilot said.

"But the weather isn't bad," I said.

Guy was praying, saying the Hail Mary over and over again. I did what I always do when I'm scared: I sang songs to myself. The same lyric again and again. I was singing "Just One of Those Things." But I must have been singing aloud because Vic told me, "Will you knock it off about them gossamer wings, Bease?"

"Where are you guys going?" the pilot asked.

I told him, "Vic's supposed to be at the Pantages Theater in about ten minutes."

"Where's that?"

"In Los Angeles! I told you we were going there!"

"No, I mean, where in the city is it? I'll take you right there."

Vic took a big swig and handed him the bottle and I looked out the window and we were coming down through the clouds. We were in Hollywood, going right over Argyle. I could make out Vine up ahead and I told the pilot to hang a right there.

"I'm gonna die," Hunny said again. "I always thought I'd die in the ring."

I could make out Hollywood Boulevard and then the theater came into view. Traffic was light and we were descending very, very quickly. The long line into the Pantages was snaking in. Then there was a tremendous bump when we hit the asphalt and we were right behind a Cadillac. I wish you could have seen the expressions on all the drivers' faces! The plane skidded and turned around two times and then stopped . . . we were about ten yards from the theater. And you can't imagine how many people were staring at us and how many horns were honking!

"Hey, thanks, buddy!" Vic said and he handed the pilot some money.

Vic and I had to jostle Hunny awake because he'd fainted. I nudged Vic in the ribs because I saw about a half a dozen photographers running toward us. When he saw that, Vic grabbed the tequila from the pilot.

We were soon surrounded by photographers snapping Vic's picture, the lights going off in our faces, dazzling us. Properly sensing the moment, Vic made exactly like John Wayne getting out of the plane and strutting with manly bravado to the theater with the bottle of tequila . . . oh my, you should have seen it. It was right out of Douglas Sirk's *The Tarnished Angels!*

We went around the back and the man at the door recognized Vic and let us in. Vic was combing his hair back and dusting himself off on his way to his dressing room. I saw a tall shadow with a cigar down the corridor. It was Arnie Latchkey. He was holding a tuxedo and he handed it to Vic and said, "Awful *muy grande* of you to show up."

"Where's Zig?" Vic asked, slipping into the tux.

"He's onstage now. Dying a horrible death. Oh, just forget the goddamn cummerbund!"

SALLY KLEIN: "I'll kill him! I'll kill him!" Ziggy was hissing to me in his dressing room. "Sal, if I go on alone, I'll die. I'll *die!*"

We waited and waited for Vic and I never told Ziggy that he was in Mexico. I said to him, "I have to ask you a tough question." He looked like he didn't have one drop of energy inside of him, like he was drained by all his waiting and worrying. I said, "How long do you think Fountain and Bliss is going to last? Do you want to be with him for thirty years?"

"I don't know if I can take another thirty days of this, Sal. Why?"

"Let's say you two split up . . . what do you imagine yourself doing?"

"Honest, I never thought about it."

"Well, think about it. Because if you're not with Vic, then you're going to be alone. So you better get used to performing alone. Or else you're stuck here. Why don't you just give it a shot?"

"No!"

"Please. Just try it!"

"No!"

I picked up a copy of the *Examiner* off the table and turned to the interview he'd done with Bobby Hale. I started reading him back excerpts from it, how *he* was the funny guy, how *he* got the laughs, how *he* did all the work. "This is all a load of malarkey!" I said. "Look at you, Ziggy! Without Vic, you're nothing!" And I stormed out.

One minute later he walked out of his dressing room, wiping his forehead, and ambled onto the stage. Poor Billy Ross didn't know what to do. He started up "Malibu Moon" and Ziggy actually sang the song . . . *imitating Vic!* It got some laughs but still, people were wondering: Where's Vic? Ziggy stood by the mike and kept adjusting it . . . he pulled it up, he pushed it down, he brought it here and there. He kept wiping his head with a handkerchief. He twitched a little, kept shaking his head and blinking his eyes. I'd seen this before and knew we were in big trouble.

"We have to get him off, Arnie," I whispered backstage. "He'll have a stroke."

"Sally, listen to that . . . LISTEN!" he said to me.

The audience was going crazy for it! They thought it was part of the routine. His gestures, his twitches and eye blinks—they thought he was doing a pansy act! Every time he moved his head they burst out laughing! The microphone picked up these faint wheezing sounds and when they heard that, they were on the floor.

I heard a loud commotion from outside the theater—horns honking, people cheering—and Arnie slipped backstage. Ziggy was frozen and pale and the crowd kept eating it up, and all of a sudden Vic was standing next to me.

"Oh, if it isn't the Italian cavalry just in time," I said to him.

"Hey, Ziggy's doing great without me," Vic said. He wasn't too pleased.

Arnie pushed Vic out there and it was a while before Ziggy even noticed him.

"Nice of you to show up, Vic," Ziggy said to him.

"I thought I'd just drop in, see how you were doing."

"And?"

"It looks like you don't need me no more."

"I guess I don't."

"Except maybe to clean that puddle you made that you're standing in."

About four thousand eyes all looked to Ziggy's feet. (Of course, there *was* no puddle.)

"I sunged 'Malibu Moon' without you, Vic," Ziggy said, "I'll have you know."

"Oh yeah? How'd it go over?"

"Well, for the first time ever, the audience was awake at the end of it."

It only took two minutes before they began to click and when they clicked, it was explosive.

The Pantages shows were all sold out, every night. There were fights outside the theater to get tickets. Vic told everybody—including dozens of reporters—that *he* had flown the plane from Mexico because the pilot was too drunk, that he had landed the plane on Hollywood Boulevard to get to the theater on time. Morty Geist said, "Gee, I wish I'd thought that one up!" The photo of Vic getting out of the plane with the bottle was everywhere! The *Examiner* had a headline "ON A SING AND A PRAYER!" and *Variety* went "CROONER'S CRAFT CRASHES PANTAGES BASH." Estelle called from New York to tell me the *Daily News* ran the photo on their cover with the headline "40 SECONDS OVER JOKE-E-O."

DANNY McGLUE: Every few years I'd ask Vic, "Did you really fly the plane that night?" And he'd tell me that he did. When I asked Guy and Hunny, they'd shrug and tell me to ask Vic.

Betsy arrived in L.A. only a few days before the plane thing and she stayed with me at the hotel. She had quit *A Date With Judy*—they were giving her only a line a week now—and it was a very rough time for her.

"So is it *always* this exciting with Ziggy and Vic?" she asked me.

"Unfortunately, yes."

I took Betsy to Vendôme . . . we ordered a bottle of expensive wine and were just about to enjoy a pleasant dinner when the waiter told me I had a phone call. I went to the bar and it was Ziggy on the other end.

"This plane thing is blowing up in our faces, Danny!" he told me. "That was some stunt Vic pulled!"

"You're sold out at the Pantages, you've been extended a week at Ciro's, and Arnie is cooking up something in Vegas . . . if this is blowing up, then maybe we should have more of it."

"Well, I'm all for it if the plane crashes a little harder next time," he said.

"Don't talk like that. I really don't think Vic crashed the plane to boost his career. If he was really flying it, that is."

"It worked for Knute Rockne, Danny," he said to me. "If Rockne's plane don't crash, they don't make that movie with Pat O'Brien."

"Ziggy, my snails just showed up . . . I'm with Betsy," I told him.

"I put an ad in *Variety,* a full-page ad," he told me. "And it's gonna run elsewheres too. The *Globe* in New York and—"

"An ad?" I said.

"Yeah, you'll see it. Enjoy your snails."

When I got back to the table, the snails were indeed there but most of the wine wasn't. Betsy had knocked back about two-thirds of it. "Sorry about that, honey," I said to her.

"About what?" she asked me, her eyes already sinking.

ARNIE LATCHKEY: The paper was slipped under my door at the hotel . . . I woke up to it. Why not wake me up with the news that they dropped the H-bomb on my living room in New York and Estelle was blown to smithereens!? Because this hit me the same way.

There weren't too many words to the thing. On the top of the ad it said, "VIC IS MY COPILOT." There was a photo beneath that of Ziggy and Vic, one of those publicity photos Bertie and Morty hand out to a million places. And then Ziggy Bliss tells the world how much he loves Vic Fountain and how he thanks God Vic didn't bite it on Hollywood Boulevard. "I have been blessed with many things," the ad said, "with beautiful, loving parents and with that most underrated and underappreciated of all of God's gifts: the gift to make people laff." By the time I'm on this sentence I had already lost my appetite for the whole day and the next few to come. "But of all the gifts I am thankful for, it is for my fellow yukster and trouper extraordinaire Vic Fountain. You may have crashed into Hollywood but in my heart, Vic, it's always a safe landing." And there was Ziggy's big, loopy, five-year-old's signature.

My jaw was dropping in disbelief and I'd spilled my coffee over the floor and then the phone rang. I knew it would be Sally asking me, "Can you believe this thing?!" so I picked up the phone and said, "No, Sally, I can*not* believe this goddamn thing!"

"Where does he get the chutzpah for this? Where?" she asked.

"I'd fire him," I told her, "but then where the hell would we be?"

In addition to all this airplane *mishegoss* there was also the matter of Vicki Fountain being born. Vic was getting letters, telegrams, and flowers sent to his room all the time. The fact that he wasn't with Lulu and hadn't seen the baby, Morty Geist was able to put a lid on; he just released it to the press that "mother, baby, and warbler are doing fine." Nobody bothered to ask where Lulu was because they just naturally assumed Vic was by her side, not that Hunny and Guy were.

When Morty found out that Vic and Ginger Bacon were living together at the Beverly Hills Hotel, he hit the ceiling. "What if this gets out?!" he was saying. "What is it with these two guys?! I'm gonna hang myself!" I told him it was his job to see that it didn't get out. He told me that cleaning up after Fountain and Bliss was like being a stable boy at an elephant circus. I told him I knew exactly what he meant but that; nevertheless, he should get sweepin'.

Hey, in the same edition of *Variety* that they ran Ziggy's ad in, you know what also ran? It was a small story, maybe a paragraph. It said that Galaxy Pictures had terminated its contract with its young blond starlet Veda Lankford.

GUY PUGLIA: We had to keep it completely hush-hush about Lulu. We checked her into French Hospital in New York under the name of Jane Q.

Doakes—Arnie come up with that name. She didn't know this though . . . I mean, Morty Geist is telling us to muffle this thing big time and Lulu's got enough worries right now, right, what with it being her first kid. So we get her her own room and the nurses and residents keep calling her Mrs. Doakes. But she's so out of it she don't even notice. Once in a while she'd ask if Vic was comin' and I told her I didn't know. Hey, I *knew!* I knew that Vic was three thousand miles away shacked up in a bungalow with Ginger Bacon.

Hunny was the one who really took care of Lu, not me. He was up till five in the morning the night Vicki was born . . . and he had a fight in Sunnyside the next day too. He didn't sleep a wink and twelve hours later he gets knocked out cold in the ring. And that fight wasn't fixed neither. He was out cold for two days, then he snapped out of it. But he wasn't really the same afterward.

SNUFFY DUBIN: I came home one night at like four in the morning from some joint called Nick's Lagoon in Roosevelt [Long Island] and there's a telegram waiting for me from Ziggy. It's telling me to fly to Los Angeles—he's marrying Jane White. He tells me he'll pay my expenses, he wants me to be his best man. He'll put me up at the Ambassador. He tells me they're going to play a fancy club soon in L.A. and do a few shows at the Oceanfront in Vegas and he'll see to it that I open for him.

I didn't even bother to call the manager of the club I was playing to tell him I couldn't finish out the week. That fucking *chozzer* hadn't paid me a dime. My agent called him up and said, "My guy isn't being paid." And this pig says, "Your guy isn't being funny either." I was playing to the same thirty drunks for two weeks and you could hear the sound of men vomiting in the bathroom every five minutes. That'll tend to throw your timing off, you know.

Now, we all know why Ziggy married Jane when he did. This is no government state secret. It was *murdering* him inside, all the attention Vic was getting—Vic piloting the plane and Vicki being born. Well, Ziggy wasn't about to stage his own airplane crash—although I bet he thought about it—so this is how he gets even. He does a quickie marriage in Nevada, invites some of his Hollywood big-shot buddies, and makes sure every reporter from Tehachapi to Timbuk-fucking-tu knows about it.

I show up with my beat-up old valise at the Ambassador—the only time I'd ever been to Los Angeles before this was right before I got sent overseas—and they didn't have me registered there. I went to the phone booth in the lobby and tried to reach Ziggy at the Beverly Hills but they wouldn't put me through. Oh Christ, I'm thinking, was this some practical joke being playing on me? What the fuck am I doing in Tinseltown with two pair of underwear and forty bucks in my wallet? I call the WAT offices in L.A. and Hank Stanco's girl says Hank will call me back right away. She asks me where I'm staying. *Where I'm staying?!* I'm staying in this fucking phone booth! And how long am I supposed to wait for an agent to call me back?!

So twenty minutes later I'm in some fleabag like the Hotel Cucaracha on Franklin. I fluff the pillows and bedbugs sprinkle out like there's snow flurries. And then I realized: Damn it, I only have five more bennies left to my name.

I called the Beverly Hills again and this time I reached Arnie. "Is Ziggy really getting married or is this a gag?" And Arnie said, "Of course he is! And Vic just cut a record yesterday with Pacific Coast Records!"

"Wha—?" I said.

"Yeah," Arnie said, "there was all this stuff about Ziggy getting married to Jane White, so Vic went out and recorded a song with Billy Ross's band. 'The Hang of It.' Bease's number. Boy, this seesaw for attention is veering out of control, Snuff. Every day some new dung is hitting the fan."

"Look," I said to him, "this hotel I'm—even the desk clerk has got antennas. Ziggy told me he'd put me up at the Ambassador, but I go there and they don't know me from Judge Crater."

"I'll make some calls. Go back to the Ambassador. The wedding is tomorrow."

"So tell me: What do I have to do as Ziggy's best man?"

"Huh?"

"I'm Ziggy's best man . . . ain't I?"

"No . . . so far as I know it," he said to me, "Vic is."

REYNOLDS CATLEDGE IV: I was in my office in Omaha when Ziggy called me from California. I asked him how he was, and he told me that he wanted me to do something. He gave me the phone number of two reporters; one man was named Bobby Hale and the other was a woman named Hilda Fleury in New York.

Ziggy wanted me to call these two journalists and tell them that someone named Ginger Bacon was living with Vic Fountain in a bungalow at the Beverly Hills Hotel. I asked him why he wanted me to do this, and he told me that Vic's wife had recently given birth, that Vic was out of control and needed to settle down. "It'd be good for the act, sure," Ziggy said, "but most of all, it'd truly be the best thing for his family."

"I just don't know if this is right," I said to him.

"Oh, it ain't right, Cat," Ziggy concurred, "but that don't mean you shouldn't do it." He then proceeded to give me a lecture on loyalty and friendship.

When I contacted Mr. Hale he was quite brusque with me. He said to me, "I know this already and I don't care! And you can tell Ziggy Bliss I said so!"

It took a while before I could actually reach Mrs. Fleury in New York City—her secretary was not easy to get past. Mrs. Fleury, when I finally was conversing with her, did seem genuinely interested in the information I possessed. She asked me who I was, how I had come upon this information, and I followed Ziggy's instructions and told her, "It's me . . . Hunny Gannett, the prizefighter," and hung up.

• • •

ERNIE BEASLEY: The recording session was very professional. Bobby Bishop got Hal Gordon to produce, and they used Billy Ross's arrangements. Vic did the tune in two takes. Billy wanted the song to really, really swing so he brought in a few extra musicians. And one of them knew Vic from a previous band.

"Cueball Swenson! You sonuvabitch, give us a hug," Vic said when he saw this bald man, a trombonist.

"Vic," Cueball said, giving him a big bear hug, "when I heard this recording date was for you I jumped at the chance."

They talked about the old days for a minute or two, and I recall Vic telling Cueball that he was going to make sure that Bobby Bishop and Hal Gordon would pay him three times what they would normally pay. Cueball was up to date on the success of Fountain and Bliss and said to Vic, "I even saw that short movie you two did."

"What? That *Gotta Dunce* thing?" Vic said. "You know, I didn't think it was as bad as everyone said." (When people say things like that, I've found, it usually was as bad.)

"So . . ." Cueball asked him, indicating Ginger Bacon, who was in the studio that day, "is that the missus? Is that Lulu Fountain?"

"That's just a friend. Lu's with the kid. So whattaya hear about Pip Grundy? And those Siamese twins?"

"Ah, they all split up soon after you left us, Vic. But you know, I ran into Floyd Lomax in Las Vegas a few months ago . . ."

"Uh-huh. Yeah?"

"And we got to talking. He said that if I ever saw you that I should tell you he sends his regards and that he hasn't forgotten."

"Well, Cue, thanks for passing the message along. If you see Floyd again, would you tell him that I *have*?"

The band did the song and then recorded an old Harold Arlen number for the B-side. Hal and Bobby wanted Vic to do another take, but Vic said he'd get to that after we broke for lunch. He, Ginger, and I went to

Chasen's and got positively gassed over martinis and chili. Vic couldn't believe he'd recorded a song on his own. At one point he got up and phoned Lulu in New York to see how she and the kid were doing.

"Don't ever become anybody's mistress, Bease," Ginger said to me then, lighting up a cigarette. "It's just pure damn hell."

When we got back to the studio Vic had no interest in doing the Arlen song again. He simply refused. Billy Ross took Hal and Bobby aside and said to them, "I know Vic . . . he won't do it." So Hal said, "Okay, then . . . can we do 'Malibu Moon' now?" Well, that's such a slow, languid, torpid song that I chimed in and said that since Vic was half in his cups, now would be the perfect time. So Billy busted out the charts for 'Moon,' the band went over it a few times, and then Ginger woke up Vic and he did it in one take. I was slightly annoyed that he slurred over a word here and there but he really captured the essence of the song. It's one of my best lyrics, one of my best songs: *"It must have been the Malibu moon, that made me fall in love with you. It must have been that light in your eyes, those cocktails of silver and blue."* The third time he sang the words "those cocktails" he somehow turned it into one syllable.

Still, when Hal and Bobby were shaking my hands that day as Vic, Ginger, and I were leaving, Bobby Bishop said to me, "Ernie, we recorded two hits today."

JANE WHITE: I can't believe that I was ever so impulsive. Ziggy called me up one day from L.A. and said, "Jane, let's you and me make it official, how about it?" Well, I'd been envisioning a long engagement and wonderful parties and dinners with my mother and him, perhaps a cruise to Europe . . . but he said that he would have a ring over to my apartment in a matter of minutes.

I expressed my reservations and he said to me, "Janie, Shep Lane'll put you and your mother on a plane to California today. And the ring too. Except the ring'll be so big it might need a separate plane. I'll put everybody up at the Beverly Hills Hotel." I asked him about my bridesmaids and my maid of honor and he said to me, "I don't have time for this, sweets. I wanna marry you. I want you to have my kids. And I wanna do it now."

The buzzer rang from the lobby and my mother spoke to the doorman. Ziggy was cajoling me and painting these wonderful pictures, and, well, I *knew* how big he was! I mean, you could not read a Walter Winchell or Earl Wilson column without seeing something about him or Vic in it. My mother walked in with a large white box and a small blue one and I asked her what it was. She told me they were from Shep Lane's office on Lexington Avenue. I tore open the large box . . . inside was the most beautiful wedding gown from Saks. I tore open the small box and ripped away all the tissue paper and there was just the most magnificent diamond ring. There were also airline tickets for my mother and me. I picked the phone back up and told Ziggy how much I loved him, and we were in California the next day.

SALLY KLEIN: Ziggy told me at the Polo Lounge: "I proposed to Jane and she said yeah."

"Then why don't you look so happy?"

"When are you and Jack gonna tie the old Gordian knot?"

I noticed that he changed the subject but I let him. I told him, "Oh, you never know . . ."

"Jack's a good guy. Jack's all right."

"So's Danny."

"Aw, come on, Sal," he said, "that's all water unner the bridge."

Ziggy told me that Janie was already on the way to California with her mother, that he wanted to get married as soon as he could. He had already called up Rabbi Gershon Susskind, the "rabbi to the stars." Morty was calling every paper and reporter he could and was still burning up the lines. He told me they were going to fly to Reno in a few days, Vic would be the best man, and—then I interrupted him.

"How do you think Jane White—née Judith Weissblau—is going to feel about someone named Rabbi Gershon Susskind performing this ritual?"

"*Oy vey,*" he said. "You're right."

"And are you and Vic even speaking to each other?"

"Ah, it's good press that he's my best man. He'll do it. You watch. Don't forget, I'm godfather to his child."

"No you're not! That's just what we're telling everybody. You haven't even seen Vic's kid."

"Yeah but neither has he."

He finished his drink and got up, said he had more arrangements to make. I said to him, "This wedding of yours . . . it has nothing to do with Vic getting all this press over the crash landing or anything, doesn't it?"

He said with a smile, "Come on, Sally, give your cousin some credit."

"I thought I was."

ARNIE LATCHKEY: After one of the final shows at the Pantages, Vic calls me from his bungalow, says he wants to see me. I'm bushed, I'm about to hit the hay. But Vic, he's on a different schedule than most Homo sapiens, up to five in the morning most nights.

I went to his bungalow, making sure to avoid going past Ziggy's—the very last thing I needed was Ziggy seeing me going to Vic's. Anyway, if my memory serves me well, Jane was already there with him then . . . and she'd just had that, uh, "work" done by Dr. Howie Baer so I'm sure they were quite occupied with matters of the flesh.

"Sit down, Latch," Vic tells me.

"Can I get you a drink, Arnie?" Ginger asks me and I told her that it depended on what Vic had to tell me.

"I recorded a song today," he said. "Two of 'em. Actually, four, but two of those were B-sides and I didn't really give it my all."

Quickly, I asked Ginger to make me a scotch and soda.

"Vic, there's the little matter of the round, red, fat, soap-pad-tressed, freckled Sigmund Blissman that is your partner."

"Well, that's why I'm comin' to you first."

I told him that, no, in fact he had not come to me first. As a matter of fact, he came to me *second to last,* it seemed!

"Well," I said, "we can't keep this a secret from him—that would be amoral—as much as I'd like to."

"Am I gonna get sued for this?" he asked me. You know, he seemed like the old, somewhat vulnerable Vic Fontana when he asked me this. "I mean, alls I did was sing."

I told him I didn't think so. I told him that Shep Lane and Hank Stanco would look at the paperwork but that I was sure everything would be okay.

"You know," he said, "me and Zig, we got quite a thing goin' . . . the clubs and the shows and whole deal and all. I don't wanna lose this! I swear it, Arn, really. But sometimes I feel—I don't know. You know?"

"Yeah. I know. Sure."

The big lug couldn't have a heart-to-heart talk even if someone had transplanted a brand-new ticker into him.

He and Ginger stood up and put on their coats, about to go somewhere.

"Listen," I told him. "I got some bad news too."

"Hold on, puddin'," he said to her.

"Morty just called me in my room," I told him. "Hilda Fleury knows that you and Ginger are shacked up here. So does Louella [Parsons]."

"So?" he said.

"So? Well, let's examine this . . . if you had once had Hunny Gannett work *my* butler over, I might want to disseminate bad dope on you to the entire universe too."

"Yeah, but don't you think she'll be scared Hunny'll do it again? I mean, that's how this leanin' on people stuff is supposed to work."

"I'll take care of Louella. And Morty's on a plane to New York now," I told him. I reminded him that Morty had also had to go back to Seattle from Frisco, to Mexico from L.A., to Detroit from Chicago, to Miami

Beach from Atlanta, and made other similar journeys just to mop up with extra-strength ammonia the swath that Vic was cutting across the country.

"Ah," Vic said, "the kid is probably lovin' all that luscious scenery!"

The kid was a nervous wreck, the kid had lost twenty pounds in the last six months, the kid was sleeping three hours a night and talkin' suicide.

I finished the scotch and made for the door. Ginger and Vic were leaving too . . . they had a chauffeur now and a Rolls they tooled around in. I asked them where they were going and Ginger said, "Johnny D'Antibes has a club in Santa Monica." Boy, those two knew about joints nobody else did, they danced and drank and did it all. They knew how to live, all right, and at times I thought it might kill the both of 'em.

Vic put Ginger in the car and came over to me and whispered, "Arn, if my music sells, if these songs go places, I'm thinkin' about maybe leaving the act."

"Don't say this to me," I hissed. "You'll kill me."

"I just need to get out on my own. You know, like the old days. I feel sorta stuck." He dropped his Chesterfield to the ground and put it out with his shoe. "So you're gonna smooth this record thing out with Zig?"

"Yeah sure," I told him. "I'll have Sally do it."

MILLIE ROTH: Hilda Fleury ran the item in her column. Morty Geist had tried everything he could to prevent it but nothing was good enough. She pointed her nose straight up in the air and said, "Mr. Geist, I am a journalist and cannot be swayed from printing the truth!" Morty Geist asked her if she was going to actually mention Vic's name, as well as Ginger Bacon's, and she said she most certainly would. "Wild horses or five thousand dollars could not prevent me from doing so," she said.

The day that Hilda Fleury printed that column, Morty was ready with a prepared statement from Vic, which ran all over town. It said: "I have many friends, and Miss Ginger Bacon happens to be one of them. That Hilda Fleury would choose to besmirch my family at a time when I just became a new father is shocking to me. This is an insult to my wife, to my child, and, most importantly, to me. I struggled all my life to get where I am today. Maybe Mrs. Fleury would like to wake up at four A.M. and go fishing for cod. But no, she's not man enough for that or man enough to make these accusations to my face. And she can tell her butler I said so."

The next day, after Morty got $6,000 in cash over to her apartment, Mrs. Fleury was kind enough to print a retraction. But Hunny Gannett told me that Ginger Bacon was let go from the Latin Quarter.

GUY PUGLIA: I was pullin' triple duty: I'd take care of Hunny at Lenox Hill [Hospital] and then I'd rush over to the Hunny Pot to make sure nobody was stealing from the till and then I'd go to Vic's apartment to check on Lulu and Vicki. I was running myself ragged—it was like *I'd* been knocked out cold for two days and given birth. In addition to all this, I had to prevent Lulu from readin' the papers and the columns.

One time I'm in the apartment and I'm changing Vicki's diaper and I hear Lulu on the phone with Vic. She was screaming at him, and I thought, Uh-oh, she knows about Ginger. Or, uh-oh, she knows about Veda. Or, uh-oh, she knows about everything else. But alls I heard was Lu saying, "Why does it say 'Victoria Catherine Doakes' on little Vicki's birth certificate?!" Vic told her, I guess, it was some hospital mistake and that it didn't matter any. Then he asked her to put me on in another room.

"Tell Vicki to say hello to her papa," he says to me.

"The kid don't know 'hello' yet, she ain't even two weeks old," I told him.

"How's the Hun?" he asked me.

"Hunny's kind of in bad shape still, Vic," I said. "All woozy, you know?"

Vic said, "Aw, he ain't in bad shape, he's just Hunny."

"We gotta get him to stop fightin'."

"Listen," he said, "I'm maybe thinking of going solo."

I thought about it for a second and then said, "Hey, pal, you and Ziggy . . . you're the kings right now. I mean, nobody's doin' better than you."

"I figure, though, if I do half as well without him, I'd still be doing the same."

"Okay, I see that. But what's so bad about being with Ziggy?"

"Being with Ziggy," he said.

Then he told me to do something. He told me to call Bud Hatch's wife, who was the biggest female drunk in New York. Face like a frog too. Bud always called her "SL" in his column, which stood for "Scintillating Lady." But everyone always said it really stood for "Slobbering Lush." Anyways, I'm supposed to call her and tell her that Ziggy's in the sack with a stripper named Myrna. She's from El Monte. I'm supposed to tell her to tell Bud. I says to Vic, "Hey, I don't wanna get involved in this. I got enough trouble with the saloon, with Hunny's coma, and your kid." He said to me, "Gaetano, just this once. For me. Okay?"

So I call the Slobbering Lush at home and pass along the news. She says thanks and that she'll call Bud when he gets in at the *Globe* office in ten minutes. I was keeping my fingers crossed hoping she was so bagged that in ten minutes she'd forget.

JANE WHITE: Our party had a whole plane to ourselves and it was so much fun! Poor Morty Geist arranged it, and he also arranged for there to be reporters at the airport in Los Angeles and in Reno too. There were about thirty bottles of Veuve Clicquot and marvelous hors d'oeuvres from Canter's of Fairfax. Frank and Ava were on the plane, so were Betty Bacall and Humphrey Bogart and Ty Power and the Van Johnsons and many others. I felt like royalty! If my mother ever objected to me marrying Ziggy, when Charles Boyer introduced himself to her on the plane and lit her cigarette, all her objections simply vanished.

Vic sat in the rear with Shep Lane and Arnie. He seemed sort of down. Lulu had just given birth to Vicki, so maybe that was it—he wanted to be with them.

ARNIE LATCHKEY: "The song is gonna hit the airwaves any minute now, Sal," I whispered. We sat together on the plane to Reno. "You gotta tell him."

"Why do *I* have to tell him?" she asked me.

"'Cause that's the way it usually is . . . I deal with Vic, you deal with Zig, and you and me deal with each other."

We were about twenty minutes from landing.

When I arrived at the Sky Lodge [in Reno], there was a message from Bertie Kahn's secretary . . . Bertie was on vacation in Paris and couldn't make the wedding. "It's in Bud Hatch's column that Ziggy and a 'model' from El Monte are involved," the note said. So I left a message at Morty Geist's office that he had to smooth things over with Bud now. I told his secretary to tell Morty to read Bud the same statement he'd read to Hilda Fleury, except jiggle the names around.

"I give Morty maybe five months to live, *tops*," I said to Sally.

DANNY McGLUE: I've been to all kinds of wedding ceremonies, Jewish, Catholic, Lutheran, large, small, shotgun. These nuptials were so hastily planned it was almost funny. Rabbi Gershon Susskind was on the plane to Reno and was schmoozing with every star he could. (I think Jack Benny said about Rabbi Susskind that he'd go to the lowest level of hell to do a bris if it was a movie star's son and there was a camera flashing.) But then Ziggy had to break the news to him that a judge would be doing the honors and not him.

The rabbi now flew into a rage. "HOW *DARE* YOU?!" he shouted out to Ziggy. He really made a big scene: He was bellowing and spitting and his eyes were crazy. He accused Ziggy of everything in the book—and that book was *Mein Kampf*!"I suppose you'll be serving pork at the reception too, you self-hating cur!" he screamed right in Ziggy's face. Jack Warner urged him to pipe down and the rabbi yelled to everyone: "I curse this marriage! I curse it and condemn it!" He put his hand on Jane and yelled, "May this Eva Braun from Lexington Avenue have five children with tails and may they all die of a slow plague!" He was spitting all over the place when he yelled, it was like he was a lawn sprinkler . . . some of it even got on Bogie. Ziggy, in a rare fit of common sense, said, "Gersh, it's just you not doing a marriage ceremony, it ain't the Temple of Jerusalem bein' sacked!" When we finally touched down, Rabbi Susskind refused to get off the plane. He didn't attend the ceremony and the pilot flew him back to Los Angeles.

SALLY KLEIN: The ceremony was fairly low-key, very simple, although there was a photographer from AP there, and UPI as well. Vic was the best man and Ziggy, who could never ever stop clowning around, kissed *him* on the cheek when the judge told him to kiss the bride. Vic and Ziggy engaged in some mugging for a few seconds and then Ziggy kissed Jane. Afterward there was a reception in Ziggy and Jane's suite. The rooms were filled with flowers, flowers from everyone. They had only one night in Reno and then Ziggy had to fly back to Los Angeles to begin the Ciro's engagement.

After the reception Arnie and I were in the lobby of the Sky Lodge and I heard Vic behind me singing "The Hang of It." Both Arnie and I turned around but Vic wasn't there.

It was the radio.

I went upstairs. I knocked on Ziggy's door and told him in the hallway that Vic had recorded two songs. I thought he'd open his mouth and fire would come shooting out, like a dragon. But he didn't do anything. I was waiting for some kind of explosion but he just stood there and thought about it and finally said, "I appreciate your telling me. The song will die. I ain't worried. And maybe now I can have my honeymoon maybe?"

SNUFFY DUBIN: "The operation took, I guess?" I asked about Jane White, and Arnie said, "Oh, it took, all right. She won't be able to stand up straight for three months." And I replied, "Bad news for her, great news for Macy's."

I hang around the Ambassador for a few days and I tell you, it was like the help there thought I was an insect. Maybe someone had tipped them off to the fact that I couldn't afford the place or maybe they could tell just by looking at me. I told Arnie that Ziggy had promised me a few gigs out there and he kept saying he'd check with him. But Ziggy told him he didn't remember saying anything like that to me. So I said, "Arnie, I came out here to stay at the Ambassador and they never heard of me. I came out to be Ziggy's best man and Vic's doing that. I also came out here to work a few joints and make some bread and I'm not doing that." He said, "It don't sound like this has been a pleasurable few days for you." I said, "Oh no, I'm having the time of my life staring at the fucking ceiling here." And he says to me, "Well, what would you be doing if you were in New York?"

And I fessed up and said, "Staring at the fucking ceiling." "Well, at least it's a different ceiling," he says.

"You guys are playing Vegas, right?" I said to him, and he said Fountain and Bliss were booked into the Oceanfront for two weeks. I said, "Look, Arnie, I *swear* to you . . . Ziggy promised me some work out there. On the grave of my mother, I swear it." And he swore on the grave of *his* mother he'd call up Pete Conifer in Vegas.

Hey, I can't be too mad. Fountain and Bliss footed the tab for the hotel. [My agent] did get me two nights at Mocambo. A guy in the crowd there had seen me at the China Doll and—guess what?—the man is an orthopedist! So I sit for a half an hour at his table with him and his wife and I make real nice and I leave there with a prescription for fifty fucking bennies.

Then I went to Vegas and saw Fountain and Bliss at the Oceanfront. They were tremendous . . . the crowd was completely mesmerized. Me and Pete Conifer have a meal together and he's just crowing how he'd laid this showgirl and that showgirl, and I'm sitting there with a big phony grin you could drive a Cadillac through. I'm just waiting for him to ask me, "Snuffy, can you give me three weeks? Snuffy, can you give me three nights? Snuffy, can you balance a lit stick of dynamite on your nose?" Nothing. I'm giving him all kinds of hints and he don't bite one fucking time. Finally I said to him, "Did Ziggy tell you that I'm available to work this place? That's why I'm here, Pete. I thought I was gonna open for Fountain and Bliss." And he said to me, "Yeah, Arnie did say something. But we're bringing in that girl singer to open for them." I asked him, "*What* girl singer?" And he said, "That Berkeley Square Nightingale girl, Julie Mansell."

●   ●   ●

ARNIE LATCHKEY: By the time the Ciro's engagement began, they weren't even talking to each other except onstage. People kept walking up to Vic and telling him things about himself that he didn't know. Things they'd read in the trades. "Hey, congratulations on extending the witch hazel show," Ann Sheridan said to him once at the Brown Derby. *Huh?* We hadn't worked out anything with Consolidated or Dickinson's! Turns out Ziggy had told a *Variety* reporter that. I'm at the House of Murphy with Vic and Ernie, and Abe Lastfogel from William Morris sashays up to us and says, "Congratulations on the musical, Vic. Broadway will *adore* you." *Huh?* "What musical?" Vic said. "Did I do a musical?" And Abe says, "It's all over Louella Parsons's column today." Abe sashayed back to his table and Vic looked into his coffee and grumbled, "Ziggy!"

Before a show at Ciro's one night, Sugar Ray Robinson comes backstage and, after he tells Vic how much he loves the "The Hang of It," he says he's sorry that Vic won't be recording any more songs. "I *won't be?*" Vic says to the greatest pound-for-pound pugilist of all time. "Well, I was at this big benefit," Robinson says, "at the Hollywood Bowl last night that Fritz Devane did for that Cedars of Lebanon Hospital . . . and Ziggy come out and he and Devane joked around for ten minutes. And then he told Fritz and all the audience how you weren't gonna record anymore." "What did Devane say to that, Ray?" Vic, quivering with rage, now asked of the sweet scientist. "Devane," Robinson said, "just said one word: 'Good.'"

Sally spoke to Zig about it. Ziggy—you know, he was floating around in the cloud nine of conjugal bliss for a little while—he apologized. He sent a telegram to Vic's bungalow even though all he really had to do was walk twenty yards and slip a note under the door. He wrote that he was very sorry, that he knew that Devane was not just a personal sore spot but was a festering one to boot. He'd crossed the line, he admitted. Vic sent back a wire telling him something like, "Don't worry about it, partner."

So for one brief, bright, shining moment there's a golden sliver of sunlight poking through the storm clouds. Sally, me, Vic, and Zig even had breakfast together one morning at some dive in Westwood. Eggs, coffee and danishes, and flapjacks and toast. And for an hour it's like the old days, all the fun and everything. You felt it, the juice, the laughter so loud it hurt your bones, the *naches!* And so that night *which* sleepy-toned, Italian, aubergine-haired, fishophobic singer does a walk-on appearance on Lenny Pearl's TV show? *Take a wild goddamn guess which one?!*

DANNY McGLUE: The atmosphere became stifling. I had to get out of Los Angeles. There was poison in the air. Betsy was drinking too much. It may have been my fault . . . I don't know. One night at Musso and Frank I let it slip that Sally and I had once been an "item," that I'd loved her very deeply and even told her we'd lived together. She was truly stunned. She had no idea and I believe she got very angry but kept it inside. This was all my mistake—I should never have told her how much I loved Sally. Now, Betsy drank before this, she drank a lot . . . but it—me and Sally—it was always a wall between us.

Betsy and I flew back to New York. I had a few meetings with Marty Miller, who was now at NBC, and with a few big shots at CBS and Dumont. CBS was offering me money to punch up a few *Life With Riley* scripts, and the money was good. I was just about to put my John Hancock on the dotted line when I realized: *I don't want to do this!* I didn't want to leave Fountain and Bliss. I didn't know where the road was going, I didn't know where or how it would end, but I knew I wanted to be bouncing up and down on it.

I'd go to the Vigorish office every day . . . I'd talk to Arnie long distance and listen to him complain about Ziggy and Vic and also listen to him *kvell* about how well the act was doing, which stars were showing up, how much money they were bringing in. I had lunch with Guy at the Hunny Pot; he told me that Lulu knew about Vic and Ginger but would never utter a word about it to Vic. I saw Hunny there and it took him about ten seconds for him to remember me.

After lunch I went back to the office and Millie Roth told me that Arnie had just called her from Los Angeles. Jack Klein and Sally had been at Ciro's the night before and Jack was laughing so much he'd had a mild heart attack. He would be okay, though, she told me, unlike the man three nights before who had seen the show, gotten in his car with his wife, and was still cracking up so much that he drove head-on into another car and killed two people.

The boys did a week in Vegas at the Oceanfront, which Pete Conifer was now running. They brought the place to its knees. Pete had Jimmy Durante booked for two weeks after Fountain and Bliss but held them over a week and took a week off Durante. The Ciro's engagement was whammo too. Arnie has always maintained that this was Fountain and Bliss in top form, at their peak. Sally said so too. Winchell was in California, so was Leonard Lyons, they both saw the show although not at the same night, thank God, and they couldn't rave enough. It all proved what Sally and Arnie and I always knew in our hearts: The boys were at their best, at their funniest, when they couldn't stand the very sight of each other.

GUY PUGLIA: I'm in my place, Hunny's at his girl Maria G.'s place. Bruno and Violetta are staying over with Lulu and Vicki, helpin' out. It's four in the morning and the phone rings. My first thought is: Hunny's broad tossed him out and he don't know where he left his keys even though they're probably bobbing up and down in his pants pockets. I pick up the phone and it's Vic in California. He's yellin' and whoopin' it up. "What happened?" I says to him. "Did Ziggy die or something?"

And he says to me, "Oh, it's even better than that!" I hear Ginger pop open a bottle of champagne in the background. Vic asks me, "Remember Gus Kahn? The Galaxy big shot?"

I said to him, "No, Vic, I fly in a Jew movie mogul's private plane to Mexico *every* day." Like, sarcastic, you know?

Vic tells me, "Guy, he just signed me and Ziggy to a big movie deal with Galaxy!"

"Wasn't you gonna break up with Ziggy, Vic? Wasn't you gonna bust up the act and go solo?"

"Oh yeah," he said. "I guess them plans are on hold, huh?"

GUY PUGLIA: In 1953 my old man bent down to lift a crate of clams and never stood back up again. I was in Los Angeles when it happened, settin' up my seafood restaurant, and had to fly to New York and then drive to Codport. I called Vic at the Beverly Wilshire, where he had his bachelor spread even though he was married, and he said to me, "*Goomba,* whatever you want, whatever you need me to do for you, you know I won't let you down." He asked me where and when the funeral was. "It's at Ciampini's Funeral Home on Tuesday at noon," I told him, "and the burial is at the Catholic cemetery on Haddock Road."

Well, yeah, the guy sent I don't know how many hundreds of flowers to the funeral parlor, and the hearse he sprang for could've fit the whole town in it. But he was too busy playing golf to actually attend the thing.

The morning after the funeral I go over to Vic's old house. Vic's mom made me so much food I thought I was gonna burst apart—all that escarole and lasagna, Jesus Christ. His old man ain't sayin' anything, as usual. All the years I known that guy, he was just quiet, lookin' at you with them icy eyes. Now, I'd seen Bruno a few times since Straccio cut off my nose, but we'd never really spent this kind of time together, there was always other people around, right? So Bruno points to my nose and makes a gesture with his chin, like to say, "What's the real story, huh? What happened with that thing anyways?" And I says to him, "It was Rocco Straccio, that goddamn *stronzo.*" And he shook his head slow, like to say it was a shame. I told him that Rocco had been asking questions about Vic, about maybe gettin' some dough from Vic, and that I'd talked back to him.

I went back to my old man's house. [My sister] Franny was there with her husband and their two kids. I spent the night there. The next morning Tony Ferro calls me up, it's maybe 9:00 A.M. He says to me, "Didja hear, Guy? Rocky Straccio died . . . he had a heart attack and died last night." I said to him, "Hey, this ain't the worst news to wake up to, Tony boy."

About a year later Vic's folks move to California. Me and Joe Yung [Vic's valet] picked them up at the airport and we was gonna drive them straight to their new spread, right? But Violetta tells me that they have to go to the police department first and I asked her why. I could see that Bruno didn't want her to tell me the story, but that didn't ever stop Vic's mom. Turns out Bruno had knocked on Straccio's door that night, the night after my old man's funeral, and Straccio invited him in. Bruno didn't say one single fuckin' word to him—he just stared at him, just fixed his ice blue eyes at Straccio. That scumbag rat couldn't look anywhere else, he was hypnotized. And he started tremblin' and sweatin' and goin' pale. And then his heart stopped cold he was so fuckin' frightened to death.

Why was Vic's parents goin' to the police station? 'Cause they had to. See, every time Bruno went to a new city, he had to register his eyes as dangerous weapons.

* * *

ARNIE LATCHKEY: We were all in Vegas when Murray called me from New York. Paramount was champing at the bit to ink Fountain and Bliss to a multipicture deal. And Jack Warner had seen the act at Ciro's and he too was drooling to sign them up. Harry Cohn caught wind of this, had a big confab with his underlings, and before you know it he was salivating as well. Well, with all this important, high-powered spittle bubbling like lava, who now starts dribbling all his spit glands dry? Gussie Kahn.

Murray told me the ins and the outs of the deal and my heart was pumping like an oil gusher. The boys would be locked in for eight pictures; they'd split four hundred grand for the first five, six hundred for the final three. If they renewed after the eight pictures were done, Galaxy would double the numbers. They'd be guaranteed top billing in the movies—it didn't matter if Jesus Christ or Joan of Arc was their costar. In addition, Murray said, Vigorish Productions would get a percentage of the gross after the picture broke even, and it was a handsome enough chunk too. Handsome enough for me to buy a wonderful house on Cañon Drive and keep Estelle in Christian Dior for perpetuity. It was Murray's expert opinion that what Galaxy was offering was a perfect package. He said this was a fan*tab*ulous offer.

"Where are they right now?" he asked me on the phone.

"Vic's probably playing dice, and Ziggy could be anywhere," I told him.

"Well, you tell them all the particulars, Arn, and if they don't snap at this bait, then those two fish are clinically dead."

"There's this slight problem, Murray," I said rather hesitatingly.

"Oh yeah? How slight?"

"Well, they don't really talk to each other anymore."

I went down to the casino and sure enough there was Vic shooting craps. I see him, I see a brunette, not Lulu and not Ginger, sidling up close to him, and I see he's got a grand on the pass line. He rolls a five and then places another thousand in bets all around. The very next roll he craps out.

"Vic, could I get in a word here?" I say to him.

"Not now, Latch, I'm hot," he said.

"Hot? You just lost two grand, Vic!"

"Yeah but ten minutes ago I lost three."

I pulled him away from the dice table and I related Murray's news. He was nodding as I was rattling off the numbers. "This is swell," he'd say. "This is marvelous." I told him that Murray and Hank Stanco were gaga over the deal and he said, "This is just marvelous." When I informed him there was no escape clause, he said, "Who needs one of those?"

"So are you in?" I asked him.

"You just tell me what you want me to do, I'll do it."

"Look, if you're locked into this deal," I said as his eyes veered from the dice table to a seat opening up at a blackjack table, "it means you're locked into Ziggy. You realize that, right?"

"How much dough is it a picture again?" he asked.

SALLY KLEIN: I found Ziggy at the bar at the Flamingo. He was with Red Buttons, Rose Marie, Buzzy Brevetto, just shooting the breeze. I told him I had some news for him and he and I went into the lobby. I related everything to him that Arnie had told me. He was very, very attentive. He told me that he wanted to see the contracts, he wanted the paperwork sent to him. He wanted to know how much control Fountain and Bliss would have over the movies, the scripts, directors. I told him that was something between WAT and Vigorish and Galaxy.

"What about you and Vic?" I asked him. "I don't think you should put your signature on this unless you and he iron out your problems."

"What problems? Me and Vic don't have any problems."

"You don't get along," I said. "You're not friends, you bicker and go behind each other's backs, and you get spiteful and try to destroy each other."

"I don't see how this is a problem though. I think it makes us click."

That night Arnie and I were having dinner. Estelle was there . . . she'd flown out from New York. The three of us barely touched on business; we were just having a pleasant dinner. Estelle said, "Look who just walked in . . ." Arnie and I turned and saw Vic checking in with the maitre d', who showed him to a secluded table. "I bet you a ten-spot tonight he's with a blonde," Arnie said.

"Redhead," Estelle said. "Pay up, honey." Arnie and I turned around again and there was Ziggy, being shown to Vic's table. The two of them sat down and had their dinner.

I remember two days later, Arnie and I were taking a drive around Las Vegas. It was a sunny day, not a cloud in the sky. There wasn't much to do in the daytime, really—there was just Fountain and Bliss at night. So we drove to Hoover Dam and then around a golf course and then headed back to the Oceanfront. When we pulled up, a valet offered to park the car. Arnie handed him the keys and we saw it was Vic! I saw a few yards away that Ziggy was also dressed as a valet and was parking people's cars too. The two of them were working the guests, they were *tummeling!* The four of us then stood out there together and Ziggy and Vic were just going off on these wonderful tangents, joking around, making no sense. All of a sudden there was a tremendous flash of light in the sky and the ground beneath us shook like there were twenty subways underneath us. I don't remember if I heard anything—I don't think so.

"Jesus, what the fuck wazzat?" Vic asked.

"That, my friends," Arnie said, "was the army. They test atomic bombs out here, didn't you know that?"

*   *   *

DANNY McGLUE: The day I married Betsy was the happiest day of my life, because that was also the day that Fountain and Bliss canceled their radio show. I know that might seem mean, but at the small, simple ceremony we had—Betsy insisted that Sally not be invited, and Sally understood—I had this nagging sense of doubt. About the marriage, not the radio show.

Film scripts started arriving by the truckload. You should see some of the garbage I was reading. Galaxy would send us everything, even if it wasn't tailored for Fountain and Bliss. We'd get swashbuckler scripts, war scripts, sports scripts, tons of romance scripts, scripts that may have been perfect for Vic and a romantic lead actress but not for Vic and Ziggy. I remember Sally read one, came into my office, and said, "This is a musical comedy about dying—it's *Dark Victory* with Ziggy as Bette Davis and Vic as George Brent!" She was exaggerating, I think.

Sid Stone and Norman White, meanwhile, had reworked *The Three of Us*—the play that would've been drop-dead perfect for Fountain and Bliss—into a comedy script for the movies. They'd added characters, opened it up, taken out some of the music. It was a wonderful screenplay. For Fountain and Bliss, you could do no better. It was silly yet mature, sophisticated but also slapstick, and it would have played perfectly on the tension between Ziggy and Vic. Sid and Norman asked me to add some jokes and I did. Murray Katz sent it to Galaxy and a week later we got it back with not even a note.

ARNIE LATCHKEY: Oh, the boys would have loved that to be their first picture! They *adored* the script. "This is us, Latch, this is us," Ziggy said. When we sent it to Gus Kahn, it didn't even occur to me that the script would get rejected.

Dissolve. Two weeks later. Murray calls me, tells me that Gus and Ezra Gorman, the producer, had decided on a script titled *Robin Hood and His Merry Morons* for the boys. When I heard the name of this vehicle it was like someone was trying to sell me a berth on the *Lusitania*. I told Murray, "This sounds like *The Dunce of Life* to me all over again!" And he said, "It was called *Shall We Dunce?* and anyway, Ezra swears it's not."

But how did Ezra Gorman know it wasn't? I mean, nobody had ever seen that picture!

ERNIE BEASLEY: I was going through a rough time. I had money coming in from Vic's records—they were huge hits—but my personal life was falling apart. My lover Mike and I were no longer together. What happened was, I'd been invited to a party at a certain movie producer's house in Bel Air. Well, this producer was gay, I knew that—everybody pretty much knew that. I brought Mike along and when we went to the swimming pool in the back, I couldn't believe my eyes. There were boys on the patio and the pool was filled with boys, gorgeous, tanned blond boys with blue eyes, all very muscular. Something out of a Leni Riefenstahl movie! Also in the pool were some older, flabbier men, who certainly did not mind sharing the water.

I went into the house and had a few Manhattans. I really got smashed. There was a piano there and when I've had a few I simply cannot resist a piano. I sang a few songs and mingled and it began to get dark. I made my way back to the patio and was looking for Mike to take me home. I couldn't find him . . . I was asking people where my date was. Then I saw Mike in the pool and was about to say, "Hey, there you are!" when I noticed James J. Pierce, a sixty-three-year old producer at MGM who resembled a fat chipmunk, right behind him. They were both in the deep end. And I don't have to tell you what Jimmy Pierce was doing to Mike.

I was terribly upset. I drove back to the Beverly Hills Hotel and I'm lucky I made it there in one piece, I was so smashed. I went to Vic's bungalow and only Ginger was there. I bawled like a baby, for hours. Ginger was so sweet . . . she was a tough broad but had a good heart. I remember saying to her, "What's Mike doing with that ugly man?" But then I realized: I'm five foot five, I'm completely bald, I wear glasses, and I'm thirty pounds overweight. Mike was young and handsome. What was Mike doing with *me?!*

Ginger and I had a few and we were just complaining about our lives . . . I knew it was over with me and Mike, and she just didn't know what to do. "I know Vic's married, Bease," she said, "but I just love him to death." I told her I thought Vic should leave Lulu and marry her. I told her I wasn't the only one who thought that.

Vic walked in and saw the shape we were in and said immediately, "Okay, who died?" Ginger told him what had happened. He saw how badly I was doing. And do you know what he said? "Aw, just write me a song about it. That'll make you feel better." *That was it!* Not another word. I'd been his buddy, his confidant, from New York to Florida to Chicago to L.A., and here I am falling to pieces and he tells me to write him a song.

"Puddin', let's go to Johnny D'Antibes's joint," he said to Ginger.

The thing is, I did write a song about it. I wrote "Lost and Lonely Again" for him. I couldn't listen to that song for years, it was so sad. When I played it for Vic the first time he said, "Great weepy number, Bease. It'll sell like hot cakes." He was right. But Vic never really got it.

Sometimes he was so shallow I thought he might implode at any given second. But still, you couldn't help but love him somehow. He simply was what he was, and there aren't too many people about whom you can say that.

Last year at an ASCAP dinner for me, a reporter asked me how I felt that millions of men all across the world have put on "Lost and Lonely Again" when they were heartbroken, when their wives and girlfriends broke up with them. I told him I thought it was nifty. But let me tell you: I always got a secret thrill out of it, that here's some sorry lug crying his eyes out in his bed, pitying himself and drinking himself silly over a woman, and he's listening to a song about a guy getting fucked up the ass in a pool in Bel Air.

LULU FOUNTAIN: What? You think I didn't know about the girls? All those whores he ran around with?

Vic was in Hollywood filming his first picture and Hunny drops by the apartment with presents for Vicki. I was pregnant with Vincent then. He was playing on the floor with her and we were eating Chinese food and I said, "I hope Vic is doing good out there in Hollywood."

And Hunny, who was starting to lose his marbles, said, "Aw, I'm sure Ginger's treatin' him real good."

"Oh yeah?" I said. This was the first whiff I ever got of her. "You think so?"

"Oh yeah, sure," he said.

"Who's Ginger?"

"That broad he met on your honeymoon night. At the Latin Quarter."

But you know, I didn't care. I didn't say nothin'. We had this apartment and Vic was providing for the kids. He wants to run around with whores, the less I knew about that the better. I knew he had the suite at the St. Regis. He never told me what it was for and I never asked. It was a good marriage. The most important thing to me was that he be a good father to his kids.

See, I knew that Vic loved me, and the others was just garbage to him. Garbage. I knew he'd come back to me.

JANE WHITE: I got pregnant on my honeymoon and before I was even showing, everybody could tell because I was looking so radiant! Dr. Baer really saved my life.

Ziggy and I moved to a large apartment on Central Park West and Seventieth Street. We would go out for dinner often, sometimes with Danny and Betsy, but she used to upset me because she drank so much. She was a wonderful girl when she was sober but after a few glasses of wine she became nasty. She'd embarrass Danny, humiliate him and say the meanest things. We'd eat with Lulu and Vic sometimes—that was good for Fountain and Bliss because it gave them a chance to see that not only did *they* not always get along, but their wives really did not like each other, either. Ziggy and I would eat with Garson Kanin and Ruth Gordon or the Frank Loessers. We'd go over to the [Broadway producer] Norman Barasches too. One time Gloria Barasch, such a dear, called us after we got home and told Ziggy that some of their silverware was missing. He looked at me and somehow some knives and forks had fallen into my pocketbook.

Ziggy went to Los Angeles to film *The Moron the Merrier* [*sic*] and I stayed in New York. He offered to take me along but I didn't want to be a burden. I trusted him.

ARNIE LATCHKEY: Ziggy banged Mandy Crane the first day he met her. In his dressing room. It was like Ezra Gorman and Gus Kahn had a map of the innermost recesses of Ziggy's mind or of some other parts of him, that she was cast for this picture. Here's a platinum blonde with blue eyes and bazoombas in a different time zone than her back. She could've had ZIGGY stenciled on her forehead. And that Tweety Bird voice of hers, like a six-year-old. Well, the word was all around Hollywood about Ziggy's *shvantz*, let me tell you. Producers, agents, actors, and directors, they would walk up to me in restaurants, ask me how everything was going, tell me they'd seen Fountain and Bliss at Mocambo, tell me they'd had the most marvelous time, and then ask, "Hey, is it true that Ziggy's got a *putz* like a Louisville Slugger?"

George S. Collier directed the picture; he'd been at Warners for years and had moved over to Galaxy. He was the typical rugged, silver-haired, professional director. The man had the classic look—he even used a cigarette holder—everything but the eye patch and jodhpurs. He had a deft touch for comedy but, to tell you the truth, I don't think he liked comedians per se. Or actors. Or anybody. "I've heard about these two," he said to me on the very first day of filming. "If there's any troublemaking on this set, I'll nail 'em so hard they won't be able to breathe. I've worked with the best and these two sons of bitches are rookies. I'm running the shots here and they better realize that. They wanna raise Cain after hours, I don't give a rat's ass. But I run a tight ship on my sets."

"Look," I said, "there were no hijinx when they did that dunce film with Clarence Gilbert."

"They made a movie with Ned?"

"Yeah, a while ago. A short."

"I didn't know that. Jesus, that's too bad."

Some script girl or continuity girl brings something over to George to sign and all of a sudden there's this yelp that comes from down a hallway. It sounded like a toy poodle getting its foot stepped on by a sumo wrestler. And then there's another.

"Will someone see what the hell that's about?" George snapped.

So a flunky goes behind the set and this yelping continues. And the guy comes back a minute later and says—and it was obvious he was lying—he couldn't find the source. Then the yelping stops and a minute later out steps Mandy Crane fixing her hair and her makeup, and ten seconds after that, enter Ziggy Bliss.

"Oh, Jesus Christ, it's already starting," George Collier groaned.

For this picture Collier got off easy. Except for the final day of shooting—when Ziggy and Vic really got to goofing on everybody and wound up destroying the set—there was really no untoward behavior. "I don't think we should get a reputation as mischievous scamps yet," Ziggy said to me and Vic one day, and we agreed. Well, that was a remarkable display of maturity on his part, but I soon was witness to the ulterior brilliant strategy: We won't wreak havoc and raise hell on our *own* set, but who's to say what we can do elsewhere? So whenever there was a break in shooting, they'd go driving around the Galaxy lot and pretty much destroy every other thing being filmed. Robert Spivey was directing *Me, Nero* and every day Ziggy and Vic would sneak on over there. It was one of those "cast of thousands" epics and the boys would don togas and sandals and just sneak into the background. But when filming began they would run to the foreground and disrupt the shoot. Spivey was not amused and neither were the two leads, but that cast of thousands behind them was in hysterics!

SALLY KLEIN: Vic bought the house in Beachwood Canyon. Jack handled that deal and he waived his fee for Vic. Vic also had his "rumpus suite" at the Beverly Wilshire. Ziggy got a place in Beverly Hills, also thanks to Jack. I was living with Jack at his house in Malibu—we were engaged now—and Estelle and Arn were living at the Hollywood Plaza until they could close on the Cañon Drive house.

Howard Leeds, the head of production at Galaxy, called me one day and said there was a problem with Vic, that he was having problems with his lines. Not only remembering them but *saying* them. Now, I knew that Vic was never ever going to be big on reading the script and committing it to memory—if they made a movie about someone rattling off a horse's past performances from the *Daily Racing Form,* then maybe Vic would've won an Oscar. But I didn't understand what Howie meant.

Merry Morons was a Robin Hood spoof. Vic was Robin Hood and Ziggy was—well, Danny, who did a wonderful job punching up the script, called the character "Sir John Falstaff of Grossinger's," but the character was really named Little John. The movie took place in Plotzingham, in Sherman Forest and in and around a castle. (Sherman Forest was a Hollywood in-joke because he was a production designer at Galaxy.) Now, Ziggy was superb with dialects, but Vic was having trouble. He could imitate Cary Grant or Ronald Colman but he couldn't for the life of him come up with his own voice. George Collier would have them do a few takes and they thought they had it in the can, but then someone would say, "George, Vic dropped the British accent the last five takes." So it was ultimately decided that Vic would do the entire picture with his normal American accent.

"His normal American accent?" Arnie said when he heard about this. "He don't *have* a normal American accent!"

They closed the set down for a week. Very expensive. And they brought in Clotilde Sturdivandt.

DANNY McGLUE: She made Margaret Dumont look like Jean Harlow. She was what they called a *couthier.* There were a few of these Emily Post/Amy Vanderbilt-like women in Hollywood. They taught couth; that is, they taught people how to not be uncouth. These women were all society grande dames . . . one of them, I heard, had even had an operation on her pinkie to get that perfect teacup-lift pose. Harry Cohn called these women "silk purses," because what they were paid to do was essentially make silk purses out of sow's ears.

So a few days a week Miss Sturdivandt would meet Vic at the Beverly Wilshire and for about two hours a day she would work him over from the toes to the hair. "This fat old dame's like a fuckin' drill sergeant, Danny boy," he said to me. She threw out his personal wardrobe—said it made him look like a gangster—and he bought about two hundred new suits. She had him walking down the hall at the hotel balancing a pea on his nose.

She told him how to cut steak, fowl, and fish at the proper angles. Every time he said "eatin'" or "takin'" instead of "eating" or "taking," she would rap him on the knuckles with a ruler and call him a silly goose. She had him saying "Ramiro Rodriguez rarely river-rafts down the roaring Raritan River" ten times, trying to get him to roll his *r*'s, and when he couldn't pull it off, she had him do it with three eagle talons under his tongue. She would show him movies of Herbert Marshall smoking cigarettes and say that this was the correct way to inhale. Every rule of etiquette there was, she taught him.

"I tell you what that fat dame needs, Ziggy," he said one day on the set, grabbing his crotch. "She needs Mr. Baciagaloop."

"Gee, I guess them lessons ain't really takin'," Ziggy said.

But Ziggy was having his own problems.

Collier, Gus Kahn, and some production people were looking at the rushes one day and Kahn stood up and said, "Hey! What the goddamn hell is that?!" And Collier said, "What the hell is *what?*" Kahn yelled to the projectionist to stop and they froze on this one frame of Ziggy in costume with Mandy Crane and Vic—it was a scene on a bridge going over a moat.

"Look at that, goddamn it!" Kahn barked out. "This is a disaster! The little fat red basketball's got a prick like a Shmulka Bernstein salami!"

And all eyes shifted to Ziggy's crotch.

"This is a goddamn catastrophe!" Kahn screamed.

They then looked at *all* the scenes they'd shot. As Little John, Ziggy had to wear these very tight green leotards, and you could see it in every scene he was in. It really did look like he had a big salami stuffed in his tights.

They shut down for a week. Monsieur Joffre—he was the Galaxy costume designer—had to go back to the drawing board. (How he had not noticed this, I don't know.) A week later they had a new costume. Ziggy wore a codpiece in some scenes or a long green waistcoat that went down to his knees, where things were "safe," in others. And they reshot all the old scenes.

ARNIE LATCHKEY: Bertie Kahn calls me and says that everybody and his kid sister knows about Ziggy and Mandy Crane. Mandy's blabbing about it like she'd just won the lottery, which, if you're a nymphomaniac, maybe you had. Now, don't forget, Jane is about to give birth to Freddy. Grayling Greene calls Millie in New York one day and tells her he's going to print it that Ziggy and Mandy are engaging in "she-nanigans," as he called it, that fat *momzer*.

Morty Geist, who meanwhile is trying to gloss over a fight that Vic had with a reporter at Romanoff's, flies to New York and he's telling Greene that if he prints this story—albeit this true story—then who knows what's going to happen to Jane? Does Grayling Greene, Morty asks him, want it on his conscience that Jane gives birth early and the baby dies?

"*What* conscience, Morty?" Greene says to him, "I'm a gossip columnist."

So the item runs in about a dozen Scripps-Howard papers across the country.

And it worked out beautifully, in the end. Jane saw it, she read it, and she gave birth to Freddy about one month too soon. By now, Morty had written what he called "The Ten Standard Denials and Apologies for Fountain and Bliss." For this situation he picked Denial Number Three, fiddled with it here and there to adapt it to the situation, and issued it. "Lots of stuff is being said about me and Miss Crane. Fortunately I do not read the papers. But Janie does. She knows that all this stuff is garbage. Janie and I are as happy a couple as can be. And a certain columnist has to live with himself that he almost killed my baby boy. Freedom of speech is one thing. Infanticide is another."

When Morty flew back to Hollywood he called me and said, "Latch, these two have got me at the end of my rope." I could hear his teeth grinding together.

"Then you gotta get a new rope, *bubeleh,*" I said to him.

JANE WHITE: I was so mad at that Grayling Greene. To go and print that rubbish at such a time! All he had to do was wait another four weeks.

When Freddy was a month old and strong enough, I took him to Los Angeles. We kept the place in New York. Galaxy sent a limo to the airport to pick us up. I loved the new house, it was a dream come true. When the limousine pulled in, there was a Mercedes-Benz with a big red ribbon around it and a sign that said FOR LIL' FREDDY. AND JANIE TOO. I opened the door and waited for Ziggy to run up and shower Freddy and me with hugs and kisses, but he was filming the *Merry Moron* movie.

ERNIE BEASLEY: The dynamic had changed. Vic and Ziggy were husbands and fathers now—Vincent was born when the Robin Hood movie wrapped shooting. Everybody but Danny McGlue had moved to Los Angeles. Vic spent as many nights at the Beverly Wilshire with Ginger as he did at his home with Lulu, probably more. But then Vic figured out that he really didn't have a place all his own, so he got another suite at the Ambassador.

This wasn't easy for anyone involved. I had to constantly be on my toes. I'd eat with Vic and Lu and have to keep mum about Ginger. I'd go out with Vic and Ginger, and Lu was pretty much a forbidden topic, and so were Lana Turner and Deena Moore and Sheila Owens. Vic would drag me to a nightclub with Sheila Owens, a contract player at Warners and a gal who cursed like a sailor, and I wasn't allowed to talk about Ginger or Lana or Deena. There was a different protocol every night!

At the premiere in Los Angeles, Fountain and Bliss did a half hour onstage before they ran the picture. I was sitting next to Lulu. Now, Vic had secured a small part for Ginger—she's in the movie for four minutes and has about three lines. Guy Puglia had told me that Lu knew about Ginger, so when Ginger came on the screen out of the corner of my eye I was watching Lulu. She didn't change her expression, not a jot, but that could be either because she didn't realize it was Ginger or simply because she was Lulu.

ARNIE LATCHKEY: When their first motion picture was released, that was really the closest they ever were. The two couples would even have dinner one or two times a week. So the negative reviews . . . they really hurt us. But I think it also brought them closer together, like two GIs surrounded and getting shelled in a very tight foxhole. The *Times* and Bosley Crowther tore us to pieces—fortunately for us, he'd forgotten the dunce picture and did not allude to it. He said that Vic passing himself off as Robin Hood would be like Ingrid Bergman playing Lucky Luciano, which, come to think of it, don't sound like a bad idea. Archer Winsten in the *Post* mauled us like a bear, and Chester Yalburton of the *Globe*—who wouldn't have liked a Fountain and Bliss movie if we paid him a hundred grand (and we gave that serious consideration)—shredded us like confetti. Justin Gilbert of the Los Angeles *Mirror* pulverized us.

"Comics don't ever get no respect, Latch," Ziggy said to me when we had all the reviews in. "You make someone cry, you're a hero, a saint. You make someone laugh, you're a mongrel. You think *Duck Soup* and *A Night at the Opera* got good notices?"

"Actually, they did," I said to him.

"Hey, who cares if any of these no-good hack bastards like the movie, as long as the people do, you know?" Vic said.

"Good point, Vic," Ziggy said.

"I mean," Vic continued, "the most important thing is we keep audiences laughing and tapping their toes, right?"

"Amen, brother!" Ziggy yelled out. "Say it!"

"The man is right, the man is right!" I said.

"Let's face it: The picture is probably garbage," Vic said. "Like shit, it'll draw flies. But who cares? Because those flies are bringin' in tons of dough."

Ziggy and I looked at each other . . . we just couldn't go that far with Vic on that, although he was probably right.

They toured in support of the movie, went to all the big cities. They also played the Copa in New York, the Chez Paree in Chicago, the Beach-comber in Miami, did three weeks in Vegas. They missed Sally and Jack's wedding but sent her flowers and got her and Jack a Cadillac. Fountain and Bliss made the cover of *Look, Life,* and *Time.* (Morty wanted to polish over Vic's rougher edges, so he tried to spread it around how smart he was; Vic told the *Life* guy he was a crossword fanatic and a history buff. But if you look at one of the photos carefully, you can see that the puzzle Vic is working on is upside down.) They were hotter than a pistol . . . but *Time* made the mistake of calling Ziggy's parents vaudevillians of minor repute and talent. Big boo-boo, that.

Morty Geist cooked up some wonderful stunts for them—they dressed up as Robin Hood and Little John and did usher work at the theaters, Morty would get crazy people off the street and out of flophouses and tell them to shriek like they were going bananas. The movie did exceptionally well, people filled the theaters, but it didn't get one good review. Ziggy would actually read the negative reviews onstage at the nightclubs. He would read the reviews and insult whoever wrote the thing, and Vic would stand there with nothing to do but hold his mike like it was a limp *putz.* Vic could handle it for five minutes, but after that he wanted to strangle Zig with the cord. Morty would try to get Ziggy to stop—"You're really not helping your next movie's reception any, Zig," he'd say—and Ziggy would let loose at the poor kid. If Ziggy couldn't cut the throats of the reviewers, well then, he'd sure try to pop Morty's eardrums.

DANNY McGLUE: I wrote a screenplay that I thought was wonderful for Fountain and Bliss. Arnie and Ziggy agreed; they were crazy about it. But Gus Kahn and Howie Leeds, the production chief, sent it back to us. At least there was a note attached this time: "All wrong for F & B." I was baf-fled.

But Ziggy had other work for me to do.

He wanted me to write an autobiographical profile of him for *Parade* magazine. I said to him, "It's autobiographical, Ziggeleh, that usually tends to mean that *you* would do that." But he said that he was too busy. Which was true. He had Freddy and Jane, and the boys were now starting their second picture, *The Ego and the Idiot.* Plus, Vegas and New York and Miami Beach and Chicago all the time. Now, I knew that Ziggy was furi-ous about what *Time* had written about Harry and Flo, but I also knew that what *Time* had said was the truth. I wanted to impart this to Ziggy but I knew better.

"We gotta tell the whole story, Danny, we gotta set the record straight for posterior," he said. (I taught him that horrible pun, I confess.)

"And that's where I come in, is it?" I asked.

"That's where *we* come in. Don't forget, it's me writin' this, not you, even though you're writin' it."

I had two weeks to turn this thing in to him so he could turn it in to *Parade*. And for the life of me, it was the most difficult thing I ever had to do. He was asking me for Ovid's *Metamorphoses!* He wanted me to create myths, to turn him into a swan, a hyacinth, or a pomegranate! You think that's easy?! I'd sit down at my old Olympia and nothing would come out. Betsy and I were staying at the Beverly Hills Hotel then and I'd sit there from nine to five and by five o'clock there wasn't one word on the page. What am I supposed to write? How much Ziggy—or "I"—loved and worshiped "my" parents? How talented and influential and successful they were? I mean, Ted, I might as well have been trying to write Eleanor Roosevelt's memoirs and cover her years as a geisha girl in the forties. It just wasn't coming.

Betsy had landed a small role in *The Ego and the Idiot* and wasn't around in the daytime. And by nine at night she'd be smashed. She'd wake up with a throbbing hangover, then go off to the set. So she had the movie, the booze, the headaches, and all I had was a blank piece of paper. Meanwhile, Sally was pregnant and living happily with Jack. My life was not doing so well.

The night before it was due I wrote it. It was like writing a short story. I made everything up . . . I said that my parents Harry and Flo were the most talented people to ever grace a stage, "the Lunt and Fontanne of vaudeville." Burns and Allen had lifted their act from them, I wrote, biting so hard on a bullet that I could taste the gunpowder. I wrote that they were obsessed with bringing Ziggy into showbiz and always brought him on the road with them; they nurtured him and nearly spoiled him to death. I went with the line Ziggy always said: "My parents may have been small of stature, but they were titans when it came to talent and heart." Ziggy had been perpetuating a myth in the press for years now, that Harry and Flo died, not when they saw the O'Hares onstage with their son, but when they saw Vic perform with Ziggy. Now, he was actually starting to believe it. "They knew I'd be safe now, they knew I'd be successful, so they died and did so happily," I wrote, "knowing their precious boychick would hit it big." It was nonsense, it was baloney from the first letter to the last period, and Ziggy loved it. And so did *Parade*'s readers.

Not long after this I also wrote an autobiographical profile of Vic for *Parade*.

SNUFFY DUBIN: You know, the first time I played Vegas, it was at the Last Frontier. Pete the pervert wouldn't hire me for the Oceanfront. Jack Entratter wouldn't hire me for the Sands. I couldn't get arrested at the Sahara or the Dunes. So I did the Last Frontier and it was no different than some of the places back east, except this place had a western motif, so instead of just puke there was sawdust on the floor. And puke too.

I was living out of a motel in Santa Monica then, the Starbrite Inn. Small square rooms, a Philco radio, a bed like a Samsonite suitcase, and a window. Oh, there was a pool but you should see some of the swill that was floating in there. Frogs would jump in and die on the spot. I worked Strip City, the Ruby Room on La Cienega, and the Colony Club. I always tell everybody that's how I met my wife, which is true, but she was no stripper. Debbie went there with her then-boyfriend, some hard-on lawyer for Paramount, and before the week was out she was all mine. Lenny Bruce used to play these places, so did Buzzy Brevetto. The girls working the joint, they weren't bad. Marty Dahl ran the Ruby but Mickey Cohn and the Fratellis were behind it. A lot of the strippers were hookers and the stories they told me I could sell now for a million bucks.

Celebrities would come in—it wasn't just raincoat artists jackin' themselves off. Marlon Brando had just done *Julius Caesar*, he'd come by a lot. Liz Taylor, Desi Arnaz, and Nat Cole. Lots of doctors too, with their nurses. There was a motel across the street and you had lots of married couples drifting in and out, but they usually weren't married to each other.

Ziggy dropped in one Saturday night at the Ruby and, man, I really needed to put a show on. You know who's there? Jack Entratter from the Sands. Joe DeWolfe from the Aladdin. Moe Dalitz is there too, so's Lee Rosenfeld from the Tidal Wave Hotel, which had just opened on the [Vegas] Strip. All these hotshots who could book me into joints in the blink of an eye. Ziggy's with this girl who used to do blue movies, her name was Nina Mellon, but the real last name was Melendez, I think. Ziggy was addicted to these movies, he had a vault full of 'em. So all these big shots are in the crowd and I know I gotta load up all the guns, I'm gonna go all out and murder every single person in that room. And I've got the act down. I relate anecdotes, I tell stories, no punch lines, no mugging, no Catskills shtick. It's me being me and if I screw up, then execute me. And none of that flop sweat—that's when the audience sees you working so hard to make you love them that they wind up hating your fucking guts. There's none of that. I'm gonna hurt 'em so much they're gonna love me.

But I'm five minutes into my set and suddenly Ziggy bounces onto the stage. Jesus Christ, this is the last thing I need! I need this like I wanna team up with Mahatma Gandhi and we sing love songs to each other like Sandler and fucking Young. Now, what's the worst thing I can do at this point? If I tell Ziggy to take a hike, it makes me look so bad it's like I'm erased right in front of your eyes. So I gotta just roll with this. I gotta roll with it and run with it and play along. Except for this: It wasn't rolling, it wasn't running, it wasn't playing. This was death. You ever wonder why there's a straight man and a funnyman and not *two* funnymen? Well, if so, you should've been at the Ruby that night. It was like bringing Joe DiMaggio and Ted Williams up to the plate at the same time! You got a righty and a lefty and do they hit the ball? Nope, they wind up banging each other's brains to applesauce with the first swing. Absolute death.

I went to my dressing room afterward. I had my door open because I was just too *festunkt* to close it. And all these strippers are walking by with their getups, it was like I was in a bird zoo or something, all these feathers and stuff. *This could've been my night!* I had all those heavy hitters out there! And I got flattened, I'm a latke underneath a steamroller.

Ziggy came in. He said, "Snuffles, remember all them years I wanted to double with you?"

"How could I forget?" I said.

"I guess it was a good thing it never happened, huh?"

"Joe DeWolfe and Jack Entratter were in the audience tonight."

"Izzat right?"

"Yeah, they were," I said. "Lee Rosenfeld too, from the Tidal Wave."

"Tonight? Just now?"

"They were probably scouting me."

"I didn't know that, Snuff."

Well, I found out that wasn't true. Because Debbie had seen Ziggy and Joe DeWolfe talking to each other five minutes before I came on. The liar.

"Well, anyways, Snuff, maybe you'll kinda bathe in my refracted glory," he says.

Bathe? I almost got drowned in it.

"What are those?" he asked me.

"These?" I said. "Oh, they're just pep pills. I got another set to do. They help me do it."

"So what is it? It's like coffee?"

"Yeah, it's like coffee. Like lots of fuckin' coffee."

"Could I get a few of those, Snuffles? I got the movies and the clubs and everything."

I passed him about ten bennies.

"So how do you get this funny fuel?" he asked. Great name for the stuff, huh?

"Doctors come in all the time. After a set, I sit with them, make them giggle, they write me a script."

"Oh yeah? They do that for you? Just for makin' 'em laugh?"

"What, you think all those girls with big tits fuck you because they *love* you?"

Two hours later I'm all keyed up for the second set. But all of the big shots were gone.

ARNIE LATCHKEY: *The Ego and the Idiot* was a slapsticky farce about psychiatry and mistaken identities. It was the Three Stooges meet *Spellbound*—in other words, a catastrophic head-on collision. Ziggy played Sigmund Floyd, a Viennese analyst but actually a schizo bricklayer from Milwaukee. Vic was a crooner—a real stretch, huh?—who suffered from stage fright and needed help. Penny Rhodes and Sondra Webb, who Ziggy and Vic, respectively, were *shtupping* on the side, were the female leads. George Collier was helming again, but this time he never warned the boys about goofing around on the set. So they went crazy. Vic doesn't rehearse and has to do five takes to get a sentence out. Ziggy gets impatient and screws around with the camera, the script girl, the props. He did this thing with the mike boom one day; he pretended to be rowing with it and swung it around, right into Collier's eye. Smashed his glasses.

So now the man finally had the eye patch.

The boys were being overworked, no doubt about it. They took on more than they could handle. Sometimes on the weekends, they'd fly to New York to do the Copa or to Florida to play the Fontainebleau. It was crazy, believe me. They played three shows at the Hollywood Bowl. Shep Lane worked a clause into the contracts so they could break if they had a week-long club date lined up. They did, they broke, the filming was all *farkakte*.

It began to wear on them. They did a week at Ciro's during the last week of the *Idiot* flick. They were lackluster shows. I'd never seen them so off. Now, it could've been because they were just so tired from all the shooting, the drinking and carousing, and from being husbands and fathers, which they did manage to squeeze in every now and then, but it also could have been because . . . they were getting along with each other! They were allies now, they were buddies, you could almost say. *Almost.*

[George S. Collier's] lawyer called Shep Lane because he wanted damages for the eye, and I tell Shep, Okay, why fight this thing, we'll give Cyclops B. DeMille what he wants. The sum they settled on I could buy ten new eyes with! While that was going on, Bobby Hale ravaged Fountain and Bliss in the *Examiner*. He said that that they were almost as bad at Ciro's as they were on screen. Vic had just released his first LP, *Midnight With Vic*, and Hale really let him have it about that. He said Vic had three modes when he sang: sleepy, very sleepy, and fast asleep. Vic was really the target—he mostly left Ziggy alone.

GUY PUGLIA: I went to the *The Ego and the Idiot* premiere at the Egyptian [Theater]. After the movie there was a party at Johnny D'Antibes's joint, where Ziggy and Vic got up and thanked everybody for coming and for putting up with the movie, which I guess they could tell wasn't so great. I was walkin' around this party—man, there were so many famous people and beautiful girls there—and I run into Lulu, she's with Bruno, who now wears black sunglasses all the time, and Violetta. And alls of a sudden Ernie Beasley walks past and he's got Ginger on his arm.

Ernie was already pretty smashed—what else is new?—and Ginger had had a few too. Ernie introduces Ginger to everybody and says she had a bit part in the *Idiot* movie, which was true, she's in it for maybe four scenes as a nurse.

" . . . And this is Lulu Fountain, Vic's wife," Ernie said.

Ginger extended her hand and Lulu didn't shake it.

"Oh, you're Vic's whore, right?" Lu said.

Ginger looked straight down.

"You wanna screw him," Lu said, "I don't care. Do a good job, keep him happy. But don't think for a second you can take him away from my kids and me."

She and Bruno and Violetta walked away.

"Maybe we should leave, baby," Ernie said.

"Maybe we should have another drink," Ginger said.

About a week after that, Chinese Joe Yung had to drive Ginger to Mexico to get an abortion.

LULU FOUNTAIN: I felt sorry for that Ginger girl. She thought she was somethin' special to Vic, but she wasn't. She was a piece of meat. I could've sat down with her and set her straight. But, I figured, the best thing to do is just let Vic break her heart.

ERNIE BEASLEY: Guy's Seafood Joint in Malibu had been open for a few months and Vic was there one night with me, those Fratelli brothers, who always frightened me, and Hunny and Ginger. And Bobby Hale and his wife walked in.

Near the end of our meal, Vic went to the bathroom, returned to the table, and called the waiter over. He said to the waiter, "Bring this over to Mr. Hale's table, tell him it's compliments of Vic Fountain. And tell him no hard feelings." He handed the waiter a rolled-up napkin and I don't have to tell you what was in there.

"Just watch this," Vic said.

"He don't need a napkin," Hunny said. "He's already got one."

"Okay, Hunny. Sure."

The waiter presented the napkin to Bobby Hale, and Bobby raised his glass to us. For a moment he must have thought Vic the magnanimous sort. His wife snuggled up close to him, wondering what was inside. They couldn't smell it—Vic told me he'd poured some of Ginger's Chanel on it.

I will *never* as long as I live forget the look on Bobby Hale and his wife's faces when they unrolled it. Before they could stand up to leave, Vic was right over them, yelling. He yelled at Bobby Hale's wife, "You actually let this stinkin' piece of shit fuck you? 'Cause that's what he is!" and to Bobby Hale, "Who the hell do you think you are to rip me like that?! *Vafancul'!*"

For some reason, Hunny and one of the Fratellis joined Vic at the table. It became this whole macho thing, a pissing contest.

"Vic, this is disgusting," Hale said. "We're leaving."

But Vic wouldn't let the two of them go.

"You're not even man enough to fight me!" Vic said. "You insult me in your paper but now that I'm here you're too afraid to have a go at me."

I thought Vic was going to shove Bobby Hale or grab his collar but he never did.

"Come on, Bobby, be a man. Come on, pussy!" Vic said.

"Honey, let's go," Bobby said, and he and his wife stood up.

But Hunny mistook "honey" for "Hunny," I guess. He started messing with Bobby Hale. By now, Guy and some waiters are over at the table and he's urging Vic to back off. The last thing he wants is a big scene. "Just let 'em go, Vic, okay?" Guy was urging.

Before anybody knew it, Hunny had leveled Bobby Hale. He was unconscious on the floor. One of the Fratellis started kicking him in the ribs but Bobby Hale's wife restrained him and so did Guy, who was very, very strong.

It was in the papers the next day. There were pictures of the ambulance outside the restaurant, which, by the way, was just fabulous publicity for the place! And all the reporters had it that hot-tempered singer/actor Vic Fountain had gotten into a fierce brawl. Nobody had it right, that someone else had fought Vic's battle for him.

* * *

GUY PUGLIA: I had this lovely setting in Malibu, right on the water, and Vic was my big backer. For years he tried to get me to take lobster and oysters off the menu but I told him that a place called Guy's Seafood Joint that didn't serve any seafood wouldn't really draw too many people. He wasn't thrilled I served seafood but, hey, seafood is what I know. The chef would always have food special for him, like veal, steak, or pasta. I had to go along with this one thing of his, though, or he wouldn't ever have put up the dough—the place looked onto the ocean and the beach, it was a great view. People would've killed for that view. But Vic said he didn't want to see the water. Windows on the highway outside, that was fine, but none onto the water. So on that I caved in. Instead of windows, there was a mural of Mount Vesuvius erupting all over Pompeii covering the whole wall. And there was another thing: My sister Franny sent me a big plastic swordfish to hang on the wall. When we knew Vic was comin'—or when he just popped in—we had to take it off the wall.

You know, Vic pissed me off with that big fight. If I wanted to open up a goddamn arena for gladiators, I would have.

The day after Hunny decked that reporter, it was the first time I ever had to turn people away. We sat about eighty people and I'm tellin' you, three hundred people turned up all at once. It made me wonder how much business that barber shop where [Albert] Anastasia was killed did the next few weeks . . . that place must've been fuckin' *packed*.

ARNIE LATCHKEY: It was a miracle Hunny didn't kill Bobby. It was one thing to have a reputation as a hot-tempered, lethargic-voiced Italian brawler—even though Vic hadn't punched anybody—but it's another thing entirely to be a murderer.

Morty Geist went berserk over this. On the one hand, Vic really wanted it spread around that he was a tough guy and could lick anyone alive; on the other he didn't want to be charged with assault and go to jail. The *Examiner*—which didn't take too much of a shining to Vic beating one of their star reporters senseless—had found out that Vic had gotten Ginger in a family way.

We were in the Vigorish offices on Wilshire, trying to figure out how to spin this thing like a dreidel.

I said, "How do they know Vic knocked up Ginger, but they don't know that it wasn't Vic that knocked out Bobby Hale?"

Sally set us straight. She said, "It's not news that Hunny Gannett knocks out Bobby, but it is if it's Vic. Man bites dog."

"What are we gonna do?" Morty said. "We gotta do something!"

"Calm down, Morty," Sally said.

"I am calm. This is me calm." He pulls another five hairs out of his head.

He and Shep Lane, who'd just moved to Los Angeles, spelled it out. Hunny, who had really knocked out Bobby anyway, would take the fall. There were witnesses in the restaurant . . . it was only Vic crowing to the world he'd laid out Bobby, nobody else. If Bobby wanted to sue for damages, we'd give him what he wanted, which we did. (Turned out the guy needed more wiring in his jaw than Bell Telephone.) So Hunny wound up going to jail for a spell, and Vic was out a hundred grand. Morty rigged it so, yeah, Vic would pay the dough but the *Examiner* would bury the thing about Ginger. And Bobby Hale, even though he was in the hospital for a week and didn't have all his wits about him, had just enough of them to go along with it.

So a week after this whole brouhaha, Joe Yung drives Vic and Hunny to the police station to turn Hunny in.

"See ya in a few weeks, okay, buddy?" Hunny said to Vic as they took him away.

The next week Vic has to make the same trip, this time with Joe Yung. 'Cause the cops had caught Joe ushering Sondra Webb to one of those "clinics."

SALLY KLEIN: Gus Kahn was furious. Not only had Ziggy half-blinded one of his directors, but Vic—via Hunny—had knocked out a big Hollywood reporter! Galaxy was paying for the *couthier* but the lessons just weren't taking. "What is Clotilde doing with him anyways?" Gus shouted to me at the Polo Lounge. "Giving him boxing lessons?"

You know, it boosted record sales. After the fight, *Midnight With Vic* really took off. And Fountain and Bliss got so much mileage in the act out of this new "Brawling Baritone" reputation of Vic's . . . they milked it for all it was worth.

"Someone's got to put a lid on these two," Gus said. And then he said, "Or hey, you know what? We could maybe put them in a prizefighting movie!"

(Not two months later *A Couple of Lightweights* went into production.)

Arnie and I went to Vic's place at the Ambassador one afternoon. We brought up some deli food from Canter's, I remember. Vic was overextending himself, Shep had told us. He was now keeping three hotel suites, one at the Wilshire for Ginger, one at the Ambassador for himself, and another at the Biltmore for . . . well, I don't know for who or what. He had the house with Lulu and the kids and had also just bought a house in Vegas.

"Look, everything's okay with me, guys," Vic said.

"What about Hunny? Have you visited him in jail?" I asked him.

"I'll get around to that," he said. "I think the Hun's a little embarrassed. Besides, I don't think he even remembers what he's in there for."

"We're getting offers from CBS for a TV show," I told him. "But I think—"

"Hey, I think we should bite. You work one day a week, you can't beat that."

"Well," I said, "it's not really working one day a week. There are rehearsals and the show has to be written."

"One day a week, Sally. How much any other sucker wants to work, that's his problem."

Arnie opens up three bottles of Cel-Ray tonic but Vic passed on it. Instead he had Joe Yung mix him up a martini.

"It's a little early for a martini," I said. "Don't you think?"

"It's always a little early for a Cel-Ray tonic, if you ask me."

"Look, you got the boxing picture," Arnie said, "you've got the *Sullivan* show to do, you're booked for three weeks in Vegas, I'm a little hesitant about adding a TV show to the mix."

"So we won't do the boxing picture," Vic said. "We'll cancel that."

"We can't cancel that!" Arnie said. "Look, do you ever see Vicki and Vincent? How are they doing?"

"Oh, they're just the best, Latch. Vicki is the prettiest little thing you ever saw."

"And Vincent?"

"Vincent's okay. He's just a boy."

"When's the last time you saw them?"

"Jesus, it was as recent as five days ago, I'd say. Joe Yung drives her to school every day. Don't worry about me and Vicki. She'll be the princess of Hollywood."

I tried to get through to Vic. I spoke very earnestly to him, girl to boy. I told him that he should spend more time with his family, with Lulu, that he shouldn't spend all his extra time running after showgirls and actresses. Joe Yung had been in jail for a week, Hunny was in for over a month. He was hurting his wife, his kids, his mistress, his friends. I went on for about ten minutes and in this time Joe Yung made him one or maybe even two more martinis. Whenever I delivered lectures to Ziggy, it felt to me that the words went *around* him, but this time, with Vic, I felt that there was a fog around his head. The words got lost in all the smoke.

Arnie and I were leaving, we were at the door. While we were saying 'bye to Vic, the bedroom door opened. There was a girl there, she looked just like she'd stepped off the floor show at the Desert Inn. She went to the bathroom, said hello to us. Arnie nudged me and I looked into the bedroom. There was another girl in the bed.

"See ya, guys," Vic said to us.

* * *

JANE WHITE: Freddy was just the cutest, the most adorable little boy. He looked just like me, too. So many celebrities would stop on over at the house and play with him. If it wasn't Larry Olivier coming over with Vivien Leigh one night, it was him coming over with Danny Kaye the next. Claude Rains would come over too, and he and Freddy would play hide-and-seek. When Jack and Sally had little Donny, Freddy and he used to play all the time. Vicki and Vince would play with him, but I think Vicki hit him a few times. Oh, did you know that Freddy had a criminal record before he was two years old? Isn't that just the darndest thing? I was shopping for a bracelet one day in Rusar's, and Freddy's nanny Ruthie was pushing him around in his stroller. By accident, a few items fell into the stroller. Well, when the man in the store stopped us as we were going out, Ruthie and I were so offended. There was no way, I told the man, that a one-year-old could possibly have taken all that merchandise and put it into the stroller! And he said to me, "You're right, there is no way, ma'am." The manager came over and it seemed to be a choice between arresting me, Ruthie, or little Freddy. But since Freddy had the goods, they arrested him and, naturally, the charges were thrown out.

When [Ziggy found out] that Vic had recorded an album—I didn't think I could control him. He had two rooms in the back of the house that I was *never* to enter, and he just sealed himself in there. When he came out for dinner he barely said a word. I would try to engage him in normal conversation but, to tell the truth, it was always hard to engage Ziggy in normal conversation. I would spend so much time supervising the cooking of his dinners and sometimes he wouldn't take a bite. Freddy and I would sit at the table and Ziggy would be silent for twenty minutes and then say out of the blue, "How does he think he can do that to me? He thinks I'm gonna roll over and play dead?" My best friend Joanie Pierce, who lived across the street then, reminded me a few years ago that Freddy's first full sentence was "I hate Vic."

Ziggy had an autographed copy of *Midnight With Vic* . . . Vic had signed it "To my favorite partner. Hope you like it." When Ziggy got that he was beyond my control. He put it on the record player and listened to each song for about three seconds each. He was merciless, he was using such nasty words—I had to cover up Freddy's ears. And he would scratch the record to pieces with the needle while the volume was turned all the way up! It was the worst noise.

Do you know what he did? We drove all around L.A. and stopped at every single hi-fi store and bought the record. We bought up every single copy we could find. He was so irate—he must've been driving ninety miles an hour down Sunset Boulevard. I think by then he was already taking what he called "funny fuel." (I took them too, but they didn't really have an effect on me. They made me feel naturally "me," peppy and all.) We went to every record store within forty miles, I'd say. Freddy was on my lap the whole way, and Ziggy was cursing a blue streak. When we got home, Ziggy broke them or burned them or buried them.

"How can he do this to me?" he said to me. "Do you think he would put out this dreck if it wasn't for me?! Do you think he'd be in movies? Do you think he'd be living in Beverly Hills?! Do you think he'd be banging Marilyn Monroe and eating at the Trocadero and wearing all those suits he's got?!"

"Is he really banging Marilyn Monroe?" I asked him.

"*Yes!!!* And it's all on account of me! If it wasn't for me, Janie," he said, "he'd still be fishing in New England!"

"I thought you told me he never did fish in New England."

And then he got that sweet, special, impish look on his face. He was in the middle of the living room, surrounded by Vic's records, the jackets and the sleeves, dozens of them, hundreds. The fact that he was boosting Vic's sales so much—this hadn't occurred to him. But when I mentioned the fishing thing to him, all of a sudden he felt 100 percent better. And he was Ziggy again.

REYNOLDS CATLEDGE IV: Ziggy Bliss, who was then appearing at a nightclub with Vic in Florida, phoned me in Nebraska. Things were not going well for me but I shall refrain from relating just how bad it was. But it was bad. An article about Vic's childhood had appeared in *Parade*, Ziggy told me now, and was replete with errors. This article was only two pages long but there were ten pages of mistakes, he jested. Ziggy related to me all the inaccuracies. He would say something to the effect of "and in the next sentence, that's all horseshit too." I informed him that I did not have the article in question, but he did not seem to hear this. "Look at this!" he yelled, but I had nothing to look at but the phone cord.

"Someone's got to clear the air here, Cat," Ziggy said to me. And I at once knew that this someone was myself.

My letter to the magazine was two pages—Ziggy had actually written it and I fixed up the grammar and the spelling, which was quite a task. When *Parade* ran it, they edited it down to some four sentences. Mr. Fountain has never worked in any aspect of the fishing industry, I'd written. A Clotilde Sturdivandt, I also wrote, has been working with Mr. Fountain for years trying to improve his couth, to no apparent effect. Mr. Fountain's father, the letter stated, was once suspected in the murder of a mob figure in the commonwealth of Massachusetts, and Vic himself had once had a run-in with some sheriffs in Washington State. I also alluded to the tale of his missing toes and indicated that it was unlikely lobsters had bitten them off. The letter was sent anonymously from Nebraska.

Several weeks later, I received a call from Arnie Latchkey. I had not spoken to him since Vic's wedding. He and I made small talk, and then he got down to business. Vigorish Productions, he told me, needed a person in charge of security. "I have to be brutally frank with you," Arnie said, and he then proceeded to tell me that individuals in nightclubs would approach Vic Fountain and challenge him, dare him to fight them. The more that Vic's entourage would fight off such people—Tony Fratelli had recently knocked a man unconscious in Las Vegas—the more challengers there would be. "We can't win," Latch said. "Like locusts, they just keep coming." Arnie was also trying to get Vic to not commingle with the Fratellis, who apparently had some underworld connections. In addition, not only did they have to worry about protecting Vic from others, they had to protect Vic from Vic. Now, Vic had recently been swayed to hire an Andy Ravelli, the grandson of a hometown acquaintance of his, as a bodyguard. "But we need someone to really take charge of this operation," Latch said.

"I run a beer distribution business, Mr. Latchkey," I informed him. This was not true, as my company had recently gone bankrupt.

"Ziggy says you're great at these type things," he said to me.

"I do have a flair for certain sorts of intrigues," I admitted rather bashfully.

He told me that I could live in Los Angeles, that I would be given a hotel room in Las Vegas and New York when Fountain and Bliss performed there, that I would be entitled to a more than generous expense account, that my car would be paid for. He told me my starting salary would be $30,000 a year, which was certainly a very handsome sum in the mid-fifties. I said, "You're asking me to simply leave my company? And move from Nebraska to California. The people who work for me are like family." He replied, "Okay, we'll make it thirty-five grand." Three weeks later I was living in Los Angeles.

My first assignment I shall never forget. I went to Shepherd Lane's office, in the Fairfax area. He handed me a suitcase. He instructed me to bring the suitcase—there was $3,000 inside—to the Broadway, a department store. I was to hand the money to a Mr. Ronald Morganthau and say it was for Jane White.

"May I ask what this money is for?" I inquired of Mr. Lane.

"Yes, you may," Mr. Lane good-naturedly responded. "And the answer is, that woman is a serious loony bird."

ERNIE BEASLEY: Vic's first album went gold. Did you know that in Los Angeles, every copy within forty miles was sold the very first day it was available?! Vic was always saying that he now had enough cachet to go solo, although he didn't use the word "cachet." He, Ginger, and I would hang out a few times a week. We got blitzed often. Joe Yung really took good care of him—he made the best martinis I've ever had—and he shaved Vic, drove him around, dressed him. Clotilde Sturdivandt was still giving Vic his couth training but it was like trying to teach a dead puppy how to sit, stay, and come. "That man will be the very death of me!" she said to me once at the Beverly Wilshire. She told me some of the actors and actresses she'd worked with—it was quite a roster—and she'd done a great job with them. Her first case, she told me, was Cary Grant, right before he made that movie with Mae West. I told her that, yes, Vic was going to be a very tough nut to crack, and she trilled, "Mr. Beasley, I am *not* a squirrel!"

Hal Gordon, Bobby Bishop, and Billy Ross agreed that Vic's second LP should be more of an up-tempo affair. "The first one was a glass of warm brandy," Hal said, "but we should serve up some Irish coffee now, heavy on the java." When he said that I sat down at the piano and wrote "The Java Jump," which really took off when Vic released it as a single. *"You got me jumpin', bubblin' like lava, you're like twenty cups of hot black java."* "Let's Have Some Fun," which was on *Swingin' With Vic* and did very well, I also wrote. Vic's voice, I'm afraid to say, wasn't really in fine fettle during these sessions: Ginger, he, and I—and sometimes Hunny and Ices Andy [Andy Ravelli]—would be up all hours of the evening the night before. Sometimes the nights bled into the morning . . . we'd leave Johnny D'Antibes's club at six, go have breakfast at some roadside diner, and then turn up at the Pacific studios.

It wasn't easy on Billy or Hal. Because of Vic's filming schedule and because Pacific had other artists to record, they wanted to record this album quickly. But sometimes Vic was in such bad shape that they'd just have to wait for him to freshen up. Vic never thought he wasn't able to sing, though, and he insisted on getting it right—or wrong, as was the case—in one take. So there are three or four songs on that LP that sound absolutely awful. Vic had gravel in his throat—that's what it sounds like. Someone said to me they ought to call the thing *Snorin' With Vic*.

That bald trombonist named Cueball was in the studio again, and he and Vic exchanged some banter. But one day there was an unfortunate incident. To record this album Billy and Hal had to bring in extra musicians again, hence Cueball. But now Floyd Lomax was sitting in.

Vic was halfway through "Makin' Whoopee" when he noticed Floyd Lomax's presence. He was using that gravel in his voice as best he could, trying to make it sizzle, when suddenly his voice went from very deep to the Vienna Boys Choir. He pushed away the microphone and charged out and didn't return that day. He called Hal Gordon and told him that he would not record the rest of the record until the extra musicians were let go. So they were, right on the spot. Cueball said to Billy Ross, "There's got to be some kind of mistake—Vic wouldn't fire me." But he was told to leave.

Hal Gordon told me several years later that Floyd Lomax, while he was packing up his horn, told him that he had a score to settle with Vic Fountain. "I thought he was talking about a musical score," Hal said, "but then I noticed a gun with a pearl handle in his case."

There's another aspect to this which I should mention. Vic formed a music publishing company and had convinced me that I should share credits for all my songs that he recorded. I was bombed and I agreed to it. I agreed to lots of things when I was bombed and I was bombed a lot of the time. This decision, if you could call it that—is it a "decision" if a drunk driver runs over three people?—has cost me so much money. But it's not the money, it's the prestige. Vic never wrote a note of music in his life—he never wrote a lyric. He wouldn't even have been able to come up with the simple java/lava rhyme! He could barely sing the songs on certain occasions. Yet here his name was now alongside mine. It's almost a joke, isn't it, but it is just too damned sad.

BARBARA NORDQUIST [actress, stripper]: I first met Ziggy at the Velvet Rabbit in L.A. in maybe '54 or '55. I performed under the name Soozie Svenson, "The Swivelin' Swede." I did three shows a night there and would work in San Francisco too.

I guess you could say I had everything that Ziggy wanted. I was a 36D, a blonde, and I had a nice round can. I could've used a few more inches in the legs—I'm only five three—but believe me, I could do things with my chest that spun men's heads.

I used to do movies for a guy named Emmett Strang around San Diego. We filmed in an old airplane hangar. It started off with me just stripping for the camera. There was no sound; believe me, nobody watching these things cared about sound. They were 16-millimeter films. I'd shake and shimmy and take my clothing off. I'd put on all kinds of getups . . . I'd dress as Cleopatra or a Swedish nurse or a French maid and I'd get fifty bucks. After I did a few of these, he brought in another girl one day and it was the two of us stripping and shimmying. "Kiss her, kiss her!" Emmett would say. "How much do I get for that?" I'd say while the camera was rolling, and he'd say, "Seventy-five bucks." One day I dressed like a nurse and did my routine . . . I thought that was it but then Emmett said he had another movie to make. In walked this blond guy, a kid about eighteen years old, he went to UCLA. This kid was built, let me tell you—the spitting image of Buster Crabbe when he was young. Emmett started filming and a minute later this kid is kissing me, licking my ears, and he's got his hands all over me. "Just do it, just do it," Emmett said. "Touch the damn thing!" "How much for this?" I asked back—all this while the camera was filming! Emmett said he'd give me two hundred. Before I knew it this college kid was making love to me with his cock between my tits and a minute later there was a quart of sperm all over my neck. I got my two hundred and Buster Crabbe Jr. got twenty.

Snuffy introduced me to Ziggy. Snuffy wasn't playing the Velvet Rabbit—they didn't use comics, they just brought the girls out. But Snuffy knew me 'cause I'd worked the Colony Club. He and Ziggy were in the audience and after the show the two of them came backstage. Snuffy was a gentleman, he never hit on any of the girls. You wouldn't believe some of the comics I'd worked with, you've never seen men so horny. Maybe there's a lot of pressure to be funny—maybe when you bomb onstage it gets to you, and all the tension builds up down there. The girls were always with the comics, the musicians too. Chuckie Williams, the impressionist, would get made love to orally every night, sometimes as John Wayne, sometimes as Gary Cooper.

Anyway, Ziggy told me he'd seen my work and I thought he meant me stripping. But he said he'd seen me in movies and liked my acting. "Acting?" Snuffy said. "Is that what they call it?" Ziggy said to him, "You think what Soozie does is easy?" Ziggy told me that Fountain and Bliss were about to begin work on a boxing movie and could use a girl like me, to play a moll. He said I should visit him at the Biltmore, where he had an office, and we could look at the script. I asked him what day should I be there, and he said he meant I should visit him right now.

We became lovers that night. I must say, it was painful at first but also wonderful. He wasn't very romantic . . . it was just right down to business. He really liked to bury his head in my chest—a lot of men did—but he was the only one who seemed to want to be dead and buried there.

I was in *A Couple of Lightweights* for maybe two minutes. I didn't have any speaking lines. I don't think I ever said a word in any movie I ever made and I must've made a hundred of them. But Ziggy took care of me, he always took good care of me.

He had lots of my movies . . . he had many others too, believe me. He had two rooms at the Biltmore and one of them had a projector and a screen. He told me there were more movies at his house. Ziggy and I would watch the movies and he would get very excited. I didn't get that excited, to tell the truth. He'd turn off the projector eventually and we would move to the couch to make love. He was enormous, he was gigantic in his pants. I had to slather him in Crisco vegetable shortening—the Crisco had to be prewar, when it still came in tins. He liked me to get on top of him and shake, but the thing he liked most was to kiss my chest and nipples and make love to himself. He sounded like a pony when he was doing that, like a young horse whinnying. He'd finish up and three minutes later I was walking out the door. He always had a chauffeur drive me home. He was a gentleman in some respects. He also bought me a Buick Roadmaster.

We were together for maybe seven months. He wanted me to stop doing the movies. He said he'd have Emmett Strang taken in. But he decided to pay him off instead. So he wrote out a check for $10,000 and when I handed it to Emmett I told him I wasn't doing any more movies. Emmett gave me a thousand from Ziggy's ten and I made four more movies for him.

One day a man named Reynolds came to my house. He looked to me like a Bible salesman when I opened the door, but he wasn't.

He told me that I was not to see or talk to or communicate with Ziggy Bliss ever again. He told me that if it ever made it into the papers that I was involved with Ziggy Bliss, it would destroy me. I was thinking: I'm a stripper, I shimmy my bust for men beating off under the table, I do these movies they show at bachelor parties—what can possibly destroy me? He gave me five grand in cash. Well, this was nothing compared to everything that Ziggy had given me, but I got the message. He then told me that, in the course of his work, he'd seen some of my work and had admired and respected it. "You're very good at what you do, Miss Svenson," he said to me. Ha! I knew what that meant, so I closed the door on him before he tried anything. I mean, I'd just woken up, for Jesus' sake!

I figured the guy was on the level. Maybe some reporter had gotten wind that Ziggy and I were lovers and this Reynolds guy was paying me to get lost. I didn't want to end Ziggy's marriage. But then through the grapevine—all the girls at the clubs talked—I found out that Ziggy was seeing Honey Graham, a big busty girl who worked at the Diamond Mine in San Francisco. This was Ziggy's way of ditching me.

Believe me, I wasn't heartbroken. I kept all the dough and the Buick Roadmaster and the jewels and I threw out the three tins of Crisco.

SNUFFY DUBIN: It used to *kill* Vic that Ziggy had this reputation as a lady-killer. Christ, it'd kill me too! The guy was a medicine ball, sure, but he was a medicine ball with a firehose attached. The showgirls in Vegas, they all knew about it. That piece-of-crap boxing film they did? Ever wonder why Vic's boxing trunks only go down halfway to his knees, but Ziggy's go almost to the ankle? They were covering up a lot more than just his flabby knees.

I was playing in Vegas, at the Gray Grotto on the Strip. When my show was done I'd go over to the Oceanfront and catch their act. They were a little tired from everything—the movies, Vic's records, the whoring around, flying to New York, Cuba, and Florida—so I'd seen them better. After one show—Jesus, it's maybe three in the morning—me, Ziggy, and Hun are hangin' at the bar and we decide we wanna goof on Vic. Hunny told us he was with two showgirls—the old double-decker—and he gave us the room number. Ziggy goes to the guy working the desk and he gets the key. Why? How can he just do that? 'Cause he's one half of Fountain and Bliss and they're bringing in millions of bucks.

Me and Ziggy go to the room and barge in with two fire extinguishers we swiped from the hallway. Me and Ziggy were soaring on amphetamines. So we burst in and we run to the bedroom and I see one female body and then another, all these legs and arms and feet and bosoms. Then I can discern another broad . . . it's kind of like picking out letters in a bowl of alphabet soup or something, right? Then I notice there's a fifth breast and I figure this is either Ripley's Believe It or Not or Vic's got three broads in the sack. Me and Ziggy are just too stunned to start spraying them all. Somewhere underneath all that pile was Vic, I'm pretty sure of it.

Pete Conifer told me that Vic was now up to triple-deckers. Look, one is enough. Two is really pushing it. But three? If you ask me, Vic was so pissed off that Ziggy had this rhino dong reputation, he was now taking on three at a time.

DANNY McGLUE: When I got the script for *A Couple of Lightweights* there was nothing I could do with it. They were asking me to raise Lazarus from the dead, but I don't think this Lazarus had ever been alive. The first two Fountain and Bliss movies were profitable; they made about seven million each and maybe cost a tenth that to make. Somewhere under a leaning tower of dusty paper was the script that was perfect for them: *The Three of Us,* the Noël Coward *Design for Living* knockoff. But Gus Kahn wouldn't look at it again.

While *Lightweights* was being shot, Fountain and Bliss signed for the *Johnson Wax Star Parade* show for [the] Dumont [Network]. Len Coles hosted this show twice a month, and every two weeks they brought in Ziggy and Vic to host. It was done live in New York City. So Sid, Norman, and I and a few other gag writers would concoct a show, then Ziggy and Vic would fly east to put the thing on.

We wrote skits for all the usual Fountain and Bliss characters. Dr. Kablooie, Professor Gobbledygook, the Cockney Barber, the Slow-Witted Cowboy. There would be guests too, usually musicians and singers and dancers. Tony Martin, Julie Mansell, Nat Cole, Julie London, Cyd Charisse, Dinah Washington, Miss Leslie Wilson, when she was only sixteen years old. People like that. But we had a problem: Ziggy and Vic could rarely get any rehearsals in. They were filming the movie, they were playing Vegas. They had their personal lives. By the time they came to New York there was barely any time. Not that Vic would rehearse anyway. He went from one rehearsal per show to just reading things fresh off the TelePrompTer. He did that better than anyone; unless you caught him squinting, you wouldn't have known he was doing it.

Ed Kapler was our director. He and the writers would work and work and we'd get the skits and everything into place, razor sharp. But when Ziggy saw the script he'd have a fit! He'd yell how lousy the material was. "You're gonna crucify me on live TV!" Now, this was bad enough . . . but we were doing the show in two days. So back to the drawing board we'd go.

Ziggy was very cruel. Writers would get called at four in the morning to get bawled out, they'd get fired by a note slipped under their doors, or Ziggy would actually go to their buildings and tell their doormen to tell them they'd been let go. One poor guy had turned in very poor material and Ziggy decided they would use it, just to embarrass him on national TV. Well, not only was the guy humiliated and forced to quit, but this skit made Vic look very bad too.

With all this craziness, the show initially had great ratings.

You know, any time anything they were doing got them in trouble, they could just toss out the script. That was the incredible talent they had. Ziggy could just wing it and Vic could play along. Sometimes, though, Vic didn't realize that Ziggy was ad-libbing and Vic would still be reading off the TelePrompTer. When that happened Vic and Ziggy would engage in the nastiest fighting after the show was done. They'd be in Vic's dressing room and they'd be yelling at the top of their lungs. "You do that to me again, I'll fuckin' kill ya!" Vic would yell. And Ziggy would yell right back at him, "You're lost up there! You're an embarrassment!" The crew would go silent . . . we would just listen to them going at it. "I don't need you, Ziggy! I could make twice as much doing half the work!" And Ziggy yelled back at him, "You're not doing *any* work! How do you divide zero in half?!"

They did this show for four seasons. By the third season the ratings began to fade. Of course, their movies still did well. No Fountain and Bliss movie ever lost a quarter, did you know that? And no Fountain and Bliss movie ever was any good, you could add that to the equation.

In the third season, Arnie thought we should aim for a younger crowd. We put on, finally, a rock 'n' roll act—Cody Lee Jarrett and the Magnificats. Their big hit was "(Let's Make) The Rubble Bounce." Jarrett was maybe nineteen years old, very handsome. Vic was dead set against having any rock 'n' and roller on the show—he hated the music. Detested it. "It just ain't music," Vic would say. But Arnie, the Dumont people, and [producer] Artie Conway prevailed.

Ziggy and Vic did a skit, they brought out a ventriloquist, did a Louie Kablooie routine. After another sketch, which Vic pretty much sleepwalked through, they brought on Cody and the Magnificats. Ziggy did the intro and Vic kept purposely yawning and sneering. The group came on, did their "Rubble" song, and it went over well. When it went back to Ziggy and Vic, Vic was curled up on the floor pretending to be asleep. Backstage, Cody told Artie Conway he was insulted. "I'd never do that to him, he shouldn't do it to me," he said. Artie said what any producer would say: "It's their show, kid. Sorry."

Twenty minutes later Ziggy and Vic bring out the group again, and Cody did a slower, softer song, very twangy and sultry. While he was singing this, *behind* him and the Magnificats, were Ziggy and Vic dancing close to each other! And the group didn't realize it. Toward the end—when he heard laughter—Cody Lee turned around and caught them. Then he slammed down his guitar and stormed off the stage, on live TV. Much to the delight of Fountain and Bliss.

Well, it didn't end there. As everyone knows.

Cody Lee Jarrett was angry; he was humiliated, hurt, and furious. His motorcycle was parked right outside the studio and he hopped onto this beautiful red machine and sped away in the pouring rain. He made it to White Plains and kept going north. People say he was going over a hundred miles an hour. It was dark and very wet and he drove right into a lamppost in Mount Kisco. The papers couldn't run a picture of it, it was so gruesome, but the police photo did eventually leak out years later in a book called *They Died With Their Leather On*. Cody Jarrett's corpse, all in slick black, is laid out near a fence and his head, with no helmet, is about ten yards away, impaled on a fence.

What made it worse was that, after Jarrett had stormed off, to kill the minute that would've been taken up by the rest of the song, Ziggy and Vic said some really insulting things. They made fun of his voice and his outfit, his hair and his music. Now, they had no idea that Cody Lee Jarrett was going to die in thirty minutes. But when the world woke up the next day to find out about it, well, it just did not play well. Not at all.

Morty Geist issued a heartfelt apology for the boys. He looked over the Ten Standard Denials and Apologies but there wasn't anything in there that quite fit. "This one is a real humdinger, guys," he said. So now there were eleven.

● ● ●

DOMINICK MANGIAPANE: I would go to Los Angeles once a year to see Lulu and Vicki and Vincent. To me, family is everything—there's nothing more important than your own blood. I would've given my arms and legs for those two kids. And they weren't even my own.

Vic would offer to pay my way to California, he'd offer to put me up at some fancy hotel. But I was making enough now, I didn't need his help. Besides, it wasn't even him offering—it was one of his "crowd."

Fountain and Bliss were working on that lousy boxing picture when I was there once. I brought his kids to Knott's Berry Farm and to Disneyland. This gave Lu a chance to go shopping with Ziggy's wife and to visit Vic's mother, who had her psychic business going now on Santa Monica Boulevard. When I got home Vic was there with Ices Andy, Hunny Gannett, a few others. Now you gotta understand: I'd already been there three days and this was the first time Vic had been home. And he was acting very tenderly, like a father with the kids. But still: First time in three days, don't forget that.

I'd tried to bring up this subject with Lulu but she wouldn't answer none of my questions. The more she didn't talk the angrier I got. Vic didn't scare me, he never did. Even when he was a kid he'd have other people fight his battles for him. I can't tell you how many times Guy Puglia would go after another kid and Vic would just watch.

When I saw him pinching Vicki's cheek I felt my blood boiling. I didn't care that his buddies were there. I said to him, "Vic, you sure do love those kids, don't you?"

"They're everything to me, Dommy," he said.

"I mean, I look at you now," I said, "and it's like you ain't seen 'em for a week."

He gave me a dirty look and said, "What do you know? Huh?"

"I know that these kids need a father and that you ain't ever there for 'em."

Vic turned to Hunny and said, "Get a load of this fuckin' guy, Hun. A guy works on a dock for a living, he can tell me how to run my life." Then he turned to me and said, "Go shuck an oyster, Dommy."

Cursin' like that in front of his own kids.

I said to him, "Why? You'll be outta here soon and you won't be back for who knows how long!"

Vic said to Andy, "Throw this guy out on his ass, Ices." (Andy's *nonno* sold ices to us kids when we was growing up, on the boardwalk.)

Andy was a big kid. Six foot three, very strong. Twenty years younger than me too. I didn't have a chance. He grabbed me by my collar and was draggin' me toward the front door. I was yelling at Vic. "You're the worst! You destroy my sister's life? I'll destroy yours! What kind of man are you, huh?!" Next thing I knew I was bouncing down Vic and Lulu's front lawn.

•   •   •

ARNIE LATCHKEY: *A Couple of Lightweights* has the distinction of being not only the worst Fountain and Bliss movie but also the worst boxing motion picture ever made. We should have had that movie done in four weeks. It took three months. There was always something going on, always someplace the boys had to be. Vic got Hunny a small part in the picture and for the life of him, Hunny couldn't remember a line. It drove George S. Collier up the wall . . . and this was the *other* side of the same wall that he'd already been driven up on the previous two pictures. There was one scene when Ziggy, who works as a janitor in a gymnasium and who eventually winds up winning a championship prizefight, asks Hunny a question. All

Hunny had to do was say the word "yeah." But it took about seventy takes, I exaggerate not. He either didn't know precisely when to say it, or he did know when to say it but couldn't remember precisely what to say.

Collier and [producer] Ezra Gorman took Vic aside and said to him, "Do we absolutely need Hunny in this movie?" and Vic said, "He's a pal of mine, so yeah, we do." The more times Hunny flubbed his lines, the more Vic would crack up. Vic's entourage would crack up too. But everybody else there—and I include myself among their number—was getting fed up.

Ziggy would complain to me, "We could find a rock and it'd do better than Hunny!" What could I say? I side with him, I'm in Vic's bad graces. I defend Vic, I got Ziggy starin' daggers to my heart. He really had it in for Vic then . . . Vic had been named the number two vocalist in a *Metronome* and *Downbeat* poll and he was second in *Billboard*. "Let's Have Some Fun," the tune he wrote with Ernie, went to number one and was on the *Hit Parade* for something like three centuries. Reporters were always asking Ziggy to his face, "Are you jealous? What do you think of Vic's success?" and Zig always had the same response: "Hey, I'm Vic's biggest fan." But it was eating up his insides like that eagle peckin' at Prometheus's innards every day.

Lightweights got eviscerated. The *L.A. Times* disemboweled it. Justin Gilbert of the *Mirror* wrote that it was featherweight entertainment, and every other *shmegegie* with a pencil wrote that the movie scored no knockout. How imaginative, huh? But they were right. *Intrusion* [magazine] ran an article about Ginger and Vic and about Vic and girls in Vegas, and Morty denied everything a hundred times and threatened to sue. Ginger was humiliated. Vic didn't really give a damn. He told Reynolds Catledge to find out who was leaking all this stuff out. I told Cat to not waste his time: Nobody was leaking it, it was common knowledge. Millie Roth in New York told me she thought Ziggy had told *Intrusion* everything, but I don't know. Vic showed up all over town with Ginger on his arm, and when he was in Vegas putting together those double- and triple-decker heros of his, he probably did it with the door open. So Vic lowered the boom on Morty Geist big time. He threatened to fire him, called him all kinds of names. You ever see a grown man wilt to the size of an M & M? That's what this was like.

"It's my job to get you in the papers and magazines," Morty said to him, "and now you've got it so it's my job to keep you out."

"Hey, you don't even have a job anymore, Morty!" Vic said.

"So I'm fired, Vic? Is that it?" Morty's knees are knocking so hard the furniture is rattlin'.

"Nah," Vic said.

Confidential and *Intrusion* had both mentioned that Joe Yung was running a one-man ferry service to Mexico, getting abortions for Vic's girl-friends. Well, this was news to me but it was the kind of news like you hear it's going to snow in February in Vermont. I wasn't terribly startled.

Gus Kahn gave me a brutal keelhauling in his office. The man yelled for an hour straight and he must have had some hidden oxygen tank hooked up to his lungs because he didn't stop one time to take a breath. And this while huffing on a Cohiba, no less! George S. Collier had lost a hand helming *Lightweights* and was suing the studio. "I don't blame him!" Gus screamed. "He's got an eye patch already and now he's got a hook for a hand! You're turnin' the man into a goddamn pirate!" I said I was sorry on behalf of the boys. "Why don't they just kill the man all at once," Gus yelled, "instead of this whittlin' him down to nothing?!"

Vic was showing up late [on the set]. He was sleeping late, he was golfing early, the hangovers—he had all the excuses. So Ziggy would get the crew all riled up . . . he was always manipulating. "Can you believe how unprofessional Vic is?" he'd ask the property master. "Have you ever worked with anyone this bad before?" he'd ask the script girl. And when Vic did show up, Ziggy's mood would change to rotten and surly just like *that,* because there went his excuse to stir up trouble. You didn't want to be within a mile of him. The worst days were when Vic showed up on time and acted professional! That really made Ziggy miserable.

At the time we had five more movies left on the contract.

"Hey, Latch," Vic asked me one day, "is there any kind of escape clause in this thing?"

SALLY KLEIN: Several times I thought about quitting. Jack did very well for himself as a real-estate lawyer in Los Angeles, you can imagine. I had a son now. Donny. I even tried it once for a month . . . I took a leave of absence. We had a wonderful house in Malibu and I adored being around Donny. But after a few weeks, I missed it all. With Ziggy and Vic, you never knew what was going to happen. Every second a disaster might hit. On *Anchors Oy Vey* George Collier had to get a peg leg after Ziggy accidentally shot him with a prop cannon that turned out to not be a prop cannon, and the next day Vic destroyed a hotel room at the Oceanfront because Pete Conifer forget to paint the walls turquoise and have matching sheets and pillowcases and carpets.

When they began work on *Anchors* Jack and I invited both Ziggy and Vic, their wives, and kids over for a big dinner. Arnie and Estelle were in Paris on vacation at the time, and we invited Danny and Betsy but Danny told me he had personal business and couldn't come.

Vic showed up without Lulu, but Hunny and Ernie Beasley came. Ziggy was with Jane and little Freddy. I tried to get Donny to play with Freddy but they didn't really get along. Freddy was always lonely and shy, even then.

We were eating dinner and I tried everything to get conversation going, talking about politics, and Jack was talking about football and the track and we talked about celebrities and the old days in New York. Vic and Ziggy had recently crashed Fritz Devane's TV show, which was live, and Devane was absolutely outraged. It was in the middle of a sketch and after thirty seconds the whole thing was ruined. We laughed about that. Vic started talking to me and Jack about singing "Ain't She Sweet" with this trio or quartet back in Boston, and then Ziggy was talking to me about some of the places he played with Harry and Flo in the Catskills.

Ted, we were at that dinner table for close to three hours and there wasn't one second when somebody wasn't talking.

Jack and I were cleaning up after everyone had left, and Jack said to me, "Honey, did you notice something weird about Ziggy and Vic tonight? They didn't say one single word to each other, not the entire night."

He was right. They had not directly spoken to each other.

An hour later Jack and I were settling into bed and he told me he didn't feel too well. Now, when a man who's had three heart attacks tells you this, you take notice. Ten minutes later he tells me he's having chest pains, so we get into the car and I'm racing toward Cedars of Lebanon. I checked him in and, yes, he was having a mild heart attack.

I was walking around the hospital, just going from hallway to hallway, floor to floor, I was in a daze. And who do I run into? Danny! He saw me and he figured it out instantly—he said right away, "Is Jack okay?"

"It's a mild one, Danny, this time," I said. "He'll live."

"Should I go in and say hello?"

"Maybe tomorrow."

We sat down in a lounge, like a waiting area.

"Why are you here?" I asked him.

"It's Betsy," he told me.

"Is she okay?"

"Yes. No. Well . . . God, I don't know." He rubbed his face with his hands.

"What is it, dahlink?" I asked him, trying anything to help.

"She starts drinking before lunch now," he said. "She's drunk almost every day." He had to put her in the hospital for a week, to dry out. "She gets crazy sometimes," he said.

I put my arm around him, I held his hand. He was crying and then I started crying too.

A nurse walked by. "She probably thinks we're brother and sister," Danny said.

"Oh, who cares what anyone thinks?" I said.

After a few minutes we both stood up and went our separate ways. I must tell you . . . it felt good to hold his hand again. Even in a hospital, even with everything going on. It felt good.

GUY PUGLIA: Hunny stopped fighting around '56. He was about forty years old then. Nobody knew how many fights he'd won or lost, even he didn't have any idea. "I probably couldn't count that high anyways," he said to me once. Jesus, you know what they called him? Jack Dempsey they once called "the Manassas Mauler." Hunny they called "the Molasses Mauler."

He thought about retiring a few times. But Vic always goaded him into fighting again. "Come on, Hun, one more shot," he'd say. "You still got it, champ."

The last fight was against Willie Ray Dixon, this colored guy out of Mississippi. Me, Ices Andy, and Vic was in the training room with Hun before the fight. He was sweating up a storm. Davey Rennick was his trainer and he had a cut man too, this guy named Jimmy "O Positive" Dobbs, not 'cause of the blood type but because he was always so optimistic. But this Dobbs guy takes me aside—he knew me and Hunny was close pals—and he says to me, "If Dixon opens up a cut on Hunny's face, it's all over. His head's a balloon but with blood and not air." And Rennick was telling Hunny his only hope was to get to Dixon early, very early. If the fight went more than one round, it was all over. "It's already all over, it seems," Hunny said while Davey was greasing him down.

"You sure you wanna fight, Hun?" I asked him. "If you don't wanna fight, you just don't fight, okay?"

"I ain't no quitter," he said to me.

I looked at him. He didn't have no muscle tone left. He had a roll of flab around his stomach and his thighs were like cheese. His chin practically had a fuckin' bulls-eye target on it.

"Vic, tell Hunny he don't have to fight if he ain't up for it," I said, and Vic said to him, "Hunny, you wanna fight?" Hunny didn't answer, and Vic said, "He wants to fight."

"Get him early, Hun, get him early," Davey told him.

The fight didn't even last a half a round. Hunny took one wild swing at Dixon and missed by a mile. Hunny lost his balance . . . he was reelin' around just from the punch he threw. Dixon stood there and watched. In Hunny's corner, O Positive was like O Negative now 'cause he was putting away his equipment, and Davey threw in the towel. Hunny went into the ropes, knocked his head against the ballast and went down. The referee counted him out.

"Was that fight fixed?" Vic asked me on the way back to the Beverly Wilshire. Joe Yung was driving us in Vic's new T-bird.

"I think if the fight was fixed," I said, "Hunny would've done a better job in losing."

We pulled up to the hotel. I said, "I'm kinda worried about Hunny. He ain't all there. Sometimes he don't even know what day it is." Vic said, "Hey, you think I do?" "Nah, I'm serious," I told him, "We gotta convince him to hang up the gloves."

He was out of the car now, bending over and talking to me in the car.

"Awright, listen," he said, "this is what we gotta do . . . "

"Yeah?"

"I got this girl in trouble. But Joe Yung can't take her to Mexico, he's doin' other stuff for me. So can you take her instead?"

* * *

ARNIE LATCHKEY: When Howard Leeds moved from Galaxy to Universal he and I went to lunch . . . we went to Guy's restaurant. This was after Fountain and Bliss had broken up. Now, Gus Kahn and Howie did not have a gentle parting of the ways, you can take my word on it, unless you consider Gussie threatening to have Howie castrated and have his balls fed to him on a piece of melba toast gentle. So what Howie told me that day I maybe take with a grain of salt.

"Did Gus ever have a falling out with Ziggy and Vic?" Howie asked me.

I thought about it. Ziggy and Vic may have loathed the sight of each other at times but they did usually get along with most other people, including Gus Kahn, who couldn't get along with Mary's little lamb.

"No, I don't think so. Ziggy entertained Gus's kids at their birthdays. So did Vic. Everything was *glatt* kosher."

"You sure about that?"

"Yeah. Sure. I think so. Why?"

"Gus had it in for them, Arnie. He did from day one."

"We're talking about Fountain and Bliss here, Howie?"

"We sure are."

"They never lost a dime for Gus. It didn't matter how bad those films were, they always made dough."

I wracked my brain . . . I thought back to our first meeting, at the racetrack. Gus bought the horse, the roan colt, then had it destroyed. All had gone well, it seemed. I thought of subsequent dealings. Nothing seemed off-kilter.

"He told me when we signed you guys," Howie said, "he was going to put them in the worst movies he could. It's only some kind of luck or happenstance or whatever that the Fountain and Bliss movies all made money."

"I am not believing what I'm hearing, Howie. You're saying Gus purposely shot himself in the foot? And missed?"

"You know that script that Sid Stone and Norman White wrote? *Three of a Kind?* Why do you think Gus always passed on it and gave them dreck like *A Couple of Lightweights* and those terrible service comedies they did? You think Gus thought *Gung Ha!* and *Two Goofballs* were going to be good movies?"

"I'm stunned at what you're telling me here, Howie. I mean, I'm taken aback here. I'm stupefied. You name it and I'm it."

"Well, I was just wondering if you knew what it was between Gus and them. But I guess you don't. See, Arn, when the boys wrapped the last picture on the deal, Gus was elated. He said, 'I wash my hands of this now and forever finally! May I never sully myself again.' I said to him, 'Hey, what did you have against them anyway?' He told me they were incorrigible, they were unprofessional, they were spiteful and childish and had not one jot of class."

"Yeah, but Gussie knew that before he signed them."

"I told him that. And then he said to me, 'You wanna know why I'm on cloud nine? I'll tell you. No, better yet, have my chauffeur drive you out to Hollywood Memorial Park, that *goyishe* cemetery. Ask the groundskeeper there or whoever to lead you to Veda Lankford's grave. And when you find it, Howie, you can ask Veda Lankford why!' "

How about that, boy? Old Gussie bearing that grudge like Gunga Din totin' a bucket of slop on his shoulders and rubbing Ziggy and Vic's faces in it. He wanted these pictures to bomb, to die, but they never did. So instead he made millions. The man couldn't lose.

Slow dissolve. Hillcrest Country Club. I run into Gus Kahn years after Howard Leeds had imparted this dope to me. He was playing gin rummy with a bunch of *alter kockers,* guys in their nineties who'd made a fortune in motion pictures going back to the silent days. He looked like a kid among them. I asked him if it was true, what Howie had told me. Gus put his cards down and said, "You really think a man of my stature, wealth, and prominence could be so easily nettled by some blond tart? You think because some sleepy dago singer with blue hair lays this broad, I'm going to jeopardize the whole operation? Shame on you, Latchkey! Shame on you!"

Fortunately the other men at the table were deaf . . . one of them had one of those old-fashioned hearing aids, like a ram's horn. I shrugged and said good-bye to Gus. But as I was moving away, he winked at me. And that little wink said to me it was all true. He'd tried to sink the ship from the get-go.

• • •

SNUFFY DUBIN: Pete Conifer ran everything at the Oceanfront. From the size of the plugs in the sinks to the temperature in the pool. And he used to audition showgirls in his office. A girl would hop off a bus in Vegas, maybe she'd won a beauty contest in Amarillo or was a dancer at some nowhere shithole in Dubuque, right? She goes into Pete's office and Pete has her slip on the outfit, the short red skirt, the black stockings, the low-cut gold lamé top. He tells her to lift up her skirt a little, to bend over and jiggle, to arch her back. Meanwhile he's soaked his thumb in Wild Turkey and he's sucking on it like a two-year-old and with the other hand he's whacking himself off under the desk. Wanda, his wife, told me this—Jesus, that's how they met.

Pete had all sorts of passageways and cameras built into the hotel. "Peeping Pete" they called him. His "thing" was watching women go to the bathroom. He would go backstage, slip into a supply closet, and watch Judy Garland, Sophie Tucker, or Dinah Shore take a dump. He ran a gigantic hotel, the casino made millions, his wife was a lovely woman, and here he is standing on a carton of coat hangers in a dark closet, looking through a hole in the wall at Totie Fields or Martha Raye wiping herself. It makes no sense to me. I just know I never let Debbie use the bathrooms there.

Fountain and Bliss *made* the Oceanfront. Sure, Pete would get other headliners—Tony Bennett, Tony Martin, Durante, Vic Damone—but when Fountain and Bliss were there, the high rollers poured in. Vic loved the place, he loved the excitement and the action. After a show and before a show too he'd gamble, he loved the dice. And blackjack too. Maybe they were making seventy-five grand a week but Vic would gamble with ten grand a night and a lot of times he lost. I saw it happen. He's rolling the dice, he's got some floozy next to him, he's got a fistful of hundreds and a drink. And in an hour all he has is the floozy. Sure, he'd sign markers with the hotel and they would extend his credit. They played the Oceanfront so often because Vic had to; he wasn't making any bread there, he was mostly just paying the casino back.

"They tear up Frank's IOUs at the Sands," Vic griped to me once. "Mine, they put up at the fuckin' post office."

They had a two-week stint there once and the place was packed. Businessmen, doctors, teamsters, Texas oil cowpokes, Jews from Florida, people tossing money around like it's air. It was the last night of the engagement. I was appearing at the Golden Nugget, opening for Eddie Fisher. I was walking through the lobby at the Oceanfront and I hear a cat say, "Hey, you're Snuffy Dubin!" I see this guy, I don't know him from John Foster fucking Dulles. He tells me he's Seymour Greenstein from Echo Beach, Ziggy's old turf. He's there with his wife and other people from the neighborhood. He was in the notions business, he told me—he manufactured buttons and stuff. He asked me if I could tell Ziggy that he was there with old friends of his. "Tell Zig ol' Stinky is here," he said. They weren't able to get tickets to the show, he told me.

So I go backstage and relayed the message and—Jesus, I just remembered it—Ziggy had about three vials of Benzedrine on his table. He nodded and said he'd take care of it. Sure enough, these six or seven people get the best seats in the house.

But you know what he did? In the middle of a Slow-Witted Cowboy sketch, he comes over to the table and starts goofing on this guy Stinky and his wife. It was funny at first but then it got serious—he started insulting button making and what the wife looked like. It got cruel. Vic came over and whispered something to him and then Ziggy let them alone. But the damage had been done.

Look, I've played every joint there is . . . and it's a law: You never insult your audience. Never. This is your cathedral, this is your flock. You lose the flock, you're dead. If Ziggy's insulting a guy who makes buttons here, then he's also insulting a nurse over there and a guy who makes thumbtacks up there and a teacher down here and so on. You're dead.

But Fountain and Bliss tore the roof off the joint that week. The two of them do an hour and a half and at the end of the set—this was par for the course—the lights go low and Ziggy steps front and center. He starts getting all choked up. The place is pitch black and all you see is his head hovering in the air, like fucking Tinkerbell dyed strawberry red. And he says the usual *shpiel*. First he apologizes if he's hurt anyone's feelings. He goes into this soppy thing and he thinks people are gonna start crying. Then he starts in about Vic: "This man here is my *rock*. This man is a giant, a Goliath, a leviathan. This man has saved my life. The Rock of Gibraltar is like a pebble compared to him. I'm nothing without this man." I can't describe to you how quiet the place would get when he did this. You could hear stomach acid gurgling. "Men are embarrassed to show love," he says. "We're embarrassed to talk about love. We hug our kids, we hug our wives, once in a while we tell them we love them. But I love this man. You cannot measure the love. There is no tool, there's no device, no measuring stick. Vic, you know how I feel. You know." And then he'd go silent for a while, while he weighed it all over and felt the love. Or maybe he was feeling the broad with big tits he'd laid the night before. But he was feeling something. And then he'd end this silence by shouting, "Good night, everybody! Thanks for coming to the Oceanfront! You're a wonderful audience!" And the band would strike up some music, the lights come on, and Ziggy and Vic go their ways, which were usually separate because, despite that orgy, the two of them were barely speaking.

You know, a couple of times he did that and Vic wasn't even on the stage anymore.

That Reynolds cat who did security for them? And Andy Ravelli? Ziggy had given them photos of Dolly Phipps! The daffy broad he ran around the Catskills with two decades previous! The two of them were told to comb the crowd every single night to see if she'd shown up. You'd see them walking up and down the aisles, looking at the picture, looking at the faces.

Hey, if I was married to Jane White I might've done the same thing.

JANE WHITE: Ziggy and Vic were touring in Miami, New York, and London for a few weeks. Freddy and I had spent a week in New York—I had a wonderful time at Tiffany's and Van Cleef & Arpels—but then we had to go back to Los Angeles so Freddy could attend school. So I was alone for a while.

There were two rooms in the back of our house which were off-limits for me. Ziggy even had two jokey signs made up that actually said OFF-LIMITS; they had that radioactive sign on it, the yellow-and-black emblem. Well, this was like Pandora's box to me—I couldn't resist it. With Freddy at school and with the house virtually to myself—Ruthie and the maid had the day off—I thought to myself, Well, it's my house too, gosh darn it. I called a locksmith and he got the doors open in such a manner that, when I closed them, Ziggy would not know they'd ever been opened.

One room was just a den, a study. There were boxes and boxes of reviews and articles about Fountain and Bliss, and also about Ziggy's parents. Every interview Ziggy had ever given, he had saved. Every interview Vic had given too. I was very meticulous as I combed through things—I didn't want him to know I'd been there. (I was good at it too, like I was a master thief!) There was a desk and a typewriter and over the desk on the wall was a framed photograph of Ziggy with his parents. It was very sweet except that his parents were just so Jewish-looking. It was unsettling. There was also a photo on the wall—it was gray and yellowed—of a thin woman with blond hair and big teeth. Maybe it was a cousin of his, I don't know.

The other room was large but sparsely designed. I only wish he would have let me furnish these rooms! (What I did for the rest of the house—I could have been one of the best interior decorators in California.) This one was a private screening room. When I opened the large metal cabinets, I saw hundreds of cans of film.

Well, I didn't know how to run a projector! I was a girl, after all. So I called my best friend, Joanie Pierce—she and I were on many charity committees together—and Joanie, who I knew would be able to run the projector, came over right away. Joan was [producer] Jimmy Pierce's wife; she grew up in Texas, was a complete tomboy, she told me. She loaded a reel and I turned off the light—oh, we were giggling just like a bunch of schoolgirls—and we watched the movie.

We couldn't believe it. I was aghast. I'd never seen anything like it. A very well-endowed woman was dancing and shaking her body parts . . . she was in a dentist's office . . . she was nude and was a nurse supposedly. "Gosh, I think I'm going to be sick, Joanie," I said. Three young men, dressed as dentists—they were not dentists, you can take my word for it—walked in and began to kiss her all over. "Please," I said, "turn it off." But Joanie said, "Let's just watch this, Janie." The dentists took their clothes off and before you know it they were on top of, underneath, and alongside this nurse. "I've had quite enough of this," I said. "Well, I sure as hell haven't!" she responded.

We watched the whole thing together and eventually I got used to it and Joanie and I had a good laugh. She rewound it and placed the movie back in the cabinet and said to me, "Hey! Let's watch this one!" and she put another movie on. This one was about two policemen and a lonely housewife. It was amazing you could even fit this woman's chest on the screen! We watched this movie too and then a few others. By the time we finished, it was like we'd been to some film festival! We wound up just laughing and giggling and hugging each other and having a good old-fashioned time.

"Let's go shopping!" I said.

We went to nearly every fancy department store that day and I could hardly fit all the bags of clothing and jewelry in the car! I'd never bought so much in my life. Then Joanie came over again the next day and we watched more movies. I gave Ruthie and the help the day off again. Well, some of those movies could get you quite hot and bothered! I would look over to Joanie and sometimes she'd be fanning herself, and this was with the air conditioner on. In the four weeks that Ziggy was on the road, Joanie and I would watch those movies every day and after that we would go shopping.

GUY PUGLIA: When Vic come back from London, I was in New York with him, Ices Andy, Hunny, and some of the usual guys. Vic had kept his suite at the St. Regis and we'd end the night there. It was a nonstop party. The only thing that stopped it was when Vic had to go perform. He was appearing at the Copa at night with Ziggy and he was recording a new album in the morning. He wasn't using the Billy Ross band on the records anymore, he said he didn't like their sound. But when he had to let Billy go, he didn't have the balls to tell Billy—he had someone else do it. Anyways, Hunny had a bartender from the Hunny Pot in Vic's suite around the clock. And there were girls coming in and out, beautiful girls. And famous people would drop by, actors and actresses and lots of athletes. Sinatra and Jilly [Rizzo] showed up one day and as they were walking out, Gleason walked in. Mickey Mantle, he come in one day and there was a hundred people in there and Mickey, who'd never met Ziggy or Vic before, asked, "Hey, where's Ziggy Bliss?" And Vic said, "Who the fuck knows or cares, Mick?" People was always asking Vic, "Where's Ziggy?" For years. Lots of people thought they were really friends.

One night Lou the Ape was up there. Lou Manganese. It was maybe five in the morning. The week before, his father-in-law, Al Pompiere, was shot in the foot getting his shoes shined on Sullivan Street. Anyway, we're all hanging around and we're just rattling off stories, stories about broads and booze and stuff. And Vic had some great ones. He told us about this one actress—I ain't gonna tell you who it was—who wanted to do it with a dog in front of Vic. He'd tell us that this one liked to get tied up, that one liked to tie other people up, these two liked to tie each other up. Ices Andy was there and he couldn't believe some of the stories. Vic and Ziggy had recently put their prints outside Grauman's Chinese Theater—it was Vic's shoes and Ziggy's hair in the cement there—and a few nights after that, Vic brings a broad to the spot at four in the morning and stands where his footprints are and gives her the sausage parmigiana standing up.

So we're all shootin' the shit and we're laughing and acting like jerks and someone—I think it was Nick Vitale, who worked the door at the Copa—says to Vic, "Hey, wasn't you once a soda jerk?" and Vic says, "Best job I ever had." And Vic laughs and slaps his knee and starts telling about how he used to do it to girls in Codport at the soda parlor. Then Nick says, "Hey, what about the guy—you laid his wife? He sold ices on the boardwalk? And paid you?" And Vic just froze up. And so did I 'cause I knew the fella who sold the ices was Joe Ravelli, Ices Andy's grandfather. Vic said, "Nah, that wasn't me. That wasn't me." And Hunny said, "Yeah, it was, Vic. You once told me you banged Ices Andy's grandma and not to ever mention it to no one." "What the hell are you talking about, you big fuckin' idiot?!" Vic snapped. "Well, that's what you told me, Vic," Hunny said.

I looked at Andy and his face was a blank. No eyes, no mouth or color. Nothin'. You couldn't tell what was going on in there.

"This party's over, guys," Vic said. "I'm gonna turn in."

But nobody stood up.

"Izzat true, Vic?" Andy said.

"Nah. It ain't."

"Come on. Izzat true?"

"Hey, Andy boy, you know Hunny. He's all stupid in the head. Ain't that right, Hunny? Too many left hooks, right?"

Hunny nodded.

Vic said, "Hunny don't know what's what, Andy. "

Andy said, "Hunny's too stupid to make things up."

Hunny nodded again.

"Stand up, Vic," Andy said.

Vic grabbed his crotch and said, "Right here, Ices . . . take a fuckin' walk."

Andy walked to the couch Vic was lyin' on and grabbed him by the collar. He lifted Vic up off the couch and stood him up.

"Hunny, come on!" Vic said. He was trying to get Hunny to protect him. But Hunny had been drinkin' six hours straight. He wasn't gonna help.

"Hey! Gaetano, come on!" Vic said to me.

"I'm tired. Hunny, let's go."

Me, Hunny, and Lou and a few others left the suite.

"Ain't that big kid Vic's bodyguard?" Lou said to me in the hallway.

I nodded.

"And his own bodyguard's beatin' him up?"

I said, "Yeah, I guess he is."

"Some hirin' practices he's got," Lou said. "Dumb fuckin' Vic."

But Ices Andy never hurt Vic. Never even hit him. Vic denied it, he lied his way out. And he doubled Andy's salary, which didn't hurt either.

REYNOLDS CATLEDGE IV: Soon after Vic Fountain's fourth album—*The Other Side of Vic*—was released, I was summoned to Ziggy Bliss's rooms at the Biltmore Hotel. I would characterize his behavior that day as extremely agitated, although I would always characterize his behavior as that. The album was doing well and it was common knowledge that Ziggy was envious of his success. I recall now that Arnie and Sally were saying things like "Batten down the hatches" when the album hit the stores; they were accustomed to Ziggy's mood swings and tantrums and knew that they often corresponded with Vic's concomitant successes and failures.

"Cat, you and me go back a long ways," Ziggy said to me at the Biltmore. It was a suite but was spartan at best, the walls were bare. One would never have surmised that the person who rented space here was a millionaire. "First time we met, remember that?"

"How could I forget?" I responded, probing my memory for the particulars of that occasion.

"You doin' okay, Cat? You like Hollywood? This kinda fast-paced life? Nuttin' bothering you?"

I informed him that these were the most content times of my life. He then asked me if I was "gettin' any" and I responded that, as I was now a member of the Fountain and Bliss entourage, I occasionally was.

"Look, you're in charge of security for this outfit," Ziggy said. "And you do a great job. And part of that work is not only keepin' Fountain and Bliss safe and alive, but keepin' Fountain and Bliss *together*. Right?"

"Yes," I responded, "that would seem of paramount importance to me."

He made an obvious, unfunny movie-related pun on the word "paramount" and then continued: "I think Vic is thinkin' of goin' solo. I'm almost sure of it. And I want you to nose around. I want you to find out everything you can. Everything. I don't care what you have to do. You see a stone left unturned, you unturn it."

"I understand."

"See, if he leaves Fountain and Bliss, there ain't no more act. And if there ain't no more act, there ain't no more me. Or you. I'm tryin' to avoid full-scale obliteration."

He told me that I should "bug" Vic's various domiciles, his house in Beverly Hills, his suites at the Beverly Wilshire and the Ambassador, and so on, his table at Guy's Seafood Joint, his room at the Oceanfront in Las Vegas, even his mother's fortune-telling business in Santa Monica. He wanted all the dope, he said.

I told him I would get right on it. He told me that this was authorized—he pronounced it "arthurized"—by Arnold and Sally, but that I should under no circumstances *ever* mention this to them, which I construed to mean that it was in fact not authorized by them.

I contacted various individuals in the small private detective community in Los Angeles. I did not reveal the name of the "client." After several days of research I settled on a man named Casper Nuñez, whose offices were in Culver City. Using an assortment of guises, a variety of clever tactics, and a plethora of cash that Ziggy had entrusted me with, we were able to gain access to the various locations. However, we were told now *not* to place a bug in Vic's house, Ziggy instructed me, because "he ain't never there for the most part ever," as Ziggy put it.

The results were as disappointing as they were entertaining. Casper Nuñez and I spent hours listening to the tapes. Some of the material was indecipherable: The technology was crude then and Vic often was inebriated and enjoying the company of several giggling women. In addition, he would have drinking parties with friends and acquaintances of his; at these gatherings, the men present would often explode in uncontrollable laughter—Vic would merely have to crack some sort of jest and the individuals present would burst into paroxysmal hysterics. As so often happens with a group of men acting childishly, the first hour of these sessions usually entailed Vic and his cohorts recapping the ribald events of their previous gathering, and this proved a labor for me to listen to as I'd already listened to the actual events themselves.

I remember that Vic watched a lot of television—he was a baseball fan—and was quite partial to Lenny Pearl's show. When I informed Ziggy of this fact, it was as if I'd told him I'd discovered an act of the highest treason. "Aha!" he shouted. "That traitor! Vic Quisling he is!" Unlike myself and Casper Nuñez, Ziggy had no interest in the various dalliances of his partner; he was much more concerned with Vic's business dealings. But, as Mr. Shepherd Lane and Arnold Latchkey were in charge of Vic's business affairs—as well as Ziggy's own—there really was nothing to listen to other than Mr. Lane telling Vic how much money was coming in. Vic owed an enormous amount of money to casinos and bookmakers in Las Vegas and California, I learned.

It was while listening to these tapes that Ziggy found out that Vic had to occasionally dye his hair a dark shade of blue, due to the recent onset of a slight salt-and-pepper effect in his hair. Too vain ever to be caught buying this dye, Vic would send someone else to effect the purchase. That someone was occasionally myself. Several times Ziggy and I listened to Vic instructing me to buy this dye.

"Why didn't you tell me about this, Cat?" Ziggy asked me.

"You never asked me," I responded.

It was also through the tapes that Ziggy found out that Vic would be recording a fifth album and also that Vic's father had been diagnosed with a brain tumor.

After a year of this surveillance, Ziggy abruptly put an end to it. He handed me a startlingly generous check to give to Casper Nuñez to ensure discretion.

I must confess that I had then what you might call a "crush" on Miss Ginger Bacon, who was Vic's primary mistress. Ginger and he would often chat about some of his other "conquests," and then, after this discussion was done, immediately engage in intercourse, as if fueled by the conversation. While engaged in coitus, Vic would tell her that he loved her, and she often told him likewise. On one such occasion they said it to each other at the exact same instant.

"You're the only one, puddin'," he would tell her. "No one else comes close."

As for the Oceanfront sessions, Vic would bring three, four, sometimes five women into bed with him. There would be soft music playing in the background. You would hear breathing, an occasional giggle, more breathing. On one tape a woman whispered, "Come on, Vic, come on." And another woman murmured, "Oh Vic, please. Come on, baby, do it to me." To which a third woman said, "Honey, Vic's not even here."

SALLY KLEIN: We were at the office on Wilshire, and Danny and Sid Stone were trying out some new material for the act. (Norman White had recently passed away.) It was fun when we got everyone together and started joking around . . . we needed to do that more. But sometimes it wasn't easy to get everybody in the same room at the same time.

In the middle of going through a new routine, Vic looked at his watch and said, "Aw, Jesus, I gotta go."

Arnie said, "But we're just getting started."

"I gotta go. I lost track of the time."

Vic went to the door. For a time he did what Jackie Gleason used to do: have two or three limos wait for him, so no matter what exit he used when leaving a building, there'd be a car there.

"This is ridiculous, Vic," Danny said. "You can't leave now."

"I gotta go, all right?! I got things, okay? Hey, who knows? I might be back in an hour."

"Aw, come on," Ziggy said, "You're gonna record a whole song in an hour?"

Vic said to him, "How did you know that's where I was goin'? I didn't tell nobody in this room I was recording a new record."

"I just guessed, Vic, that's all."

Vic looked at Ziggy up and down and shook his head. Then he left.

DANNY McGLUE: I remember one time, I was with Ziggy, Betsy, and [my son] Steve at Guy's restaurant. Betsy was doing okay then. She'd recently gotten out of the Payne Whitney [psychiatric] Clinic and things seemed to be all right for a time. Stevie's illness would often have a jarring effect on her, sometimes for the better. Sometimes not.

Vic, Ginger, and Hunny happened to be at the next table, and after they were done, they came to our table and we spoke for a while. Hunny had just been named a panelist on *What Is It?*, the old CBS game show hosted by Bob Kincaid. So we all chatted briefly and then Vic said, "I've gotta be off now." And Ziggy said, "Tell Bruno I said get well quick, Vic. I'm sure that tumor's gonna turn out to be nuttin' but a harmless golf ball."

"How'd you know about my old man?"

"Huh?"

"I didn't tell nobody my old man was sick."

Hunny said, "Vic, you told me Bruno was sick."

"Ziggy, I didn't tell nobody my old man had a tumor."

Hunny said, "You told me he had a brain tumor too, Vic. And you told me not to never tell no—"

"Quiet, Hunny. Jesus!"

Vic gave Ziggy the strangest look. Ziggy just looked down at his crab cakes and then Vic left, utterly bewildered.

REYNOLDS CATLEDGE IV: Several months into the surveillance, Vic summoned me to the Ambassador Hotel. I had to act as though I hadn't ever been on the premises before—I had been, of course, since, dressed as an exterminator, I'd placed two microphones there. This suite was entirely the antithesis of Ziggy's, in terms of decor. Some sort of martini machine was built into the wall. Vic would press an array of buttons and levers and a martini would be made; however, as this was the 1950s and automation was in its infancy, it really did seem like more work than to have merely shaken up the cocktail by hand.

At this meeting Vic was with an individual that I recognized from the newspapers as Tony Fratelli, whose brother at that time was serving time for assaulting an aggressive fan of Vic's. The fan had wanted an autograph and Jimmy, as per Vic's suggestion, took care of the woman, who was in her seventies.

"Cat, remember Los Alamos and that big party and that big bomb goin' off?" Vic said to me.

"I certainly do," I informed him.

"Man, that was some kinda blast, wasn't it?"

I said to him, "It sure was, Vic," but I could not discern whether he meant the big party in the mess hall or the actual explosion of the bomb. I knew that he was off the base for the latter, but I did not know if he was still cognizant of that fact.

He got down to business. He told me he thought that Ziggy was snooping around, spying on him. "The guy's a complete nut job, Cat," he told me. "He's got more screws loose than Tony's goddamn Edsel." Whereupon he and Tony Fratelli almost choked to death laughing. I immediately recognized Mr. Fratelli's hearty laughter from the tapes.

"Look, we spy on the Russians, right?" he asked me. "We probably got some kinda microphone in Khrushchev's vodka cabinet."

"That is probably the case," I said, "yes."

"Right. So this is what I want you to do . . ."

Within a week, Casper Nuñez and I had tapped Ziggy's house as well as his suite at the Biltmore. This was quite easy to do and we did not have to pay anyone off or dress in various guises to do so. Rather, we secreted these new bugs while Ziggy was himself occupied listening to the tapes of Vic.

Casper Nuñez and I had a problem now but it was easily rectifiable. For Vic, we had to delete the tapes of Ziggy listening to the tapes of Vic, and for Ziggy, we had to delete the tapes of Vic listening to the tapes of Ziggy.

Of particular interest to Vic—and also to myself and Casper Nuñez—was Ziggy's wife, Jane White. At the time the surveillance was under way, she was engaged in a lesbianistic relationship with a neighbor of hers named Joan Pierce. The two women, who served on assorted committees of Episcopalian women in the Los Angeles area, would watch silent movies and then proceed to enjoy sapphist relations. "Listen to this broad go—she sounds like a cowboy on a buckin' bronco," Vic would say as the Texas-born Mrs. Pierce would have coitus with Jane White. (I should mention that Jane White, after much consultation and agonizing with Mrs. Pierce, decided to surgically reverse the effects of an operation that a Dr. Howard Baer had performed on her some years before.) Of lesser interest was Ziggy ranting and railing to his wife, to his young son, and to his household staff and other individuals, about Vic. We would hear Ziggy making statements like "Do you hear this song?! He's gonna put the whole world to sleep!" and "It took Vic ten takes today to button his shirt!" I would look at Vic while he listened to this but he registered little expression. On more than one occasion he admitted, "Well, the guy's right, you know."

After eight months Vic had us remove the bugs in Ziggy's suite at the Biltmore and in the dining room, living room, and bedroom at his Beverly Hills home. After an additional two months we removed the one in Jane White's private screening room.

It was often a tricky assignment and one had to constantly be on one's toes. I played a tape to Ziggy about Vic belittling Ziggy's sexual prowess. Vic stated to his acquaintances Ernie Beasley and Hunny Gannett that Ziggy "may have the salami, but he uses it like a toothpick." Ziggy heard that and then commented to his friends, comedians Snuffy Dubin and Buzzy Brevetto, that he knew that Vic went around badmouthing his sexual technique. Casper Nuñez played that tape for Vic, who could not quite figure things out. There was also a segment, for example, wherein Ziggy told his son's nanny that Vic used blue hair dye to dye his hair. When Vic heard that, he looked at me suspiciously. Yes, it was very tricky.

When both assignments were terminated, Casper Nuñez and I were very relieved.

* * *

DANNY McGLUE: Ziggy and Vic treated the writers with so much disrespect, it nauseated you. The writers couldn't sleep, they were angry, they were humiliated constantly. I was the head writer and was spared this cruelty, but what they did to those guys was sadistic. But you know, only two guys ever quit. They were making more money than they had in their entire lives. We'd be up for three days straight sometimes without sleep, fine-tuning the script. We'd craft these funny sketches and then Ziggy would scrap them, just for the sake of scrapping them.

I'd go to bat for the writers but it was no use. In the final season, we had ten writers and none of them had ever met Fountain and Bliss face-to-face. There was this guy Tommy Orso—he wound up making a fortune in TV in the sixties and seventies. He'd been with the show since day one. After two dozen shows I went to Vic and said, "Tom Orso would really like to meet you." And he had no idea who I was talking about.

Ziggy told Artie [Conway] that he didn't want any more Dr. Louie Kablooie sketches. Artie knew not to fight Ziggy. We all did. So Artie told us and we did as Ziggy wished. Then at the last minute, two days before we went on, we got the order to come up with a Louie Kablooie sketch. Tommy Orso said, "You know, I don't need this crap. I'm walking." And the other nine writers got up and walked out too. I told Artie and he and I went to Ziggy's suite at the Sherry-Netherland. Ziggy told us to call each writer and have them come in. He would, he said, show up at the meeting tomorrow and personally apologize. He'd done wrong, he knew.

So the next day the guys are all assembled and Millie Roth pops in. She tells us to go downstairs. The writers pile into the elevator and then we're on Broadway and what's there? Ten new cars! Ziggy—who didn't ever apologize to us—had arranged it with the sponsor, which was Pontiac by then, to get ten new Bonneville convertibles, one for each of us.

"What a real sweetheart that bastard is," Tom Orso said.

ARNIE LATCHKEY: After the fourth or fifth movie in the Galaxy deal, everything caved in like an outhouse getting bombed. Nobody wanted to work on the crew; we couldn't get a cameraman or a key grip or anything. I mean, if you worked on one Fountain and Bliss picture then that was it—you wouldn't do another. Gus Kahn was livid. George Collier—or what was left of him—had given up, and we even had trouble getting a director. It took a while but Ezra Gorman, who was still producing the movies, scraped something together.

Around this same time I thought our ship might sink. The theory was that if any single one of us—Vic, Sally, Ziggy, myself—gets off the ship, then the whole damn thing would sink. And now someone—oh, we'll call him Samuel Goldwyn—approached Vic, through me, about starring in the movie version of *Guys and Dolls*. [Director] Joe Mankiewicz and [writer] Abe Burrows were really touting him to Goldwyn. Now, I could've turned it down flat and never even mentioned the offer to Vic, but I didn't do that. Why? Because of my profound conscience? Because I knew I had to do good by my talent? No. It was because I knew he'd have found out about it and chewed my head off for not telling him.

So I told him about Goldwyn's interest and, much to my dread, his face lit up. He'd seen the play. He said the Nathan Detroit role was perfectly suited to him. "That's me, baby!" he said. "I could do that part in my sleep."

Well, now my face also lit up too. "And you want I should tell them that?" I said.

"Yeah, tell them that."

I told Goldwyn that Vic felt he could do the part in his sleep. As I'd hoped, he didn't seem very happy. He relayed the line to Mankiewicz and Burrows. And Frank Sinatra—who they weren't worried about being awake or not—got the part.

•   •   •

DAVID GRAN [employee at Galaxy]: I started working at Galaxy in their commissary as a busboy. One day Arnie Latchkey plucked me out of the commissary and asked me if I'd like to work on the set of *Two Goofballs*. I said, "Wow! Sure! When can I start?!" and the man said to me, "Please . . . don't get too excited, kid."

Before you know it I was a best boy for a Fountain and Bliss movie.

Now, even in the commissary I'd heard that they could be difficult. I'd hear it when people were on line with their trays. You could tell from people's expressions that they were working on a Fountain and Bliss picture, just from their dazed looks and silences. Still, I jumped at the opportunity.

Latchkey told me my job was simple: "The director wants you to tell Ziggy and Vic something, you tell Ziggy. If Ziggy then wants you to tell Vic something, then you tell it to me first. If Vic wants to say something to Ziggy, either tell me or the director."

The director—it was Stanley London—rarely addressed them both publicly at the same time. Or privately. Ezra Gorman didn't either. Fountain and Bliss almost never talked to each other. A lot went through me. There were times when I honestly felt I was by far the most important person on the set of the movie. And I was making less than anyone there.

There was one very serious complication on this picture. Every Fountain and Bliss movie had a large musical number, but Gorman could not convince any choreographer to work on the movie. So one day a woman showed up and was introduced to us as the choreographer. She was in her late fifties and her name was Mary Beaumont. She'd choreographed some Broadway musicals and done summer stock too.

For some reason, this did not sit well with Ziggy Bliss. He refused to come out of his trailer if Mrs. Beaumont was to choreograph the big dance number. The set closed down for a week. I had to relay messages from him to Gorman to London to Arnie Latchkey and then back to Ziggy. Ziggy said that *he* would choreograph the dance. Finally he gave up. He walked onto the set to meet Mrs. Beaumont. "Hi, Mary. 'Member me?" he said, talking like a baby. And she said, "Ziggy, how could I ever, ever forget you! Please, give an old flame a kiss!" Ziggy stood on his toes to reach up to kiss her—she was in remarkable physical shape—and Mary spat on his face. "There! I've wanted to do that for years!" she said and then triumphantly walked off.

In the end, there was no big musical number in *Two Goofballs*.

• • •

VICKI FOUNTAIN: You can imagine what it was like growing up Vic Fountain's daughter. I had everything I could ever ask for. Edith Head and Irene, the MGM designer, used to design clothing for my dolls, and every day a driver would drop me off at school in a Rolls. Vincent wasn't nearly as pampered as I was. Dad really lavished most of the presents and attention on me. He always called me his little princess.

I remember when I was not named homecoming queen in my senior year. Dad went berserk. He got Tony and Jimmy Fratelli, who were in business with [gangster] Mickey Cohen, to accompany him to the school. He plucked me out of a science class and brought me down to the principal's office with the Fratellis. He was yelling at [principal] Mr. Armstrong and he was pinching my face. "How could she not be the queen?!" he was screaming. "Look at this *faccia bella!*" Mr. Armstrong was frightened, he didn't know what the Fratelli brothers would do. "It wasn't really up to me, Mr. Fountain," he told Dad. "Dad, please, it's okay!" I told him. I was in tears almost, but I appreciated his love and concern and, of course, I still wanted to be homecoming queen too. Dad told Tony Fratelli to find Katie Cornwell, the girl who'd won, and Tony went stomping off. Jimmy said, "Vic, we can't have Tony beatin' up seventeen-year-old girls he don't even know! I mean, if it was a girl he knew . . . let's get outta here!" Dad grabbed the lamp on Mr. Armstrong's desk and threw it against the wall. Then Tony burst in and he had Katie by the hair. Tony said, "Hey, you know, she *is* kinda pretty, Vic. I don't wanna have to mess anything up here." By that time Dad had lost his interest and he and the Fratellis just left.

All my girlfriends had crushes on Dad. After school, someone would ask, "So what should we do today?" And everyone else would say, "Let's go over to Vicki's!"

Dad wasn't usually there though.

FREDDY BLISS: I was not just an only child, I was a lonely child. I know how Dad had grown up and maybe that had something to do with it. Mom had many friends, she belonged to so many clubs and organizations, she was always shopping or having lunches, and Dad was Dad, performing somewhere, making a movie, on the road. I had a housekeeper named Ruthie who I was close to, but that was it.

You know, Dad wanted to have me bar mitzvahed but my mother said that was absolutely out of the question. She really put her foot down.

I don't want to give the wrong impression though. He was a good father. He always called me when he was on the road. You know, on Parent-Teacher Day Dad used to come to the school and he'd work the room. Really! He'd always make sure to be the last parent to walk in—that way, every head would turn to him when he entered. And all he had to do was appear and people were giggling. It was as if a cyclone had blown into a first-grade class. He'd put on a great show, he'd do jokes with the teacher, he'd clown around with the kids, he'd do stuff with the chalk and the eraser and that map of America that rolled down. And when I was invited to other kids' birthday parties, the parents *always* asked for Dad to bring me; that way, he would perform for the kids. He did do it, he brought me to maybe five birthday parties, and would have everyone in stitches. But when he stopped doing that, the invitations didn't come anymore.

CATHERINE RICCI: In 1961 Papa died of brain cancer. He'd been sick for a long time and he put up a good fight. It wasn't like him to go out like a coward. He refused all painkillers—he said they were for sissy boys.

Vic paid for all his hospital bills. He got him two rooms at that Cedars hospital in Los Angeles, all to himself. I'd fly out there once a month to visit him, which Vic paid for. Every time my kids saw him, they thought it was for the last time.

Mamma said to me, "He's not going to let this thing kill him." She was right.

He wore these very dark sunglasses, you know. He had to, it was the law. And he still wore them inside the hospital, even as he was wasting away every day.

They found him dead in the morning, the nurses did, when they came to check on him. He had walked to a chair, near to a mirror on the wall. He sat down, took his sunglasses off, and turned on the light. It must have been a terrible struggle. He stared at himself in the mirror and stared very hard until his heart stopped.

Vic flew the body back to Massachusetts on a private plane and Papa was buried at the Catholic cemetery. There was a wake first and even then he had to have his sunglasses on. He's got the biggest stone in the graveyard, the biggest by far. The church in charge of the cemetery didn't want it there, the priest said it was an eyesore. "It's like the Eiffel Tower!" the priest said. It *is* pretty showy. Vic came to the funeral, of course, but left the same night. He hadn't spent a night in Codport in years, and he never returned after that.

GUY PUGLIA: A few weeks [after Bruno died] there was another piece of bad news. Gino Puccio died in New York. I called Vic in Chicago and told him that. He said, "Who the fuck is Gino Puccio?" And I said, "Pooch! The guy at the Monroe! He put us up for free at the hotel and at his house in Long Beach, you fuckin' idiot!" And he said, "Oh yeah . . . *Pooch!* With that red-hot daughter of his!" I said, "*Huh?* Vic . . . she's a nun," and he said, "So how's old Pooch doin' anyways?"

Man, sometimes talkin' to him was just like talkin' to a cloud.

ARNIE LATCHKEY: Clubs were starting to close down. The Blue Beret went belly-up in '59 and the last I heard of Barney Arundel he was being pushed around in a wheelchair in Miami. Man's fate, I suppose. All the clubs were sick, dying, or dead. See, it was the idiot box, the television, that's what it was. Going out, donning your fancy threads, dancing and making merry—what was the big deal about that when you could watch *Bonanza* in your bedroom and suck down a frozen Swanson TV dinner?

Morty Geist to the rescue.

"Let's spread the rumor, Arnie, that Fountain and Bliss are calling it quits," he said.

Genius. Absolute genius.

SNUFFY DUBIN: It's four in the morning, I've just finished a big show at the Fountainebleau opening for Andy Williams, my brain is boiling like crazy on pills. I called Debbie in L.A. after a show every single night, that was the law, it didn't matter what time it was. I've got a TV in my room and who knows if there was even a show on—with all the bennies and the Jack Daniel's I could look at all them dots and static swirling around and somehow turn it into *King Lear*. So I get off the phone with Debbie and the phone rings. I picked it up and it was some newspaper reporter. At four in the fucking morning this cat is calling me! He says is it true that Fountain and Bliss are calling it quits? I said to him, "I don't know—*is it?*" It's the first I've heard about it. He said that he'd just been told Ziggy and Vic are going their separate ways. I told him, "Look, buddy, I don't know and I don't care. Adios!"

I hung up and laid my head down on the pillow. I don't know if it was all the pills and the booze but I didn't fall asleep. Not for hours. I kept thinking about Ziggy and Vic.

SALLY KLEIN: It was vintage Morty Geist. Spread the word that Fountain and Bliss were breaking up, then have them deny it. *Variety* had it as their headline. Then Ziggy and Vic called a press conference to say it was all untrue. The boys loved it. It made the press look stupid and venomous, which is what Ziggy and Vic thought they were. Bud Hatch called up Ziggy, and Ziggy unleashed a three-hour tirade on the phone. Bud made it the whole column, something he would normally reserve only for something like Gary Cooper dying. "How can they say these things about us? How? Vic says they're not even scum; I say they're not even mildew," he said. "And all 'cause we make people laugh. That's our mortal sin. It's, like, you make someone laugh so they nail you to the cross. That just don't seem fair, Bud." I was in his office when Ziggy was talking to him . . . as his tirade went on and on, he got more vehement, more agitated. By the end he was standing and his hand was in a fist.

He hung up and I said to him, "Ziggy, you know, that was very convincing. But we *did* purposely spread this rumor."

And I could tell from his face that he'd completely forgotten that.

ARNIE LATCHKEY: After Cody Lee Jarrett got killed on his bike—that really hurt the ratings. They never would book anyone for the young crowd . . . they wouldn't even put Pat Boone on. Ziggy would've put Elvis Presley or Cal [*sic*] Perkins on, I really believe that, but Vic hated that stuff; so we wound up with "the Prince of Wails," Johnny Ray, people like that. But conversely, Ziggy would never put Jan Murray, Snuffy Dubin, or Shelley Berman on the show either.

The killer was that in 1958 or so, NBC gave Fritz Devane a sitcom, *Daddy's Home.* Aptly enough, Geritol was the sponsor. That wig of his you thought any minute would sprout wings and fly off the top of his head. Every man and woman over the age of fifty years old watched the Devane show, which, of course, was in the time slot opposite us.

So this is what happened. Our show bit the dust. Their movies were bringing in less money. The last motion picture they did for Galaxy was the baseball/science-fiction movie, with the somewhat unwieldy title of *One, Two, Three Strikes, You're Out of This World.* Try fitting *that* onto your marquee, boy. See, *Damn Yankees* had done well and you had that play *Visit to a Small Planet.* So naturally the Hollywood logic is: Hey, why not make a movie about a baseball player from outer space?

This movie stank, Teddy. I mean, it reeked to the rafters. They should've fumigated the theaters after the first reel. When it wrapped, Ziggy even said, "Whew! We can breathe again!" *Variety* embalmed it, Chet Yalburton of the *Globe* put the shroud on it, the *Times* of Los Angeles dug the hole, *Time* and *Newsweek* flung it into the ground, and the *New York Times* piled the dirt onto the coffin. They insulted Vic's singing, they insulted the direction, the makeup, the costumes—they said that Ziggy Bliss swinging a bat managed to make William Bendix as Babe Ruth look like an Oscar-caliber performance. That hurt big time. I mean, in a word: *Ouch!*

Ziggy and Vic went on the road to push the movie but you can only push a dead twenty-ton carp so far. Now, this was the first time they ever went out in support of a movie separately. Ziggy I thought was gonna have an infarction when Sally came up with this masterstroke. "Two people traveling separately," she reasoned, "can cover more ground."

"She's right, Zig," Vic said.

Ziggy slumped in his chair. I thought he was gonna literally deflate.

So Vic went his way and Ziggy went his. They agreed on one thing: No performing. Vic wasn't going to sing, Ziggy wasn't going to do any stand-up, which he, emotionally, couldn't have done yet solo anyways. So Vic would go on *Jack Paar* and *Dave Garroway* and he did a surprise walk-on on *What Is It?*—it took ten minutes before Hunny recognized him—and Ziggy went on Barry Gray's [radio] show and Irv Kupcinet and Long John Nebel.

The timing was good too. Because Lulu and Vic were now legally separated. She'd had enough of Vic. Or she didn't have enough of Vic—I don't know which one it was. Lulu tells everybody—to this day—that all she wanted out of Vic was for him to be a provider . . . but he was the only man she ever loved and he broke her heart every day. Look, Vic really did love the kids, he spent as much time with Vicki as he could, but it just wasn't that much time. He'd go on golfing jags, he was always golfing with [PGA champions] Tony Newport and Tony Hampton. He'd bring Vicki and Vincent to the golf course, sometimes let them take time off from school too, which I don't think their teachers approved of. But it was Vic Fountain so it was okay.

LULU FOUNTAIN: You think I cared about all the girls? I don't care if he was keeping one *zoccola* or a thousand! I'd call him up in Vegas to tell him that Vicki got a bad report card or that Vincent had a cold . . . sometimes a broad would answer and in the background I'd hear Vic saying, "Who is it, doll?" I got used to it. I had to. What I cared about was, what made me sick was . . .

One time I was having lunch with Hunny and Joe Yung at the house. And the kids were there too . . . it must've been a weekend. At the end of the lunch, Joe got up and said, "I gotta get going now. You're going to stay around, Hunny?"

"Yeah sure, Chinese Joe," Hunny said.

Then Joe took off and Hunny started playing with Vincent's electric trains, trying to make them move.

"Why was Joe in such a rush?" I asked him.

"He's gotta bring someone to Mexico, Lu, some friend of Vic's," he said. "Vinnie, something's wrong wit' your trains."

"Why?" I asked him.

"Some doctor there fixes 'em," he told me. He said to Vincent, "Your train set is broke."

"Why do these girls need fixin'?" I asked him.

"So's they don't get babies, Lu."

Vincent put the trains back on the tracks and then they started moving.

* * *

GUY PUGLIA: Vic drives up in his new Bentley to my restaurant, he gets out with Ginger. It's one, two o'clock at night, I'm closing the place up.

I see him and what's the first thing I do? I take the big plastic swordfish off the wall.

"I need to get a word with you, *goomba*," he says to me.

I'm thinkin', Okay, what's he want me to do for him now?

We go into my little office behind the kitchen.

"Me and Lulu—it's *finito*," he said.

I opened a drawer in my desk and pulled out a bottle of bourbon and two glasses.

"I'm sorry about that," I said.

"I've known her since I was a fuckin' kid, Guy."

"So have I."

"I don't know about this whole marriage racket sometimes."

"I wouldn't know. You know?"

"Hey, you're smart not to ever get hitched," he told me. "Believe me."

"I'm smart, Vic? Nah, I ain't smart. I just don't have a fuckin' nose anymore. *Smart?* What girl you know wants to marry a guy five foot two who's got no nose?"

He drained his glass, refilled it, and shook his head.

"One day you'll get married, buddy."

"I don't know about that," I said.

"I love my kids. I love 'em. I look at Vicki, it's like she's a gift from God to me. All the stupid stuff I've done wrong in this world and still I get such an angel. And I think Vince's gonna have a better singin' voice than his old man."

I said, "Hey pal, my sick beagle's got a better singin' voice than you." I took a snort of the Jack Daniel's and said, "What about Ginger?"

"What about her?"

"She loves you, Vic. You're gonna be a free man now. Maybe you could hitch up with her eventually."

"Well, I don't know . . . I mean, maybe I wanna live a nice sweet life as a bachelor for a while, you know?"

"You been doin' that for your whole marriage!"

"Yeah, you're right. You're right. But maybe now that I'm single, it's time to settle down."

SALLY KLEIN: Have you ever seen the tape of Ed Murrow interviewing Vic at home? Morty Geist did instant damage control after the divorce and arranged for a CBS *Person to Person* interview. Lulu got the house in Beachwood Canyon so Vic was living at the Beverly Wilshire. Ernie Beasley plays piano throughout the interview; you could hear it softly in the background and sometimes make him out. Now I'll tell you: Vic didn't ever have a piano in there except for this interview. As soon as they unplugged the camera, the piano went back to the shop. The first part of the interview was Vic with Vicki and Vincent. He really did look like such a proud dad, and they were both such gorgeous children. Vicki would not get off Vic's lap when Ed Murrow wanted to interview Vic alone, it was very cute, and there was another part when Vince tries to get Vic's attention by using a cigarette, but Vic ignores him. Then Ed asks Vic to sing a song and Ernie starts up "Lost and Lonely Again," and Vic sang it and it looked like he was going to fall asleep halfway. Ed Murrow even said, "Vic . . . uh, Vic?" to stir him. Then Ed asked Vic how he was doing, living alone and being single, and Vic said, "Well, Eddie, there is a new person in my life now. A very special person." And a few seconds later, there's Ziggy in drag and they do a hilarious ten-minute bit together.

After twenty years they could still work the same old magic.

ERNIE BEASLEY: The big tour together in 1962 . . . there were all these rumors that it was going to be their last tour. At this point I didn't know if this was Morty Geist doing a publicity stunt or if they really meant it. And you couldn't tell by Ziggy and Vic. Sometimes they'd talk to each other backstage, sometimes they wouldn't. But it had been that way for years.

Ginger said to me, "You know how they communicate? Through one-upmanship. It's like they send signals to each other on their own private wavelength."

What she meant was, they had these riders built into their contracts. The soda machine on their floor in the hotels, for instance: Vic insisted that the bottles had to come out with the caps to the left, not the right. Then Ziggy wanted another machine on the floor, with the caps all to the right, not the left. Vic had to have his hotel room within a certain temperature, between 62 and 65 degrees. When Ziggy found out about that, he demanded his room be *exactly* 63½ degrees. When Vic found out that

Ziggy demanded ruby red carpeting in the hotel room as well as a ruby bath mat and matching towels, Vic had it so he'd have his own hand-picked furniture shipped from city to city—and everything turquoise, of course. The hotel would empty out his room, put in the furniture, then, when Vic moved on, the old furniture went back in. Ziggy went one up on this too. He would have Andy Ravelli or Reynolds Catledge go to the city ahead of time and *buy* new furniture for his hotel room, then, when Ziggy moved on, the hotel could keep it or throw it out.

It could get very, very ugly if their demands weren't met. Vic wanted twenty bottles of Dom Pérignon in his dressing room and if there were nineteen or twenty-one bottles, he would not go on. One time he didn't like the exact shade of turquoise so he and a few of his buddies destroyed the hotel suite. Vic called down, got another suite, and destroyed that one too.

ARNIE LATCHKEY: I'm at Chasen's one day with Sally, and Gus Kahn saunters in alone except for his Cohiba. He sits down and then he notices us and beckons me over.

"I got to hand it to your boy Vic Fountain, Latchkey, I really do," he said.

"Why's that, Gus?" I'm bracing myself.

"I got a call last night at two in the morning," he tells me. "A woman was arrested at the Sands in Las Vegas last night. She was shootin' dice. Won five grand as a matter of fact. Was cursing up a storm . . . the pit boss even had to tell her to pipe down. She was tellin' men to kiss the dice, to suck on the dice, to shove the dice down their Jockey shorts, all for good luck. She didn't pipe down. Customers were leaving, it got so dirty. *In Las Vegas it got too dirty!* They summon Jack Entratter, he tells her to kindly leave. She told him—and this is a direct quote—to 'stick his little wang in a meat grinder.'"

"Cut to the part with Vic, Gus. My red-hot chili's gettin' . . . chilly."

"Okay, so this lady, who is as drunk as you can be without passing out, moves to the blackjack tables. And she's starting to make a scene there too now. She begins losin' all the dough she made with the dice. And she starts yelling at the dealer. 'You goddamn whore!' she yells. 'You take it up the ass from Ethel Merman with a strap-on dildo!' Things such as this, things that make me blush just to repeat them to you, Latchkey, as you can no doubt see. So now a few guards mosey on over and they're going to toss her outside. And she's a big woman so it was probably more than a few guards. She sees them approaching so what does she do? Well, what would *you* do? She stands up, stands on the blackjack table, and rips the felt to shreds with her high heels, pulls down her skirt, and shows them her ass. 'Grab a good piece of it, boys, 'cause it's the best thing you'll ever have!'

she yelled out. So these ten guards lift her up and carry her out kicking and screaming onto the Strip and throw her there like she's a sack of turnips. It was quite a thud, you can imagine."

I joked, "So that was the noise I heard in my house last night on Cañon Drive, eh?"

"Do you know who this woman was?" Gus asked me, chugging on his cigar.

"Enlighten me."

"It was Clotilde Sturdivandt. Now go back to your chili. It's gettin' . . . red hot."

Dissolve. A few months later I was in New York at the WAT offices, meeting with Murray Katz. I knew the news was bad when he didn't want to take me out for lunch to the Russian Tea Room or "21." I said to him, "Murr, maybe we could go to the Automat?" But he said, "Latch, we better meet here." Very loud gulp.

The upshot was with the Galaxy deal done, the forecast was for heavy flooding, followed by famine, plague, and pestilence. Galaxy won't renew, he told me. I said to Murray, "What about this *Cleopatra* thing going on? All that money flushed right down Liz Taylor's bidet! I could finance the next three world wars for what they're wasting on that thing!" I reminded him that no Fountain and Bliss movie ever lost a penny and, boy, did he ever put me in my place. He said, "Latch, at one time people said, 'No Fountain and Bliss movie ever lost a dollar.' Then they started saying, 'No Fountain and Bliss movie ever lost a dime' Now it's down to a penny. See where we're heading on this?"

"What about we renew for three pictures? Three pictures?" I implored. "Please?"

"Gussie won't bite."

"Two. Two pictures," I begged. "They can be the worst movies ever made."

"The boys already made those. No soap."

"One picture! We'll do a one-picture-at-a-time deal. No commitment. One picture. And, Jesus Christ, if Gussie wants it, Clarence Gilbert can even direct it!"

"Ned's dead ten years, Arnie. You think I don't know that?"

"Yeah, but maybe Gussie don't. All right, all right. I refuse to beg about this thing."

He reminded me that I had indeed been begging. I agreed that, yes, I had been.

But guess what? I must have somehow found one small fraying, dangling heartstring of Murray's—he was an agent and probably didn't have too many of 'em—and tugged at it the right way. Because a week later he got the boys a deal at Paramount. One picture. Three hundred grand apiece. "What kind of material will it be?" I asked Murray. He said, "What do they want it to be?" I said, "Well, there's this thing been floatin' around since before Noah's ark washed ashore. It's called *Three of a Kind.*" "Sid and Norman's old thing?" he said. "Yep," I replied. He said, "Jesus, that thing was perfect for them," to which I tersely responded, "Precisely."

He told me he'd throw it Paramount's way. He did. And like Willie Mays goin' after Vic Wertz's fly ball, they caught it. *Finally!* Someone wanted to do it!

But if there's only one thing in this business that I've learned, it's this: Never, ever get too excited about anything. Enthusiasm can act like a poison.

JANE WHITE: After Lulu and Vic got divorced, I tried to continue being friends with her. But I really don't know why he married her. She wasn't pretty, she wasn't very smart, she wasn't terribly sweet or nice and was not pleasant company; she was like a waitress at a truck stop.

What was I saying? Oh yes. Our friendship.

I came by with Freddy one day so he could play with Vicki and Vincent. The last time I'd done this, though, do you know what happened? Vicki and Freddy were near the pool and Vicki lifted up her skirt. She was ten and he was eight. I saw it, Lulu saw it, Joe Yung saw it. And Freddy started crying. And when he was crying Vicki pushed him into the pool. That was Vicki.

So I drove up with Freddy one morning. I remember I was wearing a wonderful white Oleg Cassini dress. And a pillbox hat, just like Jackie Kennedy. I rang the door and Lulu answered. "I was just passing by," I told her, "and thought I would drop in."

"Look," she said to me, "we never liked each other. I ain't Vic's wife no more. And maybe one day you won't be Ziggy's. And maybe one day Vic and Ziggy won't be together no more. So really, Jane, you don't have to come around." And she closed the door in my face.

Well, I never!

DANNY McGLUE: I hadn't looked at the *Three of a Kind* script since well before Norman White passed away. It had really been through some kind of life. It could've been a wonderful Broadway play, a musical, a movie, a TV play. But it had never been anything except a dust magnet. So when Arnie told me that Paramount was hot to do it, I pulled it out of a file drawer.

I read it. There was something "off" about it. So I read it again. The plot was good, most of the jokes were still fresh, the characterizations were rich. But still, there was something not right about it.

I put it away and then Betsy and I went out to dinner, to Tony's on Seventy-ninth Street. She'd just spent another two weeks at Payne Whitney. I should tell you that Stevie had just died. He was gone. My poor boy had never been truly healthy. Betsy drank a lot when she was pregnant with him . . . I really would prefer not to talk about this . . .

During dinner, it hit me. I knew what was wrong. I told Betsy I had to make a phone call and went to a phone near the bar. I called Arnie in L.A. and said, "Arnie . . . Arnie . . . Listen to me."

"All ears, Danny boy," he said.

"The script . . . it's for two guys in their early twenties! It's for two guys who are twenty-two, twenty-three years old!"

"*Oy vey iz mir,*" he said. "You're right!"

"They're twice the age they need to be!"

"Well, they're more than doubly qualified then," he said. "Look, can't you rejigger things? Get an eraser, a pencil, some glue, change things around."

"Arnie, this would be like casting Rock Hudson as Lassie."

He didn't say anything for a while and I could tell he was actually thinking that might be a good idea.

"Okay," he said after a while. "I'll see what Paramount says."

"Arnie," I said, "if they do this picture, it'll kill them. Vic's put on a little weight. Ziggy isn't as perfectly round as he used to be. Did you know that Vic has to dye his hair blue now? They can't do it. It'll destroy their careers."

There was a pause again . . . maybe he was thinking that might be a good idea too.

* * *

ERNIE BEASLEY: Vic and Ginger truly loved each other, there was no doubt about that to me. She was a real "man's woman"; she could drink anyone under the table, she went to the casinos and didn't just play the slots, she knew how to have a good time. She hadn't had an easy life, growing up so poor in Kentucky. Her father was an alcoholic and abused his wife.

[We] spent more time on the phone with each other than any two people in the world. If we were hanging out with Vic's crowd, we'd go home at 3:00 A.M. and then be on the phone until five or six in the morning. You know, she had the tough exterior but she really was very sweet and girlish. *"I've got a hunch that you can take a punch, that you've got that kind of hide. But with all those hits, you break to bits, 'cause you're so tender deep inside"*—I wrote the lyrics to "The Dame Can Take It" based on her.

"He's the only guy I ever really flipped for," she told me once. She'd had boyfriends before, but they didn't mean anything to her, but Vic she was nuts for. She knew she was his mistress, of course, and she knew how devoted Vic was to the kids. But every once in a while—actually, quite often—she would say something like "Well, maybe they'll get a divorce one day." You know, Ginger knew about all of Vic's other girls. But she said to me, "Let him have his fun. Believe me, I have mine too. We're still the loves of each other's lives."

When the divorce came through, she was the happiest thing. "I'm not going to put any pressure on him," she told me on the phone. "I know men . . . if I push him, he'll fade away from me." She said those words to me and two nights later I wrote "He'll Fade Away," which was a big hit for Miss Leslie Wilson. So Ginger's plan was to lay low, to never mention marriage, and hopefully Vic would pop the question and they'd live happily ever after.

The day the divorce came through, Vic, Guy, Andy Ravelli, and I went to Johnny D'Antibes's club and went on a real bender. We got completely blind. Joe Yung had to drive us all home . . . I don't even remember that night. Or the next. Then Vic moved into his new house in Beverly Hills, a Spanish-style, stucco palace that had once belonged to Omar Caballero, the silent film star. The house was close enough to the kids but far enough so he wasn't constantly running into Lulu. He had twenty rooms and a cellar that, for some reason, he never let *anyone* into or even see. He eventually took out the swimming pool and had another one installed in the shape of a martini glass. Joe Yung lived in the guest house, which was big enough for a family of four.

A week after he moved in I got a call from Ginger. "Have you heard from Vic?" she asked me. "I'm worried about him."

"He's putting together a new record, baby," I said.

"But how long does that take each day?"

"For him? Maybe twenty minutes."

"Would you tell him to call me? I call, and the maid or Joe Yung says that he'll call back."

I saw Vic at the recording studio a few hours later and said that Ginger was worried about him. He said, "Oh, Bease, Jesus . . . I've been so busy lately . . . I got all this paperwork about the divorce and the house and stuff. I'm writing out checks to every single person Lulu ever looked at. Tell her I'll call her."

So I called Ginger right away and told her that. But two or three days later she told me he hadn't called.

"She's still waiting for you to call," I told Vic. He told me he'd tried calling her but I could tell he hadn't.

Two weeks went by and he didn't call her. She told me one night at

Romanoff's that she had the idea to drive up to Vic's new pad and just barge in and confront him. "But if I do that then I reduce myself to nothing," she said. "That shows no class." I held her hand on the table that night—she seemed very fragile. "Lulu always said I was Vic's whore, I know that," she said. "But she has no idea how happy we made each other." I said to her, "Look, baby, maybe it's not over . . . you know, he just went through the divorce. Give him some time."

The next day I was at Vic's suite at the Ambassador, which he still kept. He said to me, "You're still close with Ginger, right?"

"I am."

"Look, can you tell her I don't wanna see her anymore?"

"Um, that's for you to do, Vic."

"Come on, Bease. I say it, she'll get mad at me. You say it, she won't get mad at you."

"Well, that's true, yes. But it's not me that's getting rid of her—it's you."

"Just do it for me. Tell her if she wants me to take care of her, you know, like with dough and stuff, I'll do it. She wants a planet, I'll get her one."

"I don't think she'd take a cent from you."

"Yeah, she was always a classy broad," Vic said. "You gotta hand it to her."

Vic never called her. He didn't send a letter. He tried to deposit $10,000 in her bank account, but she got the money back to him through Shep Lane. After three months—and she was a wreck that time, an absolute wreck, on pills and vodka all the time—she moved back to New York. She gave me her phone number and we spoke often. I went to New York and we had dinner at "21." A week later I called and the number had been disconnected. I called information and they didn't have a listing for her. I called up Millie Roth and had her go to Ginger's apartment, on Fifty-fourth Street off Lexington. But she didn't live there anymore. She'd disappeared.

I'm sorry if I keep plugging my own songs but I wrote the song "Vanishing Lady" about her. It was sort of bittersweet and very Jacques Brel-y and is, in my opinion, my best song. Vic had a big hit with it. Serge Ballard was now Vic's arranger—it was a lovely, lush, ambient production. The song was in the Top 10 for over fifteen weeks. He sang that song hundreds and hundreds of times. But I don't think he had any idea who or what it was about.

REYNOLDS CATLEDGE IV: In September of 1963 Vic Fountain and I had lunch in his suite at the Beverly Wilshire. Also present at this encounter were Andy Ravelli, Ernie Beasley, and three other individuals.

"I wanna do a solo thing, Cat," he told me. "I wanna just get a taste of it."

"A solo show?" I asked. "This means without Ziggy?"

When I said this all of the others present burst out laughing, and I felt momentarily shamed. I merely had been trying to ascertain the facts.

"Solo, Cat," he said. "When Lindbergh flew to Paris, did he have Ziggy in the cockpit with him feeding him coffee and one-liners?"

"No, he did not."

"See, I haven't told anybody about this thing yet," he said (despite the five other people present). "It's all set for the Cal-Neva Lodge in Tahoe. They got me penciled in for five nights. But nobody knows about it. Latch don't know, neither does Sally or Shep Lane. If I had a goddamn psychiatrist, I wouldn't have even told him. That's how secret this thing is."

"I understand."

"Although I might tell my bartender or caddy."

This caused most of those present to incur another fit of annoying, inexplicable laughter.

"Is there a way we could keep this from them?" Vic asked me.

I informed him that if he performed at such a venue, there would no doubt be many hundreds of people present, thousands over the course of the five nights. Newspapers and magazines would surely find out about it, as would television and radio.

"So it don't sound too promising then?" he said.

"If you wanted to perform in Siberia in a frozen tundra," I told him, "if it was without Ziggy, the news would get out, I'm afraid."

"Nah, I don't want to play any tundra in Siberia," he said. "Although who knows how many shekels they'll pay . . ."

"You mean, I believe, rubles."

"Yeah, Cat. Rubles."

He walked me to the door and slapped me on the back. He said, "Well, I guess if it's gonna happen, it's inevitable."

SALLY KLEIN: Bertie Kahn called me in L.A. at three in the morning, his time. I hated getting calls late like that . . . Jack would always wake up in a panic and I never knew what it would do to his heart.

"Vic's doing a solo," he told me. "At Tahoe."

"He told you this?"

"Earl Wilson did. Ten minutes ago."

"Maybe he got it wrong."

"SL just called. She backs it up."

"Who?"

"The Slobbering Lush."

"I don't know, Bert," I said. "Maybe this is one of Morty's stunts."

"It's legit. I feel it."

"I better call Morty right away."

"I did. He's shaking like a leaf."

"How could Vic just do this?"

"Pretty easily, it seems," Bertie said.

"Oh, this is bad. This is very bad." I think I was actually groaning, like I was in physical agony. "Who the hell is going to tell Ziggy this?"

"Sally?" Bertie said.

"Yes?"

"I have to go."

ARNIE LATCHKEY: By the time Sally called me at seven in the morning, four people had already called me. Mickey Rudin, Sinatra's lawyer, called me, because Frank had such a big stake in the Cal-Neva. Pete Conifer called me—the guy was probably tied up with a diaper on and being spanked as he was talking. Shep Lane called too.

"Honey, if four people know, then twenty people know," Estelle told me over my morning grapefruit. "And if twenty people know, then a thousand people know."

Sally called Ziggy's house and Jane answered the phone. By then, Ziggy knew. I don't know who had the *baytsim* to call him, but someone did, and Ziggy probably never spoke to the man again.

I called the house and asked Jane, "How's he takin' it?"

"Oh, he'll be all right, Arnie."

"Yeah, but how's he doing *now*?"

"I don't know. He's sealed himself in the bedroom. But he'll be all right."

"Well, can you go outside and peek in through the window and see if he's alive?"

I told her that just 'cause Vic was doing one little solo gig, it didn't mean that Fountain and Bliss were kaput. But she said that Ziggy hadn't seen it that way.

Ziggy I didn't hear from for three days. Jane would call us, we'd call Jane, and it was generally agreed that he was still among the living. He relayed a message to us through her: "I can't believe he'd do this to me. Vic Iscariot is who he is."

Vic never said a word, never mentioned it. He knew we knew, and we knew he knew we knew. It was like they'd found a blood clot the size of a couch in his brain and we weren't supposed to mention it, out of politesse or something. So we didn't.

Jesus Christ, Ziggy looked like he was going to die. He had no idea what his future was.

They had five nights at the Oceanfront the following week. Billy Wilder had passed on *Three of a Kind*—so had Blake Edwards. From there we moved down to the hacks, guys who directed *Beach Brisket Bongo* movies, but no guy who knew how to yell the words "action" and "cut" would bite. We'd tried to get Marilyn Monroe interested for the Miriam Hopkins role, but she died on us so she passed too. Ziggy was hot to get Jayne Mansfield—no surprise, that—but she wasn't taken with it. Still the gears were churning, albeit at a deathly sluggish tempo.

The movie never got made.

A day before the Oceanfront shows, we were all together at the office. Shep advised Vic to avoid the casinos in Vegas . . . the only reason they were playing the Oceanfront at all was because Vic had lost so much dough there. He loses forty grand, he does another week. That's how it went.

Frank Gorshin was opening for the boys. The place was buzzing. Everyone had heard that Vic was doing a solo at the Cal-Neva. Were they breaking up? Weren't they? Everybody was asking me and I told them the God's honest truth: I had no idea.

Gorshin does his show, then the band begins and Vic comes out. He sings "The Hang of It," then launches into another song. This is the song that Ziggy is supposed to interrupt. Five bars into the number there's no Ziggy. Ziggy was in his room, or maybe he was skinny-dipping in Lake Mead. I don't know. Vic was left holding his *shlong*. The band only knew four songs for Vic and they did them all, three times over.

He came offstage, raging, and he said to me, "Okay . . . where is he?! Where is he?!"

"I don't know."

"How could he do this to me?!"

"Well, he's asking the same thing about you, most likely."

The next night Vic went on after Gorshin and in the second song, as planned, Ziggy interrupted him. They did the act. They did about two and a half goddamn hours in fact. They were cookin', they were burnin', they were torchin' that whole room, boy. That was the only show they ever did where more than two people died at the same show. Three people, two men and a women, died from laughing so much that night. Blood vessels were burstin' like balloons on New Year's Eve.

The night after that, Ziggy came on at the exact same second he had the night before. They did their first routine and then the lights went down for a brief costume change, so Ziggy could dress as a football player. The lights come up and Ziggy's onstage . . . but there's no Vic. No sign of him. So this is Vic's revenge now, in this eternal Ping-Pong game. Ziggy's onstage alone and when's the last time something like *this* happened? It's Panic Time.

He stood there for a minute and didn't make a peep other than the wheezes escaping from the pit of his guts. People start laughing . . . they're chuckling and giggling, they think it's the bit.

Sally was with me and she said, "They've got to bring the lights down now. Somebody tell the—"

Then Ziggy started talking. He began with an imitation. He imitated Eddie Fisher. Then he imitated Richard Burton and Cary Grant. (Sally whispered to me, "He used to do this in school. When he had to answer a question but was too scared . . . he used other voices.") He did President Kennedy. Then he imitated Vic singing "Malibu Moon" and falling asleep and snoring while singing, and everybody was in stitches. Gradually he eased into his own voice. It took a while but he got there. And then, once he'd found it, he did an hour's worth of material. *All by himself!* What is that line, something about "a terrible beauty is born"? Well, this was a beautiful terror, let me tell you! And it was hatched right before our eyes.

When he got off the stage I don't think I've ever in my whole life seen anyone so exhilarated. It was like he'd met his true love, married her, had a baby, another one, and then had an affair with a hot, gorgeous mistress all in one shot! "Lemme back out there, Sally, lemme back out there," he said. He was like a prizefighter, running in place, dancing like Ali, shadowboxing and snorting up smoke like some papal [sic] bull.

Vic called me in my room late that night. "How'd he do?" he asked me.

"He did terrific, Vic. The place was jumpin'."

"You gotta be kiddin' me."

"I'm not. He was terrif."

"Hey, did he ask you anything, like how could I do this to him?"

"He never did. Vic, what are you doin' to us? We've been on top of the world for years. You crack up this combo, you'll break your old pal Latch's heart."

"Look, I—"

"Vic, can you hear my heart breaking? Can you? I'm holding the phone to my ribs. Can you hear the springs poppin' out and the gears fallin' off? You hear that noise just then?! That's all the crankcase oil gluggin' out. Don't do this to me, Vic."

"I gotta do what's right for me."

"But since when have you ever known what that is?"

A few nights later he sings two songs on Lenny Pearl's TV show. The unkindest cut of all, right?

LENNY PEARL: How exquisite was this?! You talk about "just desserts"—this was a strawberry shortcake with Ziggy's name written in cyanide on the top and a bomb inside it! That fat red thing and his midget parents destroy my radio show, he runs rampant and creates havoc . . . you think you can do that to Lenny Pearl?! That I'm some helpless little schnook who don't fight back?! When Vic Fountain was crooning those two songs of his on my TV show, I didn't care *how* goddamn comatose he was sounding . . . this was the music of the gods to me! Because I knew that in some corner of the world somewhere, Sigmund Blissman's face was turning blue and he was choking on his vomit! If I had dropped dead at that second, I would have died a happy man.

* * *

SALLY KLEIN: Vic never told Arnie or me he was leaving Ziggy, and Ziggy never told Arnie or me he was leaving Vic. Did Vic and Ziggy ever tell each other? Nobody knows.

It just happened. It was in the newspapers. Nobody was communicating, they just told the papers. Nobody ever told anyone anything.

Vic told Arnie that Ziggy had slipped a note under his door at the Oceanfront. The note said something like, "It's been a blast. Hope to see you around. Arrivederci and shalom." So according to Vic, Ziggy ended it. But for years Ziggy told every reporter and columnist and Johnny Carson and Merv Griffin and Mike Douglas and Barry Gray and every single person in the world it was the other way around. "He sent a bellhop to my door at the Oceanfront with a note," the story went. The bellhop read Ziggy the note aloud, supposedly. "Ziggeleh. No hard feelings, but you've been a nightmare to be with. And I've been one for you, too. So, baby, it's all over. I'm spreading my wings and taking off. Shalom and arrivederci." That's what the note said. But each time Ziggy told the story, he added to it, enhanced it to make himself look more like the injured party and make Vic look more like Adolf Eichmann.

I honestly do not think there were any notes. I think—*pffft*—it just happened.

REYNOLDS CATLEDGE IV: I got a phone call late one evening in Los Angeles. It was Ziggy calling from Las Vegas. He sounded as though he might be in a panic. "Cat," he said, "do you know *anything* about Fountain and Bliss breakin' up?" I told him I didn't. He instructed me to call Vic immediately in his hotel room, which was only one floor down from his own, and to tell Vic to not announce a breakup until the two of them could sit down man-to-man and talk about it, *after* Vic's solo engagement at the Cal-Neva Lodge. He also told me to inform Vic that he—Ziggy—would be agreeable to Vic working solo *as well as* in tandem with him. "Make that call, Cat," he ordered.

But Vic was not in his room. I finally reached him at 4:00 A.M. I relayed

Ziggy's message and he said to me, "That seems square to me. Yeah, tell Zig we'll have a powwow." Whereupon I called Ziggy back and told him.

"I hope the discussions are fruitful," I said.

"Discussions?" he said mockingly. "Ha! You think he and I are actually gonna meet? Cat, I just won a big, big hand of poker."

The next day it was announced that Fountain and Bliss had split up.

SNUFFY DUBIN: People usually never remember where they were when they heard that Fountain and Bliss had broken up, and that's 'cause it happened on the same day that Jack Kennedy was killed. Arnie used to say, "The sheer chutzpah of that Oswald, huh? His aim may have been great but his timing was lousy." Me, I was at a hotel in Philly . . . I had an engagement at the Red Hill Inn.

I'm there in the afternoon, signing some paperwork, and I get handed the phone.

"It's horrible, Snuffy," Ziggy tells me on the phone.

"I know. I know."

"It's horrible. It's all over."

"I know," I said. "Jesus, they blew the man's brains out all over that car."

"No, not that. I meant me and Vic."

"Oh. Oh. Well. it was quite a ride, though, wasn't it?"

"Wha—? In Dallas? Yeah, I guess."

"No, I meant you and Vic."

"Yeah, it was. But all marriages have to end sometime, right?"

They do?

DANNY McGLUE: I was driving around in my car and I heard it on the radio, on the news. I couldn't believe it! I thought: *They couldn't possibly do this without anybody telling me first, could they?* But then I realized: *Of course they could!*

I'd been with them for almost twenty-five years. I was a kid when I started, I was a bellhop who wrote nonsense songs when I met Ziggy! Jesus, I looked like a lawn ornament.

I pulled over to the side of the road and started blubbering. But then the great relief of it all struck me and I began laughing and laughing, and I was bawling my eyes out and laughing at the same time. I must have looked completely nutso.

ERNIE BEASLEY: I picked up a paper and there was Vic in Leonard Lyons's column talking about the split. "Zig is the closest thing I have to a brother," Vic said. "There's no bad blood. What he wants to do is fine with

me. And Ziggy's behind me all the way too. Hey, I'm Ziggy's biggest fan."
A few hours later I read Bud Hatch, and Vic said the same thing to Bud,
word for word. Then in Earl Wilson's column Ziggy said, "Vic is the closest
thing I have to a brother. There's no bad blood. What he wants to do is fine
with me. And Vic's behind me all the way too. Hey, I'm Vic's biggest fan."

When you see something like that, you realize that it's probably Morty
Geist at work.

SALLY KLEIN: I was at the Malibu house . . . I was watering plants on the
porch. It was about midnight. Jack and Donny were asleep. A car pulls up
and I see it's Ziggy's Lincoln Continental convertible. He gets out and then
so does Danny.

"You're awake?" Ziggy called out to me.

I put a finger to my lips to tell him that I may be awake but everyone
else wasn't. He made his way to the porch, and I looked at Danny, who
was shrugging. He didn't know what they were doing here any more than
I did.

"Let's go to the beach, Sal," Ziggy said.

"Now?" I said to him.

"Yeah. The three of us. Got a beach towel in there?"

So I went to the linen closet and got out this big beach towel, and Danny,
Ziggy, and I walked down to the beach. It was a clear night, no clouds, and
the moon was full. Ziggy made like a highfalutin' waiter at some fancy
French restaurant, whipping the towel like he was setting a table and then
laying it down, and the three of us sat down on it. Ziggy was in the middle,
naturally; I was on his right and to Ziggy's left was Danny.

"So it's all over," Ziggy said.

"You never know," Danny said.

"Oh, I know. I know."

"It might not be such a bad thing," I said.

"They said that about Pearl Harbor, Sal," Ziggy said.

"No," Danny said, "I don't think they did."

"*It must have been the Malibu Moon,*" Ziggy sang, "*that made me fall
in love with you. It must have been that light in your eyes, those cocktails
of silver and blue.*"

"Hey, if the comedy thing doesn't work out," Danny joked, "you could
always try your hand at singing."

Ziggy lay back, it was like it was daytime and he was trying to get a
tan . . . he had his arms behind him and his head in his hands. Then he sat
back up and said, "So how miserable has it been? How miserable?" I
looked at him, didn't say anything. "For twenty-five years now. This is a
nightmare for you, for the two people who're the closest to me."

"Ziggeleh, this isn't the time for this," Danny said.

"What? You want we all should go surfing now?!"

Danny took some sand in his hands and let it sift out.

Ziggy said, "About ten years ago Vic and I were playing Baltimore. We're between shows. A stagehand comes to my dressing room and says to me, 'There's a fella here says he'd like to meet you.' I say to him, 'There's lotsa fellas like that.' The stagehand says, 'This guy says he knew your parents. He knew them from vaudeville.' I looked at my watch . . . I had a half hour to kill and nuttin' to kill it with, so I say, sure, show the fella in."

A cloud passed by the moon and Ziggy started humming "Malibu Moon" again for a few bars.

"So this little fella comes in and he's maybe in his seventies or eighties and he's in a tux. But this tux had seen much better days, like in maybe 1830. He's very shy. I tell him to sit down anywheres, even though there's only one place to sit down. The old man has a handlebar mustache and this thing had more wax on it than a candle factory. He says to me, 'I've wanted to meet you for the longest time.' And I said, 'Oh yeah. Why's that?' But he didn't answer. He says to me he knew my parents, he knew them a long time ago. He was a magician, he says, way back when, in that vaudeville troupe Harry and Flo used to bomb in regularly."

"The Bratton company?" I said.

"Yeah. Them. So this little guy—and what kinda accent he's got, I don't know—asks me if I ever by any chance saw him perform his magic act. I told him the truth, I said, 'Uh-uh. My parents never took me on the road. I saw 'em perform only once and that was the night I got my start. As I unnerstand it, I wasn't missin' nuttin'.' He sort of grimaced and said, 'You shouldn't talk that way about them. They were nice people. They worked very hard.' I said to him, 'Well, now *I'm* workin' hard, carrying on the tradition.' He told me he'd been following my career, he'd seen me perform up and down the East Coast, from Miami Beach to Boston. 'Your parents would be very proud of you,' he said to me. I says to him, 'They wouldn't even recognize me, pal.' He started tellin' me about some of the other acts in the troupe . . . he talked about this brother-and-sister regurgitating act; they could swallow anything and bring it back up and had even worked it out somehow so's the brother swallows a champagne glass and then the sister brings it up. I say to him, 'Jesus, I am sure glad I've made it in the big time.' And he says to me, 'And so am I.' He stood up and buttoned his jacket . . . except the button fell to the floor. I say to this little old guy, 'Buddy, why don't you let me get you a new tuxedo?' and I pull out a wad as thick as *Webster's Dictionary*. But he waved his hands over it. He don't want my dough. Then he put his hand on my shoulder and—can you believe this?—he reaches down and kisses my head! He kissed my hair! This guy did that! I looked up at him and he was crying. Not like sobbin' or nuttin', just crying."

"This guy had been a magician since before the dawn of time," Ziggy said. "He'd probably been makin' rabbits disappear on the boat over, wherever he came from. Can you imagine that? Probably never made more than ten bucks a show and he stuck at it."

"Whatever happened to him?" I asked. "Did you ever see him again?"

"No. He was on his last legs. You could tell he'd be dead in a year."

I heard footsteps behind me. I looked back. It was Jack in his black pajamas. He saw me with Danny and Ziggy. I told him everything was all right, that I'd be in soon, and he went back to bed.

"I ruined you guys' lives, didn't I?" Ziggy said.

I swallowed, I heard Danny swallow. Danny started to say something but Ziggy said, "Nah, it's the truth. I ruined you guys' lives."

"I happen to be very happy with Jack," I said.

"But if it wasn't for me, you could be with Danny." He shook his head, then said, "Hey, look at me! I got a wife who didn't even let me circumcise my own son and who's got magnets on her fingers when she walks into Bergdorf Goodman. I make whores laugh, I buy 'em chinchilla and sable and diamond earrings and make 'em laugh, and they permit me to sleep with 'em. What a life I've got. But you two . . . Jesus, I'm sorry."

"Things have worked out," Danny said. "They have."

He didn't say anything for a while. Then he said, "What am I gonna do?"

"About what?" Danny asked him.

"About everything. I gotta chart the rest of my life out. I gotta make a map. And I've started on it. And right now, all roads are leadin' me straight into the grave."

"That is nonsense," I said. "That is utter nonsense."

"Then where do I go? Where the hell do I go?"

"Ziggy, I really believe," Danny said, "that you can go as far as you want to."

"I do. Sally?"

"I think so too," I said.

Ziggy said, "Straight into the grave."

VI

ARNIE LATCHKEY: For over twenty years, a hundred times a day I got asked the same damn question: "Will Fountain and Bliss ever get back together again?" I answered it the same way every single time: "God, I hope not."

After Vic did the Cal-Neva engagement he and I had dinner. I wanted to get everything straight, I wanted to know where I stood with him or if I still stood at all. He was with some girl, I don't even remember who she was, I don't think she said a word the entire meal.

"Latch, you're still my guy," he told me. "We go back a long ways."

"We sure do, Vic," I said to him. "Remember jumping off that train in the Catskills together?"

"I think I still got the black-and-blue marks," he said. "So, uh, are you my guy, Latch? You'll still handle me and all?"

"What? I got something else going on in my life?"

But I did. I did.

Because the night before, I'm in bed and the phone rings and Estelle tells me, "It's Ziggy."

"Ziggeleh, darling," I said.

"Arnie, you spoken to Vic of late?"

"Well, uh, you know, I, uh . . ." I was new at this thing, this high-wire balancing act. I didn't know what to say, what not to say, and to whom to say it and not say it to.

"Are you still gonna be my guy, Latch?" Ziggy asked me.

And I said to him, "What? I got something else going on in my life?"

You know, one thing that's very important to an entertainer is consistency. You need a sense of flow. Any change you make, it can't be one inch bigger than a nuance. And that's what Vic did in his movie career: He kept the flow. The motion pictures he made with Ziggy were at best passable and at worst unwatchable, and now he picked up just where he left off. He did three Johnny Venice private-dick movies with Paramount. The first one wasn't all that bad, the second one wasn't terrible, the third one wasn't god-awful. Johnny Venice was this ex-L.A. cop, kicked out of the force for banging the commissioner's daughter or something, and now he takes on all kinds of sordid cases and clients. Skullduggery, shoot-outs, fistfights, high jinks, and kissing ensue. "I'm gonna be professional, Latch," Vic told me before they started shooting the first one, *Johnny Venice.* "None of that destructive behavior or anything." And he was true to his word. Not a camera, not a prop, not a lens or the body part of a director was destroyed. He had a reputation by then, thanks to the Fountain and Bliss pictures, and it was as if the crew was showing up on the set with bulletproof vests, clenching their teeth and bracing themselves for a hail of bullets or a pie fight. But it never happened. I think a lot of that was due to the fact that Vic *knew* he had to make a good impression. Another factor was he was maybe too gassed to do too much damage a lot of the time. In these movies, Johnny Venice walks around with a flask in his holster instead of a pistol. Well, that wasn't Cel-Ray tonic in that flask, you can take my word for it.

BILLY WILSON [body double for Vic Fountain]: I'd been knocking around Hollywood for a few years. My first flick was *The Naked and the Dead,* the Aldo Ray film. I get killed in that movie; a shell explodes and I drop my rifle and crumple to the ground, in that order. I did lots of war pictures, cowboy pictures, some beach and biker movies, a biblical epic now and then. Once in a while I got to say a line too. I was just a big lug but I knew how to draw a gun, ride a horse, and throw and take a punch. God, I must've crumpled to the ground in a hundred pictures.

Someone from Paramount saw me in *Cry of Battle*—this was the flick that Lee Harvey Oswald was seeing when he got caught, did you know that?—and must have said, "Hey, that galoot's the spitting image of Vic Fountain!" So I was sent to [director] William Calloway's office and I read for the first Johnny Venice flick. After flubbing a few lines I said to him, "Mr. Calloway, I usually don't speak in the movies—I just fall a lot." "Well," Bill said, "there'll probably be a lot of falling in this movie too."

I had the reputation of a "guy's guy" in Hollywood, a Ben Johnson, Steve McQueen, or Slim Pickens type, just 'cause I could ride a horse or race a Harley. I could stay out with the boys all night and get wasted. Well, all that was true, but I was and am still very gay. I was married and had two kids but my wife and I had an arrangement. And everything worked out fine for us.

I'd heard that working with Vic Fountain could be an ordeal; he doesn't ever rehearse his lines and he only does one take, people said, he shows up late, he doesn't show up at all. Well, all this was sounding good to me, I must say. The less he did, the better it would be for me. And I was right. I have *Johnny Venice, The Case of the Boom-Boom Brunette,* and *The Killer Wore Go-Go Boots* on videotape and I can show you which one is me and which one is Vic in the scenes. By the third movie, I'd say there's barely any Vic. Johnny Venice has his back turned to the camera or is in profile in half the scenes, when he's talking to Dina Merrill, Elke Sommer, and Jay C. Flippen—well, that was me. The car chases, the shoot-outs and fistfights, the kissing scenes with Dina and Elke . . . all me. (Elke nearly choked me with that tongue of hers.) Johnny Venice's hobby was golfing; everybody thought Vic would've wanted to film those scenes but he passed on those too. It was tons of fun, it really was, making those movies because after years of being ignored by John Ford, Howard Hawks, Duke Wayne, and Ward Bond, here I am being treated like a star because *I'm* doing all the work! As a joke, people were calling me Vic Fountain on the set and at parties. It was fun for a while. But, you know, I had a little thing with a very, *very* famous actor one night and after we were through he said to me, "Gee, I always suspected Vic Fountain was sort of gay."

By the final movie in the series—I'd say this was maybe '67—Vic had put on a few pounds, so they taped a little pillow to my stomach and also on the back. For the love handles. Vic found out about that and hit the ceiling. Vanity, I guess. So most of that movie was shot from the waist up. And it was very dark, even though it was in color. I remember someone telling me that the French critics loved that flick, they thought it was "noirish" and existential or some kind of claptrap, I don't know. Also, for that movie, I was given a wig to wear, something with very dark, almost blue hair. This was because Vic was starting to lose his hair. He saw me in this contraption one day and I thought, Uh-oh, he's going to put the kibosh on this too, but instead he wound up ordering a few of the wigs for himself.

GUY PUGLIA: When Ziggy and Vic called it quits, I really did think that Vic was gonna somehow settle down. I was hoping so, 'cause sometimes those late nights and all that drinkin' and going to this club and that one, it can wear you down. I wasn't no kid anymore. But maybe he still was, 'cause he didn't settle down any.

One thing that really got to him was the divorce. This is a guy that grew up with no money, who worked himself up from nowhere, and now he's turnin' over every buck he makes to Lulu. And what's she doin' with it? Nothing. She didn't buy clothes, she didn't buy cars. She did buy a small house in Palm Springs, near where Vic'd recently got one, and another very small one in Vegas . . . and that was just so when Vic decided he wanted to be her husband again and run back into her arms, her arms would be conveniently located nearby. But Lulu was basically socking all the dough away for the kids. "If she's hoping my career will hit the skids and I'll have to go back to her," Vic said, "fat chance."

I met this makeup gal on the set of *Johnny Venice*. She was a nice girl and was small, like maybe five feet. Her name was Edie Smith, which was funny 'cause she looked a little bit like that French singer Edith Piaf when she was young. And me and this Edie, we hit it off good. You know, I didn't ever once have a girlfriend. I'd wind up with whores or with Vic's girlfriends' girlfriends. And then when I lost my nose, that was it for me. So I just kept it up: Vegas showgirls and hookers and fat married broads who thought if they slept with me they could sleep with Vic. His rejects. I didn't know their names, they didn't know mine, and Vic wanted to nail these slobs like he wanted to nail a porcupine. And now here's this Edie Smith and she don't care how little I am or what my face looks like or nothin' like that. We hit it off and finally, here I am in my forties, and I got a girlfriend.

One thing I liked about Edie was, I knew she wasn't with me just on account of Vic. She already knew Vic from the movie set, although she said to me he was hardly ever there. She's the one who told me that Vic wore a wig now. I didn't believe it at first. You know how, like, you see someone every single day for a hundred years and you don't ever notice anything different—they're eighty but still they look like they're seventeen to you? That's what this was like. But then I noticed, yeah, what happened to that bald spot of his?

SALLY KLEIN: The premiere of *Johnny Venice* was a very big deal. Vic was on the cover of *Look* and this was the first time he was on a major magazine cover without Ziggy. A lot of stars turned out; Elizabeth Taylor and Richard Burton were there, so were Dean Martin, Natalie Wood, Sidney Poitier, Burt Bacharach and Angie Dickinson, and Army Archerd was interviewing everybody walking in. Ziggy was invited but he told me to tell Vic that he had a prior commitment.

"What's the prior commitment?" I asked him a week before the event.

"The prior commitment," he told me, "is that I'm stayin' home."

The very first minute of the movie was very arresting: It's just Vic against a pitch-black background. He's got on a white dress shirt and his tie is undone. He lifts a pistol up and points it close up into the camera, just like *The Great Train Robbery*. He shoots the gun and then he's surrounded by clouds and clouds of smoke. He disappears in the smoke, and they run the opening credits. "She's Dangerous" was the song, which Ernie wrote and was almost a hit for Vic—it did make it into the Top 20. After that, though, the movie goes downhill very quickly.

When the lights came up at the premiere, I said to Jack, "So? What did you think?"

He whispered, "Exactly as bad as I thought it'd be."

Jack and I went home that night—we skipped the party—and sure enough Ziggy called and wanted a review. "Do I look like Charles Champlain?" I asked. He said, "Well? Is it a bomb?" And I told him it wasn't very good and it wasn't terrible. Well, he could read between the lines of that and was overjoyed.

JANE WHITE: He was disconsolate as soon as he heard Vic had signed a movie deal. He felt it was an utter act of betrayal. "How could he do this to me?" he said. "Victor Benedict Arnold he is!" I reminded him that he and Vic were no long partners; I said that it was like a divorce, that once a couple broke up, each person was free to do as he and she pleased. "But I ain't Lulu," he said. "I'm Ziggy."

Frankly, I felt he was being very hypocritical. Because he'd made the rounds of the studios and tried to land a movie deal. Arnie, Sally, and Murray Katz tried everything. He was offered a few things here and there—he turned down [Vincente Minnelli's] *Good-bye, Charlie*—but it was never a starring role. This crushed him. Hank Stanco from WAT sent him the script for *A Distant Trumpet* and he read it and told Hank, "The part of the lieutenant is perfect for me! Let's do it!" Hank had to tell Ziggy, "Well, uh, that's the lead role . . . that's Troy Donahue's. Your part is on page thirteen and the lower half of page forty-two." He was just crushed.

I remember Joanie Pierce telling me that it was Ziggy's "tragic flaw"— his success was backfiring on him. What had made him so famous was his ability to be anything, to go from character to character, but in the long run he was *no* character. So they would send him *I'll Take Sweden* or *Muscle Beach Party* and there was nothing there for him. "Bob Hope gets the lead role and I'm supposed to play a goddamn smorgasbord chef!" he yelled. "This is criminal!"

When the Johnny Venice movies came out, though, Ziggy was overjoyed. They weren't any good. Vic was trying to be Paul Newman or Michael Caine but couldn't pull it off—they were younger than him. And a lot thinner.

[Ziggy was] offered a part in *What a Way to Go,* that Shirley MacLaine movie. He read for the role and they liked what he'd done. "This is it, honey," he said. He was as happy as a lark! But when the word got around that Ziggy might be in the picture, the other actors said they didn't want to work with him. That reputation of his. So the offer was withdrawn and Dick Van Dyke got the part.

"There's just no hope for me," he said. And for a long time he had trouble getting out of bed or doing anything but looking at the wall and walking around in a trance.

SNUFFY DUBIN: Buzzy Brevetto was booked into the Hungry i in San Francisco but he came down with some kind of virus and had to cancel. He calls me up and says, Snuffy, can you sub for me? But I couldn't—I had something going in Miami Beach and I was filming a bit part of a nightclub owner in that horrible *Go-Go Boots* thing that Vic did, the Johnny Venice vehicle. So I said to Buzzy, "Hey, what about Ziggy?" Buzzy asked me what Ziggy was doing lately and I said nothing whatsoever. So I called Sally Klein and she said she would extend the offer.

"He says he'll do it," she said to me.

That surprised the living piss out of me, Ziggy going on alone.

Let me tell you . . . when Ziggy found out I was doing that movie with Vic, he hit the ceiling. Now, we'd had our run-ins over the years but he really let me have it this time. In the past he would call me a lousy, dirty, stinkin', no-good, unfunny, joke-stealing sonuvabitch bastard and then hang up on me, but then ten minutes later we're on the phone talking about everything under the fucking sun. But this was bad . . . he took it real, real personal that I was doing this picture. I say to him, "I do three days' work, I get fifteen grand," and he says, "You're a backstabbing, buddy-fucking shitheel, Snuffles, to do this to me!" He thought I was doing this to *him*! He thought I was doing this lousy five minutes of work to sink a knife into *his* back! The fifteen grand? Nothing to do with it? A movie career? Nothing to do with it? It was all about him. Well, let me tell you: I *was* getting back at him! I was! I was offered the degenerate part in *The Dirty Dozen,* the part that went to Telly [Savalas], and I turned it down just to be in a movie with Vic. It's true, and if that makes me Satan or Lucifer or a bad person, then God strike me down right now. Yep, I did it on purpose and, man, did it ever feel good.

ARNIE LATCHKEY: Ziggy tells me he'll play the Hungry i and I told him he had a few days to put an act together. "We gotta circle the wagons," I told him. But to tell the truth, there weren't too many wagons left. Sid Stone was dead and there was just Danny McGlue, so it wasn't much of a circle either. Betsy was in and out of the hospital, still having problems, but Danny pulled through for us and we put together some semblance of an act for Ziggy. "Look," Ziggy told us, "alls I need is the frame. You give me that, I'll supply the picture." I couldn't believe how confident he was. It was fan*tab*ulous!

MICKEY KNOTT: My band was playing the Hollywood Bowl and Ziggy rings me up at my hotel and we talk old times. I was always closer to Vic than to Ziggy so to be honest, some of these old times, I didn't know what the hell he was talking about, man. Then he asks me if I had a pill connection. I told him I didn't mess with that stuff, I was just into grass. He said to me, "Aw, come on, Mick, you're a musician . . . you gotta know where I can score some pills." And I said to him, "Ziggy, that's a slur against musicians the world over." He said, "I apologize. You really don't know *one* person who could get me some amphetamines?" I thought about it and said, "Well, there's the trumpeter, the bass player, two of the sax men . . ."

Huffy Davis, my bassist, comes to me that night and tells me he'd just come back from the airport. Ziggy was about to board a place for San Francisco. Huffy handed him two pounds of pills and Ziggy gave him a grand. "Man," Huffy said to me, "that motherfucker was so keyed up, he didn't even need to take no goddamn plane to get there!"

SALLY KLEIN: Except for an appearance on a Fritz Devane TV special and two minutes goofing around with Herman's Hermits on *Hollywood Palace*, this was pretty much Ziggy's first thing since he and Vic had broken up. I went up to San Francisco with Arnie and Estelle. Jack had business in Los Angeles. I cannot tell you how crucial this was, for Ziggy's career, for his self-esteem, for everyone. Ziggy said it best: "I gotta blast off on the right foot here."

Well, there was a lot of hubbub about it. Morty Geist was really playing it up. He was spreading rumors in Herb Caen's column that there was a chance that Vic was going to surprise everyone and get onstage with Ziggy. But he also told Dean Corolla of the *Chronicle* that there was a good chance that Ziggy wouldn't be able to perform. "He's so heartbroken about Vic," Morty told him, "that he doesn't think he can do more than ten minutes. It's gonna be a nervous collapse, live onstage." So the room was filled every night, both shows; half the people were there to see if Vic would pop in, the other half to see if Ziggy would pop apart.

Arnie and I were in the dressing room before he went on and Ziggy was rarin' to go. Now I know—and Arnie knows—that he was taking those pills. So that was maybe a part of it. But I don't think the pills gave him anything that he didn't already have to begin with—it just maybe gave him a lot more of it.

We killed a few minutes by talking about the old times, some of the places Ziggy had played, with Vic and with Harry and Flo. He brought up Dolly Phipps . . . he did that often. He even told me to look for her in the crowd. He said, "Maybe Dolly moved to Frisco years and years ago, Sal, and she just wants a little look-see at her first beau. You never know." Arnie asked me a few minutes later, when Ziggy was out of earshot, "So this Dolly Phipps dame . . . was she all she's cracked up to be?" I told him she wasn't, that she was sort of Ziggy Bliss's Rosebud, and Arnie said, "Oh, she looked like a sled, did she?"

The lights came down and Ziggy was introduced and the lights stayed down. It was pitch-black . . . people couldn't even see their own cigarettes except when they inhaled. Ziggy played it so perfect . . . the timing was just wonderful. He waited for the applause to die down and then he didn't say another word. I have to admit, I was getting nervous. I didn't even really know if he was on the stage. "Jesus, *do* something," Arnie softly muttered. But Ziggy was so funny that he could make silence hysterical, and people started laughing. And he let them laugh. "It was like the silence was his partner now"—Dean Corolla wrote that, not Sally Klein—"and so who needed Vic Fountain?" Then when the laughs settled down, all of a sudden you heard Vic singing "The Hang of It." But it wasn't Vic, it was Ziggy! He sang "The Hang of It" and he was just imitating and caricaturing Vic and the crowd loved it. The spotlight came on and he finished the song and now it was time for the act. And it was just as he said; Danny and he had come up with the frame but Ziggy did the artwork. He went off in tangents, he did a little political stuff, he did impressions, told some off-color stories. He did lots of two-man routines, but he was only one person. You know, you had Bob Newhart, who was brilliant, and Shelley Berman, and they would do their acts on an imaginary phone, but Ziggy would be *both* people—he'd do both voices. I guess he was still very scared of going on alone.

It was that night when it first started, when he brought himself to the point of cracking up. He'd be talking about something and then he'd stop and he'd start giggling. Giggling like a kid. He'd try to get the joke out but every time he said a word, he giggled more. And his face got all flushed and sweaty. He was thinking about something and it was so hysterical that he couldn't utter it. So he waited for that to settle down and then he went on with the act. This kept happening; almost every time he did stand-up there was a point when he was cracking up inside.

And he talked endlessly about Vic. As if Vic was still there. He did a parody of a Johnny Venice movie and did an imitation of some other person in this imaginary scene—Lyndon Johnson, Everett Dirkson, or Cary Grant. He'd try to veer the material away from Vic, but it always got back to him. Dean Corolla wrote that he sounded like a jilted lover, talking about Vic so much, but then Ziggy just used that to make fun of Dean. You simply could not criticize him.

The other bad thing was that *Variety* mentioned in the review that Ziggy had sung "The Hang of It." So Vic—don't forget: Vigorish was still handling Vic—had Shep Lane fire off a very threatening letter to Ziggy, who Vigorish was also still handling. The letter was sent from our office on Wilshire Boulevard to our office on Wilshire Boulevard! Ernie Beasley I don't think gave a damn if Ziggy was singing it or if even Madame Chiang Kai-shek was singing it, but Vic insisted Ziggy cease and desist. Which he didn't.

We got Ziggy booked in New York—Lanie Kazan opened for him, I think—and in Boston, Miami, and Chicago. Pete Conifer booked him for the Oceanfront. It was the beginning of a whole new life for him. You know how some comics have tag lines? Rodney Dangerfield has "I don't get no respect," and Marty Allen had "Hello, dere." Well, in the ads for Ziggy's shows, sometimes there was a little black-and-white picture of him, with his hair and his eyes going all over the place, and then it said in quotes under his name: "And another thing about Vic . . ."

LULU FOUNTAIN: Vic and I, even though we were divorced, we still were close. Some couples, they divorce, and then it's all over between them, like they was never married. But with us, it was like we weren't divorced. We went to a few premieres together, we went to some charity events, and we took care of the kids. We never stopped talking to each other.

He'd be seeing some actress or some girl from Vegas, but I didn't want to hear about it. He dated [actress] Lynda Wills Benson for a few months, she was never brought up once. He had a fling with Faye Kendall—I found out about it in the paper, not from him. One time Vicki came home and she was wearing this little blue cap and I asked her where she got it. She told me that Faye Kendall got it for her. That cap was in the garbage can in ten seconds.

More than the girls, it was the gambling that worried me. He spent months in Vegas, when he wasn't on the road or makin' a film. Every time he performed there he lost more money. He'd tell me when he won, he'd call me up and say, "Honey, I won twenty grand last night at the Silver Slipper," but he never told me that the next night he lost twice that. Hunny or Guy or Ices Andy would tell me. I told his mom about it one time, I told her to talk to Vic, but she didn't really seem to care. "He grew up with no money," Violetta said, "so what if he maybe die with no money?" But she was livin' in the lap of luxury in Santa Monica, she had a Rolls and a driver. And, believe me, she wasn't spending a dime.

One time I was home and Tony Fratelli shows up at my front door. I invite him in, I make him a peanut butter and jelly sandwich. He tells me how much Vic owes one of his bookies. It's over a hundred grand. "And this is just one of 'em, Lu," he tells me. "There's plenty others out there too." I say to him, "What are you gonna do if he don't pay? Break Vic Fountain's legs, Tony? You gonna shoot him in his kneecaps?" He chewed almost as loud as Arnie and said to me, "It's crossed my mind at times, Lu, I gotta admit that to you."

So I talked to Vic about it on the phone. He was in Vegas. He didn't like it that Tony had dropped in on me at home. More than that, he didn't like it that Tony was talkin' his own personal business to me. But even more than that, he didn't like it that Tony had thought about shooting his kneecaps. "They're the Fratellis, not the Patellas," he said, but he was scared. I said to him, "Look, could you just try to not gamble so much? Not for me, but for the kids." And he said he'd try. Then he said he had to go, he had a show to put on. "How long are you there for," I asked, and he said a week. I asked him how much he was getting for the week—maybe he could turn it over to the Fratelli brothers and his knees'd be safe. But Vic told me he wasn't gettin' a dime. He was doing it 'cause he owed the casino.

He'd try to reassure me . . . he'd say, "Look, any time I'm ever short of dough, I'll just make another lousy movie. All right? So don't you worry."

REYNOLDS CATLEDGE IV: With Fountain and Bliss no longer a partnership, with them not speaking to each other, it made my tasks all the more difficult. Arnie and Sally put me in charge of keeping them away from each other, not because they feared violence, but because they feared unpleasantness. For example, if Vic was playing a venue in Miami Beach and if, at the same time Ziggy was performing at, say, the Saxony Club there, I had to keep both of them informed of their close proximity. If Ziggy made dinner reservations at a particular restaurant, I had to inform Vic so that he would not make reservations for the same time. It was understood that Vic took three hours to eat and that Ziggy took at the most forty-five minutes, so there was some leeway. There was one occasion, I recall, in 1967 when Vic was taping a Christmas special for CBS and was singing "Hooray for Hollywood" near the famed Hollywood sign. And Ziggy, ironically, was also taping there immediately afterward, for a Christmas special for ABC. It was my task to make sure that there was no overlapping. Weddings and funerals were the most difficult to manage. When Murray Katz died, it was a logistical nightmare.

Arnie and I met at the Polo Lounge one afternoon and we chatted about Vic's gambling problems. As a celebrity, Vic attracted many people to the tables at which he was betting. He would—as he was losing thousands of dollars—engage in witty repartee with them; he was always jesting with them, keeping them entertained. There were many occasions when, at a blackjack table, say, drawing a card on seventeen and losing over a thousand dollars, he would include Ziggy in his jokes. "Oh well, I guess I gotta team up with the fat kid again," he'd say to much laughter. He would also make alimony jokes too. He would crap out at a dice table and say, "There goes Lulu's next sable coat." But the barbs were usually reserved for his ex-partner.

"Is there any way," Arnie now asked me at the Polo Lounge, "that you could prevent Vic from gambling?"

"Well," I replied, "he does play Las Vegas a lot and this, naturally, places him just an elevator ride away from the gaming areas. So I would say that the only way to keep him from gambling is to handcuff him to the bed."

"Hey, you're funny, Cat! Hangin' around with us is finally rubbing off on you."

"Thank you. But I wasn't joking."

"Handcuffs, huh? Hmm, maybe you got a point."

On the set of his first western—it was *The Return of Jack Slade*—Vic told me in his trailer, "The Fratellis are givin' me all kinds of trouble. They think I owe 'em a ton of money."

"And what is the veracity of that?"

"Huh? The wha—?"

"Do you in fact owe them money?"

"Well, sort of but not really. Like, I'll make a bet on a football game and the Browns don't cover the spread 'cause Ernie Greene fumbles and they think that means I owe 'em dough. But, Cat, it's a football game, see? It's a game, that's all. A buncha guys in helmets runnin' around. And besides, I thought the Fratellis were my pals."

I couldn't follow his reasoning. For it seemed to me that he *did* owe them money.

"And where do I come in?" I inquired.

"Well, they're runnin' this illegal operation, right? They run most of the bookmaking rackets around here. So they could go to jail."

"Are you thinking of going to the police?"

"Well, gee, Cat, yeah. I am. I mean, I owe 'em a ton. They *say*. But if they get tossed into the slammer, then I don't owe 'em nothin', is the way I see it."

"I think this is problematic," I told him. I said that by turning them in and testifying against them, he not only enhanced the chances of some sort of violent retaliation against his person—particularly his kneecaps—but that he also would furthermore engender the possibility of bad public relations. It would be detrimental to his career.

"You know, there's another bad thing about it too," he said, putting out his Chesterfield and getting ready to film a scene. "If the Fratellis go to jail, who the hell am I gonna bet with?"

ARNIE LATCHKEY: He was starring with Faye Kendall in that oater that Preston Coover directed and he was seeing her too. I never liked her, Teddy, and to tell the truth, I don't think Vic was too crazy about her either. But lemme tell ya: In tight pants on top of a horse, with blond hair flying around and her drawing a six-gun, she stole your breath away and kept it. I think one reason Vic wanted to do *The Return of Jack Slade* so bad was because it meant a lot of horseback riding, a lot of fighting in saloons, and shoot-outs . . . which meant a lot of Billy Wilson, his double. Jack Slade was this character that'd been around since I don't know when—Sonny Tufts was the last guy to play him. But by the time Jack Slade returned, nobody really remembered that he'd ever gone away or had even been there in the first place.

"She don't really like you, Vic," Hunny said to him one day about Faye Kendall. "She just likes bein' around Vic Fountain."

"Hey, I ain't marrying her, Hun," Vic said. "And besides, don't *you* just like being around Vic Fountain?"

"I don't know. Who's Vic Fountain?"

Vic looked at me and said, "One too many shots to the dome, huh?"

"Nah, that ain't it," Hunny said. "I meant it. Who's Vic Fountain? Really?"

Snuffy Dubin was in this Slade picture; he does a two-minute traveling salesman bit; you know, he's dressed like a dandy, selling elixirs, trying to pick up the local lasses too. Oh yeah . . . in the original script, one of the elixirs was made of Gila monster saliva, which would grow your hair back supposedly. But since Vic was now sportin' a rug, he forced them to change it so it would *stop* hair growth. [Snuffy was] on the road a lot with Vic now. He'd open up for Vic in Vegas, the Fontainebleau, in Westbury [Long Island], in Tahoe, all over. And Ziggy was incensed . . . oh, he was really steaming, boy. Ziggy was playing clubs too, he had a schedule that gave you goose bumps. But he'd play smaller rooms than Vic. You know, they had the rock music now, the Beatles and the Beards [*sic*] and the Stones, and Vic wasn't selling as much as he used to. He'd very, very stealthily sneak a song into the Top 20, but then the next week it would just as stealthily sneak out. He cut a bossa nova album called *Vic-a-Nova* but the only place it went was nowhere. But he still had the charisma, he was still a big draw in the clubs.

Anyway, these rumors start percolating about Snuffy Dubin. From nowhere. I pick up a Bud Hatch column and it says that Snuffy and Debbie are on the rocks because he's cavorting with a showgirl. Nonsense, I said. (Snuffy and Debbie Dubin is one of the great, great marriages in this business.) I pick up another paper, I see that Snuffy's got a gambling problem and that Vic is as magnanimous as Jesus Christ because he's helping him earn all the dough to pay back the loan sharks at his door. Snuffy goes to whores, Snuffy's a dope fiend, Snuffy raped the Sabine women and shot McKinley, Archduke Ferdinand, and JFK.

I called Morty Geist and I said to him, "Morty, if you're putting this into the papers for Ziggy, this is the end of our business and personal relationship."

"I'm not doing it, Latch," he said. "I swear on my mother's grave."

"Okay then, you're off the hook."

"But he did ask me to."

SNUFFY DUBIN: All this stuff starts coming out and after the fifth or sixth time, it became a joke. I'd pick up Earl Wilson or Sidney Skolsky's

"Tintypes" and ask myself, Okay, which ten-year-old boy did I molest today? Which poodle am I leaving my wife for now? The thing that hurt the most was the pill thing. That really stung. I mean, I was the one who told Ziggy about them in the first place! He'd have never started taking that crap if it wasn't for me! And here he is blabbing to everyone about it. That was the unkindest cut of all. And so that was when I kicked. It was the worst week of my life. This was when the Democratic [National] Convention was goin' on, all those riots in Chicago. Well, I missed out on all the fun 'cause I was in my bed shaking like a fucking leaf and my pores were churning out more water than the Bay of fucking Bengal. So yeah, I owe Ziggy big time, right? He saved my life by trying to destroy it.

DANNY McGLUE: Ziggy and Jane were over at Sally and Jack's house for lunch. So was I . . . Betsy was [at the hospital in] in Santa Barbara. Jack had retired from real estate . . . he was just taking it slow, reading a lot, going to the track occasionally. Ziggy had brought over three huge scrapbooks with every tidbit and snippet in it ever written about Harry and Flo. It was some transformation; years and years ago they were the bane of his existence and now he had canonized them.

It was Jack's fault, I guess, but it started innocently enough. He said, "Someone should make a movie about those two."

"What kind of movie?" Ziggy asked.

"Oh, you know, some biographical thing. Like *The Story of Vernon and Irene Castle* or *The Seven Little Foys.*"

"Hmmm. Who would you get to play my dad?" Ziggy asked. He was on the couch but leaning in, intently. He was already hooked on the idea.

"Paul Muni maybe?" Jack said. "He was great as Louis Pasteur and Alexander Graham Bell."

"Sweetie," Sally said, "Don Ameche played Alexander Graham Bell, and Paul Muni's dead."

Jack was slow now . . . don't forget: the four heart attacks, and he had twenty years on Sally to begin with.

"A movie about my parents," Ziggy said. "I think that's a great idear. What do you think, Janie?"

"I don't know," Jane said. "Who wants to pay three bucks to see a bunch of tiny Jews from fifty years ago who never amounted to anything?"

"But what about *Funny Girl?*" Ziggy said, ignoring her. "Hey, Streisand'd be perfect for Flo. And if it was a musical, that'd add more punch. What do you think, Danny?"

I was afraid I'd get drawn into this. So I stalled and said, "And who would play Harry? What with Paul Muni being so unavailable."

"What about Paul Newman maybe? Or Peter O'Toole?"

"Uh-huh . . ." And why not cast Wilt Chamberlain as Lenny Pearl? I was thinking.

Sally and I were glancing at each other. We knew that Ziggy was hooked.

For the next few weeks, for the next few *months,* this was all he could talk about, although he did manage to take some time out to insult Vic's new albums and movies. He met with every producer, every director, every big actor and actress. See, even though he wasn't making movies anymore, he still had the reputation, the cachet, and could get these meetings. He met with people at Paramount, United Artists, MGM, everyone. He always brought along the scrapbook too. Listen, the story of two struggling, old-time, married troupers is not a bad idea for a movie. But not these two. There was no arc. A flat line from nowhere to nowhere is just not an arc. Ziggy had me concoct a treatment and he'd show that to people. After Ziggy saw *Who's Afraid of Virginia Woolf?* he got it into that silly head of his that Liz Taylor and Richard Burton were absolutely perfect for the roles, and he arranged a meeting with them in London. He met them at the bar at Claridge's and kept them there for six hours! They kept trying to sneak off—they had an event to go to—but he would not let them go. "I got on my knees, Danny," he told me. "I was on my knees and beggin' 'em to get interested in this thing. I thought I almost had 'em at one point too—I seen Burton's eyes light up like a baseball park at night—but it was just him eyeballing a delivery of a case of Chivas."

The people at Columbia got so tired of him bothering them that they commissioned a screenplay to be written, just to shut him up. I read the thing and, you know, it wasn't bad for what it was, but Ziggy hated it. And now he was bothering them more than he'd been before.

Ziggy would go on *The Tonight Show* often, maybe four times a year, to plug an appearance. If he was opening up for Phil Ford and Mimi Hines, say, he'd go on Carson, yuk it up on the couch, then plug the appearance. And he'd go on *Steve Allen, Merv Griffin,* or Joey Bishop's show when Joey had a show on ABC. But now all he was doing was talking about Harry and Flo. (Oh, he would do this funny thing though; if he was the first guest he'd point to the empty space on the couch next to him and say, "Uh, Merv, me and Vic broke up a few years ago." That always got a big laugh.) The stuff about his parents was endless . . . he'd relate tale after tale of their lives and of them schlepping him around from town to town, putting him onstage when he was three . . . *and it was all nonsense! It was all made up!* And I should know because I spun most of these tales for him. Ziggy would say how he was putting together *The Story of Harry and Florence Blissman,* and whoever was hosting the show, well, their eyes would glaze over. He did a skit once on *The Mike Douglas Show* one day—he was Harry, and Ethel Merman was Flo—and Douglas, Buddy Greco, Skiles and Henderson, and Jackie Susann, who were guests that day, winced as one. "He keeps bringing up his parents and this nonexistent motion picture," Arnie muttered to me and Sally when we were watching him on *The Tonight Show,* "they won't even let him on *Captain Kangaroo.*" It was sad to see . . . you have to remember how truly knockout, drop-dead, paralyzingly funny Ziggy was. But he was becoming something that I thought it was impossible for him ever to be: He was tiresome.

I felt bad for Morty Geist. Ziggy got Morty to plant it in Earl Wilson and Grayling Greene that Paul Newman and Joanne Woodward had agreed to play Harry and Flo. And then, of course, they both vehemently denied it. He did the same with Peter O'Toole and Maggie Smith and then Dustin Hoffman and Goldie Hawn and finally Burt Reynolds and Sally Field. Every major and minor league actor and actress had to publicly deny they were playing Harry and Flo—it became like a badge of honor. For every time he got his foot in a door, ten other doors would slam shut on him. The bangs were deafening.

Jack, Sally, and I were watching Ziggy go on about his parents on the *Griffin* show, and Jack said, "Jesus, guys, I apologize for ever bringing this up."

ARNIE LATCHKEY: I'll tell you why this movie thing crawled into his brain and started feeding off his soul. Guilt. Guilt over the way he'd treated his parents. No doubt about it. And the other reason is because he heard that Vic was now taking a "serious" turn in his acting career.

You know, Sinatra did all those serious motion pictures like *The Man With the Golden Arm,* and Tony Bennett was in *The Oscar.* Bobby Darin did this jail movie, *Pressure Point*—I got a memory like a steel cage, don't I?—and Dean [Martin] had actually done a picture with Marlon Brando. So after the Johnny Venice trilogy and two westerns—oh yeah, he did *The Brigade from Hell* with George Peppard, Senta Berger, and Richard Harris—some agent drops Hunny Gannett's book *Punch Drunk* into his lap. And you could practically measure the wattage on the lightbulbs goin' off over Vic's head when he read it. *If* he read it. (Well, you know, Hunny didn't really write it, so turnabout is fair play.) This thing grabbed him though. He *had* to play Hunny in the movie, if they ever made one. Which they did.

Ziggy calls me up at the Vigorish office and says to me, "You know about Hunny's book?"

"I'm aware of it," I said to him.

"And Vic is tryin' to play Hunny in the movie . . ."

"I'm familiar with it."

"This is a joke, Arn. It's gotta be a joke. Look, I know there's a lotta water under the bridge wit' me and Vic. But some of the water, it ain't flowed all the way under the bridge yet. See, I still like the guy. I mean, he was my rock, a Goliath, a levia—"

"Yeah, I've heard you indicate that in the past."

"So I say this out of love for the guy . . . he does that picture, the reviewers'll schmear him—it'll be like a Mack truck goin' over a slab of cream cheese."

"He really wants to do this, Zig," I told him.

"Arnie, they'll fill his footprints outside Grauman's Chinese Theater with new cement and it'll be like he never was."

"And all this is something you *don't* want?"

Ziggy, to his own glee, was right. Vic couldn't pull it off. He took the Paul Newman-being-Rocky Graziano approach but it came off like Vic being Newman being Brando being Graziano being Hunny. Vincent Canby of the *Times* was merciless. Every reviewer said Vic's movie career was down for the count or that he should throw in the towel. Chester Yalburton wrote that if Vic Fountain can play a boxer then Jack Dempsey can play Timon of Athens. Teddy, if Lee Strasberg or Stella Adler had seen this movie, they would've shut down their acting schools and opened up a dry-cleaning outfit.

GUY PUGLIA: Hunny said to me after he seen the movie for the first time, "I should've played myself, Guy. Jackie Robinson done it. Audie Murphy too." I said to him, "Was that ever an option?" And he said that, yeah, he tried out for the role but he had trouble memorizing the lines and besides, he could never inhabit the character.

BILLY WILSON: The worst thing I had to do was double for Vic playing Hunny Gannett in *Punch Drunk*. I resented it when I read interviews and when I saw Vic on *The Tonight Show* plugging the movie; he was crowing about all the boxing technique he had to learn, how he'd been in more than a few brawls in his life but now he had to retrain himself to fight like a real pugilist. He told *Life* that he ran five miles at six in the morning for weeks, but I knew from [costars] Janet Leigh and Woody Strode that he was just crawling into bed at that time. Only one time that I knew of did he strap on the Everlasts and attempt to learn how to box: He made a wisecrack and said, "How am I supposed to mix a martini with these things on?" and he shuffled a few times, worked up a sweat, and then the gloves came off. But I had to work myself into very serious shape for this movie. I'd be at Gleason's Gym in New York and at Vic Tanny's [gym] in L.A. every single day for hours. You know, it was my body doubling for Vic's body in the early part of the flick, when Hunny Gannett was young, but in the last half hour, when Hunny's washed-up and out of shape, it's Vic's body doubling for mine. Vic even told Johnny Carson he got a broken nose in the movie and they had to halt filming. *Well, that was my broken nose!* Julie [Jules] Cassell was the director and he was infuriated by Vic's lack of cooperation . . . he really thought when Vic signed for the movie that he would give it his all. But Vic's "all" amounted to one bead of sweat.

I felt bad for Hunny Gannett. I wasn't a buddy of his but I did get to spend some time with him. He was really a sad figure. His bar, the Hunny Pot, had just closed down, and the game show he'd been on was canceled too. He lived in a one-room apartment now. Didn't have any family. I realize he didn't write his autobiography, but whoever did, he probably got more money for it than Hunny did. Julie Cassell said to me at the premiere, "Poor guy . . . he's going to end up shining shoes one day. You watch." And then we turned around and Hunny was right there. He'd heard us. "Nah, guys," he said. "Too dumb to shine shoes."

Now, here's an ironic story for your book. I had that "fat pillow" back on for this movie. Vic was about twenty or thirty pounds overweight now . . . he said he had to drink chocolate milk shakes and eat french fries for the part but, well, I knew from the westerns and from the Johnny Venice flicks that he liked to drink chocolate milk shakes and eat french fries before. I was having lunch one day at a Chinese restaurant in West Hollywood with my then-lover, Pete Golyadkin, who, by the way, had been Cary Grant and Randolph Scott's doubles. And I had the pillow on. And the wig too. Well, who walks in but Ziggy Bliss! When he walked by our table I stopped him and told him who I was—well, not actually who I really was, but who I was supposed to be. "Vic's double, huh?" Ziggy said in that babyish way he had. "Hey, maybe your double and my double could team up." He noticed the rug I had on and I also told him about the fat pillow. Now, Ziggy had lost weight over the years, I guess. Maybe twenty, twenty-five pounds—he wasn't nearly as round as he'd been in the Fountain and Bliss flicks. His face was even thinner, and so was his hair. So he asked me about the pillow and you know what I did? I let him have it! I unstrapped it from my belly and gave it to him! He said that now that he was thinner he didn't look like himself anymore so he needed it. "You sure you can spare this spare tire?" he asked me. And I said there were about twenty more where that came from. So for the next few years Ziggy wore Vic Fountain's fat pillow when he performed on TV and in clubs.

And he wanted the name of the place that made the toupee too.

ERNIE BEASLEY: For *Punch Drunk*, guess who crawled out of the woodwork? They needed someone to play a woman in her mid- to late sixties. They tried to get Shirley Booth but she passed, and so did Thelma Ritter. It was a very important scene; Hunny kills a handsome fighter from Ohio in the ring, and the fighter's mother drops by where Hunny works out, to make peace. ("Never happened," Hunny told me. "Them writer fellas made it up.") So a week before they start shooting, Jules Cassell tells Vic, "I'm bringing in a lady for this meaty scene . . . she's classically trained. She's done theater in England, done radio too. I think she can pull it off."

"It's a boxin' picture," Vic says, "it ain't *Anne of the Thousand Days*." The next day, Miss Constance Tuttle walks in and reads for the part.

"Bease, I was so goddamn scared she was gonna pour a dollop of relish on me," Vic said to me, "and bite off Mr. Baciagaloop's head. I couldn't even tell Julie Cassell to get rid of her. I just sat there with the script on my lap, wishin' it was made of steel."

She got the part, and I really think she did put the fear of God into Vic. In the movie, you can tell by his expression he's absolutely scared stiff of her. He's supposed to be shadowboxing in the gym in the scene, but he's only using one hand—the other was covering his crotch.

GUY PUGLIA: I brought Edie to the premiere of *Punch Drunk*. For years we'd been goin' out and you know what? Nobody knew. I told Hunny but that was it—I never told Vic. "Are you embarrassed of me?" Edie asked me one day and when she said that, Jesus, I almost started cryin'. I says to her, "Edie, doll, it ain't you I'm embarrassed of. It's me." And I stared weepin' like a baby . . . I had to put a fuckin' pillow to my eyes. I was embarrassed 'cause of the life I led and 'cause of what I looked like. And she thought I was embarrassed of *her*.

You know what she done? Don't forget, she worked in a makeup department. She had some people at Paramount make a nose, a fake nose. It was very convincing . . . it was made of latex and a little plaster or putty or something. But I couldn't bring myself to put it on. I'm a fuckin' jerk is what I am. She would ask me to try it on and I'd get angry . . . I said, "No! I won't do it!" For years and years I had the Band-Aid over my face, where the schnoz would be. So this phony nose was in my kitchen drawer for weeks, like it was some kind of turkey baster or something you only take out but once a year. Then one day I says to myself, Aw, what the fuck. And I put the thing on. (Now, it wasn't perfect, right? Well, that was the thing: It *was* perfect, but my real nose wasn't. But still, it looked good.) And when Edie come over that night, I answered the door with the thing on and she threw her arms around me and I'm thinking to myself, Okay, Lord, this is the girl I should marry.

And you know what she done? She had them make changes in it. The color and the shape . . . so it fit better and looked better. And I'll tell you another thing: By this time, I needed glasses, to see far, to see close, to see everything. So we went and we got me some real big fancy eyeglasses, and with those things takin' up half my mug, the nose looked even realer. And

I started wearin' that thing all the time. At work, at home, drivin' around, at the track or at the ballpark. It was strange, you know . . . I wasn't ashamed to be what I was no more.

When Vic saw me at the premiere he did a double take. He wasn't expecting me to be in the company of Edie Smith or any girl and he also wasn't expecting me to be in the company of a nose either. You know, he sort of ticked me off that night, at the party afterward. Why? 'Cause he didn't spend too much time with his old buddy. I saw him for twenty seconds, tops.

"Edie, you know Vic, right?" I said, reintroducing them. "Edie's my girl."

"Hi, Vic," Edie said.

"What's up with the schnoz, Guy?" Vic said.

"It's just—" I began.

"I gotta go talk to someone over there," Vic said. "I'll catch up with you two later."

But he didn't.

● ● ●

VICKI FOUNTAIN: Mom never wanted me to go into show business. If it was up to her I'd have just become a married mother of ten. But one time Dad was driving me and Vincent to a golf course and Louis Armstrong singing "Hello, Dolly" came on the radio and I began singing along. "Hey, princess, you got a great set of pipes," Dad said to me. And then my brother started imitating Armstrong, and Daddy said to him, "Hush up back there, wouldja?"

He started me on piano and singing lessons when I was about thirteen. I couldn't stand the piano and had no talent for it, but I liked singing. I didn't like having to be at some voice coach's house after school though; the boys were crazy for me and, to tell the truth, I was crazy for them too. [TV star] Vernon Blaine's son went to my school and we had the biggest crushes on each other. Tommy Deakins, whose father had produced *Route 66* and *77 Sunset Strip*, was in love with me too. Another problem was that Dad wanted me to sing the songs that *he* sang, but nobody under twenty listened to those anymore. I would listen to records by the Beatles and Pet Clark, and Dad would look at them and say, "What is this garbage?"

He had Arnie and Sally make a bunch of phone calls and I auditioned for Larry Galen of Mendocino Records. (His father, Noël, had been a bandleader years before, someone told me.) I was seventeen and had just graduated from high school. They had a song for me to sing called "It Could Be Me," which was sort of slow, sort of Leslie Gore. There was a band, maybe seven guys, and the guitarist was cute—so was the bassist— and the drummer was very muscular and dangerous-looking in a nice way.

We did about ten takes of the song, and then Larry, who was eyeing me up and down the whole time, said we'd gotten it right. "Hey, I've got this other thing here," he said, "a Steinberg and Jones tune, we could do." Well, that song was "Come Frug With Me" and it wound up selling two million copies and being in the Top 10 for fourteen weeks! And I wound up going out not only with the guitarist, but the bassist and drummer too.

Before I knew it I had a stylist, a makeup artist, and a hairdresser working me over all the time. It was like having surgery every day. They had me wearing the sixties clothing, the boots, the miniskirt, and hoop earrings that nearly pulled my ears off. I was in *Vogue* and *She* and *Seventeen*. I went on *Laugh-In* and *Shindig* and Clay Cole and Lloyd Thaxton's shows and I did *Hullabaloo* too. And, of course, I was on Daddy's TV specials. Morty Geist and Bursley-Bates were my publicists and they got my name all over the place, in everyone's columns. In London I started dating Keith, who'd had that hit song "98.6." Mmmm mmm, he was a real dreamboat, a very sweet bloke, as they say. But I also started seeing the former manager of Wayne Fontana [no relation] and the Mindbenders. It really was a crazy time for me. I went to Europe again with "Come Frug Some More With Me," the follow-up hit, and I had a little thing going with Jean-Luc Henault, the French pop singer. And with Gunter Böll, who I think was a skier or a race car driver or something and was so gorgeous.

"When am I gonna get my shot?" Vince asked Dad one night. "I can sing too." We were having our Thanksgiving dinner, me, Grandma, Vincent, Mom, and Dad, who was sometimes there for the holidays. Hunny was there, too . . . I remember that Mom had to cut his turkey for him.

"Your shot?" Dad said to Vince. "You want a shot? Get over here."

And Vince got up and went to where Dad was sitting and Daddy punched him in the shoulder. "That's your shot right there. Now go finish your lasagna."

SALLY KLEIN: I thought it was horrible what they did to Vicki. Lulu thought so too, but she wanted to make her daughter happy. Besides, she knew this was what Vic wanted and she figured if Vic was happy with Vicki then he'd come back to her. "They're dressing her up like a cheap *puttana!*" Lulu said when Vicki went on *Shindig*. "That skirt barely makes it below her belly button!"

But the horrible thing was we all knew it wouldn't last. Vicki did not have a great voice . . . she'll read this and never talk to me again, but I think she knows it's true. Larry Galen would do things with her voice in the studio, to fix it, and she had the backup singers too, who actually could sing. Poor girl, she must have sung those frug songs a hundred thousand times.

She was the most boy-crazy girl I've ever seen. I told Danny that once and he said, "Boy crazy? Ha! That's a very polite way of putting it." Maybe he was right. She went from man to man, and most of them treated her like dirt. I think they got a big kick out of it, that she was Vic Fountain's daughter. Men, right? She had a fling with a married movie star, an actor who was then in his late forties—I won't say his name. He used her for a few days and then passed her along to a friend, a less famous actor. It was sad. But let me tell you . . . the one she really wanted was Vic. No, I don't mean it that way, not at all. Vic was hardly ever at home when Vicki was growing up, and she utterly craved his attention. So she tried to make up for it with other men and, boy, did she ever succeed. All over town and the rest of the world she succeeded!

The sad thing was Vincent. Vic never gave him a moment's thought. He was such a nice boy. His father was Vic Fountain, the actor and the singer, the great womanizer and boozer, and now his older sister is on *Laugh-In* and is topping the charts. Vincent had by far the best singing voice of anyone in that family. I wasn't surprised that he started doing all those drugs.

ARNIE LATCHKEY: Vic was more concerned with Vicki's career than his own, let me tell you. He hated the music she was doing, but it was selling. As a matter of fact, it was selling a lot better than Vic's. They did a Steinberg & Jones tune together ["Hey You, You're My Angel"], which went into the Top 20 for a moment. Morty had the idea to get Vicki's name in the papers by linking her with this fella and that fella and so he called all the columnists, but then we found out that we didn't have to really work too hard at this, she was doing a fine enough job on her own. Boy, was she ever! After a year, Morty was going the opposite route: He was denying relationships. They had her with some fella on *Peyton Place* and with Joe Namath when he was filming *C.C. and Company* and then a week later she'd never met either one of them. "No, Vicki and Mike [*sic*] Jagger are not an item," he'd have to tell everyone. "No, Vicki Fountain is not seeing the drummer from the 13th Floor Elevators." The problem was, most of the time, it was true. So Morty pulled out all the stops, but then he had to plug them all right back in again.

Vincent was another case entirely. Now, unless you have balls of tungsten and have four of 'em, don't *ever* bring up Vincent and the drug thing to Lulu. She'll shoot you.

He didn't ask for his old man's help or for mine or Sally's. You got to respect that. He wanted to go the rock 'n' roll route too, but nobody would let him. But not the Vicki Fountain or Petula Clark thing; he was more like that Joe [*sic*] Morrison of the Doors or somebody. "You're name is Vince Fountain," they'd remind him, "not Vince Hendrix." He put together some kind of psychedelic rock combo but they couldn't get a record deal. They played the Whiskey-A-Go-Go a few times and the Philmont [*sic*]. I offered to help him out, so did Morty and Hank Stanco, but he didn't want our help. From what I understand—Sally's son saw them perform—they were good, if that sort of sound was to your taste. But nobody would give them a contract.

I asked Vic if he ever saw Vince sing with Shocking Turquoise—that was his combo's name—and Vic said to me, "That ain't singin', that's howling."

Now, I don't believe everything I hear. I don't even believe half of what I hear, and the half I *do* believe, I don't even believe that. But someone told me that those two hoodlums Tony and Jimmy Fratelli had gone around with satchels full of Vic's dough to get record companies to *not* sign Vince. It was a "Lady or the Tiger" thing—the dough was the lady and the Fratelli brothers were the tiger. Everybody went with the lady, you can take my word for it.

Now, why would Vic do that, you inquire? Why would he gum up the works for his own son? Look, I'm no socio-anthropologist but it could've been because he was the big dominant male in his family—the king bee, if you will—the chief of his tribe, and here's the young potent male trying to seize the throne. Here was Vic, starting to lose his hair and his voice, gaining weight and losing his audience, and here was the young stud, the handsome young buck in leather pants and love beads with the smooth voice. And so the old man slays the pretender to the throne. Yeah, it could've been that.

Or maybe he did it just because Vic was Vic.

DANNY McGLUE: Vincent moved into some flophouse apartment in San Francisco; he tried to make it with his rock band, but it didn't happen. And he started doing LSD all the time. I ran into him in Los Feliz one night and who knows what he was seeing when he was looking at me? Maybe he saw thirty of me. He was the one who got Donny Klein into the drugs too. It's just a shame. They'd smoke pot and take the drugs and disappear for days at a time.

Did you know a cop picked Vincent up in Berkeley once? He had some drugs on him, I think it was pot. The cop recognized his name and said to him, "Hey, you're Vic Fountain's kid, aren't you?" And Vincent said, "No." The cop says to him, "Sure you are." "If I am, does that mean you're not going to arrest me?" Vincent asked, and the cop said, "I'm your dad's biggest fan. I've seen him at Harrah's in Tahoe three times. I conceived my son to 'Malibu Moon' and when my wife left me I listened to 'Lost and Lonely Again' a hundred times." "Look, Vic Fountain's not my old man," Vincent said to the cop, "so just bust me, okay? I don't give a fuck about anything." But the cop wouldn't do it. He even gave him the pot back.

The poor kid couldn't get a break.

"I made it on my own," Vic said to me once, "so can he, even though he won't."

FREDDY BLISS: There was pressure on me ever since I was a kid. Adults would meet me and bend over and tickle me and say, "You goin' to become a comic too?" I heard that a million times. Even if I fell down while trying to walk or if someone threw a ball to me and I dropped it—I was a very klutzy kid—people would laugh and say, "He's gonna be just as funny as Ziggy." Often I didn't even have to do something funny or stupid and people would laugh. I'd be trying to do homework and maybe Van Johnson was at the house or George Burns or Agnes Moorehead, who was close friends with Mom, and they'd look at me and laugh. But I wasn't funny, there really wasn't anything funny about me. If I tried to be funny, probably no one would laugh. By the time I was a teenager I was ready to punch the next person who said I was funny or who asked me if I was going to become a comic. But, you know, even if I punched them, they'd probably start laughing.

Dad sent me to a military academy in Massachusetts when I was fifteen years old. I don't know why; I thought you only did that to kids who are either potential generals or potential criminals, and I was neither. It probably was my mother's idea. It's very possible she just wanted me out of the house for some reason. So I was never a part of the "Hollywood kids" scene. I didn't go to parties with Frank Sinatra's or Liz Taylor's kids. I didn't go driving around with Tuesday Weld or Ann-Margret or Peter Fonda or anyone like that. As a matter of fact I never went to parties and rarely drove around with anyone.

But I don't want to give the wrong impression. I saw the way Vic Fountain was with Vince, and Dad was not like that with me. He wasn't distant, he wasn't unaffectionate. He was there for me when he could be and was very nurturing. The one person in the entire world who never once asked if I was going to become a comedian was Dad.

You know, Ted, there's a lot of pressure on a famous person's kid to follow in his father or his mother's footsteps. I don't know if you realize that. A lot of time the pressure comes from within, but a lot of times it comes from other people. Mom and Dad—they'd rather I become a doctor or a lawyer, I think, than start singing or telling jokes.

Well, what I found out is this: I couldn't do anything. I'm a pretty incompetent guy . . . I've always been that. I went to UCLA and for a year I was premed, but I just couldn't get the biology down. So I switched majors and took lots of politics classes, thinking maybe I'd go to law school. But my grades were pretty bad. I worked hard, I studied and studied, but I just wasn't any good. The other kids would invite me out, to clubs and bars and places, but they were all expecting me to pop my eyes out and make funny faces. Which I didn't do. They wanted me to tell jokes and be funny. When I didn't, they stopped asking me out.

I did graduate, barely. But—well, I guess I'll never know if this is true or not—I maybe graduated only because my dad made a very generous bequest to the university. He donated about a half million dollars to start a comedy library there. The Harry Blissman and Florence Blissman Memorial Comedy Library, it was called. It was supposed to cover the history of comedy and comedians from Aristophanes to vaudeville to the present day. Dad was very involved in the planning of this, and I. M. Pei was brought in to design a building. There was talk about a fellowship and establishing a permanent "chair" or something, where they would bring in a visiting professor to teach. (Dad had a typical idea for him: "The chair should have, like, a whoopee cushion on it!" he said.) I think the only person they could get was Henny Youngman, but finally he passed on it. Lenny Pearl, the old-time comic, had given millions to the university too over the years; as I understand it, though, he scuttled the entire project. They never did start the library or the fellowship. And the building was never built. But somehow I did manage to graduate.

Eventually something was built. Ziggy Bliss's Harry Blissman and Florence Blissman Museum of the Comedic Arts was opened up in Loch Sheldrake in 1990. It's full of all kinds of interesting history about the Catskills, the whole entertainment scene, and the history of American comedy. We've got thousands of tapes and records and articles. It's actually quite a marvelous place. I should know. I manage it. Finally, I found something I can do.

●　●　●

SNUFFY DUBIN: You know, Ziggy did maybe two specials a year for ABC. There was always a Christmas show and sometimes one in the spring too. The geniuses at the networks more than a few times would put Ziggy's Christmas special up against Vic's. Vic would outdraw Ziggy two to one sometimes . . . later it was three to one. And then it was no contest because Oldsmobile, which sponsored Zig's shows, dropped out. But by that time, Andy Williams's or Perry Como's specials were mopping the floor with both Ziggy *and* Vic. A few times my agent tried to book me on Ziggy's shows, but not one time did Zig ever let me on. And I was getting hot in the late sixties; instead of me opening up for Sandler and Young, now those two Canadian *putzes* were opening up for me! But I never got on a Ziggy show. So I did what anyone would've done: I started going on Vic's specials. That cat never turned me down one time. He also never turned up for rehearsal one time either. He wouldn't even read from the TelePrompTer anymore! It was his TV show but he put in a total of five minutes work on it. He'd started that syndicated golf program of his and that sapped up a lot of his energy, which shows you just how much energy he had.

When Ziggy found out I was doing Vic's show he hit the roof. And believe me, I enjoyed every minute of it.

When Olds dumped Ziggy in '68, nobody would go near him. Nobody was watching the show—Marlin Perkins tickling a gerbil was outdrawing him. He did this sketch in his last Christmas show . . . it was him and Mitzi Gaynor dressed up as a quarreling couple, two vaudevillians in their living room. And the sketch was something about her lousy cooking, about how her brisket stunk up the entire northern half of New York State. It was Harry and Flo they were playing, this was his tribute, and it stank worse than that brisket.

When he lost his TV shows, that's when a lot of other things went bad. He still had engagements all around the country. If I was around and had free time I'd stop in and watch. Half of Ziggy's act was him talking about Vic. Imitating Vic, relating funny stories about Vic, putting Vic in weird situations, like on the moon or in the White House or something. Couple times I saw him and he did something real unprofessional: He started laughing at his own material. Actually it wasn't material that he said aloud; it was stuff up in his brain. He never did get it out, he just thought about it and I thought he was gonna completely explode. Very unprofessional.

He told reporters he was taking a break from the clubs for a while. Taking a break. But, you know, he'd been playing the Latin Casino in Cherry Hill [New Jersey] or the Royal Box in New York and the joints were empty. Except for the hecklers. " . . . And another thing about Vic," Ziggy would say, and some drunk from Paramus would throw an ice cube at him and yell out, "No. *Enough* about Vic!" People were taking a break from *him*.

PERNILLA BORG [Ziggy's second wife]: It is famous story of how Ziggy meets me. I was Miss Sweden in 1964. I was twenty-three years old. From this I get to do commercials for the Top Brass, the hair cream. Some man is putting the Top Brass in his hair at his gym and I appear in a white towel and I put the Top Brass over him. I say one line: "I want to get it all over you." It was very steamy, very hot. When I sign for this Top Brass campaign, Earl Wilson prints my picture in the *Post*. "Bustacious, chestacious, bosomicious, lustacious Pernilla Borg will be steaming things up for Top Brass," it says. The picture of me is with the white towel and my cleavages. Ziggy calls up Earl Wilson and he gets my publicist's phone number from him. Then Ziggy calls me up at home! I did not believe it was Ziggy Bliss. The funny half of Fountain and Bliss. We are on phone for an hour and he has me laughing so much it is hurting me. He tells me he will be in New York sometime soon and would like to meet me. I say to him, "When will you be in New York?" and he says, "Will you be there tomorrow?" and I say to him yes and then he says, "Then so will I." And he was.

ARNIE LATCHKEY: Morty calls me, tells me we got trouble: Ziggy's been seen around New York with Pernilla Borg. *Who?* I mean, at this point, I don't know Pernilla Borg from Ingmar Bergman. He tells me, "It's that big Swede in the Top Brass ads." Do you remember that campaign? In the locker room with all the steam and the white towel? Jesus, ten million boys must have gotten their first hard-ons watching a stupid commercial for hair cream. I bet you some of them haven't even subsided yet, it was that hot. (Christ, that whole campaign backfired too, because nobody could tell what the commercial was for: hair cream, towels, Swedish tourism, or steam.) Anyway, as soon as I realized who Pernilla Borg is, I said to Morty, "This has got to be it for Jane White. She's dead in the water."

"Arnie," he says to me, "do you have any idea how much I've done for Fountain and Bliss?"

"Yes I do, because I've asked you to do most of it."

"I just can't take this anymore."

"Morty," I said, "I know you're gonna cover this lousy burnt flank steak with rich luscious icing, with fresh strawberries and sweet sugary flowers and fluffy cream and we're gonna make it through. I just know it. So, please, get bakin'."

So the next day Ziggy calls me up from New York. He's in a rage. He's yelling so goddamn loud, his spit was practically squirtin' through my ear piece. "Morty's fired!" Ziggy said. "I want Morty fired and I want him to never work at any job anywhere ever again!" I told Ziggy this would be a little tough to arrange and asked him what had happened. He read to me from Bud Hatch's column. Guess what Morty Geist had done? He'd called up columnists all over New York and L.A. and told them that Ziggy Bliss was having an adulterous sexual relationship with Pernilla Borg, she of the Top Brass ads, and that his wife didn't know about it and it would proba- bly be the end of their marriage even though he'd cheated on her numerous times, and that nobody really thought this would be injurious to Ziggy's career because his career wasn't doing particularly good anyway. That's what Morty told everyone. *The truth!* And they went with it.

"Morty told me," I said to Ziggy, "that he was at the end of his rope."

"Did you tell him to get a new—" he started to ask me.

"Yes, I most certainly did."

"I want him dead, Latch."

"Look, do you have any idea how much he's done for us? Covering up the abortions and the shoplifting, George S. Collier's peg leg, the dozens of fights, the girls, all the hanky-panky and *mishegoss.*"

"Okay . . . okay," he said. "I unnerstand."

"You do?" I said, for it did not seem characteristic of him.

Maybe a week after this, what happens? Vic was filming *Monza: 180 MPH* with Camilla Sparv, Omar Sharif, and Alain Delon, and he began a dalliance with Taffy McBain, who's in that forgettable racecar picture for about two laps. Taffy and Vic were seen all over the place, holding hands, smooching, actin' like kids. The paparazzi were all over them like potato on a knish. He'd be singing in Vegas and they'd bring the lights down except for one soft light on her in the crowd and he'd sing to her. Very tender, very sweet, very sickening. After four weeks of this relationship he tells Morty to announce to the world he's marrying Taffy McBain, who, by the way, is twenty years younger than him. So do you know what Morty does? He calls up every columnist there is and—for no reason whatsoever known to mankind—he issues the Eleven Standard Denials and Apologies! About the marriage, about the relationship, about gambling and drinking. About everything under the goddamn sun, it was like! All Vic wanted him to do was to call up Bud or Earl or the Slobbering Lush and say, "Taffy McBain and I are deeply in love and will be getting married in a private ceremony at an undisclosed location at Harrah's in Tahoe next month." But Morty—you gotta love him—he just flipped out! "I am not marrying Taffy McBain because she is expecting my child," he had Vic saying. But nobody had ever said that! Grayling Greene ran this: "My marriage to Taffy, whom I love and adore, is not an act of bigamy. I was never married to Faye Kendall." But nobody ever said that Vic and Faye Kendall had ever tied the knot!

"Latch," Vic says to me on the phone from Palm Springs, "my kids'll read this, Lulu'll read this, my mother'll read this. I want him dead. He's dead. Morty's in Forest Lawn."

"Do you have any idea how much—"

"Even if I wasn't gonna strangle him, even if my mother wasn't gonna chew his Adam's apple, do you honestly think that the Fratellis won't go after him?! Look, this is my second marriage, Latch. That's really important. It should be the second happiest day of my life."

"I'll talk to him. Maybe he can apologize for the denials and deny the apologies."

Poor Morty Geist. He *made* Fountain and Bliss. And he remade them, over and over again, whenever there was trouble. All the stunts he pulled. I don't know when it was but in Philly once he'd gotten hold of three people who were in the hospital for trying to kill themselves by jumping. And he puts them all up in the balcony and in the middle of a Fountain and Bliss sketch, all three of them dive off at once. Tell me that isn't genius.

Dissolve. Four nights later. I get a phone call in the middle of the night, it's Bertie Kahn. Bertie's retired, he's livin' in Fort Lauderdale, he moseys about with a solid-gold, diamond-studded walker. Bertie tells me that Morty had committed suicide.

"Why now?" I asked. "I mean, I see why he'd kill himself, Bertie, but why now and not five years or ten years ago?"

"The accumulation, Arnie."

All the dozens, the hundreds of things. They had all piled up and collapsed on him. The poor guy. Never married, never had a girl. The kid had no family that we knew of, and Vic and Ziggy—separately, of course—picked up the tab for the funeral.

"How'd he do it, by the way?" I asked Bertie.

"Hanged himself."

"Damn," I said. "With what?"

"A rope. It took two though. The first one snapped."

SALLY KLEIN: When I read that Vic was marrying Taffy McBain my first thought was: Poor Lulu. That flame was still burning inside her, but it must have died down when Vic told her what he was doing. Although I think he didn't tell her; Joe Yung did. That's what personal valets are for, huh?

I said to Jack, "I give this marriage three years. Not a day more."

Well, I was off by a year. Because it was over in two.

REYNOLDS CATLEDGE IV: When the nature of Ziggy and Pernilla Borg's "friendship" became common knowledge, I was contacted by Shep Lane and Merwyn Swick, the prominent Los Angeles divorce lawyer. Mr. Swick informed me that this case could get unsightly or ugly or hideous. "We want to keep it down to unsightly at best, ugly at worst," he said.

Mr. Swick asked me what I knew about Jane White. Did she ever fool around, he wanted to know, did she drink, use narcotics, or take pills?

I was in quite a bind, for I knew from the surveillance years before that Jane White had had a lesbianistic affair with Joan Pierce. If I told Mr. Swick this, it would have compromised my position. It opened up a can of worms, if you will. However, I did feel that it was my duty to tell the truth and I did so.

I detailed as best as I remembered—and I remembered it virtually blow by blow—what I had heard on the tapes. They sat spellbound while I told them, while I reenacted verbatim their ardent lovemaking. Both Mr. Swick and Shep Lane were very eager to know if the tapes were still extant and seemed equally disappointed—depressed, almost—to find out that they were not.

"So they did this after watching *silent* movies?" Mr. Swick asked incredulously. "As in, *The Gold Rush* and *Birth of a Nation*?"

"There was no sound to these movies," I told them. "Whether they were classics of the silent screen or home movies, I do not know."

"Hey, Mer," Shep Lane interjected, "Ziggy was always fooling around with strippers and girls like that. You should see the headlights on some of these dames. Bet you anything it wasn't Murnau's *Sunrise* they were watching."

"Why did Ziggy have you bugging his own house anyway, Mr. Reynolds?" Mr. Swick inquired of me.

I refrained from reminding him that I was Mr. Catledge and not Mr. Reynolds and instead replied, "Ziggy wasn't bugging his own house. Vic was. Vic Fountain."

They both shifted uncomfortably in their chairs, and their faces registered what I would characterize as an amalgam of distress and amazement.

"Vic bugged Ziggy's house?" Shep said, picking up the pile of papers he'd dropped to the floor.

"Yes. That is correct," I replied.

They huddled with each other in a corner of the office and chatted. I suppose they were discussing the admissibility of the evidence. Or perhaps they were still stunned that Vic would bug Ziggy's domicile.

"Mr. Reynolds, is there anything else you know?" Mr. Swick asked.

"Yes, Ziggy had bugs in several of Vic's places of residence, his suites and such."

This time Mr. Swick's paperwork fell to the floor.

"What happened in Vic's hotel rooms and in his bedroom," Mr. Swick stated, "would be of no use in Ziggy's divorce; however, I really would like to talk to you about that at a later date."

Shep Lane and I detailed other aspects of Jane White's "character." He and I had assiduously kept copious notation on her "shopping." For example, she would enter the I. Magnin department store and purchase a floor-length chinchilla coat, but actually exited the store with not only this new coat but with a mink stole or another coat, a sable, for example, which she had not purchased. As best we could, Shep and I kept track of every item that Jane White had purloined.

When I was shown the door, Mr. Swick said, "With the dyke thing and the shoplifting, this thing is going to be as easy as pie."

As I understand it, Mr. Swick immediately called Arnie Latchkey, probably within moments of my leaving his office. Informed of the various tasks I had performed for Fountain and Bliss, Mr. Latchkey granted me a most generous severance package and I was let go.

"You need to learn something about loyalty, Cat," he said to me.

"I consider myself loyal," I told him, "to a fault."

"Exactly," he said.

ARNIE LATCHKEY: Letting the Cat go wasn't easy. First time we met him, he was just a young soldier boy in New Mexico. But we had to do it. Spying on each other—that was bad. I know he was only doing what he was asked, but you had to draw the line somewhere.

He was devastated. He was the straightest arrow you ever saw. Hardly drank a drop, never gambled, didn't run around with girls. Christ, he still looked like a soldier.

"I don't know what I'm going to do," he said.

"Cat, don't make this tougher on me than it is," I said.

"These years with Fountain and Bliss . . . it's the only exciting thing that's ever happened to me." He was clutching the arm of his chair. I thought he might faint.

"I understand," I told him. "Without Fountain and Bliss I'd have just been a poor schnook. But they made me a rich one."

"I guess I should go," he said. He stood up and we shook hands.

"What are you gonna do? With your life?"

"I don't know. I suppose I should move back to Nebraska and pick up my life where I left it. It was in pieces then. I only hope I can still find them . . . so I can throw them out."

"Ha! You know, I do think being with us has rubbed off on you."

He told me he would keep track of Fountain and Bliss, that he'd keep tabs on them. I told him not to bother.

JANE WHITE: When I found out about Pernilla, I was stunned. Stunned. I couldn't speak. I couldn't move. I knew he had those dirty movies . . . but I thought that by having the movies and watching them, he wouldn't be tempted to fool around. After Dr. Baer operated on me the first time, I thought that all our problems were solved. Maybe the mistake was the second operation. After that, we drifted apart in so many ways.

Buford Chatham was my lawyer. I think he was very frustrated with me the first few times we met . . . I was crying all the time. My life had suddenly come crashing down. He was a very, very flamboyant lawyer, from South Carolina. Always wore white. White everything. He told me that Ziggy was the adulterer, he'd abandoned me, and that there was no way in the world I could come out of a divorce hurting for anything. "We'll take him to the cleaners, Mrs. Bliss," he said to me, "and shrink him down to extra-extra-small, so don't you worry."

He and Ziggy's lawyer met several times, trying to work out a settlement. Every day Mr. Chatham would tell me how well things were going, that Merwyn Swick was shrinking right before his eyes. "We got them at subpetite now, Jane. We're gonna keep shrinking them down to munchkin size." But one day everything suddenly changed. "They may have us by the nuts, I'm afraid," he said. "Do you want to tell me a little bit more about your marriage?"

I will not discuss any more aspects of the case with you. I've told you enough.

ARNIE LATCHKEY: The case never went to court. Thank *God*. That would've been the ugliest thing to hit Hollywood since Fatty Arbuckle and the bottle of sarsaparilla or whatever it was. Ziggy never talked about it, Shep never talked about it, and as for Jane, well, with her out of Ziggy's life now, there was never a reason for me or Estelle to utter so much as a phoneme to her ever again, that loony *gonif*.

What I think happened is that Merwyn Swick was about to unload some sort of gargantuan dump truck on Jane. All over her. It's like she was on her driveway on her back, on the ground, and the truck was slowly, slowly lowering the load, about to let loose. But just when the gate was about to open, she leaned back and lifted the garage door and there was a dump truck in there with Ziggy's name on it. And there was enough dirt in there, my friend, to sift over the entire Himalayas like so much parmigiana cheese, two times over.

So after months—nay, years—of bickering and threatening and then sober, earnest discussion, and, finally, putting cocked bazookas to each other's heads, Ziggy raised the white flag. His legal fees were killing him. It was eating away at him emotionally. Jane made away with the whole ball of wax. She got a living allowance that the Sultan of Brunei would have refused as too generous. Ziggy had to sell stock, he had to mortgage his pension fund and future. The house in Vegas? Gone. The house in Beverly Hills? Jane's. Ziggy wound up getting a one-story spread on North Irving. If Pernilla Borg was expecting a mansion, a palatial manor, she didn't get it. And if she was expecting a big-time celebrity husband, well, she didn't get much of that soon either.

SALLY KLEIN: By the early seventies no talk show would have Ziggy on. Merv Griffin's producer told me they'd rather get a ticking H-bomb on their couch. It was Ziggy talking about Harry and Flo, it was him going on about Vic. He went on with Pernilla a few times and they certainly cut an interesting figure; her bust practically shattered the glass of your television screen. And she towered over him; his head came right up to her chest. It was funny for a while, her Swedish accent and blond hair, and his New York accent and red hair, which was starting to thin a bit. Danny would write stuff for them, he would write malapropisms for Pernilla to say purposely, but she couldn't pull it off. Instead of saying something cute like "Oh, I would Kaopectate my Ziggy with a one-two brunch" as she was supposed to, she'd say "kayo" and "punch" so there was no laughter at all. It was a sort of [humorist] Jack Douglas and [wife] Reiko act. Ziggy and Pernilla did the *Tattletales* game show with Bert Convy a few times too, but they had trouble even getting on that after a while. They also filmed two *Love, American Style* episodes but only one was aired.

But I don't want to give the wrong impression about Pernilla. She really did love Ziggy, she took care of him. I loved her and still do. And, unlike with Jane, when Jack and I had them over for dinner, I didn't have to count the forks afterward.

After the divorce—it was right around when the whole Watergate craziness was going on—Ziggy got sent a play called *Bam-Bam-Bamboozled*. It was a very cheesy sex farce, lots of girls running around with their tops falling off. Lots of jiggling and bumping. Arnie and I read it and it was very depressing—not the play but the fact that this was what Ziggy was being sent. Oh, he'd do guest spots on some TV shows now and then. He did *That's Life,* with Bobby Morse and E. J. Peaker, a few times, and he did a *Marcus Welby* episode and an *Owen Marshall*. And he'd still do the stand-up act but now fewer and fewer people wanted him to open for them. Once he got going he would run a half hour over, an hour over. Now, if you're the main attraction, that's all right—who's going to complain if Frank Sinatra decides he wants to sing four or five extra songs? But he'd be opening up for Enzo Stuarti somewhere and then he begins a thirty-minute tirade against the hotel he's staying at, and it louses up everything for Enzo and the band and the club. Vic Damone didn't want him, neither did Sergio Franchi or Julie Mansell.

So this *Bamboozled* play—it was promising for him, even though it was absolute dreck.

"We could tell Zig the truth, that the play should be in the sewer, or we could let him just do it," Arnie said to me and Danny.

"Doesn't he know it should be in the sewer?" Danny asked him. "He can't possibly think it's any good, can he?"

There comes a time when you can't tell those sorts of things about people anymore. It's usually the same time when you can't tell those sorts of things *to* people either.

We never told him that the play was the pits. He was the lead, Jack Harris played the evil Lothario, and there were tons of girls in it. The show went to all the small-time theaters, all over the country. In some places it did well, it some places it didn't get noticed. The ad was Ziggy dressed up as a doctor—he's got the white coat on and the stethoscope and that round surgical mirror on his forehead—and three blondes are popping out of their tight white uniforms. And, of course, Ziggy's eyes were popping out too. It was a naughty romp and it wasn't funny and I bet you he played it two thousand times. I saw the show once, in Warren, Pennsylvania. It was a dinner theater, maybe two hundred people there. Sometimes you couldn't hear the dialogue above the plates and silverware and belching. There was a lot of laughter when Ziggy had to pass himself off as a nurse—he put on a blond wig and put two cantaloupes in his dress. I didn't laugh though.

"What did you think, Sal?" he said to me backstage, when he was taking his makeup off.

"It was . . . good, Ziggy," I said.

"And how was I?"

He still wanted to be told he was funny . . . decades and decades he'd been doing this and he still needed to hear those words.

"You were very, very funny," I told him, and when I got into my car I almost started to cry.

VICKI FOUNTAIN: Taffy McBain was nice to me, but I didn't like her. But I was polite about it. She would get me all sorts of things, jewelry and shoes and clothing. "She's a *zoccola*, a *troia*," Grandma would tell me. A slut. I would tell Grandma that Dad was married to her and so we had to be nice, but Grandma would say, "Okay then. Be nice. But she's still a *zoccola.*"

I don't think that Taffy was really buying the gifts for me—I'm pretty sure it was Ices Andy or Joe Yung, that Taffy would tell Joe what to get and then he'd go to the Broadway or to Greene's [Jewelers] and get it for me. Mom once insisted I return some earrings that Taffy had given me and when I took them back, the man at the counter said, "That Chinese guy was certain you were going to like them."

After a year of this—I don't know if she ever got Vince anything (maybe Daddy told her not to)—Mommy just started taking the stuff and throwing it away. Taffy gave me two beautiful ruby earrings and Mom pulled them off my ears and literally flushed them down the toilet . . . "Where they belong!"

"So didn't you simply adore those emerald earrings, darling?" Taffy said to me the next time I saw her. She, Daddy, and I were having dinner at Musso and Frank.

"Yes, I did," I told her, "but my mother flushed them down the toilet. And they were ruby earrings, Taffy."

"Vic," she said, "did you hear what Lulu did? My God!"

"Huh? What?" Daddy said.

He hadn't been listening to a word of it.

When it was on the news that he and Taffy were divorcing, my mother danced around the house. "I knew it!" she shrieked with joy. "I knew it! He'll come crawlin' back to me."

GUY PUGLIA: What was it? Two years with Taffy McBain? Three? Vic dropped out of my life then. They'd go all over the world together, those two. Paris, Rome, Spain. All over. She wanted something, she points at it, it's hers. Look, you know what Vic liked to do most of all when he hit fifty? Golf. Like lots of guys. He had no interest in goin' to France and staying at the most expensive hotel in the history of the world. If he went to London, it was 'cause he had an engagement there, to sing or to film a picture. But now she was dragging him up and down the world just so she could buy stuff and hang around with famous people.

Once, he come back from staying in London for a week and told me that him and Taffy had met the queen. I says—like I could give a shit—to him, "Oh yeah. How's Her Majesty doin' anyway?" And he says to me, "Saggy tits."

He and Taffy was on their way to Italy one time. This wasn't a trip so's she could buy more Yves Saint Laurent or Pucci, it was 'cause he was filming a cowboy movie there with George Kennedy, Fred "The Hammer" Williamson, and Diane Cilento. And what's-his-face, the guy who did them pictures and looked like he just stepped out of a deep fryer? Lee Van Cleef. And Vic and Taffy are at the Los Angeles Airport and who do they run into? Ziggy Bliss and Pernilla.

"I just stood there, Guy," Vic says to me. "He looked at me, I looked at him. And we both just stood there. It was like a boxin' match, but with no boxin'."

"You didn't say nothing to each other?" I asked him.

"I couldn't think of anything to say. And neither could he."

Vic and Taffy . . . it was just like when the first marriage ended. He come to my restaurant at closing time. Chinese Joe [Yung] drove him. Vic was bagged, it was maybe 2:00 A.M.

I see him gettin' out of his Rolls, I go to take the big plastic swordfish off the wall. But then I say to myself, Aw, what the hell? And I leave it up.

"It's over," he says to me.

"What is?" 'Cause by this time I didn't know if he meant his marriage or the TV specials or the record contract.

"Me and Taff. Dead and buried. *Morto.*"

"I can't say that I'm too surprised. Or too upset."

"My mother was right," he told me. "Taffy and I have a big fight, we scream at each other, then I buy her a big necklace to make up for it. And she goes out and bangs a thirty-year-old."

"Hey, if it was up to your mother, you'd be married to Lulu still. Or to Angie Crosetti."

"Yeah. Remember her? Goddamn Angie Crosetti. Firmest tits in Codport."

I did some paperwork for a few seconds and he said to me, "What's up with you and that makeup girl, huh? That Frieda girl?"

"You mean Edie. Yeah, you know, we still go out and all."

"Uh-huh," he said. "Hey, when are you gonna make this place a steak or pasta joint? I never could stand it that this place does seafood."

"Vic, you know, the place has been successful so far. I'm goin' through some tough times here lately and—"

"Don't forget, Gaetano, I was the backer here. I put up most of the dough. And I come in and what do I see? I gotta look at the goddamn Pacific Ocean. You know how I hate that."

"Vic, it ain't the Pacific Ocean. It's Mount Vesuvius explodin' over the Adriatic. And it's a mural. We're on the water. The customers could at least have a mural of the water."

"I wish you'd get rid of the thing. I really do. And that goddamn sword-fish on the wall."

"I don't wanna get rid of it. It's up to me, I get rid of the mural and I put windows there and people can see the real goddamn water, which is only twenty fuckin' yards away! And I'd have twenty fuckin' fish on the wall."

"Hey, maybe I should get rid of *you*," he said, "maybe that's what I should do."

BILLY WILSON: Vicki Fountain made a movie called *Motor Psycho Nightmare* for Roger Corman. By coincidence, I was in this flick too. It was sort of a hippies-meet-Hell's Angels thing and it was a pretty big mess. Vicki was one of the hippie chicks on a commune and I was one of the badass bikers who invade the commune. There was this two-minute psychedelic trip sequence in it . . . the cameraman had different color gels and jellies and squirted them at the camera and blurred everything while Vicki took her top off and danced in slow motion—you couldn't tell if you were looking at Vicki's nipples or at two splotches of raspberry jam.

Vicki knew me because Vic had introduced us a few times on the set of his movies or while filming *Golfing With Vic.* (Did you know that a lot of the time that you saw Vic golfing, driving the ball, or putting from far away, with Tony Hampton, that was really me driving and putting?) There were no drugs on the set of *Motor Psycho Nightmare*—we were all pretty straitlaced, but there was tons of drinking. And Vicki was after me. In the worst way. She was seeing Tip Farlow at the time. We were filming out in Death Valley and there wasn't much to do except drink tequila. Vicki knew I was gay and that I was married, but that didn't stop her. And she looked fantastic in tight shiny leather pants, just like Marlon Brando in *The Wild One.* She'd come over to my motel room at night and we'd have a few shots of tequila—we did some flaming shots too—and then she'd start to seduce me. We were both sloshed and it got a little funny. She damn near succeeded one time . . . we were in the bed with our tops off and were kissing. The damnedest thing . . . she wanted to know if I had Vic's wig and the fat pillow too. I said to her, "We're doing a biker and hippie flick, not a Vic film. Why would I have the rug and the pillow?" She said to me, slurring her words, "Come on, Billy. Put it on. Put it on for Princess Vicki." I told her I didn't have the stuff. She wobbled over to the dresser and was flinging the drawers open, looking for the blue toup and the pillow. She was really disappointed she couldn't find them. "Can you call someone," she asked me, "and have them send you the stuff?" We did a few more shots and she was near unconscious. I carried her to her motel room and put her to bed there. "Call me 'puddin'," she said when I set her down. She kept coming on to me until we finished the movie, but she gave up on the rug and the pillow.

She wound up marrying Tip Farlow. That "young rebel attorney" TV show he did was hot for a spell, but then died. I think they divorced after three years. I heard he used to mistreat her. I believe it. I remember hearing on the *Golfing With Vic* set that he'd hit her, slapped her around. I felt really, really bad for her. Vic's kids—I felt bad for both of them.

● ● ●

ANNA LIPSCOMBE [actress; Clive Bonteen's widow]: My husband was an enormous fan of the American cinema, especially the comedies. Growing up poor in Liverpool, Clive had found solace in Laurel and Hardy, the Marx Brothers, Buster Keaton, *His Girl Friday* and *Bringing Up Baby,* Fountain and Bliss. His first play, *Disease Puddle Cripple Swimming,* would have been unimaginably different were it not for his deep affection for those wonderful clowns; the interplay of violence between Pudd, Dudd, and Thudd really does smack of the Three Stooges, whom Clive also adored. *Bitch Plague Sonata,* as many a critic has noted, is essentially a Laurel and Hardy scenario set during an horrific epidemic.

When Fountain and Bliss broke up, Clive told me that he would love to write a play for Ziggy Bliss, who he said was the one true child of Chaplin, Keaton, Groucho. His publisher at Webber & Holdsclaw, Desmond Thornton, contacted Ziggy Bliss's agents but Ziggy didn't seem interested and had not—or so he claimed—ever heard of my husband or his plays, a fact which delighted Clive to no end. "This only proves how truly perfect he is," Clive said.

We were living in Paris at the time and Ziggy was in Germany filming a movie called, I believe, *Honkers Over Heidelberg*—that was the English title of the movie, at least. One weekend Clive and I drove to Germany in our red Renault and met Ziggy Bliss there. This was 1974 and the movie was being filmed outside Munich, despite the title. We were at first startled by Ziggy's appearance—he was much thinner in person and his famed mop of blazing red hair was sparse in places. He also had thick grayish bags under his eyes. Perhaps it was from popping his eyes out and crossing them, I suggested to Clive. "It's perfect, it's so brilliant," Clive said. "The tragic clown, the wretched court jester to the cosmos knocked down by the gods. Food for worms, a can of laughter for vermin. So perfect." And thus was his next play born.

PERNILLA BORG: I did not ever see any Clive Bonteen's plays but when Ziggy signed to do the *Can of Hell Laughter* play, I made sure to catch *Drama: Mean* in London. It is a very depressing and sad play, yes? Eddie Bramshill was in this play when Ziggy and I saw it—he was once the boyfriend of Julie Mansell, who had performed with Ziggy. We go backstage after play to talk to Eddie but he will not speak to us, because of some sort of thing between Julie and Ziggy and what it is, I don't know. But when Ziggy sees all the applause at the theater he says to me that he will do the *Laughter in Can* play. I warned Ziggy that this was complete switch in his life, to do *Honkers Over Heidelberg* movie and then do this drama about life on earth after atom bombs wipe out everyone but one man. But he said that he had "range," that he can do Japanese accent, Spanish accent, German accent, he can play young baby boy and senile old woman, so why cannot he play one survivor of apocalypse then?

ARNOLD LATCHKEY: Ziggy with that loony British playwright? *Oy vey!* I'll tell ya something: If Ziggy Bliss ever wrote an autobiography he would never have mentioned it—it wouldn't have gotten one sentence. Why? Because he was ashamed? Because he was embarrassed? No. The reason is because I don't think he ever remembered a second of it. He was really taking those pills then, the pep pills and then the antipep pills, like he was on a seesaw.

You know, a lot of comedians are hung up on being taken seriously. So you've got Gleason doing that dumb clown *Gigot* movie and Jerry Lewis with his concentration camp movie that never came out. But that wasn't Ziggy . . . he didn't care if anybody took him seriously. I mean, at this point in his career he just wanted to be *taken,* period.

ANNA LIPSCOMBE: We met Ziggy in the lobby bar of his hotel, and he and Clive hit it off splendidly. We'd met Olivier, Gielgud, Burton, and Scofield but Clive always regarded them as toffs and was humbled now to be in the presence of a man he regarded as a genuine, instinctual artist.

Clive mentioned Pinter, Derek Bond, Beckett, and Ionesco to Ziggy, and Ziggy expertly feigned never having heard of them. "What sort of theater do you go in for then, Mr. Bliss?" Clive asked him, and Ziggy cleverly responded, *"Hellzapoppin',"* which we'd never heard of but which immediately struck Clive as some sort of dark, postapocalyptic farce—*King Lear* amidst glowing radioactive ashes. "Hellzapoppin'!" Clive responded. "Yes, of course! Brilliant!" When we returned to our hotel room, Clive kept saying, "Hellzapoppin'!" For days he said it and he would erupt in childish giggles at the very uttering of the word. Ziggy, I remember, had told us his favorite movie ever was *The Horn Blows at Midnight,* a Jack Benny movie; he told us that he'd been trying to remake the movie but that nobody in Hollywood would finance or consider the project. "It bombed for Jack," he told us, "but I just know I could make it click." Clive asked what the movie was about, and Ziggy said it was about angels, fallen angels and musicians and blowing a trumpet and ending the world. "God, that does sound utterly magnificent," Clive said, "angels and the end of the world." "But it bombed for Jack," Ziggy reminded us.

When we returned to Paris, Clive immediately began writing *A Can of Laughter in Hell.* Like many great artists, he enjoyed a drink every now and then and often in the moments in-between too. So, fueled by rye, espressos, and Gauloises and ultimately by Dilaudid, Clive finished the play in fourteen hours. We sent the play to Munich but did not hear from Ziggy for a week. It turned out that he had to fly to the States for a funeral. But perhaps two weeks later we received a phone call at our apartment on Rue Mabillon. "This stuff is kooky, Clive," Ziggy told my husband, "it's completely cockamamie." I shall never forget the sight of my husband on the phone, his beautiful long fingers stroking his long, slightly matted black beard, his eyes opening and closing almost spasmodically. "Do you not like it then, Ziggy?" he asked. "Like it?!" Ziggy replied. "I don't even *get* it!" And my husband burst out in laughter and said, "Yes, of course. Of course, yes."

It was the first play that Clive ever directed. By then, he had come to feel that he and he alone could truly animate his own vision, only he could understand it and translate it from his soul, to his words, to the stage. Also, at this time, not too many directors wished to work with Clive. He resented—he detested—any slight change from the text. On one infamous occasion he stopped in at the Haymarket Theatre to see how his "trilogy" of short plays [*Corpse, Coffin, Crypt*] was doing; in *Coffin* he noticed that instead of the semihemidemiquaver pause he'd written in at one point in the dialogue, the actor had turned it into only a semidemi pause. He got up from his seat and stormed the stage and closed the play down. He was like that, a difficult perfectionist, yes, but he was truly a brilliant, inspired artist.

A Can of Laughter in Hell is a one-man play and so Clive explained to

Ziggy that he, Ziggy, was a living, moving, breathing extension of Clive's soul on the stage. "You are my words, my thoughts, my nightmares become flesh, my very breath," he told Ziggy. "Okay, Clive," Ziggy said, "but maybe you wanna try some mouthwash then." Ziggy was always making Clive laugh—I can still see him laughing, the saliva cackling out of his mouth, cascading down his beard, dousing his Gauloise.

[Ziggy had to] affect a Cockney accent in the play and he did not need any coaching at all—it was miraculous how he just did it. And he had no problem committing the words to memory. Even though he was the only actor in the play, there was much for him to say—he interacts with props, such as chairs, shoes, a wireless, a broom, and with unseen creatures such as mice, cockroaches, and the ghosts of his lover and others. It's no exaggeration to say that after reading the play three times and rehearsing it but twice, he knew the play as well as the playwright himself. "It's almost as if he himself had written it," Clive told Ken Tynan. "At last, I have found my amanuensis [*sic*]! He makes my words sing, he dances my dance with limbs of fire."

There were two weeks of previews and things went very well in the first week. An audience usually left a Clive Bonteen play disturbed and dismayed, sometimes disgusted even, and this was Clive's desired effect. "No person should ever desire to see one of my plays twice," he once said. "If that happens, I have failed miserably." He told John Osborne once that he knew he'd succeeded if he ever saw a patron retching immediately upon leaving the theater. However, just a few days before the play opened—it was at the Old Vic, by the way—Ziggy granted an interview to the *Evening Standard* and told the reporter that he had no idea what the play was about, other than a man talking to a broom. "No idea at all, Mr. Bliss?" the reporter inquired. "Can you not even tell us the basic thrust?" "It's basically about me making a paycheck," Ziggy said. Clive read this but was not bothered by it—he even told Ziggy he appreciated that sort of ironical detachment. "He entirely inhabits his character off the stage," he wrote to Ken Tynan, "and it is frightening." However, two nights before the play opened, Ziggy gave another interview—it was to the *Guardian* this time—and he took it several steps further. He said that Clive had tried to write slapstick and vaudevillianesque sight gags but had failed embarrassingly. "I'm supposed to dance with a broom in a certain way, to do like a tango," Ziggy said, "and I do, just like Bonteen tells me to. But if it was up to me, I'd do it my own way and I'd get five times the laughs." The reporter asked him, "Mr. Bliss, do you know what the play is *about*?" and Ziggy Bliss replied, "Oh yeah . . . it's about forty-five minutes too long."

Well, Clive and he had a real, old-fashioned row about it the night before the premiere, a slanging match the likes of which I'd never seen

before or since. When Ziggy raised his voice, it really was like a cannon-
ade . . . he even broke the stage manager's glasses. Ziggy stuck to his guns;
he told Clive that he really did not understand the play, that he thought
when it tried to be tragic it was funny, and when it tried to be funny it was
tragic. Clive at first refused to believe this but then he accepted it and said,
"All right . . . but please do not tell every person in London that you do not
understand it! It makes you look the *idjit* you apparently are!" Further com-
plicating the matter, Ziggy was refusing to wear the cushion he was supposed to wrap around his waist; he said it was making him sweat too much.
But Clive insisted that he wear it. "Without the cushion," Clive screamed at
him, "you just look like any fifty-five-year-old Yid wasting away!"

They shouted and railed at each other for nearly an hour. It was brutal,
absolutely brutal. Clive could not stop stroking his beard, and Ziggy said
to him, "Keep lookin', Bonteen—maybe you'll find a cigarette in there."
"You were my vision and now you're nothing but an arsehole!" Clive
yelled at him, and Ziggy yelled back, "Hey, maybe it ain't me, maybe it's
your vision."

Well, Ziggy wore the lard cushion for opening night. For the first act
only. Actually, he took it off in the *middle* of the first act . . . and I must say,
this got the most laughter all night. "I don't need this girdle," he said as he
stripped himself of it. The audience thought it was part of the play and
erupted in laughter. I whispered to Clive, "Perhaps you should keep that in,
darling." But he said, "Shut the bloody hell up, Annie."

* * *

SALLY KLEIN: In 1973 my son and Vince were on LSD together in Los
Angeles, at a friend of their's house. I knew that Vince was doing drugs and
I knew that Donny and he were friends, but it didn't occur to me that
Donny was into that garbage too. He didn't dress like a hippie, he didn't
talk like one. He had a job, he had short hair, he wore a suit and tie, and
was a college graduate. It just didn't occur to me. When a policeman called
me and told me that my son was in the hospital because he had jumped out
of a window—even then it didn't occur to me.

Donny had severed his spine—he'd broken his legs and ruptured his
spleen too. He was paralyzed. I didn't tell Jack that night . . . it would've
killed him for sure. I went to the hospital alone and I saw Donny in his bed
and he didn't open his eyes and I kissed him on his hair—he had such beautiful brown curly hair. I spent the whole night holding his hand. Vince was
there and they had him on tranquilizers. The policeman told me what had
happened . . . there was a party, there were drugs, Donny was having a bad
LSD trip and freaking out or whatever you call it. And he jumped out the

window. My beautiful, wonderful boy lived for six months more but then he caught pneumonia and died.

When I told Jack that Donny was paralyzed he took it like he always took bad news. He kept it in. He didn't scream, he didn't cry or throw anything. He just withdrew into himself. To tell you the truth, after this happened, he didn't really say much afterward. He just kept to himself. He stopped going to the track, stopped reading the papers. He was a sad, broken man.

Ziggy was in Germany when Donny died and flew over with Pernilla for the funeral. Vic was at the funeral, so were his sister Cathy and his mother and many people from the old days: Billy Ross, Mickey Knott, Marty Miller. Vic and Ziggy did not exchange a word to each other, they didn't shake hands or hug or anything. Vince had trouble looking me in the face. He felt guilty and I don't blame him. Ziggy came over and hugged me. I looked at him and it was the first time I saw him as an adult, as a man, not as my funny-looking cousin from Echo Beach who peed on my father's couch. He was crying and he said, "Sally . . . poor Cousin Sally. I love you so much." He was devastated. Me, I wasn't devastated. You know what I was? I was dead inside.

Vic sent Guy Puglia over to me. Guy was also in tears. He and Donny had played softball and run on the beach together when Donny was a kid. And when we'd eat at Guy's restaurant he always put Donny on his shoulders and brought him into the kitchen. Guy gave me a hug and said he'd come over to sit shivah but that Vic couldn't. Because he knew that Ziggy would be there and that he didn't want to create an awkward situation. "He doesn't want to create one or he doesn't want to *be* in one?" I asked, and Guy shrugged.

Three months after this, I went to London to see Ziggy in that silly play he was doing for that nutty playwright. It had gotten tepid reviews. I'd seen a Clive Bonteen play in Los Angeles years before; it was about two mental patients in an insane asylum who turn out to be the same person, I think. Leaving the theater I'd asked Jack, "So? What did you think?" And he said, "I was thinking about the Dodgers, frankly."

But by the time I saw *Laughter in the Can* it wasn't really a Bonteen play anymore. He'd disavowed it, he had his name taken off the marquee and off the ads in the papers. You really would have thought that nobody wrote the play; the marquee just said ZIGGY BLISS IN . . . The play would never be staged again—no great loss. And it was funny now! I suppose Ziggy sort of kept to the script at first but then he just made the play his own. He gave it all he had—well, he was taking the pills then and I think that was a big part of it. He'd be dancing with a broom and then he'd toss the broom down and then he'd bring girls from the audience up on the stage and dance with them. He would lead games of Simon Says with the audience, and you know what else he did? He would sing "The Itty-Bitty Ditty," Danny's old song. And, of course, he'd toss in a few Vic references as well, like putting a noose around his head and singing "The Hang of It." Ziggy would be doing some of the original Bonteen dialogue—I guess you'd call it a monologue, since it was a one-man play—and then break into Yiddish or other accents. There were some people who'd seen the show four or five times, Ziggy told me, because you never did know what would happen. But after three months, Clive Bonteen closed it down—it wasn't his show anymore. And it was a good thing because I think it was exhausting Ziggy.

He came back to the States and toured with *Bam-Bam-Bamboozled* again. He had Hank Stanco contact Bonteen—for a brief while it looked like Ziggy might be able to put together a musical version of the Jack Benny bomb *The Horn Blows at Midnight*. Ziggy for some reason thought that Clive Bonteen might want to write the book for it. "The man loved it," Ziggy told me. "He said it was utterly magnificent." But Bonteen never returned Hank's calls.

DANNY McGLUE: Ziggy was always coming up with projects, with ideas. He tried to get a revival of *A Funny Thing Happened on the Way to the Forum* going but couldn't. He wanted to do something with *The Shop Around the Corner* but nobody would talk to him. He and I would meet at his house and start writing a play, but after a few scenes he'd lose interest. We tried TV, we tried movies, but he always eventually lost interest. He'd do a *Love Boat* or *Fantasy Island* once in a while. One time he did a *Circus of the Stars* show and I couldn't look at it, it was too excruciating to watch. Don Rickles had that *CPO Sharkey* show for a few seasons and that really burned Ziggy because he'd wanted to do a *Sergeant Bilko*-type show, but he couldn't get any network people to show interest. He couldn't get one meeting. So he'd tour with the *Bamboozled* play and open up for Steve and Eydie or for [singer] Julie Budd somewhere. That's how he put food on the table. That and those silly German movies, with all the blondes leaning over, holding beer steins and jiggling, and him doing voices, making faces and crossing his eyes.

 •   •   •

VICKI FOUNTAIN: You know, despite the rock 'n' roll and those psychedelic motorcycle movies I made, I never once took any drug other than penicillin. But Andy Ravelli told me that Dad took LSD two times. Before he married Taffy McBain, he had a wild year or two. You know, he once substitute-hosted *The Tonight Show* for Johnny Carson and came out in a Nehru jacket and love beads. People forget that. Now, he hated rock 'n' roll music but this was like a second childhood for him. He was going out with Imogen Driscoll, the British model, at the time—she was the famous Rodolfo Negri model. Cary Grant had told Daddy about LSD and Dad had said, "Sounds like a few Manhattans too many. That don't scare me." He asked Vincent if he knew where he could get some and, an hour later, Daddy had some. He made sure, though, to never tell the press that he'd taken it. I guess he understood that he was a role model; back then you expected your role models to drink a lot, to chase girls and gamble and fight, but that was it.

He and Imogen took the LSD together. "This stuff has got me all wacky," he said. Ices Andy was there with them—he didn't take anything, just in case there was trouble.

"You okay, Vic?" Andy would ask him.

"Oh, baby, I'm soarin' all over the place over here, man," Dad said.

Everybody said Imogen was gorgeous, they called her the British Verushka, but I thought she was just a little too stringy. And it would've helped, a shower every now and then.

"You okay, Imogen?" Andy asked her.

"Everything's just smashing over here, luv," she said.

"Hey, puddin'," Vic suggested, "let's fly to Vegas. Right now."

"Oh, God no," Imogen said. "Let's not."

"Hey, Ices, put on some of my old music," Daddy said. "Let's see how 'Malibu Moon' sounds on this zany stuff."

"Oh, God no," Imogen said again. "Let's not."

I think after that experience, he got rid of Imogen Driscoll.

I married Johnny Hylan in 1973. Dad didn't like Johnny, but I don't think he ever approved of any of my boyfriends or husbands. Johnny was a child star, he'd been on *The Big Ranch* on NBC when he was a kid and had done a couple of movies since then. He was very, very handsome but he drank a lot. He was moody and had a horrible temper.

We'd been married for two years and one night, for no reason at all, Johnny hit me. Well, it wasn't for no reason—I knew he was cheating on me with [actress] Pam Newford. Now, to be honest, I'd been no angel either, *but he had no idea about that!* So I accused him about Pam—who was my friend—and he hit me and then, as soon as he hit me, he ran out of the house. I called Dad and he wasn't home but Joe Yung picked me up and brought me over. When Andy Ravelli saw the way I looked, well, he knew what'd happened. I asked him where Daddy was and he said that Pete Conifer had died and that Daddy was in Vegas. (Pete had died in one of those autoerotic stunts; he was doing something to himself with a toaster and another thing with panties around his neck.) Joe Yung put some ice on my face to ease the swelling, and I asked him, "So what's in the cellar here?" He said, "I not know, I not know. No one allow down there." I said, "Let's go check it out." He shook his head and waved his hands and said, "No one allow down there." I asked Joe if my father ever went down there and he said, "Yes. Many times. He in cellar many times. But he always alone."

Ices Andy called Dad at the Oceanfront and told him about me and Johnny.

It was sad how he reacted . . . it revealed to me how old people were getting. Daddy called Hunny and told him to work over Johnny so he never could get an acting part again unless it was in a commercial for mashed potatoes. But Hunny was in such bad shape—*he couldn't beat anyone up!* He couldn't even swat a mosquito anymore. It was sad to me that Daddy still thought that Hunny could hurt anyone.

It went all wrong. A week later I was back home, with Johnny. The doorbell rang and Johnny got it and it was Hunny at the door. Hunny had tried to sort of "goon" himself up; he had a black woolen ski mask on his head. But his head was so big that he had to slit the mask so it fit, and you could completely see his face. Johnny even said to him when he answered the door, "Hey, Hunny. What are you doing here?"

Hunny said, "I wanna speak to Johnny Hylan."

"It's me—Johnny," Johnny said. "What's with the Halloween getup?"

"Is this 430 South Holt?" Hunny said. "I'm lookin' for Vicki Fountain's home."

"Hunny," Johnny said, "it's me. Johnny Hylan. Vicki's on the couch."

"Hi," I said with a wave to him. "Why are you wearing a ski mask that's split open?"

And then Hunny threw a punch at Johnny. He missed him by two feet and fell to the ground. He hit his head against the open door. Johnny and I dragged Hunny into the house and put towels on his forehead. His head felt so strange—it wasn't like touching a person's flesh, it was more like foam padding, like in a car seat.

GUY PUGLIA: You know, before Hunny got the job as a greeter in Vegas, he moved back to New York, back to Yorkville. *What Is It?*, that game show he did for years, had been off the air for, Jesus, it had to be fifteen years by then. But you know what he'd do? At nine o'clock in the morning, which is when they used to tape that show, he'd still show up. He'd go to the theater to tape the show and the guard at the front desk would have to tell him that the show wasn't on the air no more. For five years, that went on.

And it was the same thing with his bar. For years after it closed, he still showed up at the Hunny Pot, thinking he had business to do. But it'd become a Chinese takeout joint by then. This big palooka with no teeth and with scars all over his big square head shows up every day at this place, and the Chinese guys—they didn't know what to make of Hunny—they had to turn him away. Once in a while they even called the cops. "My bar was right here," Hunny told the cops. "It was here yesterday, I swear it."

SNUFFY DUBIN: Who got Hunny the greeter gig? You think it was Vic? No way. Uh-uh. Vic never got anything for Hunny but girls and another round. I did it. When Pete Conifer bought the fucking farm with the toaster and the soiled panty hose, Wanda [Mrs. Pete Conifer] took over as entertainment director. First thing she did was hire Hunny as a greeter. No, that was the second thing. The first thing she did was have workmen seal up and plug up all the little peepholes and secret nooks and crannies that Pete had been using. The man had cameras over beds and over toilet stalls, for Christsake. It was a big job undoing all that.

So Hunny became a greeter. And it was pretty sad. He stands in front of the entrance to the casino with his gold silk robe on and championship belt. On the robe it said in red stitching THE MOLASSES MAULER. "Hey, champ," people would say to him and then slip a few casino chips into his jacket pocket. Five-dollar chips usually. And the thing is, Hunny'd never been a champion. He never contended for the crown. But still, they had this big gold belt and jewels made up for him, and there was more paste in that belt than in the Elmer's glue factory.

"Thanks for coming to the Oceanfront," he would say when he shook people's hands as they walked in or walked out. "Good to see ya here. Please come again." Jesus, it took the guy two weeks before he could even commit that to memory.

ARNIE LATCHKEY: *Golfing With Vic* was the one constant, the port in the storm. And it was Vic's idea too. See, Minnesota Fats had this *Celebrity Billiards* TV show for a while and each week he'd take on a celebrity in pool. Believe me, it wasn't Laurence Olivier or Dame Edith Evans chalking up their pool cues every week. Vic called me up one morning and told me to watch this show. I turned it on and said, "Yeah? So what? Dan Blocker is shootin' eight ball. Big deal." And he said to me, "Latch, we move this thing outdoors, you put a six-iron in my hands and replace Blocker with Jimmy Stewart, it's a gold mine."

He was right. And he could have used a gold mine at that point because the records were dying. Pacific Records dropped him and there were actually two years that Vic didn't have a contract, before we signed with Sherm Kaplan's Lodestar label. But those records didn't move either. You know,

Frank Sinatra, when his career was in the dumps, recorded a song with a barking dog. And Vic was worried that this was also his fate. "Latch, if it ever comes to that," he said to me once, "just have me put to sleep." But in the seventies he was saying, "Latch, if it ever comes to that, just make sure the dog don't sing better than me."

We took the *Golfing With Vic* idea to all the networks and nobody bit on it. "Come on," I said to some hotshot programming virtuoso at ABC half my age, "*Vic Fountain on a golf course!* Golfing with Hank Fonda! Talkin' Tinsel Town and tee shots! This couldn't sink if you filmed it aboard the *Andrea Doria!*" The guy wouldn't go for it, that *shmendrick*. And ABC was the one with that *American Sportsman* show! You had Curt Gowdy and some guest like Ernie Borgnine or Chad Everett stalking the wild Chihuahua in the wilds off Baffin Bay. I said to this Einstein in a Pierre Cardin suit, "Look, no rifles, no bullets, no carcasses, just fairways and greens and Vic." Nope. Threw us out on our asses. For years we shopped this around, knowing that this was beluga caviar at the end of our fishing line, not chopped liver. In 1972 I got a phone call from MIS-TV, which syndicated a few shows here and there, and they said they were interested. They were very wary, however, of working with Vic; they'd heard all the rumors about the drinking and gambling and skirt-chasing. I said to the man, "Look, that's the old Vic. You put Vic on a golf course and it's like you're working with a baby on sedatives with a pacifier in his mouth."

Within a year this show was on in every state in the country, including Alaska, and who knows if Alaska even has golf? Or grass! The show usually ran on Saturday mornings and was a half hour long. We got some big-name people too . . . Vic called in a lot of favors he'd done for people over the years. After the first two seasons, Vic got his golf buddy Tony Hampton to join up, to ease his burden. And then the next season we put Joe Yung on to drive them around in a cart and make everyone highballs. It was a fan*tab*ulous arrangement. You film for four days a month, you bring in George Peppard or Joey Heatherton, and then you edit and play around with the thing to give it some shape, texture, and *oomph*. A lot of times we'd have to bring Vic back in to the studio to do some narration since there really wasn't much going on at all. Or we'd film his half of a conversation he'd supposedly been having with a guest.

Like I said, this was a godsend for us, for Vic. It was an easy buck. And by the late seventies and early eighties, Vic was only taping one special a year for CBS. It used to be Vic would have an Easter special, a Christmas special, a Super Bowl special, a Thanksgiving special. Little by little they whittled it down. "They're takin' all the holidays away from me," Vic bemoaned to me once. They always let him do a Christmas show though. But then they finally took that one away too.

* * *

ERNIE BEASLEY: I'm an alcoholic. I was even an alcoholic as far back as the Brill Building days, when I heard all that laughter and jollity coming from the Vigorish offices. I lived in Greenwich Village then, on Jane Street in a little walk-up, and I had three things in that apartment: a mattress, a radio, and *always* a bottle of Jim Beam.

I needed to get help now. My money was going. I was just pissing it all away. For years I hung around with Vic, rode along on his coattails, and believe me that roller-coaster ride was a ball, but it was first-class and expensive. We'd go to Paris and stay at the Ritz or some other place and, sure, Vic footed the tab for the room but, still, I'm in Paris and I'm eating the best food and buying antiques and wining and dining boys. One week in 1964, we stayed at the Crillon and I met this beautiful boy named Phillippe, maybe nineteen years old. What a face this boy had, what gorgeous, smooth skin. We went everywhere together; I bought him clothing, furniture, anything he wanted; when Vic went back to California, Phillippe and I went to Honfleur together and spent a marvelous five days there, driving along the coast in a Citroën, drinking and eating and buying little tchotchkes. On the last morning, I woke up in our room and the bed was empty except for the bottle of Dom Pérignon I was cuddling. It was windy and the balcony doors were open and the curtains were blowing around. I went out to the balcony but Phillippe wasn't there either. He wasn't anywhere and there was no note and my wallet was empty.

Vic's music publishing company was called Straight Up With a Twist Music. Every song I wrote after 1952 was for Straight Up Music and was a Beasley and Fountain tune. Once in a while Vic would pass on a song and someone else would do it—Miss Leslie Wilson, Andy Williams, Vic Damone, Barbara McNair—but Vic always had the right of first refusal. Leslie Wilson had a hit with "He'll Fade Away" and when Vic found out I'd written it, he hit the roof.

"Why didn't you give me this song, Bease!?" he yelled at me. "Why didn't you show me this song first?! That's our deal!"

"I did," I told him. "I played it for you at the Ambassador two months ago. You said you weren't interested."

"Well . . .*yeah!* I mean, the song is that '*he'll* fade away.' I sing this song, they'll think I'm some kind of candy-assed *finocchio*. No offense."

"When I sang it for you, Vic," I told him, "it was '*she'll* fade away.' You passed on it, Miss Leslie Wilson's people liked it, and I changed the lyrics and retailored it for her."

"Well, enough of these alterations with my lyrics!"

But, of course, they were not his lyrics. They were mine. All of them.

When the hits dried up for him, when his records failed and when others succeeded, I was the whipping boy. When "Moon River" came out and was a huge hit, Vic took it personally.

"Why didn't you write this song?!" he called me on the phone and yelled.

"Because Henry Mancini already did," I explained to him.

"This is gonna be a smash for Andy Williams! And my last single didn't even make it past forty on the charts."

"I'm sorry. I'm trying."

"'Moonlight in Vermont.' 'Malibu Moon.' You used to do swell songs about the moon, Bease," he said to me. "What happened?"

"I don't know, Vic. I guess the moon dried up for me. And I didn't write 'Moonlight in Vermont.'"

"See! That's what I mean!"

And, my God, when the Rolling Stones or the Beatles had a big hit, he would let me have it even then too. He loathed that music. He had [folk singer] Melanie sing one of her hits on his Christmas special once—he mistakenly called her *Melanzane*—and I thought he was going to barf backstage. He always thought if I could get him the right song, he could top them.

So in the late sixties he stopped recording my songs. I tried everything I could for him, bossa nova, calypso, even a few country-and-western tunes for his *A Nashville Kind of Vic* LP. But it didn't work. So he passed on everything. And—and this was what destroyed me—he used his right of first refusal to prevent me from passing anything on to anybody else. He merely had to say he would *consider* recording a song, and then nobody else would be able to hear it. And nobody else did. Or, if someone wished to record one of my older standards, Vic used his power as "lyricist" to deny them use. If you've ever wondered why Sinatra never recorded "Someone Such as You," this is why.

It was a low point for me. I could not succeed and after a while, I could not write. I had a boy named Bradley living with me then, helping me around the house, driving me, dining with me. My weight was out of control . . . I was drinking morning to night and through the night if I couldn't sleep, which was the usual case. My weight—I went from a balloon to a blimp. Bradley left me too . . . he drove off in my Mercedes one day and was gone. You know, many of Vic's big songs were "signature" songs. "The Hang of It" was his "I Left My Heart in San Francisco"—you rarely hear anyone but Tony Bennett sing that song because who else would *dare* to? So nobody else was singing these songs but Vic. And the money was drying up.

Well, it was time for me to dry up too. My physician told me about the Hope Springs Clinic just outside Los Alamos, New Mexico, and, after much deliberation, denial, and, yes, getting blitzed, I packed my bag and went. I was there for six weeks and haven't had a drop to drink since.

One day at the clinic, I was talking to one of the orderlies there, a tall, goateed black man from Alabama named John Timmons. Big John, everyone called him. I was bragging about all the famous people I knew and somehow I mentioned Vic and Ginger Bacon. When I said Ginger Bacon I saw a tiny silvery twinkle in John Timmons's eye, and I said, "Do you know her?" He was reluctant to talk about it, probably because of patient confidentiality and all that rigmarole, but I kept pressing him.

[He told me] that Ginger Bacon had been a patient at Hope Springs about three years before. How do I know it was the same Ginger? Big John described her; the Ginger he described was a chain smoker, a mess of wrinkles and furrows and gray hair—which was *not* my Ginger, except for the smoking—but she had, he said, the longest legs he'd ever seen. And she still was a strawberry blonde. She'd gone through their rehab program and was just a week from being discharged when she bolted. They issued an APB for her but the police and state troopers couldn't find her. A week after she'd vanished, the clinic got a phone call from the Albuquerque police. Ginger had been found in a cathouse in Reno, Nevada . . . she'd worked there almost ten years before, it seems, and had fled back there. But poor Ginger—she was one of the dearest friends I ever had—had slit her wrists and was dead.

When I was discharged from the clinic, I went back to L.A. I sold my house in Malibu and moved to West Hollywood, to a much less grand place. I gave up the cars, the binge buying, and got a simple gray Honda Accord. I still had some money coming in—I never was broke, I'm glad to say. I lived within my means. I stopped letting younger men use me, except for every once in a while when the loneliness became too unbearable.

One day I was driving past the Riviera Country Club and I saw a location van; they were filming one of those horrendous *Golfing With Vic* shows. I got out of my car and made it to where they were filming . . . and there was Vic with Helen Reddy. I hadn't seen Vic for months. He came over to me and gave me a big hug and we did some brief catching up. A makeup girl was working him over and someone else took off his rug and replaced it with a new one. His real hair, I saw, was thinning and receding and was turning silver. But I only got a quick peek because there was only a half a second when he didn't have a toup on.

"So you cleaned up, huh, Bease?" he said to me. "No more booze."

I shrugged. I was proud of being clean but also, in Vic's presence, strangely embarrassed.

"You look good," he told me. "You must've lost a few pounds in that joint."

"I did. And I try to exercise too," I said.

"You should try this," he said, brandishing a putter. "This'll keep you in shape."

I refrained from mentioning that he was about thirty-five pounds overweight and that golfing seemed to me as much a means to losing weight as did eating cheesecake.

"Ginger Bacon," I said. "Remember her?"

"Oh sure," he said. "How could I ever forget Ginger? Gams like knitting needles."

"Well, she—" I began.

"And nipples just like nectarines too. How could I ever forget Ginger? Baby, we used to rip the town up, every single night. You couldn't stop me and her with quicksand."

"She's dead. I found out that she's dead."

He leaned forward in the canvas chair he was sitting in. The chair said VIC on the back of it in turquoise-blue lettering; the V was two crossed golf clubs and the i was dotted with a golf ball.

"Ginger's dead?" Already he was pale.

I nodded to him. I could feel tears welling in my eyes. It was a hot, sunny, cloudless day and I was sweating and so was Vic.

"Oh, Jesus," he said.

He wanted to know how she died and I told him I didn't know. But I am not a good liar, so he insisted on knowing. When I told him, I could see that he was shaken, genuinely shaken.

The director told him that it was time to start filming. Vic stood up and started walking away from where they were supposed to film. He was doubling over . . . it was like he was in pain, his stomach must have been cramping or throbbing with agony. He made it to his trailer and had to lean on it for a second, then he walked in, slammed the door, and didn't come out.

SALLY KLEIN: After I don't know how many performances of the *Bamboozled* play, Ziggy took some time off. He'd head over to Germany once in a while to make one of those silly sex farces, he'd appear in a lounge someplace, he'd tape a *Love Boat* episode. He did a little turn on a *Cannon* episode and he really did think he'd get an Emmy nomination for it, but they passed him by and he was disconsolate. He also did a *Baretta* and hoped that the role would be recurring, but at the very last minute they decided to kill off his character. Then he began touring in something called *Va-Va-Vamoose*. More jiggling, more bulging eyes.

After years and years of being banished from the talk shows, radio as well as TV, we got a call from people working for someone named Rick Dees, who had a late-night talk show for a few minutes on ABC, I think.

They would love to have Ziggy go on the show, they said. "When do you want him?" Arnie asked, and they said, "What's he doing tonight?" "Did someone drop out of your lineup or something?" Arnie asked them, and the guy admitted that, yes, some young comic had had to cancel at the last second. Ziggy did the show and he was okay for a few minutes, on the couch talking. He wore a red wig now and it was pretty obvious it was a wig. And he'd lost weight . . . he wasn't round, he was barely oval. He had a slight paunch and that was all. He sweated up a storm as he spoke and, sure enough, after five or so minutes he started carping about Vic. At one point he got up and began talking to the audience and he was very funny and then it happened: He wanted to say something, he had a joke inside his head and it was hysterical, but he couldn't bring himself to say it.

When he was talking about Vic and making fun of him and his movies—and Vic hadn't done a movie for years—you could practically hear every television producer and every booking agent take their hands off their phones and lose interest.

ARNIE LATCHKEY: The more fathoms their careers sank, the closer they got to the bottom of the sea, the more people would ask if Fountain and Bliss would ever reunite. When Pacific Coast Records dumped Vic, a few reporters asked him, "Does this mean you and Ziggy might consider teaming up again?" Vic shot them a look that took ten years off their lives.

But Ziggy, he made up these stories, that he and Vic were still close buddies. I saw him on Dinah Shore's show, I couldn't believe it. "Do you ever see Vic?" Dinah asked Ziggy, and Ziggy said that he and Vic had had dinner together only a few weeks ago. I called up Vic and asked him, "Did you have dinner with Ziggy recently?" And Vic said, "Yeah, as recently as twenty-three years ago."

DANNY McGLUE: Brillo was going to ink Ziggy to do commercials for them in the mid-eighties but the deal fell through at the last second. I don't know what it was. It could have been because they realized his hair wasn't really his hair anymore, and that was the whole connection with Brillo to begin with. It would have been a great thing for Zig, the commercials, it would've put him right back in the public consciousness. There's also the possibility that the old Ziggy resurfaced, the Ziggy who raised hell on the set, who would spray the director with seltzer or something. I don't know what happened.

I kept seeing comics all the time on TV who owed so, so much to Ziggy. They'd grown up seeing him on television, they'd seen the movies. All the comics who switch characters in the blink of an eye, who just start riffing away to the edge of nowhere, who get up there and *shpritz* themselves dry to the point that it's like bleeding—they all, every single one of them, owe a great big debt to Ziggy Bliss.

JANE WHITE: Ziggy and I were always very courteous with each other, after the divorce. When you love someone, I don't know if you ever can really stop loving that person. Whenever I needed him, he was always there for me. And I tried to be there for him. One time I went to his house on North Irving—I couldn't believe how humble it was. It wasn't a house, it was one of those smallish apartment complexes. He had only three rooms there and there was a small pool that everyone in the building shared. The pool Ziggy had put in when we were married, at the house where I was living and still live, was in the shape of a great big smile. But this pool was like a postage stamp! And he had a Ford, I think, an Escort.

Pernilla and I got along, considering. We wanted to make things easy for Freddy. But . . . Freddy and I drifted apart. He pretty much stopped speaking to his mother. (As I understand it, a year or two ago he even had himself circumcised and bar mitzvahed. Can you believe that?)

I was at a spa one day and I saw a headline in one of those horrible tabloids. The headline was something like "FORMER FUNNYMAN FOUND FILMING X-FLIX." I was stunned.

He was arrested in Oklahoma, at a motel, where he was touring with the *Vamoose* play. He'd been making those nasty, atrocious movies with video equipment, with a camera. The girls in the play were the actresses and I guess there was no trouble getting actors to do that sort of thing, the way that most men are. But what must have been terrible to Ziggy was that he was in some of the movies too. And there were pictures of him in the paper—in many papers all over the country—naked with some young woman. It was very sad, seeing the way he looked. I was only three years younger than he but he had wrinkles and, even though he was surprisingly thin, he still had pockets of flab all over his thighs. Fortunately, they blacked out his private parts. Someone told me you could send away for a bootleg tape for $29.99.

He got out on bail and returned to Los Angeles. I called him and told him that I would do anything I could for him, that I didn't believe what I was reading. I asked him if Pernilla—who was not involved—was "standing by her man," and he told me she'd left him. He sounded very depressed to me. He didn't even sound like him. There was no anger—it was just resignation.

I said if he needed anything, to just let me know. He said, "I want my old life back."

PERNILLA BORG: I knew that Ziggy once had liked the dirty movies. He had told me this once, when we first were a couple. But he told me that I was his "dream come true"—that was the words he used. And that he did not need another woman because of me. I believed him.

Always I had men trying to be close with me. Always. Football players, actors, businessmen. Ever since the Top Brass ads. A man walked up to me once in a grocery store and asked me to say my line from that commercial— "I want to get it all over you." I said it to this man and I see he is playing with himself. I remember one time in Atlantic City, Ziggy did a show in a lounge there. I did a little thing with him for five minutes, what you call a "bit." And then a half hour later when the show is over, I hear some man in the audience say to another man, "How does an ugly Jew like that get a beautiful broad like her?" And I suppose this is what many men think.

When Ziggy and I married, he tells me that many years ago there was a woman. His first girlfriend. He tells me he used to think about her a lot, he thinks she is the only woman who ever really liked him. But now he does not think of her anymore. Because he knows I love him. I do not care if he performs in a room with one person in it or one million or if he works in a gas station. He is my Ziggy.

When I find out about Ziggy making these movies my heart is broken. I cried and cried and cried. I did everything for him. Some of those football players, maybe I should have married them, yes? But I stayed with Ziggy. And now he is making these dirty movies.

"Is it true?" I asked him on the phone. "Do you make these movies?"

"Yeah. It's true," he said.

"Why? Why? I thought you love me."

"I do. I swear to God I do."

"Then why?"

"Why? I don't know. Maybe because I'm a man, I guess is the answer. And there isn't a man alive who ain't some kinda pig deep down inside."

I moved out. I got a lawyer who is telling me to divorce him. But I think of my life without Ziggy, without him making me laugh, singing silly songs to each other and eating meals and waking each other up, without all the funny times we have, and it's a very sad life. I did not want to divorce Ziggy and a year later I am living with him again.

SALLY KLEIN: It came on the news that night, it was the last story. I couldn't watch. They played some old footage from *Anchors Oy Vey*, they showed Ziggy performing with Vic at a nightclub, then they showed a few seconds of one of the movies he was making, the dirty movies.

There was no Morty Geist anymore to clean this mess up. There wasn't even a Bertie Kahn. And now my husband was dead too.

I had nobody to talk to. I would wake up and the bed was empty, it was just me. I'd go to bed at night and there was no one. Just me. Everyone thought that Jack would die of a heart attack, but somehow that didn't happen. But he went quickly and painlessly, thank God.

When Jack passed away, Jane White called me up, tried to offer me some solace, a few friendly words. She said that after I was through with my mourning we should go out for lunch, maybe go someplace for a few days, like Acapulco or Palm Springs. She said we should go shopping. And when she said that, it came back to me: I had never liked this woman. So I told her I would call her and I never did.

But Lulu, sweet Lulu . . . she was so nice to me. She came over every day with food, with flowers. She cleaned the house, she answered the mail and the phone. She cooked for me. And all the time talking as though Vic would come back to her.

One day she was making me a sandwich and the news came over the radio: The Fratelli brothers were dead. It was some big mob thing. They'd rubbed each other out, shot each other in the kneecaps and died. Lulu didn't seem too upset about it.

DANNY McGLUE: Ziggy called me up one night, put on Oliver Hardy's voice, and said, "Now look at the fine mess I've gotten myself into." I told him this wasn't a mess, it was a landfill.

"I'm the world's biggest idiot," he said to me.

"If that didn't sound like the name of one of your old movies," I told him, "I might agree with you."

"Where did I go wrong?" he asked me. "Exactly where?"

"I think we might need a world atlas to work that one out," I answered.

SNUFFY DUBIN: Jesus fucking Christ, I'm thinking when this story breaks, how the hell did they black out that *shvantz* of his in the papers? There must be a massive shortage of black ink in the world right now!

I was headlining at Caesar's in Vegas at the time . . . Vic was playing somewhere, I think the MGM Grand, I'm not sure. He calls me up and we spoke about the whole thing.

"He's going through a bad time right now, Vic," I said.

"He must be. That big Swede he's married to. You'd think that'd be enough for him."

"*You're* telling me this?! You of all people! There's a hundred chicks in this town with your fingerprints permanently embedded into their shoulder blades!"

I asked him if it had occurred to him to call up Ziggy and maybe offer a word of support and all he said was, "Yeah, it occurred to me."

But this is America, the Land of the Second Chance. A few months after this whole porno thing, Ziggy becomes a hot commodity again. It actually boosted his career. I'm playing Caesar's again and he's working the lounge there. And he hadn't played Vegas in years!

I stopped in and saw the act. Life is one strange fucking journey, ain't it? Ziggy's not telling jokes, there's no punch lines, no one-liners. He's talkin' about Vic, he's talkin' about growing up and playing the Catskills years ago, he's telling funny stories about the whole porno movie thing, poking fun at himself. Christ, at one point he was about to say something and I thought he was gonna blow to bits, it seemed so funny. What he's doing is excavating his life, digging way, way deep into the wounds and sores that hurt if you even look at them. Decades ago, Ziggy would call me up in a panic 'cause he needed jokes. He wanted me to help him out. And here he was, in front of maybe seventy people, and he was doing my act!

• • •

VICKI FOUNTAIN: I'd put out two albums and then a *Greatest Hits* LP but things weren't going well: two failed marriages, two failed children. *The Spy from B.L.O.N.D.E.*, which I did for NBC and which I thought would last forever, was canceled in its second season. So the last thing I needed in my life was to be worrying about what Vincent was up to. There were times when he vanished, when we didn't know where he was for weeks at a time. Daddy would hire private detectives to find him, but they never could. He would resurface every once in a while—he looked terrible, like he hadn't slept for a week—and tell me he was trying to put another band together, and then he'd disappear again.

But Donny Klein dying was one great big slap in the face for Vincent. He did a complete U-turn in his life.

He cut his hair. He put all his hippie clothes into a garbage can and burned them. He and Daddy spent a long weekend together in Palm Springs. Me, Mom, Grandma, Vincent, and Daddy had dinner a few times together too. He gave up smoking, he wouldn't even drink coffee . . . he was very serious about cleaning himself up.

You wouldn't know it was the same Vincent. He lost his baby fat, was lean, handsome, and serious. Daddy was almost proud of him. There'd always been this tension between the two of them—it's that way a lot between fathers and sons. Daddy and Arnie made a few phone calls, and Vince did a demo for Pacific Coast Records. It wasn't the acid hard rock he'd been doing; it was the kind of classic American standards that Daddy sang. Vincent had a beautiful voice. I heard Daddy once say, "The kid sings better than me." But he never admitted that in public or to the newspapers.

Vincent cut an album—*Vince on Vic*—and did a lot of interviews to promote it. He told all the stories about what it was like to be Vic Fountain's kid, he told about the rock music and the drugs. He looks great on the album cover, in a tuxedo holding a cocktail, underneath a photo of Daddy. The record is Vincent singing all of Vic's big hits, "The Hang of It," "Malibu Moon," "Lost and Lonely Again," "Moonlight in Vermont." There are moments, many of them, when you could swear it was Daddy singing. It was eerie.

But the album didn't sell and neither did the next one, *In-Vince-ibly Yours,* which was for RCA Victor. He toured all over the country, he knocked his brains out. He'd play some club in the middle of nowhere and there'd be only twenty people there. Daddy put him on his final Christmas special . . . but Daddy always had to get a dig in. After they finished a duet, he said, "Hey, you ain't bad, kid." And Vince said, "Gee, thanks, Pop." And Dad said, "You ain't bad, you're *terrible!*"

The charade went on for years. He married Patti, they had a son [Little Guy]. They lived in Venice, had a small place there near the beach. Only rarely did I get a hint that something was wrong. If we had a lunch date, for instance, he'd turn up late or cancel at the last minute. After RCA let him go he left Patti for a month, vanished, then went back to her. Snuffy Dubin would do favors for him and have Vincent open for him often, in Vegas, Tahoe, Atlantic City. But usually Vincent was opening for worse, a lot worse. The hecklers were merciless; they'd shout to him in the middle of the song, "Get lost, kid! Where's your father?" Or sometimes even, "Where's Ziggy?" There were no record deals. One clue that let me know something was wrong was that he'd ask me for money. It'd be $200 one week, $30 the next. There'd be a few weeks when he didn't need any, then he'd call me up and tell me he needed another hundred. In 1985 or '86, he left Patti and moved into a small motel in Redondo Beach. Patti would call me up, telling me that Vincent wasn't giving her money for Little Guy, so I'd call Daddy and Daddy would have Shep Lane write her a check. "What's with that crazy boy sometimes?" Daddy said to me.

I got a phone call in 1989 at three in the morning. It was a reporter from the *Los Angeles Times* and he wanted my reaction to my brother's death. I thought it was a prank. (Do you have any idea how many people would call me at some ungodly hour and ask me to frug with them and then hang up the phone?!) I said to this piece of dirt, "My brother's *what?*" And he told me Vincent had been found dead of a heroin overdose in the front seat of his white Buick LeSabre.

DANNY McGLUE: My one wish is that Vince would have succeeded with his rock 'n' roll band or at least been given a chance. Vic should've been more supportive. *So he didn't like the music!* Big deal! It was his son. You only get so many opportunities with your kids.

I saw Vince perform his lounge thing a few times. I caught up with him in New York, at the Rainbow Room, and I saw him at Harrah's once, with Guy and Edie. Now, I'm no mind reader or anything, but I could sense something wasn't right. I just felt it. He'd sing maybe fifteen songs, he'd snap his fingers, or close his eyes and turn on the charm and romance for a slow number. But it didn't seem remotely authentic to me. It only seemed remote.

"He's just goin' through the motions," Guy whispered to me while Vince was singing some torch song.

"He's got great pipes," Edie said. "But there's something's missing."

"It's called conviction," I said.

Patti told me only a year ago that Vincent didn't like the music he was singing. It was all an act. He hated what he was doing, he despised it. He must've been on autopilot. "It's like it's not me that the voice is coming out of," he told her.

ERNIE BEASLEY: Vincent's death destroyed Vic. It did. Joe Yung drove us to the funeral and Vic was so shaken up, he'd left the house without his rug on. We had to go back and get it. It put ten years on his face in one day—he was a wreck. He moved back in with Lulu the day after Vincent died.

Any chance father and son would ever truly connect was now gone forever.

Vic took a year off from performing. He stayed in the house a lot, watched game shows, talk shows, and soap operas. After a few months Guy and I tried to rouse his interest—we said, "Hey, let's go to Vegas, we'll shoot some dice, we'll goof around with Hunny." And he almost went. But he said, "Nah, I'll just stay here and watch *General Hospital*. Maybe next week."

You couldn't bring up Vince . . . you could never mention his name or allude to him. It was the most forbidden of all subjects. His old bandleader, Billy Ross, once expressed his condolences and Vic never spoke to him again.

Ziggy called Vic. A few days after Vince died. He called Lulu's house and asked to speak to him, and Vic told her he'd call Ziggy back. But she insisted he get on the phone. They spoke for a minute. Ziggy offered his condolences, asked him if there was anything he could do for him. Lulu told me that Vic said, "No . . . but thanks for calling me, buddy. I really do appreciate it."

A few days later Vic moved out of Lulu's place.

ARNIE LATCHKEY: The press are jackals, they're vultures—sure, everyone knows that. But the key in this business is to make them *your* jackals, *your* vultures. So, Vincent isn't in the ground one week and already here come all the goddamn vultures. The press found out what we'd been doing on Vic's TV specials. I don't know who the leak was, I got no idea if it was someone on the set or in the orchestra, but if I ever find out who the Deep Throat was I'll wring it so hard it won't be so deep anymore, let me tell you, my friend! What we'd been doing, see, was that Vincent had been singing the songs. For maybe four years. And Vic was lip-synching to them. Vic didn't have the time or the energy to sit down with a band and sing "Silent Night" or "Have Yourself a Merry Little Christmas," which, by the way, is not such an easy tune to warble. But Vincent did. And, besides, he sounded a lot more like Vic now than Vic did. So we'd bring Vincent in and he'd record the songs. Even on Vic's final record with the Lodestar label, it's Vince on four or five numbers. The press found out about it and printed it.

To reveal to the world that we were doing this, only a week after Vic lost his son, was the lowest of the low. In the old days, when these termites had some measure of class, they would have waited. Vic was down, he was in the real lower depths, boy. And now they were kicking him again and again. You get kicked in the head a hundred times like this, you're never the same.

He disappeared for a while. I'd get a call every now and then from him. He told me he was taking it slow. I ran into Ices Andy one day and he told me that Vic had had a colostomy only two weeks before. I had no idea.

The next time I saw him perform—it was a year later, in Tahoe—he was having trouble remembering the words. To songs he'd sung hundreds, thousands of times. He was slurring the words, he was making up lyrics or jumbling them. I noticed that the hand holding the mike was trembling too. When he came to the part when he had to sing "*Now, I've got the hang of it, I've got that Sturm and Drang of it, I've got the yin and yang of it,*" he garbled it, stopped the band, and then said, "So who the hell were Yin and Yang anyways, some Peking comedy team?" It got a laugh but Estelle and I were mortified.

I know what you're thinking: Vic often slurred his words, he often forgot lyrics, that was his style. But this was different. This was an older man now. An old man. This was a guy who'd been around, who'd drank a lot and lived hard and who'd rocked and rolled atop the world, but now that very same world had run him over like a goddamn eighteen-wheeler.

GUY PUGLIA: Nobody was coming to my seafood joint anymore. If I could get twenty people in there on a Saturday night, that was to me a good night. A lot of my usual customers, they got old, they retired, or they moved or died. And I'll be honest with you—the place was an old-style restaurant. The decor, the menu, the waiters. Me. Nobody drank old-fashioneds anymore, or Manhattans. You had all these new restaurants springing up, all these clubs, and half the patrons are in the bathroom snorting that cocaine or doing who-knows-what.

We changed the place around a little. We livened the joint up as best we could, we spruced the menu up. But nobody knew about it because they drove right by us on the highway. I tried to get some publicity, and this reporter says to me, "Oh, is that the place with no windows, where Vic Fountain once beat up a reporter?" I hung up on the sonuvabitch bastard.

With the banks and my suppliers closing in, I shut the place down. It was a sad day for me. Thirty years of my life. Gone. I'd had some good fuckin' times in there. It used to be quite a place—the celebrities, the athletes, reporters, politicians, cops, and robbers. And now the place was boarded up and there's a crane taking off the sign that said GUY'S SEAFOOD JOINT.

Vic—he was part owner—had been tellin' me for years to close the joint down. But I resisted. One reason was the place was like my home, it was like *me*. It was all I knew. But I was married to Edie now, so, you know, when it happened, it happened.

Edie and me, we didn't do nothin' for a while, we just drove around, went to movies and stuff. We was godparents to Vincent's little boy and we spent a lot of time with Patti and Little Guy. But alls of a sudden Edie says to me, she says, "You know, you could open up another restaurant, a smaller place."

"Yeah? What kind of place?"

"Seafood, Guy. But maybe a shack or something. Something small."

"Yeah," I says to her, "we had these places on the boardwalk in Codport. Lobster rolls, fried clams and steamers, oysters, all that stuff."

"It's not a bad idea, is it?" she said to me.

I told her that maybe I'd give it some thought.

For months that was all I thought about. I kept seein' me in this little seafood hut, slapping together an oversize lobster roll for someone, shuckin' some oysters, maybe scoopin' some Italian ices. I didn't think of nothing else. It was like when you're fifteen years old and alls you think of is girls, but now, Christ, I'm in my sixties and I'm dreaming about lobster rolls.

I says to Edie one day, "All right, I'm gonna mention it to Vic about this Guy's Seafood Shack idea."

"You don't have to mention it to Vic!" she says to me.

"Whaddaya mean? He's gotta know about this."

"Why?"

"Huh?"

"Why?" she said. "Why does he have to know?"

And for the life of me, I couldn't answer her question.

I opened up the shack right on Venice Beach. No publicity, no press, no big ballyhoo, as Arnie would call it. Just great food, a few benches and a sign, and me in my kitchen whites. And I'll kiss your ass right now if me and Edie didn't nail that big plastic swordfish to the wall.

Oh yeah . . . you look out the little window of the hut and what do you sea? The ocean, the great big blue Pacific Ocean. 'Cause it's all around the joint.

A month later Vic finds out about it, finds out I've got this operation goin', he hits the roof.

EDIE PUGLIA: It might have been Hunny who told Vic. Guy and I went to Las Vegas to check up on Hunny. He was doing his greeting thing at the Oceanfront. It took him a while to remember us . . . Guy said to him, "Hey, Hunny, what's goin' on?" and Hunny said, "Thanks for coming to the Oceanfront. Good to see ya here." "Hunny, it's me—Guy," Guy said. "Good to see ya here," Hunny said. "Welcome to the Oceanfront. Please come again."

After a few minutes he realized who we were, and Guy told him about the seafood shack. I don't gamble and Guy hadn't placed a bet for years, except very rarely at the track. (He and Jack Klein would go but after Jack stopped going, Guy stopped too.) Hunny said the next time he was in Los Angeles he would stop by and get some steamers. "They're on the house, Hun," Guy said. Then we said good-bye and Hunny said to us, "Thanks for coming to the Oceanfront. Please come again."

Maybe it wasn't Hunny who told Vic, because maybe Hunny didn't remember it.

You know, a few months later we stopped in on him again. He wasn't standing on his own power anymore. But he wasn't sitting either. People were slipping betting chips into his jacket, tipping him, and he was tilting. Guy told me that Hunny had too much pride to be piled like an old coat into a wheelchair, so they put a hook on his gold championship belt and fastened that to the wall behind him, and that kept Hunny standing.

And he was saying less and less. He was just saying, "Good to see ya here" and nothing else. That way, Guy explained to me, he didn't have to keep track of whether people were walking into the casino or walking out.

* * *

PERNILLA BORG: The moneys from the movies kept Ziggy going. The movies he has done with Vic, the movies he has done in Germany. But he was hardly ever making these movies now. The reason is because he did not look like himself anymore. Yes, he had the wig and he also had the fat pillow, but he still did not look like him.

There was going to be some sort of [a roast for] him in New York by the Friars Club and he gets very happy for this. But it is then canceled. They wanted to get Vic for the dais but he says he has previous engagement. Without Vic they do not salute Ziggy.

Some people would come to us with offers. There is talk of bringing back the *Tattletales* game show, but this fizzles. So does bringing back the *Win, Lose, or Draw* game show. There is talk of Ziggy in little roles in many movies, but this fizzles too.

In 1992 Ziggy woke up and has pain hurting his left eye. He could not see out of this eye. I drive him to Cedars-Sinai and he is brought into the emergency room. Many hours later a doctor tells me that we have to take out the eye right away. Does Ziggy know this? I ask, and this doctor—I did not like the way he is looking at me; he knows me from the Top Brass commercials, I can see this—tells me, no, he was unconscious. It is very tough decision for me. But I know that I have done right thing. So they operate on him and then he has a glass eye.

When I bring him home he's very sad. For a very long time. Cousin Sally comes over, Danny comes over, Arnie and Estelle come over. He does not want to see them. They are showing his old Robin Hood movie on the television one day but he wants me to shut it off. He loses more weight, walks out of house without the wig on. His head . . . there are now only a few little red hairs on it. Sally comes over one day and tells him that Vic Fountain had called her and said he hopes that Ziggy is feeling better. "Did he really say this, Sal?" Ziggy asks. "Yes, he did," Sally says. Ziggy smiled and then he starts feeling better.

A few months later he is in Germany to make a movie. He flies to Munich but is told at his hotel they do not need him anymore. I tell him he can go to Sweden and visit my mother.

He flies to Stockholm and there they try to kill him.

ARNIE LATCHKEY: Estelle and I did everything to get him out of the funk. But some funks, when they're self-inflicted, it's like a pair of really tight pants: You got yourself into them, only you can get yourself out. There was an offer from some company to do a wacky Ziggy Bliss exercise video. We tossed that his way and he said no. He actually passed on something! That's how low he was.

But he calls me one day and says, "Arnie, is there any slight, vague, faint ghost of a chance that Vic and me could team up together?"

I say to him, "Was there ever a chance that Adolf Hitler and Golda Meir would wed?"

"Nah, serious. Think about it. Me and him was lightning in a bottle."

"Well, this is true, Zig," I told him, "but that bottle is old and shattered and I think the lightning might now be a firefly on dialysis."

"I disagree, Latch. When you got it once, you never lose it. And me and him, we got it. 'Member what Westbrook Pegler called us? 'Table tennis with a comet.'"

"People still ask me every day if you two are gonna ever hook back up . . ."

"People ask me too. I bet they ask Vic. What do you tell them?"

"I tell 'em to leave me the hell alone."

"Look, imagine how much publicity it'd generate. We do two weeks in Vegas, it'd be the biggest thing ever hit that burg since those A-bomb tests. We'd be all over the news, everywhere. People would be getting sick of us all over again."

"I just don't know about this, Ziggy."

"Just mention it to Vic. Would ya? Do that for me?"

I didn't do it. I couldn't bring myself. I couldn't bring myself to have to call Ziggy back up and tell him that Vic had turned him down.

Maybe he understood my untenable position because he calls me a week later and asks me, "Hey, I got an idear: Vic plays in Vegas and I open up for him. I do my *shpritz* for thirty minutes and then he comes on. He and I wouldn't even have to share a stage."

I screwed up my courage and said, "Zig, I can't do it."

ERNIE BEASLEY: There was still some demand for Vic, even into the nineties. The old records still sold, the old Pacific Coast label material. And anyone in their fifties or sixties or even their forties, if they were in Vegas or Atlantic City, or if Vic was performing in their town, they were curious to see him, to see if he still "had it."

But he didn't still have it. Everything caught up with him all at once. The booze and the Chesterfields, the broads, the late nights. He went to a doctor and they turned him inside out. He went on the talk shows—they were old Danny McGlue jokes—and said, "Traces of blood were found in my alcohol," or "They found a liver on my spot." The doctor told Vic to lose some weight, to give up the sauce, and Vic said he'd try, but he didn't, not right away. After they fiddled with his prostate gland, they found that there really wasn't one thing in particular that was ailing Vic, except the whole package was slowly breaking down. The only thing life-threatening was his life, I guess, and the way he'd lived it.

He was a mess in concert. At first he didn't know it. He thought it was funny. But when a man cannot remember to sing the word "moon" after singing the word "Malibu . . ."

He tried to coast on the old Vic Fountain charisma, and it worked for a while. When he screwed up, he'd just glide over it, make a booze joke. He'd say something like, "How do you expect me to know this song? I've only had four martinis!" But then, with the quivering hand and the liver spots coming in, he couldn't coast anymore.

I remember one time in Atlantic City when he couldn't get through

"Lost and Lonely Again," a heckler stood up and yelled, "Hey, Vic! You sure *are* lost! Maybe you should get your son to sing for you!" It was a horrible, horrible thing to say, on so many levels. And I'll never forget the look on Vic's face. He was frazzled, anguished—he looked utterly devastated. He walked off and canceled the rest of the engagement.

"I don't have it anymore, Bease," he said to me.

"Sure you do," I said.

"Nah," he said. "It's over. I lost it, baby."

GUY PUGLIA: Vic hated it, that I was runnin' my seafood shack. It really got under his skin. He didn't like that it was seafood, that it was on the beach; he didn't like that it was doing well. Mostly, I think he didn't like it that I was finally doing something without him. But he didn't ever come out and say that.

"You should come check the place out, Vic," I said to him once.

"I'll pass, thank you."

I'd been seein' him less and less. That all started when Vince died. I tried to help him out. I tried but he didn't want no help. He just wanted to watch soap operas and game shows and drink. And I understood that.

Now, me and Vic, we'd had a few blowups over the years. We had 'em when we was at the Monroe, we had 'em when he was on the road with Don Leslie's band and with Ziggy. We had 'em back in Codport, too, way back when. But the biggest one ever was about Hunny.

Me and him flew to Vegas to see Hunny one night. Vic downed about nine scotches on the plane, he just kept 'em coming. I'd heard that Hunny was havin' some problems, even more so than usual. He was in his usual spot, at the casino door, fastened there. But even with the hook to his belt, he could hardly stand up. All those chips in his jacket pockets was weighin' him down, sure, but he was having trouble even without that. And he couldn't talk no more, he couldn't say the thing they had him sayin'. Alls he could say was, "Good." He couldn't even say, "Good to see ya here."

"Hunny, it's me and Vic," I says.

"Good," he says.

"What's shakin', Hun?" Vic asked him.

"Good," Hunny says.

Vic and me flew back that night. And I had all kinds of thoughts in my head. Vic had about seven more drinks on the plane. He was as bagged as I'd ever seen him.

We were on the front steps of his house. He was wobbling even though he wasn't walking.

"Hunny's in bad shape, Vic," I said.

"Yeah. He is."

"We gotta put him in a hospital. We gotta give him some dignity."

"Hey, he's happy. He's got that belt and the robe, all those chips."

"That ain't dignity."

He said, "He's so far out of it he don't know what's goin' on."

I felt myself get all red. I felt nerves in my fingertips light up.

"I'm worried about you too, buddy," I says to him.

"You're worried about *me?*" he says.

"Yeah. You don't care about Hunny!"

"What? I gotta listen to some guy steams clams for a living telling me he's worried about *me?!*"

"What's wrong with you?" I said.

"Go shower somewhere, get that smell off—"

"Look, can we maybe—"

"Why do you think Bogart and you once got gassed together, huh? Why do you think that you and Gleason went to the fights a few times or all those big shots went to your lousy fuckin' restaurant? Why did all those fat broads let you fuck them? Did you ever wonder why? You had lunch with Rita Hayworth once, remember? Ever think why? You think they all wanted to be with some dumb, sawed-off dago without a nose? Nah . . . it's 'cause you was with me. These people didn't want to have nothing to do with Gaetano Puglia from Codport. Nothing. But you were my buddy so they put up with you. You and your fuckin' no nose."

"Hey, do you know why I lost my nose, Vic? Do you have any idea?"

"Yeah, it was Straccio . . ."

"But do you know *why?* I lost my nose because I was trying to protect *you.* I lost years and years of my goddamn life because of you. I never had a life until a few years ago, because I had *your* life! Why do you think Hunny's the way he is, how he don't even know his own name? 'Cause you kept him fighting when he should've hung up the gloves! Why is your son dead? Why do men treat Vicki like she's a piece of meat and Ginger wound up dead in a whorehouse?! I got no nose and Vincent's dead and Hunny is a goddamn vegetable, all because of *you!* I don't give a fuck about any big shots and never did. I just wish I'd never given a fuck about you too."

I looked at him. His face said nothing to me. He's like a piece of fuckin' stone. Me, I was shakin' pretty bad.

I says to him, "You ever wanna see me . . . you know where my shack is," and I left.

But you know what happened? He kept drinking that night. Joe Yung finds him on the floor pukin' his guts out, pukin' out all kinds of things. "He piss in pants," Joe told me. "He see things and talk to himself, start screaming." I asked him what kind of things Vic was seeing, whether they was pink elephants, and Joe said, "No pink elephant, Guy, just ants . . . many thousand ants eating him, talking to him. He very sick."

Joe and Ices Andy put him in the hospital. He doesn't get any booze and he gets the DTs and I think they put him in a straitjacket. "I'm all alone!" he was yellin'. "Someone help me! I'm all alone!" He went crazy in there, completely fuckin' nuts . . . ants with sunglasses on were singin' his songs to him and nibbling on his body.

And then he went off to that clinic in New Mexico.

SNUFFY DUBIN: I've done only two smart things in my life: marry Debbie and kick the pills. Debbie is my savior, my angel, my messiah. If she don't come into the Colony Club that night, if I don't meet her, I'm a dead man. I'm dead by 1975, I guarantee it. You know why I never had kids? You wanna know why Debbie never wanted to have kids? Because we already had one. We had *me*. I was the world's biggest kid, I was Debbie Dubin's bouncing baby boy.

Two shows a night, five, six nights a week, forty cities a year for almost fifty years. You think that's easy? I play Caesar's Palace for a week and then the next night I'm doing the Westbury Music Fair with Miss Leslie Wilson or Lana Cantrell and I look out into the crowd and I recognize twenty faces from Caesar's. So now how'm I gonna make these cats laugh again?

Funny fuel. That's what it was. Look, I needed them. I'm not gonna lie to you. I must've needed 'em, to spend eight hundred grand on the stuff. Thirty to get up, thirty goofballs to get down, thirty to smooth me out and transition me. I get home at four in the morning, I'm shaking like I'm Julius and Ethel Rosenberg getting electrocuted—how you think I'm gonna sleep? So I got the barbs, the Valiums, the Libriums. My body was like the Smith, Kline & French factory.

So yeah, cold turkey. I didn't do it in any hospital or in any Betty Ford kind of outfit, I did it in my bedroom in Vegas. And the only one around was Debbie. Nurse Debbie. One day I was runnin' on two hours sleep and was about to head off for the Oceanfront and I fell flat on my face as I'm opening up my car door. Next thing I know I'm in my bed, Debbie's kissing my cheeks. I reach into the night table drawer, where I keep my stash, and the only thing that's there is Kleenex, a *TV Guide,* and a tub of Vaseline. Debbie had called Pete Conifer and canceled for me. I had three days of sheer hell on earth and the only pill I've taken since then is Tums.

Ziggy, he hit rock bottom too.

I think it was '91. He was supposed to film another dumb R-rated cleavage romp in Germany, of all places—Christ, he must've made ten Big Bavarian Booby movies in Deutschland; he's got lederhosen, a monocle, and an elf's cap on in most of them. How the mighty have fallen, right? Ziggy does his lines in English, afterward they dub the German in. If the movie's released in America, they dub English back into Zig's mouth, but it's not even his own voice. Anyway, Ziggy's in Sweden now, all alone, and it's a holiday weekend there and he's clean out of pills. He'd been through customs in Munich and he'd left his little black toiletry kit on that conveyer belt thing that goes through security. He wakes up in Stockholm in a fucking panic . . . he calls Lufthansa but it's early and they don't pick up the phone. He calls the American Embassy in Sweden, they don't believe he's really Ziggy Bliss. He's calling every embassy in Europe, all to track down that little black bag in the Munich airport. "I was on the phone for four hours, Snuffles," he told me, "sweatin' like a wild boar." He took a taxi to the American Embassy in Stockholm and showed them his passport to prove he was Ziggy Bliss, and the pathetic thing was the young marine guards hadn't ever heard of him. They let him in, though, and he speaks to some guy, some liaison or attaché. The guy wants to know what was in this bag that was so important that he's got to call security at the Munich airport, and Ziggy thinks for a second and says, "My material." "Your material?" this guy asks him, and Ziggy says, "Yeah, my jokes." The guy—just out of curiosity—asks him, "What movie were you filming in Germany?" and Ziggy answers, *Titanic Teutonic Titties of the Tyrol* or whatever it was called.

Ziggy watches as this guy makes one, maybe two phone calls. Now, nobody knows or cares where this bag is—how much time are they gonna spend on this has-been comic with a red wig when they got Libyan terrorists to worry about?

So Ziggy tells this embassy cat he needs a doctor and he's given the address of a hospital. At the hospital he tries every trick in the book; he wants uppers, he says to them, "Alls I do is sleep nowadays, I can't get myself motivated to perform." He wants downers so he says to them, "Alls I do is perform, I can't get myself motivated to sleep." He ends up leaving there with two aspirin.

He goes back to his hotel and he's whimpering and shivering and is tearing apart the fabric of all his suitcases, hoping that maybe a few years ago half an amphetamine slipped underneath there. The poor guy even tore apart the soles of his shoes. Oh yeah . . . he takes off the red mop wig 'cause his scalp is a sweaty mess now and he fills up the sink and lets the rug sit in there for a spell. He gets a Stockholm phone book and looks in the doctor section and starts calling every doctor's answering service in town and says he's Ziggy Bliss and he can't get motivated. Nothing. Nowhere. He gets the bellhop and asks him, "Where do I go to get some pills in this town? If I don't get pills I'm gonna die," and he hands the kid twenty marks or kroner or shillings or whatever it is they've got. The kid tells him to go around the main train station and ten minutes later that's where Ziggy is. He's walking up to every shady-lookin' character, every creep with a dangling tongue or who's scratching themselves funny, and telling them he's Ziggy Bliss and he needs pills. No one believes he's Ziggy Bliss. Why? 'Cause Ziggy's wig was still bobbing up and down in the sink! He's just some little bald American with bags under his eyes like a basset hound and about ten coats of perspiration over his skin. No one's helping him out, nobody at all. "I swear I'm Ziggy Bliss," he's yelling. "I swear to God I am!"

He takes a walk and winds up in some seedy part of town . . . there's these hookers, these men dressed up as women, junkies all of 'em. Okay, he can smell it now: pay dirt. He walks up to this one tall guy with a blond wig in a long braid and with soccer balls stuffed into his blouse—Anita Ekberg with a mustache—and asks him, "Where can I get some pills? Any pills? I got dough. Help me out." This guy, who had pockmarks as big as nickels all over his face, asks to look at his wallet. Ziggy flashes the wallet, he's got around three hundred bucks' worth of foreign currency in there. They go to some little hotel, walk up three flights. Now, Ziggy is there to get his pills and that's *all* he's there to get—he knows this guy is a guy, right? So they go into this small room and the door closes behind him. Ziggy sits on the bed and before you know it he's got a switchblade to his throat. "Take the money! Take the money!" Ziggy says. Well, uh, that was a given, wouldn't you say? The guy, who's got his wig off now—one of the soccer balls had slipped out, too—and is about as blond and Swedish in real life as Fidel Castro, takes the wallet and takes the dough. He looks at the driver's license and sees the name Ziggy Bliss and he says, "You're Ziggy Bliss?" And Ziggy, who's wiping his head with his hanky, says, "Yeah, I guess." The hooker says, "My father loved your movies. He was a big fan in Bulgaria." Or Romania or Bratislava or wherever.

"Can I go now?" Ziggy asks.

He's heading for the door now and all of a sudden he's thrown to the floor. This cat is on top of him and tearing his pants down. "He was biting my neck like it was a medium rare porterhouse," Ziggy said. "And he was trying to slip his *shlong* into my heinie." But, see, Ziggy was one strong motherfucker. Still. So he throws this creep off his back and he opens the door. But he ain't outta the woods just yet, uh-uh. There's these two junkie slimeballs in leather jackets—maybe they were the hooker's pimps, who knows?—and they start punching and kicking Ziggy, they're kicking him in the stomach and the balls and they break a few ribs. Then they do that Richard Widmark thing, in *Kiss of Death*: They toss Ziggy right down the stairs. He's unconscious and a few hours later some cop finds him and takes him to the hospital.

"They gave me antibiotics and patched me up," he told me. "I had a few teeth knocked out too. I could hardly walk, every bone in me ached.

Pernilla flew over. She brought over two fresh rugs for me. One day I'm in the hospital room and the doctor comes in, asks how I feel. I say, 'Doc, I'm havin' trouble gettin' motivated. I got no get-up-and-go.' And this doctor, the spittin' image of Max Von Sydow, says, 'Pep pills? You want pep pills?' and writes me out a few prescriptions and leaves the room. I look at these prescriptions and I look up and the ceiling and the walls are closin' in on me quick. And I yelled—I yelled so loud, Snuffy, that it cracked the mirror in the room, just like Flo singin'—I yelled out these three words: 'I HATE MYSELF!' "

Rock fucking bottom, man. Everybody gets there one way or another.

JOHN TIMMONS [orderly]: Well, I don't work there no more. They can't fire me. I wouldn't have told you nothin' three years ago—they'd have fired me. Can't do that now. Don't work there no more.

Vic Fountain, he checked in first. Had some little Chinese man drive him up in a limousine. This driver started getting Vic's bags from the trunk and I said to him, "Oh no, Vic's got to do everything by himself here and that starts right now."

Vic was always tryin' to bribe us. The orderlies, the doctors and counselors. Offered me a thousand bucks just to sneak him in some Genoa salami once, offered me a Mercedes-Benz to let him walk out, said something about showgirls in Vegas. I always pretended like he was gonna get to me if he kept upping the offer, but after a while he realized he wasn't gettin' anywhere.

He wouldn't do nothing at first. Wouldn't make his bed, wouldn't clean his bathroom. Wanted his own room. They had him in a room with some twenty-three-year-old kid addicted to heroin. Nobody in Hope Springs has their own room . . . the queen of motherfuckin' France was to be in there, she'd be rooming with some dope addict. Vic didn't like the pajamas, he wanted his own satin ones flown in. Too damn bad. He had KP duty one week; didn't want to do it. Shit, it turned out he'd never cleaned a goddamn dish in his whole goddamn life. Didn't wanna take out the garbage. Well, I got in his face about that. I got in real close and real loud and I let his ass have it. I tell him if he don't take out the goddamn motherfuckin' garbage he'll *wear* the goddamn motherfuckin' garbage and you know what he did? Started to cry. Shit. Seventy-year-old man and he's on his bed and he's cryin' like I just took his goddamn yo-yo away from him. When he was doing that I noticed a picture on his night table—at the clinic that was the only thing you was allowed to have. No books, no radio, no TV. I said to Vic, "Who's that?" He said, "My son." "He a singer like you?" I asked him. "Nah," he said, "he was in a rock band. And he's dead." "You think he'd be proud of his old pops cryin' in his bed?" I asked him.

Well, he wound up takin' the garbage out, and makin' his bed and cleaning plates.

Two weeks after Vic Fountain checked in, who the hell shows up at that rehab clinic but Ziggy Bliss? Now that's some serious fate for you. The director of the place said to me the day before Ziggy come in, he say, "Big John, we might have a little problem here," and he explains to me about Vic Fountain and Ziggy Bliss. I tell him I don't care about all that Hollywood shit. I don't care if you had Olivia de Havilland and Joan Fontaine or the Hatfields and the McCoys in there at the same goddamn time.

You should have seen Ziggy Bliss when we took his wig away from him. Heh heh! "They didn't tell me you'd do this here," he's cryin' to me, and I yell at him and say, "This ain't nothin', Izzy!" I called him Izzy, Iggy, and Squiggy just to get on his ass. He's grabbin' onto his wig like it's his whole life I'm pullin' away from him. Three other orderlies come by and jump on him and he was a strong little man, but we got that big Brillo pad offa him. He looked just like an old bloodhound dog without that wig. Hell, when we asked for Vic's wig, when *he* checked in, he wasn't too happy either. But we got it. He said, "Must I?" and I said, "You must." And he handed it over. Looked like a dead raccoon in my hands. A dead *blue* raccoon. He was embarrassed without it, wouldn't show himself for a few days.

I saw them in the dining hall, Ziggy's second day there. Vic was sitting with his young roommate, working on his London broil. Then he sees Ziggy on the buffet line all alone with his tray. Nobody'd told Vic that Ziggy was comin'—he didn't have any idea. You should've seen Vic's face, man . . . thought he was having the DTs all over again. Know what Vic done? Got up in the middle of his meal and went back to his room and didn't show his face again until the next morning when we caught him trying to escape his ass.

"You gotta let me outta here, Timmons," he said to me.

"I don't have to do shit," I said to him. "Except force you to clean your bathroom."

"Look, forget the Mercedes. I'll make it a Bentley."

"You will? A Bentley? Really, my brother?"

"Yeah. I swear."

"I still don't have to do shit. Clean your bathroom. Now!"

He and Ziggy ran into each other that day, in the Sunset Lounge. They had Ziggy on medication, to take him off all them pills he was taking. He didn't look any more like the Ziggy I'd seen on the TV than I did. He just looked like a little bent-over bald Jewish man to me. All them freckles he had? They'd all faded and his skin looked like rust. But now in the lounge he was like a zombie. That's what Hope Springs did if you was hooked on pills: They took you off what you was on, put you on something else, then slowly took you off that, then kicked your ass outside into the real world. And it usually worked.

Ziggy saw Vic settin' there playing cards with someone and he didn't believe his own eyes. Thought he was hallucinating. He was doin' that "Thorazine shuffle" dance, taking two-inch steps and teetering back and forth . . . but when he saw Vic he come to a complete stop. Tilted his head like a dog listening to a police siren. Then he just shuffles on.

I checked up on him that night. He was lyin' in bed on his back, like a dead man, his hands folded over his chest. I said, "You all right?" He said, "I'm alive." He asked me if that was really Vic Fountain he'd seen, and I told him it was. I asked him, "Who are they?" and he turned to the picture on his night table and said, "They were my parents. And that's my wife."

"Whoa, she look like that girl in the old towel commercial."

"Yeah. That's her."

I was looking at him looking at her and he said, "I let her down. I let everyone I've ever known down."

The next night Vic didn't even go to dinner 'cause he didn't want to see Ziggy. You know what he done? He had that roommate of his sneak him his London broil dinner, into the room. With the au jus. I told Vic's counselor about that right away and he say to me, "Big John, next time that happens, you drag Vic by his neck into the dining hall and you set his ass right beside Ziggy Bliss's." I looked forward to doing that and, sure enough, the next night I got my chance.

Me and another orderly carried Vic kickin' and screamin' into the dining room and we threw him right next to Ziggy. Ziggy was still all zombied out—he had his tray but there wasn't no food on the thing. Ziggy looked at Vic, still thought he was seein' things. Two old bald men who've known each other fifty goddamn years. Vic said to him, "Try the London broil. Heavy on the 'oh juice.' And the strawberry Jell-O." And Ziggy Thorazine-shuffled over and got some London broil and extra au jus and some Jell-O and sat right back next to Vic Fountain.

"Strawberry Jell-O," Ziggy said to Vic. (Sounded like a croaking, dying frog. That's what all the medication did.) "You thinkin' the same thing that I'm thinkin'?"

"Goofin' off on fat Kate Smith's show?" Vic said. "Hell yeah."

For the next few weeks, until Vic checked out, they was together quite often. I'd see 'em playing cards in the Sunset Lounge. That lounge had a great view, man. Real sunny. Big picture window lookin' out into the desert and the mountains on the horizon and the sun and blue sky. That's what I miss most about that place, that view. That's about the *only* thing I miss. And here they were every day, right near that window, the sun streaming in right on 'em, them just playin' pinochle and gin rummy or talkin' or fuckin' around.

They'd play some jokes on some of the other people and we sometimes had to put a stop to it. One day I caught the two of 'em trying to hustle another patient at pool. We had to stop that. No gambling. There was an exercise room too; the clinic was big on that. I seen the two of 'em on treadmills together once. They wasn't doin' much work on them treadmills, you can take my word for it. Had 'em in neutral or some shit like that. I said to 'em, "Man, these treadmills ain't but hummin'. Why not try moving a little?" I turned the thing up just a little and they got all sweaty and started farting and so I turned 'em back down again quick. Another time I saw Ziggy holdin' a punching bag while Vic took a few hits on it. Vic punchin' that bag in the shape he was in, he wasn't gonna beat up a gnat. But they were funny: Vic would punch the bag and Ziggy, who was holding it, would pretend that he was the one got hit. I know I seen that in one of the lousy movies they did.

Both of 'em cleaned up. Did the therapy. Spoke to the doctors, to the other patients. Did what had to be done. Vic got real close to that junkie roommate he had, that young kid. The kid left before Vic did and I saw the two of 'em huggin' when the car come to take the kid away.

"Man, you was ready to have that kid deported when you first checked in," I reminded him.

"I was?"

"You don't even remember that, do you?"

"I was all screwy, Timmons," he said. Said somethin' 'bout ants crawling over him and eatin' him. Then he looked at the car taking the kid away and said, "He's a good kid. A good kid. I hope he's okay."

"Did he know who you are?"

"He's got no idea who Vic Fountain is. He thought I was just some old lush. And he was right."

Few days later, I was playing gin with Vic and he asked me how long I'd been working there. I tell him twenty-five years. He asked me if I remembered a woman name Ginger with long legs who'd once busted out. Tall and strawberry blond. Well, I did. But I didn't tell him I did. Didn't want to upset him. "You sure?" he asked me. And I told him I was.

His doctor told me, just two days before Vic was gonna be released, that Vic's mother had died. But they wasn't gonna tell Vic while he was inside; his ex-wife or someone like that was gonna tell him when he got out. So for two days every time I saw him I was thinkin': This man's moms is dead and he don't even know it.

The limousine come to take Vic away on a Sunday. The Chinese driver pulls in and I had to go get Vic from the Sunset Lounge. What a view. That sun was so bright and big it made the mountains look gold and violet and like they was movin'. I seen Vic, he had his little bag all packed right next to him. The night table picture of his son was in his hands. I said to him, "Your ride's here." He stood up, Ziggy stood up, and they hugged for a few seconds.

Vic checked out at the front desk. Got all his personal effects back. He say to me, "Hey, Timmons, all that dough and the broads I offered you? Well, you can forget about it."

"A thousand dollars for some salami?" I said to him. "Shit."

"Well, it'll only cost me five bucks now. Your loss. Okay, see ya."

"You forgot this, Vic."

I held out my hand and he took the dead blue raccoon from me and he set it on his head. Had it lopsided, the wrong way and crooked, and I straightened it out for him. When I did that I seen him gulp hard, all choked up, like he just swallowed a baseball. I told him, "Okay, man, better get goin'. Now." And he walked out the place.

I went back to the lounge and Ziggy was all alone. I looked out that big picture window and I seen Vic Fountain's black limousine beating its way down the highway, toward the mountains, and then the sun swallowing it up like it was on fire.

I heard some sniffling. It was Ziggy. He'd seen the car going down the road too, into the sun. I said to him, "You gonna be all right?" And he told me he didn't have no idea.

Until Ziggy was discharged he mostly kept to himself. The other patients—we was supposed to call 'em "guests"—they'd try to get him to be funny. They was always trying to do that. Get him to do this voice, that voice, make a ugly face, tell a joke or some shit like that. But he didn't want to. He always said the same thing to them:

"I'm too tired to be funny."

* * *

GUY PUGLIA: When Vic got out, I kept waiting for him to come to my shack. Every day I'm in there on the beach and I think Joe Yung's gonna drive him up. Now that his head was screwed on straight. Every time I see a Mercedes roll by, I think it might be him.

But it didn't happen.

You know, I went to his mom's funeral. He had dark glasses on. Everybody there did. That was some vicious one-two punch for Vic: drying out in New Mexico and then Violetta dying. Lots of people were walking up to him, kissin' him, patting his shoulders. I don't think he knew who half of 'em were. I snuck up to him from behind and squeezed his shoulder, but he didn't know it was me.

She was buried right alongside Vince, at Forest Lawn. When they was putting her into the earth I thought of how she was the one who got Vic the singing lessons. I remembered busting into that office in Boston and her waving around that rolling pin like a machete. She believed in him and fought for him.

Andy told me that a few days after Vic got out of New Mexico, [Vic] and Lulu had gone out to dinner a few times but that they didn't say too much to each other. Vicki dropped by and it was the same thing. Then he told me that Vic had an old flame of his, a Vegas showgirl named Kiki, come by. Vic had told me once she was a real pro in the sack. Knew all the tricks, he said, could do things with her fingernails that'd blast you off to Mars. Guys in Vegas and Tahoe called her "the Specialist." Well, Kiki was forty now but Ices Andy told me she still packed a wallop. "My asshole slammed shut like a Venus flytrap when I saw her," he told me.

Vic and Kiki went straight into the sack. He's in his bedroom with her for two hours, which is a long time for a fella at that age. Finally, the door opens and Kiki comes out, she gets in her Toyota, and drives off. Ices Andy and Joe Yung wait for Vic to come out, and he doesn't.

"I went into the bedroom, Guy," Andy tells me, "to see if Vic was all right. I mean, I was worried, right? And he's in there, in the bed facedown with his robe on, and he's whimpering. I say to him, 'Boss, what's wrong? You need a doctor?' And he says to me, 'What's wrong? Nothing.' So I said to him, 'Well, if nothing's wrong, what's wrong then?'"

The "nothing" that was wrong was that Vic couldn't do nothin' with Kiki. If you know what I mean. And she was the expert too. She tried every trick in the book and when that book didn't work, she went to the rest of the encyclopedia. She tried the tongue, the nails, her eyelashes, she had things in her pocketbook she was usin', devices and gizmos and whatnot. And she couldn't get a rise out of him.

Ices Andy makes a couple of phone calls, to this doctor and that doctor, and he gets the phone number of this one guy in Santa Monica. Vic goes to this guy, he gives him some pills, like, some herbal kinda stuff, and then he starts him in on these injections. And these wasn't injections in his arm, you know? It was some kinda wheat germ solution, or oatmeal or wheat grass. I dunno. Alls I know is, it didn't work. Not one inch.

A few months go by, I don't see or call Vic and he don't see or call me, and I call up Joe Yung and he tells me that Vic's got a girlfriend now. This was good news, I thought. I ask Joe Yung who the girl is and he tells me her name is Reina Harbin. I says, "What the hell is a Reina Harbin?" "I don't know," Chinese Joe says, "but she Vic's girlfriend now. She live here now. And she not nice to me."

ARNIE LATCHKEY: Nobody knows where Reina Harbin came from. They have no idea. All of a sudden, she was just *there*. She was there and she didn't let anybody else get near Vic. She was a goddamn witch, that's what she was.

If you ask me, she found out that Vic had gone to Hope Springs. She read it in the papers—oh, it was all over the columns and the tabloid TV shows—and probably circled his name with a red Magic Marker. Her in her goddamn coven with three boiling cauldrons of God-knows-what.

I don't know what Vic saw in her. But once she was there, she wouldn't leave.

VICKI FOUNTAIN: I hated her. From the moment I saw her I hated her. Now, I'd met all of Vic's wives and all of his girlfriends. And I gave them a chance, I really did. But the very second I saw Reina I felt like I was going to convulse. That woman scared me.

We were at a Hamburger Hamlet. Daddy wanted to order a diet salad but she wouldn't let him. She ordered him something else, a pastrami and cheese sandwich. "I don't want pastrami and cheese," he said to her. "Oh, yes you do, darling," Reina said. And she ordered it for him.

After that meal I saw them to their car . . . Daddy had bought her a new Mercedes. Reina was driving, it wasn't Joe Yung. Reina started the car and, out of her earshot, Daddy said to me, "I hope you like her." I told him that I didn't trust her. "You never liked any of them, Vicki," he said to me. I said that this one—Reina—I just did not trust. "What do you know about her? Anything?" I asked him. He was thinking about it and Reina said, "Can we go already?!" And Daddy said to me, "All I know is, she takes care of me, honey."

It's very sad. Mommy said she was the devil. I really, really wished that Vincent was still around. Reina fired Ices Andy Ravelli after she moved in with Daddy. Andy told me that Reina—who now was controlling the checkbook—had written him a check for $500 and handed it to him. "Vic wants you to have this," she said to him. Andy ripped up the check, told her to kiss his dago ass, and left.

SALLY KLEIN: Oh, she was an operator all right, a real pro. Shep Lane was dead and his sons David and Jerome had taken over handling the money. But they get a phone call from Reina's lawyer one day and then four months, five court dates, and three truckloads of paperwork later, Shep Lane's kids aren't handling Vic's finances anymore.

I was having dinner with Danny at the Polo Lounge one night. And a few booths away were Reina and Vic. Vic looked very tired. He lifted up a fork to his mouth and the food fell off, onto his lap or the floor. And she started berating him. Calling him an impotent old has-been. "Can't you even eat anymore?!" she screamed. Publicly yelling at him so everyone could hear it. And Vic just took it. She was saying just the worst things. He looked petrified of her.

Danny courageously went over to their booth and said, "Vic, are you okay?"

"Hi, Danny," Vic said.

Danny put his hand on his shoulder and asked again, "Are you okay? Sally's here with me. Do you want us to take you away?"

Reina ripped Danny's hand off of Vic and said, "I beg your pardon, but can you *please* get away from us?! My God, I hate it when people come over and ask for Vic's autograph!!"

GUY PUGLIA: I heard all kinds of terrible stories. From all over the place. They got married in Reno and none of the old gang was invited. I saw a picture in the paper: The rock she had on was the biggest, ugliest diamond you ever saw. Raoul Mouchette, the guy who went over to Vic's house a few times a week to spruce up the wigs, he told me he'd seen Reina hit Vic. She slapped him in the face, called him some kinda name. And the chef that Reina had hired, he told me he knew that Reina was banging this young guy who did their landscaping.

Joe Yung tells me Reina wants to get to the cellar of the house. The place where no one but Vic was ever allowed to go. She wanted the key to the door. But Joe didn't let her know where it was. She threatened to fire him. "I no have key, I no have key," he told her.

Me and Edie went out with Arnie and Estelle one night. I says, "What can we do? We gotta get him outta her clutches. She'll kill him."

"I think that's the idea, I'm afraid," Estelle said.

Vicki got a lawyer. She wound up getting about five lawyers. Nobody could do nothin'. They were husband and wife.

VICKI FOUNTAIN: I went on two USO tours to Vietnam with Bob Hope, but the single worst thing I've ever seen was the pictures of Vic by his pool, in the back of the house. Reina had hired a photographer, then sold the pictures to the *Enquirer*. And *Hard Copy* ran the photos too. And there's Daddy lying in a chaise longue in his baggy swimming trunks and with his exposed belly, and—I know it was on purpose, just to humiliate him—you could see his colostomy bag. It was so horrible.

* * *

ARNIE LATCHKEY: It was one of the weirder coincidences of all time. I'm reading the *USA Today* about how they're going to dynamite the

Oceanfront in a few weeks to make way for some gigantic theme hotel like the MGM Mesopotamia Cradle of Civilization Casino and Resort or something, and the phone rings. It's Ziggy. I'm just about to tell him about the Oceanfront when he says to me, all excited, "Arnie? Didja hear?" And I say, "What? About the Oceanfront?" And he says, "No. Vic! It's Vic! He called me up an hour ago! He wants to get back together!"

I felt like all my blood cells were dancing a mambo. Was this good news? Bad news? My head was spinning.

"He wants to reunite with you, Ziggy? You sure somebody wasn't goofin' on you?"

"Arnie, it was Vic. We're back in business. Line up something for us." He started singing, "*That ol' Latch magic's got me in its spell . . .*"

I called Wanda Conifer. I expressed my most half-sincere condolences about the hotel. She said, "Arnie, I've had a blast here for more time than I can remember." I said, "Yeah, but wait till all that TNT brings it down, that'll be a blast." (She didn't laugh.)

"So, uh, who you got booked for your final week?" I politely inquired of her.

"It's pretty bad, Arn. We've got an illusionist and an impressionist. Hopefully both of them can combine their talents and make it seem as though there's really an audience."

"If I offered you Fountain and Bliss for five nights, what would you say?"

I think her heart pounded so goddamn loud that it almost brought the whole hotel down right then and there.

We were in, my friend.

DANNY McGLUE: I knew quite well that lightning couldn't strike twice in the same place. I knew in advance that it wasn't going to be like old times. But I was lonely. I was very lonely and I needed something. Betsy had been in the asylum for a long time now. I would visit her twice a month, but after a few years she didn't even recognize me. I'd try to have a conversation with her, to talk about anything, the weather, what she'd eaten that day, the movies they showed there, and sometimes she was coherent. But that was rare. And she may as well have been speaking to a complete stranger.

It was so rough on me, going there, driving to Santa Barbara, seeing her. I would pull over to the side of the road on the way back and just stare off into space. It would take me thirty minutes sometimes to pull myself back together. It wasn't easy.

I wish that I'd married Sally. That's what was killing me. For years and years it killed me. It was killing me to even think such a thing. I felt that I was a bad, evil person just to think it.

I married Betsy and she was a drunk. She was drunk when she was carrying Stevie. And Stevie was in the hospital all the time and he died. Then she had an operation so there would be no more kids, but she didn't need to. Because I didn't want to have any more kids with her. I didn't even want to be near her.

Sally was the love of my life. I'd felt a connection with her decades ago and it hadn't ever left. So much would've been different. It's not just pie in the sky. I would have had healthy children, a good, happy marriage, maybe become a proud grandfather. But for years and years, I'd been alone. Me and my dumb gags.

We all met at the office on Wilshire. It was me, Arnie, Sally, Ziggy, and Vic. And Reina too, she was there unfortunately. She would try to chime in, to take part, but she had the sense of humor of a CPA. That was embarrassing, her trying to be funny and everything landing like a big fat dud. Secretly we all enjoyed it, despite our cringes. But we had to be nice to her. We all knew it was her who'd convinced Vic to reunite with Ziggy.

We worked out some routines, we updated them. Dr. Louie Kablooie, the Slow-Witted Cowboy, the Cockney Barber . . . we brought them all out and shook the dust off. Ziggy had done a Japanese gardener bit during the war—that was a little racist, so we canned that. A lot of times we just sat around and reminisced about the old days. The stories we told! Vic mentioned this one incident in Washington with some sheriffs and we were all in stitches, and Ziggy told us about the time that, when Hilda Fleury died, he literally went out to Greenwood Cemetery in Brooklyn to pee on her grave and stumbled upon Snuffy Dubin who was already at her grave zipping up. "The puddle was still smokin', guys," Ziggy said. We spoke about how Ziggy and Vic had gradually turned George S. Collier into a pirate with all their antics on the set. Pernilla would pop in on us with Ziggy's medicine and some food from Canter's for all of us and, you know, she was just the perfect wife for him. She would join in with us too.

I asked Vic one day there, "So was it really you who crash-landed the plane outside the Pantages Theater? Come on. Tell."

"Me? Ha!" Vic said, slapping me on the back. "Danny boy, you gotta be kidding me."

The only bad thing was, the more we had fun, the more we started clicking and meshing, the worse mood Reina got in.

But we came up with about an hour's worth of new stuff. And Ernie was there and Vic was singing too. There was a piano in the office. "Are they gonna have a big band at the Oceanfront?" Vic asked. "'Cause if it's okay, maybe just Ernie could accompany me. I don't need all them horns and stuff." We all agreed. And it was strange, because we realized that Ernie and Vic had never once performed together live.

Ziggy and Vic . . . they still had it. The chemistry. The stuff you couldn't bottle or sell or manufacture or concoct. They still had it.

We were sure they'd be socko.

SNUFFY DUBIN: It was my retirement year. My last year in the business. You know, in all the years I did comedy, all the hundreds of clubs and thousands of people I performed for, I never took more than a week off. Not once. But in '93 Debbie says to me, "You know, Snuff, I'd like to go to Italy for a while. With you." I say, "Okay, get Yvette"—our travel agent—"on the phone and we'll go to Rome and Florence for three days." "Darling, I said a *while*," she said to me. "You know, maybe spend more than ten minutes in one town?" And then it hit me like a fucking freight train. This woman saved my life, a thousand times she saved my life . . . it's time Snuffy Dubin did something for her other than buy her her tenth mink coat or a new BMW. So I call up Yvette and tell her to book us into the Italy— Christ, even my vacations sounded like nightclub engagements!—*into* Italy, I mean, not for three days, not for a week, but a half a year. And what the hell, while I was at it, I'd buy Debbie a new mink coat and a BMW too, just for the hell of it.

Two months before my final performance of all time—it was at Caesar's— Arnie calls me and tells me Fountain and Bliss are performing at the Oceanfront. Well, thank God they didn't time their swan song with mine—I would've cashed in a few mob favors and had the both of 'em rubbed out.

"Why are they doing this?" I asked Arnie.

"Snuffles," he says, "I haven't the vaguest idea in the world."

ARNIE LATCHKEY: A day before the engagement I check in with Wanda Conifer, in her office. We talked about the usual stuff, the money, sound and lighting, how many songs Vic would sing. "Do we still have to get everything done in turquoise for Vic?" she asked me, and I said, "I don't think he can tell turquoise from mauve anymore."

When the news hit that Fountain and Bliss were reuniting, it was gigantic. It was bigger than gigantic. It was mammoth. All the networks covered it, all the papers and magazines. Every channel showed clips of their old movies and TV shows, they showed old black-and-white stills of them mugging and goofing around. It gave me a chill to watch it, not only because of all the fantastic ballyhoo it was creating, but because I knew that when Ziggy or Vic passed away, they would show these same clips and pictures. Here they were, being reborn, but it was like they'd already died.

Wanda also told me that the explosives experts, the demolitionists, were still finding some of her late husband's little trap doors, double mirrors, and passageways around the hotel. "They found a camera in a toilet bowl on the fourth floor, Latch," she said. "And they uncovered some juicy videotapes from Vic's suite." "Do me a favor, Wanda," I bade her, "could you toss those tapes out?" And she said, "Half the time, Vic isn't even there anyway. He's with four broads, then he gets up and leaves and lets them finish up with one another."

In one week to the very minute, Wanda told me, the hotel complex we were standing in would be blown to dust.

GUY PUGLIA: I didn't go. I had no desire to. Sally calls me, says she can get me and Edie in, can fly us there for free, get us a great room. I says to her, "No thanks, Sal, I got a business to run." You know who was helping me out now? Little Guy, Vic's grandkid. Me and him in the shack. I tell him, "You wanna see your granddad perform, you can take a few days off." He says to me it's okay, he'd rather work. But I told him that he had to go—Vic was his *nonno* and it was his duty.

Edie says to me, "You sure you don't want to go?"

Not after those things he said to me, I didn't.

SALLY KLEIN: I was with Ziggy, Pernilla, and Danny in Ziggy's dressing room backstage and we could hear the crowd, we could hear the electricity brewing. Wanda and her staff knew not to send any booze in. There was no champagne. There was fruit, tea, and ginger ale. Ziggy had his wigs out, his two red Brillo ones and the others he needed for the rest of the act. He was a little nervous and Danny and I tried to relax him, to keep him talking. Pernilla was very reassuring to him. She'd gotten a Swedish masseur to come in and work over his back for ten minutes, to loosen him up. "I'm loosened up, sure," Ziggy said after the guy left, "but I think that Masseur de Sade just fractured three of my vertebras."

Someone knocked on the door and said, "Five minutes, Mr. Bliss." I saw Ziggy swallow. I poured him some tea and he drank it. "Everything's going to be all right," Pernilla said to him. She kissed him on the cheek and then left to take her seat in the audience.

"Thank God for her," Ziggy said when she left. "Thank God."

"She's a great gal," Danny said.

"I slipped up a few times in my life," Ziggy said. "I was great at it. But marrying her was my salivation."

Danny and I didn't say anything. Ziggy put a dab of makeup on. He adjusted his wig.

"I only wish," he said, "I hadn't been so wrong with you two. I don't know what was wrong wit' me. I wasn't happy, so I didn't want no one else to be happy. I was funny-lookin', I was miserable, and so everybody else had to be miserable too."

"I wasn't miserable," I said.

He put some makeup under his eyes.

"If I could take one thing back in my life," he said, "that's what it would be. That you two would have had just a happy marriage as I got now. That's the one thing."

Danny said to Ziggy, "Well, I moved in with Sally a few weeks ago."

"You did?" Ziggy asked Danny. "He did?" Ziggy asked me.

We both nodded.

"God love ya," Ziggy said to us.

I reminded him that in a week he'd be in New York; the Friars Club had finally agreed to roast him, with or without Vic.

There was a knock at the door. "You ready for this, partner?" Vic said from behind the door.

"Nah," Ziggy joked, "but let's do it anyways."

A minute later from the stage I heard Ernie tickling the ivories, as they say. Then Vic started singing "The Hang of It."

Ziggy got up and went to the door. "Jeez," he said, "I gotta remember to not pop my eyes out. I'm ascared the glass one might actually shoot at someone."

"Don't worry," I said.

"Oh well. Here goes nuttin'."

DANNY McGLUE: I stood with Arnie and Sally backstage. We had a great view. The place was packed. And it wasn't just old-timers and senior citizens, people trying to revive their fond memories; there were hundreds and hundreds of people in their forties and thirties and so on. But the front tables, it was Celebrity Row. Bob and Dolores Hope were there. So were Frank and Barbara Sinatra, Milton Berle, Lenny Pearl and Jerry Lewis and Alan King and Bill Cosby, everyone. Jan Murray, Corbett Monica and Richard Pryor were there, Vic Damone, Rickles, Liza Minnelli, Buzzy Brevetto, Tony Bennett, Miss Leslie Wilson, Shecky and Buddy, Barbra Streisand. Arnie and Wanda had to turn people away!

Vic does "The Hang of It" and then launches into another song and, just as planned, in walks Ziggy. When that happened every single person who could stand—and there were a few people in that room who couldn't—stood up and started applauding. It was like drumming, like thunder, it was completely deafening. It went on for five minutes.

Arnie looked at Sally and me . . . he noticed that our hands were clasped.

"A bunch of sweet lovebirds, you two," he said, sticking his cigar in his big smiling mouth. "If it wasn't so goddamn sickening, I'd almost be really happy for you."

ARNIE LATCHKEY: I'm not going to lie to you. I could tell you it was as if they'd *never* broken up, that Fountain and Bliss didn't miss a beat. But it wasn't like that. It was like they'd been apart for only a minute, that's how goddamn tight they still were.

Ziggy waddled onto the stage in the middle of Vic's chirping. When the place erupted, Vic pretended for a minute that the applause was for him. We didn't plan that. He just did it. And it was goddamn hysterical, boy. The applause dies down and Vic sees Ziggy and does a double take that you could have sent to the Smithsonian, it was so classic. And he says, "You . . . *again?*"

Ziggy doesn't say anything. He's got the sheepish look on, the baby look. He starts inching toward Vic, centerstage. "Yeah, me again," he says.

Vic said, "So, uh, Zig . . . exactly *why* are we doing this?"

"I know why, Vic," Ziggy said.

"You do?"

"Yeah. I know why."

"Why?"

"'Cause we're desperate and flat fuckin' broke, that's why!"

More yuks, followed by guffaws, followed by chuckles. That big long train of theirs was just gettin' a-rolling.

"It's working," Danny whispered to me.

"Oh my God," Sally said. She gasped slightly.

"What?" I said.

"I just realized it!" she said. "Look at them! Ziggy is now skinnier than Vic! Vic is the round one."

It was true. God, I hadn't noticed it until then.

"So why did we break up again?" Vic was asking Ziggy. "I forgot."

"Oh, nothin' personal . . . except we couldn't stand the sight of each other."

"But things have changed now, Zig."

"They sure have . . . now we can't stand the sight of ourselves either."

"You know, Zig," Vic said, "I just heard that another comedy team was playing here tonight."

"Oh yeah?"

"Yeah."

"And which comedy team was that?"

"Stugatz and Bubkes. I just heard a guy outside saying that Stugatz and Bubkes were playing here tonight."

"That's us, Vic."

"It is?"

"Yeah. 'Cause you don't got *stugatz* and I've got *bubkes.*"

They did ten minutes, made fun of each other, they made fun of the marriages, the booze, the lousy movies, all the problems. Just when you thought it was getting too personal, too nasty, one of 'em would crack a joke, and the whole room started to shake. I could hear the ghosts, boy, ghosts from that hotel and from all the hotels and from every joint they ever played. Ghosts the world over. And these ghosts were locked and lost in such paralyzing laughter that they couldn't do anything but laugh their goddamn ghostly heads off.

Ziggy went off and changed into a costume while Vic did another song. Yeah, he screwed up on the lyrics and both of his hands were trembling, but he made it through. Ziggy came back on and they did a Louie Kablooie routine. It wasn't getting the same-size yuks as just Ziggy and Vic, but it was working. Ziggy goes off, Vic tries another song. They do another bit.

When Ziggy went off, Vic started acknowledging some of the people there. He'd joke around with them. He noticed Fritz Devane's widow and said to her, "You know, your husband was very instrumental in helping my career. Really. Many years ago, do you know what he did? I was a kid, not even twenty, and I wanted to tell him how much I admired him. And he called me a greaseball. He did. And when he did that, that's when I knew I was gonna make it in this business. 'Cause I was gonna make it so nobody could ever treat me like dirt again. So to your late husband I not only say thank you but I say, '*Vafancul'!*'" And you know what? People stood up and applauded! Well, everyone but the Widow Devane, that is, who couldn't have stood up even if she wanted to, which she certainly didn't.

The lights went down and Ziggy came on, as Ziggy. Solo. We were about two-thirds the way done. It was going over much, much better than we'd hoped. Ziggy thanked some people. Pernilla stood up and people applauded. He saluted some of the younger comics and said, "I wanna sincerely thank you guys for rippin' me off and makin' tons more dough at it than me."

Then he told the lighting guy to turn the lights down and shine the spotlight on Lenny Pearl. "Lenny, I just wanna tell you," Ziggy said, "they canceled your career thirty years ago—so it's okay for you to drop dead now." When he got off that line, he was cooking. Yeah, they were best when they were together, Ziggy and Vic, but still, this was working.

Then . . . in the middle of a sentence he stopped talking. Right in the middle. He was looking at the crowd, staring. Just fixated. This wasn't in the plan, this wasn't part of the bit. His face started getting all flushed . . . it was as red as a tomato, boy. He was sweating, *shvitzing* like a typhoon. And he was giggling! He was giggling and laughing and staring. I looked at his stomach, at his legs. They were rattling! The man had something funny to say, something downright hilarious was going on in that brain of his. But it was inside there, he wasn't letting it out. He was in hysterics but only within himself.

He froze up. There was no noise now. There was just the staring and his face frozen in a smile. The lights didn't come down. They thought it was the act—people were even laughing. But after he didn't move for a minute, they realized it wasn't any act.

He dropped to the ground. It hardly made a noise. He toppled like a house of cards, like the cards at the bottom had been kicked out from underneath.

The lights came down at once. There were murmurs, there was darkness. He was dead.

A few hours later a doctor tells me what I'd suspected. Ziggy had had a stroke.

Jesus, I thought of all those people, years and years ago . . . Fountain and Bliss had been so goddamn funny that people literally had died laughing watching them. And now Ziggy had done the same thing to himself.

He was buried in the same mausoleum as his parents, at Home of Peace Memorial Park. We kept it a low-key affair. Vic showed up. He threw a pebble into the grave and crossed himself. He was in tears and had to be helped around. I'm not kiddin' you when I tell you he was more shaken up than anyone else there.

Carved into the mausoleum under a Star of David it now says: THE BLISSMANS. COMEDIANS. FAMILY.

SNUFFY DUBIN: I cried for days. I had known this cat for fifty years. You know, he was the funniest performer I ever saw. Hands down. Nobody but nobody could touch him, onstage or off. Look, some nights, Jan Murray was the best comic in the world. Another night it might be Buddy or Shecky. Some other night, hey, maybe it was even me. But night for night, pound for pound, the funniest was Ziggy Bliss, and it ain't even close to a contest. We'd had our run-ins, we hated each other at times. The guy said terrible things about me behind my back, but he also said them to my face too. When he died, an enormous chunk of me died with him.

I never told anybody this. I'll tell you now. Some people think that Ziggy laughed himself to death, that he had a joke in his mind and that's what caused him to die. And that might be true. It might be. I believed it. And to some extent I still do. But what I wanna know is: What the hell was he staring at?

A few days after it happened, the day before they blew the Oceanfront to smithereens, Wanda Conifer showed me the list of people in the audience, the names of everyone who'd reserved a seat. I wanted it as a souvenir to send to Freddy Bliss, for that comedy museum of his.

So I'm lookin' this thing over and one name sticks out like the sorest fucking thumb in a forest of sore thumbs: D. Phipps.

What the hell. Who knows? Who knows anything?

I had a few more shows to do, then it was all over for me. And, man, I couldn't wait.

* * *

ERNIE BEASLEY: After Ziggy died, Vic's health got worse. I see things like this in the obituaries often. A couple that's been married for forty years—the wife dies and then a week later, even though he'd been in perfect health, the husband dies. I had two cats, one was twelve, the other four. The older one died and a month later the younger one was gone.

Vic retreated. He disappeared. The crone he was married to kept a tight leash on him. And that's what it was like too, a leash. Joe Yung told me horror stories. She was a tyrant. "She yell at him all day," Joe told me. "She make him sleep on floor." She'd humiliate him in public. Vic had health problems and she wouldn't take him to a doctor. But Joe did, when Reina would leave the house. Vic had a small stroke, a tiny one. A year after that, he had a pacemaker installed.

I tried to visit him but Reina and her household staff wouldn't let me. She tried to fire Joe Yung but good old Joe, loyal to the end, simply pretended he didn't understand her. She fired a maid and the maid told me that Reina was always, always snooping around, trying to find the key to the cellar. "She must think Vic's got Fort Knox down there," the maid said to me. "What is down there, do you know?" I asked. But nobody knew.

The worse Vic's health got, the more she pushed him. A few months after his second stroke—and this one was not so tiny—she began dragging him around the country. *A Night With Vic* was the name of the show. At first he could do his shows standing up but then—I read about it in *People*—he had to do them sitting down on the stage, with the microphone pulled halfway down. He would sing, tell jokes. Sometimes you could hardly hear him, he spoke in a hoarse whisper, very slowly. All the cigarettes, all the drinks, the strokes, his age. People would leave his shows and they hadn't been entertained, they'd been horrified.

Vicki tried lawyer after lawyer. Vic's remaining brother and sister did the same. They spent so much money. They tried to show that Vic was being tortured, abused. Joe Yung was the only one of the household staff to testify to that effect, the others just fell in line with Reina. Of course they did!—she controlled the purse strings. They wheeled Vic up to the witness stand, and the attorneys and the judge spoke to him. He denied being abused. He said he loved Reina. They asked him if Reina forced him to perform at clubs and in theaters against his will, and Vic summoned up enough strength to say, "You call that performing?"

"Apparently, Mr. Fountain," the judge said, "you fall asleep sometimes while singing?"

"Your Honor," Vic replied, "I was doing that forty years ago too."

The court ruled for Reina.

I think it was in 1996 . . . Reina launched a Vic Fountain Web site. I don't have a computer but I was told that for $19.99 you could watch tapes of Vic from thirty years ago at the Oceanfront, tapes from Pete Conifer's stash. The tapes were of him gallivanting about in bed with a few showgirls. They had videotapes of him alone with Ginger too, them telling each other how much they loved each other.

I had dinner with Lulu a few weeks before Vic did that celebrity cruise. Poor Lu. "He's lost to me now," she cried. "I've been lying to myself my whole life."

ARNIE LATCHKEY: I couldn't believe when I saw the ad in the paper. Don't forget how Vic hated the water! The man never ate seafood in his life, not so much as a prawn. I remember I once said to him, "The world is your oyster," and he told me never to use that expression ever again. He was serious. He'd been living in Los Angeles for almost fifty years and the closest he'd ever been to the beach was when Gussie Kahn's chauffeur took us there. And I pick up a paper now and I see that Vic Fountain is going to perform on some celebrity cruise ship?!

Estelle and I drove to Guy's shack one day, in Venice. Except now it was called Two Guys Seafood Shack, 'cause Vincent's kid, Little Guy, worked there. I showed Guy the ad in the paper. I said, "How the hell is Vic going to go on a boat?! We couldn't get him to do swashbuckler movies and that wasn't even real water! How's he gonna do this?!" All Guy could do was shake his head.

FREDDY BLISS: I boarded the ship in New York, and the first time I saw Vic was in the dining room. He and Reina Harbin had a table all to themselves. So did the other talent. Vic was the biggest name of all the entertainers, by far—there was an impressionist who couldn't even imitate himself, he was so bad, and a few other lesser talents. Reina would wheel Vic around the ship and the passengers would walk up to him, ask him for his autograph. There weren't too many young passengers, to tell the truth. "I really love you, Vic," an elderly woman would say as she shook his hand. "I saw you sing once at the Smokestack Lounge, Vinegar Hill,

Brooklyn," a man said, "and now here we are on a big ship." But Vic had no idea what or where the Smokestack Lounge was. Some old guy would grab Vic by the shoulder and say, "Mr. Fountain, I want to thank you for recording 'Lost and Lonely Again.' It saved my life." And Vic would nod and try to smile. But by then the right half of his face was paralyzed. After three days at sea, nobody would approach Vic anymore—they just watched Reina wheel him around, and the passengers would look at each other. They couldn't believe how old he looked. They were pitying him, putting their hands to their hearts, shaking their heads and pitying him.

Reina would wheel him over to the edge of the deck and leave him there. She'd go off for as much as an hour at a time. Sometimes she put the brake on the wheelchair, so he wouldn't slide around. But two times she didn't. The first time, I caught him . . . just as the chair was sliding back. He looked completely terrified. His eyes . . . he looked so helpless and scared. I caught the chair and turned him away from the water and put the brake on. He didn't recognize me. The second time it happened, I saw a man pop out of nowhere and catch the chair. He put the brake on and turned Vic away from the water, just as I'd done.

I walked up to him the next day and said, "I saw what you did for Vic Fountain. Thanks."

He shrugged and walked away.

I went up to the ship's captain the next day. I told him that I thought Vic's wife was trying to scare him into having a heart attack. He didn't believe me. He thought I was crazy.

The next night in the lounge, it was "Vic Fountain Night." Reina wheeled Vic up to the stage. He got lots of applause. I was surrounded by a bunch of *alter kockers*, Italians and Jews and Irish and everything else. I was the youngest person at the table by thirty years.

"His wig is backwards," an old man said. "She's got his wig on backwards."

Vic told some jokes, told some stories, sang three songs. I don't think he got too many words right. Before the last song Reina and Vic tried to engage in some funny banter, but it just didn't work. They had this bit about how she was hard up for sex and he was too old to perform. It didn't get too many laughs from that crowd. Then they sang a duet of "Makin' Whoopee" and Vic moved his hands up and down, like a baby in a high-chair. Reina was really hamming it up, shaking her hips and swinging her chest and her gold necklace, and Vic was just moving his lips. That necklace of hers was straight out of *The Land of the Pharaohs* and her hips were nothing to be shaking, believe me. Especially on a boat.

There was a small band. A drummer, a bassist, a pianist, a trumpeter and a saxophonist, and a guitarist.

The boat was going to pull into Florida the next morning, and after the show I was walking around, keeping an eye on everything. We were on the top deck . . . I saw Reina wheel Vic out. It was drizzling out and very windy and there was nobody else outside. All I could make out were a half-moon and shadows. She put the brake on the chair. I heard Vic trying to say something, something like, "Please . . . don't . . . please . . . oh, God . . ."

A few seconds later I heard steps coming up the stairs and another shadow appeared with Reina. It was a tall man, tall and round. The two of them whispered to each other, I couldn't hear a thing. The man was carrying something. It was—I didn't make it out at the time but it all came out in the investigation afterward—a trumpet case. He opened it and pulled out a pearl-handled gun.

I had to do something. I had to. This was it. But it was a gun! When Guy had called me from Los Angeles and told me to take this celebrity cruise and keep an eye on Vic, I had no idea it was going to be like this! You have to remember: I'm a klutz. I can barely tie my own shoes or balance a checkbook or do anything!

I started to step toward them, toward their shadows. I heard her say, "Don't use a gun! We'll use this." And she took her belt off. They were going to strangle him and throw him overboard. But Floyd Lomax, who I recognized as the trumpeter in the band I'd seen an hour before, said, "I wanna use the gun. This is unfinished business."

I was about ten feet away. I wasn't thinking . . . I was just scared. I said, "Freeze! Don't move."

Floyd Lomax said, "Fuck off."

Reina wrapped the belt around Vic's neck and I heard Floyd cock the gun. He was aiming it at me.

From out of nowhere, from out of the drizzle and the darkness and the wind, I saw another shadow . . . Floyd Lomax turned to it and the shadow kicked him in the crotch. I ran up to Vic's wheelchair and pulled Reina and her belt off of Vic. I heard Vic wheezing, gasping. I wrestled Reina to the ground, right near where Lomax was doubled over with the pain from the kick.

I was out of breath. Vic was okay. I think I was more out of breath than he was.

"Vic, it's me, Freddy. Freddy Bliss."

"Ziggy's boy?"

"Yeah. Him."

"Freddy!" he said feebly. A tear was in his eye. "Freddy . . ."

He smiled and reached for my wrist and gave it a squeeze.

In the small red EXIT light on the wall near us, I could make out the face of the man who had kicked Floyd Lomax. It was the same old guy who'd stopped Vic's chair from rolling a few days before.

"Who are you?" this man asked me.

"My name's Freddy Bliss."

"Ziggy Bliss's son?" he said. "I knew your father. Years ago."

"What's your name?"

"Your father and Vic," he told me, "used to call me Cat."

GUY PUGLIA: Freddy Bliss sure come through all right, didn't he? He come to Los Angeles a few weeks afterwards and the old gang showed him the best time he ever had. Reina and Lomax were in jail, and Vicki and Joe Yung and Ices Andy was taking care of Vic again. That Reynolds Catledge was a big hero too, he was all over the papers. I think it's the first time the guy ever cracked a smile in his life, and it must have lasted a whole week.

A few months after the cruise, me and Little Guy are in the shack. It's about six at night and the sun is setting. Little Guy, he always has the radio on, and him and me, we argue about the music. He listens to the rock 'n' roll thing and me, I like the oldies. So we were doing that and he was steamin' some clams and out our little window I see a van drive up. It comes to a stop and Joe Yung and Andy Ravelli get out. "Hey, Ices Andy!" I yell out, and the two of 'em look at me. Joe Yung opens up the rear door and meanwhile Ices Andy is helping Vic Fountain out of his seat. Joe pulls out the wheelchair and Ices Andy lifts Vic up and they put him in it, real delicate-like.

They wheel Vic up to the shack. Little Guy's mouth is dropped open, he can't believe it any more than me.

I hadn't seen Vic in a while, a really long while. And he didn't look too good.

"Hey, *paisan*," I said.

"*Goomba* Guy," he says to me very weakly. "*Goomba* Guy."

I put my hand on his shoulder and he put his hand on my hand. His hand was trembling and I started to tremble too. I clutched his hand with mine, I gave it a tight squeeze.

He nodded his head . . . he was lookin' at something. I turned around. He was looking at the swordfish on the outside of the shack. I saw half of his face smile. His hand and my hands were still clutching.

"That old fish," he said. I could hardly hear him, I had to lean in real close.

"Hey, Gramps," Little Guy said, and he kissed his granddad's forehead and Vic smiled again, as much as he could.

"What'll it be, Vic?" I said. I could hardly talk, the lump in my throat was so big.

Vic said something but I couldn't hear it. I says to him, "Can you say that again?" I leaned in real close so's I could hear him.

"A bucket of steamers," he whispered, "and a lobster roll, please."

He could barely eke it out.

Three minutes later, Joe Yung was opening a steamer for him and dipping it in the butter, and Ices Andy was putting it in his mouth. They were sliding down his throat like liquid pearls. Vic nodded. Little Guy put the tip of the lobster roll in his mouth and Vic chewed on it. We watched him. Vic widened his eyes and we could tell he wanted another bite. Hell, he wanted the whole goddamn thing! "This is marvelous," he whispered to me slowly.

They wheeled him up to the beach. Little Guy got a blanket from the van and wrapped it around his *nonno*'s shoulders. He was still eatin' that lobster roll.

He looked out at the beach. There were boys and girls, men and women, walkin' around, running around, in their bathing suits. Some kids were playing volleyball. The waves were big, big and very blue and gray, and they made that thunder sound when they smacked down, and it was the biggest reddest sunset you ever seen in your life. Vic looked out at the ocean and at that red sun settin' and he shook his head and said again, "This is just marvelous."

When they put him back in the van I said to him, "You be sure and come here again."

But that was the last time I ever seen my best friend. Five days later he was dead.

ARNIE LATCHKEY: Vic's funeral was just as he would've wanted it, with more than just a touch of the opulent about it. Garish might even be the word. But Vic would've loved it, he would've eaten it up. Ernie Beasley even said at the memorial, "Vic said to me, 'Make sure it's a blast, baby.'" They sent out invites to every single celebrity who ever was and most of 'em turned out. Vic, Shep Lane's kids told me, had wanted to be buried at the Pebble Beach golf course but they wouldn't allow that up there, those *momzers*. So Vic's buried next to Vince and his mother, at Forest Lawn, three generations of Fontanas all in a row. Vic's stone is made of Iranian turquoise, and once a week for the next thousand years, they'll polish it. The man took care of everything.

On the stone it says IL RAGAZZO CON I CAPELLI BLU COME LA NOTTE.

Hunny Gannett was flown in from his hospital in Vegas. Guy and Edie wheeled him up to the tombstone and Hunny let drop a red rose.

Vic was paying all of Hun's hospital bills, it turned out. Danny said to me that Hunny will probably outlive all of us—he just won't realize it.

Lulu stood with Sally. Sally had her arm around her. Did you know that in the last three days of Vic's life, he'd moved back in with Lu? It's true. The woman finally got her wish, and he died in her arms.

Some wiseass in the press said that Vic had died as he sang: in his sleep. I gotta admit: It's a great line. But Vic Fountain wrung more out of one second of life, asleep or awake, than most people do in twenty years. It's just that, I admit it, sometimes he wrung it the wrong way.

He got about two minutes on the newscast the night he died. They played his records, his hits, for a few seconds. They showed him when he was a kid, they had a picture of him with that barbershop quartet trio he was in, then with the Don Leslie band; they showed clips from all the lousy movies.

"He was so gorgeous," Estelle said to me.

Yeah. He sure was.

A few days after Vic was buried, his sister and his brother were going through the mansion in Beverly Hills. Vicki was there, so was Joe Yung. They came to the cellar door and couldn't open it. "Where's the key?" Cathy asked, and Joe Yung went to the liquor cabinet and found it. He tells them he's never been down there either. Joe opens the door and they walk down these steps, it's like a goddamn horror movie, boy, they don't know what or who's down there.

Joe Yung feels for a light switch and finds one and flicks it. One by one, lights go on. Their eyes were almost blinded by the glowing silver and white. There wasn't one speck of dust, and everything—the red leather stools, the long shiny counter, the tiles—was perfect and in its place and the chrome was radiant.

"Oh, my God," Cathy gasped. She and her brother Ray couldn't believe their eyes.

"It was a soda fountain," Cathy told me. "A soda fountain right out of the 1930s. It was an exact copy of the one he used to work at. Jiggs Cudahy's place."

When Vic died, my phone rang off the hook for a few days. Every vulture and jackal and termite wanted to know about Vic, about Ziggy, about Fountain and Bliss; they're asking me this question and that question. How'd they meet? When was it? Did they ever get along? What made them click? I realized, after the ten thousandth question, Hey, I don't even have to answer this stuff anymore. What the hell? So I didn't.

However, this one reporter asked me one particular question. And it was something that hadn't ever occurred to me, which is rare, because a lot occurs to Arnold Latchkey, which is maybe my problem.

He said, "A lot of entertainers are not very happy people. They're insecure and lonely, they're often miserable."

"I'm well aware of it," I said.

"A lot of comedians aren't very happy. Or funny."

"I'm quite, quite familiar with it."

And he asked me if I thought that Ziggy and Vic were funny—that *any-one* at all is funny—because of the pain. Because of some searing pain deep inside. Do people become funny because of some inner agony, some gnawing emptiness or torment?

I said to him, "Who do I look like to you? Henri Bergson? Sigmund Freud you think I am? I'm just a goddamn business manager!"

After I hung up on the guy, I started thinking about it. Was it so? Is that what makes people funny? I've known a lot of funny people who weren't ever in any kind of agony, who weren't ever miserable or lonely, and I've known lots of unfunny people, believe me, who were.

So the answer to this $64 question is this: No, being miserable and knowing pain, torment, loneliness, and emptiness does *not* make you funny. It doesn't.

But, you know, it probably helps.

IMPORTANT PEOPLE
WHO APPEAR IN THIS TEXT

Enzo Aquilino—voice teacher
Barney Arundel—nightclub owner
Ginger Bacon—dancer, Vic's mistress
Harry/Harriet Bacon—musician
"Big" Sid Baer—Rosie McCoy's husband, a hotelier
Dr. Howard Baer—gynecologist
Rosie McCoy Baer—hoofer, entertainment director, and wife of "Big" Sid Baer
Ernie Beasley—songwriter, friend of Vic's
Billy and Mary Beaumont—dancing partners
Hugh Berridge—member, with Teddy Duncan, Rowland Toomey, and Vic Fountain, of the Three Fours
Louis Bingham—bandleader, radio host
Bobby Bishop—record executive
Freddy Bliss—Ziggy's son
Harry and Florence Blissman—Ziggy's parents, entertainers
Ziggy Bliss, born Sigmund Blissman—entertainer
Mike Boley—guitarist
Thalia Boneem—Floyd Lomax's girlfriend
Clive Bonteen—playwright, existentialist
Pernilla Borg—Ziggy's second wife
Archibald Bratton—president of Bratton Theater Ventures
Buzzy Brevetto—comedian
Kid Burcham—boxer
Betsy Cantwell—actress, Danny McGlue's wife
Reynolds Catledge IV—soldier, employee of Vigorish, Inc.
Charlotte Charlot—chanteuse, Nazi
Maeve Clarity—Jack Enright's secretary
Father Claro—a Codport priest

Mickey Cohen—mobster
Harry Cohn—movie mogul
George S. Collier—director
Pete Conifer—entertainment director, entrepreneur
Wanda Conifer—Pete Conifer's widow
Artie Conway—TV producer
Mandy Crane—actress
Angie Crosetti—childhood friend of Vic's
Jiggs Cudahy—Vic's boss, owner of a soda fountain and pharmacy
Betsy Cunningham—General Woodling's mistress
Pops Deegan—trainer
Fritz Devane—singer, actor, legend
Roger Dillard—trumpeter
Debbie Dubin—Snuffy Dubin's wife
Snuffy Dubin—comedian
Teddy Duncan—member of The Three Threes
Jack Enright—agent
Dick Fain—vocalist
Ferdinand the Fantastiq—magician
Enrico Fermi—physicist
Tony Ferro—Vic's friend
Hilda Fleury—columnist
Ursula Fischer—physicist
Bruno and Violetta Fontana—Vic's parents
Ray Fontana—Vic's brother
Sal Fontana—Vic's brother
Louise "Lulu" Mangiapane Fountain—Vic's first wife
Vic Fountain, born Vittorio Fontana—entertainer
Vicki Fountain—Vic's daughter
Vincent Fountain—Vic's son
Tommy and Jimmy Fratelli—mobsters
Tony Friedman—Lenny Pearl's producer
Hunny Gannett—pugilist, raconteur, saloon keeper, greeter
Morty Geist—publicist
Joe Gersh—agent at MCA
Clarence L. "Ned" Gilbert—director
Hal Gordon—record producer
Ezra Gorman—movie producer
Grayling Greene—columnist
Seymour Greenstein—childhood friend of Ziggy's
Pip Grundy—polydactyl guitarist
Bobby Hale—columnist
Tony Hampton—golfer
Vern Hapgood—musical arranger

Reina Harbin—Vic's third wife
Bud Hatch—columnist
Jean Hatch—Bud Hatch's wife, also known as "SL"
Bernie Heine—Catskills hotelier
Cody Lee Jarrett—musician
Timothy Jones—FBI agent
Bertie Kahn—publicist
Gus Kahn—movie mogul
Ed Kapler—TV director
Murray Katz—agent at WAT
Faye Kendall—actress
Donny Klein—Sally and Jack's son
Jack Klein—real-estate lawyer, Sally Klein's husband
Sally Klein—Ziggy Bliss's cousin, co-manager of Fountain and Bliss
Mickey Knott—drummer
Shep Lane—accountant, Fountain and Bliss's money manger
Veda Lankford—actress
Arnie Latchkey—co-manager of Fountain and Bliss
Estelle Latchkey—Arnie Latchkey's secretary and wife
Howard Leeds—production chief
Don Leslie—bandleader
Anna Lipscombe—actress, Clive Bonteen's wife
Floyd Lomax—bandleader
Lou Manganese—Al Pompiere's son-in-law
Dominick Mangiapane—Lulu's older brother
Julie Mansell—singer
Louis B. Mayer—movie mogul
Taffy McBain—actress, Vic's second wife
Ed J. McDowell—journalist
Danny McGlue—joke writer
Stevie McGlue—Danny and Betsy's son
Marty Miller—radio and TV producer
Jerome Milton—Harry and Flo Blissman's agent
Larry and Stu Morrell—musicians
"Myrna"—stripper
Cecil Newcombe—radio host
Tony Newport—golfer
Barbara Nordquist—actress, stripper
Casper Nuñez—private detective
The O'Hares—vaudevillians
J. Robert Oppenheimer—physicist
Lenny Pearl—comedian, fellow trouper with Harry and Florence
Westbrook Pegler—columnist
Dolly Phipps—Ziggy's girlfriend, comedienne

Joan Pierce—neighbor of Ziggy and Jane White
Al Pompiere—mob boss
Jimmy Powell—nightclub employee
Gino Puccio—hotel employee, Guy Puglia's cousin
Kathy Puccio—his wife
Theresa and Paul Puccio—their children
Gaetano "Guy" Puglia—Vic's best friend, restaurateur
Billy Quinn—Lenny Pearl's radio announcer
Ices Andy Ravelli—bodyguard
Joe Ravelli—ices salesman, grandfather of Ices Andy
Carmine Ricci—Cathy Ricci's husband
Catherine Ricci—Vic's sister
Scarlet Robideaux—Ferdinand the Fantastiq's assistant
Billy Ross—bandleader for Fountain and Bliss
Millie Roth—secretary at Vigorish, Inc.
Barry and Manny Singer—writers
Edmund Sligh—radio actor, producer, director, and writer
Baldwyn Sloate—FBI agent
Edie Smith—Guy Puglia's wife
Hank Stanco—agent at WAT
Sid Stone—writer
Rocco Straccio—hoodlum
Emmett Strang—movie director
Clotilde Sturdivandt—couthier
Gershon Susskind—rabbi to the stars
Cueball Swenson—musician
Merwyn Swick—lawyer
"Steady" Eddie Teller—physicist, putative pugilist
John Timmons—orderly
Rowland Toomey—member of the Three Threes
Constance Tuttle—actress, lover of Vic
The Macy Twins—songstresses
Bubbles Van Boven—waitress
Joseph Weissblau—Jane White's father
Grace Wheelwright—Constance Tuttle's roommate
Jane White—Ziggy's first wife
Norman White—writer
Ruth Whitley—vocalist
Billy Wilson—Vic Fountain's double
Earl Wilson—columnist
Walter Winchell—columnist
General Emmett Woodling—U.S. Army general
Lucinda Woodling, née Hodge—his wife
Joe Yung—Vic's valet